SECTION I. EXISTENCE

1. BEING, IN THE ABSTRACT %

#1. Existence. — N. existence, being, entity, ens[Lat], esse[Lat], subsistence.

reality, actuality; positiveness &c. adj.; fact, matter of fact, sober reality; truth &c. 494; actual existence.

presence &c. (existence in space) 186; coexistence &c. 120.

stubborn fact, hard fact; not a dream &c. 515; no joke.

center of life, essence, inmost nature, inner reality, vital principle.

[Science of existence], ontology.

V. exist, be; have being &c. n.; subsist, live, breathe, stand, obtain, be the case; occur &c. (event) 151; have place, prevail; find oneself, pass the time, vegetate.

consist in, lie in; be comprised in, be contained in, be constituted by.

come into existence &c. n.; arise &c. (begin) 66; come forth &c. (appear) 446.

become &c. (be converted) 144; bring into existence &c. 161.

abide, continue, endure, last, remain, stay.

Adj. existing &c. v.; existent, under the sun; in existence &c. n.; extant; afloat, afoot, on foot, current, prevalent; undestroyed.

real, actual, positive, absolute; true &c. 494; substantial, substantive; self-existing, self-existent; essential.

well-founded, well-grounded; unideal[obs3], unimagined; not potential &c. 2; authentic.

Adv. actually &c. adj.; in fact, in point of fact, in reality; indeed; de facto, ipso facto.

Phr. ens rationis[Lat]; ergo sum cogito: "thinkest thou existence doth depend on time?" [Lat][Byron].

#2. Inexistence. — N. inexistence[obs3]; nonexistence, nonsubsistence; nonentity, nil; negativeness &c. adj.; nullity; nihility[obs3], nihilism; tabula rasa[Lat], blank; abeyance; absence &c. 187; no such thing &c. 4; nonbeing, nothingness, oblivion.

annihilation; extinction &c. (destruction) 162; extinguishment, extirpation, Nirvana, obliteration.

V. not exist &c. 1; have no existence &c. 1; be null and void; cease to exist &c. 1; pass away, perish; be extinct, become extinct &c. adj.; die out; disappear &c. 449; melt away, dissolve, leave not a rack behind; go, be no more; die &c. 360.

annihilate, render null, nullify; abrogate &c. 756; destroy &c. 162; take away; remove &c. (displace) 185; obliterate, extirpate.

Adj. inexistent[obs3], nonexistent &c. 1; negative, blank; missing, omitted; absent &c. 187; insubstantial, shadowy, spectral, visionary.

unreal, potential, virtual; baseless, in nubibus[Lat]; unsubstantial &c. 4; vain.

unborn, uncreated[obs3], unbegotten, unconceived, unproduced, unmade.

perished, annihilated, &c. v.; extinct, exhausted, gone, lost, vanished, departed, gone with the wind; defunct &c. (dead) 360.

fabulous, ideal &c. (imaginary) 515, supposititious &c. 514.

Adv. negatively, virtually &c. adj.

Phr. non ens[Lat].

#3. Substantiality. — N. substantiality, hypostasis; person, being, thing, object, article, item; something, a being, an existence; creature, body, substance, flesh and blood, stuff, substratum; matter &c. 316; corporeity[obs3], element, essential nature, groundwork, materiality, substantialness, vital part. [Totality of existences], world &c. 318; plenum. Adj. substantive, substantial; hypostatic; personal, bodily, tangible &c. (material) 316; corporeal. Adv. substantially &c. adj.; bodily, essentially.

#4. Unsubstantiality. — N. unsubstantiality[obs3], insubstantiality; nothingness, nihility[obs3]; no degree, no part, no quantity, no thing. nothing, naught, nil, nullity, zero, cipher, no one, nobody; never a one, ne'er a one[contr]; no such thing, none in the world; nothing whatever, nothing at all, nothing on earth; not a particle &c. (smallness) 32; all talk, moonshine, stuff and nonsense; matter of no importance, matter of no consequence, thing of naught, man of straw, John Doe and Richard Roe, faggot voter; nominis umbra[Lat], nonentity; flash in the pan, vox et praeterea nihil[Lat]. shadow; phantom &c.(fallacy of vision) 443; dream &c. (imagination) 515; ignis fatuus &c. (luminary) 423[Lat]; "such stuff as dreams are made of" [Tempest]; air, thin air, vapor; bubble &c. 353; "baseless fabric of a vision" [Tempest]; mockery. hollowness, blank; void &c. (absence) 187. inanity, fool's paradise. V. vanish, evaporate, fade, dissolve, melt away; disappear &c. 449. Adj. unsubstantial; baseless, groundless; ungrounded; without foundation, having no foundation. visionary &c. (imaginary) 515; immaterial &c. 137; spectral &c. 980; dreamy; shadowy; ethereal, airy; cloud built, cloud formed; gossamery, illusory, insubstantial, unreal. vacant, vacuous; empty &c. 187; eviscerated; blank, hollow; nominal; null; inane. Phr. there's nothing in it; "an ocean of dreams without a sound" [Shelley].

% 3. FORMAL EXISTENCE

Internal conditions %

#5. Intrinsicality. — N. intrinsicality[obs3], inbeing[obs3], inherence, inhesion[obs3]; subjectiveness; ego; egohood[obs3]; essence, noumenon; essentialness[obs3] &c. adj.; essential part, quintessence, incarnation, quiddity, gist, pith, marrow, core, sap, lifeblood, backbone, heart, soul; important part &c. (importance) 642. principle, nature, constitution, character, type, quality, crasis[obs3], diathesis[obs3]. habit; temper, temperament; spirit, humor, grain; disposition. endowment, capacity; capability &c. (power) 157. moods, declensions, features, aspects; peculiarities &c. (speciality) 79; idiosyncrasy, oddity; idiocrasy &c. (tendency) 176[obs3]; diagnostics. V. be in the blood, run in the blood; be born so; be intrinsic &c. adj. Adj. derived from within, subjective; intrinsic, intrinsical[obs3]; fundamental, normal; implanted, inherent, essential, natural; innate, inborn, inbred, ingrained, inwrought; coeval with birth, genetous[obs3], haematobious[obs3], syngenic[obs3]; radical, incarnate, thoroughbred, hereditary, inherited, immanent; congenital, congenite; connate, running in the blood; ingenerate[obs3], ingenite; indigenous; in the grain &c. n.; bred in the bone, instinctive; inward, internal &c. 221; to the manner born; virtual. characteristic &c. (special) 79, (indicative) 550; invariable, incurable, incorrigible, ineradicable, fixed. Adv. intrinsically &c. adj.; at bottom, in the main, in effect, practically, virtually, substantially, au fond; fairly. Phr. "character is higher than intellect" [Emerson]; "come give us a taste of your quality" magnos homines virtute metimur non fortuna [Lat][Hamlet][Nepos]; non numero haec judicantur sed pondere [Lat][Cicero]; "vital spark of heavenly flame" [Pope].

% External conditions %

#6. Extrinsicality.— N. extrinsicality[obs3], objectiveness, non ego; extraneousness &c. 57; accident; appearance, phenomenon &c. 448.

Adj. derived from without; objective; extrinsic, extrinsical[obs3]; extraneous &c. (foreign) 57; modal, adventitious; ascititious[obs3], adscititious[obs3]; incidental, accidental, nonessential; contingent, fortuitous.

implanted, ingrafted[obs3]; inculcated, infused.

outward, apparent &c. (external) 220.

Adv. extrinsically &c. adj.

<— p. 2 —>

% 4. MODAL EXISTENCE

Absolute %

#7. State. — N. state, condition, category, estate, lot, ease, trim, mood, pickle, plight, temper; aspect &c. (appearance) 448, dilemma, pass, predicament.

constitution, habitude, diathesis[obs3]; frame, fabric &c. 329; stamp, set, fit, mold, mould.

mode, modality, schesis[obs3]; form &c. (shape) 240.

tone, tenor, turn; trim, guise, fashion, light, complexion, style, character.

V. be in a state, possess a state, enjoy a state, labor under a state &c. n.; be on a footing, do, fare; come to pass.

Adj. conditional, modal, formal; structural, organic.

Adv. conditionally &c. adj.; as the matter stands, as things are; such being the case &c. 8.
% Relative %

#8. Circumstance. — N. circumstance, situation, phase, position, posture, attitude, place, point; terms; regime; footing, standing, status.

occasion, juncture, conjuncture; contingency &c. (event) 151.

predicament; emergence, emergency; exigency, crisis, pinch, pass, push; occurrence; turning point.

bearings, how the land lies.

surroundings, context, environment 229a[TE 232]; location 184.

contingency, dependence (uncertainty) 475; causation 153, attribution 155.

Adj. circumstantial; given, conditional, provisional; critical; modal; contingent, incidental; adventitious &c. (extrinsic) 6; limitative[obs3].

Adv. in the circumstances, under the circumstances &c. n., the circumstances, conditions &c. 7; thus, in such wise.

accordingly; that being the case, such being the case, in view of the circumstances; that being so, sith[obs3], since, seeing that.

as matters stand; as things go, as times go.

conditionally, provided, if, in case; if so, if so be, if it be so; depending on circumstances, in certain circumstances, under certain conditions; if it so happen, if it so turn out; in the event of; in such a contingency, in such a case, in such an event; provisionally, unless, without.

according to circumstances, according to the occasion; as it may happen, as it may turn out, as it may be; as the case may be, as the wind blows; pro re nata[Lat].

Phr. "yet are my sins not those of circumstance" [Lytton].
<— p. 3 —>

% SECTION II. RELATION

1. ABSOLUTE RELATION %

#9. Relation. — N. relation, bearing, reference, connection, concern, cognation; correlation &c. 12; analogy; similarity &c. 17; affinity, homology, alliance, homogeneity, association; approximation &c. (nearness) 197; filiation &c. (consanguinity) 11[obs3]; interest; relevancy &c. 23; dependency, relationship, relative position. comparison &c. 464; ratio, proportion. link, tie, bond of union. V. be related &c. adj.; have a relation &c. n.; relate to, refer to; bear upon, regard, concern, touch, affect, have to do with; pertain to, belong to, appertain to; answer to; interest. bring into relation with, bring to bear upon; connect, associate, draw a parallel; link &c. 43. Adj. relative; correlative &c. 12; cognate; relating to &c. v.; relative to, in relation with, referable or referrible to[obs3]; belonging to &c. v.; appurtenant to, in common with. related, connected; implicated, associated, affiliated, allied to; en rapport, in touch with. approximative[obs3], approximating; proportional, proportionate, proportionable; allusive, comparable. in the same category &c. 75; like &c. 17; relevant &c. (apt) 23; applicable, equiparant[obs3]. Adv. relatively &c. adj.; pertinently &c. 23. thereof; as to, as for, as respects, as regards; about; concerning &c. v.; anent; relating to, as relates to; with relation, with reference to, with respect to, with regard to; in respect of; while speaking of, a propos of[Fr]; in connection with; by the way, by the by; whereas; for as much as, in as much as; in point of, as far as; on the part of, on the score of; quoad hoc[Lat]; pro re nata[Lat]; under the head of &c. (class) 75 of; in the matter of, in re. Phr. "thereby hangs a tale" [Taming of the Shrew].

#10. [Want, or absence of relation.] Irrelation. — N. irrelation[obs3], dissociation; misrelation[obs3]; inapplicability; inconnection[obs3]; multifariousness; disconnection &c. (disjunction) 44; inconsequence, independence; incommensurability; irreconcilableness &c. (disagreement) 24; heterogeneity; unconformity &c. 83; irrelevancy, impertinence, nihil ad rem[Lat]; intrusion &c. 24; non-pertinence. V. have no relation to &c. 9; have no bearing upon, have no concern with &c. 9, have no business with; not concern &c. 9; have no business there, have nothing to do with, intrude &c. 24. bring in head and shoulders, drag in head and shoulders, lug in head and shoulders. Adj. irrelative[obs3], irrespective, unrelated; arbitrary; independent, unallied; unconnected, disconnected; adrift, isolated, insular; extraneous, strange, alien, foreign, outlandish, exotic. not comparable, incommensurable, heterogeneous; unconformable &c. 83. irrelevant, inapplicable; not pertinent, not to the, purpose; impertinent, inapposite, beside the mark, a propos de bottes[Fr]; aside from the purpose,, away from the purpose,, foreign to the purpose, beside the purpose, beside the question, beside the transaction, beside the point; misplaced &c. (intrusive) 24; traveling out of the record. remote, far-fetched, out of the way, forced, neither here nor there, quite another thing; detached, segregate; disquiparant[obs3]. multifarious; discordant &c. 24. incidental, parenthetical, obiter dicta, episodic. Adv. parenthetically &c. adj.; by the way, by the by; en passant[Fr], incidentally; irrespectively &c. adj.; without reference to, without regard to; in the abstract &c. 87; a se.

#11. [Relations of kindred.] Consanguinity. — N. consanguinity, relationship, kindred, blood; parentage &c. (paternity) 166; filiation[obs3], affiliation; lineage, agnation[obs3], connection, alliance; family connection, family tie; ties of blood; nepotism. kinsman, kinfolk; kith and kin; relation, relative; connection; sibling, sib; next of kin; uncle, aunt, nephew, niece; cousin, cousin- german[obs3]; first cousin, second cousin; cousin once removed, cousin twice &c. removed; near relation, distant relation; brother, sister, one's own flesh and blood. family, fraternity; brotherhood, sisterhood, cousinhood[obs3]. race, stock, generation; sept &c. 166; stirps, side; strain; breed, clan, tribe, nation. V. be related to &c. adj. claim relationship with &c. n. with. Adj. related, akin, consanguineous, of the blood, family, allied, collateral; cognate, agnate, connate; kindred; affiliated; fraternal.

<— p. 4 —>

intimately related, nearly related, closely related, remotely related, distantly related, allied; german.

#12. [Double or reciprocal relation.] Correlation. — N. reciprocalness &c. adj[obs3].; reciprocity, reciprocation; mutuality, correlation, interdependence, interrelation, connection, link, association; interchange &c. 148; exchange, barter. reciprocator, reprocitist. V. reciprocate, alternate; interchange &c. 148; exchange; counterchange[obs3]. Adj. reciprocal, mutual, commutual[obs3], correlative, reciprocative, interrelated, closely related; alternate; interchangeable; interdependent; international; complemental, complementary. Adv. mutually, mutatis mutandis[Lat]; vice versa; each other, one another; by turns &c. 148; reciprocally &c. adj. Phr. "happy in our mutual help" [Milton].

#13. Identity. — N. identity, sameness; coincidence, coalescence; convertibility; equality &c. 27; selfness[obs3], self, oneself; identification. monotony, tautology &c. (repetition) 104. facsimile &c. (copy) 21; homoousia; alter ego &c. (similar) 17[obs3]; ipsissima verba &c. (exactness) 494[Lat]; same; self, very, one and the same; very thing, actual thing; real McCoy; no other; one and only; in the flesh. V. be identical &c. adj.; coincide, coalesce, merge. treat as the same, render the same, identical; identify; recognize the identity of. Adj. identical; self, ilk; the same &c. n. selfsame, one and the same, homoousian[obs3]. coincide, coalescent, coalescing; indistinguishable; one; equivalent &c. (equal) 27; tweedle dee and tweedle dum[Lat]; much the same, of a muchness[obs3]; unaltered. Adv. identically &c. adj.; on all fours.

#14. [Noncoincidence.] Contrariety.— N. contrariety, contrast, foil, antithesis, oppositeness; contradiction; antagonism &c. (opposition) 708; clashing, repugnance. inversion &c. 218; the opposite, the reverse, the inverse, the converse, the antipodes, the antithesis, the other extreme. V. be contrary &c. adj.; contrast with, oppose; diller toto coelo[Lat]. invert, reverse, turn the tables; turn topsy-turvy, turn end for end, turn upside down, turn inside out. contradict, contravene; antagonize &c. 708. Adj. contrary, contrarious[obs3], contrariant[obs3]; opposite, counter, dead against; converse, reverse; opposed, antithetical, contrasted, antipodean, antagonistic, opposing; conflicting, inconsistent, contradictory, at cross purposes; negative; hostile &c. 703. differing toto coelo[Lat]; diametrically opposite; diametrically opposed; as opposite as black and white, as opposite as light and darkness, as opposite as

4

fire and water, as opposite as the poles; as different as night and day; "Hyperion to a satyr"[Hamlet]; quite the contrary, quite the reverse; no such thing, just the other way, tout au contraire[Fr]. Adv. contrarily &c. adj.; contra, contrariwise, per contra, on the contrary, nay rather; vice versa; on the other hand &c. (in compensation) 30. Phr. "all concord's born of contraries" [B. Jonson]. Thesis, antithesis, synthesis [Marx].

#15. Difference. — N. difference; variance, variation, variety; diversity, dissimilarity &c. 18; disagreement &c. 24; disparity &c. (inequality) 28; distinction, contradistinction; alteration. modification, permutation, moods and tenses. nice distinction, fine distinction, delicate distinction, subtle distinction; shade of difference, nuance; discrimination &c. 465; differentia. different thing, something else, apple off another tree, another pair of shoes; horse of a different color; this that or the other. V. be different &c. adj.; differ, vary, abludel, mismatch, contrast; divaricate; differ toto coelo[Lat], differ longo intervallo[It]. vary, modify &c. (change) 140. discriminate &c. 465. Adj. differing &c. v.; different, diverse, heterogeneous, multifarious, polyglot; distinguishable, dissimilar; varied, modified; diversified, various, divers, all manner of, all kinds of; variform &c. 81[obs3]; daedal[obs3]. other, another, not the same; unequal &c. 28. unmatched; widely apart, poles apart, distinctive, characteristic; discriminative; distinguishing. incommensurable, incommensurate. Adv. differently &c. adj. Phr. il y a fagots et fagots.

<— p. 5 —>

% 2. CONTINUOUS RELATION %

#16. Uniformity. — N. uniformity; homogeneity, homogeneousness; consistency; connaturality[obs3], connaturalness[obs3]; homology; accordance; conformity &c. 82; agreement &c. 23; consonance, uniformness. regularity, constancy, even tenor, routine; monotony. V. be uniform &c. adj.; accord with &c. 23; run through. become uniform &c. adj.; conform to &c. 82. render uniform, homogenize &c. adj.; assimilate, level, smooth, dress. Adj. uniform; homogeneous, homologous; of a piece[Fr], consistent, connatural[obs3]; monotonous, even, invariable; regular, unchanged, undeviating, unvaried, unvarying. unsegmented. Adv. uniformly &c. adj.; uniformly with &c. (conformably) 82; in harmony with &c. (agreeing) 23. always, invariably, without exception, without fail, unfailingly, never otherwise; by clockwork. Phr. ab uno disce omnes[Lat].

#16a. [Absence or want of uniformity.] Nonuniformity. — N. diversity, irregularity, unevenness; multiformity &c. 81; unconformity &c. 83; roughness &c. 256; dissimilarity, dissimilitude, divarication, divergence. Adj. diversified varied, irregular, uneven, rough &c. 256; multifarious; multiform &c. 81; of various kinds; all manner of, all sorts of, all kinds of. Adv. variously, in all manner of ways, here there and everywhere.

% 3. PARTIAL RELATION %

#17. Similarity. — N. similarity, resemblance, likeness, similitude, semblance; affinity, approximation, parallelism; agreement &c. 23; analogy, analogicalness[obs3]; correspondence, homoiousia[obs3], parity. connaturalness[obs3], connaturality[obs3]; brotherhood, family likeness. alliteration, rhyme, pun. repetition &c. 104; sameness &c. (identity) 13; uniformity &c. 16; isogamy[obs3]. analogue; the like; match, pendant, fellow companion, pair, mate, twin, double, counterpart, brother, sister; one's second self, alter ego, chip of the old block, par nobile fratrum[Lat], Arcades ambo[obs3], birds of a feather, et hoc genus omne[Lat]; gens de meme famille[Fr]. parallel; simile; type &c. (metaphor) 521; image &c. (representation) 554; photograph; close resemblance, striking resemblance, speaking resemblance, faithful likeness, faithful resemblance. V. be similar &c. adj.; look like, resemble, bear resemblance; smack of, savor of; approximate; parallel, match, rhyme with; take after; imitate &c. 19; favor, span [U. S.]. render similar &c. adj.; assimilate, approximate, bring near; connaturalize[obs3], make alike; rhyme, pun. Adj. similar; resembling &c. v.; like, alike; twin. analogous, analogical; parallel, of a piece[Fr]; such as, so; homoiousian[obs3]. connatural[obs3], congener, allied to; akin to &c. (consanguineous) 1 1. approximate, much the same, near, close, something like, sort of, in the ballpark, such like; a show of; mock, pseudo, simulating, representing. exact &c. (true) 494; lifelike, faithful; true to nature, true to life, the very image, the very picture of; for all the world like, comme deux gouttes d'eau[Fr]; as like as two peas in a pod, as like as it can stare; instar omnium[Lat], cast in the same mold, ridiculously like. Adv. as if, so to speak; as it were, as if it were; quasi, just as, veluti in speculum[Lat]. Phr. et sic de similibus[Lat]; tel maitre tel valet[Fr]; tel pere tel fils[Fr]; like master, like servant; like father, like son; the fruit doesn't fall far from the tree; a chip off the old block

<— p. 6 —>

#18. Dissimilarity. — N. dissimilarity, dissimilaritude[obs3]; unlikeness, diversity, disparity, dissemblance[obs3];

divergence, variation.; difference &c. 15; novelty, originality; creativeness; oogamy[obs3]. V. be unlike &c. adj.; vary &c. (differ) 15; bear no resemblance to, differ toto coelo[Lat]. render unlike &c. adj.; vary &c. (diversify) 140. Adj. dissimilar, unlike, disparate; divergent; of a different kind &c. (class) 75 unmatched, unique; new, novel; unprecedented &c. 83; original. nothing of the kind; no such thing, quite another thing; far from it, cast in a different mold, tertium quid[Lat], as like a dock as a daisy, "very like a whale" [Hamlet]; as different as chalk from cheese, as different as Macedon and Monmouth; lucus a non lucendo[Lat]. diversified &c. 16a. Adv. otherwise. Phr. diis aliter visum[Lat]; "no more like my father than I to Hercules" [Hamlet].

#19. Imitation. — N. imitation; copying &c. v.; transcription; repetition, duplication, reduplication; quotation; reproduction; mimeograph, xerox, facsimile; reprint, offprint. mockery, mimicry; simulation, impersonation, personation; representation &c. 554; semblance; copy &c. 21; assimilation. paraphrase, parody, take-off, lampoon, caricature &c. 21. plagiarism; forgery, counterfeit &c. (falsehood) 544; celluloid. imitator, echo, cuckool, parrot, ape, monkey, mocking bird, mime; copyist, copycat; plagiarist, pirate. V. imitate, copy, mirror, reflect, reproduce, repeat; do like, echo, reecho, catch; transcribe; match, parallel. mock, take off, mimic, ape, simulate, impersonate, personate; act &c. (drama) 599; represent &c. 554; counterfeit, parody, travesty, caricature, lampoon, burlesque. follow in the steps of, tread in the steps, follow in the footsteps of, follow in the wake of; take pattern by; follow suit, follow the example of; walk in the shoes of, take a leaf out of another's book, strike in with, follow suit; take after, model after; emulate. Adj. imitated &c. v.; mock, mimic; modelled after, molded on. paraphrastic; literal; imitative; secondhand; imitable; aping, apish, mimicking.

Adv. literally, to the letter, verbatim, literatim[Lat], sic, totidem verbis[Lat], word for word, mot a mot[Fr]; exactly, precisely.
Phr. like master like man; "like - but oh! how different!" [Wordsworth]; "genius borrows nobly" [Emerson]; "pursuing echoes calling 'mong the rocks" [A. Coles]; "quotation confesses inferiority" [Emerson]; "Imitation is the sincerest form of flattery".
#20. Nonimitation. — N. no imitation; originality; creativeness. invention, creation.
Adj. unimitated[obs3], uncopied[obs3]; unmatched, unparalleled; inimitable &c. 13; unique, original; creative, inventive, untranslated; exceptional, rare, sui generis uncommon[Lat], unexampled.
#20a. Variation. — N. variation; alteration &c. (change) 140. modification, moods and tenses; discrepance[obs3], discrepancy. divergency &c. 291[obs3]; deviation &c. 279; aberration; innovation. V. vary &c. (change) 140; deviate &c. 279; diverge &c. 291; alternate, swerve. Adj. varied &c. v.; modified; diversified &c. 16a.

#21. [Result of imitation.] Copy. — N. copy, facsimile, counterpart, effigies, effigy, form, likeness.
image, picture, photo, xerox, similitude, semblance, ectype[obs3], photo offset, electrotype; imitation &c. 19; model, representation, adumbration, study; portrait &c. (representation) 554; resemblance.
duplicate, reproduction; cast, tracing; reflex, reflexion[Brit], reflection; shadow, echo.
transcript[copy into a non-visual form], transcription; recording, scan.
chip off the old block; reprint, new printing; rechauffe[Fr]; apograph[obs3], fair copy.
parody, caricature, burlesque, travesty, travestie[obs3], paraphrase.
[copy with some differences] derivative, derivation, modification, expansion, extension, revision; second edition &c. (repetition) 104.
servile copy, servile imitation; plagiarism, counterfeit, fake &c.(deception) 545; pasticcio[obs3].
Adj. faithful; lifelike &c. (similar) 17; close, conscientious.
unoriginal, imitative, derivative.
#22. [Thing copied.] Prototype. — N. prototype, original, model, pattern, precedent, standard, ideal, reference, scantling, type; archetype, antitype[obs3]; protoplast, module, exemplar, example, ensample[obs3], paradigm; lay-figure. text, copy, design; fugleman[obs3], keynote; die, mold; matrix, last, plasm[obs3]; proplasm[obs3], protoplasm; mint; seal, punch, intaglio, negative; stamp. V. be an example, be a role model, set an example; set a copy. Phr. a precedent embalms a principle [Disraeli]; exempla sunt odiosa[Lat].

<— p. 7 —>

% 4. GENERAL RELATION %

#23. Agreement. — N. agreement; accord, accordance; unison, harmony; concord &c. 714; concordance, concert; understanding, mutual understanding. conformity &c. 82; conformance; uniformity &c. 16; consonance, consentaneousness[obs3], consistency; congruity, congruence; keeping; congeniality; correspondence, parallelism, apposition, union. fitness, aptness &c. adj.; relevancy; pertinence, pertinencey[obs3]; sortancel; case in point; aptitude, coaptation[obs3], propriety, applicability, admissibility, commensurability, compatibility; cognation &c. (relation) 9. adaption[obs3], adjustment, graduation, accommodation; reconciliation, reconcilement; assimilation. consent &c. (assent) 488; concurrence &c. 178; cooperation &c. 709. right man in the right place, very thing; quite the thing, just the thing. V. be accordant &c. adj.; agree, accord, harmonize; correspond, tally, respond; meet, suit, fit, befit, do, adapt itself to; fall in with, chime in with, square with, quadrate with, consort with, comport with; dovetail, assimilate; fit like a glove, fit to a tittle, fit to a T; match &c. 17; become one; homologate[obs3]. consent &c. (assent) 488. render accordant &c. adj.; fit, suit, adapt, accommodate; graduate; adjust &c. (render, equal) 27; dress, regulate, readjust; accord, harmonize,. reconcile; fadge[obs3], dovetail, square. Adj. agreeing, suiting &c. v.; in accord, accordant, concordant, consonant, congruous, consentaneous[obs3], correspondent, congenial; coherent; becoming; harmonious reconcilable, conformable; in accordance with, in harmony with, in keeping with, in unison with, &c. n.; at one with, of one mind, of a piece[Fr]; consistent, compatible, proportionate; commensurate; on all fours. apt, apposite, pertinent, pat; to the point, to the purpose; happy, felicitous, germane, ad rem[Lat], in point, on point, directly on point, bearing upon, applicable, relevant, admissible. fit adapted, in loco, a propos[Fr], appropriate, seasonable, sortable, suitable, idoneous[obs3], deft; meet &c. (expedient) 646.

at home, in one's proper element.
Adv. a propos of[Fr]; pertinently &c. adj.
Phr. rem acu tetigisti[Lat][obs3]; if the shoe fits, wear it; the cap fits; auxilia humilia firma consensus facit [Lat][Syrus]; discers concordia [Lat][Ovid].
<— p. 8 —>

#24. Disagreement. — N. disagreement; discord, discordance; dissonance, dissidence, discrepancy; unconformity &c. 83; incongruity, incongruence[obs3]; discongruity[obs3], mesalliance; jarring &c. v.; dissension &c. 713; conflict &c. (opposition) 708; bickering, clashing, misunderstanding, wrangle. disparity, mismatch, disproportion; dissimilitude, inequality; disproportionateness &c. adj[obs3].; variance, divergence, repugnance. unfitness &c. adj.; inaptitude, impropriety; inapplicability &c. adj.; inconsistency, inconcinnity[obs3]; irrelevancy &c. (irrelation) 10[obs3]. misjoining[obs3], misjoinder[obs3]; syncretism[obs3], intrusion, interference; concordia discors[Lat]. fish out of water. V. disagree; clash, jar &c. (discord) 713; interfere, intrude, come amiss; not concern &c. 10; mismatch; humano capiti cervicem jungere equinam[Lat]. Adj. disagreeing &c. v.; discordant, discrepant; at variance, at war; hostile, antagonistic, repugnant, incompatible, irreconcilable, inconsistent with; unconformable, exceptional &c. 83; intrusive, incongruous; disproportionate, disproportionated[obs3]; inharmonious, unharmonious[obs3]; inconsonant, unconsonant[obs3]; divergent, repugnant to. inapt, unapt, inappropriate, improper; unsuited, unsuitable; inapplicable, not to the point; unfit, unfitting, unbefitting; unbecoming; ill-timed, unseasonable, mal a propos[Fr], inadmissible; inapposite &c. (irrelevant) 10. uncongenial; ill-assorted, ill-sorted; mismatched, misjoined[obs3], misplaced, misclassified; unaccommodating, irreducible, incommensurable, uncommensurable[obs3]; unsympathetic. out of character, out of keeping, out of proportion, out of joint, out of tune, out of place, out of season, out of its element; at odds with, at variance with. Adv. in defiance, in contempt, in spite of; discordantly &c. adj.; a tort et a travers[obs3]. Phr. asinus ad lyram[Lat].

% SECTION III. QUANTITY

1. SIMPLE QUANTITY %

#25. [Absolute quantity.] Quantity. — N. quantity, magnitude; size &c. (dimensions) 192; amplitude, magnitude, mass, amount, sum, quantum, measure, substance, strength, force.
[Science of quantity.] mathematics, mathesis[obs3].
[Logic.] category, general conception, universal predicament.

[Definite or finite quantity.] armful, handful, mouthful, spoonful, capful; stock, batch, lot, dose; yaffle[obs3].

V. quantify, measure, fix, estimate, determine, quantitate, enumerate.

Adj. quantitative, some, any, aught, more or less, a few.

Adv. to the tune of, all of, a full, the sum of, fully, exactly, precisely.

#26. [Relative quantity.] Degree. — N. degree, grade, extent, measure, amount, ratio, stint, standard, height, pitch; reach, amplitude, range, scope, caliber; gradation, shade; tenor, compass; sphere, station, rank, standing; rate, way, sort. point, mark, stage &c. (term) 71; intensity, strength &c. (greatness) 31. Adj. comparative; gradual, shading off; within the bounds &c. (limit) 233. Adv. by degrees, gradually, inasmuch, pro tanto[It]; however, howsoever; step by step, bit by bit, little by little, inch by inch, drop by drop; a little at a time, by inches, by slow degrees, by degrees, by little and little; in some degree, in some measure; to some extent; di grado in grado[Lat].

% 2. COMPARATIVE QUANTITY %

#27. [Sameness of quantity or degree.] Equality. — N. equality, parity, coextension[obs3], symmetry, balance, poise; evenness, monotony, level. equivalence; equipollence[obs3], equipoise, equilibrium, equiponderance[obs3]; par, quits, a wash; not a pin to choose; distinction without a difference, six of one and half a dozen of the other; tweedle dee and tweedle dum[Lat]; identity &c. 13; similarity &c. 17. equalization, equation; equilibration, co*ordination, adjustment, readjustment; drawn game, drawn battle; neck and neck race; tie, draw, standoff, dead heat. match, peer, compeer, equal, mate, fellow, brother; equivalent. V. be equal &c. adj.; equal, match, reach, keep pace with, run abreast; come to, amount to, come up to; be on a level with, lie on a level with; balance; cope with; come to the same thing. render equal &c. adj.; equalize level, dress, balance, equate, handicap, give points, spot points, handicap, trim, adjust, poise; fit, accommodate; adapt &c. (render accordant) 23; strike a balance; establish equality, restore equality, restore equilibrium; readjust; stretch on the bed of Procrustes. Adj. equal, even, level, monotonous, coequal, symmetrical, coordinate; on a par with, on a level with, on a footing with; up to the mark; equiparant[obs3]. equivalent, tantamount; indistinguishable; quits; homologous; synonymous &c. 522; resolvable into, convertible, much at one, as broad as long, neither more nor less.; much the same as, the same thing as, as good as; all one, all the same; equipollent, equiponderant[obs3], equiponderous[obs3], equibalanced[obs3]; equalized &c. v.; drawn; half and half; isochronal, isochronous isoperimetric[obs3], isoperimetrical[obs3]; isobath[Oceanography], isobathic[Oceanography]. Adv. equally &c. adj.; pari passu[Lat], ad eundum[Lat], caeteris paribus[Lat]; in equilibrio[Lat]; to all intents and purposes.

Phr. it comes to the same thing, it amounts to the same thing; what is sauce for the goose is sauce for the gander.

#28. [Difference of quantity or degree.] Inequality. — N. inequality; disparity, imparity; odds; difference &c. 15; unevenness; inclination of the balance, partiality, bias, weight; shortcoming; casting weight, make- weight; superiority &c. 33; inferiority &c. 34; inequation[obs3]. V. be unequal &c. adj.; countervail; have the advantage, give the advantage; turn the scale; kick the beam; topple, topple over; overmatch &c. 33; not come up to &c. 34. Adj. unequal, uneven, disparate, partial; unbalanced, overbalanced; top-heavy, lopsided, biased, skewed; disquiparant[obs3]. Adv. haud passibus aequis [Latin][Vergil].

<— p. 9 —>

#29. Mean. — N. mean, average; median, mode; balance, medium, mediocrity, generality; golden mean &c. (mid-course) 628; middle &c. 68; compromise &c. 774; middle course, middle state; neutrality.

mediocrity, least common denominator.

V. split the difference; take the average &c. n.; reduce to a mean &c. n.; strike a balance, pair off.

Adj. mean, intermediate; middle &c. 68; average; neutral.

mediocre, middle-class; commonplace &c. (unimportant) 643.

Adv. on an average, in the long run; taking one with another, taking all things together, taking it for all in all; communibus annis[Lat], in round numbers.

Phr. medium tenuere beati[Lat].

#30. Compensation. — N. compensation, equation; commutation; indemnification; compromise &c. 774 neutralization, nullification; counteraction &c. 179; reaction; measure for measure, retaliation &c. 718 equalization &c. 27;

robbing Peter to pay Paul. set-off, offset; make-weight, casting-weight; counterpoise, ballast; indemnity, equivalent, quid pro quo; bribe, hush money; amends &c. (atonement) 952; counterbalance, counterclaim; cross-debt, cross-demand. V. make compensation; compensate, compense[obs3]; indemnify; counteract, countervail, counterpoise; balance; outbalance[obs3], overbalance, counterbalance; set off; hedge, square, give and take; make up for, lee way; cover, fill up, neutralize, nullify; equalize &c. 27; make good; redeem &c. (atone) 952. Adj. compensating, compensatory; countervailing &c. v.; in the opposite scale; equivalent &c. (equal) 27. Adv. in return, in consideration; but, however, yet, still, notwithstanding; nevertheless, nathless[obs3], none the less; although, though; albeit, howbeit; mauger[obs3]; at all events, at any rate; be that as it may, for all that, even so, on the other, hand, at the same time, quoad minus[Lat], quand meme[Fr], however that may be; after all is said and done; taking one thing with another &c. (average) 29. Phr. "light is mingled with the gloom" [Whittier]; every dark cloud has a silver lining; primo avulso non deficit alter [Lat][obs3][Vergil]; saepe creat molles aspera spina rosas [Lat][Ovid].

% QUANTITY BY COMPARISON WITH A STANDARD %

#31. Greatness. — N. greatness &c. adj.; magnitude; size &c. (dimensions) 192; multitude &c. (number) 102; immensity; enormity; infinity &c. 105; might, strength, intensity, fullness; importance &c. 642. great quantity, quantity, deal, power, sight, pot, volume, world; mass, heap &c. (assemblage) 72; stock &c. (store) 636; peck, bushel, load, cargo; cartload[obs3], wagonload, shipload; flood, spring tide; abundance &c. (sufficiency) 639. principal part, chief part, main part, greater part, major part, best part, essential part; bulk, mass &c. (whole) 50. V. be great &c. adj.; run high, soar, tower, transcend; rise to a great height, carry to a great height; know no bounds; ascend, mount. enlarge &c. (increase) 35, (expand) 194. Adj. great; greater &c. 33; large, considerable, fair, above par; big, huge &c. (large in size) 192; Herculean, cyclopean; ample; abundant &c. (enough) 639 full, intense, strong, sound, passing, heavy, plenary, deep, high; signal, at its height, in the zenith. world-wide, widespread, far-famed, extensive; wholesale; many &c. 102. goodly, noble, precious, mighty; sad, grave, heavy, serious; far gone, arrant, downright; utter, uttermost; crass, gross, arch, profound, intense, consummate; rank, uninitiated, red-hot, desperate; glaring, flagrant, stark staring; thorough-paced, thoroughgoing; roaring, thumping; extraordinary.; important &c. 642; unsurpassed &c. (supreme) 33; complete &c. 52. august, grand, dignified, sublime, majestic &c. (repute) 873. vast, immense, enormous, extreme; inordinate, excessive, extravagant, exorbitant, outrageous, preposterous, unconscionable, swinging, monstrous, overgrown; towering, stupendous, prodigious, astonishing, incredible; marvelous &c. 870. unlimited &c. (infinite) 105; unapproachable, unutterable, indescribable, ineffable, unspeakable, inexpressible, beyond expression, fabulous. undiminished, unabated, unreduced[obs3], unrestricted. absolute, positive, stark, decided, unequivocal, essential, perfect, finished. remarkable, of mark, marked, pointed, veriest; noteworthy; renowned. Adv. truly &c. (truth) 494[in a positive degree]; decidedly, unequivocally, purely, absolutely, seriously, essentially, fundamentally, radically, downright, in all conscience; for the most part, in the main. [in a complete degree] entirely &c. (completely) 52; abundantly &c. (sufficiently) 639; widely, far and wide. [in a great or high degree] greatly &c. adj.; much, muckle[obs3], well, indeed, very, very much, a deal, no end of, most, not a little; pretty, pretty well; enough, in a great measure, richly; to a large extent, to a great extent, to a gigantic extent; on a large scale; so; never so, ever so; ever so dole; scrap, shred, tag, splinter, rag, much; by wholesale; mighty, power-fully; with a witness, ultra[Lat], in the extreme, extremely, exceedingly, intensely, exquisitely, acutely, indefinitely, immeasurably; beyond compare, beyond comparison, beyond measure, beyond all bounds; incalculably, infinitely. [in a supreme degree] preeminently, superlatively &c. (superiority) 33. [in a too great degree] immoderately, mon-strously, preposterously, inordinately, exorbitantly, excessively, enormously, out of all proportion, with a vengeance. [in a marked degree] particularly, remarkably, singularly, curiously, uncommonly, unusually, peculiarly, notably, signally, strikingly, pointedly, mainly, chiefly; famously, egregiously, prominently, glaringly, emphatically, <gr/kat exochin/>[Grl], strangely, wonderfully, amazingly, surprisingly, astonishingly, incredibly, marvelously, awfully, stupen-dously. [in an exceptional degree] peculiarly &c. (unconformity) 83. [in a violent degree] furiously &c. (violence) 173; severely, desperately, tremendously, extravagantly, confoundedly, deucedly, devilishly, with a vengeance; a outrance[obs3], a toute outrance[Fr][obs3]. [in a painful degree] painfully, sadly, grossly, sorely, bitterly, piteously, grievously, miserably, cruelly, woefully, lamentably, shockingly, frightfully, dreadfully, fearfully, terribly, horribly. Phr. a maximis ad minima[Lat]; "greatness knows itself" [Henry IV]; "mightiest powers by deepest calms are fed" [B. Cornwall]; minimum decet libere cui multum licet [Lat][Seneca]; "some are born great, some achieve greatness, and some have greatness thrust upon them" [Twelfth Night].

<— p. 10 —><— to a limited degree should be broken out to a section near to qualification 469 —>

#32. Smallness. — N. smallness &c. adj.; littleness &c. (small size) 193; tenuity; paucity; fewness &c (small number) 103; meanness, insignificance (unimportance) 643; mediocrity, moderation. small quantity, modicum, trace, hint, minimum; vanishing point; material point, atom, particle, molecule, corpuscle, point, speck, dot, mote, jot, iota, ace;

minutiae, details; look, thought, idea, soupcon, dab, dight[obs3], whit, tittle, shade, shadow; spark, scintilla, gleam; touch, cast; grain, scruple, granule, globule, minim, sup, sip, sop, spice, drop, droplet, sprinkling, dash, morceau[obs3], screed, smack, tinge, tincture; inch, patch, scantling, tatter, cantlet[obs3], flitter, gobbet[obs3], mite, bit, morsel, crumb, seed, fritter, shive[obs3]; snip, snippet; snick[obs3], snack, snatch, slip, scrag[obs3]; chip, chipping; shiver, sliver, driblet, clipping, paring, shaving, hair. nutshell; thimbleful, spoonful, handful, capful, mouthful; fragment; fraction &c. (part) 51; drop in the ocean. animalcule &c. 193. trifle &c. (unimportant thing) 643; mere nothing, next to nothing; hardly anything; just enough to swear by; the shadow of a shade. finiteness, finite quantity. V. be small &c. adj.; lie in a nutshell. diminish &c. (decrease) 36; (contract) 195. Adj. small, little; diminutive &c. (small in size) 193; minute; fine; inconsiderable, paltry &c. (unimportant) 643; faint &c. (weak) 160; slender, light, slight, scanty, scant, limited; meager &c. (insufficient) 640; sparing; few &c. 103; low, so-so, middling, tolerable, no great shakes; below par, under par, below the mark; at a low ebb; halfway; moderate, modest; tender, subtle. inappreciable, evanescent, infinitesimal, homeopathic, very small; atomic, corpuscular, microscopic, molecular, subatomic. mere, simple, sheer, stark, bare; near run. dull, petty, shallow, stolid, ungifted, unintelligent. Adv. to a small extent[in a small degree], on a small scale; a little bit, a wee bit; slightly &c. adj.; imperceptibly; miserably, wretchedly; insufficiently &c. 640; imperfectly; faintly &c. 160; passably, pretty well, well enough. [in a certain or limited degree] partially, in part; in a certain degree, to a certain degree; to a certain extent; comparatively; some, rather in some degree, in some measure; something, somewhat; simply, only, purely, merely; at least, at the least, at most, at the most; ever so little, as little as may be, tant soit peu[Fr], in ever so small a degree; thus far, pro tanto[It], within bounds, in a manner, after a fashion, so to speak. almost, nearly, well-nigh, short of, not quite, all but; near upon, close upon; peu s'en faut[Fr], near the mark; within an ace of, within an inch of; on the brink of; scarcely, hardly, barely, only just, no more than; about [in an uncertain degree], thereabouts, somewhere about, nearly, say; be the same, be little more or less; no ways [in no degree], no way, no wise; not at all, not in the least, not a bit, not a bit of it, not a whit, not a jot, not a shadow; in no wise, in no respect; by no means, by no manner of means; on no account, at no hand. Phr. dare pondus idonea fumo [Lat][Persius]; magno conatu magnas nugas [Lat][Terence]; "small sands the mountain, moments make the year" [Young].

<— p. 11 —> % QUANTITY BY COMPARISON WITH A SIMILAR OBJECT %

#33. Superiority. [Supremacy.] — N. superiority, majority; greatness &c. 31; advantage; pull; preponderance, preponderation; vantage ground, prevalence, partiality; personal superiority; nobility &c. (rank) 875; Triton among the minnows, primus inter pares[Lat], nulli secundus[Lat], captain; crackajack * [obs3][U. S.]. supremacy, preeminence; lead; maximum; record; <gr/trikumia/>[obs3], climax; culmination &c. (summit) 210; transcendence; ne plus ultra[Lat]; lion's share, Benjamin's mess; excess, surplus &c. (remainder) 40; (redundancy) 641. V. be superior &c. adj.; exceed, excel, transcend; outdo, outbalance[obs3], outweigh, outrank, outrival, out-Herod; pass, surpass, get ahead of; over-top, override, overpass, overbalance, overweigh, overmatch; top, o'ertop, cap, beat, cut out; beat hollow; outstrip &c. 303; eclipse, throw into the shade, take the shine out of, outshine, put one's nose out of joint; have the upper hand, have the whip hand of, have the advantage; turn the scale, kick the beam; play first fiddle &c. (importance) 642; preponderate, predominate, prevail; precede, take precedence, come first; come to a head, culminate; beat &c. all others, bear the palm; break the record; take the cake * [U. S.]. become larger, render larger &c. (increase) 35, (expand) 194. Adj. superior, greater, major, higher; exceeding &c. v.; great &c. 31; distinguished, ultra[Lat]; vaulting; more than a match for. supreme, greatest, utmost, paramount, preeminent, foremost, crowning; first-rate &c. (important) 642, (excellent) 648; unrivaled peerless, matchless; none such, second to none, sans pareil[Fr]; unparagoned[obs3], unparalleled, unequalled, unapproached[obs3], unsurpassed; superlative, inimitable facile princeps[Lat], incomparable, sovereign, without parallel, nulli secundus[Lat], ne plus ultra[Lat]; beyond compare, beyond comparison; culminating &c. (topmost) 210; transcendent, transcendental; plus royaliste que le Roi[Fr], more catholic than the Pope increased &c. (added to) 35; enlarged &c. (expanded) 194. Adv. beyond, more, over; over the mark, above the mark; above par; upwards of, in advance of; over and above; at the top of the scale, at its height. [in a superior or supreme degree] eminently, egregiously, preeminently, surpassing, prominently, superlatively, supremely, above all, of all things, the most, to crown all, <gr/kat exochin/gr>[Grl], par excellence, principally, especially, particularly, peculiarly, a fortiori, even, yea, still more.

Phr. "I shall not look upon his like again" [Hamlet]; deos fortioribus addesse [Lat][Tacitus].

<— p. 12 —>

#34. Inferiority. — N. inferiority, minority, subordinacy; shortcoming, deficiency; minimum; smallness &c. 32; imperfection; lower quality, lower worth. [personal inferiority] commonalty &c. 876. V. be inferior &c. adj.; fall short of, come short of; not pass, not come up to; want. become smaller, render smaller &c. (decrease) 36, (contract) 195; hide its diminished head, retire into the shade, yield the palm, play second fiddle, be upstaged, take a back seat. Adj. inferior, smaller; small &c. 32; minor, less, lesser, deficient, minus, lower, subordinate, secondary; second-rate &c. (imperfect) 651; sub, subaltern; thrown into the shade; weighed in the balance and found wanting; not fit to hold a candle to, can't hold a candle to. least, smallest &c. (see little, small &c. 193); lowest. diminished &c. (decreased) 36; reduced &c. (contracted) 195; unimportant &c. 643. Adv. less; under the mark, below the mark, below par; at the bottom of the scale, at a low ebb, at a disadvantage; short of, under.

% CHANGES IN QUANTITY %

#35. Increase. — N. increase, augmentation, enlargement, extension; dilatation &c. (expansion) 194; increment, accretion; accession &c. 37; development, growth; aggrandizement, aggravation; rise; ascent &c. 305; exaggeration, exacerbation; spread &c. (dispersion) 73; flood tide; gain, produce, product, profit. V. increase, augment, add to, enlarge; dilate &c. (expand) 194; grow, wax, get ahead, gain strength; advance; run up, shoot up; rise; ascend &c. 305; sprout &c. 194. aggrandize; raise, exalt; deepen, heighten; strengthen; intensify, enhance, magnify, redouble; aggravate, exaggerate; exasperate, exacerbate; add fuel to the flame, oleum addere camino[Lat], superadd &c. (add) 37[obs3]; spread &c. (disperse) 73. Adj. increased &c. v.; on the increase, undiminished; additional &c. (added) 37. Adv. crescendo. Phr. vires acquirit eundo [Lat][Vergil].

#36. Nonincrease, Decrease. — N. decrease, diminution; lessening &c. v.; subtraction &c. 38; reduction, abatement, declension; shrinking &c. (contraction.) 195; coarctationl; abridgment &c. (shortening) 201; extenuation. subsidence, wane, ebb, decline; ebbing; descent &c. 306; decrement, reflux, depreciation; deterioration &c. 659; anticlimax; mitigation &c. (moderation) 174. V. decrease, diminish, lessen; abridge &c. (shorten) 201; shrink &c. (contract) 195; drop off, fall off, tail off; fall away, waste, wear; wane, ebb, decline; descend &c. 306; subside; melt away, die away; retire into the shade, hide its diminished head, fall to a low ebb, run low, languish, decay, crumble. bate, abate, dequantitatel; discount; depreciate; extenuate, lower, weaken, attenuate, fritter away; mitigate &c. (moderate) 174; dwarf, throw into the shade; reduce &c. 195; shorten &c. 201; subtract &c. 38. Adj. unincreased &c. (see increase &c.35)[obs3]; decreased &c. v.; decreasing &c. v.; on the wane &c. n. Phr. "a gilded halo hovering round decay" [Byron]; "fine by degrees and beautifully less" [Prior].

<— p. 13 —> % 3. CONJUNCTIVE QUANTITY %

#37. Addition. — N. addition, annexation, adjection[obs3]; junction &c. 43; superposition, superaddition, superjunction[obs3], superfetation; accession, reinforcement; increase &c. 35; increment, supplement; accompaniment &c. 88; interposition &c. 228; insertion &c. 300. V. add, annex, affix, superadd[obs3], subjoin, superpose; clap on, saddle on; tack to, append, tag; ingraft[obs3]; saddle with; sprinkle; introduce &c. (interpose) 228; insert &c. 300. become added, accrue; advene[obs3], supervene. reinforce, reenforce, restrengthen[obs3]; swell the ranks of; augment &c. 35. Adj. added &c. v.; additional; supplemental, supplementary; suppletory[obs3], subjunctive; adjectitious[obs3], adscititious[obs3], ascititious[obs3]; additive, extra, accessory. Adv. au reste[Fr], in addition, more, plus, extra; and, also, likewise, too, furthermore, further, item; and also, and eke; else, besides, to boot, et cetera; &c.; and so on, and so forth; into the bargain, cum multis aliis[Lat], over and above, moreover. with, withal; including, inclusive, as well as, not to mention, let alone; together with, along with, coupled with, in conjunction with; conjointly; jointly &c. 43. Phr. adde parvum parvo magnus acervus erit[Lat].

#38. Nonaddition. Subtraction. — N. subtraction, subductionl!; deduction, retrenchment; removal, withdrawal; ablation, sublation[obs3]; abstraction &c. (taking) 789; garbling,, &c. v. mutilation, detruncation[obs3]; amputation; abscission, excision, recision; curtailment &c. 201; minuend, subtrahend; decrease &c. 36; abrasion. V. subduct, subtract; deduct, deduce; bate, retrench; remove, withdraw, take from, take away; detract. garble, mutilate, amputate, detruncate[obs3]; cut off, cut away, cut out; abscind[obs3], excise; pare, thin, prune, decimate; abrade, scrape, file; geld, castrate; eliminate. diminish &c. 36; curtail &c. (shorten) 201; deprive of &c. (take) 789; weaken. Adj. subtracted &c. v.; subtractive. Adv. in deduction &c. n.; less; short of; minus, without, except, except for, excepting, with the exception of, barring, save, exclusive of, save and except, with a reservation; not counting, if one doesn't count.

#39. [Thing added] Adjunct. — N. adjunct; addition, additament[obs3]; additum[Lat], affix, appelidage[obs3], annexe[obs3], annex; augment, augmentation; increment, reinforcement, supernumerary, accessory, item; garnish, sauce; accompaniment &c. 88; adjective, addendum; complement, supplement; continuation. rider, offshoot, episode, side issue, corollary; piece[Fr]; flap, lappet, skirt, embroidery, trappings, cortege; tail, suffix &c. (sequel) 65; wing. Adj. additional &c. 37. alate[obs3], alated[obs3]; winged. Adv. in addition &c. 37.

#40. [Thing remaining.] Remainder. — N. remainder, residue; remains, remanent, remnant, rest, relic; leavings, heeltap[obs3], odds and ends, cheesepairings[obs3], candle ends, orts[obs3]; residuum; dregs &c. (dirt) 653; refuse &c. (useless) 645; stubble, result, educt[obs3]; fag-end; ruins, wreck, skeleton., stump; alluvium. surplus, overplus[obs3], excess; balance, complement; superplus[obs3], surplusage[obs3]; superfluity &c.(redundancy) 641; survival, survivance[obs3]. V. remain; be left &c. adj.; exceed, survive; leave.

Adj. remaining, left; left behind left over; residual, residuary; over, odd; unconsumed, sedimentary; surviving; net; exceeding, over and above; outlying, outstanding; cast off &c. 782; superfluous &c. (redundant) 641.

#40a. [Thing deducted.] Decrement. — N. decrement, discount, defect, loss, deduction; afterglow; eduction[obs3]; waste.

<— p. 14 —>

#41. [Forming a whole without coherence.] Mixture. — N. mixture, admixture, commixture, commixtion[obs3]; commixion[obs3], intermixture, alloyage[obs3], matrimony; junction &c. 43; combination &c. 48; miscegenation. impregnation; infusion, diffusion suffusion, transfusion; infiltration; seasoning, sprinkling, interlarding; interpolation &c. 228 adulteration, sophistication. [Thing mixed] tinge, tincture, touch, dash, smack, sprinkling, spice, seasoning, infusion, soupcon. [Compound resulting from mixture] alloy, amalgam; brass, chowchow[obs3], pewter; magma, half-and-half, melange, tertium quid[Lat], miscellany, ambigul, medley, mess, hotchpot[obs3], pasticcio[obs3], patchwork, odds and ends, all sorts; jumble &c. (disorder) 59; salad, sauce, mash, omnium gatherum[Lat], gallimaufry, olla-podrida[obs3], olio, salmagundi, potpourri, Noah's ark, caldron texture, mingled yarn; mosaic &c. (variegation) 440.

half-blood, half-caste, mulatto; terceron[obs3], quarteron[obs3], quinteron &c.[obs3]; quadroon, octoroon; griffo[obs3], zambo[obs3]; cafuzo[obs3]; Eurasian; fustee[obs3], fustie[obs3]; griffe, ladino[obs3], marabou, mestee[obs3], mestizo, quintroon, sacatra zebrule[obs3][U. S.]; catalo[obs3]; cross, hybrid, mongrel.

V. mix; join &c. 43; combine &c. 48; commix, immix[obs3], intermix; mix up with, mingle; commingle, intermingle, bemingle[obs3]; shuffle &c. (derange) 61; pound together; hash up, stir up; knead, brew; impregnate with; interlard &c. (interpolate) 228; intertwine, interweave &c. 219; associate with; miscegenate[obs3]. be mixed &c.; get among, be entangled with. instill, imbue; infuse, suffuse, transfuse; infiltrate, dash, tinge, tincture, season, sprinkle, besprinkle, attemper[obs3], medicate, blend, cross; alloy, amalgamate, compound, adulterate, sophisticate, infect.

Adj. mixed &c. v.; implex[obs3], composite, half-and-half, linsey- woolsey, chowchow, hybrid, mongrel, heterogeneous; motley &c. (variegated) 440; miscellaneous, promiscuous, indiscriminate; miscible. Adv. among, amongst, amid, amidst; with; in the midst of, in the crowd.

#42. [Freedom from mixture.] Simpleness. — N. simpleness &c. adj.;
purity, homogeneity.
    elimination; sifting &c. v.; purification &c. (cleanness) 652.
    V. render simple &c. adj.; simplify.
    sift, winnow, bolt, eliminate; exclude, get rid of; clear; purify &c.
(clean) 652; disentangle &c. (disjoin) 44.
    Adj. simple, uniform, of a piece[Fr], homogeneous, single, pure,
sheer, neat.
    unmixed, unmingled[obs3], unblended, uncombined, uncompounded;
elementary, undecomposed; unadulterated, unsophisticated, unalloyed,
untinged[obs3], unfortified, pur et simple[Fr]; incomplex[obs3].
    free from, exempt from; exclusive.
    Adv. simple &c. adj. only.
#43. Junction. — N. junction; joining &c. v.; joinder[Law], union connection, conjunction, conjugation; annexion[obs3], annexation, annexment[obs3]; astriction[obs3], attachment, compagination[obs3], vincture[obs3], ligation, alligation[obs3]; accouplement[obs3]; marriage &c. (wedlock,) 903; infibulation[obs3], inosculation[obs3], symphysis[Anat], anastomosis, confluence, communication, concatenation; meeting, reunion; assemblage &c. 72. coition, copulation; sex, sexual congress, sexual conjunction, sexual intercourse, love-making. joint, joining, juncture, pivot, hinge, articulation, commissure[obs3], seam, gore, gusset, suture, stitch; link &c. 45; miter mortise. closeness,

tightness, &c. adj.; coherence &c. 46; combination &c. 48. annexationist. V. join, unite; conjoin, connect; associate; put together, lay together, clap together, hang together, lump together, hold together, piece together[Fr], tack together, fix together, bind up together together; embody, reembody[obs3]; roll into one. attach, fix, affix, saddle on, fasten, bind, secure, clinch, twist, make fast &c. adj.; tie, pinion, string, strap, sew, lace, tat, stitch, tack, knit, button, buckle, hitch, lash, truss, bandage, braid, splice, swathe, gird, tether, moor, picket, harness, chain; fetter &c. (restrain) 751; lock, latch, belay, brace, hook, grapple, leash, couple, accouple[obs3], link, yoke, bracket; marry &c. (wed) 903; bridge over, span. braze; pin, nail, bolt, hasp, clasp, clamp, crimp, screw, rivet; impact, solder, set; weld together, fuse together; wedge, rabbet, mortise, miter, jam, dovetail, enchase[obs3]; graft, ingraft[obs3], inosculate[obs3]; entwine, intwine[obs3]; interlink, interlace, intertwine, intertwist[obs3], interweave; entangle; twine round, belay; tighten; trice up, screw up. be joined &c.; hang together, hold together; cohere &c. 46. Adj. joined &c. v.; joint; conjoint, conjunct; corporate, compact; hand in hand. firm, fast, close, tight, taut, taught, secure, set, intervolved l; inseparable, indissoluble, insecable[obs3], severable. Adv. jointly &c. adj.; in conjunction with &c. (in addition to) 37; fast, firmly, &c. adj.; intimately. Phr. tria juncta in uno[Lat].

<— p. 15 —>

#44. Disjunction. — N. disjunction, disconnection, disunity, disunion, disassociation, disengagement; discontinuity &c. 70; abjunction[obs3]; cataclasm[obs3]; inconnection[obs3]; abstraction, abstractedness; isolation; insularity, insulation; oasis; island; separateness &c. adj.; severalty; disjecta membra[Lat]; dispersion &c. 73; apportionment &c. 786. separation; parting &c. v.; circumcision; detachment, segregation; divorce, sejunction l, seposition l, diduction[obs3], diremption[obs3], discerption[obs3]; elision; caesura, break, fracture, division, subdivision, rupture; compartition l; dismemberment, dislocation; luxation[obs3]; severance, disseverance; scission; rescission, abscission; laceration, dilaceration[obs3]; disruption, abruption[obs3]; avulsion[obs3], divulsion[obs3]; section, resection, cleavage; fission; partibility[obs3], separability.

fissure, breach, rent, split, rift, crack, slit, incision. dissection anatomy; decomposition &c. 49; cutting instrument &c (sharpness) 253; buzzsaw, circular saw, rip saw. separatist. V. be disjoined &c.; come off, fall off, come to pieces, fall to pieces; peel off; get loose. disjoin, disconnect, disengage, disunite, dissociate, dispair[obs3]; divorce, part, dispart[obs3], detach, separate, cut off, rescind, segregate; set apart, keep apart; insulate,, isolate; throw out of gear; cut adrift; loose; unloose, undo, unbind, unchain, unlock &c. (fix) 43, unpack, unravel; disentangle; set free &c. (liberate) 750. sunder, divide, subdivide, sever, dissever, abscind[obs3]; circumcise; cut; incidel, incise; saw, snip, nib, nip, cleave, rive, rend, slit, split, splinter, chip, crack, snap, break, tear, burst; rend &c. rend asunder, rend in twain; wrench, rupture, shatter, shiver, cranch[obs3], crunch, craunch[obs3], chop; cut up, rip up; hack, hew, slash; whittle; haggle, hackle, discindl, lacerate, scamble[obs3], mangle, gash, hash, slice. cut up, carve, dissect, anatomize; dislimb[obs3]; take to pieces, pull to pieces, pick to pieces, tear to pieces; tear to tatters, tear piecemeal, tear limb from limb; divellicate[obs3]; skin &c. 226; disintegrate, dismember, disbranch[obs3], disband; disperse &c. 73; dislocate, disjoint; break up; mince; comminute &c. (pulverize) 330; apportion &c. 786. part, part company; separate, leave. Adj. disjoined &c. v.; discontinuous &c. 70; multipartite[obs3], abstract; disjunctive; secant; isolated &c. v.; insular, separate, disparate, discrete, apart, asunder, far between, loose, free; unattached, unannexed, unassociated, unconnected; distinct; adrift; straggling; rift, reft[obs3]. [capable of being cut] scissile[Chem], divisible, discerptible[obs3], partible, separable. Adv. separately &c. adj.; one by one, severally, apart; adrift, asunder, in twain; in the abstract, abstractedly.

#45. [Connecting medium.] Connection. — N. vinculum, link; connective, connection; junction &c. 43; bond of union, copula, hyphen, intermedium[obs3]; bracket; bridge, stepping-stone, isthmus. bond, tendon, tendril; fiber; cord, cordage; riband, ribbon, rope, guy, cable, line, halserl, hawser, painter, moorings, wire, chain; string &c. (filament) 205. fastener, fastening, tie; ligament, ligature; strap; tackle, rigging; standing rigging, running rigging; traces, harness; yoke; band ribband, bandage; brace, roller, fillet; inkle[obs3]; with, withe, withy; thong, braid; girder, tiebeam; girth, girdle, cestus[obs3], garter, halter, noose, lasso, surcingle, knot, running knot; cabestro [obs3][U. S.], cinch [U. S.], lariat, legadero[obs3], oxreim[obs3]; suspenders.

<— p. 16 —>

pin, corking pin, nail, brad, tack, skewer, staple, corrugated fastener; clamp, U-clamp, C-clamp; cramp, cramp iron; ratchet, detent, larigo[obs3], pawl; terret[obs3], treenail, screw, button, buckle; clasp, hasp, hinge, hank, catch, latch, bolt, latchet[obs3], tag; tooth; hook, hook and eye; lock, holdfast[obs3], padlock, rivet; anchor, grappling iron, trennel[obs3], stake, post. cement, glue, gum, paste, size, wafer, solder, lute, putty, birdlime, mortar, stucco, plaster, grout; viscum[obs3]. shackle, rein &c. (means of restraint) 752; prop &c. (support) 215. V. bridge over, span; connect

&c. 43; hang &c. 214.

#46. Coherence. — N. coherence, adherence, adhesion, adhesiveness; concretion, accretion; conglutination, agglutination, agglomeration; aggregation; consolidation, set, cementation; sticking, soldering &c. v.; connection; dependence. tenacity, toughness; stickiness &c. 352; inseparability, inseparableness; bur, remora. conglomerate, concrete &c. (density) 321. V. cohere, adhere, stick, cling, cleave, hold, take hold of, hold fast, close with, clasp, hug; grow together, hang together; twine round &c. (join) 43. stick like a leech, stick like wax; stick close; cling like ivy, cling like a bur; adhere like a remora, adhere like Dejanira's shirt. glue; agglutinate, conglutinate[obs3]; cement, lute, paste, gum; solder, weld; cake, consolidate &c. (solidify) 321; agglomerate. Adj. cohesive, adhesive, adhering, cohering &c. v.; tenacious, tough; sticky &c. 352. united, unseparated, unsessile[obs3], inseparable, inextricable, infrangible[obs3]; compact &c. (dense) 321.

#47. [Want of adhesion, nonadhesion, immiscibility.] Incoherence. — N. nonadhesion[obs3]; immiscibility; incoherence; looseness &c. adj.; laxity; relaxation; loosening &c. v.; freedom; disjunction &c. 44; rope of sand. V. make loose &c. adj.; loosen, slacken, relax; unglue &c. 46; detach &c. (disjoin) 44. Adj. nonadhesive, immiscible; incoherent, detached, loose, baggy, slack, lax, relaxed, flapping, streaming; disheveled; segregated, like grains of sand unconsolidated &c. 231, uncombined &c. 48; noncohesive[obs3].

#48. Combination. — N. combination; mixture &c. 41; junction &c. 43; union, unification, synthesis, incorporation, amalgamation, embodiment, coalescence, crasis[obs3], fusion, blending, absorption, centralization. alloy, compound, amalgam, composition, tertium quid[Lat]; resultant, impregnation. V. combine, unite, incorporate, amalgamate, embody, absorb, reembody[obs3], blend, merge, fuse, melt into one, consolidate, coalesce, centralize, impregnate; put together, lump together; cement a union, marry. Adj. combined &c. v.; impregnated with, ingrained; imbued inoculated.

#49. Decomposition. — N. decomposition, analysis, dissection, resolution, catalysis, dissolution; corruption &c. (uncleanness) 653; dispersion &c. 73; disjunction &c. 44; disintegration. V. decompose, decompound; analyze, disembody, dissolve; resolve into its elements, separate into its elements; electrolyze[Chem]; dissect, decentralize, break up; disperse &c. 73; unravel &c. (unroll) 313; crumble into dust. Adj. decomposed &c. v.; catalytic, analytical; resolvent, separative, solvent.

<— p. 17 —> % 4. CONCRETE QUANTITY %

#50. Whole. [Principal part.] — N. whole, totality, integrity; totalness &c. adj[obs3].; entirety, ensemble, collectiveness[obs3]; unity &c. 87; completeness &c. 52; indivisibility, indiscerptibility[obs3]; integration, embodiment; integer. all, the whole, total, aggregate, one and all, gross amount, sum, sum total, tout ensemble, length and breadth of, Alpha and Omega, "be all and end all"; complex, complexus [obs3]; lock stock and barrel. bulk, mass, lump, tissue, staple, body, compages[obs3]; trunk, torso, bole, hull, hulk, skeleton greater part, major part, best part, principal part, main part; essential part &c. (importance). 642; lion's share, Benjamin's mess; the long and the short; nearly, all, almost all. V. form a whole, constitute a whole; integrate, embody, amass; aggregate &c. (assemble) 72; amount to, come to. Adj. whole, total, integral, entire; complete &c. 52; one, individual. unbroken, intact, uncut, undivided, unsevered[obs3], unclipped[obs3], uncropped, unshorn; seamless; undiminished; undemolished, undissolved, undestroyed, unbruised. indivisible, indissoluble, indissolvable[obs3], indiscerptible[obs3]. wholesale, sweeping; comprehensive. Adv. wholly, altogether; totally &c. (completely) 52; entirely, all, all in all, as a whole, wholesale, in a body, collectively, all put together; in the aggregate, in the lump, in the mass, in the gross, in the main, in the long run; en masse, as a body, on the whole, bodily!!, en bloc, in extenso[Lat], throughout, every inch; substantially. Phr. tout bien ou rien[Fr].

#51. Part. — N. part, portion; dose; item, particular; aught, any; division, ward; subdivision, section; chapter, clause, count, paragraph, verse; article, passage; sector, segment; fraction, fragment; cantle, frustum; detachment, parcel. piece[Fr], lump, bit cut, cutting; chip, chunk, collop[obs3], slice, scale; lamina &c. 204; small part; morsel, particle &c. (smallness) 32; installment, dividend; share &c. (allotment) 786. debris, odds and ends, oddments, detritus; excerpta[obs3]; member, limb, lobe, lobule, arm, wing, scion, branch, bough, joint, link, offshoot, ramification, twig, bush, spray, sprig; runner; leaf, leaflet; stump; component part &c. 56; sarmentum[obs3]. compartment; department &c. (class) 75; county &c. (region) 181. V. part, divide, break &c. (disjoin) 44; partition &c. (apportion) 786. Adj. fractional, fragmentary; sectional, aliquot; divided &c. v.; in compartments, multifid[obs3]; disconnected; partial. Adv. partly, in part, partially; piecemeal, part by part; by installments, by snatches, by inches, by driblets; bit by bit, inch by inch, foot by foot, drop by drop; in detail, in lots.

#52. Completeness. — N. completeness &c. adj.; completion &c. 729; integration; allness[obs3]. entirety; perfection &c. 650; solidity, solidarity; unity; all; ne plus ultra[Lat], ideal, limit. complement, supplement, make-weight; filling, up &c. v. impletion[obs3]; saturation, saturityl; high water; high tide, flood tide, spring tide; fill, load, bumper, bellyful[obs3]; brimmer[obs3]; sufficiency &c. 639. V. be complete &c. adj.; come to a head. render complete &c. adj.; complete &c. (accomplish) 729; fill, charge, load, replenish; make up, make good; piece out[Fr], eke out; supply deficiencies; fill up, fill in, fill to the brim, fill the measure of; saturate. go the whole hog, go the whole length; go all lengths. Adj. complete, entire; whole &c. 50; perfect &c. 650; full, good, absolute, thorough, plenary; solid, undivided; with all its parts; all- sided. exhaustive, radical, sweeping, thorough-going; dead. regular, consummate, unmitigated, sheer, unqualified, unconditional, free; abundant &c. (sufficient) 639. brimming; brimful, topful, topfull; chock full, choke full; as full as an egg is of meat, as full as a vetch; saturated, crammed; replete &c. (redundant) 641; fraught, laden; full-laden, full-fraught, full-charged; heavy laden. completing &c. v.; supplemental, supplementary; ascititious[obs3]. Adv. completely &c. adj.; altogether, outright, wholly, totally, in toto, quite; all out; over head and ears; effectually, for good and all, nicely, fully, through thick and thin, head and shoulders; neck and heel, neck and crop; in all respects, in every respect; at all points, out and out, to all intents and purposes; toto coelo[Lat]; utterly; clean, clean as a whistle; to the full, to the utmost, to the backbone; hollow, stark; heart and soul, root and branch, down to the ground. to the top of one's bent, as far as possible, a outrance[obs3]. throughout; from first to last, from beginning to end, from end to end, from one end to the other, from Dan to Beersheba, from head to foot, from top to toe, from top to bottom, de fond en comble[Fr]; a fond, a capite ad calcem [Lat], ab ovo usque ad mala[Lat], fore and aft; every, whit, every inch; cap-a-pie, to the end of the chapter; up to the brim, up to the ears, up to the eyes; as . . . as can be. on all accounts; sous tous les rapports[Fr]; with a vengeance, with a witness. Phr. falsus in uno falsus in omnibus [Latin: false in one thing, false in everything]; omnem movere lapidem[Lat]; una scopa nuova spazza bene [Italian].

#53. Incompleteness. — N. incompleteness &c. adj.; deficiency, short measure; shortcoming &c. 304; insufficiency &c. 640; imperfection &c. 651; immaturity &c. (nonpreparation) 674; half measures.

[part wanting] defect, deficit, defalcation, omission; caret; shortage; interval &c. 198; break &c. (discontinuity) 70; noncompletion &c. 730; missing link.

missing piece, missing part, gap, hole, lacuna.

V. be incomplete &c. adj.; fall short of &c. 304; lack &c. (be insufficient) 640; neglect &c. 460.

Adj. incomplete; imperfect &c. 651; unfinished; uncompleted &c. (see complete &c. 729); defective, deficient, wanting, lacking, failing; in default, in arrear[obs3]; short of; hollow, meager, lame, halfand-half, perfunctory, sketchy; crude &c. (unprepared) 674.

mutilated, garbled, docked, lopped, truncated.

in progress, in hand; going on, proceeding.

Adv. incompletely &c. adj.; by halves.

Phr. caetera desunt[Lat]; caret.

<— p. 18 —>

#54. Composition. — N. composition, constitution, crasis[obs3]; combination &c. 48; inclusion, admission, compre- hension, reception; embodiment; formation. V. be composed of, be made of, be formed of, be made up of; consist of, be resolved into. include &c. (in a class) 76; contain, hold, comprehend, take in, admit, embrace, embody; involve, implicate; drag into. compose, constitute, form, make; make up, fill up, build up; enter into the composition of &c. (be a component) 56. Adj. containing, constituting &c.v.

#55. Exclusion. — N. exclusion, nonadmission, omission, exception, rejection, repudiation; exile &c. (seclusion) 893; noninclusion[obs3], preclusion, prohibition. separation, segregation, seposition[obs3], elimination, expulsion; cofferdam. V. be excluded from &c. exclude, bar; leave out, shut out, bar out; reject, repudiate, blackball; lay apart, put apart, set apart, lay aside, put aside; relegate, segregate; throw overboard; strike off, strike out; neglect &c. 460; banish &c. (seclude) 893; separate.&c. (disjoin) 44. pass over, omit; garble; eliminate, weed, winnow. Adj. excluding &c. v.; exclusive, excluded &c. v.; unrecounted[obs3], not included in; inadmissible. Adv. exclusive of, barring; except; with the exception of; save; bating.

#56. Component. — N. component; component part, integral part, integrant part[obs3]; element, constituent, ingredient, leaven; part and parcel; contents; appurtenance; feature; member &c. (part) 51; personnel. V. enter into, enter into the composition of; be a component &c. n; be part of, form part of &c. 51; merge in, be merged in; be implicated in; share in &c. (participate) 778; belong to, appertain to; combine, inhere in, unite. form, make, constitute, compose. Adj. forming &c. v. inclusive.

#57. Extraneousness. — N. extraneousness &c. adj.; extrinsicality &c. 6[obs3]; exteriority &c. 220[obs3]; alienage[obs3], alienism; foreign body, foreign substance, foreign element; alien, stranger, intruder, interloper, foreigner, novus homo[Lat], newcomer, immigrant, emigrant; creole, Africander[obs3]; outsider; Dago*, wop, mick, polak, greaser, slant, Easterner [U.S.], Dutchman, tenderfoot. Adj. extraneous, foreign, alien, ulterior; tramontane, ultramontane. excluded &c. 55; inadmissible; exceptional. Adv. in foreign parts, in foreign lands; abroad, beyond seas; over sea on one's travels.

<— p. 19 —> % SECTION IV. ORDER

1. ORDER %

#58. Order. — N. order, regularity, uniformity, symmetry, lucidus ordo[Lat]; music of the spheres. gradation, progression; series &c. (continuity) 69. subordination; course, even tenor, routine; method, disposition, arrangement, array, system, economy, discipline orderliness &c. adj. rank, place &c. (term) 71. V. be in order, become in order &c. adj.; form, fall in, draw up; arrange itself, range itself, place itself; fall into one's place, take one's place, take one's rank; rally round. adjust, methodize, regulate, systematize. Adj. orderly, regular; in order, in trim, in apple-pie order, in its proper place; neat, tidy, en regle[Fr], well regulated, correct, methodical, uniform, symmetrical, shipshape, business-like, systematic; unconfused &c. (see confuse &c. 61); arranged &c. 60. Adv. in order; methodically &c. adj.; in -turn, - its turn; step by step; by regular -steps, -gradations, -stages, -intervals; seriatim, systematically, by clockwork, gradatim[Lat]; at stated periods &c. (periodically) 138. Phr. natura non facit saltum[Lat]; "order is heaven's first law" [Pope]; "order from disorder sprung" [Paradise Lost]; ordo est parium dispariumque rerum sua loca tribuens dispositio [Lat][St. Augustine].

<— here we should break up 59 into disorder (randomness), and complexity. These are two different concepts. Note that simplicity, (entry 849) refers to affections or appearance, not internal complexity. We also need a corresponding entry for conceptual or organizational simplicity. —>

#59. [Absence, or want of Order, &c.] Disorder. — N. disorder; derangement &c. 61; irregularity; anomaly &c. (unconformity) 83; anarchy, anarchism; want of method; untidiness &c. adj.; disunion; discord &c. 24. confusion; confusedness &c. adj.; mishmash, mix; disarray, jumble, huddle, litter, lumber; cahotage[obs3]; farrago; mess, mash, muddle, muss [U. S.], hash, hodgepodge; hotch-potch[obs3], hotch-pot[obs3]; imbroglio, chaos, omnium gatherum[Lat], medley; mere mixture &c. 41; fortuitous concourse of atoms, disjecta membra[Lat], rudis indigestaque moles [Lat][Ovid]. complexity &c. 59a. turmoil; ferment &c. (agitation) 315; to-do, trouble, pudder[obs3], pother, row, rumble, disturbance, hubbub, convulsion, tumult, uproar, revolution, riot, rumpus, stour[obs3], scramble, brawl, fracas, rhubarb [baseball], fight, free-for-all, row, ruction, rumpus, embroilment, melee, spill and pelt, rough and tumble; whirlwind &c. 349; bear garden, Babel, Saturnalia, donnybrook, Donnybrook Fair, confusion worse confounded, most admired disorder, concordia discors[Lat]; Bedlam, all hell broke loose; bull in a china shop; all the fat in the fire, diable a' quatre[Fr], Devil to pay; pretty kettle of fish; pretty piece of work[Fr], pretty piece of business[Fr]. [legal terms] disorderly person; disorderly persons offence; misdemeanor. [moral disorder] slattern, slut (libertine) 962. V. be disorderly &c. adj.; ferment, play at cross-purposes. put out of order; derange &c. 61; ravel &c. 219; ruffle, rumple. Adj. disorderly, orderless; out of order, out of place, out of gear; irregular, desultory; anomalous &c. (unconformable) 83; acephalous[obs3], deranged; aimless; disorganized; straggling; unmethodical, immethodical[obs3]; unsymmetric[obs3], unsystematic; untidy, slovenly; dislocated; out of sorts; promiscuous, indiscriminate; chaotic, anarchical; unarranged &c. (see arrange &c. 60)[obs3]; confused; deranged &c. 61; topsy-turvy &c. (inverted) 218; shapeless &c. 241; disjointed, out of joint. troublous[obs3]; riotous &c. (violent) 173. complex &c. 59a. Adv. irregularly &c. adj.; by fits, by fits and snatches, by fits and starts; pellmell; higgledy-piggledy; helter-skelter, harum-scarum; in a ferment; at sixes and sevens, at cross-purposes; upside down &c. 218. Phr. the cart before the horse; <gr/hysteron proteron/gr>[Grk][Grk]; chaos is come again; "the wreck of matter and the crush of worlds" [Addison].

#59a. Complexity — N. complexity; complexness &c. adj.; complexus[obs3]; complication, implication; intricacy, intrication[obs3]; perplexity; network, labyrinth; wilderness, jungle; involution, raveling, entanglement; coil &c. (convolution) 248; sleave[obs3], tangled skein, knot, Gordian knot, wheels within wheels; kink, gnarl, knarl[obs3];

16

webwork[obs3]. [complexity if a task or action] difficulty &c. 704. V. complexify[obs3], complicate. Adj. gnarled, knarled[obs3]. complex, complexed; intricate, complicated, perplexed, involved, raveled, entangled, knotted, tangled, inextricable; irreducible.

<— p. 20 —>

#60. [Reduction to Order.] Arrangement. — N. arrangement; plan &c. 626; preparation &c. 673; disposal, disposition; collocation, allocation; distribution; sorting &c. v.; assortment, allotment, apportionment, taxis, taxonomy, syntaxis[obs3], graduation, organization; grouping; tabulation. analysis, classification, clustering, division, digestion. [Result of arrangement] digest; synopsis &c. (compendium) 596; syntagma[Gram], table, atlas; file, database; register &c. (record) 551; organism, architecture. [Instrument for sorting] sieve, riddle, screen, sorter. V. reduce to order, bring into order; introduce order into; rally. arrange, dispose, place, form; put in order, set in order, place in order; set out, collocate, pack, marshal, range, size, rank, group, parcel out, allot, distribute, deal; cast the parts, assign the parts; dispose of, assign places to; assort, sort; sift, riddle; put to rights, set to rights, put into shape, put in trim, put in array; apportion. class, classify; divide; file, string together, thread; register &c. (record) 551; catalogue, tabulate, index, graduate, digest, grade. methodize, regulate, systematize, coordinate, organize, settle, fix. unravel, disentangle, ravel, card; disembroil[obs3]; feaze[obs3]. Adj. arranged &c. v.; embattled, in battle array; cut and dried; methodical, orderly, regular, systematic. Phr. "In vast cumbrous array" [Churchill].

#61. [Subversion of Order; bringing into disorder.] Derangement. — N. derangement &c. v.; disorder &c. 59; evection[obs3], discomposure, disturbance; disorganization, deorganization[obs3]; dislocation; perturbation, interruption; shuffling &c. v.; inversion &c. 218; corrugation &c. (fold) 258; involvement. interchange &c. 148. V. derange; disarrange, misarrange[obs3]; displace, misplace; mislay, discompose, disorder; deorganize[obs3], discombobulate, disorganize; embroil, unsettle, disturb, confuse, trouble, perturb, jumble, tumble; shuffle, randomize; huddle, muddle, toss, hustle, fumble, riot; bring into disorder, put into disorder, throw into disorder &c. 59; muss [U.S.]; break the ranks, disconcert, convulse; break in upon. unhinge, dislocate, put out of joint, throw out of gear. turn topsy-turvy &c. (invert) 218; bedevil; complicate, involve, perplex, confound; imbrangle[obs3], embrangle[obs3], tangle, entangle, ravel, tousle, towzle[obs3], dishevel, ruffle; rumple &c. (fold) 258. litter, scatter; mix &c. 41. rearrange &c. 148. Adj. deranged &c. v.; syncretic, syncretistic[obs3]; mussy, messy; flaky; random, unordered [U.S.].

% 2. CONSECUTIVE ORDER %

#62. Precedence. — N. precedence; coming before &c. v.; the lead, le pas; superiority &c. 33; importance &c. 642; antecedence, antecedency[obs3]; anteriority &c. (front) 234[obs3]; precursor &c. 64; priority &c. 116; precession &c. 280; anteposition[obs3]; epacme[obs3]; preference. V. precede; come before, come first; head, lead, take the lead; lead the way, lead the dance; be in the vanguard; introduce, usher in; have the pas; set the fashion &c. (influence) 175; open the ball; take precedence, have precedence; have the start &c. (get before) 280. place before; prefix; premise, prelude, preface. Adj. preceding &c. v.; precedent, antecedent; anterior; prior &c. 116; before; former; foregoing; beforementioned[obs3], abovementioned[obs3], aforementioned; aforesaid, said; precursory, precursive[obs3]; prevenient[obs3], preliminary, prefatory, introductory; prelusive, prelusory; proemial[obs3], preparatory. Adv. before; in advance &c. (precession) 280. Phr. seniores priores[Lat]; prior tempore prior jure[Lat].

#63. Sequence. — N. sequence, coming after; going after &c. (following) 281; consecution, succession; posteriority &c. 117.
continuation; order of succession; successiveness; paracme[obs3].
secondariness[obs3]; subordinancy &c. (inferiority) 34[obs3].
afterbirth, afterburden[obs3]; placenta, secundines[Med].
V. succeed; come after, come on, come next; follow, ensue, step into the shoes of; alternate.
place after, suffix, append.
Adj. succeeding &c.v.; sequent[obs3]; subsequent, consequent, sequacious[obs3], proximate, next; consecutive &c. (continuity) 69; alternate, amoebean[obs3].
latter; posterior &c. 117.
Adv. after, subsequently; behind &c. (rear) 235.

<— p. 21 —>

#64. Precursor. — N. precursor, antecedent, precedent, predecessor; forerunner, vancourier[obs3], avant-coureur[Fr], pioneer, prodromel, prodromos[obs3], prodromus[obs3], outrider; leader, bellwether; herald, harbinger; foreboding; dawn; avant-courier, avant-garde, bellmare[obs3], forelooper[obs3], foreloper[obs3], stalking-horse, voorlooper[Afrikaans], voortrekker[Afrikaans]. prelude, preamble, preface, prologue, foreword, avant-propos[Fr], protasis[obs3], proemium[obs3], prolusion[obs3], proem, prolepsis[Gram], prolegomena, prefix, introduction; heading, frontispiece, groundwork; preparation &c. 673; overture, exordium[Lat], symphony; premises. prefigurement &c. 511; omen &c. 512. Adj. precursory; prelusive, prelusory, preludious[obs3]; proemial[obs3], introductory, prefatory, prodromous[obs3], inaugural, preliminary; precedent &c. (prior) 116. Phr. "a precedent embalms a principle" [Disraeli].

#65. Sequel. — N. sequel, suffix, successor; tail, queue, train, wake, trail, rear; retinue, suite; appendix, postscript; epilogue; peroration; codicil; continuation, sequela[obs3]; appendage; tail piece[Fr], heelpiece[obs3]; tag, more last words; colophon. aftercome[obs3], aftergrowth[obs3], afterpart[obs3], afterpiece[obs3], aftercourse[obs3], afterthought, aftergame[obs3]; arriere pensee[Fr], second thoughts; outgrowth.

#66. Beginning.— N. beginning, commencement, opening, outset, incipience, inception, inchoation[obs3]; introduction &c. (precursor) 64; alpha, initial; inauguration, debut, le premier pas, embarcation[Fr], rising of the curtain; maiden speech; outbreak, onset, brunt; initiative, move, first move; narrow end of the wedge, thin end of the wedge; fresh start, new departure. origin &c. (cause) 153; source, rise; bud, germ &c. 153; egg, rudiment; genesis, primogenesis[obs3], birth, nativity, cradle, infancy; start, inception, creation, starting point &c. 293; dawn &c. (morning) 125; evolution. title-page; head, heading; van &c. (front) 234; caption, fatihah[obs3]. entrance, entry; inlet, orifice, mouth, chops, lips, porch, portal, portico, propylon[obs3], door; gate, gateway; postern, wicket, threshold, vestibule; propylaeum[obs3]; skirts, border &c. (edge) 231. first stage, first blush, first glance, first impression, first sight. rudiments, elements, outlines, grammar, alphabet, ABCE. V. begin, start, commence; conceive, open, dawn, set in, take its rise, enter upon, enter; set out &c. (depart) 293; embark in; incept[obs3]. [transitive] initiate, launch, inaugurate. [intransitive] inchoate, rise, arise, originate. usher in; lead off, lead the way; take the lead, take the initiative; head; stand at the head, stand first, stand for; lay the foundations &c. (prepare) 673; found &c. (cause) 153; set up, set on foot, agoing[obs3], set abroach[obs3], set the ball in motion; apply the match to a train; broach; open up, open the door to. [intransitive] get underway, set about, get to work, set to work, set to; make a beginning, make a start. handsel; take the first step, lay the first stone, cut the first turf; break ground, break the ice, break cover; pass the Rubicon, cross the Rubicon; open fire, open the ball; ventilate, air; undertake &c. 676. come into existence, come into the world; make one's debut, take birth; burst forth, break out; spring up, spring forth, crop up, pop up, appear, materialize. begin at the beginning, begin ab ovo[Lat]. begin again, begin de novo; start afresh, make a fresh start, take it from the top, shuffle the cards, reshuffle the cards, resume, recommence. Adj. beginning &c. v.; initial, initiatory, initiative; inceptive, introductory, incipient; proemial[obs3], inaugural; inchoate, inchoative[obs3]; embryonic, rudimental; primogenial[obs3]; primeval, primitive, primordial &c. (old) 124; aboriginal; natal, nascent. first, foremost, leading; maiden. begun &c. v.; just begun &c. v. Adv. at the beginning, in the beginning, &c. n.; first, in the first place, imprimis[Lat], first and foremost; in limine[Lat]; in the bud, in embryo, in its infancy; from the beginning, from its birth; ab initio[Lat], ab ovo[Lat], ab incunabilis[Lat], ab origine[Lat]. Phr. let's get going! let's get this show on the road! up and at 'em! aller Anfang ist schwer [Ger]; dimidium facti qui coepit habet [Lat][Cicero]; omnium rerum principia parva sunt [Lat][Cicero].

<— p. 22 —>

#67. End. — N. end, close, termination; desinence[obs3], conclusion, finis, finale, period, term, terminus, endpoint, last, omega; extreme, extremity; gable end, butt end, fag-end; tip, nib, point; tail &c. (rear) 235; verge &c. (edge) 231; tag, peroration; bonne bouche[Fr]; bottom dollar, tail end, rear guard. consummation, denouement; finish &c. (completion) 729; fate; doom, doomsday; crack of doom, day of Judgment, dies irae, fall of the curtain; goal, destination; limit, determination; expiration, expiry[obs3], extinction, extermination; death &c. 360; end of all things; finality; eschatology. break up, commencement de la fin, last stage, turning point; coup de grace, deathblow; knock-out, -blow; sockdolager* [obs3][U.S.]. V. end, close, finish, terminate, conclude, be all over; expire; die &c. 360; come to a close, draw to a close &c. n.; have run its course; run out, pass away, bring to an end &c. n.; put an end to, make an end of; determine; get through; achieve &c. (complete) 729; stop &c. (make to cease) 142; shut up shop; hang up one's fiddle. Adj. ending &c. v.; final, terminal, definitive; crowning &c. (completing) 729; last, ultimate; hindermost[obs3]; rear &c. 235; caudal; vergent[obs3]. conterminate[obs3], conterminous, conterminable[obs3]. ended &c. v.; at an end; settled, decided, over, played out, set at rest; conclusive, penultimate; last but one, last but two, &c. unbegun, uncommenced[obs3]; fresh. Adv. finally &c. adj.; in fine; at the last; once for all. Phr. "as high as Heaven and as deep as hell" [Beaumont & Fletcher]; deficit omne quod nascitur [Lat][Quintilian]; en toute chose il faut considerer la fin[Fr][obs3]; finem respice[Lat][obs3]; ultimus Romanorum[Lat].

#68. Middle. — N. middle, midst, medietyl, mean &c. 29; medium, middle term; center &c. 222, mid-course &c. 628; mezzo termine[It]; juste milieu &c. 628[Fr]; halfway house, nave, navel, omphalos[obs3]; nucleus, nucleolus. equidistance[obs3], bisection, half distance; equator, diaphragm, midriff; intermediate &c. 228. Adj. middle, medial, mesial[Med], mean, mid, median, average; middlemost, midmost; mediate; intermediate &c. (interjacent) 228[obs3]; equidistant; central &c. 222; mediterranean, equatorial; homocentric. Adv. in the middle; midway, halfway; midships[obs3], amidships, in medias res.

#69. [Uninterrupted sequence.] Continuity. — N. continuity; consecution, consecutiveness &c. adj.; succession, round, suite, progression, series, train chain; catenation, concatenation; scale; gradation, course; ceaselessness, constant flow, unbroken extent. procession, column; retinue, cortege, cavalcade, rank and file, line of battle, array. pedigree, genealogy, lineage, race; ancestry, descent, family, house; line, line of ancestors; strain. rank, file, line, row, range, tier, string, thread, team; suit; colonnade. V. follow in a series, form a series &c. n.; fall in. arrange in a series, collate &c. n.; string together, file, thread, graduate, organize, sort, tabulate. Adj. continuous, continued; consecutive; progressive, gradual; serial, successive; immediate, unbroken, entire; linear; in a line, in a row &c. n.; uninterrupted, unintermitting[obs3]; unremitting, unrelenting (perseverence) 604a; perennial, evergreen; constant. Adv. continuously &c. adj.; seriatim; in a line &c. n.; in succession, in turn; running, gradually, step by step, gradatim[Lat], at a stretch; in file, in column, in single file, in Indian file.

#70. [Interrupted sequence.] Discontinuity.— N. discontinuity; disjunction &c. 44; anacoluthon[obs3]; interruption, break, fracture, flaw, fault, crack, cut; gap &c. (interval) 198; solution of continuity, caesura; broken thread; parenthesis, episode, rhapsody, patchwork; intermission; alternation &c. (periodicity) 138; dropping fire. V. be discontinuous &c. adj.; alternate, intermit, sputter, stop and start, hesitate. discontinue, pause, interrupt; intervene; break, break in upon, break off; interpose &c. 228; break the thread, snap the thread; disconnect &c. (disjoin) 44; dissever. Adj. discontinuous, unsuccessive[obs3], broken, interrupted, dicousu[Fr]; disconnected, unconnected; discrete, disjunctive; fitful &c. (irregular) 139; spasmodic, desultory; intermitting, occasional &c. v., intermittent; alternate; recurrent &c. (periodic) 138. Adv. at intervals; by snatches, by jerks, by skips, by catches, by fits and starts; skippingly[obs3], per saltum[Lat]; longo intervallo[It]. Phr. like "angel visits few and far between" [Campbell].

<— p. 23 —>

#71. Term. — N. term, rank, station, stage, step; degree &c. 26; scale, remove, grade, link, peg, round of the ladder, status, position, place, point, mark, pas, period, pitch; stand, standing; footing, range. V. hold a place, occupy a place, find a place, fall into a place &c. n.

% 3. COLLECTIVE ORDER %

#72. Assemblage. — N. {opp. 73} assemblage; collection, collocation, colligation[obs3]; compilation, levy, gathering, ingathering, muster, attroupement[obs3]; team; concourse, conflux[obs3], congregation, contesserationl, convergence &c. 290; meeting, levee, reunion, drawing room, at home; conversazione &c. (social gathering) 892[It]; assembly, congress; convention, conventicle; gemote[obs3]; conclave &c. (council) 696; posse, posse comitatus[Lat]; Noah's ark. miscellany, collectanea[obs3]; museum, menagerie &c. (store) 636; museology[obs3]. crowd, throng, group; flood, rush, deluge; rabble, mob, press, crush, cohue[obs3], horde, body, tribe; crew, gang, knot, squad, band, party; swarm, shoal, school, covey, flock, herd, drove; atajo[obs3]; bunch, drive, force, mulada [obs3][U.S.]; remuda[obs3]; roundup [U.S.]; array, bevy, galaxy; corps, company, troop, troupe, task force; army, regiment &c. (combatants) 726; host &c. (multitude) 102; populousness. clan, brotherhood, fraternity, sorority, association &c. (party) 712. volley, shower, storm, cloud. group, cluster, Pleiades, clump, pencil; set, batch, lot, pack; budget, assortment, bunch; parcel; packet, package; bundle, fascine[obs3], fasces[obs3], bale; seron[obs3], seroon[obs3]; fagot, wisp, truss, tuft; shock, rick, fardel[obs3], stack, sheaf, haycock[obs3]; fascicle, fascicule[obs3], fasciculus[Lat], gavel, hattock[obs3], stook[obs3]. accumulation &c. (store) 636; congeries, heap, lump, pile, rouleau[obs3], tissue, mass, pyramid; bing[obs3]; drift; snowball, snowdrift; acervation[obs3], cumulation; glomeration[obs3], agglomeration; conglobation[obs3]; conglomeration, conglomerate; coacervate[Chem], coacervation[Chem], coagmentation[obs3], aggregation, concentration, congestion, omnium gaterum[Lat], spicilegium[obs3], black hole of Calcutta; quantity &c. (greatness) 31. collector, gatherer; whip, whipper in. V. assemble[be or come together], collect, muster; meet, unite, join, rejoin; cluster, flock, swarm, surge, stream, herd, crowd, throng, associate; congregate, conglomerate, concentrate; precipitate; center round, rendezvous, resort; come together, flock get together, pig together; forgather; huddle; reassemble. [get or bring together] assemble, muster; bring together, get together, put together, draw together, scrape together, lump together; collect, collocate, colligate[obs3]; get, whip in; gather; hold a meeting; convene, convoke, convocate[obs3]; rake up, dredge; heap, mass, pile; pack, put up, truss, cram; acervate[obs3]; agglomerate, aggregate; compile; group, aggroup[obs3], concentrate, unite; collect into a focus, bring into a focus; amass, accumulate &c. (store) 636; collect in a dragnet; heap Ossa upon Pelion. Adj. assembled &c. v.; closely packed, dense, serried, crowded to suffocation, teeming, swarming, populous; as thick as hops; all of a heap, fasciculated, cumulative. Phr. the plot thickens; acervatim[Lat]; tibi seris tibi metis[Lat].

#73. Nonassemblage. Dispersion. — N. {opp. 72} dispersion; disjunction &c. 44; divergence &c. 291; aspersion; scattering &c. v.; dissemination, diffusion, dissipation, distribution; apportionment &c. 786; spread, respersion[obs3], circumfusion[obs3], interspersion, spargefaction[obs3]; affusion[obs3]. waifs and estrays[obs3], flotsam and jetsam, disjecta membra[Lat], [Hor.]; waveson[obs3]. V. disperse, scatter, sow, broadcast, disseminate, diffuse, shed, spread, bestrew, overspread, dispense, disband, disembody, dismember, distribute; apportion &c. 786; blow off, let out, dispel, cast forth, draught off; strew, straw, strow[obs3]; ted; spirtle[obs3], cast, sprinkle; issue, deal out, retail, utter; resperse[obs3], intersperse; set abroach[obs3], circumfuse[obs3]. turn adrift, cast adrift; scatter to the winds; spread like wildfire, disperse themselves. Adj. unassembled &c. (see assemble &c. 72); dispersed &c. v.; sparse, dispread, broadcast, sporadic, widespread; epidemic &c. (general) 78; adrift, stray; disheveled, streaming. Adv. sparsim[obs3], here and there, passim.

<— p. 24 —>

#74. [Place of meeting.] Focus. — N. focus; point of convergence &c. 290; corradiation[obs3]; center &c. 222; gathering place, resort haunt retreat; venue; rendezvous; rallying point, headquarters, home, club; depot &c. (store) 636; trysting place; place of meeting, place of resort, place of assignation; point de reunion; issue. V. bring to a point, bring to a focus, bring to an issue.

% 4. DISTRIBUTIVE ORDER %

#75. Class. — N. class, division, category, categorema[obs3], head, order, section; department, subdepartment, province, domain.
kind, sort, genus, species, variety, family, order, kingdom, race, tribe, caste, sept, clan, breed, type, subtype, kit, sect, set, subset; assortment; feather, kidney; suit; range; gender, sex, kin.
manner, description, denomination, designation, rubric, character, stamp predicament; indication, particularization, selection, specification.
similarity &c. 17.
#76. Inclusion. [Comprehension under, or reference to a class.] — N. {opp. 77} inclusion, admission, comprehension, reception. composition &c. (inclusion in a compound) 54. V. be included in &c.; come under, fall under, range under; belong to, pertain to; range with; merge in. include, comprise, comprehend, contain, admit, embrace, receive; inclose &c. (circumscribe) 229; embody, encircle. reckon among, enumerate among, number among; refer to; place with, arrange with, place under; take into account. Adj. included, including &c. v.; inclusive; congener, congenerous; of the same class &c. 75; encircling. Phr. a maximis ad minima[Lat], et hoc genus omne[Lat], &c., etc.; et coetera[Lat].

#77. Exclusion. — N. {opp. 76} exclusion &c. 55. <— The same set of words are used to express Exclusion from a class and Exclusion from a compound. Reference is therefore made to the former at 55. This identity does not occur with regard to Inclusion, which therefore constitutes a separate category. —>

#78. Generality. — N. {opp. 79} generality, generalization; universality; catholicity, catholicism; miscellany, miscellaneousness[obs3]; dragnet; common run; worldwideness[obs3].
everyone, everybody; all hands, all the world and his wife; anybody, N or M, all sorts.
prevalence, run.
V. be general &c. adj.; prevail, be going about, stalk abroad.
render general &c. adj.; generalize.
Adj. general, generic, collective; broad, comprehensive, sweeping; encyclopedical[obs3], widespread &c. (dispersed) 73.
universal; catholic, catholical[obs3]; common, worldwide;

ecumenical, oecumenical[obs3]; transcendental; prevalent, prevailing, rife,
epidemic, besetting; all over, covered with.

 Pan-American, Anglican[obs3], Pan-Hellenic, Pan-Germanic, Slavic;
panharmonic[obs3].

 every, all; unspecified, impersonal.

 customary &c. (habitual) 613.

 Adv. whatever, whatsoever; to a man, one and all.

 generally &c. adj.; always, for better for worse; in general,
generally speaking; speaking generally; for the most part; in the long run
&c. (on an average) 29.

<— p. 25 —>

#79. Speciality. — N. {opp. 78} speciality, specialite[obs3]; individuality, individuityl; particularity, peculiarity; idiocrasy
&c. (tendency) 176[obs3]; personality, characteristic, mannerism, idiosyncrasy; specificness &c. adj[obs3].; singular-
ity &c. (unconformity) 83; reading, version, lection; state; trait; distinctive feature; technicality; differentia. particulars,
details, items, counts; minutiae. I, self, I myself; myself, himself, herself, itself. V. specify, particularize, individualize,
realize, specialize, designate, determine; denote, indicate, point out, select. descend to particulars, enter into detail,
go into detail, come to the point. Adj. special, particular, individual, specific, proper, personal, original, private,
respective, definite, determinate, especial, certain, esoteric, endemic, partial, party, peculiar, appropriate, several,
characteristic, diagnostic, exclusive; singular &c. (exceptional) 83; idiomatic; idiotypical; typical. this, that; yon,
yonder. Adv. specially, especially, particularly &c. adj.; in particular, in propria persona[Lat]; ad hominem[Lat]; for my
part. each, apiece, one by one, one at a time; severally, respectively, each to each; seriatim, in detail, in great detail,
in excruciating detail, in mind-numbing detail; bit by bit; pro hac vice[Lat], pro re nata[Lat]. namely, that is to say, for
example, id est, exemplia gratia[Lat], e.g., i.e., videlicet, viz.; to wit. Phr. le style est l'homme meme[Fr].

% 5. ORDER AS REGARDS CATEGORIES %

 #80. Normality. — N. normality, normalcy, normalness[obs3];
familiarity, naturalness; commonness (frequency) 136; rule, standard
(conformity) 82; customary (habit) 613; standard, pattern (prototype) 22.

 V. normalize, standardize.

 Adj. normal, natural, unexceptional; common, usual (frequency) 136;
#81. Multiformity. — N. multiformity, omniformity[obs3]; variety, diversity; multifariousness &c. adj.; varied assort-
ment. dissimilarity &c. 18. Adj. polymorphous, multiform, multifold, multifarious, multigenerous[obs3], multiplex;
heterogeneous, diversified, dissimilar, various, varied, variform[obs3]; manifold, many-sided; variegated, motley,
mosaic; epicene, indiscriminate, desultory, irregular; mixed, different, assorted, mingled, odd, diverse, divers; all
manner of; of every description, of all sorts and kinds; et hoc genus omne[Lat]; and what not? de omnibus rebus et
quibusdam aliis [Lat]. jumbled, confused, mixed up, discordant; inharmonious, unmatched, unrelated, nonuniform.
omniform[obs3], omnigenous[obs3], omnifarious[obs3]; protean (form) 240. Phr. "harmoniously confused" [Pope];
"variety's the very spice of life" [Cowper].

#82. Conformity. — N. {opp. 83} conformity, conformance; observance; habituation; naturalization; conventionality
&c. (custom) 613; agreement &c. 23. example, instance, specimen, sample, quotation; exemplification, illustration,
case in point; object lesson; elucidation. standard, model, pattern &c. (prototype) 22. rule, nature, principle; law;
order of things; normal state, natural state, ordinary state, model state, normal condition, natural condition, ordinary
condition, model condition; standing dish, standing order; Procrustean law; law of the Medes and Persians; hard and
fast rule.

V. conform to, conform to rule; accommodate oneself to, adapt oneself to; rub off corners. be regular &c. adj.; move
in a groove; follow observe the rules, go by the rules, bend to the rules, obey the rules, obey the precedents; comply
with, tally with, chime in with, fall in with; be guided by, be regulated by; fall into a custom, fall into a usage; follow the
fashion, follow the crowd, follow the multitude; pass muster, do as others do, hurler avec les loups [Fr]; stand on
ceremony; when in Rome do as the Romans do; go with the stream, go with the flow, swim with the stream, swim
with the current, swim with the tide, blow with the wind; stick to the beaten track &c. (habit) 613; keep one in
countenance. exemplify, illustrate, cite, quote, quote precedent, quote authority, appeal to authority, put a case;
produce an instance &c. n.; elucidate, explain. Adj. conformable to rule; regular &c. 136; according to regulation,
according to rule, according to Hoyle, according to Cocker, according to Gunter; en regle [Fr], selon les regles[Fr],
well regulated, orderly; symmetric &c. 242. conventional &c. (customary) 613; of daily occurrence, of everyday

occurrence; in the natural order of things; ordinary, common, habitual, usual, everyday, workaday. in the order of the day; naturalized. typical, normal, nominal, formal; canonical, orthodox, sound, strict, rigid, positive, uncompromising, Procrustean. secundum artem[Lat], shipshape, technical; exemple[Fr]. illustrative, in point. Adv. conformably &c. adj.; by rule; agreeably to; in conformity with, in accordance with, in keeping with; according to; consistently with; as usual, ad instar[Lat], instar omnium[Lat]; more solito[Lat], more-majorum. for the sake of conformity; as a matter of course, of course; pro forma[Lat], for form's sake, by the card. invariably, &c. (uniformly) 16. for example, exempli gratia[Lat], e. g.; inter alia[Lat], among other things; for instance. Phr. cela va sans dire[Fr]; ex pede Herculem[Lat]; noscitur a sociis [Lat]; ne e quovis ligno Mercurius fiat [Lat][Erasmus]; "they are happy men whose natures sort with their vocations" [Bacon]. "The nail that sticks up will get hammered down" [Japanese saying]; "Stick your neck out and it may get cut off."

<— p. 26 —>

#83. Unconformity.— N. {opp. 82} nonconformity &c. 82; unconformity, disconformity; unconventionality, informality, abnormity[obs3], abnormality, anomaly; anomalousness &c. adj[obs3].; exception, peculiarity; infraction of law, breach, of law, violation of law, violation of custom, violation of usage, infringement of law, infringement of custom, infringement of usage; teratism[obs3], eccentricity, bizarrerie[obs3], oddity, je ne sais quoi[Fr], monster, monstrosity, rarity; freak, freak of Nature, weirdo, mutant; rouser, snorter* [U.S.]. individuality, idiosyncrasy, originality, manner-ism. aberration; irregularity; variety; singularity; exemption; salvo &c. (qualification) 469. nonconformist; nondescript, character, original, nonesuch, nonsuch[obs3], monster, prodigy, wonder, miracle, curiosity, flying fish, black sheep, black swan, lusus naturae[Lat], rara avis[Lat], queer fish; mongrel, random breed; half-caste, half-blood, half-breed; metis[Lat], crossbreed, hybrid, mule, hinny, mulatto; tertium quid[Lat], hermaphrodite. [mythical animal] phoenix, chimera, hydra, sphinx, minotaur; griffin, griffon; centaur; saggittary[obs3]; kraken, cockatrice, wyvern, roc, dragon, sea serpent; mermaid, merman, merfolk[obs3]; unicorn; Cyclops, "men whose heads do grow beneath their shoul-ders" [Othello]; teratology. [unconformable to the surroundings] fish out of water; neither one thing nor another, neither fish nor fowl, neither fish flesh nor fowl nor good red herring; one in a million, one in a way, one in a thou-sand; outcast, outlaw; off the beaten track; oasis. V. be uncomfortable &c. adj.; abnormalize[obs3]; leave the beaten track, leave the beaten path; infringe a law, infringe a habit, infringe a usage, infringe a custom, break a law, break a habit, break a usage, break a custom, violate a law, violate a habit, violate a usage, violate a custom; drive a coach and six through; stretch a point; have no business there; baffle all description, beggar all description. Adj. uncomfortable, exceptional; abnormal, abnormous[obs3]; anomalous, anomalistic; out of order, out of place, out of keeping, out of tune, out of one's element; irregular, arbitrary; teratogenic; lawless, informal, aberrant, stray, wander-ing, wanton; peculiar, exclusive, unnatural, eccentric, egregious; out of the beaten track, off the beaten track, out of the common, out of the common run; beyond the pale of, out of the pale of; misplaced; funny. unusual, unaccus-tomed, uncustomary, unwonted, uncommon; rare, curious, odd, extraordinary, out of the ordinary; strange, mon-strous; wonderful &c. 870; unexpected, unaccountable; outre[Fr], out of the way, remarkable, noteworthy; queer, quaint, nondescript, none such, sui generis[Lat]; unfashionable; fantastic, grotesque, bizarre; outlandish, exotic, tombe des nues[Fr], preternatural; denaturalized[obs3]. heterogeneous, heteroclite[Gram], amorphous, mongrel, amphibious, epicene, half blood, hybrid; androgynous, androgynal[obs3]; asymmetric &c. 243; adelomorphous[obs3], bisexual, hermaphrodite, monoclinous[obs3]. qualified &c. 469. singular, unique, one-of-a-kind. newfangled, novel, non-classical; original, unconventional, unheard of, unfamiliar; undescribed, unprecedent-ed, unparalleled, unexampled. Adv. unconformably &c. adj.; except, unless, save barring, beside, without, save and except, let alone. however, yet. but. once in a blue moon, once in a million years. Int. what on earth! what in the world! What the devil! Holy cow! Can you top that?; Sacre bleu [Fr]. Phr. never was seen the like, never was heard the like, never was known the like. I could hardly believe it; I saw it, but I didn't believe it.

<— p. 27 —> % SECTION V. NUMBER

1. NUMBER, IN THE ABSTRACT %

#84. Number. — N. number, symbol, numeral, figure, cipher, digit,
integer; counter; round number; formula; function; series.
    sum, difference, complement, subtrahend; product; multiplicand,
multiplier, multiplicator[obs3]; coefficient, multiple; dividend, divisor,
factor, quotient, submultiple[Math]; fraction, rational number; surd,
irrational number; transcendental number; mixed number, complex number,
complex conjugate; numerator, denominator; decimal, circulating decimal,
repetend; common measure, aliquot part; prime number, prime, relative

prime, prime factor, prime pair; reciprocal; totient[obs3].

binary number, octal number, hexadecimal number[Comp].

permutation, combination, variation; election.

ratio, proportion, comparison &c.464; progression; arithmetical progression, geometrical progression, harmonical progression[obs3]; percentage, permilage.

figurate numbers[obs3], pyramidal numbers, polygonal numbers.

power, root, exponent, index, logarithm, antilogarithm; modulus, base.

differential, integral, fluxion[obs3], fluent.

Adj. numeral, complementary, divisible, aliquot, reciprocal, prime, relatively prime, fractional, decimal, figurate[obs3], incommensurable.

proportional, exponential, logarithmic, logometric[obs3], differential, fluxional[obs3], integral, totitive[obs3].

positive, negative; rational, irrational; surd, radical, real; complex, imaginary; finite; infinite; impossible.

Adv. numerically; modulo.

#85. Numeration. — N. numeration; numbering &c. v.; pagination; tale, recension[obs3], enumeration, summation, reckoning, computation, supputation[obs3]; calculation, calculus; algorithm, algorism[obs3], rhabdology[obs3], dactylonomy[obs3]; measurement &c. 466; statistics. arithmetic, analysis, algebra, geometry, analytical geometry, fluxions[obs3]; differential calculus, integral calculus, infinitesimal calculus; calculus of differences. [Statistics] dead reckoning, muster, poll, census, capitation, roll call, recapitulation; account &c. (list) 86. [Operations] notation, addition, subtraction, multiplication, division, rule of three, practice, equations, extraction of roots, reduction, involution, evolution, estimation, approximation, interpolation, differentiation, integration. [Instruments] abacus, logometer[obs3], slide rule, slipstick[coll.], tallies, Napier's bones, calculating machine, difference engine, suanpan[obs3]; adding machine; cash register; electronic calculator, calculator, computer; [people who calculate] arithmetician, calculator, abacist[obs3], algebraist, mathematician; statistician, geometer; programmer; accountant, auditor.
V. number, count, tally, tell; call over, run over; take an account of, enumerate, muster, poll, recite, recapitulate; sum; sum up, cast up; tell off, score, cipher, compute, calculate, suppute[obs3], add, subtract, multiply, divide, extract roots; algebraize[obs3]. check, prove, demonstrate, balance, audit, overhaul, take stock; affix numbers to, page. amount to, add up to, come to. Adj. numeral, numerical; arithmetical, analytic, algebraic, statistical, numerable, computable, calculable; commensurable, commensurate; incommensurable, incommensurate, innumerable, unfathomable, infinite. Adv. quantitatively; arithmetically; measurably; in numbers.

#86. List. — N. list, catalog, catalogue, inventory; register &c.
(record) 551.

account; bill, bill of costs; terrier; tally, listing, itemization; atlas; book, ledger; catalogue raisonne[Fr]; tableau; invoice, bill of lading; prospectus; bill of fare, menu, carte[Fr]; score, census, statistics, returns.

[list of topics in a document] contents, table of contents, outline; synopsis.

[list of topics in a protracted activity (frame)] program, programme[Brit]; syllabus; agenda, schedule, calendar, docket.

[computer-generated list] listing, printout, output.

[written list used as an aid to memory] checklist.

table, chart, database; index, inverted file, word list, concordance.

dictionary, lexicon; vocabulary, glossary; thesaurus.

file, card index, card file, rolodex, address book.

Red book, Blue book, Domesday book; cadastre[Fr]; directory, gazetter[obs3]. almanac; army list, clergy list, civil service list, navy list; Almanach de Gotha[obs3], cadaster; Lloyd's register, nautical almanac;

who's who; Guiness's Book of World Records.

roll; check roll, checker roll, bead roll; muster roll, muster book; roster, panel, jury list; cartulary, diptych.

V. list, itemize; sort, collate; enumerate, tabulate, catalog, tally.

Adj. cadastral[obs3].

<— p. 28 —>

#87. {opp. 100} Unity. — N. unity; oneness &c. adj.; individuality; solitude &c. (seclusion) 893; isolation &c. (disjunction) 44; unification &c. 48. one, unit, ace; individual; none else, no other. V. be one, be alone &c. adj.; dine with Duke Humphrey[obs3]. isolate &c. (disjoin) 44. render one; unite &c. (join) 43, (combine) 48. Adj. one, sole, single, solitary, unitary; individual, apart, alone; kithless[obs3]. unaccompanied, unattended; solus[Lat], single-handed; singular, odd, unique, unrepeated[obs3], azygous, first and last; isolated &c. (disjoined) 44; insular. monospermous[obs3]; unific[obs3], uniflorous[obs3], unifoliate[obs3], unigenital[obs3], uniliteral[obs3], unijocular[obs3], unimodal [statistics], unimodular[obs3]. lone, lonely, lonesome; desolate, dreary, insecablel, inseverable[obs3], indiscerptible[obs3]; compact, indivisible, atomic, irresolvable[obs3]. Adv. singly &c. adj.; alone, by itself, per se, only, apart, in the singular number, in the abstract; one by one, one at a time; simply; one and a half, sesqui-[obs3]. Phr. natura il fece [It], e poi roppe la stampa[It]; du fort au faible [obs3][Fr]; "two souls with but a single thought, two hearts that beat as one".

#88. Accompaniment. — N. accompaniment; adjunct &c. 39; context; appendage, appurtenance. coexistence, concomitance, company, association, companionship; partnership, copartnership; coefficiency[obs3]. concomitant, accessory, coefficient; companion, buddy, attendant, fellow, associate, friend, colleague; consort, spouse, mate; partner, co- partner; satellite, hanger on, fellow-traveller, shadow; escort, cortege; attribute. V. accompany, coexist, attend; hang on, wait on; go hand in hand with; synchronize &c. 120; bear company, keep company; row in the same boat; bring in its train; associate with, couple with. Adj. accompanying &c. v.; concomitant, fellow, twin, joint; associated with, coupled with; accessory, attendant, obbligato. Adv. with, withal; together with, along with, in company with; hand in hand, side by side; cheek by jowl, cheek by jole[obs3]; arm in arm; therewith, herewith; and &c. (addition) 37. together, in a body, collectively. Phr. noscitur a sociis[Lat]; virtutis fortuna comes[Lat].

#89. Duality. — N. duality, dualism; duplicity; biplicity[obs3], biformity[obs3]; polarity; two, deuce, couple, duet, brace, pair, cheeks, twins, Castor and Pollux, gemini, Siamese twins; fellows; yoke, conjugation; dispermy[obs3], doublets, dyad, span. V. pair[unite in pairs], couple, bracket, yoke; conduplicate[obs3]; mate, span [U.S.]. Adj. two, twin; dual, dualistic, double; binary, binomial; twin, biparous[obs3]; dyadic[Math]; conduplicate[obs3]; duplex &c. 90; biduous[obs3], binate[obs3], diphyletic[obs3], dispermic[obs3], unijugate[obs3]; tete-a-tete. coupled &c. v.; conjugate. both, both the one and the other.

#90. Duplication. — N. duplication; doubling &c. v.; gemination, ingemination[obs3]; reduplication; iteration &c. (repetition) 104; renewal. V. double, redouble, duplicate, reduplicate; geminate; repeat &c. 104; renew &c. 660. Adj. double; doubled &c. v.; bicipital[obs3], bicephalous[obs3], bidental[obs3], bilabiate, bivalve, bivalvular[obs3], bifold[obs3], biform[obs3], bilateral; bifarious[obs3], bifacial[obs3]; twofold, two- sided; disomatous[obs3]; duplex; double-faced, double-headed; twin, duplicate, ingeminate[obs3]; second. Adv. twice, once more; over again &c. (repeatedly) 104; as much again, twofold; secondly, in the second place, again.

#91. [Division into two parts.] bisection. — N. bisection, bipartition; dichotomy, subdichotomy[obs3]; halving &c. v.; dimidiation[obs3].

bifurcation, forking, branching, ramification, divarication; fork, prong; fold; half, moiety.

V. bisect, halve, divide, split, cut in two, cleave dimidiate[obs3], dichotomize.

go halves, divide with.

separate, fork, bifurcate; branch off, out; ramify.

Adj. bisected &c. v.; cloven, cleft; bipartite, biconjugate[obs3], bicuspid, bifid; bifurcous[obs3], bifurcate, bifurcated; distichous, dichotomous, furcular[obs3]; semi-, demi-, hemi[obs3].

<— p. 29 —>

#92. Triality. — N. Triality[obs3], trinity; triunity[obs3].

three, triad, triplet, trey, trio, ternion[obs3], leash; shamrock, tierce[obs3], spike-team [U.S.], trefoil; triangle, trident, triennium[obs3], trigon[obs3], trinomial, trionym[obs3], triplopia[obs3], tripod, trireme, triseme[obs3], triskele[obs3], triskelion, trisula[obs3].

third power, cube; cube root.

Adj. three; triform[obs3], trinal[obs3], trinomial; tertiary; ternary; triune; triarch, triadie[obs3]; triple &c. 93.

Pref. tri-, tris-.

Phr. tria juncta in uno[Lat].

#93. Triplication. — N. triplication, triplicity[obs3]; trebleness[obs3], trine.

V. treble, triple; triplicate, cube.

Adj. treble, triple; tern, ternary; triplicate, threefold, trilogistic[obs3]; third; trinal[obs3], trine.

Adv. three times, three fold; thrice, in the third place, thirdly; trebly &c. adj.

#94. [Division into three parts.] Trisection. — N. trisection, tripartition[obs3], trichotomy; third, third part. V. trisect, divide into three parts. Adj. trifid; trisected &c. v.; tripartite, trichotomous[obs3], trisulcate[obs3]. Triadelphous[obs3], triangular, tricuspid, tricapsular[obs3], tridental[obs3], tridentate, tridentiferous[obs3], trifoliate, trifurcate, trigonal[obs3], trigrammic[obs3], trigrammatic[obs3], tripetalous[obs3], tripodal, tripodic[obs3], triquetral[obs3], triquetrous[obs3].

<— note that square in the mathematical sense is more related to two than to four. Subdivide? —>

#95. Four. — N. quaternity[obs3], four, tetrad, quartet, quaternion, square, quarter.

[planar form with four sides] tetract[obs3], tetragon, quadrangle, rectangle.

[three dimensional object with four surfaces] tetrahedron.

quadrature, quadrifoil, quadriform, quadruplet; quatrefoil.

[object or animal with four legs] tetrapod.

[geographical area with four sides] quadrangle, quad[coll.].

[electromagnetic object] quadrupole.

[four fundamental studies] quadrivium.

V. reduce to a square, square.

Adj. four; quaternary, quaternal[obs3]; quadratic; quartile; tetract[obs3], tetractic[obs3], tetractinal[obs3]; tetrad, tetragonal; square, quadrate.

#96. Quadruplication. — N. quadruplication.

V. multiply by four, quadruplicate, biquadrate[obs3].

Adj. fourfold, four times; quadrable[obs3], quadrumanous[obs3], quadruple, quadruplicate, quadrible[obs3]; fourth.

quadrifoliate[obs3], quadrifoliolate[obs3], quadrigeminal[obs3], quadrigeminate[obs3], quadriplanar[obs3], quadriserial[obs3].

Adv. four times; in the fourth place, fourthly.

#97. [Division into four parts.] Quadrisection. — N. quadrisection, quadripartition[obs3]; quartering &c. v; fourth; quart; quarter, quartern[obs3]; farthing (i.e. fourthing)[obs3]; quadrant.

V. quarter, divide into four parts.

Adj. quartered &c. v.; quadrifid[obs3], quadripartite.

rectangular.

#98. Five, &c. — N. five, cinque[Fr], quint, quincux[obs3]; six, half-a-dozen, half dozen; seven; eight; nine, three times three; dicker; ten, decade; eleven; twelve, dozen; thirteen; long dozen, baker's dozen; quintuplet; twenty, score; twenty-four, four and twenty, two dozen; twenty- five, five and twenty, quarter of a hundred; forty, two score; fifty, half a hundred; sixty, three score; seventy, three score and ten; eighty, four score; ninety, fourscore and ten; sestiad[obs3]. hundred, centenary, hecatomb, century; hundredweight, cwt.; one hundred and forty-four, gross. thousand, chiliad; millennium, thousand years, grand[coll.]; myriad; ten thousand, ban[Japanese], man[Japanese]; ten thousand years, banzai[Japanese]; lac, one hundred thousand, plum; million; thousand million, milliard, billion, trillion &c. V. centuriate[obs3]; quintuplicate. Adj. five, quinary[obs3], quintuple; fifth; senary[obs3], sextuple; sixth; seventh; septuple; octuple; eighth; ninefold, ninth; tenfold, decimal, denary[obs3], decuple[obs3], tenth; eleventh; duodenary[obs3], duodenal; twelfth; in one's 'teens, thirteenth. vicesimal[obs3], vigesimal; twentieth; twenty-fourth &c. n.; vicenary[obs3], vicennial[obs3]. centuple[obs3], centuplicate[obs3], centennial, centenary, centurial[obs3];

secular, hundredth; thousandth, &c.

#99. Quinquesection, &c. — N. division by five &c. 98; quinquesection &c.; decimation; fifth &c. V. decimate; quinquesect. Adj. quinquefid, quinquelateral, quinquepartite; quinqevalent, pentavalent; quinquarticular[obs3]; octifid[obs3]; decimal, tenth, tithe; duodecimal, twelfth; sexagesimal[obs3], sexagenary[obs3]; hundredth, centesimal; millesimal &c. [obs3]

<— p. 30 —>

#100. {opp. 87} [More than one.] Plurality. — N. plurality; a number, a certain number; one or two, two or three &c.; a few, several; multitude &c. 102; majority.
[large number] multitude &c. 102.
Adj. plural, more than one, upwards of; some, several, a few; certain; not alone &c. 87.
Adv. et cetera, &c., etc.
among other things, inter alia[Lat].
Phr. non deficit alter [Lat].
% 3. Indeterminate Number %

#100a. [Less than one.] Fraction — N. fraction, fractional part; part &c. 51.
Adj. fractional, fragmentary, inconsiderable, negligible, infinitesimal.
#101. Zero. — N. zero, nothing; null, nul, naught, nought, void; cipher, goose egg; none, nobody, no one; nichts[Ger.], nixie*, nix*; zilch, zip, zippo [all slang]; not a soul; ame qui vive[Fr]; absence &c. 187; unsubstantiality &c. 4[obs3]. Adj. not one, not a one, not any, nary a one [dial.]; not a, never a; not a whit of, not an iota of, not a drop of, not a speck of, not a jot; not a trace of, not a hint of, not a smidgen of, not a suspicion of, not a shadow of, neither hide nor hair of.

#102. Multitude. — N. multitude; numerous &c. adj.; numerosity, numerality; multiplicity; profusion &c. (plenty) 639; legion, host; great number, large number, round number, enormous number; a quantity, numbers, array, sight, army, sea, galaxy; scores, peck, bushel, shoal, swarm, draught, bevy, cloud, flock, herd, drove, flight, covey, hive, brood, litter, farrow, fry, nest; crowd &c. (assemblage) 72; lots; all in the world and his wife. [Increase of number] greater number, majority; multiplication, multiple. V. be numerous &c. adj.; swarm with, teem with, creep with; crowd, swarm, come thick upon; outnumber, multiply; people; swarm like locusts, swarm like bees. Adj. many, several, sundry, divers, various, not a few; Briarean; a hundred, a thousand, a myriad, a million, a quadrillion, a nonillion, a thousand and one; some ten or a dozen, some forty or fifty &c.; half a dozen, half a hundred &c.; very many, full many, ever so many; numerous; numerose[obs3]; profuse, in profusion; manifold, multiplied, multitudinous, multiple, multinominal, teeming, populous, peopled, crowded, thick, studded; galore. thick coming, many more, more than one can tell, a world of; no end of, no end to; cum multis aliis[Lat]; thick as hops, thick as hail; plenty as blackberries; numerous as the stars in the firmament, numerous as the sands on the seashore, numerous as the hairs on the head; and what not, and heaven knows what; endless &c. (infinite) 105. Phr. their name is "legion"; acervatim[Lat]; en foule[Fr]; "many- headed multitude" [Sidney]; "numerous as glittering gems of morning dew" [Young]; vel prece vel pretio[Lat] [obs3].

#103. Fewness. — N. fewness &c. adj.; paucity, small number; small quantity &c. 32; rarity; infrequency &c. 137; handful, maniple; minority; exiguity. [Diminution of number] reduction; weeding &c. v.; elimination, sarculationl, decimation; eradication. V. be few &c. adj. render few &c. adj.; reduce, diminish the number, weed, eliminate, cull, thin, decimate. Adj. few; scant, scanty; thin, rare, scattered, thinly scattered, spotty, few and far between, exiguous; infrequent &c. 137; rari nantes[Latin]; hardly any, scarcely any; to be counted on one's fingers; reduced &c. v.; unrepeated[obs3]. Adv. rarely, here and there.

<— p. 31 —>

#104. Repetition. — N. repetition, iteration, reiteration, harping, recurrence, succession, run; battology, tautology; monotony, tautophony; rhythm &c. 138; diffuseness, pleonasm, redundancy. chimes, repetend, echo, ritornello[obs3], burden of a song, refrain; rehearsal; rechauffe[Fr], rifacimento[It], recapitulation. cuckoo &c. (imitation) 19; reverberation &c. 408; drumming &c. (roll) 407; renewal &c. (restoration) 660. twice-told tale; old story, old song; second edition, new edition; reappearance, reproduction, recursion [Comp]; periodicity &c. 138. V. repeat, iterate, reiterate, reproduce, echo, reecho, drum, harp upon, battologize[obs3], hammer, redouble. recur, revert, return, reappear, recurse [Comp]; renew &c. (restore) 660. rehearse; do over again, say over again; ring the changes on; harp on the same string; din in the ear, drum in the ear; conjugate in all its moods tenses and inflexions[obs3], begin again, go over the same ground, go the same round, never hear the last of; resume, return to, recapitulate, reword. Adj. repeated &c. v.; repetitional[obs3], repetitionary[obs3]; recurrent, recurring; ever recurring, thick coming; frequent, incessant; redundant, pleonastic. monotonous, harping, iterative, recursive [Math, Comp], unvaried; mocking, chiming; retold; aforesaid, aforenamed[obs3]; above-mentioned, above-said; habitual &c. 613; another. Adv. repeatedly, often, again, anew, over again, afresh, once more; ding-dong, ditto, encore, de novo, bis[obs3], da capo[It]. again and again; over and over, over and over again; recursively [Comp]; many times over; time and again, time after time; year after year; day by day &c.; many times, several times, a number of times; many a time, full many a time; frequently &c. 136. Phr. ecce iterum Crispinus[Lat]; toujours perdrix[Fr]; "cut and come again" [Crabbe]; "tomorrow and tomorrow and tomorrow" [Macbeth]; cantilenam eandem canis [Lat][Terence]; nullum est jam dictum quod non dictum sit prius [Lat][Terence].

#105. Infinity. — N. infinity, infinitude, infiniteness &c. adj.; perpetuity &c. 112; boundlessness. V. be infinite &c. adj.; know no limits, have no limits, know no bounds, have no bounds; go on for ever. Adj. infinite; immense; numberless, countless, sumless[obs3], measureless; innumerable, immeasurable, incalculable, illimitable, inexhaustible, interminable, unfathomable, unapproachable; exhaustless, indefinite; without number, without measure, without limit, without end; incomprehensible; limitless, endless, boundless, termless[obs3]; untold, unnumbered, unmeasured, unbounded, unlimited; illimited[obs3]; perpetual &c. 112. Adv. infinitely &c. adj.; ad infinitum. Phr. "as boundless as the sea" [Romeo and Juliet].

%

SECTION VI. TIME
1. ABSOLUTE TIME %

#106. Time. — N. time, duration; period, term, stage, space, span, spell, season; the whole time, the whole period; space-time; course &c. 109; snap. intermediate time, while, interim, interval, pendency[obs3]; intervention, intermission, intermittence, interregnum, interlude; respite. era, epoch; time of life, age, year, date; decade &c. (period) 108; moment, &c. (instant) 113. glass of time, sands of time, march of time, Father Time, ravages of time; arrow of time; river of time, whirligig of time, noiseless foot of time; scythe. V. continue last endure, go on, remain, persist; intervene; elapse &c. 109; hold out. take time, take up time, fill time, occupy time. pass time, pass away time, spend time, while away time, consume time, talk against time; tide over; use time, employ time; seize an opportunity &c. 134; waste time &c. (be inactive) 683. Adj. continuing &c. v.; on foot; permanent &c. (durable) 110. Adv. while, whilst, during, pending; during the time, during the interval; in the course of, at that point, at that point in time; for the time being, day by day; in the time of, when; meantime, meanwhile; in the meantime, in the interim; ad interim, pendente lite[Lat]; de die in diem[Lat]; from day to day, from hour to hour &c.; hourly, always; for a time, for a season; till, until, up to, yet, as far as, by that time, so far, hereunto, heretofore, prior to this, up to this point. the whole time, all the time; all along; throughout &c. (completely) 52; for good &c. (diuturnity)[obs3] 110. hereupon, thereupon, whereupon; then; anno Domini; A.D.; ante Christum; A.C.; before Christ; B.C.; anno urbis conditae[Lat]; A.U.C.; anno regni[Lat]; A.R.; once upon a time, one fine morning, one fine day, one day, once. Phr. time flies, tempus fugit [Lat.]; time runs out, time runs against, race against time, racing the clock, time marches on, time is of the essence, "time and tide wait for no man". ad calendas Groecas[Lat]; "panting Time toileth after him in vain" [Johnson]; "'gainst the tooth of time and razure of oblivion" [Measure for Measure]; "rich with the spoils of time" [Gray]; tempus edax rerum [Lat] [Horace]; "the long hours come and go" [C.G. Rossetti]; "the time is out of joint" [Hamlet]; "Time rolls his ceaseless course" [Scott]; "Time the foe of man's dominion" [Peacock]; "time wasted is existence, used is life" [Young]; truditur dies die [Lat][Horace]; volat hora per orbem [Lat][Lucretius]; carpe diem[Lat].

<— p. 32 —>

#107. Neverness. — N. "neverness"; absence of time, no time; dies non; Tib's eve; Greek Kalends, a blue moon. Adv. never, ne'er[contr]; at no time, at no period; on the second Tuesday of the week, when Hell freezes over; on no occasion, never in all one's born days, nevermore, sine die; in no degree.

#108. [Definite duration, or portion of time.] Period. — N. period, age, era; second, minute, hour, day, week, month, quarter, year, decade, decenniumm lustrum[obs3], quinquennium, lifetime, generation; epoch, ghurry[obs3], lunation[obs3], moon.

century, millennium; annus magnus[Lat].

Adj. horary[obs3]; hourly, annual &c. (periodical) 138.

#108a. Contingent Duration.— Adv. during pleasure, during good behavior; quamdiu se bene gesserit[Latin].

#109. [Indefinite duration.] Course. — N. corridors of time, sweep of time, vesta of time[obs3], course of time, progress of time, process of time, succession of time, lapse of time, flow of time, flux of time, stream of time, tract of time, current of time, tide of time, march of time, step of time, flight of time; duration &c. 106. [Indefinite time] aorist[obs3]. V. elapse, lapse, flow, run, proceed, advance, pass; roll on, wear on, press on; flit, fly, slip, slide, glide; run its course. run out, expire; go by, pass by; be -past &c. 122. Adj. elapsing &c. v.; aoristic[obs3]; progressive. Adv. in due time, in due season; in in due course, in due process, in the fullness of time; in time. Phr. labitur et labetur [Lat][Horace]; truditur dies die [Lat][Horace]; fugaces labuntur anni [Lat][Horace]; "tomorrow and tomorrow and tomorrow creeps in this petty pace from day to day" [Macbeth].

#110. [Long duration.] Diuturnity. — N. diuturnity[obs3]; a long time, a length of time; an age, a century, an eternity; slowness &c. 275; perpetuity &c. 112; blue moon, coon's age [U.S.], dog's age. durableness, durability; persistence, endlessness, lastingness &c. adj[obs3].; continuance, standing; permanence &c. (stability) 150 survival, survivance[obs3]; longevity &c. (age) 128; distance of time. protraction of time, prolongation of time, extension of time; delay &c. (lateness) 133. V. last, endure, stand, remain, abide, continue, brave a thousand years. tarry &c. (be late) 133; drag on, drag its slow length along, drag a lengthening chain; protract, prolong; spin out, eke out, draw out, lengthen out; temporize; gain time, make time, talk against time. outlast, outlive; survive; live to fight again. Adj. durable; lasting &c. v.; of long duration, of long-standing; permanent, endless, chronic, long-standing; intransient[obs3], intransitive; intransmutable[obs3], persistent; lifelong, livelong; longeval[obs3], long-lived, macrobi- otic, diuturnal[obs3], evergreen, perennial; sempervirent[obs3], sempervirid[obs3]; unrelenting, unintermitting[obs3], unremitting; perpetual &c. 112. lingering, protracted, prolonged, spun out &c. v. long-pending, long- winded; slow &c. 275. Adv. long; for a long time, for an age, for ages, for ever so long, for many a long day; long ago &c. (in a past time) 122; longo intervallo[It]. all the day long, all the year round; the livelong day, as the day is long, morning noon and night; hour after hour, day after day, &c.; for good; permanently &c. adj.

#111. [Short duration.] Transientness. — N. transience, transientness &c. adj[obs3].; evanescence, impermanence, fugacity[Chem], caducity[obs3], mortality, span; nine days' wonder, bubble, Mayfly; spurt; flash in the pan; temporary arrangement, interregnum. velocity &c. 274; suddenness &c. 113; changeableness &c. 149. transient, transient boarder, transient guest [U.S.]. V. be transient &c. adj.; flit, pass away, fly, gallop, vanish, fade, evaporate; pass away like a cloud, pass away like a summer cloud, pass away like a shadow, pass away like a dream. Adj. transient, transitory, transitive; passing, evanescent, fleeting, cursory, short-lived, ephemeral; flying &c. v.; fugacious, fugitive; shifting, slippery; spasmodic; instantaneous, momentaneous[obs3]. temporal, temporary; provisional, provisory; deciduous; perishable, mortal, precarious, unstable, insecure; impermanent. brief, quick, brisk, extemporaneous, summary; pressed for time &c. (haste) 684; sudden, momentary &c. (instantaneous) 113. Adv. temporarily &c. adj.; pro tempore[Lat]; for the moment, for a time; awhile, en passant[Fr], in transitu[Lat]; in a short time; soon &c. (early) 132; briefly &c. adj.; at short notice; on the point of, on the eve of; in articulo; between cup and lip. Phr. one's days are numbered; the time is up; here today and gone tomorrow; non semper erit aestas[Lat][obs3]; eheu! fugaces labuntur anni[Lat]; sic transit gloria mundi[Lat]; a schoolboy's tale, the wonder of the hour! [Byron]; dum loquimur fugerit invidia aetas[Lat][obs3]; fugit hora[Lat]; all that is transitory is but an illusion [Goethe].

<— p. 33 —>

#112. [Endless duration.] Perpetuity. — N. perpetuity, eternity, everness[obs3], aye, sempiternity[obs3], immortality, athanasia[obs3]; interminability[obs3], agelessness[obs3], everlastingness &c. adj.; perpetuation; continued exist- ence, uninterrupted existence; perennity[obs3]; permanence (durability) 110. V. last forever, endure forever, go on forever; have no end. eternize, perpetuate. Adj. perpetual, eternal; everduring[obs3], everlasting, ever-living, ever-flowing; continual, sempiternal[obs3]; coeternal; endless, unending; ceaseless, incessant, uninterrupted, indesinent[obs3], unceasing; endless, unending, interminable, having no end; unfading[obs3], evergreen, amaran- thine; neverending[obs3], never-dying, never-fading; deathless, immortal, undying, imperishable. Adv. perpetually &c. adj.; always, ever, evermore, aye; for ever, for aye, till the end of the universe, forevermore, forever and a day, for ever and ever; in all ages, from age to age; without end; world without end, time without end; in secula seculorum[Lat]; to the end of time, to the crack of doom, to the "last syllable of recorded time" [Macbeth]; till dooms- day; constantly &c. (very frequently) 136. Phr. esto perpetuum[Lat]; labitur et labetur in omne volubilis oevum [Lat]

[Horace]; "but thou shall flourish in immortal youth" [Addison]; "Eternity! thou pleasing, dreadful thought" [Addison]; "her immortal part with angels lives" [Romeo & Juliet]; ohne Rast [Ger][Goethe's motto]; ora e sempre[It].

#113. [Point of time] Instantaneity. — N. instantaneity, instantaneousness, immediacy; suddenness, abruptness. moment, instant, second, minute; twinkling, trice, flash, breath, crack, jiffy, coup, burst, flash of lightning, stroke of time. epoch, time; time of day, time of night; hour, minute; very minute &c., very time, very hour; present time, right time, true time, exact correct time. V. be instantaneous &c. adj.; twinkle, flash. Adj. instantaneous, momentary, sudden, immediate, instant, abrupt, discontinuous, precipitous, precipitant, precipitate; subitaneous[obs3], hasty; quick as thought, quick as lightning, quick as a flash; rapid as electricity. speedy, quick, fast, fleet, swift, lively, blitz; rapid (velocity) 274. Adv. instantaneously &c. adj.; in no time, in less than no time; presto, subito[obs3], instanter, suddenly, at a stroke, like a shot; in a moment &c. n. in the blink of an eye, in the twinkling of an eye, in a trice; in one's tracks; right away; toute a l'heure[Fr]; at one jump, in the same breath, per saltum[Lat], uno saltu[Lat]; at once, all at once; plump, slap; "at one fell swoop"; at the same instant &c. n.; immediately &c. (early) 132; extempore, on the moment, on the spot, on the spur of the moment; no sooner said than done; just then; slap-dash &c. (haste) 684. Phr. touch and go; no sooner said than done.

#114. [Estimation, measurement, and record of time.] Chronometry. — N. chronometry, horometry[obs3], horology; date, epoch; style, era. almanac, calendar, ephemeris; register, registry; chronicle, annals, journal, diary, chrono-gram. [Instruments for the measurement of time]; clock, wall clock, pendulum clock, grandfather's clock, cuckoo clock, alarm clock, clock radio; watch, wristwatch, pocket watch, stopwatch, Swiss watch; atomic clock, digital clock, analog clock, quartz watch, water clock; chronometer, chronoscope[obs3], chronograph; repeater; timekeeper, timepiece; dial, sundial, gnomon, horologe, pendulum, hourglass, clepsydra[obs3]; ghurry[obs3]. chronographer[obs3], chronologer, chronologist, timekeeper; annalist. calendar year, leap year, Julian calendar, Gregorian calendar, Chinese calendar, Jewish calendar, perpetual calendar, Farmer's almanac, fiscal year. V. fix the time, mark the time; date, register, chronicle; measure time, beat time, mark time; bear date; synchronize watches. Adj. chronological, chronometrical[obs3], chronogrammatical[obs3]; cinquecento[Fr], quattrocento[obs3], trecento[obs3]. Adv. o'clock.

#115. [False estimate of time.] Anachronism. — N. anachronism, metachronism, parachronism, prochronism; prolepsis, misdate; anticipation, antichronism.
disregard of time, neglect of time, oblivion of time.
intempestivity &c. 135[obs3].
V. misdate, antedate, postdate, backdate, overdate[obs3]; anticipate; take no note of time, lose track of time; anachronize[obs3].
Adj. misdated &c. v.; undated; overdue, past due; out of date.
<— p. 34 —>

% 2. RELATIVE TIME

Time with reference to Succession %

#116. Priority. — N. priority, antecedence, anteriority, precedence, pre-existence; precession &c. 280; precursor &c. 64; the past &c. 122; premises. V. precede, come before; forerun; go before &c. (lead) 280; preexist; dawn; presage &c. 511; herald, usher in. be beforehand &c. (be early) 132; steal a march upon, anticipate, forestall; have the start, gain the start. Adj. prior, previous; preceding, precedent; anterior, antecedent; pre- existing, pre-existent; former, foregoing; aforementioned, before- mentioned, abovementioned; aforesaid, said; introductory &c. (precursory) 64. Adv. before, prior to; earlier; previously &c. adj.; afore[obs3], aforehand[obs3], beforehand, ere, theretofore, erewhile[obs3]; ere then, ere now, before then, before now; erewhile[obs3], already, yet, beforehand; on the eve of. Phr. prior tempore prior jure[Lat].

#117. Posteriority. — N. posteriority; succession, sequence; following &c. 281.; subsequence, supervention; futurity &c. 121; successor; sequel &c. 65; remainder, reversion. V. follow &c. 281 after, come after, go after; succeed, supervene; ensue, occur; step into the shoes of. Adj. subsequent, posterior, following, after, later, succeeding, postliminious[obs3], postnate[obs3]; postdiluvial[obs3], postdiluvian[obs3]; puisnel!; posthumous; future &c. 121; afterdinner, postprandial. Adv. subsequently, after, afterwards, since, later; at a subsequent, at a later period, at a later date; next, in the sequel, close upon, thereafter, thereupon, upon which, eftsoonsl; from that time, from that moment; after a while, after a time; in process of time.

#118. The Present Time. — N. the present, the present time, the present day, the present moment, the present juncture, the present occasion; the times, the existing time, the time being; today, these days, nowadays, our times, modern times, the twentieth century; nonce, crisis, epoch, day, hour. age, time of life. Adj. present, actual, instant, current, existing, extant, that is; present-day, up-to-date, up-to-the-moment. Adv. at this time, at this moment &c. 113; at the present time &c. n.; now, at present; at hand. at this time of day, today, nowadays; already; even now, but now, just now; on the present occasion; for the time being, for the nonce; pro hac vice[Lat].; on the nail, on the spot; on the spur of the moment, until now; to this day, to the present day. Phr. "the present hour alone is man's" [Johnson].

#119. [Time different from the present.] Different time. — N.
different time, other time.
[Indefinite time] aorist.
Adj. aoristic; indefinite.
Adv. at that time, at which time, at that moment, at that instant;
then, on that occasion, upon; not now, some other time.
when; whenever, whensoever; upon which, on which occasion; at another,
at a different, at some other, at any- time; at various times; some one of
these days, one of these days, one fine morning; eventually, some day, by
and by, sooner or later; some time or other; once upon a time.
<— p. 35 —>

#120. Synchronism. — N. synchronism; coexistence, coincidence; simultaneousness, simultaneity &c. adj.; concurrence, concomitance, unity of time, interim. [Having equal times] isochronism[obs3]. contemporary, coetanian[obs3]. V. coexist, concur, accompany, go hand in hand, keep pace with; synchronize. Adj. synchronous, synchronal[obs3], synchronic, synchronical, synchronistical[obs3]; simultaneous, coexisting, coincident, concomitant, concurrent; coeval, coevous[obs3]; contemporary, contemporaneous; coetaneous[obs3]; coeternal; isochronous. Adv. at the same time; simultaneously &c. adj.; together, in concert, during the same time; in the same breath; pari passu[Lat]; in the interim; as one. at the very moment &c. 113; just as, as soon as; meanwhile &c. (while) 106.

#121. [Prospective time.] Futurity. — N. futurity, futurition; future, hereafter, time to come; approaching time, coming time, subsequent time, after time, approaching age, coming age, subsequent age, after age, approaching days, coming days, subsequent days, after days, approaching hours, coming hours, subsequent hours, after hours, approaching ages, coming ages, subsequent ages, after ages, approaching life, coming life, subsequent life, after life, approaching years, coming years, subsequent years, after years; morrow; millennium, doomsday, day of judgment, crack of doom, remote future. approach of time advent, time drawing on, womb of time; destiny &c. 152; eventuality. heritage, heirs posterity. prospect &c. (expectation) 507; foresight &c. 510. V. look forwards; anticipate &c. (expect) 507, (foresee) 510; forestall &c. (be early) 132. come on, draw on; draw near; approach, await, threaten; impend &c. (be destined) 152. Adj. future, to come; coming &c. (impending) 152; next, near; close at hand; eventual, ulterior; in prospect &c. (expectation) 507. Adv. prospectively, hereafter, in future; kal[obs3], tomorrow, the day after tomorrow; in course of time, in process of time, in the fullness of time; eventually, ultimately, sooner or later; proximo[Lat]; paulo post futurum[Lat]; in after time; one of these days; after a time, after a while. from this time; henceforth, henceforwards[obs3]; thence; thenceforth, thenceforward; whereupon, upon which. soon &c. (early) 132; on the eve of, on the point of, on the brink of; about to; close upon. Phr. quid sit futurum cras fuge quaerere [Latin] [Horace].

#122. [Retrospective time.] The Past — N. the past, past time; days of yore, times of yore, days of old, times of old, days past, times past, days gone by, times gone by; bygone days; old times, ancient times, former times; fore time; the good old days, the olden time, good old time; auld lang syne[obs3]; eldl. antiquity, antiqueness[obs3], status quo; time immemorial; distance of time; remote age, remote time; remote past; rust of antiquity [study of the past] paleontology, paleography, paleology[obs3]; paleozoology; palaetiologyl[obs3], archaeology; paleogeography; paleoecology; paleobotany; paleoclimatooogy; archaism, antiquarianism, medievalism, Pre-Raphaelitism; paleography. retrospect, retrospection, looking back, memory &c. 505. <— originally - preterition; priority &c. 116 —>

laudator temporis acti[Lat]; medievalist, Pre-Raphaelite; antiquary, antiquarian; archmologist &c.[obs3]; Oldbuck, Dryasdust. ancestry &c. (paternity) 166. V. be past &c. adj.; have expired &c. adj., have run its course, have had its day; pass; pass by, go by, pass away, go away, pass off, go off; lapse, blow over. look back, trace back, cast the eyes back; exhume. Adj. past, gone, gone by, over, passed away, bygone, foregone; elapsed, lapsed, preterlapsed[obs3], expired, no more, run out, blown over, has-been, that has been, extinct, antediluvian, antebellum, never to return, gone with the wind, exploded, forgotten, irrecoverable; obsolete &c. (old) 124. former, pristine, quondam, ci-devant[Fr], late; ancestral. foregoing; last, latter; recent, over night; preterperfect[obs3], preterpluperfect[obs3]. looking back &c. v.; retrospective, retroactive; archaeological &c. n. Adv. paleo-; archaeo-; formerly; of old, of yore; erst[Ger], whilom, erewhile[obs3], time was, ago, over; in the olden time &c. n.; anciently, long ago, long since; a long while, a long time ago; years ago, yesteryear, ages ago; some time ago, some time since, some time back. yesterday, the day before yesterday; last year, ultimo; lately &c. (newly) 123. retrospectively; ere now, before now, till now; hitherto, heretofore; no longer; once, once upon a time; from time immemorial, from prehistoric times; in the memory of man; time out of mind; already, yet, up to this time; ex post facto. Phr. time was; the time has been, the time hath been; you can't go home again; fuimus Troes [Lat][Vergil]; fruit Ilium [Vergil]; hoc erat in more majorum[Lat]; "O call back yesterday, bid time return" [Richard II]; tempi passati[It]; "the eternal landscape of the past" [Tennyson]; ultimus Romanorum[Lat]; "what's past is prologue" [Tempest]; "whose yesterdays look backward with a smile" [Young].

<— p. 36 —>

#123. Newness. — N. newness &c. adj.; novelty, recency; immaturity; youth &c. 127; gloss of novelty. innovation; renovation &c. (restoration) 660. modernism; mushroom, parvenu; latest fashion. V. renew &c. (restore) 660; modernize. Adj. new, novel, recent, fresh, green; young &c. 127; evergreen; raw, immature, unsettled, yeasty; virgin; untried, unhandseled[obs3], untrodden, untrod, unbeaten; fire-new, span-new. late, modern, neoteric, hypermodern, nouveau; new-born, nascent, neonatal[med.], new-fashioned, new-fangled, new-fledged; of yesterday; just out, brand-new, up to date, up to the minute, with it, fashionable, in fashion; in, hip [coll.]; vernal, renovated, sempervirent[obs3], sempervirid[obs3]. fresh as a rose, fresh as a daisy, fresh as paint; spick and span. Adv. newly &c. adj.; afresh, anew, lately, just now, only yesterday, the other day; latterly, of late. not long ago, a short time ago. Phr. di novello tutto par bello[It]; nullum est jam dictum quod non dictum est prius[Lat]; una scopa nuova spazza bene[It].

#124. Oldness. — N. oldness &c. adj[obs3].; age, antiquity; cobwebs of antiquity; maturity; decline, decay; senility &c. 128. seniority, eldership, primogeniture; archaism &c. (the past) 122; thing of the past, relic of the past; megatherium[obs3]; Sanskrit. tradition, prescription, custom, immemorial usage, common law. V. be old &c. adj.; have had its day, have seen its day; become old &c. adj.; age, fade, senesce. Adj. old, ancient, antique; of long standing, time-honored, venerable; elder, eldest; firstborn. prime; primitive, primeval, primigenous[obs3]; paleontological, paleontologic, paleoanthropological, paleoanthropic[obs3], paleolithic; primordial, primordinate[obs3]; aboriginal &c. (beginning) 66; diluvian[obs3], antediluvian; protohistoric[obs3]; prehistoric; antebellum, colonial, precolumbian; patriarchal, preadamite[obs3]; paleocrystic[obs3]; fossil, paleozoolical, paleozoic, preglacial[obs3], antemundane[obs3]; archaic, classic, medieval, Pre-Raphaelite, ancestral, black-letter. immemorial, traditional, prescriptive, customary, whereof the memory of man runneth not to the contrary; inveterate, rooted. antiquated, of other times, rococo, of the old school, after-age, obsolete; out of date, out of fashion, out of it; stale, old-fashioned, behind the age; old-world; exploded; gone out, gone by; passe, run out; senile &c. 128; time worn; crumbling &c. (deteriorated) 659; secondhand. old as the hills, old as Methuselah, old as Adam[obs3], old as history. [geological eras (list, starting at given number of years bp)] Archeozoic[5,000,000,000], Proterozoic[1,500,000,000], Paleozoic[600,000,000], Mesozoic[220,000,000], Cenozoic[70,000,000]. [geological periods (list)] Precambrian, Cambrian[600,000,000], Ordovician[500,000,000], Silurian[440,000,000], Devonian[400,000,000], Mississippian[350,000,000], Pennsylvanian[300,000,000], Permian[270,000,000], Triassic[220,000,000], Jurassic[180,000,000], Cretaceous[135,000,000]; Tertiary[70,000,000], Paleogene[70,000,000], Neocene[25,0000,000]; Quaternary[1,000,000]. [geological epochs (list, starting at 70,000,000 years bp)] Paleocene, Eocene, Oligocene, Miocene, Pliocene, Pleistocene, Recent. Adv. since the world was made, since the year one, since the days of Methuselah. Phr. vetera extollimus recentium incuriosi [Lat][Tacitus].

#125. Morning. [Noon.] — N. morning, morn, forenoon, a.m., prime, dawn, daybreak; dayspring[obs3], foreday[obs3], sunup; peep of day, break of day; aurora; first blush of the morning, first flush of the morning, prime of the morning; twilight, crepuscule, sunrise; cockcrow, cockcrowing[obs3]; the small hours, the wee hours of the morning. spring; vernal equinox, first point of Aries. noon; midday, noonday; noontide, meridian, prime; nooning, noontime. summer, midsummer. Adj. matin, matutinal[obs3]; vernal. Adv. at sunrise &c. n.; with the sun, with the lark, "when the morning dawns". Phr. "at shut of evening flowers" [Paradise Lost]; entre chien et loup[Fr]; "flames in the forehead of the morning sky" [Milton]; "the breezy call of incense-breathing morn" [Gray].

#126. Evening. [Midnight.] — N. evening, eve; decline of day, fall of day, close of day; candlelight, candlelighting[obs3]; eventide, nightfall, curfew, dusk, twilight, eleventh hour; sunset, sundown; going down of the sun, cock- shut, dewy eve, gloaming, bedtime. afternoon, postmeridian, p.m. autumn; fall, fall of the leaf; autumnal equinox; Indian summer, St. Luke's summer, St. Martin's summer. midnight; dead of night, witching hour, witching hour of night, witching time of night; winter; killing time. Adj. vespertine, autumnal, nocturnal. Phr. "midnight, the outpost of advancing day" [Longfellow]; "sable- vested Night" [Milton]; "this gorgeous arch with golden worlds inlay'd" [Young].

<— p. 37 —>

#127. Youth. — N. youth; juvenility, juvenescence[obs3]; juniority[obs3]; infancy; babyhood, childhood, boyhood, girlhood, youthhood[obs3]; incunabula; minority, nonage, teens, tender age, bloom. cradle, nursery, leading strings, pupilage, puberty, pucelage[obs3]. prime of life, flower of life, springtide of life[obs3], seedtime of life, golden season of life; heyday of youth, school days; rising generation. Adj. young, youthful, juvenile, green, callow, budding, sappy, puisne, beardless, under age, in one's teens; in statu pupillari[Lat]; younger, junior; hebetic[obs3], unfledged. Phr. "youth on the prow and pleasure at the helm" [Gray]; "youth . . . the glad season of life" [Carlyle].

#128. Age. — N. age; oldness[obs3] &c. adj.; old age, advanced age, golden years; senility, senescence; years, anility[obs3], gray hairs, climacteric, grand climacteric, declining years, decrepitude, hoary age, caducity[obs3], superannuation; second childhood, second childishness; dotage; vale of years, decline of life, "sear and yellow leaf" [Macbeth]; threescore years and ten; green old age, ripe age; longevity; time of life. seniority, eldership; elders &c. (veteran) 130; firstling; doyen, father; primogeniture. [Science of old age.] geriatrics, nostology. V. be aged &c. adj.; grow old, get old &c. adj.; age; decline, wane, dodder; senesce. Adj. aged; old &c. 124; elderly, geriatric, senile; matronly, anilel; in years; ripe, mellow, run to seed, declining, waning, past one's prime; gray, gray-headed; hoar, hoary; venerable, time-worn, antiquated, passe, effete, decrepit, superannuated; advanced in life, advanced in years; stricken in years; wrinkled, marked with the crow's foot; having one foot in the grave; doting &c. (imbecile) 499; like the last of pea time. older, elder, eldest; senior; firstborn. turned of, years old; of a certain age, no chicken, old as Methuselah; ancestral, patriarchal, &c. (ancient) 124; gerontic. Phr. "give me a staff of honor for my age" [Titus Andronicus]; bis pueri senes [Lat]; peu de gens savent elre vieux[Fr]; plenus annis abiit plenus honoribus [Lat] [Pliny the Younger]; "old age is creeping on apace" [Byron]; "slow-consuming age" [Gray]; "the hoary head is a crown of glory" [Proverbs xvi, 31]; "the silver livery of advised age" [II Henry VI]; to grow old gracefully; "to vanish in the chinks that Time has made" [Rogers].

#129. Infant.— N. infant, babe, baby, babe in arms; nurseling, suckling, yearling, weanling; papoose, bambino; kid; vagitus. child, bairn, little one, brat, chit, pickaninny, urchin; bantling, bratling[obs3]; elf; youth, boy, lad, stripling, youngster, youngun, younker[obs3], callant[obs3], whipster[obs3], whippersnapper, whiffet [obs3][U.S.], schoolboy, hobbledehoy, hopeful, cadet, minor, master; scion; sap, seedling; tendril, olive branch, nestling, chicken, larva, chrysalis, tadpole, whelp, cub, pullet, fry, callow; codlin, codling; foetus, calf, colt, pup, foal, kitten; lamb, lambkin[obs3]; aurelia[obs3], caterpillar, cocoon, nymph, nympha[obs3], orphan, pupa, staddle[obs3]. girl; lass, lassie; wench, miss, damsel, demoiselle; maid, maiden; virgin; hoyden. Adj. infantine[obs3], infantile; puerile; boyish, girlish, childish, babyish, kittenish; baby; newborn, unfledged, new-fledged, callow. in the cradle, in swaddling clothes, in long clothes, in arms, in leading strings; at the breast; in one's teens.

#130. Veteran.— N. veteran, old man, seer, patriarch, graybeard; grandfather, grandsire; grandam; gaffer, gammer; crone; pantaloon; sexagenarian, octogenarian, nonagenarian, centenarian; old stager; dotard &c. 501. preadamite[obs3], Methuselah, Nestor, old Parr; elders; forefathers &c. (paternity) 166. Phr. "superfluous lags the veteran on the stage" [Johnson].

<— p. 38 —>

#131. Adolescence. — N. adolescence, pubescence, majority; adultism; adultness &c. adj.; manhood, virility, maturity full age, ripe age; flower of age; prime of life, meridian of life, spring of life. man &c. 373; woman &c. 374; adult, no chicken. V. come of age, come to man's estate, come to years of discretion; attain majority, assume the toga virilis[Lat]; have cut one's eyeteeth, have sown one's mild oats. Adj. adolescent, pubescent, of age; of full age, of ripe age; out of one's teens, grown up, mature, full grown, in one's prime, middle-aged, manly, virile, adult; womanly, matronly; marriageable, nubile.

% Time with reference to an Effect or Purpose %

#132. Earliness. — N. {ant. 133} earliness &c. adj.; morning &c. 125. punctuality; promptitude &c. (activity) 682; haste &c. (velocity) 274; suddenness &c. (instantaneity) 113. prematurity, precocity, precipitation, anticipation; a stitch in time. V. be early &c. adj., be beforehand &c. adv.; keep time, take time by the forelock, anticipate, forestall; have the start, gain the start; steal a march upon; gain time, draw on futurity; bespeak, secure, engage, preengage[obs3]. accelerate; expedite &c. (quicken) 274; make haste &c. (hurry) 684. Adj. early, prime, forward; prompt &c. (active) 682; summary. premature, precipitate, precocious; prevenient[obs3], anticipatory; rath[obs3]. sudden &c. (instantaneous) 113; unexpected &c. 508; near, near at hand; immediate. Adv. early, soon, anon, betimes, rath[obs3]; eft, eftsoons; ere long, before long, shortly. beforehand; prematurely &c. adj.; precipitately &c. (hastily) 684; too soon; before its time, before one's time; in anticipation; unexpectedly &c. 508. suddenly &c. (instantaneously) 113; before one can say "Jack Robinson", at short notice, extempore; on the spur of the moment, on the spur of the occasion [Bacon]; at once; on the spot, on the instant; at sight; offhand, out of hand; a' vue d'oeil[Fr]; straight, straightway, straightforth[obs3]; forthwith, incontinently, summarily, immediately, briefly, shortly, quickly, speedily, apace, before the ink is dry, almost immediately, presently at the first opportunity, in no long time, by and by, in a while, directly. Phr. no sooner said than done, immediately, if not sooner; tout vient a temps pour qui sait attendre[Fr].

#132a. Punctuality — N. punctuality, promptness, immediateness.
V. be prompt, be on time, be in time; arrive on time; be in the nick of time.
Adj. timely, seasonable, in time, punctual, prompt.
Adv. on time, punctually, at the deadline, precisely, exactly; right on time, to the minute; in time; in good time, in military time, in pudding timel, in due time; time enough; with no time to spare, by a hair's breadth.
Phr. touch and go, not a minute too soon, in the nick of time, just under the wire, get on board before the train leaves the station.

#133. Lateness. — N. {ant. 132} lateness &c. adj.; tardiness &c. (slowness) 275. delay, delation; cunctation, procrastination; deferring, deferral &c. v.; postponement, adjournment, prorogation, retardation, respite, pause, reprieve, stay of execution; protraction, prolongation; Fabian policy, medecine expectante[Fr], chancery suit, federal case; leeway; high time; moratorium, holdover. V. be late &c. adj.; tarry, wait, stay, bide, take time; dawdle &c. (be inactive) 683; linger, loiter; bide one's time, take one's time; gain time; hang fire; stand over, lie over. put off, defer, delay, lay over, suspend; table [parliamentary]; shift off, stave off; waive, retard, remand, postpone, adjourn; procrastinate; dally; prolong, protract; spin out, draw out, lengthen out, stretch out; prorogue; keep back; tide over; push to the last, drive to the last; let the matter stand over; reserve &c. (store) 636; temporize; consult one's pillow, sleep on it. lose an opportunity &c. 135; be kept waiting, dance attendance; kick one's heels, cool one's heels; faire antichambre[Fr] [obs3]; wait impatiently; await &c. (expect) 507; sit up, sit up at night. Adj. late, tardy, slow, behindhand, serotine[obs3], belated, postliminious[obs3], posthumous, backward, unpunctual, untimely; delayed, postponed; dilatory &c. (slow) 275; delayed &c. v.; in abeyance. Adv. late; lateward[obs3], backward; late in the day; at sunset, at the eleventh hour, at length, at last; ultimately; after time, behind time, after the deadline; too late; too late for &c. 135. slowly, leisurely, deliberately, at one's leisure; ex post facto; sine die [parl.]. Phr. nonum prematur in annum [Lat] [Horace]; "against the sunbeams serotine and lucent" [Longfellow]; ie meglio tardi che mai[It]; deliberando saepe perit occasio [Lat][Syrus].

<— p. 39 —>

#134. Occasion. — N. {ant. 135} timeliness, occasion, opportunity, opening, room; event (eventuality) 151; suitable season, proper season, suitable time, proper time; high time; opportuneness &c. adj.; tempestivity[obs3]. crisis, turn, juncture, conjuncture; crisis, turning point, given time. nick of time; golden opportunity, well timed opportunity, fine opportunity, favorable opportunity, opening; clear stage, fair field; mollia tempora[Lat][obs3]; fata Morgana[Lat]; spare time &c. (leisure) 685. V. seize &c. (take) 789 an opportunity, use &c. 677 an opportunity, give &c. 784 an opportunity, use an occasion; improve the occasion. suit the occasion &c. (be expedient) 646. seize the occasion, strike while the iron is hot, battre le fer sur l'enclume[Fr], make hay while the sun shines, seize the present hour, take time by the forelock, prendre la balle au bond[Fr]. Adj. opportune, timely, well-timed, timeful[obs3], seasonable. providential, lucky, fortunate, happy, favorable, propitious, auspicious, critical; suitable &c. 23; obiter dicta. Adv. opportunely &c. adj.; in proper course, in due course, in proper season, in due season, in proper time, in due time; for the nonce; in the nick of time, in the fullness of time; all in good time; just in time, at the eleventh hour, now or never. by the way, by the by; en passant[Fr], a propos[Fr]; pro re nata[Lat], pro hac vice[Lat]; par parenthese[Fr], parenthetically, by way of parenthesis, incidentally; while speaking of, while on the subject; extempore; on the spur of the moment, on the spur of the occasion; on the spot &c. (early) 132. Phr. carpe diem[Lat], [Horace]; occasionem cognosce[Lat]; one's hour is come, the time is up; that reminds me, now that you mention it, come to think of it; bien perdu bien connu[Fr]; e sempre l'ora[It]; ex quovis ligno non fit Mercurius[Lat]; nosce tempus[Lat]; nunc aut nunquam[Lat].

#135. Untimeliness — N. {ant. 134} untimeliness, intempestivity[obs3], unseasonableness, inexpedience; unsuitable time, improper time; unreasonableness &c. adj; evil hour; contretemps; intrusion; anachronism &c. 115. bad time, wrong time, inappropriate time, not the right occasion, unsuitable time, inopportune time, poor timing. V. be ill timed &c. adj.; mistime, intrude, come amiss, break in upon; have other fish to fry; be busy, be occupied. lose an opportunity, throw away an opportunity, waste an opportunity, neglect &c. 460 an opportunity; allow the opportunity to pass, suffer the opportunity to pass, allow the opportunity to slip, suffer the opportunity to slip, allow the opportunity to go by, suffer the opportunity to go by, allow the opportunity to escape, suffer the opportunity to escape, allow the opportunity to lapse, suffer the opportunity to lapse, allow the occasion to pass, allow the occasion to slip by; waste time &c. (be inactive) 683; let slip through the fingers, lock the barn door after the horse is stolen. Adj. ill-timed, mistimed; ill-fated, ill-omened, ill-starred; untimely, unseasonable; out of date, out of season; inopportune, timeless, intrusive, untoward, mal a propos[Fr], unlucky, inauspicious, infelicitous, unbefitting, unpropitious, unfortunate, unfavorable; unsuited &c. 24; inexpedient &c. 647. unpunctual &c. (late) 133; too late for; premature &c. (early) 132; too soon for; wise after the event, monday morning quarterbacking, twenty- twenty hindsight. Adv. inopportunely &c. adj.; as ill luck would have it, in an evil hour, the time having gone by, a day after the fair. Phr. after death the doctor, after meat mustard.

% 3. RECURRENT TIME %

#136. Frequency. — N. frequency, oftness[obs3], oftenness[obs3], commonness; repetition &c. 104; normality &c. 80; example (conformity) 82; routine, custom (habit) 613. regularity, uniformity, constancy, clock-work precision; punctuality &c. (exactness) 494; even tenor; system; routine &c. (custom) 613; formula; rule &c. (form, regulation) 697; keynote, standard, model; precedent &c. (prototype) 22; conformity &c. 82. V. recur &c. 104; do nothing but; keep, keep on. Adj. frequent, many times, not rare, thickcoming[obs3], incessant, perpetual, continual, steady, constant, thick; uniform; repeated &c. 104; customary &c. 613 (habit) 613; regular (normal) 80; according to rule &c. (conformable) 82. common, everyday, usual, ordinary, familiar. old-hat, boring, well-known, trivial. Adv. often, oft; ofttimes[obs3], oftentimes; frequently; repeatedly &c. 104; unseldom[obs3], not unfrequently[obs3]; in quick succession, in rapid succession; many a time and oft; daily, hourly &c.; every day, every hour, every moment &c. perpetually, continually, constantly, incessantly, without ceasing, at all times, daily and hourly, night and day, day and night, day after day, morning noon and night, ever anon, invariably (habit) 613. most often; commonly &c. (habitually) 613. sometimes, occasionally, at times, now and then, from time to time, there being times when, toties quoties[Lat] [obs3], often enough, when the mood strikes, again and again.

<— p. 40 —>

#137. Infrequency. — N. infrequency, rareness, rarity; fewness &c. 103; seldomness[obs3]; uncommonness.

V. be rare &c. adj.

Adj. unfrequent[obs3], infrequent; rare, rare as a blue diamond; few &c. 103; scarce; almost unheard of, unprecedented, which has not occurred within the memory of the oldest inhabitant, not within one's previous experience; not since Adam[obs3].

scarce as hen's teeth; one in a million; few and far between.

Adv. seldom, rarely, scarcely, hardly; not often, not much, infrequently, unfrequently[obs3], unoften[obs3]; scarcely, scarcely ever, hardly ever; once in a blue moon.

once; once in a blue moon; once in a million years; once for all, once in a way; pro hac vice[Lat].

Phr. ein mal kein mal[German].

#138. Regularity of recurrence. Periodicity. — N. periodicity, intermittence; beat; oscillation &c. 314; pulse, pulsation; rhythm; alternation, alternateness, alternativeness, alternity[obs3]. bout, round, revolution, rotation, turn, say. anniversary, jubilee, centenary. catamenia[obs3]; courses, menses, menstrual flux. [Regularity of return] rota, cycle, period, stated time, routine; days of the week; Sunday, Monday &c.; months of the year; January &c.; feast, fast &c.; Christmas, Easter, New Year's day &c. Allhallows[obs3], Allhallowmas[obs3], All Saints' Day; All Souls', All Souls' Day; Ash Wednesday, bicentennial, birthday, bissextile[obs3], Candlemas[obs3], Dewali, groundhog day [U.S.],

Halloween, Hallowmas[obs3], Lady day, leap year, Midsummer day, Muharram, woodchuck day [U.S.], St. Swithin's day, natal day; yearbook; yuletide. punctuality, regularity, steadiness. V. recur in regular order, recur in regular succession; return, revolve; come again, come in its turn; come round, come round again; beat, pulsate; alternate; intermit. Adj. periodic, periodical; serial, recurrent, cyclical, rhythmical; recurring &c. v.; intermittent, remittent; alternate, every other. hourly; diurnal, daily; quotidian, tertian, weekly, hebdomadall, hebdomadaryl; biweekly, fortnightly; bimonthly; catameniall; monthly, menstrual; yearly, annual; biennial, triennial, &c.; centennial, secular; paschal, lenten, &c. regular, steady, punctual, regular as clockwork. Adv. periodically &c. adj.; at regular intervals, at stated times; at fixed established, at established periods; punctually &c. adj. de die in diem[Lat]; from day to day, day by day. by turns; in turn, in rotation; alternately, every other day, off and on, ride and tie, round and round.

#139. Irregularity of recurrence. — N. irregularity, uncertainty, unpunctuality; fitfulness &c. adj.; capriciousness, ecrhythmusl. Adj. irregular, uncertain, unpunctual, capricious, desultory, fitful, flickering; rambling, rhapsodical; spasmodic; immethodical[obs3], unmethodical, variable. Adv. irregularly &c. adj.; by fits and starts &c. (discontinuously) 70.

% SECTION VII. CHANGE

1. SIMPLE CHANGE %

#140. [Difference at different times.] Change. — N. change, alteration, mutation, permutation, variation, modification, modulation, inflexion, mood, qualification, innovation, metastasis, deviation, turn, evolution, revolution; diversion; break. transformation, transfiguration; metamorphosis; transmutation; deoxidization[Chem]; transubstantiation; mutagenesis[Genet], transanimation[obs3], transmigration, metempsychosisl; avatar; alterative. conversion &c. (gradual change) 144; revolution &c. (sudden or radical change) 146 inversion &c. (reversal) 218; displacement &c. 185; transference &c. 270. changeableness &c. 149; tergiversation &c. (change of mind) 607. V. change, alter, vary, wax and wane; modulate, diversify, qualify, tamper with; turn, shift, veer, tack, chop, shuffle, swerve, warp, deviate, turn aside, evert, intervert[obs3]; pass to, take a turn, turn the corner, resume. work a change, modify, vamp, superinduce; transform, transfigure, transmute, transmogrify, transume[obs3]; metamorphose, ring the changes. innovate, introduce new blood, shuffle the cards; give a turn to, give a color to; influence, turn the scale; shift the scene, turn over a new leaf. recast &c. 146; reverse &c. 218; disturb &c. 61; convert into &c. 144. Adj. changed &c. v.; newfangled; changeable &c. 149; transitional; modifiable; alterative. Adv. mutatis mutandis[Lat]. Int. quantum mutatus[Lat]! Phr. "a change came o'er the spirit of my dream" [Byron]; nous avons change tout cela [Fr][Moliere]; tempora mutantur nos et mutamur in illis[Lat][obs3]; non sum qualis eram [Lat][Horace]; casaque tourner[Fr]; corpora lente augescent cito extinguuntur [Lat][obs3][Tacitus]; in statu quo ante bellum[Lat]; "still ending and beginning still" [Cowper]; vox audita perit littera scripta manet[Lat].

<— p. 41 —>

#141. [Absence of change.] Permanence. — N. stability &c. 150; quiescence &c. 265; obstinacy &c. 606. permanence, persistence, endurance; durability; standing, status quo; maintenance, preservation, conservation; conservation; law of the Medes and Persians; standing dish. V. let alone, let be, let it be; persist, remain, stay, tarry, rest; stet [copy editing]; hold, hold on; last, endure, bide, abide, aby[obs3], dwell, maintain, keep; stand, stand still, stand fast; subsist, live, outlive, survive; hold one's ground, keep one's ground, hold one's footing, keep one's footing; hold good. Adj. stable &c. 150; persisting &c. v.; permanent; established; unchanged &c. (change &c. 140); renewed; intact, inviolate; persistent; monotonous, uncheckered[obs3]; unfailing. undestroyed, unrepealed, unsuppressed[obs3]; conservative, qualis ab incepto[Lat]; prescriptive &c. (old) 124; stationary &c. 265. Adv. in statu quo[Lat]; for good, finally; at a stand, at a standstill; uti possidetis[Lat]; without a shadow of turning. Phr. esto perpetua[Lat]; nolumus leges Angliae mutari[Lat][obs3]; j'y suis et j'y ereste[Fr].

#142. [Change from action to rest.] Cessation. — N. cessation, discontinuance, desistance, desinence[obs3]. intermission, remission; suspense, suspension; interruption; stop; stopping &c. v.; closure, stoppage, halt; arrival &c. 292. pause, rest, lull, respite, truce, drop; interregnum, abeyance; cloture [U.S. congress]. dead stop, dead stand, dead lock; finis, cerrado[Sp]; blowout, burnout, meltdown, disintegration; comma, colon, semicolon, period, full stop; end &c. 67; death &c. 360. V. cease, discontinue, desist, stay, halt; break off, leave off; hold, stop, pull up, stop short; stick, hang fire; halt; pause, rest; burn out, blow out, melt down. have done with, give over, surcease, shut up shop; give up &c. (relinquish) 624. hold one's hand, stay one's hand; rest on one's oars repose on one's laurels. come to a stand, come to a standstill; come to a deadlock, come to a full stop; arrive &c. 292; go out, die away; wear away, wear off; pass away &c. (be past) 122; be at an end; disintegrate, self-destruct. intromit, interrupt, suspend, interpel[obs3]; intermit, remit; put an end to, put a stop to, put a period to; derail; turn off, switch off, power down, deactivate, disconnect; bring to a stand, bring to a standstill; stop, cut short, arrest, stem the tide, stem the torrent; pull the check- string, pull the plug on. Int. hold! stop! enough! avast! have done! a truce to! soft! leave off! tenez[Fr]! Phr. "I pause for a reply" [Julius Caesar].

#143. Continuance in action. — N. continuance, continuation; run; perpetuation, prolongation; persistence &c. (perseverance) 604a; repetition &c. 104. V. continue, persist; go on, jog on, keep on, run on, hold on; abide, keep, pursue, stick to its course, take its course, maintain its course; carry on, keep up. sustain, uphold, hold up, keep on foot; follow up, perpetuate; maintain; preserve &c. 604a; harp upon &c. (repeat) 104. keep going, keep alive, keep the pot boiling, keep up the ball, keep up the good work; die in harness, die with one's boots on; hold on the even tenor of one's way, pursue the even tenor of one's way. let be; stare super antiquas vias[Lat][obs3]; quieta non movere[Lat]; let things take their course; stare decisis [Lat][Jurisprudence]. Adj. continuing &c. v.; uninterrupted, unintermitting[obs3], unvarying, unshifting[obs3]; unreversed[obs3], unstopped, unrevoked, unvaried; sustained; undying &c. (perpetual) 112; inconvertible. Int. keep it up! go to it! right away! right on! attaboy! Phr. nolumus leges Angliae mutari[Lat][obs3]; vestigia nulla retrorsum [Lat][Horace]; labitur et albetur [Lat][obs3][Horace].

<— p. 42 —>

#144. [Gradual change to something different.] Conversion. — N. conversion, reduction, transmutation, resolution, assimilation; evolution, sea change; change of state; assumption; naturalization; transportation; development [biol.], developing [photography]. [conversion of currency] conversion of currency, exchange of currency; exchange rate; bureau de change. chemistry, alchemy; progress, growth, lapse, flux. passage; transit, transition; transmigration, shifting &c. v.; phase; conjugation; convertibility. crucible, alembic, caldron, retort. convert, pervert, renegade, apostate. V. be converted into; become, get, wax; come to, turn to, turn into, evolve into, develop into; turn out, lapse, shift; run into, fall into, pass into, slide into, glide into, grow into, ripen into, open into, resolve itself into, settle into, merge into, emerge as; melt, grow, come round to, mature, mellow; assume the form of, assume the shape of, assume the state of, assume the nature of, assume the character of; illapsel; begin a new phase, assume a new phase, undergo a change. convert into, resolve into; make, render; mold, form &c. 240; remodel, new model, refound[obs3], reform, reorganize; assimilate to, bring to, reduce to. Adj. converted into &c. v.; convertible, resolvable into; transitional; naturalized. Adv. gradually, &c. (slowly) 275 in transitu &c. (transference) 270[Lat].

#145. Reversion. — N. reversion, return; revulsion. turning point, turn of the tide; status quo ante bellum; calm before a storm; alternation &c. (periodicity) 138; inversion &c. 219; recoil &c. 277; retreat, regression, retrogression &c. 283; restoration &c. 660; relapse, recidivism &c. 661; atavism; vicinism[obs3]; V. revert, turn back, regress; relapse &c. 661; recoil &c. 277; retreat &c. 283; restore &c. 660; undo, unmake; turn the tide, roll back the tide, turn the scale, tip the scale. Adj. reverting &c. v.; regressive, revulsive, reactionary; retrorse[obs3]. Adv. a rebours[Fr].

#146. [Sudden or violent change.] Revolution. — N. revolution, bouleversement, subversion, break up; destruction &c. 162; sudden change, radical change, sweeping organic change; change of state, phase change; quantum leap, quantum jump; clean sweep, coup d'etat[Fr], counter revolution. jump, leap, plunge, jerk, start, transiliencel; explosion; spasm, convulsion, throe, revulsion; storm, earthquake, cataclysm. legerdemain &c. (trick) 545. V. revolutionize; new model, remodel, recast; strike out something new, break with the past; change the face of, unsex. Adj. unrecognizable; revolutionary.

#147. [Change of one thing for another.] Substitution. — N. substitution, commutation; supplanting &c. v.; metaphor, metonymy &c. (figure of speech) 521. [Thing substituted] substitute, ersatz, makeshift, temporary expedient, replacement, succedaneum; shift, pis aller[Fr], stopgap, jury rigging, jury mast, locum tenens, warming pan, dummy, scapegoat; double; changeling; quid pro quo, alternative. representative &c. (deputy) 759; palimpsest. price, purchase money, consideration, equivalent. V. substitute, put in the place of, change for; make way for, give place to; supply the place of, take the place of; supplant, supersede, replace, cut out, serve as a substitute; step into stand in the shoes of; jury rig, make a shift with, put up with; borrow from Peter to pay Paul, take money out of one pocket and put it in another, cannibalize; commute, redeem, compound for. Adj. substituted &c.; ersatz; phony; vicarious, subditious[obs3]. Adv. instead; in place of, in lieu of, in the stead of, in the room of; faute de mieux[Fr].

#148. [Double or mutual change.] Interchange. — N. interchange, exchange; commutation, permutation, intermutation; reciprocation, transposition, rearrangement; shuffling; alternation, reciprocity; castling [at chess]; hocus-pocus.

interchangeableness[obs3], interchangeability.
recombination; combination 48[ref], 84..
barter &c. 794; tit for tat &c. (retaliation) 718; cross fire,
battledore and shuttlecock; quid pro quo.
V. interchange, exchange, counterchange[obs3]; bandy, transpose,
shuffle, change bands, swap, permute, reciprocate, commute; give and take,
return the compliment; play at puss in the corner, play at battledore and
shuttlecock; retaliate &c. 718; requite.
rearrange, recombine.
Adj. interchanged &c. v.; reciprocal, mutual, commutative,
interchangeable, intercurrent[obs3].
combinatorial[Math, Statistics].
recombinant[Biology, Genetics].
Adv. in exchange, vice versa, mutatis mutandis[Lat], backwards and
forwards, by turns, turn and turn about; each in his turn, everyone in his
turn.
Adj. substituted &c. v.; vicarious, subdititious[obs3].
Adv. instead; in place of, in lieu of, in the stead of, in the room
of; faute de mieux[Fr].
<— p. 43 —> % 2. COMPLEX CHANGE %

#149. Changeableness. — N. changeableness &c. adj.; mutability, inconstancy; versatility, mobility; instability,
unstable equilibrium; vacillation &c. (irresolution) 605; fluctuation, vicissitude; alternation &c. (oscillation) 314.
restlessness &c. adj. fidgets, disquiet; disquietude, inquietude; unrest; agitation &c. 315. moon, Proteus, chameleon,
quicksilver, shifting sands, weathercock, harlequin, Cynthia of the minute, April showers[obs3]; wheel of Fortune;
transientness &c. 111[obs3]. V. fluctuate, vary, waver, flounder, flicker, flitter, flit, flutter, shift, shuffle, shake, totter,
tremble, vacillate, wamble[obs3], turn and turn about, ring the changes; sway to and fro, shift to and fro; change and
change about; waffle, blow with the wind (irresolute) 605; oscillate &c. 314; vibrate between, two extremes, oscillate
between, two extremes; alternate; have as many phases as the moon. Adj. changeable, changeful; changing &c.
140; mutable, variable, checkered, ever changing; protean, proteiforml; versatile. unstaid[obs3], inconstant; un-
steady, unstable, unfixed, unsettled; fluctuating &c. v.; restless; agitated &c. 315; erratic, fickle; irresolute &c. 605;
capricious &c. 608; touch and go; inconsonant, fitful, spasmodic, vibratory; vagrant, wayward; desultory; afloat;
alternating; alterable, plastic, mobile; transient &c. 111; wavering. Adv. seesaw &c. (oscillation) 314; off and on. Phr.
"a rolling stone gathers no moss"; pictra mossa non fa muschis[It]; honores mutant mores[Lat]; varium et mutabile
semper femina [Lat][Vergil].

#150. Stability. — N. stability; immutability &c. adj.; unchangeability, &c. adj.; unchangeablenessl!; constancy; stable
equilibrium, immobility, soundness, vitality, stabiliment[obs3], stiffness, ankylosis[obs3], solidity, aplomb. establishment, fixture; rock, pillar, tower, foundation, leopard's spots, Ethiopia's skin. permanence &c. 141; obstinacy &c. 606.
V. be firm &c. adj.; stick fast; stand firm, keep firm, remain firm; weather the storm, stay the course, stick to the
course, keep the faith, don't give in, don't buckle under. settle, establish, stablish[obs3], ascertain, fix, set,
stabilitate[obs3]; retain, keep hold; make good, make sure; fasten &c. (join) 43; set on its legs, float; perpetuate.
settle down; strike roots, put down roots, take root; take up one's abode &c. 184; build one's house on a rock. Adj.
unchangeable, immutable; unaltered, unalterable; not to be changed, constant; permanent &c. 141; invariable, unde-
viating; stable, durable; perennial &c. (diuturnal) 110[obs3]. fixed, steadfast, firm, fast, steady, balanced; confirmed,
valid; fiducial[obs3]; immovable, irremovable, riveted, rooted; settled, established &c. v.; vested; incontrovertible,
stereotyped, indeclinable. tethered, anchored, moored, at anchor, on a rock, rock solid, firm as a rock; firmly seated,
firmly established &c. v.; deep-rooted, ineradicable; inveterate; obstinate &c. 606. transfixed, stuck fast, aground,
high and dry, stranded. [movable object rendered unmovable] stuck, jammed; unremovable; quiescent &c. 265;
deterioration &c. 659. indefeasible, irretrievable, intransmutable[obs3], incommutable[obs3], irresoluble[obs3],
irrevocable, irreversible, reverseless[obs3], inextinguishable, irreducible; indissoluble, indissolvable[obs3]; inde-
structible, undying, imperishable, incorruptible, indelible, indeciduous[obs3]; insusceptible, insusceptible of change.
Int. stet. Phr. littera scripta manet[Lat].

<— p. 44 —>

% Present Events %

#151. Eventuality. — N. eventuality, event, occurrence, incident, affair, matter, thing, episode, happening, proceeding, contingency, juncture, experience, fact; matter of fact; naked fact, bare facts, just the facts; phenomenon; advent. business, concern, transaction, dealing, proceeding; circumstance, particular, casualty, accident, adventure, passage, crisis, pass, emergency, contingency, consequence; opportunity (occasion) 143. the world, life, things, doings, affairs in general; things in general, affairs in general; the times, state of affairs, order of the day; course of things, tide of things, stream of things, current of things, run of things, march of things, course of events; ups and downs of life, vicissitudes of life; chapter of accidents &c. (chance) 156; situation &c. (circumstances) 8. V. happen, occur; take place, take effect; come, become of; come off, comeabout[obs3], come round, come into existence, come forth, come to pass, come on; pass, present itself; fall; fall out, turn out; run, be on foot, fall in; befall, betide, bechance[obs3]; prove, eventuate, draw on; turn up, crop up, spring up, pop up, arise, show up, show its face, appear, come forth, cast up; supervene, survene[obs3]; issue, arrive, ensue, arise, start, hold, take its course; pass off &c. (be past) 122. meet with; experience, enjoy, encounter, undergo, suffer, pass through, go through, be subjected to, be exposed to; fall to the lot of; be one's chance, be one's fortune, be one's lot; find; endure &c. (feel) 821. Adj. happening &c. v; going on, doing, current; in the wind, in the air, afloat; on foot, afoot, on the tapis[obs3]; at issue, in question; incidental. eventful, stirring, bustling, full of incident; memorable, momentous, signal. Adv. eventually; in the event of, in case, just in case; in the course of things; as things, times go; as the world goes, wags; as the tree falls, cat jumps; as it may turn out, happen. Phr. that's the way the ball bounces, that's the way the cookie crumbles; you never know what may turn up, you never know what the future will bring; the plot thickens; "breasts the blows of circumstance" [Tennyson]; "so runs round of life from hour to hour" "sprinkled along the waste of years" [Tennyson][Keble].

% Future Events %

#152. Destiny. — N. destiny &c. (necessity) 601; future existence, post existence; hereafter; future state, next world, world to come, after life; futurity &c. 121; everlasting life, everlasting death; life beyond the grave, world beyond the grave; prospect &c. (expectation) 507. V. impend; hang over, lie over; threaten, loom, await, come on, approach, stare one in the face; foreordain, preordain, predestine, doom, have in store for. Adj. impending &c. v.; destined; about to be, happen; coming, in store, to come, going to happen, instant, at hand, near; near, close at hand; over hanging, hanging over one's head, imminent; brewing, preparing, forthcoming; in the wind, on the cards, in reserve; that will, is to be; in prospect &c. (expected) 507; looming in the distance, horizon, future; unborn, in embryo; in the womb of time, futurity; pregnant &c. (producing) 161. Adv. in time, the long run; all in good time; eventually &c. 151; whatever may happen &c. (certainly) 474; as chance &c. 156 would have it.

% SECTION VIII. CAUSATION

1. CONSTANCY OF SEQUENCE IN EVENTS %

#153. [Constant antecedent]. Cause.— N. cause, origin, source, principle, element; occasioner[obs3], prime mover, primum mobile[Lat]; vera causa[Lat]; author &c. (producer) 164; mainspring; agent; leaven; groundwork, foundation &c. (support) 215. spring, fountain, well, font; fountainhead, spring head, wellhead; fons et origo[Lat], genesis; descent &c. (paternity) 166; remote cause; influence. pivot, hinge, turning point, lever, crux, fulcrum; key; proximate cause, causa causans[Lat]; straw that breaks the camel's back. ground; reason, reason why; why and wherefore, rationale, occasion, derivation; final cause &c. (intention) 620; les dessous des cartes[Fr]; undercurrents. rudiment, egg, germ, embryo, bud, root, radix radical, etymon, nucleus, seed, stem, stock, stirps, trunk, tap-root, gemmule[obs3], radicle, semen, sperm. nest, cradle, nursery, womb, nidus, birthplace, hotbed. causality, causation; origination; production &c. 161. V. be the cause &c. n of; originate; give origin to, give rise, to, give occasion to; cause, occasion, sow the seeds of, kindle, suscitate[obs3]; bring on, bring to bring pass, bring about; produce; create &c. 161; set up, set afloat, set on foot; found, broach, institute, lay the foundation of; lie at the root of. procure, induce, draw down, open the door to, superinduce, evoke, entail, operate; elicit, provoke. conduce to &c. (tend to) 176; contribute; have a hand in the pie, have a finger in the pie; determine, decide, turn the scale; have a common origin; derive its origin &c. (effect) 154. Adj. caused &c. v; causal, original; primary, primitive, primordial; aboriginal; protogenal[obs3]; radical; embryonic, embryotic[obs3]; in embryo, in ovo[Lat]; seminal, germinal; at the bottom of; connate, having a common origin. Adv. because &c. 155; behind the scenes. Phr. causa latet vis est notissima [Lat] [Ovid]; felix qui potuit rerum cognoscere causas [Lat][Vergil].

<— p. 45 —>

#154. [Constant sequent.] Effect.— N. effect, consequence; aftergrowth[obs3], aftercome[obs3]; derivative, derivation; result; resultant, resultance[obs3]; upshot, issue, denouement; end &c. 67; development, outgrowth, fruit, crop, harvest, product, bud. production, produce, work, handiwork, fabric, performance; creature, creation; offspring, offshoot; firstfruits[obs3], firstlings; heredity, telegony[obs3]; premices premises[obs3]. V. be the effect of &c. n.; be due to, be owing to; originate in, originate from; rise -, arise, take its rise spring from, proceed from, emanate from, come from, grow from, bud from, sprout from, germinate from, issue from, flow from, result from, follow from, derive its origin from, accrue from; come to, come of, come out of; depend upon, hang upon, hinge upon, turn upon. take the consequences, sow the wind and reap the whirlwind. Adj. owing to; resulting from &c. v.; derivable from; due to; caused by &c. 153; dependent upon; derived from, evolved from; derivative; hereditary; telegonous[obs3]. Adv. of course, it follows that, naturally, consequently; as a consequence, in consequence; through, all along of, necessarily, eventually. Phr. cela va sans dire[Fr], "thereby hangs a tale" [Taming of the Shrew].

#155. [Assignment of cause] Attribution — N. attribution, theory, etiology, ascription, reference to, rationale; accounting for &c. v; palaetiologyl, imputation, derivation from. filiation[obs3], affiliation; pedigree &c. (paternity) 166. explanation &c. (interpretation) 522; reason why &c. (cause) 153. V. attribute to, ascribe to, impute to, refer to, lay to, point to, trace to, bring home to; put down to, set down to, blame; charge on, ground on; invest with, assign as cause, lay at, the door of, father upon; account for, derive from, point out the reason &c. 153; theorize; tell how it comes; put the saddle on the right horse. Adj. attributed &c. v.; attributable &c. v.; referable to, referrible to[obs3], due to, derivable from; owing to &c. (effect) 154; putative; ecbatic[obs3]. Adv. hence, thence, therefore, for, since, on account of, because, owing to; on that account; from this cause, from that cause; thanks to, forasmuch as; whence, propter hoc[Lat]. why? wherefore? whence? how comes it, how is it, how happens it? how does it happen? in some way, in some such way; somehow, somehow or other. Phr. that is why; hinc illae lachrymae [Lat][Horace]. <— —————————————————————————————————————— 1. Whewell History of the inductive Sciences, book xviii vol. iii.p. 397 (3d edit.). 2 The word Chance has two distinct meanings: the first, the absence of assignable cause, as above; and the second, the absence of design — for the latter see 621. —>

#156. [Absence of assignable cause.] Chance. 2 — N. chance, indetermination, accident, fortune, hazard, hap, haphazard, chance medley, random, luck, raccroc[obs3], casualty, contingence, adventure, hit; fate &c. (necessity) 601; equal chance; lottery; tombola[obs3]; toss up &c. 621; turn of the table, turn of the cards; hazard of the die, chapter of accidents, fickle finger of fate; cast of the dice, throw of the dice; heads or tails, flip of a coin, wheel of Fortune; sortes[obs3], sortes Virgilianae[obs3]. probability, possibility, odds; long odds, run of luck; accidentalness; main chance, odds on, favorable odds. contingency, dependence (uncertainty) 475; situation (circumstance) 8. statistics, theory of Probabilities, theory of Chances; bookmaking; assurance; speculation, gaming &c. 621. V. chance, hap, turn up; fall to one's lot; be one's -fate &c. 601; stumble on light upon; take one's chance &c. 621. Adj. casual, fortuitous, accidental, adventitious, causeless, incidental, contingent, uncaused, undetermined, indeterminate; random, statistical; possible &c. 470; unintentional &c. 621. Adv. by chance, accidentally, by accident; casually; perchance &c. (possibly) 470; for aught one knows; as good would have it, as bad would have it, as luck would have it, as ill-luck would have it, as chance would have it; as it may be, as it may chance, as it may turn up, as it may happen; as the case may be. Phr. "grasps the skirts of happy chance" [Tennyson]; "the accident of an accident" [Lord Thurlow]. "There but for the grace of God go I."

<— p. 46 —> % 2. CONNECTION BETWEEN CAUSE AND EFFECT % <— "power" contains the concepts of both efficacy and efficiency —>

#157. Power.— N. power; potency, potentiality; jiva[obs3]; puissance, might, force, energy &c. 171; dint; right hand, right arm; ascendency[obs3], sway, control; prepotency, prepollencel; almightiness, omnipotence; authority &c. 737; strength &c. 159. ability; ableness &c. adj[obs3].; competency; efficacy; efficiency, productivity, expertise (skill) 698; validity, cogency; enablement[obs3]; vantage ground; influence &c. 175. pressure; conductivity; elasticity; gravity, electricity, magnetism, galvanism, voltaic electricity, voltaism, electromagnetism; atomic power, nuclear power, thermonuclear power; fuel cell; hydraulic power, water power, hydroelectric power; solar power, solar energy, solar panels; tidal power; wind power; attraction; vis inertiae[Lat], vis mortua[Lat], vis viva [Latin]; potential energy, dynamic energy; dynamic friction, dynamic suction; live circuit, live rail, live wire. capability, capacity; quid valeant humeri quid ferre recusent [obs3][Latin]; faculty, quality, attribute, endowment, virtue, gift, property, qualification, susceptibility. V. be powerful &c. adj.; gain power &c. n. belong to, pertain to; lie in one's power, be in one's power; can, be able. give power, confer power, exercise power &c. n.; empower, enable, invest; indue[obs3], endue; endow, arm; strengthen &c. 159; compel &c. 744. Adj. powerful, puissant; potential; capable, able; equal to, up to; cogent, valid; efficient, productive; effective, effectual, efficacious, adequate, competent; multipotent[obs3], plenipotent[obs3], omnipotent; almighty. forcible &c. adj. (energetic) 171; influential &c. 175; productive &c. 168. Adv. powerfully &c. adj.; by virtue of, by dint of. Phr. a toute force[Fr]; <gr/dos moi pou sto kai kino ten gen/gr>[Sp][Grk]

[Grk][Grk][Grk][Grk]; eripuit coelo fulmen sceptrumque tyrannis [Latin]; fortis cadere cedere non potest [Latin].

#158. Impotence.— N. impotence; inability, disability; disablement, impuissance, imbecility; incapacity, incapability; inaptitude, ineptitude, incompetence, unproductivity[obs3]; indocility[obs3]; invalidity, disqualification; inefficiency, wastefulness. telum imbelle[Lat], brutum fulmen[Lat], blank, blank cartridge, flash in the pan, vox et proeterea nihil[Lat], dead letter, bit of waste paper, dummy; paper tiger; Quaker gun. inefficacy &c. (inutility) 645[obs3]; failure &c. 732. helplessness &c. adj.; prostration, paralysis, palsy, apoplexy, syncope, siderationl, deliquiuml[Lat], collapse, exhaustion, softening of the brain, inanition; emasculation, orchiotomy [Med], orchotomy[Med]. cripple, old woman, muff, powder puff, creampuff, pussycat, wimp, mollycoddle; eunuch. V. be impotent &c. adj.; not have a leg to stand on. vouloir rompre l'anguille au genou [French], vouloir prendre la lune avec les dents [French]. collapse, faint, swoon, fall into a swoon, drop; go by the board, go by the wayside; go up in smoke, end in smoke &c. (fail) 732. render powerless &c. adj.; deprive of power; disable, disenable[obs3]; disarm, incapacitate, disqualify, unfit, invalidate, deaden, cramp, tie the hands; double up, prostrate, paralyze, muzzle, cripple, becripple[obs3], maim, lame, hamstring, draw the teeth of; throttle, strangle, garrotte, garrote; ratten[obs3], silence, sprain, clip the wings of, put hors de combat[Fr], spike the guns; take the wind out of one's sails, scotch the snake, put a spoke in one's wheel; break the neck, break the back; unhinge, unfit; put out of gear. unman, unnerve, enervate; emasculate, castrate, geld, alter, neuter, sterilize, fix. shatter, exhaust, weaken &c. 160. Adj. powerless, impotent, unable, incapable, incompetent; inefficient, ineffective; inept; unfit, unfitted; unqualified, disqualified; unendowed; inapt, unapt; crippled, disabled &c. v.; armless[obs3]. harmless, unarmed, weaponless, defenseless, sine ictu[Lat], unfortified, indefensible, vincible, pregnable, untenable. paralytic, paralyzed; palsied, imbecile; nerveless, sinewless[obs3], marrowless[obs3], pithless[obs3], lustless[obs3]; emasculate, disjointed; out of joint, out of gear; unnerved, unhinged; water-logged, on one's beam ends, rudderless; laid on one's back; done up, dead beat, exhausted, shattered, demoralized; graveled &c. (in difficulty) 704; helpless, unfriended[obs3], fatherless; without a leg to stand on, hors de combat[Fr], laid on the shelf. null and void, nugatory, inoperative, good for nothing; ineffectual &c. (failing) 732; inadequate &c. 640; inefficacious &c. (useless) 645. Phr. der kranke Mann[Ger]; "desirous still but impotent to rise" [Shenstone]; the spirit is willing but the flesh is weak.

<— p. 47 —>

#159. [Degree of power.] Strength.— N. strength; power &c. 157; energy &c. 171; vigor, force; main force, physical force, brute force; spring, elasticity, tone, tension, tonicity. stoutness &c. adj.; lustihood[obs3], stamina, nerve, muscle, sinew, thews and sinews, physique; pith, pithiness; virtility, vitality. athletics, athleticism[obs3]; gymnastics, feats of strength. adamant, steel, iron, oak, heart of oak; iron grip; grit, bone. athlete, gymnast, acrobat; superman, Atlas, Hercules, Antaeus[obs3], Samson, Cyclops, Goliath; tower of strength; giant refreshed. strengthening &c. v.; invigoration, refreshment, refocillation[obs3]. [Science of forces] dynamics, statics. V. be strong &c. adj., be stronger; overmatch. render strong &c. adj.; give strength &c. n.; strengthen, invigorate, brace, nerve, fortify, sustain, harden, case harden, steel, gird; screw up, wind up, set up; gird up one's loins, brace up one's loins; recruit, set on one's legs; vivify; refresh &c. 689; refect[obs3]; reinforce, reenforce &c. (restore) 660. Adj. strong, mighty, vigorous, forcible, hard, adamantine, stout, robust, sturdy, hardy, powerful, potent, puissant, valid. resistless, irresistible, invincible, proof against, impregnable, unconquerable, indomitable, dominating, inextinguishable, unquenchable; incontestable; more than a match for; overpowering, overwhelming; all powerful, all sufficient; sovereign. able-bodied; athletic; Herculean, Cyclopean, Atlantean[obs3]; muscular, brawny, wiry, well-knit, broad-shouldered, sinewy, strapping, stalwart, gigantic. manly, man-like, manful; masculine, male, virile. unweakened[obs3], unallayed, unwithered[obs3], unshaken, unworn, unexhausted[obs3]; in full force, in full swing; in the plenitude of power. stubborn, thick-ribbed, made of iron, deep-rooted; strong as a lion, strong as a horse, strong as an ox, strong as brandy; sound as a roach; in fine feather, in high feather; built like a brick shithouse; like a giant refreshed. Adv. strongly &c. adj.; by force &c. n.; by main force &c. (by compulsion) 744. Phr. "our withers are unwrung" [Hamlet]. Blut und Eisen[Ger]; coelitus mihi vires[Lat]; du fort au diable[Fr]; en habiles gens[Lat]; ex vi termini; flecti non frangi[Lat]; "he that wrestles with us strengthens our nerves and sharpens our skill" [Burke]; "inflexible in faith invincible in arms" [Beattie].

#160. Weakness.— N. weakness &c. adj.; debility, atony[obs3], relaxation, languor, enervation; impotence &c. 158; infirmity; effeminacy, feminality[obs3]; fragility, flaccidity; inactivity &c. 683. anaemia, bloodlessness, deficiency of blood, poverty of blood. declension of strength, loss of strength, failure of strength; delicacy, invalidation, decrepitude, asthenia[obs3], adynamy[obs3], cachexy[obs3], cachexia[Med], sprain, strain. reed, thread, rope of sand, house of cards. softling[obs3], weakling; infant &c. 129; youth &c. 127. V. be weak &c. adj.; drop, crumble, give way, totter, tremble, shake, halt, limp, fade, languish, decline, flag, fail, have one leg in the grave. render weak &c. adj.; weaken, enfeeble, debilitate, shake, deprive of strength, relax, enervate, eviscerate; unbrace, unnerve; cripple, unman &c. (render powerless) 158; cramp, reduce, sprain, strain, blunt the edge of; dilute, impoverish; decimate; extenuate; reduce in strength, reduce the strength of; mettre de l'eau dans son vin[Fr]. Adj. weak, feeble, debilel; impotent &c. 158; relaxed, unnerved, &c. v.; sapless, strengthless[obs3], powerless; weakly, unstrung, flaccid, adynamic[obs3], asthenic[obs3]; nervous. soft, effeminate, feminate[obs3], womanly. frail, fragile, shattery[obs3]; flimsy, unsubstantial, insubstantial, gimcrack, gingerbread; rickety, creaky, creaking, cranky; craichy[obs3]; drooping, tottering &c. v.. broken, lame, withered, shattered, shaken, crazy, shaky; palsied &c. 158; decrepit. languid, poor, infirm; faint, faintish[obs3]; sickly &c. (disease) 655; dull, slack, evanidl, spent, short-winded, effete; weather-beaten; decayed, rotten, worn, seedy, languishing, wasted, washy, laid low, pulled down, the worse for wear. unstrengthened &c. 159[obs3], unsupported, unaided, unassisted; aidless[obs3], defenseless &c. 158; cantilevered (support) 215. on its last legs; weak as a child, weak as a baby, weak as a chicken, weak as a cat, weak as a rat; weak as water, weak as water gruel, weak as gingerbread, weak as milk and water; colorless &c. 429. Phr. non sum qualis eram[Lat].

<— p. 48 —>

% 3. POWER IN OPERATION %

#161. Production.— N. {ant. 162, 158} production, creation, construction, formation, fabrication, manufacture; building, architecture, erection, edification; coinage; diaster[obs3]; organization; nisus formativus[Lat]; putting together &c. v.; establishment; workmanship, performance; achievement &c. (completion) 729. flowering, fructification; inflorescence. bringing forth &c. v.: parturition, birth, birth-throe, childbirth, delivery, confinement, accouchement, travail, labor, midwifery, obstetrics; geniture[obs3]; gestation &c. (maturation) 673; assimilation; evolution, development, growth; entelechy[Phil]; fertilization, gemination, germination, heterogamy[Biol], genesis, generation, epigenesis[obs3], procreation, progeneration[obs3], propagation; fecundation, impregnation; albumen &c. 357. spontaneous generation; archegenesis[obs3], archebiosis[obs3]; biogenesis, abiogenesis[obs3], digenesis[obs3], dysmerogenesis[obs3], eumerogenesis[obs3], heterogenesis[obs3], oogenesis, merogenesis[obs3], metogenesis[obs3], monogenesis[obs3], parthenogenesis, homogenesis[obs3], xenogenesisl[obs3]; authorship, publication; works, opus, oeuvre. biogeny[obs3], dissogeny[obs3], xenogeny[obs3]; tocogony[obs3], vacuolization. edifice, building, structure, fabric, erection, pile, tower, flower, fruit. V. produce, perform, operate, do, make, gar, form, construct, fabricate, frame, contrive, manufacture; weave, forge, coin, carve, chisel; build, raise, edify, rear, erect, put together, set up, run up; establish, constitute, compose, organize, institute; achieve, accomplish &c. (complete) 729. flower, bear fruit, fructify, teem, ean[obs3], yean[obs3], farrow, drop, pup, kitten, kindle; bear, lay, whelp, bring forth, give birth to, lie in, be brought to bed of, evolve, pullulate, usher into the world. make productive &c. 168; create; beget, get, generate, fecundate, impregnate; procreate, progenerate[obs3], propagate; engender; bring into being, call into being, bring into existence; breed, hatch, develop, bring up. induce, superinduce; suscitatel; cause &c. 153; acquire &c. 775. Adj. produced, producing &c. v.; productive of; prolific &c. 168; creative; formative, genetic, genial, genital; pregnant; enceinte, big with, fraught with; in the family way, teeming, parturient, in the straw, brought to bed of; puerperal, puerperous[obs3]. digenetic[obs3], heterogenetic[obs3], oogenetic, xenogenetic[obs3]; ectogenous[obs3], gamic[obs3], haematobious[obs3], sporogenous[Biol], sporophorous[Biol]. architectonic. Phr. ex nihilo nihil[Lat]; fiat lux[Lat]; materiam superabat opus [Lat][Ovid]; nemo dat quod non habet [Latin].

<— p. 49 —>

#162. [Nonproduction.] Destruction.— N. {ant. 161} destruction; waste, dissolution, breaking up; diruption[obs3], disruption; consumption; disorganization. fall, downfall, devastation, ruin, perdition, crash; eboulement[French], smash, havoc, delabrement[French], debacle; break down, break up, fall apart; prostration; desolation, bouleversement[Fr], wreck, wrack, shipwreck, cataclysm; washout. extinction, annihilation; destruction of life &c. 361; knock-down blow; doom, crack of doom. destroying &c. v.; demolition, demolishment; overthrow, subversion, suppression; abolition &c. (abrogation) 756; biblioclasm[obs3]; sacrifice; ravage, razzia[obs3]; inactivation; incendiarism; revolution &c. 146; extirpation &c. (extraction) 301; beginning of the end, commencement de la fin[French], road to ruin; dilapidation &c. (deterioration) 659; sabotage. V. be destroyed &c.; perish; fall to the ground; tumble, topple; go to pieces, fall to pieces; break up; crumble to dust; go to the dogs, go to the wall, go to smash, go to shivers, go to wreck, go to pot, go to wrack and ruin; go by the board, go all to smash; be all over, be all up, be all with; totter to its fall. destroy; do away with, make away with; nullify; annual &c. 756; sacrifice, demolish; tear up; overturn, overthrow, overwhelm; upset, subvert, put an end to; seal the doom of, do in, do for, dish*, undo; break up, cut up; break down, cut down, pull down, mow down, blow down, beat down; suppress, quash, put down, do a job on; cut short, take off, blot out; dispel, dissipate, dissolve; consume. smash, crash, quell, squash, squelch, crumple up, shatter, shiver; batter to pieces, tear to pieces, crush to pieces, cut to pieces, shake to pieces, pull to pieces, pick to
41

pieces; laniate[obs3]; nip; tear to rags, tear to tatters; crush to atoms, knock to atoms; ruin; strike out; throw over, knock down over; fell, sink, swamp, scuttle, wreck, shipwreck, engulf, ingulf[obs3], submerge; lay in ashes, lay in ruins; sweep away, erase, wipe out, expunge, raze; level with the dust, level with the ground; waste; atomize, vaporize. deal destruction, desolate, devastate, lay waste, ravage gut; disorganize; dismantle &c. (render useless) 645; devour, swallow up, sap, mine, blast, bomb, blow to smithereens, drop the big one, confound; exterminate, extinguish, quench, annihilate; snuff out, put out, stamp out, trample out; lay in the dust, trample in the dust; prostrate; tread under foot; crush under foot, trample under foot; lay the ax to the root of; make short work of, make clean sweep of, make mincemeat of; cut up root and branch, chop into pieces, cut into ribbons; fling to the winds, scatter to the winds; throw overboard; strike at the root of, sap the foundations of, spring a mine, blow up, ravage with fire and sword; cast to the dogs; eradicate &c. 301. Adj. destroyed &c. v.; perishing &c. v.; trembling to its fall, nodding to its fall, tottering to its fall; in course of destruction &c. n.; extinct. all-destroying, all-devouring, all-engulfing. destructive, subversive, ruinous, devastating; incendiary, deletoryl; destroying &c. n. suicidal; deadly &c. (killing) 361. Adv. with crushing effect, with a sledge hammer. Phr. delenda est Carthago[Lat]; dum Roma deliberat Saguntum perit[Lat]; ecrasez l'infame [Fr][Voltaire].

#163. Reproduction.— N. reproduction, renovation; restoration &c. 660; renewal; new edition, reprint, revival, regeneration, palingenesis[obs3], revivification; apotheosis; resuscitation, reanimation, resurrection, reappearance; regrowth; Phoenix. generation &c. (production) 161; multiplication. V. reproduce; restore &c. 660; revive, renovate, renew, regenerate, revivify, resuscitate, reanimate; remake, refashion, stir the embers, put into the crucible; multiply, repeat; resurge[obs3]. crop up, spring up like mushrooms. Adj. reproduced &c. v.; renascent, reappearing; reproductive; suigenetic[obs3].

#164. Producer.— N. producer, originator, inventor, author, founder, generator, mover, architect, creator, prime mover; maker &c. (agent) 690; prime mover.

#165. Destroyer.— N. destroyer &c. (destroy &c. 162); cankerworm &c. (bane) 663; assassin &c. (killer) 361; executioner &c. (punish) 975; biblioclast[obs3], eidoloclast[obs3], iconoclast, idoloclast[obs3]; nihilist.

#166. Paternity.— N. paternity; parentage; consanguinity &c. 11. parent; father, sire, dad, papa, paterfamilias, abba[obs3]; genitor, progenitor, procreator; ancestor; grandsire[obs3], grandfather; great- grandfather; fathership[obs3], fatherhood; mabap[obs3]. house, stem, trunk, tree, stock, stirps, pedigree, lineage, line, family, tribe, sept, race, clan; genealogy, descent, extraction, birth, ancestry; forefathers, forbears, patriarchs. motherhood, maternity; mother, dam, mamma, materfamilias[Lat], grandmother. Adj. paternal, parental; maternal; family, ancestral, linear, patriarchal. Phr. avi numerantur avorum[Lat]; "happy he with such a mother" [Tennyson]; hombre bueno no le busquen abolengo[Sp][obs3]; philosophia stemma non inspicit [Lat][Seneca].

<— p. 50 —>

#167. Posterity.— N. posterity, progeny, breed, issue, offspring, brood, litter, seed, farrow, spawn, spat; family, grandchildren, heirs; great-grandchild. child, son, daughter; butcha[obs3]; bantling, scion; acrospire[obs3], plumule[obs3], shoot, sprout, olive-branch, sprit[obs3], branch; off-shoot, off-set; ramification; descendant; heir, heiress; heir-apparent, heir- presumptive; chip off the old block; heredity; rising generation. straight descent, sonship[obs3], line, lineage, filiation[obs3], primogeniture. Adj. filial; diphyletic[obs3]. Phr. "the child is father of the man" [Wordsworth]; "the fruit doesn't fall far from the tree", "like father, like son".

#168. Productiveness — N. productiveness &c. adj.; fecundity, fertility, luxuriance, ubertyl. pregnancy, pullulation, fructification, multiplication, propagation, procreation; superfetation. milch cow, rabbit, hydra, warren, seed plot, land flowing with milk and honey; second crop, aftermath; aftercrop, aftergrowth[obs3]; arrish[obs3], eddish[obs3], rowen[obs3]; protoplasm; fertilization. V. make -productive &c. adj.; fructify; procreate, generate, fertilize, spermative[obs3], impregnate; fecundate, fecundify[obs3]; teem, multiply; produce &c. 161; conceive. Adj. productive, prolific; teeming, teemful[obs3]; fertile, fruitful, frugiferous[obs3], fruit-bearing; fecund, luxuriant; pregnant, uberous[obs3]. procreant[obs3], procreative; generative, life-giving, spermatic; multiparous; omnific[obs3], propagable. parturient &c. (producing) 161; profitable &c. (useful) 644.

#169. Unproductiveness.— N. unproductiveness &c. adj.; infertility, sterility, infecundity[obs3]; masturbation; impotence &c. 158; unprofitableness &c. (inutility) 645. waste, desert, Sahara, wild, wilderness, howling wilderness. V. be - unproductive &c. adj.; hang fire, flash in the pan, come to nothing. [make unproductive] sterilize, addle; disable, inactivate. Adj. unproductive, acarpous[obs3], inoperative, barren, addled, infertile, unfertile, unprolific[obs3], arid, sterile, unfruitful, infecund[obs3]; sine prole; fallow; teemless[obs3], issueless[obs3], fruitless; unprofitable &c. (useless) 645; null and void, of no effect.

#170. Agency. — N. agency, operation, force, working, strain, function, office, maintenance, exercise, work, swing, play; interworking[obs3], interaction; procurement.

causation &c. 153; instrumentality &c. 631; influence &c. 175; action &c. (voluntary) 680; modus operandi &c. 627.

quickening power, maintaining power, sustaining power; home stroke.

V. be -in action &c. adj.; operate, work; act, act upon; perform, play, support, sustain, strain, maintain, take effect, quicken, strike.

come play, come bring into operation; have play, have free play; bring to bear upon.

Adj. operative, efficient, efficacious, practical, effectual.

at work, on foot; acting &c. (doing) 680; in operation, in force, in action, in play, in exercise; acted upon, wrought upon.

Adv. by the -agency &c. n.- of; through &c. (instrumentality) 631; by means of &c. 632.

Phr. "I myself must mix with action lest I wither by despair" [Tennyson].

<— p. 51 —>

#171. Physical Energy. — N. energy, physical energy, force, power &c. 157; keenness &c. adj.; intensity, vigor, strength, elasticity; go; high pressure; fire; rush.

acrimony, acritude[obs3]; causiticity[obs3], virulence; poignancy; harshness &c. adj.; severity, edge, point; pungency &c. 392.

cantharides; seasoning &c. (condiment) 393.

activity, agitation, effervescence; ferment, fermentation; ebullition, splutter, perturbation, stir, bustle; voluntary energy &c. 682; quicksilver.

resolution &c. (mental energy) 604; exertion &c. (effort) 686; excitation &c. (mental) 824.

V. give -energy &c. n.; energize, stimulate, kindle, excite, exert; sharpen, intensify; inflame &c. (render violent) 173; wind up &c. (strengthen) 159.

strike home, into home, hard home; make an impression.

Adj. strong, energetic, forcible, active; intense, deep-dyed, severe, keen, vivid, sharp, acute, incisive, trenchant, brisk.

rousing, irritation; poignant; virulent, caustic, corrosive, mordant, harsh, stringent; double-edged, double-shotted[obs3], double-distilled; drastic, escharoticl; racy &c. (pungent) 392.

potent &c. (powerful) 157; radioactive.

Adv. strongly &c. adj.; fortiter in re[Lat]; with telling effect.

Phr. the steam is up; vires acquirit eundo[Lat]; "the race by vigor not by vaunts is won" [Pope].

#172. Physical Inertness. — N. inertness, dullness &c. adj.; inertia, vis inertiae[Latin], inertion[obs3], inactivity, torpor, languor; quiescence &c. 265; latency, inaction; passivity.

mental inertness; sloth &c. (inactivity) 683; inexcitability &c. 826[obs3]; irresolution &c. 605; obstinacy &c. 606; permanence &c. 141.

rare gas, paraffin, noble metal, unreactivity.

V. be -inert &c. adj.; hang fire, smolder.

Adj. inert, inactive, passive; torpid &c. 683; sluggish, dull, heavy, flat, slack, tame, slow, blunt; unreactive; lifeless, dead, uninfluential[obs3].

latent, dormant, smoldering, unexerted[obs3].

Adv. inactively &c. adj.; in suspense, in abeyance.

<— separate force from violence? —> #173. Violence.— N. violence, inclemency, vehemence, might, impetuosity; boisterousness &c. adj.; effervescence, ebullition; turbulence, bluster; uproar, callithump [obs3][U. S.], riot, row, rumpus, le diable a quatre[Fr], devil to pay, all the fat in the fire. severity &c. 739; ferocity, rage, fury; exacerbation, exasperation, malignity; fit, paroxysm; orgasm, climax, aphrodisia[obs3]; force, brute force; outrage; coup de main; strain, shock, shog[obs3]; spasm, convulsion, throe; hysterics, passion &c. (state of excitability) 825. outbreak, outburst; debacle; burst, bounce, dissilience[obs3], discharge, volley, explosion, blow up, blast, detonation, rush, eruption, displosionl, torrent. turmoil &c. (disorder) 59; ferment &c. (agitation) 315; storm, tempest, rough weather; squall &c. (wind) 349; earthquake, volcano, thunderstorm. berserk, berserker; fury, dragon, demon, tiger, beldame, Tisiphone[obs3], Megaera, Alecto[obs3], madcap, wild beast; fire eater &c. (blusterer) 887. V. be -violent &c. adj.; run high; ferment, effervesce; romp, rampage, go on a rampage; run wild, run amuck, run riot; break the peace; rush, tear; rush headlong, rush foremost; raise a storm, make a riot; rough house*; riot, storm; wreak, bear down, ride roughshod, out Herod, Herod; spread like wildfire. [(person) shout or act in anger at something] explode, make a row, kick up a row; boil, boil over; fume, foam, come on like a lion, bluster, rage, roar, fly off the handle, go bananas, go ape, blow one's top, blow one's cool, flip one's lid, hit the ceiling, hit the roof; fly into a rage (anger) 900.. break out, fly out, burst out; bounce, explode, go off, displodel, fly, detonate, thunder, blow up, crump[obs3], flash, flare, burst; shock, strain; break open, force open, prize open. render violent &c. adj.; sharpen, stir up, quicken, excite, incite, annoy, urge, lash, stimulate, turn on; irritate, inflame, kindle, suscitatel, foment; accelerate, aggravate, exasperate, exacerbate, convulse, infuriate, madden, lash into fury; fan the flame; add fuel to the flame, pour oil on the fire, oleum addere camino[Lat]. explode; let fly, fly off; discharge, detonate, set off, detonize[obs3], fulminate. Adj. violent, vehement; warm; acute, sharp; rough, rude, ungentle, bluff, boisterous, wild; brusque, abrupt, waspish; impetuous; rampant. turbulent; disorderly; blustering, raging &c. v.; troublous[obs3], riotous; tumultuary[obs3], tumultuous; obstreperous, uproarious; extravagant; unmitigated; ravening, inextinguishable, tameless; frenzied &c. (insane) 503. desperate &c. (rash) 863; infuriate, furious, outrageous, frantic, hysteric, in hysterics. fiery, flaming, scorching, hot, red-hot, ebullient. savage, fierce, ferocious, fierce as a tiger. excited &c. v.; unquelled[obs3], un-quenched, unextinguished[obs3], unrepressed, unbridled, unruly; headstrong, ungovernable, unappeasable, immitigable, unmitigable[obs3]; uncontrollable, incontrollable[obs3]; insuppressible, irrepressible; orgastic, orgas-matic, orgasmic. spasmodic, convulsive, explosive; detonating &c. v.; volcanic, meteoric; stormy &c. (wind) 349. Adv. violently &c. adj.; amain[obs3]; by storm, by force, by main force; with might and main; tooth and nail, vi et armis[Lat], at the point of the sword, at the point of the bayonet; at one fell swoop; with a high hand, through thick and thin; in desperation, with a vengeance; a outrance[obs3], a toute outrance[Fr][obs3]; headlong, head foremost. Phr. furor arma ministrat[Lat]; "blown with restless violence round about the pendent world" [Measure for Measure].

<— p. 52 —>

#174. Moderation.— N. moderation, lenity &c. 740; temperateness, gentleness &c. adj.; sobriety; quiet; mental calmness &c. (inexcitability) 826[obs3]. moderating &c. v.; anaphrodisia[obs3]; relaxation, remission, mitigation, tranquilization[obs3], assuagement, contemporation[obs3], pacification. measure, juste milieu[Fr], golden mean, <gr/ ariston metron/gr>[Grk]. moderator; lullaby, sedative, lenitive, demulcent, antispasmodic, carminative, laudanum; rose water, balm, poppy, opiate, anodyne, milk, opium, "poppy or mandragora"; wet blanket; palliative. V. be -moder-ate &c. adj.; keep within bounds, keep within compass; sober down, settle down; keep the peace, remit, relent, take in sail. moderate, soften, mitigate, temper, accoyl; attemper[obs3], contemper[obs3]; mollify, lenify[obs3], dulcify[obs3], dull, take off the edge, blunt, obtund[obs3], sheathe, subdue, chasten; sober down, tone down, smooth down; weaken &c. 160; lessen &c. (decrease) 36; check palliate. tranquilize, pacify, assuage, appease, swag, lull, soothe, compose, still, calm, calm down, cool, quiet, hush, quell, sober, pacify, tame, damp, lay, allay, rebate, slacken, smooth, alleviate, rock to sleep, deaden, smooth, throw cold water on, throw a wet blanket over, turn off; slake; curb &c. (restrain) 751; tame &c. (subjugate) 749; smooth over; pour oil on the waves, pour oil on the troubled waters; pour balm into, mattre de l'eau dans son vin[Fr]. go out like a lamb, "roar you as gently as any sucking dove," [Midsummer-Night's Dream]. Adj. moderate; lenient &c. 740; gentle, mild, mellow; cool, sober, temperate, reasonable, measured; tempered &c. v.; calm, unruffled, quiet, tranquil, still; slow, smooth, untroubled; tame; peaceful, peaceable; pacific, halcyon. unexciting, unirritating[obs3]; soft, bland, oily, demulcent, lenitive, anodyne; hypnotic &c. 683; sedative; antiorgastic[obs3], anaphrodisiac[obs3]. mild as mother's milk; milk and water. Adv. moderately &c. adj.; gingerly; piano; under easy sail, at half speed; within bounds, within compass; in reason. Phr. est modue in rebus[obs3]; pour oil on troubled waters.

% 4. Indirect Power %

#175. Influence.— N. influence; importance &c. 642; weight, pressure, preponderance, prevalence, sway; predomi-nance, predominancy[obs3]; ascendency[obs3]; dominance, reign; control, domination, pull*; authority &c.737;

capability &c. (power) 157; effect &c. 154; interest. synergy (cooperation) 709. footing; purchase &c. (support) 215; play, leverage, vantage ground. tower of strength, host in himself; protection, patronage, auspices. V. have -influence &c. n.; be -influential &c. adj.; carry weight, weigh, tell; have a hold upon, magnetize, bear upon, gain a footing, work upon; take root, take hold; strike root in. run through, pervade; prevail, dominate, predominate; out weigh, over weigh; over-ride, over-bear; gain head; rage; be -rife &c. adj.; spread like wildfire; have the upper hand, get the upper hand, gain the upper hand, have full play, get full play, gain full play. be recognized, be listened to; make one's voice heard, gain a hearing; play a part, play a leading part, play a leading part in; take the lead, pull the strings; turn the scale, throw one's weight into the scale; set the fashion, lead the dance. Adj. influential, effective; important &c. 642; weighty; prevailing &c. v.; prevalent, rife, rampant, dominant, regnant, predominant, in the ascendant, hegemonical[obs3]. Adv. with telling effect. Phr. tel maure tel valet[Fr].

#175a. Absence of Influence.— N. impotence &c. 158; powerlessness;
inertness &c. 172; irrelevancy &c. 10.
    V. have no -influence &c. 175.
    Adj. uninfluential[obs3], ineffective; inconsequential, nugatory;
unconducing, unconducive, unconducting to[obs3]; powerless &c. 158;
irrelevant &c. 10.
<— p. 53 —>

#176. Tendency.— N. tendency; aptness, aptitude; proneness, proclivity, bent, turn, tone, bias, set, leaning to; predisposition, inclination, propensity, susceptibility; conatus[Lat], nisus[Lat]; liability &c. 177; quality, nature, temperament; idiocrasy[obs3], idiosyncrasy; cast, vein, grain; humor, mood; drift &c. (direction) 278; conduciveness, conducement[obs3]; applicability &c. (utility) 644; subservience &c. (instrumentality) 631. V. tend, contribute, conduce, lead, dispose, incline, verge, bend to, trend, affect, carry, redound to, bid fair to, gravitate towards; promote &c. (aid) 707. Adj. tending &c. v.; conducive, working towards, in a fair way to, calculated to; liable &c. 177; subservient &c. (instrumental) 631; useful &c. 644; subsidiary &c. (helping) 707. Adv. for, whither.

#177. Liability.— N. liability, liableness[obs3]; possibility, contingency; susceptivity[obs3], susceptibility, exposure. V. be -liable &c. adj.; incur, lay oneself open to; run the chance, stand a chance; lie under, expose oneself to, open a door to. Adj. liable, subject; in danger &c. 665; open to, exposed to, obnoxious to; answerable; unexempt from[obs3]; apt to; dependent on; incident to. contingent, incidental, possible, on the cards, within range of, at the mercy of.

% 5. Combinations of Causes %

#178. Concurrence.— N. concurrence, cooperation, coagency[obs3];
union; agreement &c. 23; consilience[obs3]; consent, coincidence &c.
(assent) 488; alliance; concert, additivity, synergy &c. 709; partnership
&c. 712.
    common cause.
    V. concur, conduce, conspire, contribute; agree, unite; hang together,
pull together, join forces, make common cause.
 &c. (cooperate) 709; help to &c. (aid) 707.
    keep pace with, run parallel; go with, go along with, go hand in hand
with, coincide.
    Adj. concurring &c. v.; concurrent, in alliance with, banded together,
of one mind, at one with, coinciding.
    Adv. with one consent.
#179. Counteraction.— N. counteraction, opposition; contrariety &c. 14; antagonism, polarity; clashing &c. v.; collision, interference, inhibition, resistance, renitency, friction; reaction; retroaction &c. (recoil) 277; counterblast[obs3]; neutralization &c. (compensation) 30; vis inertiae[Lat]; check &c. (hindrance) 706. voluntary opposition &c. 708, voluntary resistance &c. 719; repression &c. (restraint) 751. opposites, action and reaction, yang and yin, yang-yin (contrariety) 14. V. counteract; run counter, clash, cross; interfere with, conflict with; contravene; jostle; go against, run against, beat against, militate against; stultify; antagonize, block, oppose &c. 708; traverse; withstand &c. (resist) 719; hinder &c. 706; repress &c. (restrain) 751; react &c. (recoil) 277. undo, neutralize; counterpoise &c. (compensate) 30; overpoise[obs3]. Adj. counteracting &c. v.; antagonistic, conflicting, retroactive, renitent, reactionary; contrary &c. 14. Adv. although &c. 30; in spite of &c. 708; against. Phr. "for every action there is a reaction, equal in force and opposite in direction" [Newton].

<— p. 54 —>

%

CLASS II
WORDS RELATING TO SPACE
SECTION I. SPACE IN GENERAL

1. ABSTRACT SPACE % <— dimensions must be broken down separately —>

#180. [Indefinite space.] Space.— N. space, extension, extent, superficial extent, expanse, stretch, hyperspace; room, scope, range, field, way, expansion, compass, sweep, swing, spread. dimension, length &c. 200; distance &c. 196; size &c. 192; volume; hypervolume. latitude, play, leeway, purchase, tolerance, room for maneuver. spare room, elbow room, house room; stowage, roomage[obs3], margin; opening, sphere, arena. open space, free space; void &c. (absence) 187; waste; wildness, wilderness; moor, moorland; campagna[obs3]. abyss &c. (interval) 198; unlimited space; infinity &c. 105; world; ubiquity &c. (presence) 186; length and breadth of the land. proportions, acreage; acres, acres and perches, roods and perches, hectares, square miles; square inches, square yards, square centimeters, square meters, yards (clothing) &c.; ares, arpents[obs3]. Adj. spacious, roomy, extensive, expansive, capacious, ample; widespread, vast, world-wide, uncircumscribed; boundless &c. (infinite) 105; shoreless[obs3], trackless, pathless; extended. Adv. extensively &c. adj.; wherever; everywhere; far and near, far and wide; right and left, all over, all the world over; throughout the world, throughout the length and breadth of the land; under the sun, in every quarter; in all quarters, in all lands; here there and everywhere; from pole to pole, from China to Peru [Johnson], from Indus to the pole [Pope], from Dan to Beersheba, from end to end; on the face of the earth, in the wide world, from all points of the compass; to the four winds, to the uttermost parts of the earth.

#180a. Inextension.— N. inextension[obs3], nonextension[obs3], point; dot; atom &c. (smallness) 32.

#181. [Definite space.] Region.— N. region, sphere, ground, soil, area, field, realm, hemisphere, quarter, district, beat, orb, circuit, circle; reservation, pale &c. (limit) 233; compartment, department; clearing.
[political divisions: see property &c. 780 and Government &c. 737a.].
arena, precincts, enceinte, walk, march; patch, plot, parcel, inclosure, close, field, court; enclave, reserve, preserve; street &c. (abode) 189.
clime, climate, zone, meridian, latitude.
biosphere; lithosphere.
Adj. territorial, local, parochial, provincial, regional.
#182. [Limited space.] Place.— N. place, lieu, spot, point, dot; niche, nook &c. (corner) 244; hole; pigeonhole &c. (receptacle) 191; compartment; premises, precinct, station; area, courtyard, square; abode &c. 189; locality &c. (situation) 183. ins and outs; every hole and corner. Adv. somewhere, in some place, wherever it may be, here and there, in various places, passim.

% 2. RELATIVE SPACE %

#183. Situation.— N. situation, position, locality, locale, status, latitude and longitude; footing, standing, standpoint, post; stage; aspect, attitude, posture, pose.
environment, surroundings (location) 184; circumjacence &c. 227[obs3].
place, site, station, seat, venue, whereabouts; ground; bearings &c. (direction) 278; spot &c. (limited space) 182.
topography, geography, chorography[obs3]; map &c. 554.
V. be situated, be situate; lie, have its seat in.
Adj. situate, situated; local, topical, topographical &c. n.
Adv. in situ, in loco; here and there, passim; hereabouts, thereabouts, whereabouts; in place, here, there.
in such and such surroundings, in such and such environs, in such and such entourage, amidst such and such surroundings, amidst such and such environs, amidst such and such entourage.
#184. Location.— N. location, localization; lodgment; deposition, reposition; stowage, package; collocation; packing,

lading; establishment, settlement, installation; fixation; insertion &c. 300. habitat, environment, surroundings (situation) 183; circumjacence &c. 227[obs3]. anchorage, mooring, encampment. plantation, colony, settlement, cantonment; colonization, domestication, situation; habitation &c. (abode) 189; cohabitation; "a local habitation and a name" [Midsummer Night's Dream]; endenization[obs3], naturalization. V. place, situate, locate, localize, make a place for, put, lay, set, seat, station, lodge, quarter, post, install; house, stow; establish, fix, pin, root; graft; plant &c. (insert) 300; shelve, pitch, camp, lay down, deposit, reposit[obs3]; cradle; moor, tether, picket; pack, tuck in; embed, imbed; vest, invest in. billet on, quarter upon, saddle with; load, lade, freight; pocket, put up, bag. inhabit &c. (be present) 186; domesticate, colonize; take root, strike root; anchor; cast anchor, come to an anchor; sit down, settle down; settle; take up one's abode, take up one's quarters; plant oneself, establish oneself, locate oneself; squat, perch, hive, se nicher[Fr], bivouac, burrow, get a footing; encamp, pitch one's tent; put up at, put up one's horses at; keep house. endenizen[obs3], naturalize, adopt. put back, replace &c. (restore) 660. Adj. placed &c. v.; situate, posited, ensconced, imbedded, embosomed[obs3], rooted; domesticated; vested in, unremoved[obs3]. moored &c. v.; at anchor.

#185. Displacement.— N. displacement, elocation[obs3], transposition.
ejectment &c. 297[obs3]; exile &c. (banishment) 893; removal &c. (transference) 270.
misplacement, dislocation &c. 61; fish out of water.
V. displace, misplace, displant[obs3], dislodge, disestablish; exile
&c. (seclude) 893; ablegate[obs3], set aside, remove; take away, cart away; take off, draft off; lade &c. 184.
unload, empty &c. (eject) 297; transfer &c. 270; dispel.
vacate; depart &c. 293.
Adj. displaced &c. v.; unplaced, unhoused[obs3], unharbored[obs3], unestablished[obs3], unsettled; houseless[obs3], homeless; out of place, out of a situation; in the wrong place.
misplaced, out of its element.
% 3. EXISTENCE IN SPACE %

#186. Presence.— N. presence; occupancy, occupation; attendance; whereness[obs3].
permeation, pervasion; diffusion &c. (dispersion) 73.
ubiety[obs3], ubiquity, ubiquitariness[obs3]; omnipresence.
bystander &c. (spectator) 444.
V. exist in space, be present &c. adj.; assister[obs3]; make one of, make one at; look on, attend, remain; find oneself, present oneself; show one's face; fall in the way of, occur in a place; lie, stand; occupy; be there.
people; inhabit, dwell, reside, stay, sojourn, live, abide, lodge, nestle, roost, perch; take up one's abode &c. (be located) 184; tenant.
resort to, frequent, haunt; revisit.
fill, pervade, permeate; be diffused, be disseminated, be through; over spread, overrun; run through; meet one at every turn.
Adj. present; occupying, inhabiting &c. v.; moored &c. 184; resiant[obs3], resident, residentiary[obs3]; domiciled.
ubiquitous, ubiquitary[obs3]; omnipresent; universally present.
peopled, populous, full of people, inhabited.
Adv. here, there, where, everywhere, aboard, on board, at home, afield; here there and everywhere &c. (space) 180; in presence of, before; under the eyes of, under the nose of; in the face of; in propria persona[Lat].
on the spot; in person, in the flesh.
Phr. nusquam est qui ubique est [Lat][Seneca].
<— p. 56 —>

#187. [Nullibiety.1] Absence.— N. absence; inexistence &c. 2[obs3]; nonresidence, absenteeism; nonattendance, alibi.
emptiness &c. adj.; void, vacuum; vacuity, vacancy; tabula rasa[Lat];

exemption; hiatus &c. (interval) 198; lipotypel!.

truant, absentee.

nobody; nobody present, nobody on earth; not a soul; ame qui vive[Fr].

V. be absent &c. adj.; keep away, keep out of the way; play truant, absent oneself, stay away; keep aloof, hold aloof.

withdraw, make oneself scarce, vacate; go away &c. 293.

Adj. absent, not present, away, nonresident, gone, from home; missing; lost; wanting; omitted; nowhere to be found; inexistence &c. 2[obs3].

empty, void; vacant, vacuous; untenanted, unoccupied, uninhabited; tenantless; barren, sterile; desert, deserted; devoid; uninhabitable.

Adv. without, minus, nowhere; elsewhere; neither here nor there; in default of; sans; behind one's back.

Phr. the bird has flown, non est inventus[Lat].

"absence makes the heart grow fonder" [Bayley]; "absent in body but present in spirit" [1 Corinthians v, 3]; absento nemo ne nocuisse velit [Lat][Propertius]; "Achilles absent was Achilles still" [Homer]; aux absents les os; briller par son absence[Fr]; "conspicuous by his absence" [Russell]; "in the hope to meet shortly again and make our absence sweet" [B. Jonson].

#188. Inhabitant.— N. inhabitant; resident, residentiary[obs3]; dweller, indweller[obs3]; addressee; occupier, occupant; householder, lodger, inmate, tenant, incumbent, sojourner, locum tenens, commorant[obs3]; settler, squatter, backwoodsman, colonist; islander; denizen, citizen; burgher, oppidan[obs3], cockney, cit, townsman, burgess; villager; cottager, cottier[obs3], cotter; compatriot; backsettler[obs3], boarder; hotel keeper, innkeeper; habitant; paying guest; planter. native, indigene, aborigines, autochthones[obs3]; Englishman, John Bull; newcomer &c. (stranger) 57. aboriginal, American[obs3], Caledonian, Cambrian, Canadian, Canuck*, downeaster [U.S.], Scot, Scotchman, Hibernian, Irishman, Welshman, Uncle Sam, Yankee, Brother Jonathan. garrison, crew; population; people &c. (mankind) 372; colony, settlement; household; mir[obs3]. V. inhabit &c. (be present) 186; endenizen &c. (locate oneself) 184[obs3]. Adj. indigenous; native, natal; autochthonal[obs3], autochthonous; British; English; American[obs3]; Canadian, Irish, Scotch, Scottish, Welsh; domestic; domiciliated[obs3], domiciled; naturalized, vernacular, domesticated; domiciliary. in the occupation of; garrisoned by, occupied by.

<— 1. Bishop Wilkins. —>

<— p. 57 —>

#189. [Place of habitation, or resort.] Abode.— N. abode, dwelling, lodging, domicile, residence, apartment, place, digs, pad, address, habitation, where one's lot is cast, local habitation, berth, diggings, seat, lap, sojourn, housing, quarters, headquarters, resiancel, tabernacle, throne, ark. home, fatherland; country; homestead, homestall[obs3]; fireside; hearth, hearth stone; chimney corner, inglenook, ingle side; harem, seraglio, zenana[obs3]; household gods, lares et penates[Lat], roof, household, housing, dulce domum[Lat], paternal domicile; native soil, native land. habitat, range, stamping ground; haunt, hangout; biosphere; environment, ecological niche. nest, nidus, snuggery[obs3]; arbor, bower, &c. 191; lair, den, cave, hole, hiding place, cell, sanctum sanctorum[Lat], aerie, eyrie, eyry[obs3], rookery, hive; covert, resort, retreat, perch, roost; nidification; kala jagah[obs3]. bivouac, camp, encampment, cantonment, castrametation[obs3]; barrack, casemate[obs3], casern[obs3]. tent &c. (covering) 223; building &c. (construction) 161; chamber &c. (receptacle) 191; xenodochium[obs3]. tenement, messuage, farm, farmhouse, grange, hacienda, toft[obs3]. cot, cabin, hut, chalet, croft, shed, booth, stall, hovel, bothy[obs3], shanty, dugout [U.S.], wigwam; pen &c. (inclosure) 232; barn, bawn[obs3]; kennel, sty, doghold[obs3], cote, coop, hutch, byre; cow house, cow shed; stable, dovecote, columbary[obs3], columbarium; shippen[obs3]; igloo, iglu[obs3], jacal[obs3]; lacustrine dwelling[obs3], lacuslake dwelling[obs3], lacuspile dwelling[obs3]; log cabin, log house; shack, shebang*, tepee, topek[obs3]. house, mansion, place, villa, cottage, box, lodge, hermitage, rus in urbe[Lat], folly, rotunda, tower, chateau, castle, pavilion, hotel, court, manor-house, capital messuage, hall, palace; kiosk, bungalow; casa[Sp], country seat, apartment house, flat house, frame house, shingle house, tenement house; temple &c. 1000. hamlet, village, thorp[obs3], dorp[obs3], ham, kraal; borough, burgh, town, city, capital, metropolis; suburb; province, country; county town, county seat; courthouse [U.S.]; ghetto. street, place, terrace, parade, esplanade, alameda[obs3], board walk, embankment, road, row, lane, alley, court, quadrangle, quad, wynd[Scot], close, yard, passage, rents, buildings, mews. square, polygon, circus, crescent, mall, piazza, arcade, colonnade, peristyle, cloister; gardens, grove, residences; block of buildings, market place, place, plaza. anchorage, roadstead, roads; dock, basin, wharf, quay, port, harbor. quarter, parish &c. (region) 181. assembly room, meetinghouse, pump room, spa, watering place; inn; hostel, hostelry; hotel, tavern, caravansary, dak bungalow[obs3], khan, hospice; public house, pub, pot house, mug house; gin mill, gin palace; bar, bar room; barrel house* [U.S.], cabaret, chophouse; club, clubhouse; cookshop[obs3], dive [U.S.], exchange [euphemism, U.S.]; grill room, saloon [U.S.], shebeen[obs3]; coffee house, eating house; canteen, restaurant, buffet, cafe, estaminet[obs3], posada[obs3], almshouse[obs3], poorhouse, townhouse [U.S.]. garden, park, pleasure ground, plaisance[obs3], demesne. [quarters for animals] cage, terrarium, doghouse; pen, aviary; barn, stall; zoo. V. take up one's abode &c. (locate oneself) 184; inhabit &c. (be present) 186. Adj. urban, metropolitan; suburban; provincial, rural, rustic; domestic; cosmopolitan; palatial. Phr. eigner Hert ist goldes Werth[Ger]; "even cities have their graves" [Longfellow]; ubi libertas ibi patria[Lat]; home sweet home.

#190. [Things contained.] Contents.— N. contents; cargo, lading, freight, shipment, load, bale, burden, jag; cartload[obs3], shipload; cup of, basket of, &c. (receptacle) 191 of; inside &c. 221; stuffing, ullage.

#191. Receptacle. — N. receptacle; inclosure &c. 232; recipient, receiver, reservatory. compartment; cell, cellule; follicle; hole, corner, niche, recess, nook; crypt, stall, pigeonhole, cove, oriel; cave &c. (concavity) 252. capsule, vesicle, cyst, pod, calyx, cancelli, utricle, bladder; pericarp, udder. stomach, paunch, venter, ventricle, crop, craw, maw, gizzard, breadbasket; mouth. pocket, pouch, fob, sheath, scabbard, socket, bag, sac, sack, saccule, wallet, cardcase, scrip, poke, knit, knapsack, haversack, sachel, satchel, reticule, budget, net; ditty bag, ditty box; house-wife, hussif; saddlebags; portfolio; quiver &c. (magazine) 636. chest, box, coffer, caddy, case, casket, pyx, pix, caisson, desk, bureau, reliquary; trunk, portmanteau, band-box, valise; grip, grip sack [U.S.]; skippet, vasculum; boot, imperial; vache; cage, manger, rack. vessel, vase, bushel, barrel; canister, jar; pottle, basket, pannier, buck-basket, hopper, maundl, creel, cran, crate, cradle, bassinet, wisket, whisket, jardiniere, corbeille, hamper, dosser, dorser, tray, hod, scuttle, utensil; brazier; cuspidor, spittoon. [For liquids] cistern &c. (store) 636; vat, caldron, barrel, cask, drum, puncheon, keg, rundlet, tun, butt, cag, firkin, kilderkin, carboy, amphora, bottle, jar, decanter, ewer, cruse, caraffe, crock, kit, canteen, flagon; demijohn; flask, flasket; stoup, noggin, vial, phial, cruet, caster; urn, epergne, salver, patella, tazza, patera; pig gin, big gin; tyg, nipperkin, pocket pistol; tub, bucket, pail, skeel, pot, tankard, jug, pitcher, mug, pipkin; galipot, gallipot; matrass, receiver, retort, alembic, bolthead, capsule, can, kettle; bowl, basin, jorum, punch bowl, cup, goblet, chalice, tumbler, glass, rummer, horn, saucepan, skillet, posnetl, tureen. [laboratory vessels for liquids] beaker, flask, Erlenmeyer flask, Florence flask, round-bottom flask, graduated cylinder, test tube, culture tube, pipette, Pasteur pipette, disposable pipette, syringe, vial, carboy, vacuum flask, Petri dish, microtiter tray, centrifuge tube. bail, beaker, billy, canakin; catch basin, catch drain; chatti, lota, mussuk, schooner [U.S.], spider, terrine, toby, urceus. plate, platter, dish, trencher, calabash, porringer, potager, saucer, pan, crucible; glassware, tableware; vitrics. compote, gravy boat, creamer, sugar bowl, butter dish, mug, pitcher, punch bowl, chafing dish. shovel, trowel, spoon, spatula, ladle, dipper, tablespoon, watch glass, thimble. closet, commode, cupboard, cellaret, chiffonniere, locker, bin, bunker, buffet, press, clothespress, safe, sideboard, drawer, chest of drawers, chest on chest, highboy, lowboy, till, scrutoirel, secretary, secretaire, davenport, bookcase, cabinet, canterbury; escritoire, etagere, vargueno, vitrine. chamber, apartment, room, cabin; office, court, hall, atrium; suite of rooms, apartment [U.S.], flat, story; saloon, salon, parlor; by-room, cubicle; presence chamber; sitting room, best room, keeping room, drawing room, reception room, state room; gallery, cabinet, closet; pew, box; boudoir; adytum, sanctum; bedroom, dormitory; refectory, dining room, salle-a-manger; nursery, schoolroom; library, study; studio; billiard room, smoking room; den; stateroom, tablinum, tenement. [room for defecation and urination] bath room, bathroom, toilet, lavatory, powder room; john, jakes, necessary, loo; [in public places] men's room, ladies' room, rest room; [fixtures: see 653 (uncleanness)]. attic, loft, garret, cockloft, clerestory; cellar, vault, hold, cockpit; cubbyhole; cook house; entre-sol; mezzanine floor; ground floor, rez-de-chaussee; basement, kitchen, pantry, bawarchi-khana, scullery, offices; storeroom &c. (depository) 636; lumber room; dairy, laundry. coach house; garage; hangar; out-house; penthouse; lean-to. portico, porch, stoop, stope, veranda, patio, lanai, terrace, deck; lobby, court, courtyard, hall, vestibule, corridor, passage, breezeway; ante room, ante chamber; lounge; piazza [=veranda, U.S.]. conservatory, greenhouse, bower, arbor, summerhouse, alcove, grotto, hermitage. lodging &c. (abode) 189; bed &c. (support) 215; carriage &c. (vehicle) 272. Adj. capsular; saccular, sacculated; recipient; ventricular, cystic, vascular, vesicular, cellular, camerated, locular, multilocular, polygastric; marsupial; siliquose, siliquous.

% SECTION II. DIMENSIONS

1. GENERAL DIMENSIONS %

#192. Size.— N. size, magnitude, dimension, bulk, volume; largeness &c. adj.; greatness &c. (of quantity) 31; expanse &c. (space) 180; amplitude, mass; proportions. capacity, tonnage, tunnage; cordage; caliber, scantling. turgidity &c. (expansion) 194; corpulence, obesity; plumpness &c. adj.; embonpoint, corporation, flesh and blood, lustihood. hugeness &c. adj.; enormity, immensity, monstrosity. giant, Brobdingnagian, Antaeus, Goliath, Gog and Magog, Gargantua, monster, mammoth, Cyclops; cachalot, whale, porpoise, behemoth, leviathan, elephant, hippopotamus; colossus; tun, cord, lump, bulk, block, loaf, mass, swad, clod, nugget, bushel, thumper, whooper, spanker, strapper; "Triton among the minnows" [Coriolanus]. mountain, mound; heap &c. (assemblage) 72. largest portion &c. 50; full size, life size. V. be large &c. adj.; become large &c. (expand) 194. Adj. large, big; great &c. (in quantity) 31; considerable, bulky, voluminous, ample, massive, massy; capacious, comprehensive; spacious &c. 180; mighty, towering, fine, magnificent. corpulent, stout, fat, obese, plump, squab, full, lusty, strapping, bouncing; portly, burly, well-fed, full-grown; corn fed, gram fed; stalwart, brawny, fleshy; goodly; in good case, in good condition; in condition; chopping, jolly; chub faced, chubby faced. lubberly, hulky, unwieldy, lumpish, gaunt, spanking, whacking, whopping, walloping, thumping, thundering, hulking; overgrown; puffy &c. (swollen) 194. huge, immense, enormous, mighty; vast, vasty; amplitudinous, stupendous; monster, monstrous, humongous, monumental; elephantine, jumbo, mammoth; gigantic, gigantean, giant, giant like, titanic; prodigious, colossal, Cyclopean, Brobdingnagian, Bunyanesque, Herculean, Gargantuan; infinite &c. 105. large as life; plump as a dumpling, plump as a partridge; fat as a pig, fat as a quail, fat as butter, fat as brawn, fat as bacon. immeasurable, unfathomable, unplumbed; inconceivable, unimaginable, unheard-of. of cosmic proportions; of epic proportions, the mother of all, the granddaddy of all.

<— p. 59 —>

#193. Littleness.— N. littleness &c. adj.; smallness &c. (of quantity) 32; exiguity, inextension[obs3]; parvitude[obs3], parvity[obs3]; duodecimo[obs3]; Elzevir edition, epitome, microcosm; rudiment; vanishing point; thinness &c. 203. dwarf, pygmy, pigmy[obs3], Liliputian, chit, pigwidgeon[obs3], urchin, elf; atomy[obs3], dandiprat[obs3]; doll, puppet; Tom Thumb, Hop-o'-my- thumb[obs3]; manikin, mannikin; homunculus, dapperling[obs3], cock-sparrow. animalcule, monad, mite, insect, emmet[obs3], fly, midge, gnat, shrimp, minnow, worm, maggot, entozoon[obs3]; bacteria; infusoria[obs3]; microzoa[Microbiol]; phytozoaria[obs3]; microbe; grub; tit, tomtit, runt, mouse, small fry; millet seed, mustard seed; barleycorn; pebble, grain of sand; molehill, button, bubble. point; atom &c. (small quantity) 32; fragment &c. (small part) 51; powder &c. 330; point of a pin, mathematical point; minutiae &c. (unimportance) 643. micrometer; vernier; scale. microphotography, photomicrography, micrography[obs3]; photomicrograph, microphotograph; microscopy; microscope (optical instruments) 445.. V. be little &c. adj.; lie in a nutshell; become small &c. (decrease) 36, (contract) 195. Adj. little; small &c. (in quantity) 32; minute, diminutive, microscopic; microzoal; inconsiderable &c. (unimportant) 643; exiguous, puny, tiny, wee, petty, minikin[obs3], miniature, pygmy, pigmy[obs3], elfin; undersized; dwarf, dwarfed, dwarfish; spare, stunted, limited; cramp, cramped; pollard, Liliputian, dapper, pocket; portative[obs3], portable; duodecimo[obs3]; dumpy, squat; short &c. 201. impalpable, intangible, evanescent, imperceptible, invisible, inappreciable, insignificant, inconsiderable, trivial; infinitesimal, homoeopathic[obs3]; atomic, subatomic, corpuscular, molecular; rudimentary, rudimental; embryonic, vestigial. weazenl!, scant, scraggy, scrubby; thin &c. (narrow) 203; granular &c. (powdery) 330; shrunk &c. 195; brevipennate[obs3]. Adv. in a small compass, in a nutshell; on a small scale; minutely, microscopically.

#194. Expansion.— N. expansion; increase &c. 35 of size; enlargement, extension, augmentation; amplification, ampliation[obs3]; aggrandizement, spread, increment, growth, development, pullulation, swell, dilation, rarefaction; turgescence[obs3], turgidness, turgidity; dispansionl; obesity &c. (size) 192; hydrocephalus, hydrophthalmus[Med]; dropsy, tumefaction, intumescence, swelling, tumor, diastole, distension; puffing, puffiness; inflation; pandiculation[obs3]. dilatability, expansibility. germination, growth, upgrowth[obs3]; accretion &c. 35; budding, gemmation[obs3]. overgrowth, overdistension[obs3]; hypertrophy, tympany[obs3]. bulb &c. (convexity) 250; plumper; superiority of size. [expansion of the universe] big bang; Hubble constant. V. become larger &c. (large &c. 192); expand, widen, enlarge, extend, grow, increase, incrassate[obs3], swell, gather; fill out; deploy, take open order, dilate, stretch, distend, spread; mantle, wax; grow up, spring up; bud, bourgeon[Fr], shoot, sprout, germinate, put forth, vegetate, pullulate, open, burst forth; gain flesh, gather flesh; outgrow; spread like wildfire, overrun. be larger than; surpass &c. (be superior) 33. render larger &c. (large &c. 192); expand, spread, extend, aggrandize, distend, develop, amplify, spread out, widen, magnify, rarefy, inflate, puff, blow up, stuff, pad, cram; exaggerate; fatten. Adj. expanded &c. v.; larger &c. (large &c. 192; swollen; expansive; wide open, wide spread; flabelliform[obs3]; overgrown, exaggerated, bloated, fat, turgid, tumid, hypertrophied, dropsical; pot bellied, swag bellied|; edematous, oedematous[obs3], obese, puffy, pursy[obs3], blowzy, bigswoln[obs3], distended; patulous; bulbous &c. (convex) 250; full blown, full grown, full formed; big &c. 192; abdominous[obs3], enchymatous[obs3], rhipidate[obs3]; tumefacient[obs3], tumefying[obs3].

<— p. 60 —>

#195. Contraction. — N. contraction, reduction, diminution; decrease &c. 36 of size; defalcation, decrement; lessening, shrinking &c. v.; compaction; tabes[obs3], collapse, emaciation, attenuation, tabefaction[obs3], consumption, marasmus[obs3], atrophy; systole, neck, hourglass. condensation, compression, compactness; compendium &c. 596; squeezing &c. v.; strangulation; corrugation; astringency; astringents, sclerotics; contractility, compressibility; coarctation[obs3]. inferiority in size. V. become small, become smaller; lessen, decrease &c. 36; grow less, dwindle, shrink, contract, narrow, shrivel, collapse, wither, lose flesh, wizen, fall away, waste, wane, ebb; decay &c. (deteriorate) 659. be smaller than, fall short of; not come up to &c. (be inferior) 34. render smaller, lessen, diminish, contract, draw in, narrow, coarctate[obs3]; boil down; constrict, constringe[obs3]; condense, compress, squeeze, corrugate, crimp, crunch, crush, crumple up, warp, purse up, pack, squeeze, stow; pinch, tighten, strangle; cramp; dwarf, bedwarf[obs3]; shorten &c. 201; circumscribe &c. 229; restrain &c. 751. [reduce in size by abrasion or paring; see subtraction 38] abrade, pare, reduce, attenuate, rub down, scrape, file, file down, grind, grind down, chip, shave, shear, wear down. Adj. contracting &c. v.; astringent; shrunk, contracted &c. v.; strangulated, tabid[obs3], wizened, stunted; waning &c. v.; neap, compact. unexpanded &c. (expand &c. 194)[obs3]; contractile; compressible; smaller &c. (small &c.193).

#196. Distance. — N. distance; space &c. 180; remoteness, farness[obs3], far-cry to; longinquity[obs3], elongation; offing, background; remote region; removedness[obs3]; parallax; reach, span, stride. outpost, outskirt; horizon; aphelion; foreign parts, ultima Thule[Lat], ne plus ultra[Lat], antipodes; long range, giant's stride. dispersion &c.73. [units of distance] length &c. 200. cosmic distance, light-years. V. be distant &c. adj.; extend to, stretch to, reach to, spread to, go to, get to, stretch away to; range. remain at a distance; keep away, keep off, keep aloof, keep clear of, stand away, stand off, stand aloof, stand clear of, stay away, keep one's distance'. [transitive] distance; distance oneself from. Adj. distant; far off, far away; remote, telescopic, distal, wide of; stretching to &c. v.; yon, yonder; ulterior; transmarine[obs3], transpontine[obs3], transatlantic, transalpine; tramontane; ultramontane, ultramundane[obs3]; hyperborean, antipodean; inaccessible, out of the way; unapproached[obs3], unapproachable; incontiguous[obs3]. Adv. far off, far away; afar, afar off; off; away; a long way off, a great way off, a good way off; wide away, aloof; wide of, clear of; out of the way, out of reach; abroad, yonder, farther, further, beyond; outre mer[Fr], over the border, far and wide, "over the hills and far away" [Gay]; from pole to pole &c. (over great space) 180; to the uttermost parts, to the ends of the earth; out of hearing, nobody knows where, a perte de vue[Fr], out of the sphere of, wide of the mark; a far cry to. apart, asunder; wide apart, wide asunder; longo intervallo[It]; at arm's length. Phr. "distance lends enchantment" [Campbell]; "it's a long long way to Tipperary"; out of sight, out of mind.

#197. Nearness. — N. nearness &c. adj.; proximity, propinquity; vicinity, vicinage; neighborhood, adjacency; contiguity &c. 199. short distance, short step, short cut; earshot, close quarters, stone's throw; bow shot, gun shot, pistol shot; hair's breadth, span. purlieus, neighborhood, vicinage, environs, alentours[Fr], suburbs, confines, banlieue[obs3], borderland; whereabouts. bystander; neighbor, borderer[obs3]. approach &c. 286; convergence 7c. 290; perihelion. V. be near &c. adj.; adjoin, hang about, trench on; border upon, verge upon; stand by, approximate, tread on the heels of, cling to, clasp, hug; huddle; hang upon the skirts of, hover over; burn. touch &c. 199 bring near, draw near &c. 286; converge &c. 290; crowd &c. 72; place side by side &c. adv. Adj. near, nigh; close at hand, near at hand; close, neighboring; bordering upon, contiguous, adjacent, adjoining; proximate, proximal; at hand, handy; near the mark, near run; home, intimate. Adv. near, nigh; hard by, fast by; close to, close upon; hard upon; at the point of; next door to; within reach, within call, within hearing, within earshot; within an ace of; but a step, not far from, at no great distance; on the verge of, on the brink of, on the skirts of; in the environs &c. n.; at one's door, at one's feet, at one's elbow, at one's finger's end, at one's side; on the tip of one's tongue; under one's nose; within a stone's throw &c. n.; in sight of, in presence of; at close quarters; cheek by jole[obs3], cheek by jowl; beside, alongside, side by side, tete-a-tete; in juxtaposition &c. (touching) 199; yardarm to yardarm, at the heels of; on the confines of, at the threshold, bordering upon, verging to; in the way. about; hereabouts, thereabouts; roughly, in round numbers; approximately, approximatively[obs3]; as good as, well-nigh.

<— p. 61 —>

#198. Interval. — N. interval, interspace[obs3]; separation &c. 44; break, gap, opening; hole &c. 260; chasm, hiatus, caesura; interruption, interregnum; interstice, lacuna, cleft, mesh, crevice, chink, rime, creek, cranny, crack, chap, slit, fissure, scissure[obs3], rift, flaw, breach, rent, gash, cut, leak, dike, ha-ha. gorge, defile, ravine, canon, crevasse, abyss, abysm; gulf; inlet, frith[obs3], strait, gully; pass; furrow &c. 259; abra[obs3]; barranca[obs3], barranco[obs3]; clove [U.S.], gulch [U.S.], notch [U.S.]; yawning gulf; hiatus maxime[Lat], hiatus valde deflendus[Lat]; parenthesis &c. (interjacence) 228[obs3]; void 7c. (absence) 187; incompleteness &c. 53. [interval of time] period &c. 108; interim (time) 106. V. gape &c. (open) 260. Adj. with an interval, far between; breachy[obs3], rimose[obs3], rimulose[obs3]. Adv. at intervals &c. (discontinuously) 70; longo intervallo[It].

#199. Contiguity.— N. contiguity, contact, proximity, apposition, abuttal[obs3], juxtaposition; abutment, osculation; meeting, appulse[obs3], rencontre[obs3], rencounter[obs3], syzygy[Astron], coincidence, coexistence; adhesion &c. 46; touching &c. v. (see touch 379).

borderland; frontier &c. (limit) 233; tangent; abutter.

V. be contiguous &c. adj.; join, adjoin, abut on, march with; graze, touch, meet, osculate, come in contact, coincide; coexist; adhere &c. 46.

[transitive][cause to be contiguous] juxtapose; contact; join (unite) 43; link (vinculum) 45.

Adj. contiguous; touching &c. v.; in contact &c. n.; conterminous, end to end, osculatory; pertingentl; tangential.

hand to hand; close to &c. (near) 197; with no interval &c. 198.
% 2. LINEAR DIMENSIONS %

#200. Length.— N. length, longitude, span; mileage; distance &c. 196.
line, bar, rule, stripe, streak, spoke, radius.

lengthening &c. v.; prolongation, production, protraction; tension, tensure[obs3]; extension.

[Measures of length] line, nail, inch, hand, palm, foot, cubit, yard, ell, fathom, rood, pole, furlong, mile, league; chain, link; arpent[obs3], handbreadth[obs3], jornada [obs3][U.S.], kos[obs3], vara[obs3].

[astronomical units of distance] astronomical unit, AU, light-year, parsec.

[metric units of length] nanometer, nm, micron, micrometer, millimicron, millimeter, mm, centimeter, cm, meter, kilometer, km.

pedometer, perambulator; scale &c. (measurement) 466.

V. be long &c. adj.; stretch out, sprawl; extend to, reach to, stretch to; make a long arm, "drag its slow length along."

render long &c. adj.; lengthen, extend, elongate; stretch; prolong, produce, protract; let out, draw out, spin outl!; drawl.

enfilade, look along, view in perspective.

distend (expand) 194.

Adj. long, longsome[obs3]; lengthy, wiredrawn[obs3], outstretched; lengthened &c. v.; sesquipedalian &c. (words) 577; interminable, no end of; macrocolous[obs3].

linear, lineal; longitudinal, oblong.

as long as my arm, as long as today and tomorrow; unshortened &c. (shorten &c. 201)[obs3].

Adv. lengthwise, at length, longitudinally, endlong[obs3], along; tandem; in a line &c. (continuously) 69; in perspective.

from end to end, from stem to stern, from head to foot, from the crown of the head to the sole of the foot, from top to toe; fore and aft.

#201. Shortness.— N. shortness &c. adj.; brevity; littleness &c. 193; a span. shortening &c. v.; abbreviation, abbreviature[obs3]; abridgment, concision, retrenchment, curtailment, decurtationl; reduction &c. (contraction) 195; epitome &c. (compendium) 596. elision, ellipsis; conciseness &c. (in style) 572. abridger, epitomist[obs3], epitomizer[obs3]. V. be short &c. adj.; render short &c. adj.; shorten, curtail, abridge, abbreviate, take in, reduce; compress &c. (contract) 195; epitomize &c. 596. retrench, cut short, obtruncate[obs3]; scrimp, cut, chop up, hack, hew; cut down, pare down; clip, dock, lop, prune, shear, shave, mow, reap, crop; snub; truncate, pollard, stunt, nip, check the growth of; foreshorten[in drawing]. Adj. short, brief, curt; compendious, compact; stubby, scrimp; shorn, stubbed; stumpy, thickset, pug; chunky [U.S.], decurtate[obs3]; retrousse[obs3]; stocky; squab, squabby[obs3]; squat, dumpy; little &c. 193; curtailed of its fair proportions; short by; oblate; concise &c. 572; summary. Adv. shortly &c. adj.; in short &c. (concisely) 572.

#202. Breadth, Thickness.— N. breadth, width, latitude, amplitude; diameter, bore, caliber, radius; superficial extent &c. (space) 180.

thickness, crassitude[obs3]; corpulence &c. (size) 192; dilation &c. (expansion) 194.

V. be broad &c. adj.; become broad, render broad &c. adj.; expand &c. 194; thicken, widen, calibrate.

Adj. broad, wide, ample, extended; discous[obs3]; fanlike; outspread, outstretched; "wide as a church-door" [Romeo and Juliet]; latifoliate[obs3], latifolous[obs3].

thick, dumpy, squab, squat, thickset; thick as a rope.

#203. Narrowness. Thinness. — N. narrowness &c. adj.; closeness, exility[obs3]; exiguity 7c. (little) 193. line; hair's breadth, finger's breadth; strip, streak, vein. monolayer; epitaxial deposition[Engin]. thinness &c. adj.; tenuity; emaciation, macilency[obs3], marcorl. shaving, slip &c. (filament) 205; thread paper, skeleton, shadow, anatomy, spindleshanks[obs3], lantern jaws, mere skin and bone. middle constriction, stricture, neck, waist, isthmus, wasp, hourglass; ridge, ghaut[obs3], ghat[obs3], pass; ravine &c. 198. narrowing, coarctation[obs3], angustation[obs3], tapering; contraction &c. 195. V. be narrow &c. adj.; narrow, taper, contract &c. 195; render narrow &c. adj; waste away. Adj. narrow, close; slender, thin, fine; thread-like &c. (filament) 205; finespun[obs3], gossamer; paper-thin; taper, slim, slight-made; scant, scanty; spare, delicate, incapacious[obs3]; contracted &c. 195; unexpanded &c. (expand &c. 194)[obs3]; slender as a thread. [in reference to people or animals] emaciated, lean, meager, gaunt, macilent[obs3]; lank, lanky; weedy, skinny; scrawny slinky[U.S.]; starved, starveling; herring gutted; worn to a shadow, lean as a rake [Chaucer]; thin as a lath, thin as a whipping post, thin as a wafer; hatchet-faced; lantern-jawed. attenuated, shriveled, extenuated, tabid[obs3], marcidl, barebone, rawboned. monomolecular.

#204. Layer. — N. layer, stratum, strata, course, bed, zone, substratum, substrata, floor, flag, stage, story, tier, slab, escarpment; table, tablet; dess[obs3]; flagstone; board, plank; trencher, platter. plate; lamina, lamella; sheet, foil; wafer; scale, flake, peel; coat, pellicle; membrane, film; leaf; slice, shive[obs3], cut, rasher, shaving, integument &c. (covering) 223; eschar[obs3]. stratification, scaliness, nest of boxes, coats of an onion. monolayer; bilayer; trilayer[Biochem]. V. slice, shave, pare, peel; delaminate; plate, coat, veneer; cover &c. 223. Adj. lamellar, lamellated[obs3], lamelliform[obs3], layered; laminated, laminiferous[obs3]; micaceous[obs3]; schistose, schistous[obs3]; scaly, filmy, membranous, pellicular, flaky, squamous[Anat]; foliated, foliaceous[obs3]; stratified, stratiform; tabular, discoid; spathic[obs3], spathose[obs3]. trilamellar[obs3]. graphitic[obs3].

#205. Filament. — N. filament, line; fiber, fibril; funicle[obs3], vein; hair, capillament[obs3], cilium, cilia, pilus, pili; tendril, gossamer; hair stroke; veinlet[obs3], venula[obs3], venule[obs3]. wire, string, thread, packthread, cotton, sewing silk, twine, twist, whipcord, tape, ribbon, cord, rope, yarn, hemp, oakum, jute. strip, shred, slip, spill, list, band, fillet, fascia, ribbon, riband, roll, lath, splinter, shiver, shaving. beard &c. (roughness) 256; ramification; strand. Adj. filamentous, filamentiferous[obs3], filaceous[obs3], filiform[obs3]; fibrous, fibrillous[obs3]; thread-like, wiry, stringy, ropy; capillary, capilliform[obs3]; funicular, wire-drawn; anguilliform[obs3]; flagelliform[obs3]; hairy &c. (rough) 256; taeniate[obs3], taeniform[obs3], taenioid[obs3]; venose[obs3], venous.

<— p. 63 —>

#206. Height. — N. height, altitude, elevation; eminence, pitch; loftiness &c. adj.; sublimity. tallness &c. adj.; stature, procerity[obs3]; prominence &c. 250. colossus &c. (size) 192; giant, grenadier, giraffe, camelopard. mount, mountain; hill alto, butte [U.S.], monticle[obs3], fell, knap[obs3]; cape; headland, foreland[obs3]; promontory; ridge, hog's back, dune; rising ground, vantage ground; down; moor, moorland; Alp; uplands, highlands; heights &c. (summit), 210; knob, loma[obs3], pena [obs3][U.S.], picacho[obs3], tump[obs3]; knoll, hummock, hillock, barrow, mound, mole; steeps, bluff, cliff, craig[obs3], tor[obs3], peak, pike, clough[obs3]; escarpment, edge, ledge, brae; dizzy height. tower, pillar, column, obelisk, monument, steeple, spire, minaret, campanile, turret, dome, cupola; skyscraper. pole, pikestaff, maypole, flagstaff; top mast, topgallant mast. ceiling &c. (covering) 223. high water; high tide, flood tide, spring tide. altimetry &c. (angel) 244[obs3]; batophobia[obs3]. satellite, spy-in-the-sky. V. be high &c. adj.; tower, soar, command; hover, hover over, fly over; orbit, be in orbit; cap, culminate; overhang, hang over, impend, beetle, bestride, ride, mount; perch, surmount; cover &c. 223; overtop &c. (be superior) 33; stand on tiptoe. become high &c. adj.; grow higher, grow taller; upgrow[obs3]; rise &c. (ascend) 305; send into orbit. render high &c. adj.; heighten &c. (elevate) 307. Adj. high, elevated, eminent, exalted, lofty, tall; gigantic &c. (big) 192; Patagonian; towering, beetling, soaring, hanging [gardens]; elevated &c. 307; upper; highest &c. (topmost) 210; high reaching, insessorial[obs3], perching. upland, moorland; hilly, knobby [U.S.]; mountainous, alpine, subalpine, heaven kissing; cloudtopt[obs3], cloudcapt[obs3], cloudtouching[obs3]; aerial. overhanging &c. v.; incumbent, overlying, superincumbent[obs3], supernatant, superimposed; prominent &c. c. 250. tall as a maypole, tall as a poplar, tall as a steeple, lanky &c. (thin) 203. Adv. on high, high up, aloft, up, above, aloof, overhead; airwind[obs3]; upstairs, abovestairs[obs3]; in the clouds; on tiptoe, on stilts, on the shoulders of; over head and ears; breast high. over, upwards; from top to bottom &c. (completely) 52. Phr. e meglio cader dalle finistre che dal tetto[It].

#207. Lowness. — N. lowness &c. adj.; debasement, depression, prostration &c. (horizontal) 213; depression &c. (concave) 252. molehill; lowlands; basement floor, ground floor; rez de chaussee[Fr]; cellar; hold, bilge; feet, heels. low water; low tide, ebb tide, neap tide, spring tide. V. be low &c. adj.; lie low, lie flat; underlie; crouch, slouch, wallow, grovel; lower &c. (depress) 308. Adj. low, neap, debased; nether, nether most; flat, level with the ground; lying low &c. v.; crouched, subjacent, squat, prostrate &c. (horizontal) 213. Adv. under; beneath, underneath; below; downwards; adown[obs3], at the foot of; under foot, under ground; down stairs, below stairs; at a low ebb; below par.

#208. Depth. — N. depth; deepness &c. adj.; profundity, depression &c. (concavity) 252.

hollow, pit, shaft, well, crater; gulf &c. 198; bowels of the earth, bottomless pit[obs3], hell.

soundings, depth of water, water, draught, submersion; plummet, sound, probe; sounding rod, sounding line; lead.

bathymetry.

[instrument to measure depth] sonar, side-looking sonar; bathometer[obs3].

V. be deep &c. adj.; render deep &c. adj.; deepen.

plunge &c. 310; sound, fathom, plumb, cast the lead, heave the lead, take soundings, make soundings; dig &c. (excavate) 252.

Adj. deep, deep seated; profound, sunk, buried; submerged &c. 310; subaqueous, submarine, subterranean, subterraneous, subterrene[obs3]; underground.

bottomless, soundless, fathomless; unfathomed, unfathomable; abysmal; deep as a well; bathycolpian[obs3]; benthal[obs3], benthopelagic[obs3]; downreaching[obs3], yawning.

knee deep, ankle deep.

Adv. beyond one's depth, out of one's depth; over head and ears; mark twine, mark twain.

#209. Shallowness. — N. shallowness &c. adj.; shoals; mere scratch.

Adj. shallow, slight, superficial; skin deep, ankle deep, knee deep; just enough to wet one's feet; shoal, shoaly[obs3].

<— p. 64 —>

#210. Summit. — N. summit, summityl; top, peak, vertex, apex, zenith, pinnacle, acme, culmination, meridian, utmost height, ne plus utra, height, pitch, maximum, climax, culminating point, crowning point, turning point; turn of the tide, fountain head; water shed, water parting; sky, pole.

tip, tip top; crest, crow's nest, cap, truck, nib; end &c. 67; crown, brow; head, nob[obs3], noddle[obs3], pate; capsheaf[obs3].

high places, heights.

topgallant mast, sky scraper; quarter deck, hurricane deck.

architrave, frieze, cornice, coping stone, zoophorus[obs3], capital, epistyle[obs3], sconce, pediment, entablature[obs3]; tympanum; ceiling &c. (covering) 223.

attic, loft, garret, house top, upper story.

[metaphorical use] summit conference, summit; peak of achievement, peak of performance; peaks and troughs, peaks and valleys [in graphs].

V. culminate, crown, top; overtop &c. (be superior to) 33.

Adj. highest &c. (high &c. 206); top; top most, upper most; tiptop; culminating &c. v.; meridian, meridional[obs3]; capital, head, polar, supreme, supernal, topgallant.

Adv. atop, at the top of the tree.

Phr. en flute; fleur deau[Fr].

#211. Base. — N. base, basement; plinth, dado, wainscot; baseboard, mopboard[obs3]; bedrock, hardpan [U.S.]; foundation &c. (support) 215; substructure, substratum, ground, earth, pavement, floor, paving, flag, carped, ground floor, deck; footing, ground work, basis; hold, bilge. bottom, nadir, foot, sole, toe, hoof, keel, root; centerboard. Adj. bottom, undermost, nethermost; fundamental; founded on, based on, grounded on, built on.

#212. Verticality. — N. verticality; erectness &c. adj.; perpendicularity &c. 216a; right angle, normal; azimuth circle.

wall, precipice, cliff.

elevation, erection; square, plumb line, plummet.

V. be vertical &c. adj.; stand up, stand on end, stand erect, stand upright; stick up, cock up.

render vertical &c. adj.; set up, stick up, raise up, cock up; erect, rear, raise on its legs.

Adj. vertical, upright, erect, perpendicular, plumb, normal, straight, bolt, upright; rampant; standing up &c. v.; rectangular, orthogonal &c. 216a.

Adv. vertically &c. adj.; up, on end; up on end, right on end; a plomb[Fr], endwise; one one's legs; at right angles.

#213. Horizontality. — N. horizontality[obs3]; flatness; level, plane; stratum &c. 204; dead level, dead flat; level plane.

recumbency, lying down &c. v.; reclination[obs3], decumbence[obs3]; decumbency[obs3], discumbencyl; proneness &c. adj.; accubation[obs3], supination[obs3], resupination[obs3], prostration; azimuth.

plain, floor, platform, bowling green; cricket ground; croquet ground, croquet lawn; billiard table; terrace, estrade[obs3], esplanade, parterre.

[flat land area] table land, plateau, ledge; butte; mesa (plain) 344.

[instrument to measure horizontality] level, spirit level.

V. be horizontal &c. adj.; lie, recline, couch; lie down, lie flat, lie prostrate; sprawl, loll, sit down.

render horizontal &c. adj.; lay down, lay out; level, flatten; prostrate, knock down, floor, fell.

Adj. horizontal, level, even, plane; flat &c. 251; flat as a billiard table, flat as a bowling green; alluvial; calm, calm as a mill pond; smooth, smooth as glass.

recumbent, decumbent, procumbent, accumbent[obs3]; lying &c. v.; prone, supine, couchant, jacent[obs3], prostrate, recubant[obs3].

Adv. horizontally &c. adj.; on one's back, on all fours, on its beam ends.

#214. Pendency. — N. pendency[obs3], dependency; suspension, hanging &c. v.; pedicel, pedicle, peduncle; tail, train, flap, skirt, pigtail, pony tail, pendulum; hangnail

peg, knob, button, hook, nail, stud, ring, staple, tenterhook; fastening &c. 45; spar, horse.

V. be pendent &c. adj.; hang, depend, swing, dangle; swag; daggle[obs3], flap, trail, flow; beetle.

suspend, hang, sling, hook up, hitch, fasten to, append.

Adj. pendent, pendulous; pensile; hanging &c. v.; beetling, jutting over, overhanging, projecting; dependent; suspended &c. v.; loose, flowing.

having a peduncle &c. n.; pedunculate[obs3], tailed, caudate.

<— p. 65 —>

#215. Support. — N. support, ground, foundation, base, basis; terra firma; bearing, fulcrum, bait [U.S.], caudex crib[obs3]; point d'appui[Fr], <gr/pou sto/gr>[Grk][Grk], purchase footing, hold, locus standi[Lat]; landing place, landing stage; stage, platform; block; rest, resting place; groundwork, substratum, riprap, sustentation, subvention; floor &c. (basement) 211. supporter; aid &c. 707; prop, stand, anvil, fulcimentl; cue rest, jigger; monkey; stay, shore, skid, rib, truss, bandage; sleeper; stirrup, stilts, shoe, sole, heel, splint, lap, bar, rod, boom, sprit[obs3], outrigger; ratlings[obs3]. staff, stick, crutch, alpenstock, baton, staddle[obs3]; bourdon[obs3], cowlstaff[obs3], lathi[obs3], mahlstick[obs3]. post, pillar, shaft, thill[obs3], column, pilaster; pediment, pedicle; pedestal; plinth, shank, leg, socle[obs3], zocle[obs3]; buttress, jamb, mullion, abutment; baluster, banister, stanchion; balustrade; headstone; upright; door post, jamb, door jamb. frame, framework; scaffold, skeleton, beam, rafter, girder, lintel, joist, travis[obs3], trave[obs3], corner stone, summer, transom; rung, round, step, sill; angle rafter, hip rafter; cantilever, modillion[obs3]; crown post, king post; vertebra. columella[obs3], backbone; keystone; axle, axletree; axis; arch, mainstay. trunnion, pivot, rowlock[obs3]; peg &c. (pendency) 214[obs3]; tiebeam &c. (fastening) 45; thole pin[obs3]. board, ledge, shelf, hob, bracket, trevet[obs3], trivet, arbor, rack; mantel, mantle piece[Fr], mantleshelf[obs3]; slab, console; counter, dresser; flange, corbel; table, trestle; shoulder; perch; horse; easel, desk; clotheshorse, hatrack; retable; teapoy[obs3]. seat, throne, dais; divan, musnud[obs3]; chair, bench, form, stool, sofa, settee, stall; arm chair, easy chair, elbow chair, rocking chair; couch, fauteuil[Fr], woolsack[obs3], ottoman, settle, squab, bench; aparejo[obs3], faldstool[obs3], horn; long chair, long sleeve chair, morris chair; lamba chauki[obs3], lamba kursi[obs3]; saddle, pannel[obs3], pillion; side saddle, pack saddle; pommel. bed, berth, pallet, tester, crib, cot, hammock, shakedown, trucklebed[obs3], cradle, litter, stretcher, bedstead; four poster, French bed, bunk, kip, palang[obs3]; bedding, bichhona, mattress, paillasse[obs3]; pillow, bolster; mat, rug, cushion. footstool, hassock; tabouret[obs3]; tripod, monopod. Atlas, Persides, Atlantes[obs3], Caryatides, Hercules. V. be supported &c.; lie on, sit on, recline on, lean on, loll on, rest on, stand on, step on, repose on, abut on, bear on, be based on &c.; have at one's back; bestride, bestraddle[obs3]. support, bear, carry, hold, sustain, shoulder; hold up, back up, bolster up, shore up; uphold, upbear[obs3]; prop; under prop, under pin, under set; riprap; bandage &c. 43. give support, furnish support, afford support, supply support, lend support, give foundations, furnish foundations, afford foundations, supply foundations, lend foundations; bottom, found, base, ground, imbed, embed. maintain, keep on foot; aid &c. 707. Adj. supporting, supported &c. v.; fundamental; dorsigerous[obs3]. Adv. astride on, straddle.

#216. Parallelism. — N. {ant. 216a} parallelism; coextension[obs3]; equidistance[obs3]; similarity &c. 17.
  Adj. parallel; coextensive; equidistant.
  Adv. alongside &c. (laterally) 236.
  #216a. Perpendicularity — N. {ant. 216} perpendicularity, orthogonality; verticality, &c. 212.
  V. be perpendicular, be orthogonal; intersect at right angles, be rectangular, be at right angles to, intersect at 90 degrees; have no correlation.
  Adj. orthogonal, perpendicular; rectangular; uncorrelated.
<— p. 66 —>

#217. Obliquity. — N. obliquity, inclination, slope, slant, crookedness &c. adj.; slopeness[obs3]; leaning &c. v.; bevel, tilt; bias, list, twist, swag, cant, lurch; distortion &c. 243; bend &c. (curve) 245; tower of Pisa. acclivity, rise, ascent, gradient, khudd[obs3], rising ground, hill, bank, declivity, downhill, dip, fall, devexityl; gentle slope, rapid slope, easy ascent, easy descent; shelving beach; talus; monagne Russe[Fr]; facilis descensus averni[Lat]. V. intersect; lack parallelism.

#218. Inversion. — N. inversion, eversion, subversion, reversion, retroversion, introversion; contraposition &c. 237[obs3]; contrariety &c. 14; reversal; turn of the tide. overturn; somersault, somerset; summerset[obs3]; culbute[obs3]; revulsion; pirouette. transposition, transposal[obs3], anastrophy[obs3], metastasis, hyperbaton[obs3], anastrophe[obs3], hysteron proteron[Grk][Grk], hypallage[obs3], synchysis[obs3], tmesis[obs3], parenthesis; metathesis; palindrome. pronation and supination[Anat][obs3]. V. be inverted &c.; turn round, turn about, turn to the right about, go round, go about, go to the right about, wheel round, wheel about, wheel to the right about; turn over, go over, tilt over, topple over; capsize, turn turtle. invert, subvert, retrovert[obs3], introvert; reverse; up turn, over turn, up set, over set; turn topsy turvy &c. adj.; culbuter[obs3]; transpose, put the cart before the horse, turn the tables. Adj. inverted &c. v.; wrong side out, wrong side up; inside out, upside down; bottom upwards, keel upwards; supine, on one's head, topsy- turvy, sens dessus dessous[Fr]. inverse; reverse &c. (contrary) 14; opposite &c. 237. top heavy. Adv. inversely &c. adj.; hirdy-girdy[obs3]; heels over head, head over heels.

#219. Crossing. — N. crossing &c. v.; intersection, interdigitation; decussation[obs3], transversion[obs3]; convolution &c. 248; level crossing.
  reticulation, network; inosculation[obs3], anastomosis, intertexture[obs3], mortise.
  net, plexus, web, mesh, twill, skein, sleeve, felt, lace; wicker; mat, matting; plait, trellis, wattle, lattice, grating, grille, gridiron, tracery, fretwork, filigree, reticle; tissue, netting, mokes[obs3]; rivulation[obs3].
  cross, chain, wreath, braid, cat's cradle, knot; entangle &c. (disorder) 59.
  [woven fabrics] cloth, linen, muslin, cambric &c.

56

[web-footed animal] webfoot.

V. cross, decussate[obs3]; intersect, interlace, intertwine, intertwist[obs3], interweave, interdigitate, interlink.

twine, entwine, weave, inweave[obs3], twist, wreathe; anastomose[Med], inosculate[obs3], dovetail, splice, link; lace, tat.

mat, plait, plat, braid, felt, twill; tangle, entangle, ravel; net, knot; dishevel, raddle[obs3].

Adj. crossing &c. v.; crossed, matted &c, v. transverse.

cross, cruciform, crucial; retiform[obs3], reticular, reticulated; areolar[obs3], cancelled[obs3], grated, barred, streaked; textile; crossbarred[obs3], cruciate[obs3], palmiped[obs3], secant; web-footed.

Adv. cross, thwart, athwart, transversely; at grade [U.S.]; crosswise.
<— p. 67 —>

% 3. CENTRICAL DIMENSIONS % <— That is, dimensions having reference to a center —> % General. %

#220. Exteriority. — N. exteriority[obs3]; outside, exterior; surface, superficies; skin &c. (covering) 223; superstratum[obs3]; disk, disc; face, facet; extrados[obs3].

excentricity[obs3]; eccentricity; circumjacence &c. 227[obs3].

V. be exterior &c. adj.; lie around &c. 227.

place exteriorly, place outwardly, place outside; put out, turn out.

Adj. exterior, external; outer most; outward, outlying, outside, outdoor; round about &c. 227; extramural; extralimitary[obs3], extramundane.

superficial, skin-deep; frontal, discoid.

extraregarding[obs3]; excentric[obs3], eccentric; outstanding; extrinsic &c. 6; ecdemic[Med], exomorphic[obs3].

Adv. externally &c. adj.; out, with out, over, outwards, ab extra, out of doors; extra muros[Lat].

in the open air; sub Jove, sub dio[Lat]; a la belle etoile[Fr], al fresco.

#221. Interiority. — N. interiority; inside, interior; interspace[obs3], subsoil, substratum; intrados. contents &c. 190; substance, pith, marrow; backbone &c. (center) 222; heart, bosom, breast; abdomen; vitals, viscera, entrails, bowels, belly, intestines, guts, chitterings[obs3], womb, lap; penetralia[Lat], recesses, innermost recesses; cave &c. (concavity) 252. V. be inside &c. adj.; within &c. adv. place within, keep within; inclose &c. (circumscribe) 229; intern; imbed &c. (insert) 300. Adj. interior, internal; inner, inside, inward, intraregarding[obs3]; inmost, innermost; deep seated, gut; intestine, intestinal; inland; subcutaneous; abdominal, coeliac, endomorphic[Physiol]; interstitial &c. (interjacent) 228[obs3]; inwrought &c. (intrinsic) 5; inclosed &c. v. home, domestic, indoor, intramural, vernacular; endemic. Adv. internally &c. adj.; inwards, within, in, inly[obs3]; here in, there in, where in; ab intra, withinside[obs3]; in doors, within doors; at home, in the bosom of one's family.

#222. Centrality. — N. centrality, centricalness[obs3], center; middle &c. 68; focus &c. 74.

core, kernel; nucleus, nucleolus; heart, pole axis, bull's eye; nave, navel; umbilicus, backbone, marrow, pith; vertebra, vertebral column; hotbed; concentration &c. (convergence) 290; centralization; symmetry.

center of gravity, center of pressure, center of percussion, center of oscillation, center of buoyancy &c.; metacenter[obs3].

V. be central &c. adj.; converge &c. 290.

render central, centralize, concentrate; bring to a focus.

Adj. central, centrical[obs3]; middle &c. 68; azygous, axial, focal, umbilical, concentric; middlemost; rachidian[obs3]; spinal, vertebral.

Adv. middle; midst; centrally &c. adj.

#223. Covering. — N. covering, cover; baldachin, baldachino[obs3], baldaquin[obs3]; canopy, tilt, awning, tent, marquee, tente d'abri[Fr], umbrella, parasol, sunshade; veil (shade) 424; shield &c. (defense) 717. roof, ceiling, thatch, tile; pantile, pentile[obs3]; tiling, slates, slating, leads; barrack [U.S.], plafond, planchment [obs3][U.S.], tiling, shed &c. (abode) 189. top, lid, coverclel, door, operculum; bulkhead [U.S.]. bandage, plaster, lint, wrapping, dossil[obs3], finger stall. coverlet, counterpane, sheet, quilt, tarpaulin, blanket, rug, drugget[obs3]; housing; antima-cassar, eiderdown, numdah[obs3], pillowcase, pillowslip[obs3]; linoleum; saddle cloth, blanket cloth; tidy; tilpah [obs3][U.S.], apishamore [obs3][U.S.]. integument, tegument; skin, pellicle, fleece, fell, fur, leather, shagreen[obs3], hide; pelt, peltry[obs3]; cordwain[obs3]; derm[obs3]; robe, buffalo robe [U.S.]; cuticle, scarfskin, epidermis. clothing &c. 225; mask &c. (concealment) 530. peel, crust, bark, rind, cortex, husk, shell, coat; eggshell, glume[obs3]. capsule; sheath, sheathing; pod, cod; casing, case, theca[obs3]; elytron[obs3]; elytrum[obs3]; involucrum[Lat]; wrapping, wrapper; envelope, vesicle; corn husk, corn shuck [U.S.]; dermatology, conchology; testaceology[obs3]. inunction[obs3]; incrustation, superimposition, superposition, obductionl; scale &c. (layer) 204. [specific coverings: list] veneer, facing; overlay; plate, silver plate, gold plate, copper plate; engobe[obs3]; ormolu; Sheffield plate; pavement; coating, paint; varnish &c. (resin) 356a; plating, barrel plating, anointing &c. v.; enamel; epitaxial deposition[Engin], vapor deposition; ground, whitewash, plaster, spackel, stucco, compo; cerement; ointment &c. (grease) 356. V. cover; superpose, superimpose; overlay, overspread; wrap &c. 225; encase, incase[obs3]; face, case, veneer, pave, paper; tip, cap, bind; bulkhead, bulkhead in; clapboard [U.S.]. coat, paint, varnish, pay, incrust, stucco, dab, plaster, tar; wash; besmear, bedaub; anoint, do over; gild, plate, japan, lacquer, lacker[obs3], enamel, whitewash; parget[obs3]; lay it on thick. overlie, overarch[obs3]; endome[obs3]; conceal &c. 528. [of aluminum] anodize. [of steel] galvanize. Adj. covering &c. v.; superimposed, overlaid, plated &c. v.; cutaneous, dermal, cortical, cuticular, tegumentary[obs3], skinny, scaly, squamous[Anat]; covered &c. v.; imbricated, loricated[obs3], armor plated, ironclad; under cover; cowled, cucullate[obs3], dermatoid[obs3], encuirassed[obs3], hooded, squamiferous[obs3], tectiform[obs3]; vaginate[obs3].

<— p. 68 —>

#224. Lining. — N. lining, inner coating; coating &c. (covering) 223; stalactite, stalagmite.
   filling, stuffing, wadding, padding.
   wainscot, parietes[Lat], wall.
   V. line, stuff, incrust, wad, pad, fill.
   Adj. lined &c. v..
<— ++add separate entry under materials (constitution, substance); entry for types of cloth and other materials for garments —> #225. Clothing. — N. clothing, investment; covering &c. 223; dress, raiment, drapery, costume, attire, guise, toilet, toilette, trim; habiliment; vesture, vestment; garment, garb, palliamentl, apparel, wardrobe, wearing apparel, clothes, things; underclothes. array; tailoring, millinery; finery &c. (ornament) 847; full dress &c. (show) 882; garniture; theatrical properties. outfit, equipment, trousseau; uniform, regimentals; continentals [Am. Hist.]; canoni-cals &c. 999; livery, gear, harness, turn-out, accouterment, caparison, suit, rigging, trappings, traps, slops, togs, toggery[obs3]; day wear, night wear, zoot suit; designer clothes; masquerade. dishabille, morning dress, undress. kimono; lungi[obs3]; shooting-coat; mufti; rags, tatters, old clothes; mourning, weeds; duds; slippers. robe, tunic, paletot[obs3], habit, gown, coat, frock, blouse, toga, smock frock, claw coat, hammer coat, Prince Albert coat[obs3], sack coat, tuxedo coat, frock coat, dress coat, tail coat. cloak, pall, mantle, mantlet mantua[obs3], shawl, pelisse, wrapper; veil; cape, tippet, kirtle[obs3], plaid, muffler, comforter, haik[obs3], hukol, chlamys[obs3], mantilla, tabard, housing, horse cloth, burnoose, burnous, roquelaure[obs3]; houppelande[Fr]; surcoat, overcoat, great coat; surtout[Fr]; spencer[obs3]; mackintosh, waterproof, raincoat; ulster, P- coat, dreadnought, wraprascal[obs3], poncho, cardinal, pelerine[obs3]; barbe[obs3], chudder[obs3], jubbah[obs3], oilskins, pajamas, pilot jacket, talma jacket[obs3], vest, jerkin, waistcoat, doublet, camisole, gabardine; farthingale, kilt, jupe[obs3], crinoline, bustle, panier, skirt, apron, pinafore; bloomer, bloomers; chaqueta[obs3], songtag[Ger], tablier[obs3]. pants, trousers, trowsers[obs3]; breeches, pantaloons, inexpressiblesl!, overalls, smalls, small clothes; shintiyanl!; shorts, jockey shorts, boxer shorts; tights, drawers, panties, unmentionables; knickers, knickerbockers; philibeg[obs3], fillibeg[obs3]; pants suit; culottes; jeans, blue jeans, dungarees, denims. [brand names for jeans] Levis, Calvin Klein, Calvins, Bonjour, Gloria Vanderbilt. headdress, headgear; chapeau[Fr], crush hat, opera hat; kaffiyeh; sombrero, jam, tam-o-shanter, tarboosh[obs3], topi, sola topi[Lat], pagri[obs3], puggaree[obs3]; cap, hat, beaver hat, coonskin cap; castor, bonnet, tile, wideawake, billycock[obs3], wimple; nightcap, mobcap[obs3], skullcap; hood, coif; capote[obs3], calash; kerchief, snood, babushka; head, coiffure; crown &c. (circle) 247; chignon, pelt, wig, front, peruke, periwig, caftan, turban, fez, shako, csako[obs3], busby; kepi[obs3], forage cap, bearskin; baseball cap; fishing hat; helmet &c. 717; mask, domino. body clothes; linen; hickory shirt [U.S.]; shirt, sark[obs3], smock, shift, chemise; night gown, negligee, dressing gown, night shirt; bedgown[obs3], sac de nuit[Fr]. underclothes [undercloth-ing], underpants, undershirt; slip [for women], brassiere, corset, stays, corsage, corset, corselet, bodice, girdle &c. (circle) 247; stomacher; petticoat, panties; under waistcoat; jock [for men], athletic supporter, jockstrap. sweater, jersey; cardigan; turtleneck, pullover; sweater vest. neckerchief, neckcloth[obs3]; tie, ruff, collar, cravat, stock, handkerchief, scarf; bib, tucker; boa; cummerbund, rumal[obs3], rabat[obs3]. shoe, pump, boot, slipper, sandal,

galoche[obs3], galoshes, patten, clog; sneakers, running shoes, hiking boots; high-low; Blucher boot, wellington boot, Hessian boot, jack boot, top boot; Balmoral[obs3]; arctics, bootee, bootikin[obs3], brogan, chaparajos[obs3]; chavar[obs3], chivarras[obs3], chivarros[obs3]; gums [U.S.], larrigan [obs3][N. Am.], rubbers, showshoe, stogy[obs3], veldtschoen[Ger], legging, buskin, greave[obs3], galligaskin[obs3], gamache[obs3], gamashes[obs3], moccasin, gambado, gaiter, spatterdash[obs3], brogue, antigropelos[obs3]; stocking, hose, gaskins[obs3], trunk hose, sock; hosiery. glove, gauntlet, mitten, cuff, wristband, sleeve. swaddling cloth, baby linen, layette; ice wool; taffeta. pocket handkerchief, hanky[obs3], hankie. clothier, tailor, milliner, costumier, sempstress[obs3], snip; dressmaker, habitmaker[obs3], breechesmaker[obs3], shoemaker; Crispin; friseur[Fr]; cordwainer[obs3], cobbler, hosier[obs3], hatter; draper, linen draper, haberdasher, mercer. [underpants for babies] diaper, nappy[obs3][Brit]; disposable diaper, cloth diaper; Luvs[brand names for diapers], Huggies. V. invest; cover &c. 223; envelope, lap, involve; inwrap[obs3], enwrap; wrap; fold up, wrap up, lap up, muffle up; overlap; sheath, swathe, swaddle, roll up in, circumvest. vest, clothe, array, dress, dight[obs3], drape, robe, enrobe, attire, apparel, accounter[obs3], rig, fit out; deck &c. (ornament) 847; perk, equip, harness, caparison. wear; don; put on, huddle on, slip on; mantle. Adj. invested &c. v.; habited; dighted[obs3]; barbed, barded; clad, costume, shod, chausse[Fr]; en grande tenue &c. (show) 882[Fr]. sartorial. Phr. "the soul of this man is his clothes" [All's Well].

<— p. 69 —>

#226. Divestment. — N. divestment; taking off &c. v.. nudity; bareness &c. adj.; undress; dishabille &c. 225; the altogether; nudation[obs3], denudation; decortication, depilation, excoriation, desquamation; molting; exfoliation; trichosis[Med]. V. divest; uncover &c. (cover &c. 223); denude, bare, strip; disfurnish[obs3]; undress, disrobe &c. (dress, enrobe &c. 225); uncoif[obs3]; dismantle; put off, take off, cast off; doff; peel, pare, decorticate, excoriate, skin, scalp, flay; expose, lay open; exfoliate, molt, mew; cast the skin. Adj. divested &c. v.; bare, naked, nude; undressed, undraped; denuded; exposed; in dishabille; bald, threadbare, ragged, callow, roofless. in a state of nature, in nature's garb, in the buff, in native buff, in birthday suit; in puris naturalibus[Lat]; with nothing on, stark naked, stark raving naked [joc.]; bald as a coot, bare as the back of one's hand; out at elbows; barefoot; bareback, barebacked; leafless, napless[obs3], hairless.

#227. Circumjacence. — N. circumjacence[obs3], circumambience[obs3]; environment, encompassment; atmosphere, medium, surroundings. outpost; border &c. (edge) 231; girdle &c. (circumference) 230; outskirts, boulebards, suburbs, purlieus, precincts, faubourgs[obs3], environs, entourage, banlieue[obs3]; neighborhood, vicinage, vicinity. V. lie around &c. adv.; surround, beset, compass, encompass, environ, inclose, enclose, encircle, embrace, circumvent, lap, gird; belt; begird, engird[obs3]; skirt, twine round; hem in &c. (circumscribe) 229. Adj. circumjacent, circumambient[obs3], circumfluent[obs3]; ambient; surrounding &c. v.; circumferential, suburban. Adv. around, about; without; on every side; on all sides; right and left, all round, round about.

#228. Interposition. — N. interposition, interjacence[obs3], intercurrence[obs3], intervenience[obs3], interlocation[obs3], interdigitation, interjection, interpolation, interlineation, interspersion, intercalation. [interposition at a fine-grained level] interpenetration; permeation; infiltration. [interposition by one person in another's affairs, at the intervenor's initiative] intervention, interference; intrusion, obtrusion; insinuation. insertion &c. 300; dovetailing; embolism. intermediary, intermedium[obs3]; go between, bodkin!!, intruder, interloper; parenthesis, episode, flyleaf. partition, septum, diaphragm; midriff; dissepiment[obs3]; party wall, panel, room divider. halfway house. V. lie between, come between, get between; intervene, slide in, interpenetrate, permeate. put between, introduce, import, throw in, wedge in, edge in, jam in, worm in, foist in, run in, plow in, work in; interpose, interject, intercalate, interpolate, interline, interleave, intersperse, interweave, interlard, interdigitate, sandwich in, fit in, squeeze in; let in, dovetail, splice, mortise; insinuate, smuggle; infiltrate, ingrain. interfere, put in an oar, thrust one's nose in; intrude, obtrude; have a finger in the pie; introduce the thin end of the wedge; thrust in &c. (insert) 300. Adj. interjacent[obs3], intercurrent[obs3], intervenient[obs3], intervening &c. v., intermediate, intermediary, intercalary, interstitial; embolismal[obs3]. parenthetical, episodic; mediterranean; intrusive; embosomed[obs3]; merged. Adv. between, betwixt; twixt; among, amongst; amid, amidst; mid, midst; in the thick of; betwixt and between; sandwich-wise; parenthetically, obiter dictum.

<— p. 70 —>

#229. Circumscription. — N. circumscription, limitation, inclosure; confinement &c. (restraint) 751; circumvallation[obs3]; encincture; envelope &c. 232. container (receptacle) 191. V. circumscribe, limit, bound, confine, inclose; surround &c. 227; compass about; imprison &c. (restrain) 751; hedge in, wall in, rail in; fence round, fence in, hedge round; picket; corral. enfold, bury, encase, incase[obs3], pack up, enshrine, inclasp[obs3]; wrap up

&c. (invest) 225; embay[obs3], embosom[obs3]. containment (inclusion) 76. Adj. circumscribed &c. v.; begirt[obs3], lapt[obs3]; buried in, immersed in; embosomed[obs3], in the bosom of, imbedded, encysted, mewed up; imprisoned &c. 751; landlocked, in a ring fence.

#230. Outline. — N. outline, circumference; perimeter, periphery, ambit, circuit, lines tournure[obs3], contour, profile, silhouette; bounds; coast line. zone, belt, girth, band, baldric, zodiac, girdle, tyre[Brit], cingle[obs3], clasp, girt; cordon &c. (inclosure) 232; circlet, &c. 247..

#231. Edge. — N. edge, verge, brink, brow, brim, margin, border, confine, skirt, rim, flange, side, mouth; jaws, chops, chaps, fauces; lip, muzzle.
threshold, door, porch; portal &c. (opening) 260; coast, shore.
frame, fringe, flounce, frill, list, trimming, edging, skirting, hem, selvedge, welt, furbelow, valance, gimp.
Adj. border, marginal, skirting; labial, labiated[obs3], marginated[obs3].
#232. Inclosure. — N. inclosure, envelope; case &c. (receptacle) 191; wrapper; girdle &c. 230.
pen, fold; pen fold, in fold, sheep fold; paddock, pound; corral; yard; net, seine net.
wall, hedge, hedge row; espalier; fence &c. (defense) 717; pale, paling, balustrade, rail, railing, quickset hedge, park paling, circumvallation[obs3], enceinte, ring fence.
barrier, barricade; gate, gateway; bent, dingle [U.S.]; door, hatch, cordon; prison &c. 752.
dike, dyke, ditch, fosse[obs3], moat.
V. inclose, circumscribe &c. 229.
#233. Limit. — N. limit, boundary, bounds, confine, enclave, term, bourn, verge, curbstone[obs3], but, pale, reservation; termination, terminus; stint, frontier, precinct, marches; backwoods.
boundary line, landmark; line of demarcation, line of circumvallation[obs3]; pillars of Hercules; Rubicon, turning point; ne plus ultra[Lat]; sluice, floodgate.
Adj. definite; conterminatel, conterminable[obs3]; terminal, frontier; bordering.
Adv. thus far, thus far and no further.
Phr. stick to the reservation; go beyond the pale.
<— p. 71 —> % Special %

#234. Front. — N. front; fore, forepart; foreground; face, disk, disc, frontage; facade, proscenium, facia[Lat], frontis-piece; anteriority[obs3]; obverse [of a medal or coin]. fore rank, front rank; van, vanguard; advanced guard; outpost; first line; scout. brow, forehead, visage, physiognomy, phiz[obs3], countenance, mut*[obs3]; rostrum, beak, bow, stem, prow, prore[obs3], jib. pioneer &c. (precursor) 64; metoposcopy[obs3]. V. be in front, stand in front &c. adj.; front, face, confront; bend forwards; come to the front, come to the fore. Adj. fore, anterior, front, frontal. Adv. before; in front, in the van, in advance; ahead, right ahead; forehead, foremost; in the foreground, in the lee of; before one's face, before one's eyes; face to face, vis-a-vis; front a front. Phr. formosa muta commendatio est [Lat][Syrus]; frons est animi janua [Lat][Cicero]; "Human face divine" [Milton]; imago animi vultus est indices oculi [Lat][Cicero]; "sea of upturned faces" [Scott].

#235. Rear. — N. rear, back, posteriority; rear rank, rear guard; background, hinterland.
occiput[Anat], nape, chine; heels; tail, rump, croup, buttock, posteriors, backside scut[obs3], breech, dorsum, loin; dorsal region, lumbar region; hind quarters; aitchbone[obs3]; natch, natch bone.
stern, poop, afterpart[obs3], heelpiece[obs3], crupper.
wake; train &c. (sequence) 281.
reverse; other side of the shield.
V. be behind &c. adv.; fall astern; bend backwards; bring up the rear.

Adj. back, rear; hind, hinder, hindmost, hindermost[obs3]; postern, posterior; dorsal, after; caudal, lumbar; mizzen, tergal[obs3].

Adv. behind; in the rear, in the background; behind one's back; at the heels of, at the tail of, at the back of; back to back.

after, aft, abaft, astern, sternmost[obs3], aback, rearward.

Phr. ogni medaglia ha il suo rovescio[It][obs3]; the other side of the coin.

#236. Laterality. — N. laterality[obs3]; side, flank, quarter, lee; hand; cheek, jowl, jole[obs3], wing; profile; temple, parietes[Lat], loin, haunch, hip; beam.

gable, gable end; broadside; lee side.

points of the compass; East, Orient, Levant; West; orientation.

V. be on one side &c. adv.; flank, outflank; sidle; skirt; orientate.

Adj. lateral, sidelong; collateral; parietal, flanking, skirting; flanked; sideling.

many sided; multilateral, bilateral, trilateral, quadrilateral.

Eastern; orient, oriental; Levantine; Western, occidental, Hesperian.

Adv. sideways, sidelong; broadside on; on one side, abreast, alongside, beside, aside; by the side of; side by side; cheek by jowl &c. (near) 197; to windward, to leeward; laterally &c. adj.; right and left; on her beam ends.

Phr. "his cheek the may of days outworn" [Shakespeare].

#237. Contraposition. — N. contraposition[obs3], opposition; polarity; inversion &c. 218; opposite side; reverse, inverse; counterpart; antipodes; opposite poles, North and South.

antonym, opposite (contrariety) 14.

V. be opposite &c. adj.; subtend.

Adj. opposite; reverse, inverse; converse, antipodal, subcontrary[obs3]; fronting, facing, diametrically opposite.

Northern, septentrional, Boreal, arctic; Southern, Austral, antarctic.

Adv. over, over the way, over against; against; face to face, vis-a-vis; as poles asunder.

#238. Dextrality. — N. dextrality[obs3]; right, right hand; dexter, offside, starboard.

Adj. dextral, right-handed; dexter, dextrorsal[obs3], dextrorse[obs3]; ambidextral[obs3], ambidextrous; dextro-.

Adv. dextrad[obs3], dextrally[obs3].

#239. Sinistrality. — N. sinistrality[obs3]; left, left hand, a gauche; sinister, nearside[obs3], larboard, port.

Adj. left-handed; sinister; sinistral, sinistrorsal[obs3], sinistrorse[obs3], sinistrous[obs3];

Pref. laevo-.

Adv. sinistrally, sinistrously[obs3].

<— p. 72 —> % Section III. FORM 1. General Form %

#240. Form. — N. form, figure, shape; conformation, configuration; make, formation, frame, construction, cut, set, build, trim, cut of one's jib; stamp, type, cast, mold; fashion; contour &c. (outline) 230; structure &c. 329; plasmature[obs3].

feature, lineament, turn; phase &c. (aspect) 448; posture, attitude, pose.

[Science of form] morphism.

[Similarity of form] isomorphism.

forming &c. v.; formation, figuration, efformation[obs3]; sculpture; plasmation[obs3].

V. form, shape, figure, fashion, efform[obs3], carve, cut, chisel, hew, cast; rough hew, rough cast; sketch; block out, hammer out; trim; lick into shape, put into shape; model, knead, work up into, set, mold, sculpture; cast, stamp; build &c. (construct) 161.

Adj. formed &c. v.

[Receiving form] plastic, fictile[obs3]; formative; fluid.

[Giving form] plasmic[obs3].

[Similar in form] isomorphous.

[taking several forms] pleomorphic; protean; changeable, &c. 149.

#241. [Absence of form.] Amorphism. — N. amorphism[obs3], informity[obs3]; unlicked cub[obs3]; rudis indigestaque moles[Lat]; disorder &c. 59; deformity &c. 243.

disfigurement, defacement; mutilation; deforming.

chaos, randomness (disorder) 59.

[taking form from surroundings] fluid &c. 333.

V. deface[Destroy form], disfigure, deform, mutilate, truncate; derange &c. 61; blemish, mar.

Adj. shapeless, amorphous, formless; unformed, unhewn[obs3], unfashioned[obs3], unshaped, unshapen; rough, rude, Gothic, barbarous, rugged.

#242. [Regularity of form.] Symmetry. — N. symmetry, shapeliness, finish; beauty &c. 845; proportion, eurythmy[obs3], uniformity, parallelism; bilateral symmetry, trilateral symmetry, multilateral symmetry; centrality &c. 222.

arborescence[obs3], branching, ramification; arbor vitae.

Adj. symmetrical, shapely, well set, finished; beautiful &c. 845; classic, chaste, severe.

regular, uniform, balanced; equal &c. 27; parallel, coextensive.

arborescent[obs3], arboriform[obs3]; dendriform[obs3], dendroid[obs3]; branching; ramous[obs3], ramose; filiciform[obs3], filicoid[obs3]; subarborescent[obs3]; papilionaceous[obs3].

fuji-shaped, fujigata[Jap.].

#243. [Irregularity of form.] Distortion. — N. distortion, detortion[obs3], contortion; twist, crookedness &c. (obliquity) 217; grimace; deformity; malformation, malconformation[obs3]; harelip; monstrosity, misproportion[obs3], want of symmetry, anamorphosis[obs3]; ugliness &c. 846; talipes[obs3]; teratology. asymmetry; irregularity. V. distort, contort, twist, warp, wrest, writhe, make faces, deform, misshape. Adj. distorted &c. v.; out of shape, irregular, asymmetric, unsymmetric[obs3], awry, wry, askew, crooked; not true, not straight; on one side, crump[obs3], deformed; harelipped; misshapen, misbegotten; misproportioned[obs3], ill proportioned; ill-made; grotesque, monstrous, crooked as a ram's horn; camel backed, hump backed, hunch backed, bunch backed, crook backed; bandy; bandy legged, bow legged; bow kneed, knock kneed; splay footed, club footed; round shouldered; snub nosed; curtailed of one's fair proportions; stumpy &c. (short) 201; gaunt &c. (thin) 203; bloated &c. 194; scalene; simous[obs3]; taliped[obs3], talipedic[obs3]. Adv. all manner of ways. Phr. crooked as a Virginia fence [U.S.].

<— p. 73 —> % 2. Special Form %

#244. Angularity. — N. angularity, angularness[obs3]; aduncity[obs3]; angle, cusp, bend; fold &c. 258; notch &c. 257; fork, bifurcation. elbow, knee, knuckle, ankle, groin, crotch, crutch, crane, fluke, scythe, sickle, zigzag, kimbo[obs3], akimbo. corner, nook, recess, niche, oriel[Arch], coign[obs3]. right angle &c. (perpendicular) 216a, 212; obliquity &c. 217; angle of 45x, miter; acute angle, obtuse angle, salient angle, reentering angle, spherical angle. angular measurement, angular elevation, angular distance, angular velocity; trigonometry, goniometry; altimetry[obs3]; clinometer, graphometer[obs3], goniometer; theodolite; sextant, quadrant; dichotomy. triangle, trigon[obs3], wedge; rectangle, square, lozenge, diamond; rhomb, rhombus; quadrangle, quadrilateral; parallelogram; quadrature; polygon, pentagon, hexagon, heptagon, octagon, oxygon[obs3], decagon. pyramid, cone. Platonic bodies; cube, rhomboid; tetrahedron, pentahedron, hexahedron, octahedron, dodecahedron, icosahedron, eicosahedron; prism, pyramid; parallelopiped; curb roof, gambrel roof, mansard roof. V. bend, fork, bifurcate, crinkle. Adj. angular, bent, crooked, aduncous[obs3], uncinated[obs3], aquiline, jagged, serrated; falciform[obs3], falcated[obs3]; furcated[obs3], forked, bifurcate, zigzag; furcular[obs3]; hooked; dovetailed; knock kneed, crinkled, akimbo, kimbo[obs3], geniculated[obs3]; oblique &c. 217. fusiform[Microb], wedge-shaped, cuneiform; cuneate[obs3], multangular[obs3], oxygonal[obs3]; triangular, trigonal[obs3], trilateral; quadrangular, quadrilateral, foursquare; rectangular, square, multilateral; polygonal &c. n.; cubical, rhomboid, rhomboidal, pyramidal.

#245. Curvature. — N. curvature, curvity[obs3], curvation[obs3]; incurvature[obs3], incurvityl; incurvation[obs3]; bend; flexure, flexion, flection[obs3]; conflexurel; crook, hook, bought, bending; deflection, deflexion[obs3]; inflection, inflexion[obs3]; concameration[obs3]; arcuation[obs3], devexityl, turn, deviation, detour, sweep; curl, curling; bough; recurvity[obs3], recurvation[obs3]; sinuosity &c. 248. kink. carve, arc, arch, arcade, vault, bow, crescent, half-moon, lunule[obs3], horseshoe, loop, crane neck; parabola, hyperbola; helix, spiral; catenary[obs3], festoon; conchoid[obs3], cardioid; caustic; tracery; arched ceiling, arched roof; bay window, bow window. sine curve; spline, spline curve, spline function; obliquity &c. 217. V. be curved &c. adj[intrans].; curve, sweep, sway, swag, sag; deviate &c. 279; curl, turn; reenter. [trans] render curved &c. adj.; flex, bend, curve, incurvate[obs3]; inflect; deflect, scatter[Phys]; refract (light) 420; crook; turn, round, arch, arcuate, arch over, concamerate[obs3]; bow, curl, recurve, frizzle. rotundity &c. 249; convexity &c. 250. Adj. curved &c. v.; curviform[obs3], curvilineal[obs3], curvilinear; devexl; devious; recurved, recurvous[obs3]; crump[obs3]; bowed &c. v.; vaulted, hooked; falciform[obs3], falcated[obs3]; semicircular, crescentic; sinusoid[Geom], parabolic, paraboloid; luniform[obs3], lunular[obs3]; semilunar, conchoidal[obs3]; helical, double helical, spiral; kinky; cordiform[obs3], cordated[obs3]; cardioid; heart shaped, bell shaped, boat shaped, crescent shaped, lens shaped, moon shaped, oar shaped, shield shaped, sickle shaped, tongue shaped, pear shaped, fig shaped; kidney- shaped, reniform; lentiform[obs3], lenticular; bow-legged &c. (distorted) 243; oblique &c. 217; circular &c. 247. aduncated[obs3], arclike[obs3], arcuate, arched, beaked; bicorn[obs3], bicornuous[obs3], bicornute[obs3]; clypeate[obs3], clypeiform[obs3]; cymbiform[obs3], embowed[obs3], galeiform[obs3]; hamate[obs3], hamiform[obs3], hamous[obs3]; hooked; linguiform[obs3], lingulate[obs3]; lobiform[obs3], lunate, navicular[obs3], peltate[obs3], remiform[obs3], rhamphoid[obs3]; rostrate[obs3], rostriferous[obs3], rostroid[obs3]; scutate[obs3], scaphoid[obs3], uncate[obs3]; unguiculate[obs3], unguiform[obs3].

#246. Straightness. — N. straightness, rectilinearity[obs3], directness; inflexibility &c. (stiffness) 323; straight line, right line, direct line; short cut. V. be straight &c. adj.; have no turning; not incline to either side, not bend to either side, not turn to either side, not deviate to either side; go straight; steer for &c. (directions) 278. render straight, straighten, rectify; set straight, put straight; unbend, unfold, uncurl &c. 248, unravel &c. 219, unwrap. Adj. straight; rectilinear, rectilineal[obs3]; direct, even, right, true, in a line; unbent, virgate &c. v[obs3].; undeviating, unturned, undistorted, unswerving; straight as an arrow &c. (direct) 278; inflexible &c. 323. laser-straight; ramrod-straight.

#247. [Simple circularity.] Circularity. — N. circularity, roundness; rotundity &c. 249. circle, circlet, ring, areola, hoop, roundlet[obs3], annulus, annulet[obs3], bracelet, armlet; ringlet; eye, loop, wheel; cycle, orb, orbit, rundle, zone, belt, cordon, band; contrate wheel[obs3], crown wheel; hub; nave; sash, girdle, cestus[obs3], cincture, baldric, fillet, fascia, wreath, garland; crown, corona, coronet, chaplet, snood, necklace, collar; noose, lasso, lassoo[obs3]. ellipse, oval, ovule; ellipsoid, cycloid; epicycloid[Geom], epicycle; semicircle; quadrant, sextant, sector. sphere &c. 249. V. make round &c. adj.; round. go round; encircle &c. 227; describe a circle &c. 311. Adj. round, rounded, circular, annular, orbicular; oval, ovate; elliptic, elliptical; egg-shaped; pear-shaped &c. 245; cycloidal &c. n[obs3].; spherical &c. 249. Phr. "I watched the little circles die" [Tennyson].

<— p. 74 —>

#248. [Complex curvature.] Convolution. — N. winding &c. v.; convolution, involution, circumvolution; wave, undulation, tortuosity, anfractuosity[obs3]; sinuosity, sinuation[obs3]; meandering, circuit, circumbendibus[obs3], twist, twirl, windings and turnings, ambages[obs3]; torsion; inosculation[obs3]; reticulation &c. (crossing) 219; rivulation[obs3]; roughness &c. 256. coil, roll, curl; buckle, spiral, helix, corkscrew, worm, volute, rundle; tendril; scollop[obs3], scallop, escalop[obs3]; kink; ammonite, snakestone[obs3]. serpent, eel, maze, labyrinth. knot. V. be convoluted &c. adj.; wind, twine, turn and twist, twirl; wave, undulate, meander; inosculate[obs3]; entwine, intwine[obs3]; twist, coil, roll; wrinkle, curl, crisp, twill; frizzle; crimp, crape, indent, scollop[obs3], scallop, wring, intort[obs3]; contort; wreathe &c. (cross) 219. Adj. convoluted; winding, twisted &c. v.; tortile[obs3], tortivel; wavy; undated, undulatory; circling, snaky, snake-like, serpentine; serpent, anguill[obs3], vermiform; vermicular; mazy, tortuous, sinuous, flexuous, anfractuous[obs3], reclivate[obs3], rivulose[obs3], scolecoid[obs3]; sigmoid, sigmoidal[Geom]; spiriferous[obs3], spiroid[obs3]; involved, intricate, complicated, perplexed; labyrinth, labyrinthic[obs3], labyrinthian[obs3], labyrinthine; peristaltic; daedalian[obs3]; kinky, knotted. wreathy[obs3], frizzly, crepe, buckled; raveled &c. (in disorder) 59. spiral, coiled, helical; cochleate, cochleous; screw-shaped; turbinated, turbiniform[obs3]. Adv. in and out, round and round; a can of worms; Gordian knot.

#249. Rotundity. — N. rotundity; roundness &c. adj.; cylindricity[obs3]; sphericity, spheroidity[obs3]; globosity[obs3]. cylinder, cylindroid[obs3], cylindrical; barrel, drum; roll, roller; rouleau[obs3], column, rolling-pin, rundle. cone, conoid[obs3]; pear shape, egg shape, bell shape. sphere, globe, ball, boulder, bowlder[obs3]; spheroid, ellipsoid;

oblong spheroid; oblate spheroid, prolate spheroid; drop, spherule, globule, vesicle, bulb, bullet, pellet, pelote[obs3], clew, pill, marble, pea, knob, pommel, horn; knot (convolution) 248. curved surface, hypersphere; hyperdimensional surface. V. render spherical &c. adj.; form into a sphere, sphere, roll into a ball; give rotundity &c. n.; round. Adj. rotund; round &c. (circular) 247; cylindric, cylindrical, cylindroid[obs3]; columnar, lumbriciform[obs3]; conic, conical; spherical, spheroidal; globular, globated[obs3], globous[obs3], globose; egg shaped, bell shaped, pear shaped; ovoid, oviform; gibbous; rixiform[obs3]; campaniform[obs3], campanulate[obs3], campaniliform[obs3]; fungiform[obs3], bead-like, moniliform[obs3], pyriform[obs3], bulbous; tres atque rotundus[Lat]; round as an orange, round as an apple, round as a ball, round as a billiard ball, round as a cannon ball.

% 3. Superficial Form %

#250. Convexity. — N. convexity, prominence, projection, swelling, gibbosity[obs3], bilge, bulge, protuberance, protrusion; camber, cahot [obs3][N. Am.], thank-ye-ma'am [U.S.]. swell. intumescence; tumour[Brit], tumor; tubercle, tuberosity[Anat]; excrescence; hump, hunch, bunch. boss, embossment, hub, hubble [convex body parts] tooth[U.S.], knob, elbow, process, apophysis[obs3], condyle, bulb, node, nodule, nodosity[obs3], tongue, dorsum, bump, clump; sugar loaf &c. (sharpness) 253; bow; mamelon[obs3]; molar; belly, corporation!, pot belly, gut[coll]; withers, back, shoulder, lip, flange. [convexities on skin] pimple, zit [slang]; wen, wheel, papula[Med], pustule, pock, proud flesh, growth, sarcoma, caruncle[obs3], corn, wart, pappiloma, furuncle, polypus[obs3], fungus, fungosity[obs3], exostosis[obs3], bleb, blister, blain[obs3]; boil &c. (disease) 655; airbubble[obs3], blob, papule, verruca. [convex body parts on chest] papilla, nipple, teat, tit [vulgar], titty [vulgar], boob [vulgar], knocker[vulgar], pap, breast, dug, mammilla[obs3]. [prominent convexity on the face] proboscis, nose, neb, beak, snout, nozzle, schnoz[coll]. peg, button, stud, ridge, rib, jutty, trunnion, snag. cupola, dome, arch, balcony, eaves; pilaster. relief, relievo[It], cameo; bassorilievo[obs3], mezzorilevo[obs3], altorivievo; low relief, bas relief[Fr], high relief. hill &c. (height) 206; cape, promontory, mull; forehead, foreland[obs3]; point of land, mole, jetty, hummock, ledge, spur; naze[obs3], ness. V. be prominent &c. adj.; project, bulge, protrude, pout, bougel[Fr], bunch; jut out, stand out, stick out, poke out; stick up, bristle up, start up, cock up, shoot up; swell over, hang over, bend over; beetle. render prominent &c. adj.; raise 307; emboss, chase. [become convex] belly out. Adj. convex, prominent, protuberant, projecting &c. v.; bossed, embossed, bossy, nodular, bunchy; clavate, clavated[obs3], claviform; hummocky[obs3], moutonne[obs3], mammiliform[obs3]; papulous[obs3], papilose[obs3]; hemispheric, bulbous; bowed, arched; bold; bellied; tuberous, tuberculous; tumous[obs3]; cornute[obs3], odontoid[obs3]; lentiform[obs3], lenticular; gibbous; club shaped, hubby [obs3][U.S.], hubbly [obs3][U.S.], knobby, papillose, saddle-shaped, selliform[obs3], subclavate[obs3], torose[obs3], ventricose[obs3], verrucose[obs3]. salient, in relief, raised, repousse; bloated &c, (expanded) 194.

<— p. 75 —>

#251. Flatness. — N. flatness &c. adj.; smoothness &c. 255.
plane; level &c. 213; plate, platter, table, tablet, slab.
V. render flat, flatten; level &c. 213.
Adj. flat, plane, even, flush, scutiform[obs3], discoid; level &c.
(horizontal) 213; flat as a pancake, flat as a fluke, flat as a flounder,
flat as a board, flat as my hand.

#252. Concavity. — N. concavity, depression, dip; hollow, hollowness; indentation, intaglio, cavity, dent, dint, dimple, follicle, pit, sinus, alveolus[obs3], lacuna; excavation, strip mine; trough &c. (furrow) 259; honeycomb. cup, basin, crater, punch bowl; cell &c. (receptacle) 191; socket. valley, vale, dale, dell, dingle, combe[obs3], bottom, slade[obs3], strath[obs3], glade, grove, glen, cave, cavern, cove; grot[obs3], grotto; alcove, cul-de-sac; gully &c. 198; arch &c. (curve) 245; bay &c. (of the sea) 343. excavator, sapper, miner. honeycomb (sponge) 252a. V. be concave &c. adj.; retire, cave in. render concave &c. adj.; depress, hollow; scoop, scoop out; gouge, gouge out, dig, delve, excavate, dent, dint, mine, sap, undermine, burrow, tunnel, stave in. Adj. depressed &c. v.; alveolate[obs3], calathiform[obs3], cup-shaped, dishing; favaginous[obs3], faveolate[obs3], favose[obs3]; scyphiform[obs3], scyphose[obs3]; concave, hollow, stove in; retiring; retreating; cavernous; porous &c. (with holes) 260; infundibul[obs3], infundibular[obs3], infundibuliform[obs3]; funnel shaped, bell shaped; campaniform[obs3], capsular; vaulted, arched.

252a Sponge — N. sponge, honeycomb, network; frit[Chem], filter.
sieve, net, screen (opening) 260.
Adj. cellular, spongy, spongious[obs3]; honeycombed, alveolar;
sintered; porous (opening) 260.

#253. Sharpness. — N. sharpness &c. adj.; acuity, acumination[obs3]; spinosity[obs3]. point, spike, spine, spicule[Biol], spiculum[obs3]; needle, hypodermic needle, tack, nail, pin; prick, prickle; spur, rowel, barb; spit, cusp; horn, antler; snag; tag thorn, bristle; Adam's needle[obs3], bear grass [U.S.], tine, yucca. nib, tooth, tusk; spoke, cog, ratchet. crag, crest, arete[Fr], cone peak, sugar loaf, pike, aiguille[obs3]; spire, pyramid, steeple. beard, chevaux de frise[Fr], porcupine, hedgehog, brier, bramble, thistle; comb; awn, beggar's lice, bur, burr, catchweed[obs3], cleavers, clivers[obs3], goose, grass, hairif[obs3], hariff, flax comb, hackle, hatchel[obs3], heckle. wedge; knife edge, cutting edge; blade, edge tool, cutlery, knife, penknife, whittle, razor, razor blade, safety razor, straight razor, electric razor; scalpel; bistoury[obs3], lancet; plowshare, coulter, colter[obs3]; hatchet, ax, pickax, mattock, pick, adze, gill; billhook, cleaver, cutter; scythe, sickle; scissors, shears, pruning shears, cutters, wire cutters, nail clipper, paper cutter; sword &c. (arms) 727; bodkin &c. (perforator) 262; belduque[obs3], bowie knife[obs3], paring knife; bushwhacker [U.S.]; drawing knife, drawing shave; microtome[Microbiol]; chisel, screwdriver blade; flint blade; guillotine. sharpener, hone, strop; grindstone, whetstone; novaculite[obs3]; steel, emery. V. be sharp &c. adj.; taper to a point; bristle with. render sharp &c. adj.; sharpen, point, aculeate, whet, barb, spiculate[obs3], set, strop, grind; chip [flint]. cut &c. (sunder) 44. Adj. sharp, keen; acute; acicular, aciform[obs3]; aculeated[obs3]; acuminated[obs3]; pointed; tapering; conical, pyramidal; mucronate[obs3], mucronated[obs3]; spindle shaped, needle shaped; spiked, spiky, ensiform[obs3], peaked, salient; cusped, cuspidate, cuspidated[obs3]; cornute[obs3], cornuted[obs3], cornicultate[obs3]; prickly; spiny, spinous[obs3], spicular; thorny, bristling, muricated[obs3], pectinated[obs3], studded, thistly, briary[obs3]; craggy &c. (rough) 256; snaggy, digitated[obs3], two-edged, fusiform[Microb]; dentiform[obs3], denticulated; toothed; odontoid[obs3]; starlike; stellated[obs3], stelliform[obs3]; sagittate[obs3], sagittiform[obs3]; arrowheaded[obs3]; arrowy[obs3], barbed, spurred. acinaciform; apiculate[obs3], apiculated[obs3]; aristate[obs3], awned, awny[obs3], bearded, calamiform[obs3], cone-shaped, coniform[obs3], crestate[obs3], echinate[obs3], gladiate[obs3]; lanceolate[obs3], lanciform; awl, awl-shaped, lance-shaped, awl-shaped, scimitar-shaped, sword-shaped; setarious[obs3], spinuliferous[obs3], subulate[obs3], tetrahedral, xiphoid[obs3]. cutting; sharp edged, knife edged; sharp as a razor, keen as a razor; sharp as a needle, sharp as a tack; sharpened &c. v.; set.

<— p. 76 —>

#254. Bluntness. — N. bluntness &c. adj.
V. be blunt, render blunt &c. adj.; obtund[obs3], dull; take off the point, take off the edge; turn.
Adj. blunt, obtuse, dull, bluff; edentate, toothless.

#255. Smoothness. — N. smoothness &c. adj.; polish, gloss; lubricity, lubrication. [smooth materials] down, velvet, velure, silk, satin; velveteen, velour, velours, velumen[obs3]; glass, ice. slide; bowling green &c. (level) 213; asphalt, wood pavement, flagstone, flags. [objects used to smooth other objects] roller, steam roller, lawn roller, rolling pin, rolling mill; sand paper, emery paper, emery cloth, sander; flat iron, sad iron; burnisher, turpentine and beeswax; polish, shoe polish. [art of cutting and polishing gemstones] lapidary. [person who polishes gemstones] lapidary, lapidarian. V. smooth, smoothen[obs3]; plane; file; mow, shave; level, roll; macadamize; polish, burnish, calender[obs3], glaze; iron, hot-press, mangle; lubricate &c. (oil) 332. Adj. smooth; polished &c. v.; leiodermatous[obs3], slick, velutinous[obs3]; even; level &c. 213; plane &c. (flat) 251; sleek, glossy; silken, silky; lanate[obs3], downy, velvety; glabrous, slippery, glassy, lubricous, oily, soft, unwrinkled[obs3]; smooth as glass, smooth as ice, smooth as monumental alabaster, smooth as velvet, smooth as oil; slippery as an eel; woolly &c. (feathery) 256. Phr. smooth as silk; slippery as coonshit on a pump handle; slippery as a greased pig.

#256. Roughness. — N. roughness &c. adj.; tooth, grain, texture, ripple; asperity, rugosity[obs3], salebrosityl, corrugation, nodosity[obs3]; arborescence[obs3] &c. 242; pilosity[obs3]. brush, hair, beard, shag, mane, whisker, moustache, imperial, tress, lock, curl, ringlet; fimbriae, pili, cilia, villi; lovelock; beaucatcher[obs3]; curl paper; goatee; papillote, scalp lock. plumage, plumosity[obs3]; plume, panache, crest; feather, tuft, fringe, toupee. wool, velvet, plush, nap, pile, floss, fur, down; byssus[obs3], moss, bur; fluff. knot (convolution) 248. V. be rough &c. adj.; go against the grain. render-rough &c. adj.; roughen, ruffle, crisp, crumple, corrugate, set on edge, stroke the wrong way, rumple. Adj. rough, uneven, scabrous, scaly ,knotted; rugged, rugose[obs3], rugous[obs3]; knurly[obs3]; asperous[obs3], crisp, salebrousl, gnarled, unpolished, unsmooth[obs3], roughhewn[obs3]; craggy, cragged; crankling[obs3], scraggy; prickly &c. (sharp) 253; arborescent &c. 242[obs3]; leafy, well-wooded; feathery; plumose, plumigerous[obs3]; laciniate[obs3], laciniform[obs3], laciniose[obs3]; pappose[obs3]; pileous[obs3], pilose[obs3]; trichogenous[obs3], trichoid[Med]; tufted, fimbriated, hairy, ciliated, filamentous, hirsute; crinose[obs3], crinite[obs3]; bushy, hispid, villous, pappous[obs3], bearded, pilous[obs3], shaggy, shagged; fringed, befringed[obs3]; setousl, setose[obs3], setaceous; "like quills upon the fretful porcupine" [Hamlet]; rough as a nutmeg grater, rough as a bear. downy, velvety, flocculent, woolly; lanate[obs3], lanated[obs3]; lanuginous[obs3], lanuginose[obs3]; tomentose[obs3];

fluffy. Adv. against the grain. Phr. cabello luengo y corto el seso[Sp].

#257. Notch. — N. notch, dent, nick, cut; indent, indentation;
dimple.
embrasure, battlement, machicolation[obs3]; saw, tooth,
crenelle[obs3], scallop, scollop[obs3], vandyke; depression; jag.
V. notch, nick, cut, dent, indent, jag, scarify, scotch, crimp,
scallop, scollop[obs3], crenulate[obs3], vandyke.
Adj. notched &c. v.; crenate[obs3], crenated[obs3]; dentate, dentated;
denticulate, denticulated; toothed, palmated[obs3], serrated.
<— p. 77 —>

#258. Fold. — N. fold, plicature[obs3], plait, pleat, ply, crease; tuck, gather; flexion, flexure, joint, elbow, double,
doubling, duplicature[obs3], gather, wrinkle, rimple[obs3], crinkle, crankle[obs3], crumple, rumple, rivel[obs3],
ruck[obs3], ruffle, dog's ear, corrugation, frounce[obs3], flounce, lapel; pucker, crow's feet; plication[obs3]. V. fold,
double, plicate[obs3], plait, crease, wrinkle, crinkle, crankle[obs3], curl, cockle up, cocker, rimple[obs3], rumple, flute,
frizzle, frounce[obs3], rivel[obs3], twill, corrugate, ruffle, crimplel, crumple, pucker; turn down, double down, down
under; tuck, ruck[obs3], hem, gather. Adj. folded, fluted, pleated &c. v..

#259. Furrow. — N. furrow, groove, rut, sulcus[Anat], scratch, streak, striae, crack, score, incision, slit; chamfer,
fluting; corduroy road, cradle hole. channel, gutter, trench, ditch, dike, dyke; moat, fosse[obs3], trough, kennel;
ravine &c. (interval) 198; tajo [obs3][U.S.], thank-ye-ma'am [U.S.]. V. furrow &c. n.; flute, plow; incise, engrave, etch,
bite in. Adj. furrowed &c. v.; ribbed, striated, sulcated[Anat], fluted, canaliculated[obs3]; bisulcous[obs3],
bisulcate[obs3], bisulcated[obs3]; canaliferous[obs3]; trisulcate[obs3]; corduroy; unisulcate[obs3]; costate[obs3],
rimiform[obs3].

#260. Opening — N. hole, foramen; puncture, perforation; fontanel[obs3]; transforation[obs3]; pinhole, keyhole, loop-
hole, porthole, peephole, mousehole, pigeonhole; eye of a needle; eyelet; slot. opening; aperture, apertness[obs3];
hiation[obs3], yawning, oscitancy[obs3], dehiscence, patefactionl, pandiculation[obs3]; chasm &c. (interval) 198.
embrasure, window, casement; abatjour[obs3]; light; sky light, fan light; lattice; bay window, bow window; oriel[Arch];
dormer, lantern. outlet, inlet; vent, vomitory; embouchure; orifice, mouth, sucker, muzzle, throat, gullet,
weasand[obs3], wizen, nozzle; placket. portal, porch, gate, ostiaryl, postern, wicket, trapdoor, hatch, door; arcade;
cellarway[obs3], driveway, gateway, doorway, hatchway, gangway; lich gate[obs3]. way, path &c. 627; thoroughfare;
channel; passage, passageway; tube, pipe; water pipe &c. 350; air pipe &c. 351; vessel, tubule, canal, gut, fistula;
adjutage[obs3], ajutage[obs3]; ostium[obs3]; smokestack; chimney, flue, tap, funnel, gully, tunnel, main; mine, pit,
adit[obs3], shaft; gallery. alley, aisle, glade, vista. bore, caliber; pore; blind orifice; fulgurite[obs3], thundertube[obs3].
porousness, porosity. sieve, cullender[obs3], colander; cribble[obs3], riddle, screen; honeycomb. apertion[obs3],
perforation; piercing &c. v.; terebration[obs3], empalement[obs3], pertusionl, puncture, acupuncture, penetration. key
&c. 631, opener, master key, password, combination, passe-partout. V. open, ope[obs3], gape, yawn, bilge; fly open.
perforate, pierce, empiercel, tap, bore, drill; mine &c. (scoop out) 252; tunnel; transpierce[obs3], transfix; enfilade,
impale, spike, spear, gore, spit, stab, pink, puncture, lance, stick, prick, riddle, punch; stave in. cut a passage
through; make way for, make room for. uncover, unclose, unrip[obs3]; lay open, cut open, rip open, throw open, pop
open, blow open, pry open, tear open, pull open. Adj. open; perforated &c. v.; perforate; wide open, ajar, unclosed,
unstopped; oscitant[obs3], gaping, yawning; patent. tubular, cannular[obs3], fistulous; pervious, permeable;
foraminous[obs3]; vesicular, vasicular[obs3]; porous, follicular, cribriform[obs3], honeycombed, infundibular[obs3],
riddled; tubulous[obs3], tubulated[obs3]; piped, tubate[obs3]. opening &c. v.; aperient[obs3]. Int. open sesame!

#261. Closure. — N. closure, occlusion, blockade; shutting up &c. v.; obstruction &c. (hindrance) 706; embolus;
contraction &c. 195; infarction; constipation, obstipation[obs3]; blind alley, blind corner; keddah[obs3]; cul-de-sac,
caecum; imperforation[obs3], imperviousness &c. adj.; impermeability; stopper &c. 263. V. close, occlude, plug;
block up, stop up, fill up, bung up, cork up, button up, stuff up, shut up, dam up; blockade, obstruct &c. (hinder) 706;
bar, bolt, stop, seal, plumb; choke, throttle; ram down, dam, cram; trap, clinch; put to the door, shut the door. Adj.
closed &c. v.; shut, operculated[obs3]; unopened. unpierced[obs3], imporous[obs3], caecal[Med]; closable; imperfo-
rate, impervious, impermeable; impenetrable; impassable, unpassablel2; inviousl; pathless, wayless[obs3]; untrod-
den, untrod. unventilated; air tight, water tight; hermetically sealed; tight, snug.

<— p. 78 —>

#262. Perforator. — N. perforator, piercer, borer, auger, chisel, gimlet, stylet[obs3], drill, wimble[obs3], awl, bradawl, scoop, terrier, corkscrew, dibble, trocar[Med], trepan, probe, bodkin, needle, stiletto, rimer, warder, lancet; punch, puncheon; spikebit[obs3], gouge; spear &c. (weapon) 727; puncher; punching machine, punching press; punch pliers.

#263. Stopper. — N. stopper, stopple; plug, cork, bung, spike, spill, stopcock, tap; rammer[obs3]; ram, ramrod; piston; stop-gap; wadding, stuffing, padding, stopping, dossil[obs3], pledget[obs3], tompion[obs3], tourniquet.
cover &c. 223; valve, vent peg, spigot, slide valve.
janitor, doorkeeper, porter, warder, beadle, cerberus, ostiary[obs3].
% Section IV. MOTION 1. Motion in General %

#264. [Successive change of place.] Motion. — N. motion, movement, move; going &c. v.; unrest. stream, flow, flux, run, course, stir; evolution; kinematics; telekinesis. step, rate, pace, tread, stride, gait, port, footfall, cadence, carriage, velocity, angular velocity; clip, progress, locomotion; journey &c. 266; voyage &c. 267; transit &c. 270. restlessness &c. (changeableness) 149; mobility; movableness, motive power; laws of motion; mobilization. V. be in motion &c. adj.; move, go, hie, gang, budge, stir, pass, flit; hover about, hover round, hover about; shift, slide, glide; roll, roll on; flow, stream, run, drift, sweep along; wander &c. (deviate) 279; walk &c. 266; change one's place, shift one's place, change one's quarters, shift one's quarters; dodge; keep going, keep moving; put in motion, set in motion; move; impel &c. 276; propel &c. 284; render movable, mobilize. Adj. moving &c. v.; in motion; transitional; motory[obs3], motive; shifting, movable, mobile, mercurial, unquiet; restless &c. (changeable) 149; nomadic &c. 266; erratic &c. 279. Adv. under way; on the move, on the wing, on the tramp, on the march. Phr. eppur si muove [It] [Galileo]; es bildet ein Talent sich in der Stille[Ger], sich ein Charakter in dem Strom der Welt[Ger].

#265. Quiescence. — N. rest; stillness &c. adj.; quiescence; stagnation, stagnancy; fixity, immobility, catalepsy; indisturbance[obs3]; quietism. quiet, tranquility, calm; repose &c. 687; peace; dead calm, anticyclonel!; statue-like repose; silence &c. 203; not a breath of air, not a mouse stirring; sleep &c. (inactivity) 683. pause, lull &c. (cessation) 142; stand still; standing still &c. v.; lock; dead lock, dead stop, dead stand; full stop; fix; embargo. resting place; gite[Fr]; bivouac; home &c. (abode) 189; pillow &c. (support) 215; haven &c. (refuge) 666; goal &c. (arrival) 292. V. be quiescent &c. adj.; stand still, lie still; keep quiet, repose, hold the breath. remain, stay; stand, lie to, ride at anchor, remain in situ, tarry, mark time; bring to, heave to, lay to; pull up, draw up; hold, halt; stop, stop short; rest, pause, anchor; cast to an anchor, come to an anchor; rest on one's oars; repose on one's laurels, take breath; stop &c. (discontinue) 142. stagnate; quieta non movere[Lat]; let alone; abide, rest and be thankful; keep within doors, stay at home, go to bed. dwell &c. (be present) 186; settle &c. (be located) 184; alight &c. (arrive) 292 stick, stick fast; stand like a post; not stir a peg, not stir a step; be at a stand &c. n. quell, becalm, hush, stay, lull to sleep, lay an embargo on. Adj. quiescent, still; motionless, moveless; fixed; stationary; immotile; at rest at a stand, at a standstill, at anchor; stock, still; standing still &c. v.; sedentary, untraveled, stay-at-home; becalmed, stagnant, quiet; unmoved, undisturbed, unruffled; calm, restful; cataleptic; immovable &c. (stable) 150; sleeping &c. (inactive) 683; silent &c. 403; still as a statue, still as a post, still as a mouse, still as death; vegetative, vegetating. Adv. at a stand &c. adj.; tout court; at the halt. Int. stop! stay! avast! halt! hold hard! whoa! hold! sabr karo[obs3]!. Phr. requiescat in pace[Lat]; Deus nobis haec otia fecit [Lat][Vergil]; "the noonday quiet holds the hill" [Tennyson].

<— p. 79 —>

#266. [Locomotion by land.] Journey. — N. travel; traveling &c. v. wayfaring, campaigning. journey, excursion, expedition, tour, trip, grand tour, circuit, peregrination, discursionl, ramble, pilgrimage, hajj, trek, course, ambulation[obs3], march, walk, promenade, constitutional, stroll, saunter, tramp, jog trot, turn, stalk, perambulation; noctambulation[obs3], noctambulism; somnambulism; outing, ride, drive, airing, jaunt. equitation, horsemanship, riding, manege[Fr], ride and tie; basophobia[obs3]. roving, vagrancy, pererrationl; marching and countermarching; nomadism; vagabondism, vagabondage; hoboism [U.S.]; gadding; flit, flitting, migration; emigration, immigration, demigrationl, intermigration[obs3]; wanderlust. plan, itinerary, guide; handbook, guid, road book; Baedeker[obs3], Bradshaw, Murray; map, road map, transportation guide, subway map. procession, cavalcade, caravan, file, cortege, column. [Organs and instruments of locomotion] vehicle &c. 272; automobile, train, bus, airplane, plane, autobus, omnibus, subway, motorbike, dirt bike, off-road vehicle, van, minivan, motor scooter, trolley, locomotive; legs, feet, pegs, pins, trotters. traveler &c. 268. depot [U.S.], railway station, station. V. travel, journey, course; take a journey, go a journey; take a walk, go out for walk &c. n.; have a run; take the air. flit, take wing; migrate, emigrate; trek; rove, prowl, roam, range, patrol, pace up and down, traverse; scour the country, traverse the country; peragratel; circum-

67

ambulate, perambulate; nomadize[obs3], wander, ramble, stroll, saunter, hover, go one's rounds, straggle; gad, gad about; expatiate. walk, march, step, tread, pace, plod, wend, go by shank's mare; promenade; trudge, tramp; stalk, stride, straddle, strut, foot it, hoof it, stump, bundle, bowl along, toddle; paddle; tread a path. take horse, ride, drive, trot, amble, canter, prance, fisk[obs3], frisk, caracoler[obs3], caracole; gallop &c. (move quickly) 274. [start riding] embark, board, set out, hit the road, get going, get underway. peg on, jog on, wag on, shuffle on; stir one's stumps; bend one's steps, bend one's course; make one's way, find one's way, wend one's way, pick one's way, pick one's way, thread one's way, plow one's way; slide, glide, coast, skim, skate; march in procession, file on, defile. go to, repair to, resort to, hie to, betake oneself to. Adj. traveling &c. v.; ambulatory, itinerant, peripatetic, roving, rambling, gadding, discursive, vagrant, migratory, monadic; circumforanean[obs3], circumforaneous[obs3]; noctivagrant[obs3], mundivagrant; locomotive. wayfaring, wayworn; travel-stained. Adv. on foot, on horseback, on Shanks's mare; by the Marrowbone stage, in transitu &c. 270[Lat]; en route &c. 282. Int. come along!

#267. [Locomotion by water, or air.] Navigation. — N. navigation; aquatics; boating, yachting; ship &c. 273; oar, paddle, screw, sail, canvas, aileron. natation[obs3], swimming; fin, flipper, fish's tail. aerostation[obs3], aerostatics[obs3], aeronautics; balloonery[obs3]; balloon &c. 273; ballooning, aviation, airmanship; flying, flight, volitation[obs3]; wing, pinion; rocketry, space travel, astronautics, orbital mechanics, orbiting. voyage, sail, cruise, passage, circumnavigation, periplus[obs3]; headway, sternway, leeway; fairway. mariner &c. 269. flight, trip; shuttle, run, airlift. V. sail; put to sea &c. (depart) 293; take ship, get under way; set sail, spread sail, spread canvas; gather way, have way on; make sail, carry sail; plow the waves, plow the deep, plow the main, plow the ocean; walk the waters. navigate, warp, luff[obs3], scud, boom, kedge; drift, course, cruise, coast; hug the shore, hug the land; circumnavigate. ply the oar, row, paddle, pull, scull, punt, steam. swim, float; buffet the waves, ride the storm, skim, effleurer[Fr], dive, wade. fly, be wafted, hover, soar, flutter, jet, orbit, rocket; take wing, take a flight, take off, ascend, blast off, land, alight; wing one's flight, wing one's way; aviate; parachute, jump, glide. Adj. sailing &c. v.; volant[obs3], aerostatic[obs3]; seafaring, nautical, maritime, naval; seagoing, coasting; afloat; navigable; aerial, aeronautic; grallatory[obs3]. Adv. under way, under sail, under canvas, under steam; on the wing, in flight, in orbit. Phr. bon voyage; "spread the thin oar and catch the driving gale" [Pope].

<— p. 80 —>

#268. Traveler. — N. traveler, wayfarer, voyager, itinerant, passenger, commuter. tourist, excursionist, explorer, adventurer, mountaineer, hiker, backpacker, Alpine Club; peregrinator[obs3], wanderer, rover, straggler, rambler; bird of passage; gadabout, gadling[obs3]; vagrant, scatterling[obs3], landloper[obs3], waifs and estrays[obs3], wastrel, foundling; loafer; tramp, tramper; vagabond, nomad, Bohemian, gypsy, Arab[obs3], Wandering Jew, Hadji, pilgrim, palmer; peripatetic; somnambulist, emigrant, fugitive, refugee; beach comber, booly[obs3]; globegirdler[obs3], globetrotter; vagrant, hobo [U.S.], night walker, sleep walker; noctambulist, runabout, straphanger, swagman, swags-man [obs3][Aust.]; trecker[obs3], trekker, zingano[obs3], zingaro[obs3]. runner, courier; Mercury, Iris, Ariel[obs3], comet. pedestrian, walker, foot passenger; cyclist; wheelman. rider, horseman, equestrian, cavalier, jockey, rough-rider, trainer, breaker. driver, coachman, whip, Jehu, charioteer, postilion, postboy[obs3], carter, wagoner, drayman[obs3]; cabman, cabdriver; voiturier[obs3], vetturino[obs3], condottiere[obs3]; engine driver; stoker, fireman, guard; chauffeur, conductor, engineer, gharry-wallah[obs3], gari-wala[obs3], hackman, syce[obs3], truckman[obs3]. Phr. on the road

#269. Mariner. — N. sailor, mariner, navigator; seaman, seafarer, seafaring man; dock walloper*; tar, jack tar, salt, able seaman, A. B.; man-of-war's man, bluejacket, galiongee[obs3], galionji[obs3], marine, jolly, midshipman, middy; skipper; shipman[obs3], boatman, ferryman, waterman[obs3], lighterman[obs3], bargeman, longshoreman; bargee[obs3], gondolier; oar, oarsman; rower; boatswain, cockswain[obs3]; coxswain; steersman, pilot; crew. aerial navigator, aeronaut, balloonist, Icarus; aeroplanist[obs3], airman, aviator, birdman, man-bird, wizard of the air, aviatrix, flier, pilot, test pilot, glider pilot, bush pilot, navigator, flight attendant, steward, stewardess, crew; astronaut, cosmonaut; parachutist, paratrooper.

#270. Transference. — N. transfer, transference; translocation, elocationl; displacement; metastasis, metathesis; removal; remotion[obs3], amotion[obs3]; relegation; deportation, asportation[obs3]; extradition, conveyance, draft, carrying, carriage; convection, conduction, contagion; transfer &c. (of property) 783. transit, transition; passage, ferry, gestation; portage, porterage[obs3], carting, cartage; shoveling &c. v.; vectionl, vecturel, vectitationl; shipment, freight, wafture[obs3]; transmission, transport, transportation, importation, exportation, transumption[obs3], trans-plantation, translation; shifting, dodging; dispersion &c. 73; transposition &c. (interchange) 148; traction &c. 285. [Thing transferred] drift. V. transfer, transmit, transport, transplace[obs3], transplant, translocate; convey, carry, bear, fetch and carry; carry over, ferry over; hand pass, forward; shift; conduct, convoy, bring, fetch, reach; tote [U.S.];

port, import, export. send, delegate, consign, relegate, turn over to, deliver; ship, embark; waft; shunt; transpose &c. (interchange) 148; displace &c. 185; throw &c. 284; drag &c. 285; mail, post. shovel, ladle, decant, draft off, transfuse, infuse, siphon. Adj. transferred &c. v.; drifted, movable; portable, portative[obs3]; mailable [U.S.]; contagious. Adv. from hand to hand, from pillar to post. on the way, by the way; on the road, on the wing, under way, in transit, on course; as one goes; in transitu[Lat], en route, chemin faisant[Fr], en passant[Fr], in mid progress, in mid course.

<— p. 81 —>

#271. Carrier. — N. carrier, porter, bearer, tranterl, conveyer; cargador[obs3]; express, expressman; stevedore, coolie; conductor, locomotive, motor. beast, beast of burden, cattle, horse, nag, palfrey, Arab[obs3], blood horse, thoroughbred, galloway[obs3], charger, courser, racer, hunter, jument[obs3], pony, filly, colt, foal, barb, roan, jade, hack, bidet, pad, cob, tit, punch, roadster, goer[obs3]; racehorse, pack horse, draft horse, cart horse, dray horse, post horse; ketch; Shetland pony, shelty, sheltie; garran[obs3], garron[obs3]; jennet, genet[obs3], bayard[obs3], mare, stallion, gelding; bronco, broncho[obs3], cayuse [U.S.]; creature, critter [rural U.S.]; cow pony, mustang, Narraganset, waler[obs3]; stud. Pegasus, Bucephalus, Rocinante. ass, donkey, jackass, mule, hinny; sumpter horse, sumpter mule; burro, cuddy[obs3], ladino [obs3][U.S.]; reindeer; camel, dromedary, llama, elephant; carrier pigeon. [object used for carrying] pallet, brace, cart, dolley; support &c. 215; fork lift. carriage &c. (vehicle) 272; ship &c. 273. Adj. equine, asinine.

#272. Vehicle. — N. vehicle, conveyance, carriage, caravan, van; common carrier; wagon, waggon[obs3], wain, dray, cart, lorry. truck, tram; cariole, carriole[obs3]; limber, tumbrel, pontoon; barrow; wheel barrow, hand barrow; perambulator; Bath chair, wheel chair, sedan chair; chaise; palankeen[obs3], palanquin; litter, brancard[obs3], crate, hurdle, stretcher, ambulance; black Maria; conestoga wagon, conestoga wain; jinrikisha, ricksha, brett[obs3], dearborn [obs3][U.S.], dump cart, hack, hackery[obs3], jigger, kittereen[obs3], mailstate[obs3], manomotor[obs3], rig, rockaway[obs3], prairie schooner [U.S.], shay, sloven [Can.], team, tonga[obs3], wheel; hobbyhorse, go-cart; cycle; bicycle, bike, two-wheeler; tricycle, velocipede, quadricycle[obs3]. equipage, turn-out; coach, chariot, phaeton, break, mail phaeton, wagonette, drag, curricle[obs3], tilbury[obs3], whisky, landau, barouche, victoria, brougham, clarence[obs3], calash, caleche[French], britzka[obs3], araba[obs3], kibitka[obs3]; berlin; sulky, desobligeant[French], sociable, vis-a-vis, dormeuse[Fr]; jaunting car, outside car; dandi[obs3]; doolie[obs3], dooly[obs3]; munchil[obs3], palki[obs3]; roller skates, skate; runabout; ski; tonjon[obs3]; vettura[obs3]. post chaise, diligence, stage; stage coach, mail coach, hackney coach, glass coach; stage wagon, car, omnibus, fly, cabriolet[obs3], cab, hansom, shofle[obs3], four-wheeler, growler, droshki[obs3], drosky[obs3]. dogcart, trap, whitechapel, buggy, four-in-hand, unicorn, random, tandem; shandredhan[obs3], char-a-bancs[French]. motor car, automobile, limousine, car, auto, jalopy, clunker, lemon, flivver, coupe, sedan, two-door sedan, four-door sedan, luxury sedan; wheels [coll.], sports car, roadster, gran turismo[It], jeep, four-wheel drive vehicle, electric car, steamer; golf cart, electric wagon; taxicab, cab, taxicoach[obs3], checker cab, yellow cab; station wagon, family car; motorcycle, motor bike, side car; van, minivan, bus, minibus, microbus; truck, wagon, pick-up wagon, pick-up, tractor-trailer, road train, articulated vehicle; racing car, racer, hot rod, stock car, souped-up car.. bob, bobsled, bobsleigh[obs3]; cutter; double ripper, double runner [U.S.]; jumper, sled, sledge, sleigh, toboggan. train; accommodation train, passenger train, express trail, special train, corridor train, parliamentary train, luggage train, freight train, goods train; 1st class train, 2nd class train, 3rd class train, 1st class carriage, 2nd class carriage, 3rd class carriage, 1st class compartment, 2nd class compartment, 3rd class compartment; rolling stock; horse box, cattle truck; baggage car, express car, freight car, parlor car, dining car, Pullman car, sleeping car, sleeper, dome car; surface car, tram car, trolley car; box car, box wagon; horse car [U.S.]; bullet train, shinkansen [Jap.], cannonball, the Wabash cannonball, lightning express; luggage van; mail, mail car, mail van. shovel, spool, spatula, ladle, hod, hoe; spade, spaddle[obs3], loy[obs3]; spud; pitchfork; post hole digger. [powered construction vehicles] tractor, steamshovel, backhoe, fork lift, earth mover, dump truck, bulldozer, grader, caterpillar, trench digger, steamroller; pile driver; crane, wrecking crane.

#273. Ship. — N. ship, vessel, sail; craft, bottom. navy, marine, fleet, flotilla; shipping. man of war &c. (combatant) 726; transport, tender, storeship[obs3]; merchant ship, merchantman; packet, liner; whaler, slaver, collier, coaster, lighter; fishing boat, pilot boat; trawler, hulk; yacht; baggala[obs3]; floating hotel, floating palace; ocean greyhound. ship, bark, barque, brig, snow, hermaphrodite brig; brigantine, barkantine[obs3]; schooner; topsail schooner, for and aft schooner, three masted schooner; chasse-maree[Fr]; sloop, cutter, corvette, clipper, foist, yawl, dandy, ketch, smack, lugger, barge, hoy[obs3], cat, buss; sailer, sailing vessel; windjammer; steamer, steamboat, steamship, liner, ocean liner, cruisp, flap, dab, pat, thump, beat, blow, bang, slam, dash; punch, thwack, whack; hit hard, strike hard; swap, batter, dowsel, baste; pelt, patter, buffet, belabor; fetch one a blow; poke at, pip, ship of the line; destroyer, cruiser, frigate; landing ship, LST[abbr]; aircraft carrier, carrier, flattop[coll.], nuclear powered carrier; submarine, submersible, atomic submarine. boat, pinnace, launch; life boat, long boat, jolly boat, bum boat, fly boat, cock boat, ferry oat, canal boat; swamp boat, ark, bully [Nfld.], bateau battery[Can.], broadhorn[obs3], dory, droger[obs3], drogher; dugout, durham boat, flatboat, galiot[obs3]; shallop[obs3], gig, funny, skiff, dingy, scow, cockleshell, wherry, coble[obs3], punt, cog, kedge, lerret[obs3]; eight oar, four oar, pair oar; randan[obs3]; outrigger; float, raft, pontoon; prame[obs3]; iceboat, ice canoe, ice yacht. catamaran, hydroplane, hovercraft, coracle, gondola, carvel[obs3], caravel; felucca, caique[obs3], canoe, birch bark canoe, dugout canoe; galley, galleyfoist[obs3]; bilander[obs3], dogger[obs3], hooker, howker[obs3]; argosy, carack[obs3]; galliass[obs3], galleon; polacca[obs3], polacre[obs3], tartane[obs3], junk, lorcha[obs3], praam[obs3], proa[obs3], prahu[obs3], saick[obs3], sampan, xebec, dhow; dahabeah[obs3]; nuggah[obs3]; kayak, keel boat [U.S.], log canoe, pirogue; quadrireme[obs3], trireme; stern-wheeler [U.S.]; wanigan[obs3], wangan [obs3][U.S.], wharf boat. balloon; airship, aeroplane; biplane, monoplane, triplane[obs3]; hydroplane; aerodrome; air balloon, pilot balloon, fire balloon, dirigible, zeppelin; aerostat, Montgolfier; kite, parachute. jet plane, rocket plane, jet liner, turbojet, prop-jet, propeller plane; corporate plane, corporate jet, private plane, private aviation; airline, common carrier; fighter, bomber, fighter-bomber, escort plane, spy plane; supersonic aircraft, subsonic aircraft. Adv. afloat, aboard; on board, on ship board; hard a lee, hard a port, hard a starboard, hard a weather.

<— p. 82 —> % 2. Degrees of Motion %

#274. Velocity. — N. velocity, speed, celerity; swiftness &c. adj.; rapidity, eagle speed; expedition &c. (activity) 682; pernicityl; acceleration; haste &c. 684. spurt, rush, dash, race, steeple chase; smart rate, lively rate, swift rate &c. adj.; rattling rate, spanking rate, strapping rate, smart pace, lively pace, swift pace, rattling pace, spanking pace, strapping pace; round pace; flying, flight. lightning, greased lightning, light, electricity, wind; cannon ball, rocket, arrow, dart, hydrargyrum[Lat], quicksilver; telegraph, express train; torrent. eagle, antelope, courser, race horse, gazelle, greyhound, hare, doe, squirrel, camel bird, chickaree[obs3], chipmunk, hackee [obs3][U.S.], ostrich, scorcher*. Mercury, Ariel[obs3], Camilla[obs3], Harlequin. [Measurement of velocity] log, log line; speedometer, odometer, tachometer, strobe, radar speed detector, radar trap, air speed gauge, wind sock, wind speed meter; pedometer. V. move quickly, trip, fiskl; speed, hie, hasten, post, spank, scuttle; scud, scuddle[obs3]; scour, scour the plain; scamper; run like mad, beat it; fly, race, run a race, cut away, shot, tear, whisk, zoom, swoosh, sweep, skim, brush; cut along, bowl along, barrel along, barrel; scorch, burn up the track; rush &c. (be violent) 173; dash on, dash off, dash forward; bolt; trot, gallop, amble, troll, bound, flit, spring, dart, boom; march in quick time, march in double time; ride hard, get over the ground. hurry &c. (hasten) 684; accelerate, put on; quicken; quicken one's pace, mend one's pace; clap spurs to one's horse; make haste, make rapid strides, make forced marches, make the best of one's way; put one's best leg foremost, stir one's stumps, wing one's way, set off at a score; carry sail, crowd sail; go off like a shot, go like a shot, go ahead, gain ground; outstrip the wind, fly on the wings of the wind. keep up with, keep pace with; outstrip &c. 303; outmarch[obs3]. Adj. fast, speedy, swift, rapid, quick, fleet; aliped[obs3]; nimble, agile, expeditious; express; active &c. 682; flying, galloping &c. v.; light footed, nimble footed; winged, eagle winged, mercurial, electric, telegraphic; light-legged, light of heel; swift as an arrow &c. n.; quick as lightning &c. n., quick as a thought. Adv. swiftly &c. adj.; with speed &c. n.; apace; at a great rate, at full speed, at railway speed; full drive, full gallop; posthaste, in full sail, tantivy[obs3]; trippingly; instantaneously &c. 113. under press of sail, under press of canvas, under press of sail and steam; velis et remis[Lat], on eagle's wing, in double quick time; with rapid strides, with giant strides; a pas de geant[Fr]; in seven league boots; whip and spur; ventre a terre[Fr]; as fast as one's legs will carry one, as fast as one's heels will carry one; as fast as one can lay legs to the ground, at the top of one's speed; by leaps and bounds; with haste &c. 684. Phr. vires acquirit eundo[Lat]; "I'll put a girdle about the earth in forty minutes" [M.N.D.]; "swifter than arrow from the Tartar's bow" [M.N.D.]; go like a bat out of hell; tempus fugit[Lat].

#275. Slowness. — N. slowness &c. adj.; languor &c. (inactivity) 683; drawl; creeping &c. v., lentor[obs3]. retardation; slackening &c. v.; delay &c. (lateness) 133; claudicationl. jog trot, dog trot; mincing steps; slow march, slow time. slow goer[obs3], slow coach, slow back; lingerer, loiterer, sluggard, tortoise, snail; poke* [U.S.]; dawdle &c. (inactive) 683. V. move slowly &c. adv.; creep, crawl, lag, slug, drawl, linger, loiter, saunter; plod, trudge, stump along, lumber; trail, drag; dawdle &c. (be inactive) 683; grovel, worm one's way, steal along; job on, rub on, bundle on; toddle, waddle, wabble[obs3]; slug, traipse, slouch, shuffle, halt, hobble, limp, caludicatel, shamble; flag, falter, trotter, stagger; mince, step short; march in slow time, march in funeral procession; take one's time; hang fire &c. (be late) 133. retard, relax; slacken, check, moderate, rein in, curb; reef; strike sail, shorten sail, take in sail; put on the drag, apply the brake; clip the wings; reduce the speed; slacken speed, slacken one's pace; lose ground. Adj. slow, slack; tardy; dilatory &c. (inactive) 683; gentle, easy; leisurely; deliberate, gradual; insensible, imperceptible; glacial, languid, sluggish, slow paced, tardigradel!, snail-like; creeping &c. v.; reptatorial[obs3]. Adv. slowly &c. adj.; leisurely; piano, adagio; largo, larghetto; at half speed, under easy sail; at a foots pace, at a snail's pace, at a funeral pace; in slow time, with mincing steps, with clipped wings; haud passibus aequis [Lat][Vergil]. gradually &c. adj.;

gradatim[Lat]; by degrees, by slow degrees, by inches, by little and little; step by step, one step at a time; inch by inch, bit by bit, little by little, seriatim; consecutively. Phr. dum Roma deliberat Saguntum perit[Lat]; at a glacial pace.

<— p. 83 —> % 3. Motion conjoined with Force % <— distinguish between impact, collision, and impulse imparted thereby? 12-13-90 —>

#276. Impulse. — N. impulse, impulsion, impetus; momentum; push, pulsion[obs3], thrust, shove, jog, jolt, brunt, booming, boost [U.S.], throw; explosion &c. (violence) 173; propulsion &c. 284. percussion, concussion, collision, occursionl, clash, encounter, cannon, carambole[obs3], appulse[obs3], shock, crash, bump; impact; elan; charge &c. (attack) 716; beating &c. (punishment) 972. blow, dint, stroke, knock, tap, rap, slap, smack, pat, dab; fillip; slam, bang; hit, whack, thwack; cuff &c. 972; squash, dowse, swap, whap[obs3], punch, thump, pelt, kick, puncel, calcitration[obs3]; ruade[obs3]; arietationl; cut, thrust, lunge, yerkl; carom, carrom[obs3], clip *, jab, plug*, sidewinder* [U.S.], sidewipe[obs3], sideswipe [U.S.]. hammer, sledge hammer, mall, maul, mallet, flail; ram, rammer[obs3]; battering ram, monkey, pile-driving engine, punch, bat; cant hook; cudgel &c. (weapon) 727; ax &c. (sharp) 253. [Science of mechanical forces] dynamics; seismometer, accelerometer, earthquake detector. V. give an impetus &c. n.; impel, push; start, give a start to, set going; drive, urge, boom; thrust, prod, foin[Fr]; cant; elbow, shoulder, jostle, justle[obs3], hustle, hurtle, shove, jog, jolt, encounter; run against, bump against, butt against; knock one's head against, run one's head against; impinge; boost [U.S.]; bunt, carom, clip y; fan, fan out; jab, plug *. strike, knock, hit, tap, rap, slap, flap, dab, pat, thump, beat, blow, bang, slam, dash; punch, thwack, whack; hit hard, strike hard; swap, batter, dowsel, baste; pelt, patter, buffet, belabor; fetch one a blow; poke at, pink, lunge, yerk[obs3]; kick, calcitrate[obs3]; butt, strike at &c. (attack) 716; whip *c. (punish) 972. come into a collision, enter into collision; collide; sideswipe; foul; fall foul of, run foul of; telescope. throw &c. (propel) 284. Adj. impelling &c. v.; impulsive, impellent[obs3]; booming; dynamic, dynamical; impelled &c. v. Phr. "a hit, a very palpable hit" [Hamlet].

#277. Recoil. — N. recoil; reaction, retroaction; revulsion; bounce, rebound, ricochet; repercussion, recalcitration[obs3]; kick, contrecoup[Fr]; springing back &c. v.; elasticity &c. 325; reflection, reflexion[Brit], reflex, reflux; reverberation &c. (resonance) 408; rebuff, repulse; return.
    ducks and drakes; boomerang; spring, reactionist[obs3].
    elastic collision, coefficient of restitution.
    V. recoil, react; spring back, fly back, bounce back, bound back; rebound, reverberate, repercuss[obs3], recalcitrate[obs3]; echo, ricochet.
    Adj. recoiling &c. v.; refluent[obs3], repercussive, recalcitrant, reactionary; retroactive.
    Adv. on the rebound, on the recoil &c. n.
    Phr. for every action there is a reaction equal in force and opposite in direction [Newton].
<— p. 84 —> % 4. Motion with reference to Direction %

#278. Direction. — N. direction, bearing, course, vector; set, drift, tenor; tendency &c. 176; incidence; bending, trending &c. v.; dip, tack, aim, collimation; steering steerage. point of the compass, cardinal points; North East, South, West; N by E, ENE, NE by N, NE, &c; rhumb[obs3], azimuth, line of collimation. line, path, road, range, quarter, line of march; alignment, allignment[obs3]; air line, beeline; straight shoot. V. tend towards, bend towards, point towards; conduct to, go to; point to, point at; bend, trend, verge, incline, dip, determine. steer for, steer towards, make for, make towards; aim at, level at; take aim; keep a course, hold a course; be bound for; bend one's steps towards; direct one's course, steer one's course, bend one's course, shape one's course; align one's march, allign one's march[obs3]; to straight, go straight to the point; march on, march on a point. ascertain one's direction &c. n.; s'orienter[French], see which way the wind blows; box the compass; take the air line. Adj. directed &c. v. directed towards; pointing towards &c. v.; bound for; aligned, with alligned with[obs3]; direct, straight; undeviating, unswerving; straightforward; North, Northern, Northerly, &c. n. Adv. towards; on the road, on the high road to; en avant; versus, to; hither, thither, whither; directly; straight as an arrow, forwards as an arrow; point blank; in a bee line to, in a direct line to, as the crow flies, in a straight line to, in a bee line for, in a direct line for, in a straight line for, in a bee line with, in a direct line with, in a straight line with; in a line with; full tilt at, as the crow flies. before the wind, near the wind, close to the wind, against the wind; windwards, in the wind's eye. through, via, by way of; in all directions, in all manner of ways; quaquaversum[Lat], from the four winds. Phr. the shortest distance between two points is a straight line.

#279. Deviation. — N. deviation; swerving &c. v.; obliquationl, warp, refraction; flection[obs3], flexion; sweep; deflection, deflexure[obs3]; declination. diversion, digression, depart from, aberration; divergence &c. 291; zigzag; detour &c. (circuit) 629; divagation. [Desultory motion] wandering &c. v.; vagrancy, evagation[obs3]; bypaths and crooked ways; byroad. [Motion sideways, oblique motion] sidling &c. v.; knight's move at chess. V. alter one's course, deviate, depart from, turn, trend; bend, curve &c. 245; swerve, heel, bear off; gybe[obs3], wear. intervert[obs3]; deflect; divert, divert from its course; put on a new scent, shift, shunt, draw aside, crook, warp. stray, straggle; sidle; diverge &c. 291; tralineatel; digress, wander; wind, twist, meander; veer, tack; divagate; sidetrack; turn aside, turn a corner, turn away from; wheel, steer clear of; ramble, rove, drift; go astray, go adrift; yaw, dodge; step aside, ease off, make way for, shy. fly off at a tangent; glance off; wheel about, face about; turn to the right about, face to the right about; waddle &c. (oscillate) 314; go out of one's way &c. (perform a circuit) 629; lose one's way. Adj. deviating &c. v.; aberrant, errant; excursive, discursive; devious, desultory, loose; rambling; stray, erratic, vagrant, undirected, circuitous, indirect, zigzag; crab-like. Adv. astray from, round about, wide of the mark; to the right about; all manner of ways; circuitously &c. 629. obliquely, sideling, like the move of the knight on a chessboard.

#280. [Going before.] Precession. — N. precession, leading, heading; precedence &c. 62; priority &c. 116; the lead, le pas; van &c. (front) 234; precursor &c. 64. V. go before, go ahead, go in the van, go in advance; precede, forerun; usher in, introduce, herald, head, take the lead; lead the way, lead the dance; get the start, have the start; steal a march; get before, get ahead, get in front of; outstrip &c. 303; take precedence &c. (first in order) 62. Adj. leading, precedent &c. v. Adv. in advance, before, ahead, in the van, in the lead; foremost, headmost[obs3]; in front; at the head, out in front; way out in front, far ahead. Phr. seniores priores[Lat], ahead of his time.

#281. [Going after.] Sequence. — N. sequence; coming after &c. (order) 63; (time) 117; following pursuit &c. 622. follower, attendant, satellite, shadow, dangler, train. V. follow; pursue &c. 622; go after, fly after. attend, beset, dance attendance on, dog; tread in the steps of, tread close upon; be in the wake of, be in the trail of, be in the rear of, go in the wake of, go in the trail of, go in the rear of, follow in the wake of, follow in the trail of, follow in the rear of; follow as a shadow, hang on the skirts of; tread on the heels of, follow on the heels of; camp on the trail. Adj. subsequent, next, succeeding; following &c. v.. Adv. behind; in the rear &c. 235, in the train of, in the wake of; after &c. (order) 63, (time) 117.

<— p. 85 —>

#282. [Motion forward; progressive motion.] Progression. — N. progress, progression, progressiveness; advancing &c. v.; advance, advancement; ongoing; flood, tide, headway; march &c. 266; rise; improvement &c. 658. V. advance; proceed, progress; get on, get along, get over the ground; gain ground; forge ahead; jog on, rub on, wag on; go with the stream; keep one's course, hold on one's course; go on, move on, come one, get on, pass on, push on, press on, go forward, move forward, come forward, get forward, pass forward, push forward, press forward, go forwards, move forwards, come forwards, get forwards, pass forwards, push forwards, press forwards, go ahead, move ahead, come ahead, get ahead, pass ahead, push ahead, press ahead; make one's way, work one's way, carve one's way, push one's way, force one's way, edge one's way, elbow one's way; make progress, make head, make way, make headway, make advances, make strides, make rapid strides &c. (velocity) 274; go ahead, shoot ahead; distance; make up leeway. Adj. advancing &c. v.; progressive, profluent[obs3]; advanced. Adv. forward, onward; forth, on, ahead, under way, en route for, on one's way, on the way, on the road, on the high road, on the road to; in progress; in mid progress; in transitu &c. 270[Lat]. Phr. vestigia nulla retrorsum[Lat]; "westward the course of empire takes its way" [Berkeley].

#283. [Motion backwards.] Regression. — N. regress, regression; retrocession[obs3], retrogression, retrograduation[obs3], retroaction; reculade[obs3]; retreat, withdrawal, retirement, remigration[obs3]; recession &c. (motion from) 287; recess; crab-like motion. refluence[obs3], reflux; backwater, regurgitation, ebb, return; resilience reflection, reflexion (recoil) 277[Brit]; flip-flop, volte- face[Fr]. counter motion, retrograde motion, backward move- ment, motion in reverse, counter movement, counter march; veering, tergiversation, recidivationl, backsliding, fall; deterioration &c. 659; recidivism, recidivity[obs3]. reversal, relapse, turning point &c.(reversion) 145. V. recede, regrade, return, revert, retreat, retire; retrograde, retrocede; back out; back down; balk; crawfish* [U.S.], crawl*; withdraw; rebound &c. 277; go back, come back, turn back, hark back, draw back, fall back, get back, put back, run back; lose ground; fall astern, drop astern; backwater, put about; backtrack, take the back track; veer round; double, wheel, countermarch; ebb, regurgitate; jib, shrink, shy. turn tail, turn round, turn upon one's heel, turn one's back upon; retrace one's steps, dance the back step; sound a retreat, beat a retreat; go home. Adj. receding &c. v.; retrograde, retrogressive; regressive, refluent[obs3], reflex, recidivous, resilient; crab-like; balky; reactionary &c. 277. Adv. back, backwards; reflexively, to the right about; a reculons[Fr], a rebours[Fr]. Phr. revenons a nos moutons[Fr], as you were.

#284. [Motion given to an object situated in front.] Propulsion. — N. propulsion, projection; propelment[obs3]; vis a tergo[Lat: force from behind]; push, shove &c. (impulse) 276; ejaculate; ejection &c. 297; throw, fling, toss, shot, discharge, shy; launch, release.

[Science of propulsion] projectiles, ballistics, archery.

[devices to give propulsion] propeller, screw, twin screws, turbine, jet engine.

[objects propelled] missile, projectile, ball, discus, quoit, brickbat, shot;

[weapons which propel] arrow, gun, ballista &c. (arms) 727[obs3].

[preparation for propulsion] countdown, windup.

shooter; shot; archer, toxophilite[obs3]; bowman, rifleman, marksman; good shot, crack shot; sharpshooter &c. (combatant) 726.

V. propel, project, throw, fling, cast, pitch, chuck, toss, jerk, heave, shy, hurl; flirt, fillip.

dart, lance, tilt; ejaculate, jaculate[obs3]; fulminate, bolt, drive, sling, pitchfork.

send; send off, let off, fire off; discharge, shoot; launch, release, send forth, let fly; put in orbit, send into orbit, launch into orbit dash.

put in motion, set in motion; set agoing[obs3], start; give a start, give an impulse to; impel &c. 276; trundle &c. (set in rotation) 312; expel &c. 297.

carry one off one's legs; put to flight.

Adj. propelled &c. v.; propelling &c. v..; propulsive, projectile.

#285. [Motion given to an object situated behind.] Traction. — N. traction; drawing &c. v.; draught, pull, haul; rake; "a long pull a strong pull and a pull all together"; towage[obs3], haulage.

V. draw, pull, haul, lug, rake, drag, tug, tow, trail, train; take in tow.

wrench, jerk, twitch, tousel; yank [U.S.].

Adj. drawing &c. v.; tractile[obs3], tractive.
<— p. 86 —>

#286. [Motion towards.] Approach. — N. approach, approximation, appropinquation[obs3]; access; appulse[obs3]; afflux[obs3], affluxion[obs3]; advent &c. (approach of time) 121; pursuit &c. 622. V. approach, approximate, appropinquate[obs3]; near; get near, go near, draw near; come to close quarters, come near; move towards, set in towards; drift; make up to; gain upon; pursue &c. 622; tread on the heels of; bear up; make the land; hug the shore, hug the land. Adj. approaching &c. v.; approximative[obs3]; affluent; impending, imminent &c. (destined) 152. Adv. on the road. Int. come hither! approach! here! come! come near! forward!

#287. [Motion from.] Recession. — N. recession, retirement, withdrawal; retreat; retrocession &c. 283[obs3]; departure, &c. 293; recoil &c. 277; flight &c. (avoidance) 623.

V. recede, go, move back, move from, retire; withdraw, shrink, back off; come away, move away, back away, go away, get away, drift away; depart &c. 293; retreat &c. 283; move off, stand off, sheer off; fall back, stand aside; run away &c. (avoid) 623.

remove, shunt, distance.

Adj. receding &c. v.

Phr. distance oneself from a person.

#288. [Motion towards, actively; force causing to draw closer.] Attraction. — N. attraction, attractiveness; attractivity[obs3]; drawing to, pulling towards, adduction[obs3].

electrical attraction, electricity, static electricity, static, static cling; magnetism, magnetic attraction; gravity, attraction of gravitation.

[objects which attract by physical force] lodestone, loadstone, lodestar, loadstar[obs3]; magnet, permanent magnet, siderite, magnetite; electromagnet; magnetic coil, voice coil; magnetic dipole; motor coil, rotor, stator.

electrical charge; positive charge, negative charge.

magnetic pole; north pole, south pole; magnetic monopole.

V. attract, draw; draw towards, pull towards, drag towards; adduce.

Adj. attracting &c. v.; attrahent[obs3], attractive, adducent[obs3], adductive[obs3].

centrifugal.

Phr. ubi mel ibi apes [Latin][Plautus].

#289. [Motion from, actively; force driving apart.] Repulsion. — N. repulsion; driving from &c. v.; repulse, abduction.

magnetic repulsion, magnetic levitation; antigravity.

V. repel, push from, drive apart, drive from &c. 276; chase, dispel; retrude[obs3]; abduce[obs3], abduct; send away; repulse.

keep at arm's length, turn one's back upon, give the cold shoulder; send off, send away with a flea in one's ear.

Adj. repelling &c. v.; repellent, repulsive; abducent[obs3], abductive[obs3].

centripetal

Phr. like charges repel; opposite charges attract; like poles repel, opposite poles attract.

#290. [Motion nearer to.] Convergence. — N. convergence, confluence, concourse, conflux[obs3], congress, concurrence, concentration; convergency; appulse[obs3], meeting; corradiation[obs3].

assemblage &c. 72; resort &c. (focus) 74; asymptote.

V. converge, concur, come together, unite, meet, fall in with; close with, close in upon; center round, center in; enter in; pour in.

gather together, unite, concentrate, bring into a focus.

Adj. converging &c. v.; convergent, confluent, concurrent; centripetal; asymptotical, asymptotic; confluxible[obs3].

#291. [Motion further off.] Divergence. — N. divergence, divergency[obs3]; divarication, ramification, forking; radiation; separation &c. (disjunction) 44; dispersion &c. 73; deviation &c. 279; aberration. V. diverge, divaricate, radiate; ramify; branch off, glance off, file off; fly off, fly off at a tangent; spread, scatter, disperse &c. 73; deviate &c. 279; part &c. (separate) 44. Adj. diverging &c. v.; divergent, radiant, centrifugal; aberrant.

#292. [Terminal motion at.] Arrival. — N. arrival, advent; landing; debarkation, disembarkation; reception, welcome, vin d'honneur[Fr].

home, goal, goalpost; landing placc, landing stage; bunder[obs3]; resting place; destination, harbor, haven, port, airport, spaceport; terminus, halting place, halting ground, landing strip, runway, terminal; journey's end; anchorage &c. (refuge) 666.

return, remigration[obs3]; meeting; rencounter[obs3], encounter.

completion &c. 729.

recursion[Math, Comp].

V. arrive; get to, come to; come; reach, attain; come up with, come up to; overtake, make, fetch; complete &c. 729; join, rejoin.

light, alight, dismount; land, go ashore; debark, disembark; put in, put into; visit, cast anchor, pitch one's tent; sit down &c. (be located) 184; get to one's journey's end; make the land; be in at the death; come back, get back, come home, get home; return; come in &c. (ingress) 294; make one's appearance &c. (appear) 446; drop in; detrain, deplane; outspan; de-orbit.

come to hand; come at, come across; hit; come upon, light upon, pop upon, bounce upon, plump upon, burst upon, pitch upon; meet; encounter, rencounter[obs3]; come in contact.

Adj. arriving &c. v.; homeward bound.

Adv. here, hither.

Int. welcome! hail! all Hail! good-day, good morrow!

Phr. any port in a storm.

<— p. 87 —>

#293. [Initial motion from.] Departure. — N. departure, decession[obs3], decampment; embarkation; outset, start; removal; exit &c. (egress) 295; exodus, hejira, flight. leave taking, valediction, adieu, farewell, goodbye, auf wiedersehen[Ger], sayonara, dosvidanya[Russ], ciao, aloha, hasta la vista[Sp]; stirrup cup; valedictorian. starting point, starting post; point of departure, point of embarkation, place of departure, place of embarkation; port of embarkation; airport, take-off point, taxiing runway, runway, launching pad, spaceport. V. depart; go away; take one's departure, set out; set off, march off, put off, start off, be off, move off, get off, whip off, pack off, go off, take oneself off; start, issue, march out, debouch; go forth, sally forth; sally, set forward; be gone; hail from. leave a place, quit, vacate, evacuate, abandon; go off the stage, make one's exit; retire, withdraw, remove; vamoose*, vamose* [obs3] [U.S.]; go one's way, go along, go from home; take flight, take wing; spring, fly, flit, wing one's flight; fly away, whip away; embark; go on board, go aboard; set sail' put to sea, go to sea; sail, take ship; hoist blue Peter; get under way, weigh anchor; strike tents, decamp; walk one's chalks, cut one's stick; take leave; say good bye, bid goodbye &c. n.; disappear &c. 449; abscond &c. (avoid) 623; entrain; inspan[obs3]. Adj. departing &c. v.; valedictory; outward bound. Adv. whence, hence, thence; with a foot in the stirrup; on the wing, on the move. Int. begone! &c. (ejection) 297; farewell! adieu! goodbye! good day! au revoir[Fr]! fare you well! God bless you! God speed! all aboard! auf wiedersehen[Ger]! au plaisir de vous revoir[Fr]! bon voyage! gluckliche Reise[Ger]! vive valeque[Fr]!

#294. [Motion into.] Ingress. — N. ingress; entrance, entry; introgression; influx, intrusion, inroad, incursion, invasion, irruption; ingression; penetration, interpenetration; illapse[obs3], import, infiltration; immigration; admission &c. (reception) 296; insinuation &c. (interjacence) 228[obs3]; insertion &c. 300. inlet; way in; mouth, door, &c. (opening) 260; barway[obs3]; path &c. (way) 627; conduit &c. 350; immigrant. V. have the entree; enter; go into, go in, come into, come in, pour into, pour in, flow into, flow in, creep into, creep in, slip into, slip in, pop into, pop in, break into, break in, burst into, burst in; set foot on; ingress; burst in upon, break in upon; invade, intrude; insinuate itself; interpenetrate, penetrate; infiltrate; find one's way into, wriggle into, worm oneself into. give entrance to &c. (receive) 296; insert &c. 300. Adj. incoming.

#295. [Motion out of.] Egress. — N. egress, exit, issue; emersion, emergence; outbreak, outburst; eruption, proruption[obs3]; emanation; egression; evacuation; exudation, transudation; extravasation[Med], perspiration, sweating, leakage, percolation, distillation, oozing; gush &c. (water in motion) 348; outpour, outpouring; effluence, effusion; effluxion[obs3], drain; dribbling &c. v.; defluxion[obs3]; drainage; outcome, output; discharge &c. (excretion) 299. export, expatriation; emigration, remigration[obs3]; debouch, debouche; emunctory[obs3]; exodus &c. (departure) 293; emigrant. outlet, vent, spout, tap, sluice, floodgate; pore; vomitory, outgate[obs3], sally port; way out; mouth, door &c. (opening) 260; path &c. (way) 627; conduit &c. 350; airpipe &c. 351[obs3]. V. emerge, emanate, issue; egress; go out of, come out of, move out of, pass out of, pour out of, flow out of; pass out of, evacuate. exude, transude; leak, run through, out through; percolate, transcolatel; egurgitate[obs3]; strain, distill; perspire, sweat, drain, ooze; filter, filtrate; dribble, gush, spout, flow out; well, well out; pour, trickle, &c. (water in motion) 348; effuse, extravasate[Med], disembogue[obs3], discharge itself, debouch; come forth, break forth; burst out, burst through; find vent; escape &c. 671. Adj. effused &c. v.; outgoing.

<— p. 88 —>

#296. [Motion into, actively.] Reception. — N. reception; admission, admittance, entree, importation; introduction, intromission; immission[obs3], ingestion, imbibation[obs3], introception[obs3], absorption, ingurgitation[obs3], inhalation; suction, sucking; eating, drinking &c. (food) 298; insertion &c. 300; interjection &c. 228; introit. V. give entrance to, give admittance to, give the entree; introduce, intromit; usher, admit, receive, import, bring in, open the door to, throw in, ingest, absorb, imbibe, inhale, breathe in; let in, take in, suck in, draw in; readmit, resorb, reabsorb; snuff up, swallow, ingurgitate[obs3]; engulf, engorge; gulp; eat, drink &c. (food) 298. Adj. admitting &c. v., admitted &c. v.; admissable; absorbent.

#297. [Motion out of, actively.] Ejection. — N. ejection, emission, effusion, rejection, expulsion, exportation, eviction, extrusion, trajection[obs3]; discharge. emesis, vomiting, vomition[obs3]. egestion[obs3], evacuation; ructation[obs3], eructation; bloodletting, venesection[Med], phlebotomy, paracentesis[obs3]; expuition, exspuition; tapping, drainage; clearance, clearage[obs3]. deportation; banishment &c. (punishment) 972; rouge's march; relegation, extradition; dislodgment. bouncer [U.S.], chucker-out*[obs3]. [material vomited] vomit, vomitus[Med], puke, barf[coll]. V. give exit, give vent to; let out, give out, pour out, squeeze out, send out; dispatch, despatch; exhale, excernl, excrete;

embogue[obs3]; secrete, secern[obs3]; extravasate[Med], shed, void, evacuation; emit; open the sluices, open the floodgates; turn on the tap; extrude, detrude[obs3]; effuse, spend, expend; pour forth; squirt, spirt[obs3], spurt, spill, slop; perspire &c. (exude) 295; breathe, blow &c. (wind) 349. tap, draw off; bale out, lade out; let blood, broach. eject, reject; expel, discard; cut, send to coventry, boycott; chasser[Fr]; banish &c. (punish) 972; bounce * [U.S.]; fire *, fire out *; throw &c. 284 throw out, throw up, throw off, throw away, throw aside; push &c. 276 throw out, throw off, throw away, throw aside; shovel out, shovel away, sweep out, sweep away; brush off, brush away, whisk off, whisk away, turn off, turn away, send off, send away; discharge; send adrift, turn adrift, cast adrift; turn out, bundle out; throw overboard; give the sack to; send packing, send about one's business, send to the right about; strike off the roll &c. (abrogate) 756; turn out neck and heels, turn out head and shoulders, turn out neck and crop; pack off; send away with a flea in the ear; send to Jericho; bow out, show the door to. turn out of doors, turn out of house and home; evict, oust; unhouse, unkennel; dislodge; unpeople[obs3], dispeople[obs3]; depopulate; relegate, deport. empty; drain to the dregs; sweep off; clear off, clear out, clear away; suck, draw off; clean out, make a clean sweep of, clear decks, purge. embowel[obs3], disbowel[obs3], disembowel; eviscerate, gut; unearth, root out, root up; averuncatel; weed out, get out; eliminate, get rid of, do away with, shake off; exenterate[obs3]. vomit, throw up, regurgitate, spew, puke, keck[obs3], retch, heave, upchuck, chuck up, barf; belch out; cast up, bring up, be sick, get sick, worship the porcelain god. disgorge; expectorate, clear the throat, hawk, spit, sputter, splutter, slobber, drivel, slaver, slabber[obs3]; eructate; drool. unpack, unlade, unload, unship, offload; break bulk; dump. be let out. spew forth, erupt, ooze &c. (emerge) 295. Adj. emitting, emitted, &c. v. Int. begone! get you gone! get away, go away, get along, go along, get along with you, go along with you! go your way! away with! off with you! get the hell out of here![vulg.], go about your business! be off! avaunt[obs3]! aroynt[obs3]! allez-vous-en[Fr]! jao[obs3]! va-t'en[Fr]!

<— p. 89 —>

#298. [Eating.] Food. — N. eating &c. v.; deglutition, gulp, epulation[obs3], mastication, manducation[obs3], rumination; gluttony &c. 957. [eating specific foods] hippophagy[obs3], ichthyophagy[obs3]. [CAUSED BY: appetite &c. 865]. mouth, jaws, mandible, mazard[obs3], chops. drinking &c. v.; potation, draught, libation; carousal &c. (amusement) 840; drunkenness &c. 959. food, pabulum; aliment, nourishment, nutriment; sustenance, sustentation, sustention; nurture, subsistence, provender, corn, feed, fodder, provision, ration, keep, commons, board; commissariat &c. (provision) 637; prey, forage, pasture, pasturage; fare, cheer; diet, dietary; regimen; belly timber, staff of life; bread, bread and cheese. comestibles, eatables, victuals, edibles, ingesta; grub, grubstake, prog[obs3], meat; bread, bread stuffs; cerealia[obs3]; cereals; viands, cates[obs3], delicacy, dainty, creature comforts, contents of the larder, fleshpots; festal board; ambrosia; good cheer, good living. beef, bisquit[obs3], bun; cornstarch [U.S.]; cookie, cooky [U.S.]; cracker, doughnut; fatling[obs3]; hardtack, hoecake [U.S.], hominy [U.S.]; mutton, pilot bread; pork; roti[obs3], rusk, ship biscuit; veal; joint, piece de resistance[Fr], roast and boiled; remove, entremet[obs3]; releve[Fr], hash, rechauffe[Fr], stew, ragout, fricassee, mince; pottage, potage[obs3], broth, soup, consomme, puree, spoonmeat[obs3]; pie, pasty, volauvent[obs3]; pudding, omelet; pastry; sweets &c. 296; kickshaws[obs3]; condiment &c. 393. appetizer, hors d'oeuvre[Fr]. main course, entree. alligator pear, apple &c., apple slump; artichoke; ashcake[obs3], griddlecake, pancake, flapjack; atole[obs3], avocado, banana, beche de mer[Fr], barbecue, beefsteak; beet root; blackberry, blancmange, bloater, bouilli[obs3], bouillon, breadfruit, chop suey [U.S.]; chowder, chupatty[obs3], clam, compote, damper, fish, frumenty[obs3], grapes, hasty pudding, ice cream, lettuce, mango, mangosteen, mince pie, oatmeal, oyster, pineapple, porridge, porterhouse steak, salmis[obs3], sauerkraut, sea slug, sturgeon ("Albany beef"), succotash [U.S.], supawn [obs3][U.S.], trepang[obs3], vanilla, waffle, walnut. table, cuisine, bill of fare, menu, table d'hote[Fr], ordinary, entree. meal, repast, feed, spread; mess; dish, plate, course; regale; regalement[obs3], refreshment, entertainment; refection, collation, picnic, feast, banquet, junket; breakfast; lunch, luncheon; dejeuner[Fr], bever[obs3], tiffin[obs3], dinner, supper, snack, junk food, fast food, whet, bait, dessert; potluck, table d'hote[Fr], dejeuner a la fourchette[Fr]; hearty meal, square meal, substantial meal, full meal; blowout*; light refreshment; bara[obs3], chotahazri[obs3]; bara khana[obs3]. mouthful, bolus, gobbet[obs3], morsel, sop, sippet[obs3]. drink, beverage, liquor, broth, soup; potion, dram, draught, drench, swill*; nip, sip, sup, gulp. wine, spirits, liqueur, beer, ale, malt liquor, Sir John Barleycorn, stingo[obs3], heavy wet; grog, toddy, flip, purl, punch, negus[obs3], cup, bishop, wassail; gin &c. (intoxicating liquor) 959; coffee, chocolate, cocoa, tea, the cup that cheers but not inebriates; bock beer, lager beer, Pilsener beer, schenck beer[obs3]; Brazil tea, cider, claret, ice water, mate, mint julep [U.S.]; near beer, 3.2 beer, non-alcoholic beverage. eating house &c. 189. [person who eats] diner; hippophage; glutton &c. 957. V. eat, feed, fare, devour, swallow, take; gulp, bolt, snap; fall to; despatch, dispatch; discuss; take down, get down, gulp down; lay in, tuck in*; lick, pick, peck; gormandize &c. 957; bite, champ, munch, cranch[obs3], craunch[obs3], crunch, chew, masticate, nibble, gnaw, mumble. live on; feed upon, batten upon, fatten upon, feast upon; browse, graze, crop, regale; carouse &c. (make merry) 840; eat heartily, do justice to, play a good knife and fork, banquet. break bread, break one's fast; breakfast, lunch, dine, take tea, sup. drink in, drink up, drink one's fill; quaff, sip, sup; suck, suck up; lap; swig; swill*, chugalug[slang], tipple &c. (be drunken) 959; empty one's glass, drain the cup; toss off, toss one's glass; wash down, crack a bottle, wet one's whistle. purvey &c. 637. Adj. eatable, edible, esculent[obs3], comestible, alimentary; cereal, cibarious[obs3]; dietetic; culinary; nutritive, nutritious; gastric; succulent; potable, potulentl; bibulous. omnivorous, carnivorous, herbivorous, granivorous[obs3], graminivorous, phytivorous[obs3]; ichthyivorous[obs3]; omophagic[obs3], omophagous[obs3]; pantophagous[obs3], phytophagous[obs3], xylophagous Phr[Biol]. "across the walnuts and the wine" [Tennyson]; "blessed hour of our dinners!" [O. Meredith]; "now good digestion wait on appetite, and health on both!" [Macbeth]; "who can cloy the hungry edge of appetite?" [Richard II]

<— p. 90 —>

#299. Excretion — N. excretion, discharge, emanation; exhalation, exudation, extrusion, secretion, effusion, extravasation[Med], ecchymosis[Med]; evacuation, dejection, faeces, excrement, shit, stools, crap[vulg.]; bloody flux; cacation[obs3]; coeliac-flux, coeliac-passion; dysentery; perspiration, sweat; subation[obs3], exudation; diaphoresis; sewage; eccrinology[Med]. saliva, spittle, rheum; ptyalism[obs3], salivation, catarrh; diarrhoea; ejecta, egesta[Biol], sputa; excreta; lava; exuviae &c. (uncleanness) 653[Lat]. hemorrhage, bleeding; outpouring &c. (egress) 295. V. excrete &c. (eject) 297; emanate &c. (come out) 295.

#300. [Forcible ingress.] Insertion. — N. insertion, implantation, introduction; insinuation &c. (intervention) 228; planting, &c. v.; injection, inoculation, importation, infusion; forcible ingress &c. 294; immersion; submersion, submergence, dip, plunge; bath &c. (water), 337; interment &c. 363.
   clyster[Med], enema, glyster[obs3], lavage, lavement[obs3].
   V. insert; introduce, intromit; put into, run into; import; inject; interject &c. 298; infuse, instill, inoculate, impregnate, imbue, imbrue.
   graft, ingraft[obs3], bud, plant, implant; dovetail.
   obtrude; thrust in, stick in, ram in, stuff in, tuck in, press, in, drive in, pop in, whip in, drop in, put in; impact; empiercel &c. (make a hole) 260[obs3].
   imbed; immerse, immerge, merge; bathe, soak &c. (water) 337; dip, plunge &c. 310.
   bury &c. (inter) 363.
   insert &c itself; plunge in medias res.
   Adj. inserted &c. v.
#301. [Forcible egress.] Extraction. — N. extraction; extracting &c. v.; removal, elimination, extrication, eradication, evolution.
   evulsion[obs3], avulsion[obs3]; wrench; expression, squeezing; extirpation, extermination; ejection &c. 297; export &c. (egress) 295.
   extractor, corkscrew, forceps, pliers.
   V. extract, draw; take out, draw out, pull out, tear out, pluck out, pick out, get out; wring from, wrench; extort; root up, weed up, grub up, rake up, root out, weed out, grub out, rake out; eradicate; pull up by the roots, pluck up by the roots; averruncatel; unroot[obs3]; uproot, pull up, extirpate, dredge.
   remove; educe, elicit; evolve, extricate; eliminate &c. (eject) 297; eviscerate &c. 297.
   express, squeeze out, press out.
   Adj. extracted &c. v.
#302. [Motion through.] Passage. — N. passage, transmission; permeation; penetration, interpenetration; transudation, infiltration; endosmose exosmose[obs3]; endosmosis[Chem]; intercurrence[obs3]; ingress &c. 294; egress &c. 295; path &c. 627; conduit &c. 350; opening &c. 260; journey &c. 266; voyage &c. 267. V. pass, pass through; perforate &c. (hole) 260; penetrate, permeate, thread, thrid[obs3], enfilade; go through, go across; go over, pass over; cut across; ford, cross; pass and repass, work; make one's way, thread one's way, worm one's way, force one's way; make a passage form a passage; cut one's way through; find its way, find its vent; transmit, make way, clear the course; traverse, go over the ground. Adj. passing &c. v.; intercurrent[obs3]; endosmosmic[obs3], endosmotic[Chem]. Adv. en passant &c. (transit) 270[Fr].

<— p. 91 —>

#303. [Motion beyond] Transcursion — N. transcursionl, transiliency[obs3], transgression; trespass; encroachment, infringement; extravagationl, transcendence; redundancy &c. 641. V. transgress, surpass, pass; go beyond, go by; show in front, come to the front; shoot ahead of; steal a march upon, steal a gain upon. overstep, overpass, over-reach, overgo[obs3], override, overleap, overjump[obs3], overskip[obs3], overlap, overshoot the mark; outstrip, outleap, outjump, outgo, outstep[obs3], outrun, outride, outrival, outdo; beat, beat hollow; distance; leave in the lurch, leave in the rear; throw into the shade; exceed, transcend, surmount; soar &c. (rise) 305. encroach, trespass, infringe, trench upon, entrench on, intrench on[obs3]; strain; stretch a point, strain a point; cross the Rubicon. Adj. surpassing &c. v. Adv. beyond the mark, ahead.

#304. [motion short of] Shortcoming — N. shortcoming, failure; falling short &c v.; default, defalcation; leeway; labor in vain, no go. incompleteness &c. 53; imperfection &c. 651; insufficiency &c. 640; noncompletion &c. 730; failure &c. 732. V. 303, come short of, fall short of, stop short of, come short, fall short, stop short; not reach; want; keep within bounds, keep within the mark, keep within the compass. break down, stick in the mud, collapse, flat out [U.S.], come to nothing; fall through, fall to the ground; cave in, end in smoke, miss the mark, fail; lose ground; miss stays. Adj. unreached; deficient; short, short of; minus; out of depth; perfunctory &c. (neglect) 460. Adv. within the mark, within the compass, within the bounds; behindhand; re infecta[Lat]; to no purpose; for from it. Phr. the bubble burst.

#305. [Motion upwards] Ascent. — N. ascent, ascension; rising &c. 309; acclivity, hill &c. 217; flight of steps, flight of stairs; ladder
rocket, lark; sky rocket, sky lark; Alpine Club.
V. ascend, rise, mount, arise, uprise; go up, get up, work one's way up, start up; shoot up, go into orbit; float up; bubble up; aspire.
climb, clamber, ramp, scramble, escalade[obs3], surmount; shin, shinny, shinney; scale, scale the heights.
[cause to go up] raise, elevate &c. 307.
go aloft, fly aloft; tower, soar, take off; spring up, pop up, jump up, catapult upwards, explode upwards; hover, spire, plane, swim, float, surge; leap &c. 309.
Adj. rising &c. v. scandentl, buoyant; supernatant, superfluitantl; excelsior.
Adv. uphill.
#306. [Motion downwards] Descent. — N. descent, descension[obs3], declension, declination; fall; falling &c. v.: slump; drop, plunge, plummet, cadence; subsidence, collapse, lapse; downfall, tumble, slip, tilt, trip, lurch; cropper, culbute[obs3]; titubation[obs3], stumble; fate of Icarus.
avalanche, debacle, landslip, landslide.
declivity, dip, hill.
[equipment for descending by rappeling] rappel.
V. descend; go down, drop down, come down; fall, gravitate, drop, slip, slide, rappel, settle; plunge, plummet, crash; decline, set, sink, droop, come down a peg; slump.
dismount, alight, light, get down; swoop; stoop &c. 308; fall prostrate, precipitate oneself; let fall &c. 308.
tumble, trip, stumble, titubate[obs3], lurch, pitch, swag, topple, topple over, tumble over, topple down, tumble down; tilt, sprawl, plump down, come down a cropper.
Adj. descending &c. v.; descendent; decurrent[obs3], decursive[obs3]; labent[obs3], deciduous; nodding to its fall.
Adv. downhill, downwards.
Phr. the bottom fell out.
#307. Elevation. — N. elevation; raising &c. v.; erection, lift; sublevation[obs3], upheaval; sublimation, exaltation; prominence &c. (convexity) 250.
lever &c. 633; crane, derrick, windlass, capstan, winch; dredge, dredger, dredging machine.
dumbwaiter, elevator, escalator, lift.

V. heighten, elevate, raise, lift, erect; set up, stick up, perch up,
perk up, tilt up; rear, hoist, heave; uplift, upraise, uprear,
upbear[obs3], upcast[obs3], uphoist[obs3], upheave; buoy, weigh mount, give
a lift; exalt; sublimate; place on a pedestal, set on a pedestal.

[ref] escalate (increase) 35, 102, 194.

take up, drag up, fish up; dredge.

stand up, rise up, get up, jump up; spring to one's feet; hold
oneself, hold one's head up; drawn oneself up to his full height.

Adj. elevated &c. v.; stilted, attollent[obs3], rampant.

Adv. on stilts, on the shoulders of, on one's legs, on one's hind
legs.

<— p. 92 —>

#308. Depression. — N. lowering &c. v.; depression; dip &c. (concavity) 252; abasement; detrusion[obs3]; reduction.
overthrow, overset[obs3], overturn; upset; prostration, subversion, precipitation. bow; courtesy, curtsy;
genuflexion[obs3], genuflection, kowtow, obeisance, salaam. V. depress, lower, let down, take down, let down a peg,
take down a peg; cast; let drop, let fall; sink, debase, bring low, abase, reduce, detrude[obs3], pitch, precipitate.
overthrow, overturn, overset[obs3]; upset, subvert, prostate, level, fell; cast down, take down, throw down, fling
down, dash down, pull down, cut down, knock down, hew down; raze, raze to the ground, rase to the ground[obs3];
trample in the dust, pull about one's ears. sit, sit down; couch, squat, crouch, stoop, bend, bow; courtesy, curtsy;
bob, duck, dip, kneel; bend the knee, bow the knee, bend the head, bow the head; cower; recline &c. (be horizontal)
213. Adj. depressed &c. v.; at a low ebb; prostrate &c. (horizontal) 213; detrusive[obs3]. Phr. facinus quos inquinat
aequat [Lat][Lucan].

#309. Leap. — N. leap, jump, hop, spring, bound, vault,
saltation[obs3].

ance, caper; curvet, caracole; gambadel, gambadol; capriole,
demivolt[obs3]; buck, buck jump; hop skip and jump; falcade[obs3].

kangaroo, jerboa; chamois, goat, frog, grasshopper, flea;
buckjumper[obs3]; wallaby.

V. leap; jump up, jump over the moon; hop, spring, bound, vault, ramp,
cut capers, trip, skip, dance, caper; buck, buck jump; curvet, caracole;
foot it, bob, bounce, flounce, start; frisk &c. (amusement) 840; jump about
&c. (agitation) 315; trip it on the light fantastic toe, trip the light
fantastic, dance oneself off one's legs, dance off one's shoes.

Adj. leaping &c. v.; saltatory[obs3], frisky.

Adv. on the light fantastic toe.

Phr. di salto in salto[It].

#310. Plunge — N. plunge, dip, dive, header; ducking &c. v.; diver.

V. plunge, dip, souse, duck; dive, plump; take a plunge, take a
header; make a plunge; bathe &c.(water) 337.

submerge, submerse; immerse; douse, sink, engulf, send to the bottom.

get out of one's depth; go to the bottom, go down like a stone, drop
like a lead balloon; founder, welter, wallow.

#311. [Curvilinear motion.] Circuition. — N. circuition[obs3], circulation; turn, curvet; excursion, circumvention,
circumnavigation, circumambulation; northwest passage; circuit &c. 629. turning &c. v.; wrench; evolution; coil,
corkscrew. V. turn, bend, wheel; go about, put about; heel; go round to the right about, turn round to the right about;
turn on one's heel; make a circle, make a complete circle, describe a circle, describe a complete circle; go through
180x, go through 360x, pass through 180x, pass through 360x. circumnavigate, circumambulate, circumvent; "put a
girdle round about the earth" [M.N.D.]; go the round, make the round of. wind, circulate, meander; whisk, twirl; twist
&c. (convolution) 248; make a detour &c. (circuit) 629. Adj. turning &c. v.; circuitous; circumforaneous[obs3],
circumfluent[obs3]. Adv. round about.

#312. [Motion in a continued circle.] Rotation. — N. rotation, revolution, spinning, gyration, turning about an axis,
turning around an axis, circulation, roll; circumrotation[obs3], circumvolution, circumgyration[obs3]; volutation[obs3],
circinationl, turbination[obs3], pirouette, convolution. verticityl, whir, whirl, eddy, vortex, whirlpool, gurge[obs3];
countercurrent; Maelstrom, Charybdis; Ixion. [rotating air] cyclone; tornado, whirlwind; dust devil. [rotation of an
automobile] spin-out. axis, axis of rotation, swivel, pivot, pivot point; axle, spindle, pin, hinge, pole, arbor, bobbin,

mandrel; axle shaft; gymbal; hub, hub of rotation. [rotation and translation together] helix, helical motion. [measure of rotation] angular momentum, angular velocity; revolutions per minute, RPM. [result of rotation] centrifugal force; surge; vertigo, dizzy round; coriolus force. [things that go around] carousel, merry-go-round; Ferris wheel; top, dreidel ,teetotum[obs3]; gyroscope; turntable, lazy suzan; screw, whirligig, rolling stone[obs3], water wheel, windmill; wheel, pulley wheel, roulette wheel, potter's wheel, pinwheel, gear; roller; flywheel; jack; caster; centrifuge, ultracentrifuge, bench centrifuge, refrigerated centrifuge, gas centrifuge, microfuge; drill, augur, oil rig; wagon wheel, wheel, tire, tyre[Brit][Brit]. [Science of rotary motion] trochilics[obs3]. [person who rotates] whirling dervish. V. rotate; roll along; revolve, spin; turn round; circumvolve[obs3]; circulate; gyre, gyrate, wheel, whirl, pirouette; twirl, trundle, troll, bowl. roll up, furl; wallow, welter; box the compass; spin like a top, spin like a teetotum!!. [of an automobile] spin out. Adj. rotating &c.v.; rotary, rotary; circumrotatory[obs3], trochilic[obs3], vertiginous, gyratory; vortical, vorticose[obs3]. Adv. head over heels, round and round, like a horse in a mill.

<— most of this should go under change (make a 146a)... develop not in change section!! revolution, evolution. revolution = change = #146—> #313. [Motion in the reverse circle.] Evolution. — N. evolution, unfolding, development; evolvement; unfoldment; eversion &c. (inversion) 218. V. evolve; unfold, unroll, unwind, uncoil, untwist, unfurl, untwine, unravel; untangle, disentangle; develop. Adj. evolving &c. v.; evolved &c. v.

<— p. 93 —>

#314. [Reciprocating motion, motion to and fro.] Oscillation. — N. oscillation; vibration, libration; motion of a pendulum; nutation; undulation; pulsation; pulse. alternation; coming and going &c. v.; ebb and flow, flux and reflux, ups and down. fluctuation; vacillation &c. (irresolution) 605. wave, vibratiuncle[obs3], swing, beat, shake, wag, seesaw, dance, lurch, dodge; logan[obs3], loggan[obs3], rocking-stone, vibroscope[obs3]. V. oscillate; vibrate, librate[obs3]; alternate, undulate, wave; rock, swing; pulsate, beat; wag, waggle; nod, bob, courtesy, curtsy; tick; play; wamble[obs3], wabble[obs3]; dangle, swag. fluctuate, dance, curvet, reel, quake; quiver, quaver; shake, flicker; wriggle; roll, toss, pitch; flounder, stagger, totter; move up and down, bob up and down &c. Adv.; pass and repass, ebb and flow, come and go; vacillate &c. 605; teeter [U.S.]. brandish, shake, flourish. Adj. oscillating &c. v.; oscillatory, undulatory, pulsatory[obs3], libratory, rectilinear; vibratory, vibratile[obs3]; pendulous. Adv. to and fro, up and down, backwards and forwards, hither and yon, seesaw, zigzag, wibble-wabble[obs3], in and out, from side to side, like buckets in a well.

#315. [Irregular motion] Agitation. — N. agitation, stir, tremor, shake, ripple, jog, jolt, jar, jerk, shock, succussion[obs3], trepidation, quiver, quaver, dance; jactitationl, quassationl; shuffling 7c. v.; twitter, flicker, flutter. turbulence, perturbation; commotion, turmoil, disquiet; tumult, tumultuationl; hubbub, rout, bustle, fuss, racket, subsultus[obs3], staggers, megrims, epilepsy, fits; carphology[obs3], chorea, floccillation[obs3], the jerks, St. Vitus's dance, tilmus[obs3]. spasm, throe, throb, palpitation, convulsion. disturbance, chaos &c. (disorder) 59; restlessness &c. (changeableness) 149. ferment, fermentation; ebullition, effervescence, hurly-burly, cahotage[obs3]; tempest, storm, ground swell, heavy sea, whirlpool, vortex &c. 312; whirlwind &c. (wind) 349. V. be agitated &c.; shake; tremble, tremble like an aspen leaf; quiver, quaver, quake, shiver, twitter, twire[obs3], writhe, toss, shuffle, tumble, stagger, bob, reel, sway, wag, waggle; wriggle, wriggle like an eel; dance, stumble, shamble, flounder, totter, flounce, flop, curvet, prance, cavort [U.S.]; squirm. throb, pulsate, beat, palpitate, go pitapat; flutter, flitter, flicker, bicker; bustle. ferment, effervesce, foam; boil, boil over; bubble up; simmer. toss about, jump about; jump like a parched pea; shake like an aspen leaf; shake to its center, shake to its foundations; be the sport of the winds and waves; reel to and fro like a drunken man; move from post to pillar and from pillar to post, drive from post to pillar and from pillar to post, keep between hawk and buzzard. agitate, shake, convulse, toss, tumble, bandy, wield, brandish, flap, flourish, whisk, jerk, hitch, jolt; jog, joggle, jostle, buffet, hustle, disturb, stir, shake up, churn, jounce, wallop, whip, vellicate[obs3]. Adj. shaking &c. v.; agitated, tremulous; desultory, subsultoryl; saltatoric[obs3]; quasative[obs3]; shambling; giddy-paced, saltatory[obs3], convulsive, unquiet, restless, all of a twitter. Adv. by fits and starts; subsultorilyl &c. adj[obs3].; per saltum[Lat]; hop skip and jump; in convulsions, in fits. Phr. tempete dans un verre d'eau[Fr].

<— p. 94 —>

%
CLASS III
WORDS RELATION TO MATTER
Section I. MATTER IN GENERAL
%
#316. MATERIALITY. — N. materiality, materialness; corporeity[obs3], corporality[obs3]; substantiality, substantial-

ness, flesh and blood, plenum; physical condition. matter, body, substance, brute matter, stuff, element, principle, parenchyma[Biol], material, substratum, hyle[obs3], corpus, pabulum; frame. object, article, thing, something; still life; stocks and stones; materials &c. 635. [Science of matter] physics; somatology[obs3], somatics; natural philosophy, experimental philosophy; physicism[obs3]; physical science, philosophie positive[Fr], materialism; materialist; physicist; somatism[obs3], somatist[obs3]. Adj. material, bodily; corporeal, corporal; physical; somatic, somatoscopic[obs3]; sensible, tangible, ponderable, palpable, substantial. objective, impersonal, nonsubjective[obs3], neuter, unspiritual, materialistic.

#317. Immateriality. — N. immateriality, immaterialness; incorporeity[obs3], spirituality; inextension[obs3]; astral plane.
personality; I, myself, me; ego, spirit &c. (soul) 450; astral body; immaterialism[obs3]; spiritualism, spiritualist.
V. disembody, spiritualize.
Adj. immaterial, immateriate[obs3]; incorporeal, incorporal[obs3]; incorporate, unfleshly[obs3]; supersensible[obs3]; asomatous[obs3], unextended[obs3]; unembodied[obs3], disembodied; extramundane, unearthly; pneumatoscopic[obs3]; spiritual &c. (psychical) 450[obs3].
personal, subjective, nonobjective.

#318. World. — N. world, creation, nature, universe; earth, globe, wide world; cosmos; kosmos[obs3]; terraqueous globe[obs3], sphere; macrocosm, megacosm[obs3]; music of the spheres. heavens, sky, welkinl, empyrean; starry cope, starry heaven, starry host; firmament; Midgard; supersensible regions[obs3]; varuna; vault of heaven, canopy of heaven; celestial spaces. heavenly bodies, stars, asteroids; nebulae; galaxy, milky way, galactic circle, via lactea[Lat], ame no kawa [Jap.]. sun, orb of day, Apollo[obs3], Phoebus; photosphere, chromosphere; solar system; planet, planetoid; comet; satellite, moon, orb of night, Diana, silver-footed queen; aerolite[obs3], meteor; planetary ring; falling star, shooting star; meteorite, uranolite[obs3]. constellation, zodiac, signs of the zodiac, Charles's wain, Big Dipper, Little Dipper, Great Bear, Southern Cross, Orion's belt, Cassiopea's chair, Pleiades. colures[obs3], equator, ecliptic, orbit. [Science of heavenly bodies] astronomy; uranography, uranology[obs3]; cosmology, cosmography[obs3], cosmogony; eidouranion[obs3], orrery; geodesy &c. (measurement) 466; star gazing, star gazer[obs3]; astronomer; observatory; planetarium. Adj. cosmic, cosmical[obs3]; mundane, terrestrial, terrestriousl, terraqueous[obs3], terrene, terreousl, telluric, earthly, geotic[obs3], under the sun; sublunary[obs3], subastral[obs3]. solar, heliacal[obs3]; lunar; celestial, heavenly, sphery[obs3]; starry, stellar; sidereal, sideral[obs3]; astral; nebular; uranic. Adv. in all creation, on the face of the globe, here below, under the sun. Phr. die Weltgeschichte ist das Weltergesicht[Ger]; "earth is but the frozen echo of the silent voice of God" [Hageman]; "green calm below, blue quietness above" [Whittier]; "hanging in a golden chain this pendant World" [Paradise Lost]; "nothing in nature is unbeautiful" [Tennyson]; "silently as a dream the fabric rose" [Cowper]; "some touch of nature's genial glow" [Scott]; "this majestical roof fretted with golden fire" [Hamlet]; "through knowledge we behold the World's creation" [Spenser].

<— p. 95 —>

#319. Gravity. — N. gravity, gravitation; weight; heaviness &c. adj.; specific gravity; pondorosity[obs3], pressure, load; burden, burthen[obs3]; ballast, counterpoise; lump of, mass of, weight of.
lead, millstone, mountain, Ossa on Pelion.
weighing, ponderation[obs3], trutinationl; weights; avoirdupois weight, troy weight, apothecaries' weight; grain, scruple, drachma[obs3], ounce, pound, lb, arroba[obs3], load, stone, hundredweight, cwt, ton, long ton, metric ton, quintal, carat, pennyweight, tod[obs3].
[metric weights] gram, centigram, milligram, microgram, kilogram; nanogram, picogram, femtogram, attogram.
[Weighing Instrument] balance, scale, scales, steelyard, beam, weighbridge[obs3]; spring balance, piezoelectric balance, analytical balance, two-pan balance, one-pan balance; postal scale, baby scale.
[Science of gravity] statics.
V. be heavy &c. adj.; gravitate, weigh, press, cumber, load.
[Measure the weight of] weigh, poise.
Adj. weighty; weighing &c. v.; heavy as lead; ponderous, ponderable; lumpish[obs3], lumpy, cumbersome, burdensome; cumbrous, unwieldy, massive.
incumbent, superincumbent[obs3].

#320. Levity. — N. levity; lightness &c. adj.; imponderability, buoyancy, volatility.

feather, dust, mote, down, thistle, down, flue, cobweb, gossamer, straw, cork, bubble, balloon; float, buoy; ether, air.

leaven, ferment, barm[obs3], yeast.

lighter-than-air balloon, helium balloon, hydrogen balloon, hot air balloon.

convection, thermal draft, thermal.

V. be light &c. adj.; float, rise, swim, be buoyed up.

render light &c. adj.; lighten, leaven.

Adj. light, subtile, airy; imponderous[obs3], imponderable; astatic[obs3], weightless, ethereal, sublimated; gossamery; suberose[obs3], suberous[obs3]; uncompressed, volatile; buoyant, floating &c. v.; portable.

light as a feather, light as a thistle, light as air; lighter than air; rise like a balloon, float like a balloon.

% Section II. INORGANIC MATTER 1. Solid Matter %

#321. Density.. — N. density, solidity; solidness &c. adj.; impenetrability, impermeability; incompressibility; imporosity[obs3]; cohesion &c. 46; constipation, consistence, spissitudel. specific gravity; hydrometer, areometer[obs3]. condensation; caseation[obs3]; solidation[obs3], solidification; consolidation; concretion, coagulation; petrification &c. (hardening) 323; crystallization, precipitation; deposit, precipitate; inspissation[obs3]; gelation, thickening &c. v. indivisibility, indiscerptibility[obs3], insolubility, indissolvableness. solid body, mass, block, knot, lump; concretion, concrete, conglomerate; cake, clot, stone, curd, coagulum; bone, gristle, cartilage; casein, crassamentuml; legumin[obs3]. superdense matter, condensed states of matter; dwarf star, neutron star. V. be dense &c. adj.; become solid, render solid &c. adj.; solidify, solidate[obs3]; concrete, set, take a set, consolidate, congeal, coagulate; curd, curdle; lopper; fix, clot, cake, candy, precipitate, deposit, cohere, crystallize; petrify &c. (harden) 323. condense, thicken, gel, inspissate[obs3], incrassate[obs3]; compress, squeeze, ram down, constipate. Adj. dense, solid; solidified &c. v.; caseous; pukka[obs3]; coherent, cohesive &c. 46; compact, close, serried, thickset; substantial, massive, lumpish[obs3]; impenetrable, impermeable, nonporous, imporous[obs3]; incompressible; constipated; concrete &c. (hard) 323; knotted, knotty; gnarled; crystalline, crystallizable; thick, grumousl, stuffy. undissolved, unmelted[obs3], unliquefied[obs3], unthawed[obs3]. indivisible, indiscerptible[obs3], infrangible[obs3], indissolvable[obs3], indissoluble, insoluble, infusible.

#322. Rarity. — N. rarity, tenuity; absence of solidity &c. 321; subtility[obs3]; subtilty[obs3], subtlety; sponginess, compressibility.

rarefaction, expansion, dilatation, inflation, subtilization[obs3].

vaporization, evaporation, diffusion, gassification[obs3].

ether &c. (gas) 334.

V. rarefy, expand, dilate, subtilize[obs3].

Adj. rare, subtile, thin, fine, tenuous, compressible, flimsy, slight; light &c. 320; cavernous, spongy &c. (hollow) 252.

rarefied &c. v.; unsubstantial; uncompact[obs3], incompressed[obs3]; rarefiable[obs3].

<— p. 96 —>

#323. Hardness. — N. hardness &c. adj.; rigidity; renitence[obs3], renitency; inflexibility, temper, callosity, durity [obs3]. induration, petrifaction; lapidification[obs3], lapidescence[obs3]; vitrification, ossification; crystallization. stone, pebble, flint, marble, rock, fossil, crag, crystal, quartz, granite, adamant; bone, cartilage; hardware; heart of oak, block, board, deal board; iron, steel; cast iron, decarbonized iron, wrought iron; nail; brick, concrete; cement. V. render hard &c. adj.; harden, stiffen, indurate, petrify, temper, ossify, vitrify; accrust[obs3]. Adj. hard, rigid, stubborn, stiff, firm; starch, starched; stark, unbending, unlimber, unyielding; inflexible, tense; indurate, indurated; gritty, proof. adamant, adamantine, adamantean[obs3]; concrete, stony, granitic, calculous, lithic[obs3], vitreous; horny, corneous[obs3]; bony; osseous, ossific[obs3]; cartilaginous; hard as a rock &c. n.; stiff as buckram, stiff as a poker; stiff as starch, stiff as a board.

#324. Softness. — N. softness, pliableness &c. adj.; flexibility; pliancy, pliability; sequacity[obs3], malleability; ductility, tractility[obs3]; extendibility, extensibility; plasticity; inelasticity,

82

flaccidity, laxity.

penetrability.

clay, wax, butter, dough, pudding; alumina, argil; cushion, pillow, feather bed, down, padding, wadding; foam.

mollification; softening &c.v.

V. render -soft &c. adj.; soften, mollify, mellow, relax, temper; mash, knead, squash.

bend, yield, relent, relax, give.

plasticize'.

Adj. soft, tender, supple; pliant, pliable; flexible, flexile; lithe, lithesome; lissom, limber, plastic; ductile; tractile[obs3], tractable; malleable, extensile, sequacious[obs3], inelastic; aluminous[obs3]; remollient[obs3].

yielding &c. v.; flabby, limp, flimsy.

doughy, spongy, penetrable, foamy, cushiony[obs3].

flaccid, flocculent, downy; edematous, oedematous[obs3], medullary[Anat], argillaceous, mellow.

soft as butter, soft as down, soft as silk; yielding as wax, tender as chicken.

#325. Elasticity. — N. elasticity, springiness, spring, resilience, renitency, buoyancy.

rubber, India(n) rubber, latex, caoutchouc, whalebone, gum elastic, baleen, natural rubber; neoprene, synthetic rubber, Buna-S, plastic.

flexibility, Young's modulus.

V. stretch, flex, extend, distend, be elastic &c. adj.; bounce, spring back &c. (recoil) 277.

Adj. elastic, flexible, tensile, spring, resilient, renitent, buoyant; ductile, stretchable, extendable.

Phr. the stress is proportional to the strain.

#326. Inelasticity. — N. want of elasticity, absence of elasticity &c. 325; inelasticity &c. (softness) 324,

Adj. unyielding, inelastic, inflexible &c. (soft) 324; irresilient[obs3].

#327. Tenacity. — N. {ant. 328} tenacity, toughness, strength; (cohesion) 46; grip, grasp, stickiness, (cohesion) 46; sequacity[obs3]; stubbornness &c. (obstinacy); glue, cement, glutinousness[obs3], sequaciousness[obs3], viscidity, (semiliquidity) 352.

leather; white leather, whitleather[obs3]; gristle, cartilage.

unbreakability, tensile strength.

V. be tenacious &c. adj.; resist fracture.

grip, grasp, stick (cohesion) 46.

Adj. tenacious, tough, strong, resisting, sequacious[obs3], stringy, gristly cartilaginous, leathery, coriaceous[obs3], tough as whitleather[obs3]; stubborn &c. (obstinate) 606.

unbreakable, indivisible; atomic.

#328. Brittleness. — N. {ant. 327} brittleness &c. adj.; fragility, friability, frangibility, fissibility[obs3]; house of cards, house of glass. V. be brittle &c. adj.; live in a glass house. break, crack, snap, split, shiver, splinter, crumble, break short, burst, fly, give way; fall to pieces; crumble to, crumble into dust. Adj. brittle, brash [U.S.], breakable, weak, frangible, fragile, frail, gimcrackl, shivery, fissile; splitting &c. v.; lacerable[obs3], splintery, crisp, crimp, short, brittle as glass.

#329. [Structure.] Texture. — N. structure (form) 240, organization, anatomy, frame, mold, fabric, construction; framework, carcass, architecture; stratification, cleavage.

substance, stuff, compages[obs3], parenchyma[Biol]; constitution, staple, organism.

[Science of structures] organography[obs3], osteology, myology, splanchnology[obs3], neurology, angiography[obs3], adeology[obs3];

angiography[obs3], adenography[obs3].

texture, surface texture; intertexture[obs3], contexture[obs3];
tissue, grain, web, surface; warp and woof, warp and weft; tooth, nap &c.
(roughness) 256; flatness (smoothness) 255; fineness of grain; coarseness
of grain, dry goods.

silk, satin; muslin, burlap.

[Science of textures] histology.

Adj. structural, organic; anatomic, anatomical.

textural, textile; fine grained, coarse grained; fine, delicate,
subtile, gossamery, filmy, silky, satiny; coarse; homespun.

rough, gritty; smooth.

smooth as silk, smooth as satin.

<— p. 97 —>

#330. Pulverulence. — N. powderiness[obs3][State of powder.], pulverulence[obs3]; sandiness &c. adj.; efflores-
cence; friability. powder, dust, sand, shingle; sawdust; grit; meal, bran, flour, farina, rice, paddy, spore, sporule[obs3];
crumb, seed, grain; particle &c. (smallness) 32; limaturel, filings, debris, detritus, tailings, talus slope, scobs[obs3],
magistery[obs3], fine powder; flocculi[Lat]. smoke; cloud of dust, cloud of sand, cloud of smoke; puff of smoke,
volume of smoke; sand storm, dust storm. [Reduction to powder] pulverization, comminution[obs3], attenuation,
granulation, disintegration, subaction[obs3], contusion, trituration[Chem], levigation[obs3], abrasion, detrition,
multure[obs3]; limitation; tripsis[obs3]; filing &c.v.. [Instruments for pulverization] mill, arrastra[obs3], gristmill, grater,
rasp, file, mortar and pestle, nutmeg grater, teeth, grinder, grindstone, kern[obs3], quern[obs3], koniology[obs3]. V.
come to dust; be disintegrated, be reduced to powder &c. reduce to powder, grind to powder; pulverize, comminute,
granulate, triturate, levigate[obs3]; scrape, file, abrade, rub down, grind, grate, rasp, pound, bray, bruise; contuse,
contund[obs3]; beat, crush, cranch[obs3], craunch[obs3], crunch, scranch[obs3], crumble, disintegrate; attenuate &c.
195. Adj. powdery, pulverulent[obs3], granular, mealy, floury, farinaceous, branny[obs3], furfuraceous[obs3], flocculent, dusty, sandy, sabulous[obs3], psammous[obs3]; arenose[obs3], arenarious[obs3], arenaceous[obs3]; gritty,
efflorescent, impalpable; lentiginous[obs3], lepidote[obs3], sabuline[obs3]; sporaceous[obs3], sporous[obs3].
pulverizable; friable, crumbly, shivery; pulverized &c. v.; attrite[obs3]; in pieces.

#331. Friction. — N. friction, attrition; rubbing, abrasion, scraping
&c. v.; confricationl, detrition, contritionl, affriction[obs3], abrasion,
arrosionl, limaturel, frication[obs3], rub; elbow grease; rosin; massage;
roughness &c. 256.

rolling friction, sliding friction, starting friction.

V. rub, scratch, scrape, scrub, slide, fray, rasp, graze, curry,
scour, polish, rub out, wear down, gnaw; file, grind &c. (reduce to powder)
330.

set one's teeth on edge; rosin.

Adj. anatriptic[obs3]; attrite[obs3].

#332. [Absence of friction. Prevention of friction.] Lubrication. —
N. smoothness &c. 255; unctuousness &c. 355.

lubrication, lubrification[obs3]; anointment; oiling &c. v.

synovia[Anat]; glycerine, oil, lubricating oil, grease &c. 356;
saliva; lather.

teflon.

V. lubricate, lubricitatel; oil, grease, lather, soap; wax.

Adj. lubricated &c. v.; lubricous.

% 2. FLUID MATTER Fluids in General %

#333. Fluidity. — N. fluidity, liquidity; liquidness &c. adj[obs3].;
gaseity &c. 334[obs3].

fluid, inelastic fluid; liquid, liquor; lymph, humor, juice, sap,
serum, blood, serosity[obs3], gravy, rheum, ichor[obs3], sanies[obs3];
chyle[Med].

solubility, solubleness[obs3].

[Science of liquids at rest] hydrology, hydrostatics, hydrodynamics.

V. be fluid &c. adj.; flow &c. (water in motion) 348; liquefy, melt, condense &c. 335.

Adj. liquid, fluid, serous, juicy, succulent, sappy; ichorous[obs3];
fluent &c. (flowing) 348.

liquefied &c. 335; uncongealed; soluble.

#334. Gaseity. — N. gaseity[obs3]; vaporousness &c. adj.; flatulence,
flatulency; volatility; aeration, aerification.

elastic fluid, gas, air, vapor, ether, steam, essence, fume, reek,
effluvium, flatus; cloud &c. 353; ammonia, ammoniacal gas[obs3]; volatile
alkali; vacuum, partial vacuum.

[Science of elastic fluids] pneumatics, pneumatostatics[obs3];
aerostatics[obs3], aerodynamics.

gasmeter[obs3], gasometer[obs3]; air bladder, swimming bladder, sound
(of a fish).

V. vaporize, evaporate, evanesce, gasify, emit vapor &c. 336; diffuse.

Adj. gaseous, aeriform[obs3], ethereal, aerial, airy, vaporous,
volatile, evaporable[obs3], flatulent.
<— p. 98 —>

#335. Liquefaction. — N. liquefaction; liquescence[obs3], liquescency[obs3]; melting &c. (heat) 384; colliquationl,
colliquefactionl; thaw; liquationl, deliquationl, deliquescence; lixiviation[obs3], dissolution. solution, apozem[obs3],
lixivium[obs3], infusion, flux. solvent, menstruum, alkahest[obs3]. V. render liquid &c. 333; liquefy, run; deliquesce;
melt &c. (heat) 384; solve; dissolve, resolve; liquatel; hold in solution; condense, precipitate, rain. Adj. liquefied &c.
v., liquescent, liquefiable; deliquescent, soluble, colliquative[obs3].

#336. Vaporization. — N. vaporization, volatilization; gasification,
evaporation, vaporation[obs3]; distillation, cupellation[Chem], cohobation,
sublimination[obs3], exhalation; volatility.

vaporizer, still, retort; fumigation, steaming; bay salt, chloride of
sodiuml!.

mister, spray.

bubble, effervescence.

V. render -gaseous &c. 334; vaporize, volatilize; distill, sublime;
evaporate, exhale, smoke, transpire, emit vapor, fume, reek, steam,
fumigate; cohobate[obs3]; finestill[obs3].

bubble, sparge, effervesce, boil.

Adj. volatilized &c. v.; reeking &c. v.; volatile; evaporable[obs3],
vaporizable.

bubbly, effervescent, boiling.
% Specific Fluids %

#337. Water. — N. water; serum, serosity[obs3]; lymph; rheum; diluent; agua[Sp], aqua, pani[obs3]. dilution, macera-
tion, lotion; washing &c. v.; immersionl, humectation[obs3], infiltration, spargefactionl, affusion[obs3], irrigation,
douche, balneation[obs3], bath. deluge &c. (water in motion) 348; high water, flood tide. V. be watery &c. adj.; reek.
add water, water, wet; moisten &c. 339; dilute, dip, immerse; merge; immerge, submerge; plunge, souse, duck,
drown; soak, steep, macerate, pickle, wash, sprinkle, lave, bathe, affuse[obs3], splash, swash, douse, drench;
dabble, slop, slobber, irrigate, inundate, deluge; syringe, inject, gargle. Adj. watery, aqueous, aquatic, hydrous,
lymphatic; balneal[obs3], diluent; drenching &c. v.; diluted &c. v.; weak; wet &c. (moist) 339. Phr. the waters are out.

#338. Air. — N. air &c. (gas) 334; common air, atmospheric air;
atmosphere; aerosphere[obs3].

open air; sky, welkin; blue sky; cloud &c. 353.

weather, climate, rise and fall of the barometer, isobar.

[Science of air] aerology, aerometry[obs3], aeroscopy[obs3],
aeroscopy[obs3], aerography[obs3]; meteorology, climatology; pneumatics;
eudioscope[obs3], baroscope[obs3], aeroscope[obs3], eudiometer[obs3],
barometer, aerometer[obs3]; aneroid, baroscope[obs3]; weather gauge,
weather glass, weather cock.

exposure to the air, exposure to the weather; ventilation;

aerostation[obs3], aeronautics, aeronaut.

V. air, ventilate, fan &c. (wind) 349.

Adj. containing air, flatulent, effervescent; windy &c. 349.

atmospheric, airy; aerial, aeriform[obs3]; meteorological;
weatherwise[obs3].

Adv. in the open air, a la belle etoile[Fr], al fresco; sub jove
dio[Lat].

#339. Moisture. — N. moisture; moistness &c. adj.; humidity,
humectation[obs3]; madefactionl; dew; serein[obs3]; marsh &c. 345;
hygrometry, hygrometer.

V. moisten, wet; humect[obs3], humectate[obs3]; sponge, damp, bedew;
imbue, imbrue, infiltrate, saturate; soak, drench &c. (water) 337.

be moist &c. adj.; not have a dry thread; perspire &c. (exude) 295.

Adj. moist, damp; watery &c. 337; madid[obs3], roric[obs3];
undried[obs3], humid, sultry, wet, dank, luggy[obs3], dewy; rorall, roridl;
roscid[obs3]; juicy.

wringing wet, soaking wet; wet through to the skin; saturated &c. v.

swashy[obs3], soggy, dabbled; reeking, dripping, soaking, soft, sodden,
sloppy, muddy; swampy &c. (marshy) 345; irriguous[obs3].

#340. Dryness. — N. dryness &c. adj.; siccity[obs3], aridity,
drought, ebb tide, low water.

exsiccationl, desiccation; arefactionl, dephlegmationl, drainage;
drier.

[CHEMSUB which renders dry] desiccative, dessicator.

[device to render dry] dessicator; hair drier, clothes drier, gas
drier, electric drier; vacuum oven, drying oven, kiln; lyophilizer.

clothesline.

V. be dry &c. adj..

[transitive] render dry &c. adj.; dry; dry up, soak up; sponge, swab,
wipe; drain.

desiccate, dehydrate, exsiccate[obs3]; parch.

kiln dry; vacuum dry, blow dry, oven dry; hang out to dry.

mummify.

be fine, hold up.

Adj. dry, anhydrous, arid; adust[obs3], arescentl; dried &c. v.;
undamped; juiceless[obs3], sapless; sear; husky; rainless, without rain,
fine; dry as a bone, dry as dust, dry as a stick, dry as a mummy, dry as a
biscuit.

water proof, water tight.

dehydrated, dessicated.

<— p. 99 —>

#341. Ocean — N. sea, ocean, main, deep, brine, salt water, waves,
billows, high seas, offing, great waters, watery waste, "vasty deep"; wave,
tide, &c. (water in motion) 348.

hydrography, hydrographer; Neptune, Poseidon, Thetis, Triton, Naiad,
Nereid; sea nymph, Siren; trident, dolphin.

Adj. oceanic; marine, maritime; pelagic, pelagian; seagoing;
hydrographic; bathybic[obs3], cotidal[obs3].

Adv. at sea, on sea; afloat.

#342. Land. — N. land, earth, ground, dry land, terra firma.

continent, mainland, peninsula, chersonese[Fr], delta; tongue of land,
neck of land; isthmus, oasis; promontory &c. (projection) 250; highland &c.
(height) 206.

coast, shore, scar, strand, beach; playa; bank, lea; seaboard,
seaside, seabank[obs3], seacoast, seabeach[obs3]; ironbound coast; loom of
the land; derelict; innings; alluvium, alluvion[obs3]; ancon.

riverbank, river bank, levee.

soil, glebe, clay, loam, marl, cledge[obs3], chalk, gravel, mold,
subsoil, clod, clot; rock, crag.

acres; real estate &c. (property) 780; landsman[obs3].

V. land, come to land, set foot on the soil, set foot on dry land;
come ashore, go ashore, debark.

Adj. earthy, continental, midland, coastal, littoral, riparian;
alluvial; terrene &c. (world) 318; landed, predial[obs3], territorial;
geophilous[obs3]; ripicolous.

Adv. ashore; on shore, on land.

#343. Gulf. Lake — N. land covered with water, gulf, gulph[obs3], bay, inlet, bight, estuary, arm of the sea, bayou
[U.S.], fiord, armlet; frith[obs3], firth, ostiaryl, mouth; lagune[obs3], lagoon; indraught[obs3]; cove, creek; natural
harbor; roads; strait; narrows; Euripus; sound, belt, gut, kyles[obs3]; continental slope, continental shelf. lake, loch,
lough[obs3], mere, tarn, plash, broad, pond, pool, lin[obs3], puddle, slab, well, artesian well; standing water, dead
water, sheet of water; fish pond, mill pond; ditch, dike, dyke, dam; reservoir &c. (store) 636; alberca[obs3],
barachois[obs3], hog wallow [U.S.]. Adj. lacustrine[obs3].

#344. Plain. — N. plain, table-land, face of the country; open country, champaign country[obs3]; basin, downs,
waste, weary waste, desert, wild, steppe, pampas, savanna, prairie, heath, common, wold[obs3], veldt; moor,
moorland; bush; plateau &c. (level) 213; campagna[obs3]; alkali flat, llano; mesa, mesilla [obs3][U.S.], playa;
shaking prairie, trembling prairie; vega[Sp]. meadow, mead, haugh[obs3], pasturage, park, field, lawn, green, plat,
plot, grassplat[obs3], greensward, sward, turf, sod, heather; lea, ley, lay; grounds; maidan[obs3], agostadero[obs3].
Adj. champaign[obs3], alluvial; campestral[obs3], campestrial[obs3], campestrian[obs3], campestrine[obs3].

#345. Marsh. — N. marsh, swamp, morass, marish[obs3], moss, fen, bog, quagmire, slough, sump, wash; mud,
squash, slush; baygall [obs3][U.S.], cienaga[obs3], jhil[obs3], vlei[obs3]. Adj. marsh, marshy; swampy, boggy,
plashy[obs3], poachy[obs3], quaggy[obs3], soft; muddy, sloppy, squashy; paludal[obs3]; moorish, moory; fenny.

#346. Island. — N. island, isle, islet, eyot[obs3], ait[obs3],
holf[obs3], reef, atoll, breaker; archipelago; islander.

Adj. insular, seagirt; archipelagic[obs3].
<— p. 100 —> % Fluids in Motion %

#347. [Fluid in motion.] Stream. — N. stream &c. (of water) 348, (of
air) 349.

flowmeter.

V. flow &c. 348; blow &c. 349.

#348. [Water in motion.] River. — N. running water. jet, spirt[obs3], spurt, squirt, spout, spray, splash, rush, gush, jet
d'eau[Fr]; sluice. water spout, water fall; cascade, force, foss[obs3]; lin[obs3], linn[obs3]; ghyll[obs3], Niagara;
cataract, rapids, white water, catadupel, cataclysm; debacle, inundation, deluge; chute, washout. rain, rainfall;
serein[obs3]; shower, scud; downpour; driving rain, drenching rain, cloudburst; hyetology[obs3], hyetography[obs3];
predominance of Aquarius[obs3], reign of St. Swithin; mizzle[obs3], drizzle, stillicidum[obs3], plash; dropping &c. v.;
falling weather; northeaster, hurricane, typhoon. stream, course, flux, flow, profluence[obs3]; effluence &c. (egress)
295; defluxion[obs3]; flowing &c. v.; current, tide, race, coulee. spring, artesian well, fount, fountain; rill, rivulet, gill,
gullet, rillet[obs3]; streamlet, brooklet; branch [U.S.]; runnel, sike[obs3], burn, beck, creek, brook, bayou, stream,
river; reach, tributary. geyser, spout, waterspout. body of water, torrent, rapids, flush, flood, swash; spring tide, high
tide, full tide; bore, tidal bore, eagre[obs3], hygre[obs3]; fresh, freshet; indraught[obs3], reflux, undercurrent, eddy,
vortex, gurge[obs3], whirlpool, Maelstrom, regurgitation, overflow; confluence, corrivationl. wave, billow, surge, swell,
ripple; <gr/anerythmon gelasma/gr>[obs3][Grk]; beach comber, riffle [U.S.], rollers, ground swell, surf, breakers,
white horses, whitecaps; rough sea, heavy sea, high seas, cross sea, long sea, short sea, chopping sea. [Science of
fluids in motion] hydrodynamics; hydraulics, hydraulicostatics[obs3]; rain gauge, flowmeter; pegology[obs3]. irrigation &c. (water) 337; pump; watering pot, watering cart; hydrant, syringe; garden hose, lawn spray; bhisti[obs3],
mussuk[obs3]. V. flow, run; meander; gush, pour, spout, roll, jet, well, issue; drop, drip, dribble, plash, spirtle[obs3],
trill, trickle, distill, percolate; stream, overflow, inundate, deluge, flow over, splash, swash; guggle[obs3], murmur,
babble, bubble, purl, gurgle, sputter, spurt, spray, regurgitate; ooze, flow out &c. (egress) 295. rain hard, rain in
torrents, rain cats and dogs, rain pitchforks; pour with rain, drizzle, spit, set in; mizzle[obs3]. flow into, fall into, open
into, drain into; discharge itself, disembogue[obs3]. [Cause a flow] pour; pour out &c. (discharge) 297; shower down,
irrigate, drench &c. (wet) 337; spill, splash. [Stop a flow] stanch; dam, up &c. (close) 261; obstruct &c. 706. Adj.
fluent; diffluent[obs3], profluent[obs3], affluent; tidal; flowing &c. v.; meandering, meandry[obs3], meandrous[obs3];

fluvial, fluviatile; streamy[obs3], showery, rainy, pluvial, stillicidousl; stillatitious[obs3]. Phr. "for men may come and men may go but I go on forever" [Tennyson]; "that old man river, he just keeps rolling along" [Showboat].

#349. [Air in motion] Wind. — N.. wind, draught, flatus, afflatus, efflation[obs3], eluvium[obs3]; air; breath, breath of air; puff, whiff, zephyr; blow, breeze, drift; aura; stream, current, jet stream; undercurrent. gust, blast, squall, gale, half a gale, storm, tempest, hurricane, whirlwind, tornado, samiel, cyclone, anticyclone, typhoon; simoon[obs3], simoom; harmattan[obs3], monsoon, trade wind, sirocco, mistral, bise[obs3], tramontane, levanter; capful of wind; fresh breeze, stiff breeze; keen blast; blizzard, barber [Can.], candelia[obs3], chinook, foehn, khamsin[obs3], norther, vendaval[obs3], wuther[obs3]. windiness &c. adj.; ventosityl; rough weather, dirty weather, ugly weather, stress of weather; dirty sky, mare's tail; thick squall, black squall, white squall. anemography[obs3], aerodynamics; wind gauge, weathercock, vane, weather-vane, wind sock; anemometer, anemoscope[obs3]. sufflation[obs3], insufflation[obs3], perflation[obs3], inflation, afflation[obs3]; blowing, fanning &c. v.; ventilation. sneezing &c.v.: errhine[obs3]; sternutative[obs3], sternutatory[obs3]; sternutation; hiccup, hiccough; catching of the breath. Eolus, Boreas, Zephyr, cave of Eolus. air pump, air blower, lungs, bellows, blowpipe, fan, ventilator, punkah[obs3]; branchiae[obs3], gills, flabellum[obs3], vertilabrum[obs3]. whiffle ball. V. blow, waft; blow hard, blow great guns, blow a hurricane &c. n.; wuther[obs3]; stream, issue. respire, breathe, puff; whiff, whiffle; gasp, wheeze; snuff, snuffle; sniff, sniffle; sneeze, cough. fan, ventilate; inflate, perflatel; blow up. Adj. blowing &c. v.; windy, flatulent; breezy, gusty, squally; stormy, tempestuous, blustering; boisterous &c. (violent) 173. pulmonic[Med], pulmonary. Phr. "lull'd by soft zephyrs" [Pope]; "the storm is up and all is on the hazard" [Julius Caesar]; "the winds were wither'd in the stagnant air" [Byron]; "while mocking winds are piping loud" [Milton]; "winged with red lightning and tempestuous rage" [Paradise Lost].

<— p. 101 —>

#350. [Channel for the passage of water.] Conduit. — N. conduit, channel, duct, watercourse, race; head race, tail race; abito[obs3], aboideau[obs3], aboiteau[Fr], bito[obs3]; acequia[obs3], acequiador[obs3], acequiamadre[obs3]; arroyo; adit[obs3], aqueduct, canal, trough, gutter, pantile; flume, ingate[obs3], runner; lock-weir, tedge[obs3]; vena[obs3]; dike, main, gully, moat, ditch, drain, sewer, culvert, cloaca, sough, kennel, siphon; piscina[obs3]; pipe &c. (tube) 260; funnel; tunnel &c. (passage) 627; water pipe, waste pipe; emunctory[obs3], gully hole, artery, aorta, pore, spout, scupper; adjutage[obs3], ajutage[obs3]; hose; gargoyle; gurgoyle[obs3]; penstock, weir; flood gate, water gate; sluice, lock, valve; rose; waterworks. pipeline. Adj. vascular &c. (with holes) 260.

#351. [Channel for the passage of air.] Airpipe. — N. air pipe, air tube; airhole[obs3], blowhole, breathinghole[obs3], venthole; shaft, flue, chimney, funnel, vent, nostril, nozzle, throat, weasand[obs3], trachea; bronchus, bronchia[Med]; larynx, tonsils, windpipe, spiracle; ventiduct[obs3], ventilator; louvre, jalousie, Venetian blinds; blowpipe &c. (wind) 349; pipe &c. (tube) 260; jhilmil[obs3]; smokestack. screen, window screen. artificial lung, iron lung, heart and lung machine.

% 3. IMPERFECT FLUIDS %

#352. Semiliquidity. — N. semiliquidity; stickiness &c. adj.; viscidity, viscosity; gummosity[obs3], glutinosity[obs3], mucosity[obs3]; spissitude[obs3], crassitude[obs3]; lentor[obs3]; adhesiveness &c. (cohesion) 46. inspissation[obs3], incrassation[obs3]; thickening. jelly, mucilage, gelatin, gluten; carlock[obs3], fish glue; ichthyocol[obs3], ichthycolla[obs3]; isinglass; mucus, phlegm, goo; pituite[obs3], lava; glair[obs3], starch, gluten, albumen, milk, cream, proteinl!; treacle; gum, size, glue (tenacity) 327; wax, beeswax. emulsion, soup; squash, mud, slush, slime, ooze; moisture &c. 339; marsh &c. 345. V. inspissate[obs3], incrassate[obs3]; thicken, mash, squash, churn, beat up. sinter. Adj. semifluid, semiliquid; tremellose[obs3]; half melted, half frozen; milky, muddy &c. n.; lacteal, lactean[obs3], lacteous[obs3], lactescent[obs3], lactiferous[obs3]; emulsive, curdled, thick, succulent, uliginous[obs3]. gelatinous, albuminous, mucilaginous, glutinous; glutenous, gelatin, mastic, amylaceous[obs3], ropy, clammy, clotted; viscid, viscous; sticky, tacky, gooey; slab, slabby[obs3]; lentousl, pituitous[obs3]; mucid[obs3], muculent[obs3], mucous; gummy.

#353. [Mixture of air and water.] Bubble. [Cloud.] — N. bubble, foam, froth, head, spume, lather, suds, spray, surf, yeast, barm[obs3], spindrift. cloud, vapor, fog, mist, haze, steam, geyser; scud, messenger, rack, nimbus; cumulus, woolpack[obs3], cirrus, stratus; cirrostratus, cumulostratus; cirrocumulus; mackerel sky, mare's tale, dirty sky; curl cloud; frost smoke; thunderhead. [Science of clouds] nephelognosy[obs3]; nephograph[obs3], nephology[obs3]. effervescence, fermentation; bubbling &c. v. nebula; cloudliness &c. (opacity) 426[obs3]; nebulosity &c. (dimness) 422. V. bubble, boil, foam, froth, mantle, sparkle, guggle[obs3], gurgle; effervesce, ferment, fizzle. Adj. bubbling &c.

v.; frothy, nappy[obs3], effervescent, sparkling, mousseux[French: frothy], up. cloudy &c. n.; thunderheaded[obs3]; vaporous, nebulous, overcast. Phr. "the lowring element scowls o'er the darkened landscip" [Paradise Lost].

#354. Pulpiness. — N. pulpiness &c. adj.; pulp, taste, dough, curd, pap, rob, jam, pudding, poultice, grume[obs3].
mush, oatmeal, baby food.
Adj. pulpy &c. n.; pultaceous[obs3], grumous[obs3]; baccate[obs3].
#355. Unctuousness. — N. unctuousness &c. adj.; unctuosity[obs3], lubricity; ointment &c. (oil) 356; anointment; lubrication &c. 332.
V. oil &c. (lubricate) 332.
Adj. unctuous, oily, oleaginous, adipose, sebaceous; unguinous[obs3]; fat, fatty, greasy; waxy, butyraceous, soapy, saponaceous[obs3], pinguid, lardaceous[obs3]; slippery.
#356. Oil. — N. oil, fat, butter, cream, grease, tallow, suet, lard, dripping exungel, blubber; glycerin, stearin, elaine[Chem], oleagine[obs3]; soap; soft soap, wax, cerement; paraffin, spermaceti, adipocere[obs3]; petroleum, mineral, mineral rock, mineral crystal, mineral oil; vegetable oil, colza oil[obs3], olive oil, salad oil, linseed oil, cottonseed oil, soybean oil, nut oil; animal oil, neat's foot oil, train oil; ointment, unguent, liniment; aceite[obs3], amole[obs3], Barbados tar[obs3]; fusel oil, grain oil, rape oil, seneca oil; hydrate of amyl, ghee[obs3]; heating oil, "#2 oil", No. 2 oil, distillate, residual oils, kerosene, jet fuel, gasoline, naphtha; stearin.

<— p. 102 —>

#356a. Resin. — N. resin, rosin; gum; lac, sealing wax; amber, ambergris; bitumen, pitch, tar; asphalt, asphaltum; camphor; varnish, copal[obs3], mastic, magilp[obs3], lacquer, japan.
artificial resin, polymer; ion-exchange resin, cation-exchange resin, anion exchange resin, water softener, Amberlite[obs3], Dowex[Chem], Diaion.
V. varnish &c. (overlay) 223.
Adj. resiny[obs3], resinous; bituminous, pitchy, tarry; asphaltic, asphaltite.
% SECTION III. ORGANIC MATTER

1. VITALITY

Vitality in general %

#357. Organization. — N. organized world, organized nature; living nature, animated nature; living beings; organic remains, fossils. protoplasm, cytoplasm, protein; albumen; structure &c. 329; organization, organism. [Science of living beings] biology; natural history, organic chemistry, anatomy, physiology; zoology &c. 368; botany; microbiology, virology, bacteriology, mycology &c. 369; naturalist. archegenesis &c. (production) 161[obs3]; antherozoid[obs3], bioplasm[obs3], biotaxy[obs3], chromosome, dysmeromorph[obs3]; ecology, oecology; erythroblast[Physiol], gametangium[obs3], gamete, germinal matter, invagination[Biol]; isogamy[obs3], oogamy[obs3]; karyaster[obs3]; macrogamete[obs3], microgamete[obs3]; metabolism, anabolism, catabolism; metaplasm[obs3], ontogeny, ovary, ovum, oxidation, phylogeny, polymorphism, protozoa, spermary[obs3], spermatozoon, trophoplasm[obs3], vacuole, vertebration[obs3], zoogloea[obs3], zygote. Darwinism, neo-Darwinism, Lamarkism, neoLamarkism, Weismannism. morphology, taxonomy. Adj. organic, organized; karyoplasmic[obs3], unsegmentic[obs3], vacuolar, zoogloeic[obs3], zoogloeoid[obs3].

#358. Inorganization. — N. mineral world, mineral kingdom; unorganized matter, inorganic matter, brute matter, inanimate matter.
[Science of the mineral kingdom] mineralogy, geology, geognosy[obs3], geoscopy[obs3]; metallurgy, metallography[obs3]; lithology; oryctologyl, oryctographyl.
V. turn to dust; mineralize, fossilize.
Adj. inorganic, inanimate, inorganized[obs3]; lithoidal[obs3]; azoic; mineral.
#359. Life. — N. life, vitality, viability; animation; vital spark, vital flame, soul, spirit.

respiration, wind; breath of life, breath of one's nostrils; oxygen, air.

[devices to sustain respiration] respirator, artificial respirator, heart and lung machine, iron lung; medical devices &c. 662.

lifeblood; Archeus[obs3]; existence &c. 1.

vivification; vital force; vitalization; revivification &c. 163; Prometheus; life to come &c. (destiny) 152.

[Science of life] physiology, biology; animal ecology.

nourishment, staff of life &c. (food) 298.

genetics, heredity, inheritance, evolution, natural selection, reproduction (production) 161.

microbe, aerobe, anaerobe, facultative anaerobe, obligate aerobe, obligate anaerobe, halophile[Microbiol], methanogen[Microbiol], archaebacteria[Microb], microaerophile[Microbiol].

animal &c. 366; vegetable &c. 367.

artificial life, robot, robotics, artificial intelligence.

[vital signs] breathing, breathing rate, heartbeat, pulse, temperature.

preservation of life, healing (medicine) 662.

V. be alive &c. adj.; live, breathe, respire; subsist &c. (exist) 1; walk the earth "strut and fret one's hour upon the stage" [Macbeth]; be spared.

see the light, be born, come into the world, fetch breath, draw breath, fetch the breath of life, draw the breath of life; quicken; revive; come to life.

give birth to &c. (produce) 161; bring to life, put into life, vitalize; vivify, vivificate[obs3]; reanimate &c. (restore) 660; keep alive, keep body and soul together, keep the wolf from the door; support life.

hive nine lives like a cat.

Adj. living, alive; in life, in the flesh, in the land of the living; on this side of the grave, above ground, breathing, quick, animated; animative[obs3]; lively &c. (active) 682; all alive and kicking; tenacious of life; full of life, yeasty.

vital, vitalic[obs3]; vivifying, vivified, &c. v.; viable, zoetic[obs3]; Promethean.

Adv. vivendi causa[Lat].

Phr. atqui vivere militare est [Lat][Seneca]; non est vivere sed valere vita [Lat][Marial].

<— p. 103 —>

#360. Death. — N. death; decease, demise; dissolution, departure, obit, release, rest, quietus, fall; loss, bereavement; mortality, morbidity. end of life &c. 67, cessation of life &c. 142, loss of life, extinction of life, ebb of life &c. 359. death warrant, death watch, death rattle, death bed; stroke of death, agonies of death, shades of death, valley of death, jaws of death, hand of death; last breath, last gasp, last agonies; dying day, dying breath, dying agonies; chant du cygne[Fr]; rigor mortis[Lat]; Stygian shore. King of terrors, King Death; Death; doom &c. (necessity) 601; "Hell's grim Tyrant" [Pope]. euthanasia; break up of the system; natural death, natural decay; sudden death, violent death; untimely end, watery grave; debt of nature; suffocation, asphyxia; fatal disease &c. (disease) 655; death blow &c. (killing) 361. necrology, bills of mortality, obituary; death song &c. (lamentation) 839. V. die, expire, perish; meet one's death, meet one's end; pass away, be taken; yield one's breath, resign one's breath; resign one's being, resign one's life; end one's days, end one's life, end one's earthly career; breathe one's last; cease to live, cease to breathe; depart this life; be no more &c. adj.; go off, drop off, pop off; lose one's life, lay down one's life, relinquish one's life, surrender one's life; drop into the grave, sink into the grave; close one's eyes; fall dead, drop dead, fall down dead, drop down dead; break one's neck; give up the ghost, yield up the ghost; be all over with one. pay the debt to nature, shuffle off this mortal coil, take one's last sleep; go the way of all flesh; hand in one's checks, pass in one's checks, hand in one's chips, pass in one's chips [U.S.]; join the greater number, join the majority; come to dust, turn to dust; cross the Stygian ferry, cross the bar; go to one's long account, go to one's last home, go to Davy Jones's locker, go to the wall; receive one's death warrant, make one's will, step out, die a natural death, go out like the snuff of a candle; come to an untimely end; catch one's death; go off the hooks, kick the bucket, buy the farm, hop the twig, turn up one's toes; die a violent death &c. (be killed) 361. Adj. dead, lifeless; deceased, demised, departed, defunct, extinct; late, gone, no more; exanimate[obs3], inanimate; out of the world, taken off, released; departed this life &c. v.; dead and gone; dead as a doornail, dead as a doorpost[obs3], dead as a mutton, dead as a herring, dead as nits; launched into eternity, gone to one's eternal reward, gone to meet one's maker, pushing up daisies, gathered to one's fathers, numbered with the dead. dying &c. v.; moribund, morientl; hippocratic; in articulo, in extremis; in the jaws of death, in the agony of death; going off; aux abois[Fr]; one one's last legs, on one's death bed; at the point of death, at death's door,, at the last gasp; near one's end, given over, booked; with one foot in the grave, tottering on the brink of the grave. stillborn; mortuary; deadly &c. (killing) 361. Adv. post obit, post mortem[Lat]. Phr. life ebbs, life fails, life hangs by a thread; one's days are numbered, one's hour is come, one's race is run, one's doom is sealed; Death knocks at the door, Death stares one in the face; the breath is out of the body; the grave closes over one; sic itur ad astra [Lat][Vergil]; de mortuis nil nisi bonum[Lat]; dulce et decorum est pro patria mori [Lat][Horace]; honesta mors turpi vita potior [Lat][Tacitus]; "in adamantine chains shall death be bound" [Pope]; mors ultima linea rerum est [Lat][Girace]; ominia mors aequat [Lat][Claudianus]; "Spake the grisly Terror" [Paradise Lost]; "the lone couch of this everlasting sleep" [Shelley]; nothing is certain but death and taxes.

<— p. 104 —>

#361. [Destruction of live; violent death.] Killing. — N. killing &c. v.; homicide, manslaughter, murder, assassination, trucidationl, iccusionl; effusion of blood; blood, blood shed; gore, slaughter, carnage, butchery; battue[obs3]. massacre; fusillade, noyade[obs3]; thuggery, Thuggism[obs3]. deathblow, finishing stroke, coup de grace, quietus; execution &c. (capital punishment) 972; judicial murder; martyrdom. butcher, slayer, murderer, Cain, assassin, terrorist, cutthroat, garroter, bravo, Thug, Moloch, matador, sabreur[obs3]; guet-a-pens; gallows, executioner &c. (punishment) 975; man-eater, apache[obs3], hatchet man [U.S.], highbinder [obs3][U.S.]. regicide, parricide, matricide, fratricide, infanticide, feticide, foeticide[obs3], uxoricide[obs3], vaticide[obs3]. suicide, felo de se[obs3], hara-kiri, suttee, Juggernath[obs3]; immolation, auto da fe, holocaust. suffocation, strangulation, garrote; hanging &c. v.; lapidation[obs3]. deadly weapon &c. (arms) 727; Aceldama[obs3]. [Destruction of animals] slaughtering; phthisozoics[obs3]; sport, sporting; the chase, venery; hunting, coursing, shooting, fishing; pig- sticking; sportsman, huntsman, fisherman; hunter, Nimrod; slaughterhouse, meat packing plant, shambles, abattoir. fatal accident, violent death, casualty. V. kill, put to death, slay, shed blood; murder, assassinate, butcher, slaughter, victimize, immolate; massacre; take away life, deprive of life; make away with, put an end to; despatch, dispatch; burke, settle, do for. strangle, garrote, hang, throttle, choke, stifle, suffocate, stop the breath, smother, asphyxiate, drown. saber; cut down, cut to pieces, cut the throat; jugulate[obs3]; stab, run through the body, bayonet, eviscerate; put to the sword, put to the edge of the sword. shoot dead; blow one's brains out; brain, knock on the head; stone, lapidate[obs3]; give a deathblow; deal a deathblow; give a quietus, give a coupe de grace. behead, bowstring, electrocute, gas &c. (execute) 972. hunt, shoot &c. n. cut off, nip in the bud, launch into eternity, send to one's last account, sign one's death warrant, strike the death knell of. give no quarter, pour out blood like water; decimate; run amuck; wade knee deep in blood, imbrue one's hands in blood. die a violent death, welter in one's blood; dash out one's brains, blow out one's brains; commit suicide; kill oneself, make away with oneself, put an end to oneself, put an end to it all. Adj. killing &c. v.; murderous, slaughterous; sanguinary, sanguinolent[obs3]; blood stained, blood thirsty; homicidal, red handed; bloody, bloody minded; ensanguined[obs3], gory; thuggish. mortal, fatal, lethal; dead, deadly; mortiferousl, lethiferous[obs3]; unhealthy &c. 657; internecine; suicidal. sporting; piscatorial, piscatory[obs3]. Adv. in at the death. Phr. "assassination has never changed the history of the world" [Disraeli].

#362. Corpse. — N. corpse, corse[obs3], carcass, cadaver, bones, skeleton, dry bones; defunct, relics, reliquiae[Lat], remains, mortal remains, dust, ashes, earth, clay; mummy; carrion; food for worms, food for fishes; tenement of clay this mortal coil.
shade, ghost, manes.
organic remains, fossils.
Adj. cadaverous, corpse-like; unburied &c. 363; sapromyiophyllous[obs3].

#363. Interment. — N. interment, burial, sepulture[obs3]; inhumationl; obsequies, exequies[obs3]; funeral, wake, pyre, funeral pile; cremation. funeral, funeral rite, funeral solemnity; kneel, passing bell, tolling; dirge &c. (lamenta- tion) 839; cypress; orbit, dead march, muffled drum; mortuary, undertaker, mute; elegy; funeral, funeral oration, funeral sermon; epitaph. graveclothes[obs3], shroud, winding sheet, cerecloth; cerement. coffin, shell, sarcophagus, urn, pall, bier, hearse, catafalque, cinerary urn[obs3]. grave, pit, sepulcher, tomb, vault, crypt, catacomb, mauso- leum, Golgotha, house of death, narrow house; cemetery, necropolis; burial place, burial ground; grave yard, church yard; God's acre; tope, cromlech, barrow, tumulus, cairn; ossuary; bone house, charnel house, dead house; morgue; lich gate[obs3]; burning ghat[obs3]; crematorium, crematory; dokhma[obs3], mastaba[obs3], potter's field, stupa[obs3], Tower of Silence. sexton, gravedigger. monument, cenotaph, shrine; grave stone, head stone, tomb stone; memento mori[Lat]; hatchment[obs3], stone; obelisk, pyramid. exhumation, disinterment; necropsy, autopsy, post mortem examination[Lat]; zoothapsis[obs3]. V. inter, bury; lay in the grave, consign to the grave, lay in the tomb, entomb, in tomb; inhume; lay out, perform a funeral, embalm, mummify; toll the knell; put to bed with a shovel; inurn[obs3]. exhume, disinter, unearth. Adj. buried &c. v.; burial, funereal, funebrial[obs3]; mortuary, sepulchral, cinerary[obs3]; elegiac; necroscopic[obs3]. Adv. in memoriam; post obit, post mortem[Lat]; beneath the sod. Phr. hic jacet[Lat][obs3], ci-git[Fr]; RIP; requiescat in pace[Lat]; "the lone couch of his everlasting sleep" [Shelley]; "without a grave- unknell'd, uncoffin'd, and unknown" [Byron]; "in the dark union of insensate dust" [Byron]; "the deep cold shadow of the tomb" [Moore].

<— p. 105 —> % Special Vitality %

#364. Animality. — N. animal life; animation, animality[obs3], animalization[obs3]; animalness, corporeal nature, human system; breath.
flesh, flesh and blood; physique; strength &c. 159.
Adj. fleshly, human, corporeal.
#365. Vegetabilityl. — N. vegetable life; vegetation, vegetabilityl; vegetality[obs3].
V. vegetate, grow roots, put down roots.
Adj. rank, lush; vegetable, vegetal, vegetive[obs3].
#366. Animal. — N. animal, animal kingdom; fauna; brute creation. beast, brute, creature, critter [US dialect], wight, created being; creeping thing, living thing; dumb animal, dumb creature; zoophyte. [major divisions of animals] mammal, bird, reptile, amphibian, fish, crustacean, shellfish, mollusk, worm, insect, arthropod, microbe. [microscopic animals] microbe, animalcule &c. 193. [reptiles] alligator, crocodile; saurian; dinosaur [extinct]; snake, serpent, viper, eft; asp, aspick[obs3]. [amphibians] frog, toad. [fishes] trout, bass, tuna, muskelunge, sailfish, sardine, mackerel. [insects] ant, mosquito, bee, honeybee. [arthropods] tardigrade, spider. [classification by number of feet] biped, quadruped. flocks and herds, live stock; domestic animals, wild animals; game, ferae naturae[Lat]; beasts of the field, fowls of the air, denizens of the sea; black game, black grouse; blackcock[obs3], duck, grouse, plover, rail, snipe. [domesticated mammals] horse &c. (beast of burden) 271; cattle, kine[obs3], ox; bull, bullock; cow, milch cow, calf, heifer, shorthorn; sheep; lamb, lambkin[obs3]; ewe, ram, tup; pig, swine, boar, hog, sow; steer, stot[obs3]; tag, teg[obs3]; bison, buffalo, yak, zebu, dog, cat. [dogs] dog, hound; pup, puppy; whelp, cur, mongrel; house dog, watch dog, sheep dog, shepherd's dog, sporting dog, fancy dog, lap dog, toy dog, bull dog, badger dog; mastiff; blood hound, grey hound, stag hound, deer hound, fox hound, otter hound; harrier, beagle, spaniel, pointer, setter, retriever; Newfoundland; water dog, water spaniel; pug, poodle; turnspit; terrier; fox terrier, Skye terrier; Dandie Dinmont; collie. [cats][generally] feline, puss, pussy; grimalkin[obs3]; gib cat, tom cat. [wild mammals] fox, Reynard, vixen, stag, deer, hart, buck, doe, roe; caribou, coyote, elk, moose, musk ox, sambar[obs3]. bird; poultry, fowl, cock, hen, chicken, chanticleer, partlet[obs3], rooster, dunghill cock, barn door fowl; feathered tribes, feathered songster; singing bird, dicky bird; canary, warbler; finch; aberdevine[obs3], cushat[obs3], cygnet, ringdove[obs3], siskin, swan, wood pigeon. [undesirable animals] vermin, varmint[Western US], pest. Adj. animal, zoological equine, bovine, vaccine, canine, feline, fishy; piscatory[obs3], piscatorial; molluscous[obs3], vermicular; gallinaceous, rasorial[obs3], solidungulate[obs3], soliped[obs3].

#367. Vegetable. — N. vegetable, vegetable kingdom; flora, verdure. plant; tree, shrub, bush; creeper; herb, herbage; grass. annual; perennial, biennial, triennial; exotic. timber, forest; wood, woodlands; timberland; hurst[obs3], frith[obs3], holt, weald[obs3], park, chase, greenwood, brake, grove, copse, coppice, bocage[obs3], tope, clump of trees, thicket, spinet, spinney; underwood, brushwood; scrub; boscage, bosk[obs3], ceja[Sp], chaparral, motte [obs3][U.S.].; arboretum &c. 371. bush, jungle, prairie; heath, heather; fern, bracken; furze, gorse, whin; grass, turf; pasture, pasturage; turbary[obs3]; sedge, rush, weed; fungus, mushroom, toadstool; lichen, moss, conferva[obs3], mold; growth; alfalfa, alfilaria[obs3], banyan; blow, blowth[obs3]; floret[obs3], petiole; pin grass, timothy, yam, yew, zinnia. foliage, branch, bough, ramage[obs3], stem, tigella[obs3]; spray &c. 51; leaf. flower, blossom, bine[obs3]; flowering plant; timber tree, fruit tree; pulse, legume. Adj. vegetable, vegetal, vegetive[obs3], vegitousl; herbaceous, herbal; botanic[obs3]; sylvan, silvan[obs3]; arborary[obs3], arboreous[obs3], arborescent[obs3], arboricall; woody, grassy; verdant, verdurous; floral, mossy; lignous[obs3], ligneous; wooden, leguminous; vosky[obs3], cespitose[obs3], turf-like, turfy; endogenous, exogenous. Phr. "green-robed senators of mighty woods" [Keats]; "this is the forest primeval" [Longfellow].

<— p. 106 —>

#368. [The science of animals.] Zoology. — N. zoology, zoonomy[obs3], zoography[obs3], zootomy[obs3]; anatomy; comparative anatomy; animal physiology, comparative physiology; morphology; mammalogy. anthropology, ornithology, ichthyology, herpetology, ophiology[obs3], malacology[obs3], helminthology[Med], entomology, oryctology[obs3], paleontology, mastology[obs3], vermeology[obs3]; ichthy &c. ichthyotomy[obs3]; taxidermy. zoologist &c. Adj. zoological &c. n.

#369. [The science of plants.] Botany. — N. botany; physiological botany, structural botany, systematic botany; phytography[obs3], phytology[obs3], phytotomy[obs3]; vegetable physiology, herborization[obs3], dendrology, mycology, fungology[obs3], algology[obs3]; flora, romona; botanic garden &c. (garden) 371[obs3]; hortus siccus[Lat], herbarium, herbal. botanist &c.; herbist[obs3], herbarist[obs3], herbalist, herborist[obs3], herbarian[obs3]. V. botanize, herborize[obs3]. Adj. botanical &c. n.; botanic[obs3].

#370. [The economy or management of animals.] Husbandry. — N. husbandry, taming &c. v.; circuration[obs3], zoohygiantics[obs3]; domestication, domesticity; manege[Fr], veterinary art; farriery[obs3]; breeding, pisciculture. menagerie, vivarium, zoological garden; bear pit; aviary, apiary, alveary[obs3], beehive; hive; aquarium, fishery; duck pond, fish pond. phthisozoics &c. (killing) 361[obs3][Destruction of animals]; euthanasia, sacrifice, humane destruction. neatherd[obs3], cowherd, shepherd; grazier, drover, cowkeeper[obs3]; trainer, breeder; apiarian[obs3], apiarist; bull whacker [U.S.], cowboy, cow puncher [U.S.], farrier; horse leech, horse doctor; vaquero, veterinarian, vet, veterinary surgeon. cage &c. (prison) 752; hencoop[obs3], bird cage, cauf[obs3]; range, sheepfold, &c. (inclosure) 232. V. tame, domesticate, acclimatize, breed, tend, break in, train; cage, bridle, &c. (restrain) 751. Adj. pastoral, bucolic; tame, domestic.

#371. [The economy or management of plants.] Agriculture. — N. agriculture, cultivation, husbandry, farming; georgics, geoponics[obs3]; tillage, agronomy, gardening, spade husbandry, vintage; horticulture, arboriculture[obs3], floriculture; landscape gardening; viticulture. husbandman, horticulturist, gardener, florist; agricultor[obs3], agriculturist; yeoman, farmer, cultivator, tiller of the soil, woodcutter, backwoodsman; granger, habitat, vigneron[obs3], viticulturist; Triptolemus. field, meadow, garden; botanic garden[obs3], winter garden, ornamental garden, flower garden, kitchen garden, market garden, hop garden; nursery; green house, hot house; conservatory, bed, border, seed plot; grassplot[obs3], grassplat[obs3], lawn; park &c. (pleasure ground) 840; parterre, shrubbery, plantation, avenue, arboretum, pinery[obs3], pinetum[obs3], orchard; vineyard, vinery; orangery[obs3]; farm &c. (abode) 189. V. cultivate; till the soil; farm, garden; sow, plant; reap, mow, cut; manure, dress the ground, dig, delve, dibble, hoe, plough, plow, harrow, rake, weed, lop and top; backset [obs3][U.S.]. Adj. agricultural, agrarian, agrestic[obs3]. arable, predial[obs3], rural, rustic, country; horticultural.

#372. Mankind. — N. man, mankind; human race, human species, human kind, human nature; humanity, mortality, flesh, generation. [Science of man] anthropology, anthropogeny[obs3], anthropography[obs3], anthroposophy[obs3]; ethnology, ethnography; humanitarian. human being; person, personage; individual, creature, fellow creature, mortal, body, somebody; one; such a one, some one; soul, living soul; earthling; party, head, hand; dramatis personae[Lat]; quidam[Lat]. people, persons, folk, public, society, world; community, community at large; general public; nation, nationality; state, realm; commonweal, commonwealth; republic, body politic; million &c. (commonalty) 876; population &c. (inhabitant) 188. tribe, clan (paternity) 166; family (consanguinity) 11. cosmopolite; lords of the creation; ourselves. Adj. human, mortal, personal, individual, national, civic, public, social; cosmopolitan; anthropoid. Phr. "am I not a man and a brother?" [Wedgwood].

<— p. 107 —>

#373. Man. — N. man, male, he, him; manhood &c. (adolescence) 131; gentleman, sir, master; sahib; yeoman, wightl!, swain, fellow, blade, beau, elf, chap, gaffer, good man; husband &c. (married man) 903; Mr., mister; boy &c. (youth) 129.
[Male animal] cock, drake, gander, dog, boar, stag, hart, buck, horse, entire horse, stallion; gibcat[obs3], tomcat; he goat, Billy goat; ram, tup; bull, bullock; capon, ox, gelding, steer, stot[obs3].
androgen.
homosexual, gay, queen[slang].
V. masculinize

Adj. male, he-, masculine; manly, virile; unwomanly, unfeminine.

Pron. he, him, his.

Phr. hominem pagina nostra sapit [Lat][Mar.]; homo homini aut deus aut lupus [Lat][Erasmus]; homo vitae commodatus non donatus est [Lat][Syrus].

#374. Woman. — N. woman, she, her, female, petticoat.

feminality[obs3], muliebrity[obs3]; womanhood &c. (adolescence) 131.

womankind; the sex, the fair; fair sex, softer sex; weaker vessel.

dame, madam, madame, mistress, Mrs. lady, donna belle[Sp], matron, dowager, goody, gammer[obs3]; Frau[Ger], frow[obs3], Vrouw[Dutch], rani; good woman, good wife; squaw; wife &c. (marriage) 903; matronage, matronhood[obs3].

bachelor girl, new woman, feminist, suffragette, suffragist.

nymph, wench, grisette[obs3]; girl &c. (youth) 129.

[Effeminacy] sissy, betty, cot betty [U.S.], cotquean[obs3], henhussy[obs3], mollycoddle, muff, old woman.

[Female animal] hen, bitch, sow, doe, roe, mare; she goat, Nanny goat, tabita; ewe, cow; lioness, tigress; vixen.

gynecaeum[obs3].

estrogen, oestrogen.

consanguinity &c. 166[female relatives], paternity &c. 11.

lesbian, dyke[slang].

V. feminize.

Adj. female, she-; feminine, womanly, ladylike, matronly, maidenly, wifely; womanish, effeminate, unmanly; gynecic[obs3], gynaecic[obs3].

Pron. she, her, hers.

Phr. "a perfect woman nobly planned" [Wordsworth]; "a lovely lady garmented in white" [Shelley]; das Ewig-Weibliche zieht uns hinan [Ger][Goethe]; "earth's noblest thing, a woman perfected" [Lowell]; es de vidrio la mujer[Sp]; "she moves a goddess and she looks a queen" [Pope]; "the beauty of a lovely woman is like music" [G. Eliot]; varium et mutabile semper femina [Lat][Vergil]; "woman is the lesser man" [Tennyson].

#374a. Sexuality [human] — N. sex, sexuality, gender; male, masculinity, maleness &c. 373; female, femininity &c. 374.

sexual intercourse, copulation, mating, coitus, sex; lovemaking, marital relations, sexual union; sleeping together, carnal knowledge.

sex instinct, sex drive, libido, lust, concupiscence; hots, horns [coll]; arousal, heat, rut, estrus, oestrus; tumescence; erection, hard-on, boner.

masturbation, self-gratification, autoeroticism, onanism, self-abuse.

orgasm, climax, ejaculation.

sexiness, attractiveness; sensuality, voluptuousness.

[sexual intercourse outside of marriage] fornication, adultery.

[person who is sexy] sex symbol, sex goddess; stud, hunk.

one-night stand.

pornography, porn, porno; hardcore pornography, softcore pornography; pin-up, cheesecake; beefcake; Playboy[magazines with sexual photos], Esquire, Hustler.

[unorthodox sexual activity] perversion, deviation, sexual abnormality; fetish, fetishism; homosexuality, lesbianism, bisexuality; sodomy, buggery; pederasty; sadism, masochism, sado-masochism; incest.

V. mate, copulate; make love, have intercourse, fornicate, have sex, do it, sleep together, fuck[vulg.]; sleep around, play the field..

masturbate, jerk off[coll.], jack off[coll.], play with oneself.

have the hots[coll]; become aroused, get hot; have an erection, get it up.

come, climax, ejaculate.

Adj. sexy, erotic, sexual, carnal, sensual.

hot, horny, randy, rutting; passionate, lusty, hot-blooded, libidinous; up, in the mood.

homosexual, gay, lesbian, bisexual.

% 2. SENSATION Sensation in general %

#375. Physical Sensibility. — N. sensibility; sensitiveness &c. adj.; physical sensibility, feeling, impressibility, perceptivity, aesthetics; moral sensibility &c. 822.

sensation, impression; consciousness &c. (knowledge) 490.

external senses.

V. be sensible of &c. adj.; feel, perceive.

render sensible &c. adj.; sharpen, cultivate, tutor.

cause sensation, impress; excite an impression, produce an impression.

Adj. sensible, sensitive, sensuous; aesthetic, perceptive, sentient; conscious &c. (aware) 490.

acute, sharp, keen, vivid, lively, impressive, thin-skinned.

Adv. to the quick.

Phr. "the touch'd needle trembles to the pole" [Pope].

#376. Physical Insensibility. — N. insensibility, physical insensibility; obtuseness &c. adj.; palsy, paralysis, paraesthesia[Med], anaesthesia; sleep &c. 823; hemiplegia[obs3], motor paralysis; vegetable state; coma. anaesthetic agent, opium, ether, chloroform, chloral; nitrous oxide, laughing gas; exhilarating gas, protoxide of nitrogen[ISA:chemsubcfs]; refrigeration. V. be insensible &c. adj.; have a thick skin, have a rhinoceros hide. render insensible &c. adj.; anaesthetize[obs3], blunt, pall, obtund[obs3], benumb, paralyze; put under the influence of chloroform &c. n.; stupefy, stun. Adj. insensible, unfeeling, senseless, impercipient[obs3], callous, thick-skinned, pachydermatous; hard, hardened; case hardened; proof, obtuse, dull; anaesthetic; comatose, paralytic, palsied, numb, dead.

<— p. 108 —>

#377. Physical Pleasure. — N. pleasure; physical pleasure, sensual pleasure, sensuous pleasure; bodily enjoyment, animal gratification, hedonism, sensuality; luxuriousness &c. adj.; dissipation, round of pleasure, titillation, gusto, creature comforts, comfort, ease; pillow &c. (support) 215; luxury, lap of luxury; purple and fine linen; bed of downs, bed of roses; velvet, clover; cup of Circe &c. (intemperance) 954. treat; refreshment, regale; feast; delice[Fr]; dainty &c. 394; bonne bouche[Fr]. source of pleasure &c. 829; happiness &c. (mental enjoyment) 827. V. feel pleasure, experience pleasure, receive pleasure; enjoy, relish; luxuriate in, revel in, riot in, bask in, swim in, drink up, eat up, wallow in; feast on; gloat over, float on; smack the lips. live on the fat of the land, live in comfort &c. adv.; bask in the sunshine, faire ses choux gras[Fr].. give pleasure &c. 829. Adj. enjoying &c. v.; luxurious, voluptuous, sensual, comfortable, cosy, snug, in comfort, at ease. pleasant, agreeable &c. 829. Adv. in comfort &c. n.; on a bed of roses &c. n.; at one's ease. Phr. ride si sapis [Lat][Martial]; voluptales commendat rarior usus [Lat][Juvenal].

#378. Physical Pain. — N. pain; suffering, sufferance, suffrance[obs3]; bodily pain, physical pain, bodily suffering, physical suffering, body pain; mental suffering &c. 828; dolour, ache; aching &c. v.; smart; shoot, shooting; twinge, twitch, gripe, headache, stomach ache, heartburn, angina, angina pectoris[Lat]; hurt, cut; sore, soreness; discomfort, malaise; cephalalgia[Med], earache, gout, ischiagra[obs3], lumbago, neuralgia, odontalgia[obs3], otalgia[obs3], podagra[obs3], rheumatism, sciatica; tic douloureux[Fr], toothache, tormina[obs3], torticollis[obs3]. spasm, cramp; nightmare, ephialtes[obs3]; crick, stitch; thrill, convulsion, throe; throb &c. (agitation) 315; pang; colic; kink. sharp pain, piercing pain, throbbing pain, shooting pain, sting, gnawing pain, burning pain; excruciating pain. anguish, agony; torment, torture; rack; cruciation[obs3], crucifixion; martyrdom, toad under a harrow, vivisection. V. feel pain, experience pain, suffer pain, undergo pain &c. n.; suffer, ache, smart, bleed; tingle, shoot; twinge, twitch, lancinate[obs3]; writhe, wince, make a wry face; sit on thorns, sit on pins and needles. give pain, inflict pain; lacerate; pain, hurt, chafe, sting, bite, gnaw, gripe; pinch, tweak; grate, gall, fret, prick, pierce, wring, convulse; torment, torture; rack, agonize; crucify; cruciate[obs3], excruciatel; break on the wheel, put to the rack; flog &c. (punish) 972; grate on the ear &c. (harsh sound) 410. Adj. in pain &c. n., in a state of pain; pained &c. v.; gouty, podagric[obs3], torminous[obs3]. painful; aching &c. v.; sore, raw.

% Special Sensation (1) Touch %

#379. [Sensation of pressure] Touch. — N. touch; tact, taction[obs3], tactility; feeling; palpation, palpability;

contrectation[obs3]; manipulation; massage. [Organ of touch] hand, finger, forefinger, thumb, paw, feeler, antenna; palpus[obs3]. V. touch, feel, handle, finger, thumb, paw, fumble, grope, grabble; twiddle, tweedle; pass the fingers over, run the fingers over; manipulate, wield; throw out a feeler. Adj. tactual, tactile; tangible, palpable; lambent.

<— p. 109 —>

#380. Sensations of Touch. — N. itching, pruritis &c. v[Med].; titillation, formication[obs3], aura; stereognosis[obs3].

V. itch, tingle, creep, thrill, sting; prick, prickle; tickle, titillate.

Adj. itching &c. v.; stereognostic[obs3], titillative.

#381. [insensibility to touch.] Numbness. — N. numbness &c. (physical insensibility) 376; anaesthesia; pins and needles.

V. benumb &c. 376.

Adj. numb; benumbed &c. v.; deadened; intangible, impalpable.

% (2) Heat %

#382. Heat. — N. heat, caloric; temperature, warmth, fervor, calidity[obs3]; incalescence[obs3], incandescence; glow, flush; fever, hectic. phlogiston; fire, spark, scintillation, flash, flame, blaze; bonfire; firework, pyrotechnics, pyrotechny[obs3]; wildfire; sheet of fire, lambent flame; devouring element; adiathermancy[obs3]; recalescence[Phys]. summer, dog days; canicular days[obs3]; baking &c. 384 heat, white heat, tropical heat, Afric heat[obs3], Bengal heat[obs3], summer heat, blood heat; sirocco, simoom; broiling sun; insolation; warming &c. 384. sun &c. (luminary) 423. [Science of heat] pyrology[obs3]; thermology[obs3], thermotics[obs3], thermodynamics; thermometer &c. 389. [thermal units] calorie, gram-calorie, small calorie; kilocalorie, kilogram calorie, large calorie; British Thermal Unit, B.T.U.; therm, quad. [units of temperature] degrees Kelvin, kelvins, degrees centigrade, degrees Celsius; degrees Fahrenheit. V. be hot &c. adj.; glow, flush, sweat, swelter, bask, smoke, reek, stew, simmer, seethe, boil, burn, blister, broil, blaze, flame; smolder, parch, fume, pant. heat &c. (make hot) 384; recalesce[obs3]; thaw, give. Adj. hot, warm, mild, genial, tepid, lukewarm, unfrozen; thermal, thermic; calorific; fervent, fervid; ardent; aglow. sunny, torrid, tropical, estivall!, canicular[obs3], steamy; close, sultry, stifling, stuffy, suffocating, oppressive; reeking &c. v.; baking &c. 384. red hot, white hot, smoking hot, burning &c. v. hot, piping hot; like a furnace, like an oven; burning, hot as fire, hot as pepper; hot enough to roast an ox, hot enough to boil an egg. fiery; incandescent, incalescent[obs3]; candent[obs3], ebullient, glowing, smoking; live; on fire; dazzling &c. v.; in flames, blazing, in a blaze; alight, afire, ablaze; unquenched, unextinguished[obs3]; smoldering; in a heat, in a glow, in a fever, in a perspiration, in a sweat; sudorific[obs3]; sweltering, sweltered; blood hot, blood warm; warm as a toast, warm as wool. volcanic, plutonic, igneous; isothermall!, isothermicl!, isotherall!. Phr. not a breath of air; "whirlwinds of tempestuous fire" [Paradise Lost].

#383. Cold. — N. cold, coldness &c. adj.; frigidity, inclemency, fresco. winter; depth of winter, hard winter; Siberia, Nova Zembla; wind-chill factor. [forms of frozen water] ice; snow, snowflake, snow crystal, snow drift; sleet; hail, hailstone; rime, frost; hoar frost, white frost, hard frost, sharp frost; barf; glaze [U. S.], lolly [obs3][N. Am.]; icicle, thick-ribbed ice; fall of snow, heavy fall; iceberg, icefloe; floe berg; glacier; neve, serac[obs3]; pruina[obs3]. [cold substances] freezing mixture, dry ice, liquid nitrogen, liquid helium. [Sensation of cold] chilliness &c. adj.; chill; shivering &c. v.; goose skin, horripilation[obs3]; rigor; chattering of teeth; numbness, frostbite. V. be cold &c. adj[intrans.].; shiver, starve, quake, shake, tremble, shudder, didder[obs3], quiver; freeze, freeze to death, perish with cold. [transitive] chill, freeze &c. (render cold) 385; horripilate[obs3], make the skin crawl, give one goose flesh. Adj. cold, cool; chill, chilly, icy; gelid, frigid, algid[obs3]; fresh, keen, bleak, raw, inclement, bitter, biting, niveous[obs3], cutting, nipping, piercing, pinching; clay-cold; starved &c. (made cold) 385; chilled to the bone, shivering &c. v.; aguish, transi de froid[Fr]; frostbitten, frost-bound, frost-nipped. cold as a stone, cold as marble, cold as lead, cold as iron, cold as a frog, cold as charity, cold as Christmas; cool as a cucumber, cool as custard. icy, glacial, frosty, freezing, pruinose[obs3], wintry, brumal[obs3], hibernal[obs3], boreal, arctic, Siberian, hyemal[obs3]; hyperborean, hyperboreal[obs3]; icebound; frozen out. unwarmed[obs3], unthawed[obs3]; lukewarm, tepid; isocheimal[obs3], isocheimenal[obs3], isocheimic[obs3]. frozen, numb, frost-bitten. Adv. coldly, bitterly &c. adj.; pierre fendre[Fr];

<— p. 110 —>

#384. Calefaction. — N. increase of temperature; heating &c. v.; calefaction[obs3], tepefaction[obs3], torrefaction[obs3]; melting, fusion; liquefaction &c. 335; burning &c. v.; ambustion[obs3], combustion; incensionl, accension[obs3]; concremation[obs3], cremation; scorification[obs3]; cautery, cauterization; ustulation[obs3], calcination; cracking, refining; incineration, cineration[obs3]; carbonization; cupellation[Chem]. ignition, inflammation, adustion[obs3], flagrationl [obs3]; deflagration, conflagration; empyrosis[obs3], incendiarism; arson; auto dafe[Fr]. boiling &c. v.; coction[obs3], ebullition, estuation[obs3], elixationl, decoction; ebullioscope[obs3]; geyser; distillation (vaporization) 336. furnace &c. 386; blanket, flannel, fur; wadding &c. (lining) 224; clothing &c. 225. still; refinery; fractionating column, fractionating tower, cracking tower. match &c. (fuel) 388; incendiary; petroleuse[Fr]; [biological effects resembling the effects of heat][substances causing a burning sensation and damage on skin or tissue] cauterizer[obs3]; caustic, lunar caustic, alkali, apozem[obs3], moxa[obs3]; acid, aqua fortis[Lat], aqua regia; catheretic[obs3], nitric acid, nitrochloro-hydric acid[ISA:CHEMSUB], nitromuriatic acid[ISA:CHEMSUBPREFIX]; radioactivity, gamma rays, alpha particles, beta rays, X-rays, radiation, cosmic radiation, background radiation, radio-active isotopes, tritium, uranium, plutonium, radon, radium. sunstroke, coup de soleil[Fr]; insolation. [artifacts requiring heat in their manufacture] pottery, ceramics, crockery, porcelain, china; earthenware, stoneware; pot, mug, terra cotta[Sp], brick, clinker. [products of combustion] cinder, ash, scoriae, embers, soot; slag. [products of heating organic materials] coke, carbon, charcoal; wood alcohol, turpentine, tea tree oil; gasoline, kerosene, naptha[ISA:CHEMSUB], fuel oil (fuel) 388; wax, paraffin; residue, tar. inflammability, combustibility. [Transmission of heat] diathermancy[obs3], transcalency[obs3], conduction; convection; radiation, radiant heat; heat conductivity, conductivity. [effects of heat 2.] thermal expansion; coefficient of expansion. V. heat, warm, chafe, stive[obs3], foment; make hot &c. 382; sun oneself, sunbathe. go up in flames, burn to the ground (flame) 382. fire; set fire to, set on fire; kindle, enkindle, light, ignite, strike a light; apply the match to, apply the torch to; rekindle, relume[obs3]; fan the flame, add fuel to the flame; poke the fire, stir the fire, blow the fire; make a bonfire of. melt, thaw, fuse; liquefy &c. 335. burn, inflame, roast, toast, fry, grill, singe, parch, bake, torrefy[obs3], scorch; brand, cauterize, sear, burn in; corrode, char, calcine, incinerate; smelt, scorify[obs3]; reduce to ashes; burn to a cinder; commit to the flames, consign to the flames. boil, digest, stew, cook, seethe, scald, parboil, simmer; do to rags. take fire, catch fire; blaze &c. (flame) 382. Adj. heated &c. v.; molten, sodden; rchauff; heating &c. v.; adust[obs3]. inflammable, combustible; diathermal[obs3], diathermanous[obs3]; burnt &c. v.; volcanic, radioactive.

#385. Refrigeration. — N. refrigeration, infrigidation[obs3], reduction of temperature; cooling &c. v.; congelation[obs3], conglaciationl [obs3]; ice &c. 383; solidification &c. (density) 321; ice box (refrigerator) 385.. extincteur[Fr]; fire annihilator; amianth[obs3], amianthus[obs3]; earth-flax, mountain-flax; flexible asbestos; fireman, fire brigade (incombustibility) 388a. incombustibility, incombustibleness &c. adj[obs3]. (insulation) 388a. air conditioning[residential cooling], central air conditioning; air conditioner; fan, attic fan; dehumidifier. V. cool, fan, refrigerate, refresh, ice; congeal, freeze, glaciate; benumb, starve, pinch, chill, petrify, chill to the marrow, regelate[obs3], nip, cut, pierce, bite, make one's teeth chatter, damp, slack quench; put out, stamp out; extinguish; go out, burn out (incombustibility) 388a.. Adj. cooled &c. v.; frozen out; cooling &c. v.; frigorific[obs3].

#386. Furnace. — N. furnace, stove, kiln, oven; cracker; hearth, focus, combustion chamber; athanor[obs3], hypocaust[obs3], reverberatory; volcano; forge, fiery furnace; limekiln; Dutch oven; tuyere, brasier[obs3], salaman-der, heater, warming pan; boiler, caldron, seething caldron, pot; urn, kettle; chafing-dish; retort, crucible, alembic, still; waffle irons; muffle furnace, induction furnace; electric heater, electric furnace, electric resistance heat. [steel-making furnace] open-hearth furnace. fireplace, gas fireplace; coal fire, wood fire; fire-dog, fire-irons; grate, range, kitchener; caboose, camboose[obs3]; poker, tongs, shovel, ashpan, hob, trivet; andiron, gridiron; ashdrop; frying-pan, stew-pan, backlog. [area near a fireplace] hearth, inglenook. [residential heating methods] oil burner, gas burner, Franklin stove, pot-bellied stove; wood-burning stove; central heating, steam heat, hot water heat, gas heat, forced hot air, electric heat, heat pump; solar heat, convective heat. hothouse, bakehouse[obs3], washhouse[obs3]; laundry; conservatory; sudatory[obs3]; Turkish bath, Russian bath, vapor bath, steam bath, sauna, warm bath; vaporarium[obs3].

#387. Refrigerator. — N. refrigerator, refrigeratory[obs3]; frigidarium[obs3]; cold storage, cold room, cold laboratory; icehouse, icepail, icebag, icebox; cooler, damper, polyurethane cooler; wine cooler. freezer, deep freeze, dry ice freezer, liquid nitrogen freezer, refigerator-freezer. freezing mixture[refrigerating substances], ice, ice cubes, blocks of ice, chipped ice; liquid nitrogen, dry ice, dry ice-acetone, liquid helium.

#388. Fuel. — N. fuel, firing, combustible. [solid fuels] coal, wallsend[obs3], anthracite, culm[obs3], coke, carbon, charcoal, bituminous coal, tar shale; turf, peat, firewood, bobbing, faggot, log; cinder &c. (products of combustion) 384; ingle, tinder, touchwood; sulphur, brimstone; incense; port-fire; fire-barrel, fireball, brand; amadou[obs3], bavin[obs3]; blind coal, glance coal; German tinder, pyrotechnic sponge, punk, smudge [U. S.]; solid fueled rocket. [fuels for candles and lamps] wax, paraffin wax, paraffin oil; lamp oil, whale oil. [liquid fuels] oil, petroleum, gasoline, high octane gasoline, nitromethane[ISA:CHEMSUB@fuel], petrol, gas, juice [coll.], gasohol, alcohol, ethanol, methanol, fuel oil, kerosene, jet fuel, heating oil, number 2 oil, number 4 oil, naphtha; rocket fuel, high specific impulse fuel, liquid hydrogen, liquid oxygen, lox. [gaseous fuels] natural gas, synthetic gas, synthesis gas, propane, butane, hydrogen. brand, torch, fuse; wick; spill, match, light, lucifer, congreve[obs3], vesuvian, vesta[obs3], fusee, locofoco[obs3]; linstock[obs3]. candle &c. (luminary) 423; oil &c. (grease) 356. Adj. carbonaceous; combustible, inflammable; high octane, high specific impulse; heat of combustion,.

#388a. Insulation, Fire extinction. {ant. of 388} — insulation, incombustible material, noncombustible material; fire retardant, flame retardant; fire wall, fire door.

incombustibility, incombustibleness &c. adj.

extincteur[Fr]; fire annihilator; amianth[obs3], amianthus[obs3]; earth-flax, mountain-flax; asbestos; fireman, fire fighter, fire eater, fire department, fire brigade, engine company; pumper, fire truck, hook and ladder, aerial ladder, bucket; fire hose, fire hydrant.

[forest fires] backfire, firebreak, trench; aerial water bombardment.

wet blanket; fire extinguisher, soda and acid extinguisher, dry chemical extinguisher, CO-two extinguisher, carbon tetrachloride, foam; sprinklers, automatic sprinkler system; fire bucket, sand bucket.

[warning of fire] fire alarm, evacuation alarm,

[laws to prevent fire] fire code, fire regulations, fire; fire inspector; code violation, citation.

V. go out, die out, burn out; fizzle.

extinguish; damp, slack, quench, smother; put out, stamp out; douse, snuff, snuff out, blow out.

fireproof, flameproof.

Adj. incombustible; nonflammable, uninflammable, unflammable[obs3]; fireproof.

Phr. fight fire with fire

<— p. 111 —>

#389. Thermometer. — N. thermometer, thermometrograph[obs3], mercury thermometer, alcohol thermometer, clinical thermometer, dry-bulb thermometer, wet-bulb thermometer, Anschutz thermometer[Ger], gas thermometer, telethermometer; color-changing temperature indicator; thermopile, thermoscope[obs3]; pyrometer, calorimeter, bomb calorimeter; thermistor, thermocouple. [temperature-control devices] thermostat, thermoregulator.

% (3) Taste %

#390. Taste. — N. taste, flavor, gust, gusto, savor; gout, relish; saporl, sapidity[obs3]; twang, smack, smatchl [obs3]; aftertaste, tang.

tasting; degustation, gustation.

palate, tongue, tooth, stomach.

V. taste, savor, smatch[obs3], smack, flavor, twang; tickle the palate &c. (savory) 394; smack the lips.

Adj. sapid, saporific[obs3]; gustablel, gustatory; gustful[obs3]; strong, gamy; palatable &c. 394.

#391. Insipidity. — N. insipidity, blandness; tastelessness &c. adj.

V. be tasteless &c. adj.

Adj. bland, void of taste &c. 390; insipid; tasteless, gustlessl, savorless; ingustiblel, mawkish, milk and water, weak, stale, flat, vapid, fade, wishy-washy, mild; untasted[obs3].

#392. Pungency. — N. pungency, piquance, piquancy, poignancy haut- gout, strong taste, twang, race. sharpness &c. adj.; acrimony; roughness &c. (sour) 392; unsavoriness &c. 395. mustard, cayenne, caviare; seasoning &c. (condiment) 393; niter, saltpeter, brine (saltiness) 392a; carbonate of ammonia; sal ammoniac[obs3], sal volatile, smelling salts; hartshorn (acridity) 401a. dram, cordial, nip. nicotine, tobacco, snuff, quid, smoke; segar[obs3]; cigar, cigarette; weed; fragrant weed, Indian weed; Cavendish, fid[obs3], negro head, old soldier, rappee[obs3], stogy[obs3]. V. be pungent &c. adj.; bite the tongue. render -pungent &c. adj.; season, spice, salt, pepper, pickle, brine, devil. smoke, chew, take snuff. Adj. pungent, strong; high-, full-flavored; high-tasted, high- seasoned; gamy, sharp, stinging, rough, piquant, racy; biting, mordant; spicy; seasoned &c. v.; hot, hot as pepper; peppery, vellicating[obs3], escharotic[obs3], meracious|; acrid, acrimonious, bitter; rough &c. (sour) 397; unsavory &c. 395.

#392a. Saltiness. — N. saltiness.

niter, saltpeter, brine.

Adj. salty, salt, saline, brackish, briny; salty as brine, salty as a herring, salty as Lot's wife.

salty, racy (indecent) 961.

Phr. take it with a grain of salt.

#392b. Bitterness — N. bitterness, acridness[obs3], acridity, acrimony; caustic, alkali; acerbity; gall, wormwood; bitters, astringent bitters.

[additive for alcoholic beverages]Angostura aromatic bitters.

sourness &c. 397; pungency &c. 392.

[bitter substances] alkaloids; turmeric.

Adj. bitter, bitterish, acrid, acerb, acerbic.

Phr. bitter as gall; bitter pill to take; sugar coating on a bitter pill.

#393. Condiment. — N. condiment, seasoning, sauce, spice, relish, appetizer.

[exlist] salt; mustard, grey poupon mustard; pepper, black pepper, white pepper, peppercorn, curry, sauce piquante[Fr]; caviare, onion, garlic, pickle; achar[obs3], allspice; bell pepper, Jamaica pepper, green pepper; chutney; cubeb[obs3], pimento.

[capsicum peppers] capsicum, red pepper, chili peppers, cayenne.

nutmeg, mace, cinnamon, oregano, cloves, fennel.

[herbs] pot herbs, parsley, sage, rosemary, thyme, bay leaves, marjoram.

[fragrant woods and gums] frankincense, balm, myrrh.

[from pods] paprika.

[from flower stigmas] saffron.

[from roots] ginger, turmeric.

V. season, spice, flavor, spice up &c. (render pungent) 392.

#394. Savoriness. — N. savoriness &c. adj.; good taste, deliciousness, delectability.

relish, zest; appetizer.

tidbit, titbit[obs3], dainty, delicacy, tasty morsel; appetizer, hors d'ouvres[Fr.]; ambrosia, nectar, bonne-bouche[Fr]; game, turtle, venison; delicatessen.

V. be savory &c. adj.; tickle the palate, tickle the appetite; flatter the palate.

render palatable &c. adj.

relish, like, smack the lips.

Adj. savory, delicious, tasty, well-tasted, to one's taste, good, palatable, nice, dainty, delectable; toothful[obs3], toothsome; gustful[obs3], appetizing, lickerish[obs3], delicate, exquisite, rich, luscious, ambrosial, scrumptious, delightful.

Adv. per amusare la bocca

Phr[It]. cela se laisse manger[Fr].

<— p. 112 —>

#395. Unsavoriness. — N. unsavoriness &c. adj.; amaritude[obs3]; acrimony, acridity (bitterness) 392b; roughness &c. (sour) 397; acerbity, austerity; gall and wormwood, rue, quassia[obs3], aloes; marah[obs3]; sickener[obs3]. V. be unpalatable &c. adj.; sicken, disgust, nauseate, pall, turn the stomach. Adj. unsavory, unpalatable, unsweetened, unsweet[obs3]; ill-flavored; bitter, bitter as gall; acrid, acrimonious; rough. offensive, repulsive, nasty; sickening &c. v.; nauseous; loathsome, fulsome; unpleasant &c. 830.

#396. Sweetness. — N. sweetness, dulcitude[obs3].

sugar, syrup, treacle, molasses, honey, manna; confection,

confectionary; sweets, grocery, conserve, preserve, confiture[obs3], jam, julep; sugar-candy, sugar-plum; licorice, marmalade, plum, lollipop, bonbon, jujube, comfit, sweetmeat; apple butter, caramel, damson, glucose; maple sirup[obs3], maple syrup, maple sugar; mithai[obs3], sorghum, taffy.

nectar; hydromel[obs3], mead, meade[obs3], metheglin[obs3], honeysuckle, liqueur, sweet wine, aperitif.

[sources of sugar] sugar cane, sugar beets.

[sweet foods] desert, pastry, pie, cake, candy, ice cream, tart, puff, pudding (food) 298.

dulcificationl, dulcorationl.

sweetener, corn syrup, cane sugar, refined sugar, beet sugar, dextrose; artificial sweetener, saccharin, cyclamate, aspartame, Sweet'N Low.

V. be sweet &c. adj.

render sweet &c. adj.; sweeten; edulcorate[obs3]; dulcoratel, dulcifyl; candy; mull. Adj. sweet; saccharine, sacchariferous[obs3]; dulcet, candied, honied[obs3], luscious, lush, nectarious[obs3], melliferous[obs3]; sweetened &c. v.

sweet as a nut, sweet as sugar, sweet as honey.

sickly sweet.

Phr. eau sucre[Fr]; "sweets to the sweet" [Hamlet].

#397. Sourness. — N. sourness &c. adj.; acid, acidity, low pH; acetous fermentation, lactic fermentation.

vinegar, verjuice[obs3], crab, alum; acetic acid, lactic acid.

V. be sour; sour, turn sour &c. adj.; set the teeth on edge.

render sour &c. adj.; acidify, acidulate.

Adj. sour; acid, acidulous, acidulated; tart, crabbed; acetous, acetose[obs3]; acerb, acetic; sour as vinegar, sourish, acescent[obs3], subacid[Chem]; styptic, hard, rough.

Phr. sour as a lemon.

% (4) Odor %

#398. Odor. — N. odor, smell, odoramentl, scent, effluvium; emanation, exhalation; fume, essence, trail, nidorl, redolence.

sense of smell; scent; act of smelling &c. v.; olfaction, olfactories[obs3].

[pleasant odor] fragrance &c. 400.

odorant.

[animal with acute sense of smell] bloodhound, hound.

[smell detected by a hound] spoor.

V. have an odor &c. n.; smell, smell of, smell strong of; exhale; give out a smell &c. n.; reek, reek of; scent.

smell, scent; snuff, snuff up; sniff, nose, inhale.

Adj. odorous, odoriferous; smelling, reeking, foul-smelling, strong-scented; redolent, graveolent[obs3], nidorous[obs3], pungent; putrid, foul.

[Relating to the sense of smell] olfactory, quick-scented.

#399. Inodorousness.— N. inodorousness[obs3]; absence of smell, want of smell.

deodorant, deodorization, deodorizer.

V. be inodorous &c. adj[obs3].; not smell.

deodorize.

Adj. inodorous[obs3], onodorate; scentless; without smell, wanting smell &c. 398.

deodorized, deodorizing.

#400. Fragrance. — N. fragrance, aroma, redolence, perfume, bouquet, essence, scent; sweet smell, aromatic perfume. agalloch[obs3], agallochium[obs3]; aloes wood; bay rum; calambac[obs3], calambour[obs3]; champak[obs3], horehound[ISA:plant@mint], lign-aloes[obs3], marrubium[obs3], mint, muskrat, napha water[obs3], olibanum[obs3], spirit of myrcia[obs3]. essential oil. incense; musk, frankincense; pastil[obs3], pastille; myrrh, perfumes of Arabia[obs3]; otto[obs3], ottar[obs3], attar; bergamot, balm, civet, potpourri, pulvill; nosegay; scentbag[obs3]; sachet, smelling bottle, vinaigrette; eau de Cologne[Fr], toilet water, lotion, after-shave lotion; thurification[obs3]. perfumer. [fragrant wood oils] eucalyptus oil, pinene. V. be fragrant &c. adj.; have a perfume &c. n.; smell sweet. scent[render fragrant], perfume, embalm. Adj. fragrant, aromatic, redolent, spicy, savory, balmy, scented, sweet-smelling, sweet-scented; perfumed, perfumatory[obs3]; thuriferous; fragrant as a rose, muscadine[obs3], ambrosial.

#401. Fetor. — N. fetor[obs3]; bad &c. adj. smell, bad odor; stench, stink; foul odor, malodor; empyreuma[obs3]; mustiness &c. adj.; rancidity; foulness &c. (uncleanness) 653. stoat, polecat, skunk; assafoetida[obs3]; fungus, garlic; stinkpot; fitchet[obs3], fitchew[obs3], fourmart[obs3], peccary. acridity &c. 401a. V. have a bad smell &c. n.; smell; stink, stink in the nostrils, stink like a polecat; smell strong &c. adj., smell offensively. Adj. fetid; strong-smelling; high, bad, strong, fulsome, offensive, noisome, rank, rancid, reasty[obs3], tainted, musty, fusty, frouzy[obs3]; olid[obs3], olidousl; nidorous[obs3]; smelling, stinking; putrid &c. 653; suffocating, mephitic; empyreumatic[obs3].

#401a. Acridity — N. acridity, astringency, bite. [acrid substances] tear gas; smoke, acrid fumes. Adj. acrid, biting, astringent, sharp, harsh; bitter &c. 392b.

<— p. 113 —> % (5) Sound

(i) SOUND IN GENERAL %

#402. Sound. — N. sound, noise, strain; accent, twang, intonation, tone; cadence; sonorousness &c. adj.; audibility; resonance &c. 408; voice &c. 580; aspirate; ideophone[obs3]; rough breathing. [Science, of sound] acoustics; phonics, phonetics, phonology, phonography[obs3]; diacoustics[obs3], diaphonics[obs3]; phonetism[obs3]. V. produce sound; sound, make a noise; give out sound, emit sound; resound &c. 408. Adj. sounding; soniferous[obs3]; sonorous, sonorific[obs3]; resonant, audible, distinct; stertorous; phonetic; phonic, phonocamptic[obs3]. Phr. "a thousand trills and quivering sounds" [Addison]; forensis strepitus[Lat].

#403. Silence. — N. silence; stillness &c. (quiet) 265; peace, hush, lull; muteness &c. 581; solemn silence, awful silence, dead silence, deathlike silence. V. be silent &c. adj.; hold one's tongue &c. (not speak) 585. render silent &c. adj.; silence, still, hush; stifle, muffle, stop; muzzle, put to silence &c. (render mute) 581. Adj. silent; still, stilly; noiseless, soundless; hushed &c. v.; mute &c. 581. soft, solemn, awful, deathlike, silent as the grave; inaudible &c. (faint) 405. Adv. silently &c. adj.; sub silentio[Lat]. Int. hush! silence! soft! whist! tush! chut[obs3]! tut! pax[Lat]! be quiet! be silent! be still! shut up![rude]; chup[obs3]! chup rao[obs3]! tace[It]! Phr. one might hear a feather drop, one might hear a pin drop, so quiet you could hear a pin drop; grosse Seelen dulden still [German]; le silence est la vertu de ceux qui ne sont pas sages [French]; le silence est le parti le plus sar de celui se dfie de soi-meme[French]; "silence more musical than any song" [C. G. Rossetti]; tacent satis laudant[Latin]; better to be silent and thought a fool than to speak up and remove all doubt.

#404. Loudness. — N. loudness, power; loud noise, din; blare; clang, clangor; clatter, noise, bombilation[obs3], roar, uproar, racket, hubbub, bobbery[obs3], fracas, charivari[obs3], trumpet blast, flourish of trumpets, fanfare, tintamarre[obs3], peal, swell, blast, larum[obs3], boom; bang (explosion) 406; resonance &c. 408. vociferation, hullabaloo, &c. 411; lungs; Stentor. artillery, cannon; thunder. V. be loud &c. adj.; peal, swell, clang, boom, thunder, blare, fulminate, roar; resound &c. 408. speak up, shout &c. (vociferate) 411; bellow &c. (cry as an animal) 412. rend the air, rend the skies; fill the air; din in the ear, ring in the ear, thunder in the ear; pierce the ears, split the ears, rend the ears, split the head; deafen, stun; faire le diable a quatre[Fr]; make one's windows shake, rattle the windows; awaken the echoes, startle the echoes; wake the dead. Adj. loud, sonorous; high-sounding, big-sounding; deep, full, powerful, noisy, blatant, clangorous, multisonous[obs3]; thundering, deafening &c. v; trumpet-tongued; ear-splitting, ear-rending, ear- deafening; piercing; obstreperous, rackety, uproarious; enough to wake the dead, enough to wake seven sleepers. shrill &c. 410 clamorous &c. (vociferous) 411 stentorian, stentorophonicl. Adv. loudly &c. adj. aloud; at the top of one's voice, at the top of one's lungs, lustily, in full cry. Phr. the air rings with; "the deep dread-bolted thunder" [Lear].

#405. Faintness. — N. faintness &c. adj.; faint sound, whisper, breath; undertone, underbreath[obs3]; murmur, hum, susurration; tinkle; "still small voice." hoarseness &c. adj.; raucity[obs3]. V. whisper, breathe, murmur, purl, hum, gurgle, ripple, babble, flow; tinkle; mutter &c. (speak imperfectly) 583; susurrate[obs3]. steal on the ear; melt in the air, float on the air. Adj. inaudible; scarcely audible, just audible; low, dull; stifled, muffled; hoarse, husky; gentle, soft, faint; floating; purling, flowing &c. v.; whispered &c. v.; liquid; soothing; dulcet &c. (melodious) 413; susurrant[obs3], susurrous[obs3]. Adv. in a whisper, with bated breath, sotto voce[Lat], between the teeth, aside; piano, pianissimo; d la sourdine[obs3]; out of earshot inaudibly &c. adj.

<— p. 114 —> % (ii) SPECIFIC SOUNDS %

#406. [Sudden and violent sounds.] Snap. — N. snap &c. v.; rapping
&c. v.; decrepitation, crepitation; report, thud; burst, explosion, blast,
boom, discharge, detonation, firing, salvo, volley.
  squib, cracker, firecracker, cherry bomb, M80, gun, cap, cap gun,
popgun.
  implosion.
  bomb burst, atomic explosion, nuclear explosion (arms) 727.
  [explosive substances] gunpowder, dynamite, gun cotton,
nitroglycerine, nitrocellulose, plastic explosive, plastique, TNT, cordite,
trinitrotoluene, picric acid, picrates, mercury fulminate (arms) 727.
  whack, wham, pow.
  V. rap, snap, tap, knock, ping; click; clash; crack, crackle; crash;
pop; slam, bang, blast, boom, clap, clang, clack, whack, wham;
brustle[obs3]; burst on the ear; crepitate, rump.
  blow up, blow; detonate.
  Adj. rapping &c. v.
  Int. kaboom! whamo! Heewhack! pow!
  #407. [Repeated and protracted sounds.] Roll. — N. roll &c. v.;
drumming &c. v.; berloque[obs3], bombination[obs3], rumbling; tattoo,
drumroll; dingdong; tantara[obs3]; rataplan[obs3]; whirr; ratatat, ratatat-
tat; rubadub; pitapat; quaver, clutter, charivari[obs3], racket; cuckoo;
repetition &c. 104; peal of bells, devil's tattoo; reverberation &c. 408.
  [sound of railroad train rolling on rails] clickety-clack.
  hum, purr.
  [animals that hum] hummingbird.
  [animals that purr] cat, kitten (animal sounds) 412.
  V. roll, drum, rumble, rattle, clatter, patter, clack;
bombinate[obs3].
  hum, trill, shake; chime, peal, toll; tick, beat.
  drum in the ear, din in the ear.
  Adj. rolling &c. v.; monotonous &c. (repeated) 104; like a bee in a
bottle.
<— resonance here covers 3 sound qualities; echo, low note, and ringing. They should be separated. The physical
science meanings must also be listed separately —>

#408. Resonance. — N. resonance; ring &c. v.; ringing, tintinabulation &c. v.; reflexion[Brit], reflection, reverberation;
echo, reecho; zap, zot[coll.]; buzz (hiss) 409. low note, base note, bass note, flat note, grave note, deep note; bass;
basso, basso profondo[It]; baritone, barytone[obs3]; contralto. [device to cause resonance] echo chamber, resonator.
[ringing in the ears] tinnitus[Med]. [devices which make a resonating sound] bell, doorbell, buzzer; gong, cymbals
(musical instruments) 417. [physical resonance] sympathetic vibrations; natural frequency, coupled vibration
frequency; overtone; resonating cavity; sounding board, tuning fork. [electrical resonance] tuning, squelch, frequency
selection; resonator, resonator circuit; radio &c. @2.3.1.6.8. [chemical resonance] resonant structure, aromaticity,
alternating double bonds, non-bonded resonance; pi clouds, unsaturation, double bond (valence) @2.3.2.2. V.
resound, reverberate, reecho, resonate; ring, jingle, gingle[obs3], chink, clink; tink[obs3], tinkle; chime; gurgle &c.
405 plash, goggle, echo, ring in the ear. Adj. resounding &c. v.; resonant, reverberant, tinnientl, tintinnabulary;
sonorous, booming, deep-toned, deep-sounding, deep-mouthed, vibrant; hollow, sepulchral; gruff &c. (harsh) 410.
Phr. "sweet bells jangled, out of time and harsh" [Hamlet]; echoing down the mountain and through the dell.

  #408a. Nonresonance[obs3]. — N. thud, thump, dead sound;
nonresonance[obs3]; muffled drums, cracked bell; damper; silencer.
  V. sound dead; stop the sound, damp the sound, deaden the sound,
deaden the reverberations, dampen the reverberations.

Adj. nonresonant[obs3], dead; dampened, muffled.

<— "sibilation" includes hissing and buzzing —>

#409. [Hissing sounds.] Sibilation. — N. sibilance, sibilation; zip; hiss &c. v.; sternutation; high note &c. 410.

[animals that hiss] goose, serpent, snake (animal sounds) 412.

[animals that buzz] insect, bug; bee, mosquito, wasp, fly.

[inanimate things that hiss] tea kettle, pressure cooker; air valve, pressure release valve, safety valve, tires, air escaping from tires, punctured tire; escaping steam, steam, steam radiator, steam release valve.

V. hiss, buzz, whiz, rustle; fizz, fizzle; wheeze, whistle, snuffle; squash; sneeze; sizzle, swish.

Adj. sibilant; hissing &c. v.; wheezy; sternutative[obs3].

#410. [Harsh sounds.] Stridor. — N. creak &c. v.; creaking &c. v.; discord, &c. 414; stridor; roughness, sharpness, &c. adj.; cacophony; cacoepy[obs3]. acute note, high note; soprano, treble, tenor, alto, falsetto, penny trumpet, voce di testa[It]. V. creak, grate, jar, burr, pipe, twang, jangle, clank, clink; scream &c. (cry) 411; yelp &c. (animal sound) 412; buzz &c. (hiss) 409. set the teeth on edge, corcher les oreilles[Fr]; pierce the ears, split the ears, split the head; offend the ear, grate upon the ear, jar upon the ear. Adj. creaking &c. v.; stridulous[obs3], harsh, coarse, hoarse, horrisonousl, rough, gruff, grum[obs3], sepulchral, hollow. sharp, high, acute, shrill; trumpet-toned; piercing, ear-piercing, high-pitched, high-toned; cracked; discordant &c. 414; cacophonous.

<— p. 115 —>

#411. Cry. — N. cry &c. v.; voice &c. (human) 580; hubbub; bark &c. (animal) 412. vociferation, outcry, hullabaloo, chorus, clamor, hue and cry, plaint; lungs; stentor. V. cry, roar, shout, bawl, brawl, halloo, halloa, hoop, whoop, yell, bellow, howl, scream, screech, screak[obs3], shriek, shrill, squeak, squeal, squall, whine, pule, pipe, yaup[obs3]. cheer; hoot; grumble, moan, groan. snore, snort; grunt &c. (animal sounds) 412. vociferate; raise up the voice, lift up the voice; call out, sing out, cry out; exclaim; rend the air; thunder at the top of one's voice, shout at the top of one's voice, shout at the pitch of one's breath, thunder at the pitch of one's breath; s'gosiller; strain the throat, strain the voice, strain the lungs; give a cry &c. Adj. crying &c. v.; clamant[obs3], clamorous; vociferous; stentorian &c. (loud) 404; open-mouthed.

#412. [Animal sounds.] Ululation. — N. cry &c. v.; crying &c. v.; bowwow, ululation, latration[obs3], belling; reboation[obs3]; wood-note; insect cry, fritiniancyl, drone; screech owl; cuckoo. wailing (lamentation) 839. V. cry, roar, bellow, blare, rebellow[obs3]; growl, snarl. [specific animal sounds] bark [dog, seal]; bow-wow, yelp [dog]; bay, bay at the moon [dog, wolf]; yap, yip, yipe, growl, yarrl, yawl, snarl, howl [dog, wolf]; grunt, gruntle[obs3]; snort [pig, hog, swine, horse]; squeak [swine, mouse]; neigh, whinny [horse]; bray [donkey, mule, hinny, ass]; mew, mewl [kitten]; meow [cat]; purr [cat]; caterwaul, pule [cats]; baa[obs3], bleat [lamb]; low, moo [cow, cattle]; troat[obs3], croak, peep [frog]; coo [dove, pigeon]; gobble [turkeys]; quack [duck]; honk, gaggle, guggle [obs3][goose]; crow, caw, squawk, screech, [crow]; cackle, cluck, clack [hen, rooster, poultry]; chuck, chuckle; hoot, hoo [owl]; chirp, cheep, chirrup, twitter, cuckoo, warble, trill, tweet, pipe, whistle [small birds]; hum [insects, hummingbird]; buzz [flying insects, bugs]; hiss [snakes, geese]; blatter[obs3]; ratatat [woodpecker]. Adj. crying &c. v.; blatant, latrant[obs3], remugient[obs3], mugient[obs3]; deep-mouthed, full-mouthed; rebellowing[obs3], reboant[obs3]. Adv. in full cry.

% (iii) MUSICAL SOUNDS %

#413. Melody. Concord. — N. melody, rhythm, measure; rhyme &c.(poetry) 597. pitch, timbre, intonation, tone. scale, gamut; diapason; diatonic chromatic scale[obs3], enharmonic scale[obs3]; key, clef, chords. modulation, temperament, syncope, syncopation, preparation, suspension, resolution. staff, stave, line, space, brace; bar, rest; appoggiato[obs3], appoggiatura[obs3]; acciaccatura[obs3]. note, musical note, notes of a scale; sharp, flat, natural; high note &c.(shrillness) 410; low note &c. 408; interval; semitone; second, third, fourth &c.; diatessaron[obs3]. breve, semibreve[Mus], minim, crotchet, quaver; semiquaver, demisemiquaver, hemidemisemiquaver; sustained note, drone, burden. tonic; key note, leading note, fundamental note; supertonic[obs3], mediant[obs3], dominant; submediant[obs3], subdominant[obs3]; octave, tetrachord[obs3]; major key, minor key, major scale, minor scale, major mode, minor mode; passage, phrase. concord, harmony; emmeleia[obs3]; unison, unisonance[obs3]; chime, homophony; euphony, euphonism[obs3]; tonality; consonance; consent; part. [Science of harmony] harmony, harmonics; thorough-bass, fundamental- bass; counterpoint; faburden[obs3]. piece of music &c. 415[Fr]; composer, harmonist[obs3], contrapuntist (musician) 416. V. be harmonious &c. adj.; harmonize, chime, symphonize[obs3], transpose; put in tune, tune, accord, string. Adj. harmonious, harmonical[obs3]; in concord &c. n., in tune, in concert;

unisonant[obs3], concentual[obs3], symphonizing[obs3], isotonic, homophonous[obs3], assonant; ariose[obs3], consonant. measured, rhythmical, diatonic[obs3], chromatic, enharmonic[obs3]. melodious, musical; melic[obs3]; tuneful, tunable; sweet, dulcet, canorous[obs3]; mellow, mellifluous; soft, clear, clear as a bell; silvery; euphonious, euphonic, euphonical[obs3]; symphonious; enchanting &c. (pleasure-giving) 829; fine-toned, full-toned, silver-toned. Adv. harmoniously, in harmony; as one &c. adj. Phr. "the hidden soul of harmony" [Milton].

#414. Discord. — N. discord, discordance; dissonance, cacophony, want of harmony, caterwauling; harshness &c. 410. Babel[Confused sounds]; Dutch concert, cat's concert; marrowbones and cleavers. V. be discordant &c. adj.; jar &c. (sound harshly) 410. Adj. discordant; dissonant, absonant[obs3]; out of tune, tuneless; unmusical, untunable[obs3]; unmelodious, immelodious[obs3]; unharmonious[obs3], inharmonious; singsong; cacophonous; harsh &c. 410; jarring.

<— p. 116 —>

#415. Music. — N. music; concert; strain, tune, air; melody &c. 413; aria, arietta[obs3]; piece of music[Fr], work, number, opus; sonata; rondo, rondeau[Fr]; pastorale, cavatina[obs3], roulade[obs3], fantasia, concerto, overture, symphony, variations, cadenza; cadence; fugue, canon, quodlibet, serenade, notturno [Italian], dithyramb; opera, operetta; oratorio; composition, movement; stave; passamezzo [obs3][Italian], toccata, Vorspiel [German]. instrumental music; full score; minstrelsy, tweedledum and tweedledee, band, orchestra; concerted piece[Fr], potpourri, capriccio. vocal music, vocalism[obs3]; chaunt, chant; psalm, psalmody; hymn; song &c. (poem) 597; canticle, canzonet[obs3], cantata, bravura, lay, ballad, ditty, carol, pastoral, recitative, recitativo[obs3], solfeggio[obs3]. Lydian measures; slow music, slow movement; adagio &c. adv.; minuet; siren strains, soft music, lullaby; dump; dirge &c. (lament) 839; pibroch[obs3]; martial music, march; dance music; waltz &c. (dance) 840. solo, duet, duo, trio; quartet, quartett[obs3]; septett[obs3]; part song, descant, glee, madrigal, catch, round, chorus, chorale; antiphon[obs3], antiphony; accompaniment, second, bass; score; bourdon[obs3], drone, morceau[obs3], terzetto[obs3]. composer &c. 413; musician &c. 416. V. compose, perform &c. 416; attune. Adj. musical; instrumental, vocal, choral, lyric, operatic; harmonious &c. 413; Wagnerian. Adv. adagio; largo, larghetto, andante, andantino[obs3]; alla capella[It] [obs3]; maestoso[obs3], moderato; allegro, allegretto; spiritoso[obs3], vivace[obs3], veloce[obs3]; presto, prestissimo[obs3]; con brio; capriccioso[obs3]; scherzo, scherzando[obs3]; legato, staccato, crescendo, diminuendo, rallentando[obs3], affettuoso[obs3]; obbligato; pizzicato; desto[obs3]. Phr. "in notes by distance made more sweet" [Collins]; "like the faint exquisite music of a dream" [Moore]; "music arose with its voluptuous swell" [Byron]; "music is the universal language of mankind" [Longfellow]; "music's golden tongue" [Keats]; "the speech of angels" [Carlyle]; "will sing the savageness out of a bear" [Othello]; music hath charms to soothe the savage beast.

#416. Musician. [Performance of Music.] — N. musician, artiste, performer, player, minstrel; bard &c. (poet) 597;
[specific types of musicians] accompanist, accordionist, instrumentalist, organist, pianist, violinist, flautist; harper, fiddler, fifer[obs3], trumpeter, piper, drummer; catgut scraper.
band, orchestral waits.
vocalist, melodist; singer, warbler; songster, chaunter[obs3], chauntress[obs3], songstress; cantatrice[obs3].
choir, quire, chorister; chorus, chorus singer; liedertafel[Ger].
nightingale, philomel[obs3], thrush; siren; bulbul, mavis; Pierides; sacred nine; Orpheus, Apollo[obs3], the Muses Erato, Euterpe, Terpsichore; tuneful nine, tuneful quire.
composer &c. 413.
performance, execution, touch, expression, solmization[obs3].
V. play, pipe, strike up, sweep the chords, tweedle, fiddle; strike the lyre, beat the drum; blow the horn, sound the horn, wind the horn; doodle; grind the organ; touch the guitar &c. (instruments) 417; thrum, strum, beat time.
execute, perform; accompany; sing a second, play a second; compose, set to music, arrange.
sing, chaunt, chant, hum, warble, carol, chirp, chirrup, lilt, purl, quaver, trill, shake, twitter, whistle; sol-fa[obs3]; intone.
have an ear for music, have a musical ear, have a correct ear.
Adj. playing &c. v.; musical.

Adv. adagio, andante &c. (music) 415.
<— p. 117 —>

#417. Musical Instruments. — N. musical instruments; band; string- band, brass-band; orchestra; orchestrina[obs3]. monochord[obs3][Stringed instruments], polychord[obs3]; harp, lyre, lute, archlute[obs3]; mandola[obs3], mandolin, mandoline[obs3]; guitar; zither; cither[obs3], cithern[obs3]; gittern[obs3]; rebeck[obs3], bandurria[obs3], bandura, banjo; bina[obs3], vina[obs3]; xanorphica[obs3]. viol, violin; fiddle, kit; viola, viola d'amore[Fr], viola di gamba[It]; tenor, cremona, violoncello, bass; bass viol, base viol; theorbo[obs3], double base, contrabasso[obs3], violone[obs3], *psaltery; bow, fiddlestick[obs3]. piano, pianoforte; harpsichord, clavichord, clarichord[obs3], manichord[obs3]; clavier, spinet, virginals, dulcimer, hurdy-gurdy, vielle[obs3], pianino[obs3], Eolian harp. organ[Wind instruments]; harmonium, harmoniphon[obs3]; American organ[obs3], barrel organ, hand organ; accordion, seraphina[obs3], concertina; humming top. flute, fife, piccolo, flageolet; clarinet, claronet[obs3]; basset horn, corno di bassetto[obs3], oboe, hautboy, cor Anglais[Fr], corno Inglese[obs3], bassoon, double bassoon, contrafagotto[obs3], serpent, bass clarinet; bagpipes, union pipes; musette, ocarina, Pandean pipes; reed instrument; sirene[obs3], pipe, pitch-pipe; sourdet[obs3]; whistle, catcall; doodlesack[obs3], harmoniphone[obs3]. horn, bugle, cornet, cornet-a-pistons, cornopeanl, clarion, trumpet, trombone, ophicleide[obs3]; French horn, saxophone, sax [informal], buglehorn[obs3], saxhorn, flugelhorn[obs3], althorn[obs3], helicanhorn[obs3], posthorn[obs3]; sackbut, euphonium, bombardon tuba[obs3]. [Vibrating surfaces] cymbal, bell, gong; tambourl!, tambourine, tamborine[obs3]; drum, tom-tom; tabor, tabret[obs3], tabourine[obs3], taborin[obs3]; side drum, kettle drum; timpani, tympani[obs3]; tymbal[obs3], timbrel[obs3], castanet, bones; musical glasses, musical stones; harmonica, sounding-board, rattle; tam-tam, zambomba[obs3]. [Vibrating bars] reed, tuning fork, triangle, Jew's harp, musical box, harmonicon[obs3], xylophone. sordine[obs3], sordet[obs3]; sourdine[obs3], sourdet[obs3]; mute.

% (iv) PERCEPTION OF SOUND %

#418. [Sense of sound.] Hearing. — N. hearing &c. v.; audition, auscultation; eavesdropping; audibility.

acute ear, nice ear, delicate ear, quick ear, sharp ear, correct ear, musical ear; ear for music.

ear, auricle, lug, acoustic organs, auditory apparatus; eardrum, tympanum, tympanic membrane.

[devices to aid human hearing by amplifying sound] ear trumpet, speaking trumpet, hearing aid, stethoscope.

[distance within which direct hearing is possible] earshot, hearing distance, hearing, hearing range, sound, carrying distance.

[devices for talking beyond hearing distance] telephone[exlist], phone, telephone booth, intercom, house phone, radiotelephone, radiophone, wireless, wireless telephone, mobile telephone, car radio, police radio, two-way radio, walkie-talkie[military], handie-talkie, citizen's band, CB, amateur radio, ham radio, short-wave radio, police band, ship-to-shore radio, airplane radio, control tower communication; (communication) 525, 527, 529, 531, 532; electronic devices (POINFO @.2.2.3.1.3.5.3).

[devices for recording and reproducing recorded sound] phonograph, gramophone, megaphone, phonorganon[obs3].

[device to convert sound to electrical signals] microphone,directional microphone, mike, hand mike, lapel microphone.

[devices to convert recorded sound to electronic signals] phonograph needle, stylus, diamond stylus, pickup; reading head (electronic devices).

hearer, auditor, listener, eavesdropper, listener-in.

auditory, audience.

[science of hearing] otology, otorhinolaryngology.

[physicians specializing in hearing] otologist, otorhinolaryngologist.

V. hear, overhear; hark, harken; list, listen, pay attention, take heed; give an ear, lend an ear, bend an ear; catch, catch a sound, prick up one's ears; give ear, give a hearing, give audience to.

hang upon the lips of, be all ears, listen with both ears.

become audible; meet the ear, fall upon the ear, catch the ear, reach the ear; be heard; ring in the ear &c. (resound) 4O8.

105

Adj. hearing &c. v.; auditory, auricular, acoustic; phonic.

Adv. arrectis auribus[Lat].

Int. hark, hark ye! hear! list, listen! O yes! Oyez!

listen up [coll.]; listen here! hear ye! attention! achtung [German].

#419. Deafness. — N. deafness, hardness of hearing, surdityl; inaudibility, inaudibleness[obs3].

V. be deaf &c. adj.; have no ear; shut one's ears, stop one's ears, close one's ears; turn a deaf ear to.

render deaf, stun, deafen.

Adj. deaf, earless[obs3], surd; hard of hearing, dull of hearing; deaf-mute, stunned, deafened; stone deaf; deaf as a post, deaf as an adder, deaf as a beetle, deaf as a trunkmaker[obs3].

inaudible, out of hearing.

Phr. hear no evil.

<— p. 118 —>

%

(6) Light
(i) LIGHT IN GENERAL
%

#420. Light.— N. light, ray, beam, stream, gleam, streak, pencil; sunbeam, moonbeam; aurora. day; sunshine; light of day, light of heaven; moonlight, starlight, sun &c. (luminary) 432 light; daylight, broad daylight, noontide light; noontide, noonday, noonday sun. glow &c. v.; glimmering &c. v.; glint; play of light, flood of light; phosphorescence, lambent flame. flush, halo, glory, nimbus, aureola. spark, scintilla; facula; sparkling &c. v.; emicationl, scintillation, flash, blaze, coruscation, fulguration[obs3]; flame &c. (fire) 382; lightning, levin[obs3], ignis fatuus[Lat], &c. (luminary) 423. luster, sheen, shimmer, reflexion[Brit], reflection; gloss, tinsel, spangle, brightness, brilliancy, splendor; effulgence, refulgence; fulgor[obs3], fulgidity[obs3]; dazzlement[obs3], resplendence, transplendency[obs3]; luminousness &c. adj.; luminosity; lucidity; renitencyl, nitency[obs3]; radiance,, radiation; irradiation, illumination. actinic rays, actinism; Roentgen-ray, Xray; photography, heliography; photometer &c. 445. [Science of light] optics; photology[obs3], photometry; dioptrics[obs3], catoptrics[obs3]. [Distribution of light] chiaroscuro, clairobscur[obs3], clear obscure, breadth, light and shade, black and white, tonality. reflection, refraction, dispersion; refractivity. V. shine, glow, glitter; glister, glisten; twinkle, gleam; flare, flare up; glare, beam, shimmer, glimmer, flicker, sparkle, scintillate, coruscate, flash, blaze; be bright &c. adj.; reflect light, daze, dazzle, bedazzle, radiate, shoot out beams; fulgurate. clear up, brighten. lighten, enlighten; levin[obs3]; light, light up; irradiate, shine upon; give out a light, hang out a light; cast light upon, cast light in, throw light upon, throw light in, shed light upon, shed luster upon; illume[obs3], illumine, illuminate; relume[obs3], strike a light; kindle &c. (set fire to) 384. Adj. shining &c. v.; luminous, luminiferous[obs3]; lucid, lucent, luculent[obs3], lucific[obs3], luciferous; light, lightsome; bright, vivid, splendent[obs3], nitid[obs3], lustrous, shiny, beamy[obs3], scintillant[obs3], radiant, lambent; sheen, sheeny; glossy, burnished, glassy, sunny, orient, meridian; noonday, tide; cloudless, clear; unclouded, unobscured[obs3]. gairish[obs3], garish; resplendent, transplendent[obs3]; refulgent, effulgent; fulgid[obs3], fulgent[obs3]; relucent[obs3], splendid, blazing, in a blaze, ablaze, rutilant[obs3], meteoric, phosphorescent; aglow. bright as silver; light as day, bright as day, light as noonday, bright as noonday, bright as the sun at noonday. actinic; photogenic[obs2], graphic; heliographic; heliophagous[obs3]. Phr. "a day for gods to stoop and men to soar" [Tennyson]; "dark with excessive bright" [Milton].

#421. Darkness. — N. darkness &c. adj., absence of light; blackness &c. (dark color) 431; obscurity, gloom, murk; dusk &c. (dimness) 422. Cimmerian darkness[obs3], Stygian darkness, Egyptian darkness; night; midnight; dead of night, witching hour of night, witching time of night; blind man's holiday; darkness visible, darkness that can be felt; palpable obscure; Erebus[Lat]; "the jaws of darkness" [Midsummer Night's Dream]; "sablevested night" [Milton]. shade, shadow, umbra, penumbra; sciagraphy[obs3]. obscuration; occultation, adumbration, obumbration[obs3]; obtenebration[obs3], offuscationl, caligationl; extinction; eclipse, total eclipse; gathering of the clouds. shading; distribution of shade; chiaroscuro &c. (light) 420. noctivagation[obs3]. [perfectly black objects] black body; hohlraum[Phys]; black hole; dark star; dark matter, cold dark matter. V. be dark &c. adj. darken, obscure, shade; dim; tone down, lower; overcast, overshadow; eclipse; obfuscate, offuscatel; obumbrate[obs3], adumbrate; cast into the shade becloud, bedim[obs3], bedarken[obs3]; cast a shade, throw a shade, spread a shade, cast a shadow, cast a gloom, throw a shadow, spread a shadow, cast gloom, throw gloom, spread gloom. extinguish; put out, blow out, snuff out; doubt. turn out the lights, douse the lights, dim the lights, turn off the lights, switch off the lights. Adj. dark, darksome[obs3], darkling; obscure, tenebrious[obs3], sombrous[obs3], pitch dark, pitchy, pitch black;

106

caliginous[obs3]; black &c. (in color) 431. sunless, lightless &c. (see sun[obs3], light, &c. 423); somber, dusky; unilluminated &c. (see illuminate &c. 420)[obs3]; nocturnal; dingy, lurid, gloomy; murky, murksome[obs3]; shady, umbrageous; overcast &c. (dim) 422; cloudy &c. (opaque) 426; darkened; &c. v. dark as pitch, dark as a pit, dark as Erebus[Lat]. benighted; noctivagant!!, noctivagous!!. Adv. in the dark, in the shade. Phr. "brief as the lightning in the collied night" [M. N. D.]; "eldest Night and Chaos, ancestors of Nature" [P. L.]; "the blackness of the noonday night" [Longfellow]; "the prayer of Ajax was for light" [Longfellow].

<— p. 119 —>

#422. Dimness. — N. dimness &c. adj.; darkness &c. 421; paleness &c. (light color) 429.

half light, demi-jour; partial shadow, partial eclipse; shadow of a shade; glimmer, gliming[obs3]; nebulosity; cloud &c. 353; eclipse.

aurora, dusk, twilight, shades of evening, crepuscule, cockshut time!; break of day, daybreak, dawn.

moonlight, moonbeam, moonglade[obs3], moonshine; starlight, owl's light, candlelight, rushlight, firelight; farthing candle.

V. be dim, grow dim &c. adj.; flicker, twinkle, glimmer; loom, lower; fade; pale, pale its ineffectual fire [Hamlet].

render dim &c. adj.; dim, bedim[obs3], obscure; darken, tone down.

Adj. dim, dull, lackluster, dingy, darkish, shorn of its beams, dark 421.

faint, shadowed forth; glassy; cloudy; misty &c. (opaque) 426; blear; muggy!, fuliginous[obs3]; nebulous, nebular; obnubilated[obs3], overcast, crepuscular, muddy, lurid, leaden, dun, dirty; looming &c. v.

pale &c. (colorless) 429; confused &c. (invisible) 447.

#423. [Source of light, self-luminous body.] Luminary. — N. luminary; light &c. 420; flame &c. (fire) 382. spark, scintilla; phosphorescence, fluorescence. sun, orb of day, Phoebus, Apollo[obs3], Aurora; star, orb; meteor, falling star, shooting star; blazing star, dog star, Sirius; canicula, Aldebaran[obs3]; constellation, galaxy; zodiacal light; anthelion[obs3]; day star, morning star; Lucifer; mock sun, parhelion; phosphor, phosphorus; sun dog!; Venus. aurora, polar lights; northern lights, aurora borealis; southern lights, aurora australis. lightning; chain lightning, fork lightning, sheet lightning, summer lightning; ball lightning, kugelblitz [German]; [chemical substances giving off light without burning] phosphorus, yellow phosphorus; scintillator, phosphor; firefly luminescence. ignis fatuus[Lat]; Jack o'lantern, Friar's lantern; will-o'-the-wisp, firedrake[obs3], Fata Morgana[Lat]; Saint Elmo's fire. [luminous insects] glowworm, firefly, June bug, lightning bug. [luminous fish] anglerfish. [Artificial light] gas; gas light, lime light, lantern, lanthorn[obs3]; dark lantern, bull's-eye; candle, bougie[Fr], taper, rushlight; oil &c. (grease) 356; wick, burner; Argand[obs3], moderator, duplex; torch, flambeau, link, brand; gaselier[obs3], chandelier, electrolier[obs3], candelabrum, candelabra, girandole[obs3], sconce, luster, candlestick. [non-combustion based light sources] lamp, light; incandescent lamp, tungsten bulb, light bulb; flashlight, torch[Brit]; arc light; laser; maser [microwave radiation]; neon bulb, neon sign; fluorescent lamp. [parts of a light bulb] filament; socket; contacts; filler gas. firework, fizgig[obs3]; pyrotechnics; rocket, lighthouse &c. (signal) 550. V. illuminate &c. (light) 420. Adj. self-luminous, glowing; phosphoric!!, phosphorescent, fluorescent; incandescent; luminescent, chemiluminescent; radiant &c. (light) 420. Phr. "blossomed the lovely stars, the forget-me-nots of the angels" [Longfellow]; "the sentinel stars set their watch in the sky" [Campbell]; "the planets in their station list'ning stood" [Paradise Lost]; "the Scriptures of the skies" [Bailey]; "that orbed continent, the fire that severs day from night" [Twelfth Night].

#424. Shade. — N. shade; awning &c. (cover) 223; parasol, sunshade, umbrella; chick; portiere; screen, curtain, shutter, blind, gauze, veil, chador, mantle, mask; cloud, mist, gathering. of clouds.

umbrage, glade; shadow &c. 421.

beach umbrella, folding umbrella.

V. draw a curtain; put up a shutter, close a shutter; veil &c. v.; cast a shadow &c. (darken) 421.

Adj. shady, umbrageous.

Phr. "welcome ye shades! ye bowery thickets hail" [Thomson].

#425. Transparency. — N. transparence, transparency; clarity; translucence, translucency; diaphaneity[obs3]; lucidity, pellucidity[obs3], limpidity; fluorescence; transillumination, translumination[obs3]. transparent medium, glass, crystal, lymph, vitrite[obs3], water. V. be transparent &c. adj.; transmit light. Adj. transparent, pellucid, lucid, diaphanous, translucent, tralucentl, relucent[obs3]; limpid, clear, serene, crystalline, clear as crystal, vitreous, transpicuous[obs3], glassy, hyaline; hyaloid[Med], vitreform[obs3].

#426. Opacity.— N. opacity; opaqueness &c. adj.
film; cloud &c. 353.
V. be opaque &c. adj.; obstruct the passage of light; obfuscate,
offuscatel.
Adj. opaque, impervious to light; adiaphanous[obs3]; dim &c. 422;
turbid, thick, muddy, opacousl, obfuscated, fuliginous[obs3], cloud, hazy,
misty, foggy, vaporous, nubiferous[obs3], muggyll (turbidity) 426a.
smoky, fumid[obs3], murky, dirty.
#426a. Turbidity — N. turbidity, cloudiness, fog, haze, muddiness,
haziness, obscurity.
nephelometer[instrument to measure turbidity].
Adj. turbid, thick, muddy, obfuscated, fuliginous[obs3], hazy, misty,
foggy, vaporous, nubiferous[obs3]; cloudy (cloud) 353.
smoky, fumid[obs3], murky, dirty.
<— p. 120 —>

#427. Semitransparency. — N. semitransparency, translucency,
semiopacity; opalescence, milkiness, pearliness[obs3]; gauze, muslin; film;
mica, mother-of-pearl, nacre; mist &c. (cloud) 353.
[opalescent jewel] opal.
turbidity &c. 426a.
Adj. semitransparent, translucent, semipellucid[obs3],
semidiaphanous[obs3], semiopacous[obs3], semiopaque; opalescent,
opaline[obs3]; pearly, milky; frosted, nacreous.
V. opalesce.
% (ii) SPECIFIC LIGHT %

#428. Color. — N. color, hue, tint, tinge, dye, complexion, shade, tincture, cast, livery, coloration, glow, flush; tone, key. pure color, positive color, primary color, primitive complementary color; three primaries; spectrum, chromatic dispersion; broken color, secondary color, tertiary color. local color, coloring, keeping, tone, value, aerial perspective. [Science of color] chromatics, spectrum analysis, spectroscopy; chromatism[obs3], chromatographyll, chromatology[obs3]. [instruments to measure color] prism, spectroscope, spectrograph, spectrometer, colorimeter (optical instruments) 445. pigment, coloring matter, paint, dye, wash, distemper, stain; medium; mordant; oil paint &c. painting 556. V. color, dye, tinge, stain, tint, tinct[obs3], paint, wash, ingrain, grain, illuminate, emblazon, bedizen, imbue; paint &c. (fine art) 556. Adj. colored &c. v.; colorific[obs3], tingent[obs3], tinctorial[obs3]; chromatic, prismatic; full-colored, high-colored, deep-colored; doubly- dyed; polychromatic; chromatogenous[obs3]; tingible[obs3]. bright, vivid, intense, deep; fresh, unfaded[obs3]; rich, gorgeous; gay. gaudy, florid; gay, garish; rainbow-colored, multihued; showy, flaunting, flashy; raw, crude; glaring, flaring; discordant, inharmonious. mellow, pastel, harmonious, pearly, sweet, delicate, tender, refined.

#429. [Absence of color.] Achromatism. — N. achromatism[obs3]; decoloration[obs3], discoloration; pallor, pallid-ness, pallidity[obs3]; paleness &c. adj.; etiolation; neutral tint, monochrome, black and white. V. lose color &c. 428; fade, fly, go; become colorless &c. adj.; turn pale, pale. deprive of color, decolorize, bleach, tarnish, achromatize, blanch, etiolate, wash out, tone down. Adj. uncolored &c. (see color &c. 428); colorless, achromatic, aplanatic[obs3]; etiolate, etiolated; hueless[obs3], pale, pallid; palefaced[obs3], tallow-faced; faint, dull, cold, muddy, leaden, dun, wan, sallow, dead, dingy, ashy, ashen, ghastly, cadaverous, glassy, lackluster; discolored &c. v. light-colored, fair, blond; white &c. 430. pale as death, pale as ashes, pale as a witch, pale as a ghost, pale as a corpse, white as a corpse.

#430. Whiteness. — N. whiteness &c. adj.; argent. albification[obs3], etiolation; lactescence[obs3]. snow, paper, chalk, milk, lily, ivory, alabaster; albata[obs3], eburin[obs3], German silver, white metal, barium sulphate[Chem], titanium oxide, blanc fixe[Fr], ceruse[obs3], pearl white; white lead, carbonate of lead. V. be white &c. adj. render white &c. adj.; whiten, bleach, blanch, etiolate, whitewash, silver. Adj. white; milk-white, snow-white; snowy; niveous[obs3], candid, chalky; hoar, hoary; silvery; argent, argentine; canescent[obs3], cretaceous, lactescent[obs3]. whitish, creamy, pearly, fair, blond; blanched &c. v.; high in tone, light. white as a sheet, white as driven snow, white as a lily, white as silver; like ivory &c. n.

<— p. 121 —>

#431. Blackness. — N. blackness &c. adj.; darkness &c. (want of light). 421; swartliness[obs3], lividity, dark color, tone, color; chiaroscuro &c. 420. nigrification[obs3], infuscation[obs3]. jet, ink, ebony, coal pitch, soot, charcoal, sloe, smut, raven, crow. [derogatory terms for black-skinned people] Negro, blackamoor, man of color, nigger, darkie, Ethiop, black; buck, nigger [U. S.]; coon [U. S.], sambo. [Pigments] lampblack, ivory black, blueblack; writing ink, printing ink, printer's ink, Indian ink, India ink. V. be black &c. adj.; render -black &c. adj. blacken, infuscate[obs3], denigrate; blot, blotch; smutch[obs3]; smirch; darken &c. 421. black, sable, swarthy, somber, dark, inky, ebony, ebon, atramentous[obs3], jetty; coal-black, jet-black; fuliginous[obs3], pitchy, sooty, swart, dusky, dingy, murky, Ethiopic; low-toned, low in tone; of the deepest dye. black as jet &c. n., black as my hat, black as a shoe, black as a tinker's pot, black as November, black as thunder, black as midnight; nocturnal &c. (dark) 421; nigrescent[obs3]; gray &c. 432; obscure &c. 421. Adv. in mourning.

#432. Gray. — N. gray &c. adj.; neutral tint, silver, pepper and salt, chiaroscuro, grisaille[Fr]. [Pigments] Payne's gray; black &c. 431. Adj. gray, grey; iron-gray, dun, drab, dingy, leaden, livid, somber, sad, pearly, russet, roan; calcareous, limy, favillous[obs3]; silver, silvery, silvered; ashen, ashy; cinereous[obs3], cineritious[obs3]; grizzly, grizzled; slate-colored, stone-colored, mouse-colored, ash- colored; cool.

#433. Brown. — N. brown &c. adj. bister[obs3][Pigments], ocher, sepia, Vandyke brown. V. render brown &c. adj.; tan, embrown[obs3], bronze. Adj. brown, bay, dapple, auburn, castaneous[obs3], chestnut, nut- brown, cinnamon, russet, tawny, fuscous[obs3], chocolate, maroon, foxy, tan, brunette, whitey brown[obs3]; fawn-colored, snuff-colored, liver- colored; brown as a berry, brown as mahogany, brown as the oak leaves; khaki. sun-burnt; tanned &c. v.

% - Primitive Colors %

#434. Redness. — N. red, scarlet, vermilion, carmine, crimson, pink, lake, maroon, carnation, couleur de rose[Fr], rose du Barry[obs3]; magenta, damask, purple; flesh color, flesh tint; color; fresh color, high color; warmth; gules[Heraldry]. ruby, carbuncle; rose; rust, iron mold. [Dyes and pigments] cinnabar, cochineal; fuchsine[obs3]; ruddle[obs3], madder; Indian red, light red, Venetian red; red ink, annotto[obs3]; annatto[obs3], realgar[ISA:mineral], minium[obs3], red lead. redness &c. adj.; rubescence[obs3], rubicundity, rubification[obs3]; erubescence[obs3], blush. V. be red, become red &c.adj.; blush, flush, color up, mantle, redden. render red &c. adj.; redden, rouge; rubify[obs3], rubricate; incarnadine.; ruddle[obs3]. Adj. red &c. n., reddish; rufous, ruddy, florid, incarnadine, sanguine; rosy, roseate; blowzy, blowed[obs3]; burnt; rubicund, rubiform[obs3]; lurid, stammell blood red[obs3]; russet buff, murrey[obs3], carroty[obs3], sorrel, lateritious[obs3]; rubineous[obs3], rubricate, rubricose[obs3], rufulous[obs3]. rose-colored, ruby-colored, cherry-colored, claret-colored, flame- colored, flesh-colored, peach-colored, salmon-colored, brick-colored, brick-colored, dust-colored. blushing &c. v.; erubescent[obs3]; reddened &c. v. red as fire, red as blood, red as scarlet, red as a turkey cock, red as a lobster; warm, hot; foxy.

% - Complementary Colors %

#435. Greenness. — N. green &c. adj.; blue and yellow; vert [heraldry].
emerald, verd antique[Fr], verdigris, malachite, beryl, aquamarine; absinthe, creme de menthe[Fr].
[Pigments] terre verte[Fr], verditer[obs3], verdine[obs3], copperas.
greenness, verdure; viridity[obs3], viridescence[obs3]; verditure[obs3].
[disease of eyes with green tint] glaucoma, [Jap: rokunaisho].
Adj. green, verdant; glaucous, olive, olive green; green as grass; verdurous.
emerald green, pea green, grass green, apple green, sea green, olive green, bottle green, coke bottle green.
greenish; virent[obs3], virescent[obs3].
green (learner) 541[new, inexperienced, novice], (unskillful) 699.
green [ill, sick].
Phr. green with envy; the green grass of Ireland; the wearing of the

green.

<— p. 122 —>

#436. Yellowness. — N. yellow &c. adj.; or. [Pigments] gamboge; cadmium-yellow, chrome-yellow, Indian-yellow king's-yellow, lemonyellow; orpiment[obs3], yellow ocher, Claude tint, aureolin[obs3]; xanthein[Chemsub], xanthin[obs3]; zaofulvin[obs3]. crocu s, saffron, topaz; xanthite[obs3]; yolk. jaundice; London fogl!; yellowness &c. adj.; icterus[obs3]; xantho- cyanopial!, xanthopsia[Med]. Adj. yellow, aureate, golden, flavousl, citrine, fallow; fulvous[obs3], fulvid[obs3]; sallow, luteous[obs3], tawny, creamy, sandy; xanthic[obs3], xanthous[obs3]; jaundiced-auricomous[obs3]. gold-colored, citron-colored, saffron-colored, lemon-colored, lemon yellow, sulphur-colored, amber-colored, straw-colored, primrose-colored, creamcolored; xanthocarpous[obs3], xanthochroid[obs3], xanthopous[obs3]. yellow as a quince, yellow as a guinea, yellow as a crow's foot. warm, advancing.

#437. Purple. — N. purple &c. adj.; blue and red, bishop's purple;
aniline dyes, gridelin[obs3], amethyst; purpure[Heraldry]; heliotrope.
   lividness, lividity.
   V. empurple[obs3].
   Adj. purple, violet, ultraviolet; plum-colored, lavender, lilac, puce,
mauve; livid.
   #438. Blueness. — N. blue &c. adj.; garter-blue; watchetl.
   [Pigments] ultramarine, smalt, cobalt, cyanogen[Chemsub]; Prussian
blue, syenite blue[obs3]; bice[obs3], indigo; zaffer[obs3].
   lapis lazuli, sapphire, turquoise; indicolite[obs3].
   blueness, bluishness; bloom.
   Adj. blue, azure, cerulean; sky-blue, sky-colored, sky-dyed;
cerulescent[obs3]; powder blue, bluish; atmospheric, retiring; cold.
   #439. Orange. — N. orange, red and yellow; gold; or; flame &c. color,
adj.
   [Pigments] ocher, Mars'orange[obs3], cadmium.
   cardinal bird, cardinal flower, cardinal grosbeak, cardinal lobelia[a
flowering plant].
   V. gild, warm.
   Adj. orange; ochreous[obs3]; orange-colored, gold-colored,
flame-colored, copper-colored, brass-colored, apricot-colored; warm, hot,
glowing.
#440. Variegation. — N. variegation; colors, dichroism, trichroism; iridescence, play of colors, polychrome, macula-tion, spottiness, striae. spectrum, rainbow, iris, tulip, peacock, chameleon, butterfly, tortoise shell; mackerel, mack-erel sky; zebra, leopard, cheetah, nacre, ocelot, ophite[obs3], mother-of-pearl, opal, marble. check, plaid, tartan, patchwork; marquetry-, parquetry; mosaic, tesserae[obs3], strigae[obs3]; chessboard, checkers, chequers; harle-quin; Joseph's coat; tricolor. V. be variegated &c. adj.; variegate, stripe, streak, checker, chequer; bespeckle[obs3], speckle; besprinkle, sprinkle; stipple, maculate, dot, bespot[obs3]; tattoo, inlay, damascene; embroider, braid, quilt. Adj. variegated &c. v.; many-colored, many-hued; divers-colored, party-colored; dichromatic, polychromatic; bicolor[obs3], tricolor, versicolor[obs3]; of all the colors of the rainbow, of all manner of colors; kaleidoscopic. iridescent; opaline[obs3], opalescent; prismatic, nacreous, pearly, shot, gorge de pigeon, chatoyant[obs3]; irisated[obs3], pavonine[obs3]. pied, piebald; motley; mottled, marbled; pepper and salt, paned, dappled, clouded, cymophanous[obs3]. mosaic, tesselated, plaid; tortoise shell &c. n. spotted, spotty; punctated[obs3], powdered; speckled &c. v.; freckled, flea-bitten, studded; flecked, fleckered[obs3]; striated, barred, veined; brinded[obs3], brindled; tabby; watered; grizzled; listed; embroidered &c. v.; daedal[obs3]; naevose[obs3], stipiform[obs3]; strigose[obs3], striolate[obs3].

<— p. 123 —>

% (iii) PERCEPTIONS OF LIGHT %

#441. Vision. — N. vision, sight, optics, eyesight. view, look, espial[obs3], glance, ken, coup d'oeil[Fr]; glimpse, glint, peep; gaze, stare, leer; perlustration[obs3], contemplation; conspection l, conspectuityl; regard, survey; introspection;

reconnaissance, speculation, watch, espionage, espionnage[Fr], autopsy; ocular inspection, ocular demonstration; sight-seeing. point of view; gazebo, loophole, belvedere, watchtower. field of view; theater, amphitheater, arena, vista, horizon; commanding view, bird's eye view; periscope. visual organ, organ of vision; eye; naked eye, unassisted eye; retina, pupil, iris, cornea, white; optics, orbs; saucer eyes, goggle eyes, gooseberry eyes. short sight &c. 443; clear sight, sharp sight, quick sight, eagle sight, piercing sight, penetrating sight, clear glance, sharp glance, quick glance, eagle glance, piercing glance, penetrating glance, clear eye, sharp eye, quick eye, eagle eye, piercing eye, penetrating eye; perspicacity, discernment; catopsis[obs3]. eagle, hawk; cat, lynx; Argus[obs3]. evil eye; basilisk, cockatrice [Mythical]. V. see, behold, discern, perceive, have in sight, descry, sight, make out, discover, distinguish, recognize, spy, espy, ken; get a sight of, have a sight of, catch a sight of, get a glimpse of, have a glimpse of, catch a glimpse of; command a view of; witness, contemplate, speculate; cast the eyes on, set the eyes on; be a spectator &c. 444 of; look on &c. (be present) 186; see sights &c. (curiosity) 455; see at a glance &c. (intelligence) 498. look, view, eye; lift up the eyes, open one's eye; look at, look on, look upon, look over, look about one, look round; survey, scan, inspect; run the eye over, run the eye through; reconnoiter, glance round, glance on, glance over turn one's looks upon, bend one's looks upon; direct the eyes to, turn the eyes on, cast a glance. observe &c. (attend to) 457; watch &c. (care) 459; see with one's own eyes; watch for &c. (expect) 507; peep, peer, pry, take a peep; play at bopeep[obs3]. look full in the face, look hard at, look intently; strain one's eyes; fix the eyes upon, rivet the eyes upon; stare, gaze; pore over, gloat on; leer, ogle, glare; goggle; cock the eye, squint, gloat, look askance. Adj. seeing &c. v.; visual, ocular; optic, optical; ophthalmic. clear-eyesighted &c. n.; eagle-eyed, hawk-eyed, lynx-eyed, keen-eyed, Argus-eyed. visible &c. 446. Adv. visibly &c. 446; in sight of, with one's eyes open at sight, at first sight, at a glance, at the first blush; prima facie[Lat]. Int. look! &c. (attention) 457. Phr. the scales falling from one's eyes; "an eye like Mars to threaten or command" [Hamlet]; "her eyes are homes of silent prayer" [Tennyson]; "looking before and after" [Hamlet]; "thy rapt soul sitting in thine eyes" [Milton].

#442. Blindness. — N. blindness, cecity[obs3], excecationl, amaurosis[obs3], cataract, ablepsyl, ablepsia[obs3], prestrictionl; dim- sightedness &c. 443; Braille, Braille-type; guttaserena ("drop serene"), noctograph[obs3], teichopsia[obs3]. V. be blind &c. adj.; not see; lose sight of; have the eyes bandaged; grope in the dark. not look; close the eyes, shut the eyes-, turn away the eyes, avert the eyes; look another way; wink &c. (limited vision) 443; shut the eyes to, be blind to, wink at, blink at. render blind &c. adj.; blind, blindfold; hoodwink, dazzle, put one's eyes out; throw dust into one's eyes, pull the wool over one's eyes; jeter de la poudre aux yeux[Fr]; screen from sight &c. (hide) 528. Adj. blind; eyeless, sightless, visionless; dark; stone-blind, sand- blind, stark-blind; undiscerning[obs3]; dimsighted &c. 443. blind as a bat, blind as a buzzard, blind as a beetle, blind as a mole, blind as an owl; wall-eyed. blinded &c. v. Adv. blindly, blindfold, blindfolded; darkly. Phr. "O dark, dark, dark, amid the blaze of noon" [Milton].

<— p. 124 —>

#443. [Imperfect vision.] Dimsightedness. [Fallacies of vision.] — N. dim sight, dull sight half sight, short sight, near sight, long sight, double sight, astigmatic sight, failing sight; dimsightedness &c.; purblindness, lippitude[obs3]; myopia, presbyopia[obs3]; confusion of vision; astigmatism; color blindness, chromato-pseudo-blepsis[obs3], Daltonism; nyctalopia[obs3]; strabismus, strabism[obs3], squint, blearedness[obs3], day blindness, hemeralopia[obs3], nystagmus; xanthocyanopia[obs3], xanthopsia[Med]; cast in the eye, swivel eye, goggle- eyes; obliquity of vision. winking &c. v.; nictitation; blinkard[obs3], albino. dizziness, swimming, scotomy[obs3]; cataract; ophthalmia. [Limitation of vision] blinker; screen &c. (hider) 530. [Fallacies of vision] deceptio visus[Lat]; refraction, distortion, illusion, false light, anamorphosis[obs3], virtual image, spectrum, mirage, looming, phasmal; phantasm, phantasma[obs3], phantom; vision; specter, apparition, ghost; ignis fatuus &c. (luminary) 423 specter of the Brocken magic mirror[Lat]; magic lantern &c. (show) 448; mirror lens &c. (instrument) 445. V. be dimsighted &c. n.; see double; have a mote in the eye, have a mist before the eyes, have a film over the eyes; see through a prism, see through a glass darkly; wink, blink, nictitate; squint; look askant[obs3], askant askance[obs3]; screw up the eyes, glare, glower; nictate[obs3]. dazzle, loom. Adj. dim-sighted &c. n.; myopic, presbyopic[obs3]; astigmatic moon- eyed, mope-eyed, blear-eyed, goggle-eyed, gooseberry-eyed, one-eyed; blind of one eye, monoculous[obs3]; half-blind, purblind; cock-eyed, dim-eyed, mole-eyed; dichroic. blind as a bat &c. (blind) 442; winking &c. v.

#444. Spectator. — N. spectator, beholder, observer, looker-on, onlooker, witness, eyewitness, bystander, passer by; sightseer; rubberneck, rubbernecker * [U. S.].

spy; sentinel &c. (warning) 668.

V. witness, behold &c. (see) 441; look on &c. (be present) 186; gawk, rubber *, rubberneck *[U.S.].

#445. Optical Instruments. — N. optical instruments; lens, meniscus, magnifier, sunglass, magnifying glass, hand lens; microscope, megascope[obs3], tienoscope[obs3]. spectacles, specs [coll.],glasses, barnacles, goggles, eyeglass, pince-nez, monocle, reading glasses, bifocals; contact lenses, soft lenses, hard lenses; sunglasses, shades[coll.]. periscopic lens[obs3]; telescope, glass, lorgnette; spyglass, opera glass, binocular, binoculars, field glass; burning glass, convex lens, concave lens, convexo-concave lens[obs3], coated lens, multiple lens, compound lens, lens system, telephoto lens, wide-angle lens, fish-eye lens, zoom lens; optical bench. astronomical telescope, reflecting telescope, reflector, refracting telescope, refractor, Newtonian telescope, folded-path telescope, finder telescope, chromatoscope; X-ray telescope; radiotelescope, phased-array telescope, Very Large Array radiotele-scope; ultraviolet telescope; infrared telescope; star spectroscope; space telescope. [telescope mounts] altazimuth mount, equatorial mount. refractometer, circular dichroism spectrometer. interferometer. phase-contrast microscope, fluorescence microscope, dissecting microscope; electron microscope, transmission electron microscope; scanning electron microscope, SEM; scanning tunneling electron microscope. [microscope components] objective lens, eyepiece, barrel, platform, focusing knob; slide, slide glass, cover glass, counting chamber; illuminator, light source, polarizer, [component parts of telescopes] reticle, cross-hairs. light pipe, fiber optics mirror, reflector, speculum; looking-glass, pier-glass, cheval-glass, rear-view mirror, hand mirror, one-way mirror, magnifying mirror. [room with distorting mirrors] fun house. prism, diffraction grating; beam splitter, half-wave plate, quarter- wave plate. camera lucida[Lat], camera obscura[Lat]; magic lantern &c. (show) 448; stereopticon; chromatrope[obs3], thaumatrope[obs3]; stereoscope, pseudoscope[obs3], polyscope[obs3], kaleidoscope. photometer, eriometer[obs3], actinometer[obs3], lucimeter[obs3], radiometer; ligth detector, photodiode, photomultiplier, photodiode array, photocell. X-ray diffractometer, goniometer. spectrometer, monochrometer, UV spectrometer, visible spectrometer, Infrared spectrometer, Fourier transform infrared spectrometer, recording spectrometer; densitometer, scanning densitometer, two-dimensional densitometer. abdominoscope[obs3], gastroscope[Med], helioscope[obs3], polariscope[obs3], polemoscope[obs3], spectroscope. abdominoscopy[obs3]; gastroscopy[Med]; microscopy, microscopist.

#446. Visibility. — N. visibility, perceptibility; conspicuousness, distinctness &c. adj.; conspicuity[obs3], conspicuous-ness; appearance &c. 448; bassetting[obs3]; exposure; manifestation &c. 525; ocular proof, ocular evidence, ocular demonstration; field of view &c. (vision) 441; periscopism[obs3]. V. be become visible &c. adj.; appear, open to the view; meet the eye, catch the eye; basset; present itself, show manifest itself, produce itself, discover itself, reveal itself, expose itself, betray itself; stand forth, stand out; materialize; show; arise; peep out, peer out, crop out; start up, spring up, show up, turn up, crop up; glimmer, loom; glare; burst forth; burst upon the view, burst upon the sight; heave in sight; come in sight, come into view, come out, come forth, come forward; see the light of day; break through the clouds; make its appearance, show its face, appear to one's eyes, come upon the stage, float before the eyes, speak for itself &c. (manifest) 525; attract the attention &c. 457; reappear; live in a glass house. expose to view &c. 525. Adj. visible, perceptible, perceivable, discernible, apparent; in view, in full view, in sight; exposed to view, en evidence; unclouded, unobscured[obs3], in the foreground. obvious &c. (manifest) 525; plain, clear, distinct, definite; well defined, well marked; in focus; recognizable, palpable, autoptical[obs3]; glaring, staring, conspicuous; stereoscopic; in bold, in strong relief. periscopic[obs3], panoramic. before one's eyes, under one's eyes; before one, vue d'oeil[Fr], in one's eye, oculis subjecta fidelibus[Lat]. Adv. visibly &c. adj.; in sight of; before one's eyes &c. adj.; veluti in speculum[Lat].

#447. Invisibility. — N. invisibility, invisibleness, nonappearance, imperceptibility; indistinctness &c. adj.; mystery, delitescence[obs3].

concealment &c. 528; latency &c. 526.

V. be invisible &c. adj.; be hidden &c. (hide) 528; lurk &c. (lie hidden) 526; escape notice.

render invisible &c. adj.; conceal &c. 528; put out of sight.

not see &c. (be blind) 442; lose sight of.

Adj. invisible, imperceptible; undiscernible[obs3], indiscernible; unapparent, non-apparent; out of sight, not in sight; a perte de vue[French]; behind the scenes, behind the curtain; viewless, sightless; inconspicuous, unconspicuous[obs3]; unseen &c. (see see &c. 441); covert &c. (latent) 526; eclipsed, under an eclipse.

dim &c. (faint) 422; mysterious, dark, obscure, confused; indistinct, indistinguishable; shadowy, indefinite, undefined; ill-defined, ill-marked; blurred, fuzzy, out of focus; misty &c. (opaque) 426; delitescent[obs3].

hidden, obscured, covered, veiled (concealed) 528.

Phr. "full many a flower is born to blush unseen" [Gray].

<— p. 125 —>

#448. Appearance. — N. appearance, phenomenon, sight, spectacle, show, premonstrationl, scene, species, view, coup d'oeil[Fr]; lookout, outlook, prospect, vista, perspective, bird's-eye view, scenery, landscape, picture, tableau; display, exposure, mise en scene[Fr]; rising of the curtain. phantasm, phantom &c. (fallacy of vision) 443. pageant, spectacle; peep-show, raree-show, gallanty-show; ombres chinoises[Sp]; magic lantern, phantasmagoria, dissolving views; biograph[obs3], cinematograph, moving pictures; panorama, diorama, cosmorama[obs3], georama[obs3]; coup de theatre, jeu de theatre[Fr]; pageantry &c. (ostentation) 882; insignia &c. (indication) 550. aspect, angle, phase, phasis[obs3], seeming; shape &c. (form) 240; guise, look, complexion, color, image, mien, air, cast, carriage, port, demeanor; presence, expression, first blush, face of the thing; point of view, light. lineament feature trait lines; outline, outside; contour, face, countenance, physiognomy, visage, phiz[obs3],. cast of countenance, profile, tournure[obs3], cut of one's jib, metoposcopy[obs3]; outside &c. 220. V. appear; be visible, become visible &c. 446; seem, look, show; present the appearance of, wear the appearance of, carry the appearance of, have the appearance of, bear the appearance of, exhibit the appearance of, take the appearance of, take on the appearance of, assume the appearance, present the semblance of, wear the semblance of, carry the semblance of, have the semblance of, bear the semblance of, exhibit the semblance of, take the semblance of, take on the semblance of, assume the semblance of; look like; cut a figure, figure; present to the view; show &c. (make manifest) 525. Adj. apparent, seeming, ostensible; on view. Adv. apparently; to all seeming, to all appearance; ostensibly, seemingly, as it seems, on the face of it, prima facie [Lat]; at the first blush, at first sight; in the eyes of; to the eye. Phr. editio princeps [Lat].

#449. Disappearance. — N. disappearance, evanescence, eclipse, occultation.

departure &c. 293; exit; vanishing point; dissolving views.

V. disappear, vanish, dissolve, fade, melt away, pass, go, avaunt[obs3], evaporate, vaporize; be gone &c. adj.; leave no trace, leave "not a rack behind" [Tempest]; go off the stage &c. (depart) 293; suffer an eclipse, undergo an eclipse; retire from sight; be lost to view, pass out of sight.

lose sight of.

efface &c. 552.

Adj. disappearing &c. v.; evanescent; missing, lost; lost to sight, lost to view; gone.

Int. vanish! disappear! avaunt[obs3]! get lost! get out of here &c. (ejection) 297.

<— p. 126 —>
%

CLASS IV
WORDS RELATING TO THE INTELLECTUAL FACULTIES
DIVISION (I) FORMATION OF IDEAS
Section I. OPERATIONS OF INTELLECT IN GENERAL
%

#450. Intellect. — N. intellect, mind, understanding, reason, thinking principle; rationality; cogitative faculties, cognitive faculties, discursive faculties, reasoning faculties, intellectual faculties; faculties, senses, consciousness, observation, percipience, intelligence, intellection, intuition, association of ideas, instinct, conception, judgment, wits, parts, capacity, intellectuality, genius; brains, cognitive powers, intellectual powers; wit &c. 498; ability &c. (skill) 698; wisdom &c. 498; Vernunft[Ger], Verstand[Ger]. soul, spirit, ghost, inner man, heart, breast, bosom, penetralia mentis[Lat], divina particula aurae[Lat], heart's core; the Absolute, psyche, subliminal consciousness, supreme principle. brain, organ of thought, seat of thought; sensorium[obs3], sensory; head, headpiece; pate, noddle[obs3], noggin, skull, scull, pericranium[Med], cerebrum, cranium, brainpan[obs3], sconce, upper story. [in computers] central processing unit, CPU; arithmetic and logical unit, ALU. [Science of mind] metaphysics; psychics, psychology; ideology; mental philosophy, moral philosophy; philosophy of the mind; pneumatology[obs3], phrenology; craniology[Med], cranioscopy[Med]. ideality, idealism; transcendentalism, spiritualism; immateriality &c. 317; universal concept, universal conception. metaphysician, psychologist &c. V. note, notice, mark; take notice of, take cognizance of be aware of, be conscious of; realize; appreciate; ruminate &c. (think) 451; fancy &c. (imagine) 515. Adj. intellectual[Relating to intellect], mental, rational, subjective, metaphysical, nooscopic[obs3], spiritual; ghostly; psychical[obs3], psychological; cerebral; animastic[obs3]; brainy; hyperphysical[obs3], superphysical[obs3]; subconscious, subliminal. immaterial &c. 317; endowed with reason. Adv. in petto. Phr. ens rationis [Lat]; frons est animi janua [Lat][Cicero]; locos y ninos dicen la verdad [Sp]; mens sola loco non exulat [Lat][Ovid]; "my mind is my

113

kingdom" [Campbell]; "stern men with empires in their brains" [Lowell]; "the mind, the music breathing from her face" [Byron]; "thou living ray of intellectual Fire" [Falconer].

<— differentiate between instinct and intuition. Intuition is reserved for people. —>

#450a. Absence or want of Intellect.— N. absence of intellect, want of intellect &c. 450; imbecility &c. 499.: brutality, brute force.

instinct, brute instinct, stimulus-response loop, conditioned response, instinctive reaction, Pavlovian response.

mimicry, aping (imitation) 19.

moron, imbecile, idiot; fool &c. 501; dumb animal; vegetable, brain-dead.

Adj. unendowed with reason, void of reason; thoughtless; vegetative; moronic, idiotic, brainless [all pejorative].

Adv. instinctively, like Pavlov's dog; vegetatively.

V. mimic, ape (imitate) 19; respond instinctively.

#451. Thought. — N. thought; exercitation of the intellect[obs3], exercise of the intellect; intellection; reflection, cogitation, consideration, meditation, study, lucubration, speculation, deliberation, pondering; head work, brain work; cerebration; deep reflection; close study, application &c. (attention) 457. abstract thought, abstraction contemplation, musing; brown study &c. (inattention) 458; reverie, Platonism; depth of thought, workings of the mind, thoughts, inmost thoughts; self-counsel self-communing, self- consultation; philosophy of the Absolute, philosophy of the Academy, philosophy of the Garden, philosophy of the lyceum, philosophy of the Porch. association of thought, succession of thought, flow of thought, train of thought, current of thought, association of ideas, succession of ideas, flow of ideas, train of ideas, current of ideas. after thought, mature thought; reconsideration, second thoughts; retrospection &c. (memory) 505; excogitation[obs3]; examination &c. (inquiry) 461 invention &c. (imagination) 515. thoughtfulness &c. adj. V. think, reflect, cogitate, excogitate[obs3], consider, deliberate; bestow thought upon, bestow consideration upon; speculate, contemplate, meditate, ponder, muse, dream, ruminate; brood over, con over; animadvert, study; bend -, apply mind &c. (attend) 457; digest, discuss, hammer at, weigh, perpend; realize, appreciate; fancy &c. (imagine) 515; trow[obs3]. take into consideration; take counsel &c. (be advised) 695; commune with oneself, bethink oneself; collect one's thoughts; revolve in the mind, turn over in the mind, run over in the mind; chew the cud upon, sleep upon; take counsel of one's pillow, advise with one's pillow. rack one's brains, ransack one's brains, crack one's brains, beat one's brains, cudgel one's brains; set one's brain to work, set one's wits to work. harbor an idea, entertain an idea, cherish an idea, nurture an idea &c. 453; take into one's head; bear in mind; reconsider. occur; present itself, suggest itself; come into one's head, get into one's head; strike one, flit across the view, come uppermost, run in one's head; enter the mind, pass in the mind, cross the mind, flash on the mind, flash across the mind, float in the mind, fasten itself on the mind, be uppermost in the mind, occupy the mind; have in one's mind. make an impression; sink into the mind, penetrate into the mind; engross the thoughts. Adj. thinking &c. v.; thoughtful, pensive, meditative, reflective, museful[obs3], wistful, contemplative, speculative, deliberative, studious, sedate, introspective, Platonic, philosophical. lost in thought &c. (inattentive) 458; deep musing &c. (intent) 457. in the mind, under consideration. Adv. all things considered. Phr. the mind being on the stretch; the mind turning upon, the head turning upon, the mind running upon; "divinely, bent to meditation" [Richard III]; en toute chose il faut considerer la fin[Fr][obs3]; "fresh- pluckt from bowers of never-failing thought" [O. Meredith]; "go speed the stars of Thought"[Emerson]; "in maiden meditation fancy-free" [M. N. D.]; "so sweet is zealous contemplation" [Richard III]; "the power of thought is the magic of the Mind" [Byron]; "those that think must govern those that toil" [Goldsmith]; "thought is parent of the deed" [Carlyle]; "thoughts in attitudes imperious" [Longfellow]; "thoughts that breathe and words that burn" [Gray]; vivere est cogitare [Lat][Cicero]; Volk der Dichter und Denker [Ger].

<— p. 127 —>

#452. [Absence or want of thought.] Incogitancy. — N. incogitancy[obs3], vacancy, inunderstanding[obs3]; fatuity &c. 499; thoughtlessness &c. (inattention) 458; vacuity.

couch potato, vegetable.

V. not think &c. 451; not think of; dismiss from the mind, dismiss from the thoughts &c. 451.

indulge in reverie &c. (be inattentive) 458.

put away thought; unbend the mind, relax the mind, divert the mind, veg out.

Adj. vacant, unintellectual, unideal[obs3], unoccupied, unthinking, inconsiderate, thoughtless, mindless, no-brain, vacuous; absent &c. (inattentive) 458; diverted; irrational &c. 499; narrow-minded &c. 481.

unthought of, undreamt 'of, unconsidered; off one's mind; incogitable[obs3], not to be thought of.

Phr. absence d'esprit; pabulum pictura pascit inani[Lat][obs3].

#453. [Object of thought.] Idea. — N. idea, notion, conception, thought, apprehension, impression, perception, image, <gr/eidolon/gr>[Grk], sentiment, reflection, observation, consideration; abstract idea; archetype, formative notion; guiding conception, organizing conception; image in the mind, regulative principle. view &c. (opinion) 484; theory &c. 514; conceit, fancy; phantasy &c. (imagination) 515.point of view &c. (aspect) 448; field of view.

<— p. 128 —>

<— recall distinction between objective reality and perception thereof: noumenon and phenomenon —>

#454. [Subject of thought, <gr/noemata/gr>] Topic. — N. subject of thought, material for thought; food for the mind, mental pabulum.

subject, subject matter; matter, theme, <gr/noemata/gr>[Grk], topic, what it is about, thesis, text, business, affair, matter in hand, argument; motion, resolution; head, chapter; case, point; proposition, theorem; field of inquiry; moot point, problem &c. (question) 461.

V. float in the mind, pass in the mind &c. 451.

Adj. thought of; uppermost in the mind; in petto.

Adv. under consideration; in question, in the mind; on foot, on the carpet, on the docket, on the tapis[obs3]; relative to &c. 9.
% Section II. PRECURSORY CONDITIONS AND OPERATIONS %

#455. [The desire of knowledge.] Curiosity. — N. interest, thirst for knowledge, thirst for truth; curiosity, curiousness; inquiring mind; inquisitiveness. omnivorous intellect, devouring mind. [person who desires knowledge] inquirer; sightseer; quidnunc[Lat], newsmonger, Paul Pry, eavesdropper; gossip &c. (news) 532; rubberneck; intellectual; seeker[inquirer after religious knowledge], seeker after truth. V. be curious &c. adj.; take an interest in, stare, gape; prick up the ears, see sights, lionize; pry; nose; rubberneck*[U. S.]. Adj. curious, inquisitive, burning with curiosity, overcurious; inquiring &c. 461; prying, snoopy, nosy, peering; prurient; inquisitorial, inquisitory[obs3]; curious as a cat; agape &c. (expectant) 507. Phr. what's the matter? what next? consumed with curiosity; curiosity killed the cat, satisfaction brought it back. "curiouser and curiouser" [Alice in Wonderland].

#456. [Absence of curiosity.] Incuriosity. — N. incuriosity, incuriousness &c. adj.; insouciance &c. 866; indifference, lack of interest, disinterest. boredom, ennui (weariness) 841; satiety &c. 639; foreknowledge (foresight) 510. V. be incurious &c. adj.; have no curiosity &c. 455; take no interest in &c. 823; mind one's own business. Adj. incurious, uninquisitive, indifferent; impassive &c. 823; uninterested, detached, aloof.

#457. Attention. — N. attention; mindfulness, presence of mind &c. adj.; intentness, intentiveness[obs3]; alertness; thought &c. 451; advertence, advertency[obs3]; observance, observation; consideration, reflection, perpensionl; heed; heedfulness; particularity; notice, regard &c. v.; circumspection, diligence &c. (care) 459; study, scrutiny inspection, introspection; revision, revisal. active application, diligent application, exclusive application, minute application, close application, intense application, deep application, profound application, abstract application, labored application, deliberate application, active attention, diligent attention, exclusive attention, minute attention, close attention, intense attention, deep attention, profound attention, abstract attention, labored attention, deliberate attention, active thought, diligent thought, exclusive thought, minute thought, close thought, intense thought, deep thought, profound thought, abstract thought, labored thought, deliberate thought, active study, diligent study, exclusive study, minute study, close study, intense study, deep study, profound study, abstract study, labored study, deliberate study. minuteness, attention to detail. absorption of mind &c. (abstraction) 458. indication, calling attention to &c. v. V. be attentive &c. adj.; attend, advert to, observe, look, see, view, remark, notice, regard, take notice, mark; give attention to, pay attention to, pay heed to, give heed to; incline an ear to, lend an ear to; trouble one's head about; give a thought to, animadvert to; occupy oneself with; contemplate &c. (think of) 451; look at, look to, look after, look into, look over; see to; turn the mind to, bend the mind to, apply the mind to, direct the mind to, give the mind to, turn the eye to, bend the eye to, apply the eye to, direct the eye to, give the eye to, turn the attention to, bend the attention to, apply the attention to, direct the attention to, give the attention to; have an eye to, have in one's eye; bear in mind; take into account, take into consideration; keep in sight, keep in view; have regard to, heed, mind, take cognizance of entertain, recognize; make note of, take note of; note. examine cursorily; glance at, glance upon, glance over; cast the eyes over, pass the eyes over; run over, turn over the leaves, dip into, perstringe! skim &c. (neglect) 460; take a cursory view of. examine, examine closely, examine intently; scan, scrutinize, consider; give one's mind to, bend one's mind to; overhaul, revise, pore over; inspect, review, pass under review; take stock of; fix the eye on, rivet attention on, fix attention on, devote the eye to, fix the mind on, devote the thoughts to; hear out, think out; mind one's business. revert to; watch &c. (expect) 507, (take care of) 459; hearken to, listen to; prick up the ears; have the eyes open, keep the eyes open; come to the point. meet with attention; fall under one's notice, fall under one's observation; be under consideration &c. (topic) 454. catch the eye, strike the eye; attract notice; catch the attention, awaken the attention, wake the attention, invite the attention, solicit the attention, attract the attention, claim the attention, excite the attention, engage the attention, occupy the attention, strike the attention, arrest the attention, fix the attention, engross the attention, absorb the attention, rivet the attention, catch the mind, awaken the mind, wake the mind, invite the mind, solicit the mind, attract the mind, claim the mind excite the mind, engage the mind, occupy the mind, strike the mind, arrest the mind, fix the mind, engross the mind, absorb the mind, rivet the mind, catch the thoughts, awaken the thoughts, wake the thoughts, invite the thoughts, solicit the thoughts, attract the thoughts, claim the thoughts excite the thoughts, engage the thoughts, occupy the thoughts, strike the thoughts, arrest the thoughts, fix the thoughts, engross the thoughts, absorb the thoughts, rivet the thoughts; be present to the mind, be uppermost in the mind. bring under one's notice; point out, point to, point at, point the finger at; lay the finger on, indigitate! indicate; direct attention to, call attention to; show; put a mark &c. (sign) 550 upon; call soldiers to "attention"; bring forward &c. (make manifest) 525. Adj. attentive, mindful, observant, regardful; alive to, awake to; observing &c. v.; alert, open-eyed; intent on, taken up with, occupied with, engaged in; engrossed in, wrapped in, absorbed, rapt, transfixed, riveted, mesmerized, hypnotized; glued to (the TV); breathless; preoccupied &c. (inattentive) 458; watchful &c. (careful) 459; breathless, undistracted, upon the stretch; on the watch &c. (expectant) 507. steadfast. [compelling attention] interesting, engrossing, mesmerizing, riveting. Int. see! look, look here, look you, look to it! mark! lo! behold! soho[obs3]! hark, hark ye! mind! halloo! observe! lo and behold! attention! nota bene [Latin], "N.B.", note well; I'd have you to know; notice! O yes! Oyez! dekko[obs3]! ecco[obs3]! yoho! Phr. this is to give notice, these are to give notice; dictum sapienti sat est [Latin: a word to the wise is sufficient]; finem respice[Lat]. Attention! Now hear this! Oyez!; Achtung[German]; vnimanie[Russ][Russian]; chui[Japanese].

<— p. 129 —>

#458. Inattention. — N. inattention, inconsideration; inconsiderateness &c. adj.; oversight; inadvertence, inadvertency, nonobservance, disregard. supineness &c. (inactivity) 683; etourderie[French], want of thought; heedlessness &c. (neglect) 460; insouciance &c. (indifference) 866. abstraction; absence of mind, absorption of mind; preoccupation, distraction, reverie, brown study, deep musing, fit of abstraction. V. be inattentive &c. adj.; overlook, disregard; pass by &c. (neglect) 460 not observe &c. 457; think little of. close one's eyes to, shut one's eyes to; pay no attention to; dismiss from one's thoughts, discard from one's thoughts, discharge from one's thoughts, dismiss from one's mind, discard from one's mind, discharge from one's mind; drop the subject, think no more of; set aside, turn aside, put aside; turn away from, turn one's attention from, turn a deaf ear to, turn one's back upon. abstract oneself, dream, indulge in reverie. escape notice, escape attention; come in at one ear and go out at the other; forget &c. (have no remembrance) 506. call off the attention, draw off the attention, call away the attention, divert the attention, distract the mind; put out of one's head; disconcert, discompose; put out, confuse, perplex, bewilder, moider[obs3], fluster, muddle, dazzle; throw a sop to Cerberus. Adj. inattentive; unobservant, unmindful, heedless, unthinking, unheeding, undiscerning[obs3]; inadvertent; mindless, regardless, respectless[obs3], listless &c. (indifferent) 866; blind, deaf; bird- witted; hand over head; cursory, percursory[obs3]; giddy-brained, scatter- brained, hare-brained; unreflective, unreflecting[obs3], ecervele [French]; offhand; dizzy, muzzy[obs3], brainsick[obs3]; giddy, giddy as a goose; wild, harum-scarum, rantipole[obs3], highflying; heedless, careless &c. (neglectful) 460. inconsiderate, thoughtless. absent, abstracted, distrait; absentminded, lost; lost in thought, wrapped in thought; rapt, in the clouds, bemused; dreaming on other things, musing on other things; preoccupied, engrossed &c. (attentive) 457; daydreaming, in a reverie &c. n.; off one's guard &c. (inexpectant) 508[obs3]; napping; dreamy; caught napping. disconcerted, distracted, put out &c. v. Adv. inattentively, inadvertently, absent-mindedly &c. adj[obs3].; per incuriam[Lat], sub silentio[Lat]. Int. stand at ease, stand easy! Phr. the attention wanders; one's wits gone a woolgathering, one's wits gone a bird's nesting; it never entered into one's head; the mind running on other things; one's thoughts being elsewhere; had it been a bear it would have bitten you. 129

<— p. 130 —>

#459. Care. [Vigilance.] — N. care, solicitude, heed; heedfulness &c. adj.; scruple &c. (conscientiousness) 939.

watchfulness &c. adj.; vigilance, surveillance, eyes of Argus[obs3], watch, vigil, look out, watch and ward, loeil du maitre[Fr]. alertness &c. (activity) 682; attention &c. 457; prudence &c., circumspection &c. (caution) 864; anxiety; forethought &c. 510; precaution &c. (preparation) 673; tidiness &c. (order) 58, (cleanliness) 652; accuracy &c. (exactness) 494; minuteness, attention to detail. V. be careful &c. adj.; reck[obs3]; take care &c. (be cautious) 864; pay attention to &c. 457; take care of; look to, look after, see to, see after; keep an eye on, keep a sharp eye on; chaperon, matronize[obs3], play gooseberry; keep watch, keep watch and ward; mount guard, set watch, watch; keep in sight, keep in view; mind, mind one's business. look sharp, look about one; look with one's own eyes; keep a good lookout, keep a sharp lookout; have all one's wits about one, have all one's eyes about one; watch for &c. (expect) 507; keep one's eyes open, have the eyes open, sleep with one's eye open. Adj. careful regardful, heedful; taking care &c. v.; particular; prudent &c. (cautious) 864; considerate; thoughtful &c. (deliberative) 451; provident &c. (prepared) 673; alert &c. (active) 682; sure-footed. guarded, on one's guard; on the qui vivre[Fr], on the alert, on watch, on the lookout; awake, broad awake, vigilant; watchful, wakeful, wistful; Argus-eyed; wide awake &c. (intelligent) 498; on the watch for (expectant) 507. tidy &c. (orderly) 58, (clean) 652; accurate &c. (exact) 494; scrupulous &c. (conscientious) 939; cavendo tutus &c. (safe) 664[Lat]. Adv. carefully &c. adj.; with care, gingerly. Phr. quis custodiet istos custodes? [Latin: who will watch the watchers?]; "care will kill a cat" [Wither]; ni bebas agua que no veas [Sp]; "O polished perturbation! Golden care!" [Henry IV]; "the incessant care and labor of his mind" [Henry IV].

#460. Neglect. — N. neglect; carelessness &c. adj.; trifling &c. v.; negligence; omission, oversight, laches[Law], default; supineness &c. (inactivity) 683; inattention &c. 458; nonchalance &c. (insensibility) 823; imprudence, recklessness &c. 863; slovenliness &c. (disorder) 59, (dirt) 653; improvidence &c. 674; noncompletion &c. 730; inexactness &c. (error) 495. paralipsis, paralepsis, paraleipsis [in rhetoric]. trifler, waiter on Providence; Micawber. V. be negligent &c. adj.; take no care of &c. (take care of &c. 459); neglect; let slip, let go; lay aside, set aside, cast aside, put aside; keep out of sight, put out of sight; lose sight of. overlook, disregard; pass over, pas by; let pass; blink; wink at, connive at; gloss over; take no note of, take no thought of, take no account of, take no notice of; pay no regard to; laisser aller[Fr]. scamp; trifle, fribble[obs3]; do by halves; cut; slight &c. (despise) 930; play with, trifle with; slur, skim, skim the surface; effleurer [Fr]; take a cursory view of &c. 457. slur over, skip over, jump over, slip over; pretermit[obs3], miss, skip, jump, omit, give the go-by to, push aside, pigeonhole, shelve, sink; table [parliamentary]; ignore, shut one's eyes to, refuse to hear, turn a deaf ear to; leave out of one's calculation; not attend to &c. 457, not mind; not trouble oneself about, not trouble one's head about, not trouble oneself with; forget &c. 506; be caught napping &c. (not expect) 508; leave a loose thread; let the grass grow under one's feet. render neglectful &c. adj.; put off one's guard, throw off one's guard; distract, divert. Adj. neglecting &c. v.; unmindful, negligent, neglectful; heedless, careless, thoughtless; perfunctory, remiss; feebleness &c. 575. inconsiderate; uncircumspect[obs3], incircumspect[obs3]; off one's guard; unwary, unwatchful[obs3], unguarded; offhand. supine &c. (inactive) 683; inattentive &c. 458; insouciant &c. (indifferent) 823; imprudent, reckless &c. 863; slovenly &c. (disorderly) 59, (dirty) 653; inexact &c. (erroneous) 495; improvident &c. 674. neglected &c. v.; unheeded, uncared-for, unperceived, unseen, unobserved, unnoticed, unnoted[obs3], unmarked, unattended to, unthought of, unregarded[obs3], unremarked, unmissed[obs3]; shunted, shelved. unexamined, unstudied, unsearched[obs3], unscanned[obs3], unweighed[obs3], unsifted, unexplored. abandoned; buried in a napkin, hid under a bushel. Adv. negligently &c. adj.; hand over head, anyhow; in an unguarded moment &c. (unexpectedly) 508; per incuriam[Lat]. Int. never mind, no matter, let it pass. Phr. out of sight, out of mind.

<— p. 131 —>

#461. Inquiry [Subject of Inquiry. Question] — N. inquiry; request &c. 765; search, research, quest, pursuit &c. 622. examination, review, scrutiny, investigation, indagationl; perquisition[obs3], perscrutation[obs3], pervestigationl; inquest, inquisition; exploration; exploitation, ventilation. sifting; calculation, analysis, dissection, resolution, induction; Baconian method[obs3]. strict inquiry, close inquiry, searching inquiry, exhaustive inquiry; narrow search, strict search; study &c. (consideration) 451. scire facias[Lat], ad referendum; trial. questioning &c. v.; interrogation, interrogatory; interpellation; challenge, examination, cross-examination, catechism; feeler, Socratic method, zetetic philosophy[obs3]; leading question; discussion &c. (reasoning) 476. reconnoitering, reconnaissance; prying &c. v.; espionage, espionnage[Fr]; domiciliary visit, peep behind the curtain; lantern of Diogenes. question, query, problem, desideratum, point to be solved, porism[obs3]; subject of inquiry, field of inquiry, subject of controversy; point in dispute, matter in dispute; moot point; issue, question at issue; bone of contention &c. (discord) 713; plain question, fair question, open question; enigma &c. (secret) 533; knotty point &c. (difficulty) 704; quodlibet; threshold of an inquiry. [person who questions] inquirer, investigator, inquisitor, inspector, querist[obs3], examiner, catechist; scrutator scrutineer scrutinizer[obs3]; analyst; quidnunc &c. (curiosity) 455[Lat]. V. make inquiry &c. n.; inquire, ask, seek, search. look for, look about for, look out for; scan, reconnoiter, explore, sound, rummage, ransack, pry, peer, look round; look over, go over, look through, go through; spy, overhaul. [transitive: object is a topic] ask about, inquire about. scratch the head, slap the forehead. look into every hole and corner, peer into every hole and corner, pry into every hole and corner; nose; trace up; search out, hunt down, hunt out, fish out, ferret out; unearth; leave no stone unturned. seek a clue, seek a clew; hunt, track, trail, mouse, dodge, trace; follow the trail, follow the scent; pursue &c. 662; beat up one's quarters; fish for; feel for &c. (experiment) 463. investigate; take up an inquiry, institute an inquiry, pursue an inquiry, follow up an inquiry, conduct an inquiry, carry on an inquiry, carry out an inquiry, prosecute an inquiry &c. n.; look at, look into; preexamine; discuss, canvass, agitate. [inquire into a topic] examine, study, consider, calculate; dip into, dive into, delve into, go deep into; make sure of, probe, sound, fathom; probe to the bottom, probe to the quick; scrutinize, analyze, anatomize, dissect, parse, resolve, sift, winnow; view in all its phases, try in all its phases; thresh out. bring in question, bring into question, subject to examination; put to the proof &c. (experiment) 463; audit, tax, pass in review; take into consideration &c. (think over) 451; take counsel &c. 695. [intransitive] question, demand; put the question, pop the question, propose the question, propound the question, moot the question, start the question, raise the question, stir the question, suggest the question, put forth the question, ventilate the question, grapple with the question, go into a question. question[transitive: human object], put to the question, interrogate, pump; subject to interrogation, subject to examination; cross-question, cross-examine; press for an answer; give the third degree; put to the inquisition; dodge!. catechize. require an answer; pick the brains of, suck the brains of; feel the pulse. get the lay of the land; see how the wind is blowing; put one's ear to the ground. [intransitive] be in question &c. adj.; undergo examination. Adj. inquiry &c. v.; inquisitive &c. (curious) 455; requisitivel, requisitory[obs3]; catechetical[obs3], inquisitorial, analytic; in search of, in quest of; on the lookout for, interrogative, zetetic[obs3]; all searching. undetermined, untried, undecided; in question, in dispute, in issue, in course of inquiry; under discussion, under consideration, under investigation &c. n.; sub judice[Lat], moot, proposed; doubtful &c. (uncertain) 475. Adv. what? why? wherefore? whence? whither? where? quaere? how comes it[Lat], how happens it, how is it? what is the reason? what's the matter, what's in the wind? what on earth? when? who? nicht wahr?[Ger].

#462. Answer. — N. answer, response, reply, replication, riposte, rejoinder, surrejoinder[obs3], rebutter, surrebutter[obs3], retort, repartee; rescript, rescription[obs3]; antiphon[obs3], antiphony; acknowledgment; password; echo; counter statement.
discovery &c. 480a; solution &c. (explanation) 522; rationale &c. (cause) 153; clue &c. (indication) 550.
Oedipus; oracle &c. 513; return &c. (record) 551.
V. answer, respond, reply, rebut, retort, rejoin; give for answer, return for answer; acknowledge, echo.
explain &c. (interpret) 522; solve &c. (unriddle) 522; discover &c. 480a; fathom, hunt out &c. (inquire) 461; satisfy, set at rest, determine.
Adj. answering &c. v.; responsive, respondent; conclusive.
Adv. because &c. (cause) 153; on the scent, on the right scent.
Int. eureka!

<— p. 132 —>

#463. Experiment. — N. experiment; essay &c. (attempt) 675; analysis &c. (investigation) 461; screen; trial, tentative method, ttonnement. verification, probation, experimentum crucis[Lat], proof, (demonstration) 478; criterion, diagnostic, test, probe, crucial test, acid test, litmus test. crucible, reagent, check, touchstone, pix[obs3]; assay, ordeal; ring; litmus paper, curcuma paper[obs3], turmeric paper; test tube; analytical instruments &c. 633. empiricism, rule of thumb. feeler; trial balloon, pilot balloon, messenger balloon; pilot engine; scout; straw to show the wind. speculation, random shot, leap in the dark. analyzer, analyst, assayist[obs3]; adventurer; experimenter, experimentist[obs3], experimentalist; scientist, engineer, technician. subject, experimentee[obs3], guinea pig, experimental animal. [experimental method] protocol, experimental method, blind experiment, double-blind experiment, controlled experiment. poll, survey, opinion poll. epidemiological survey[Med], retrospective analysis, retrospective survey, prospective survey, prospective analysis; statistical analysis. literature search, library research. tryout, audition. [results of experiment] discovery &c 480; measurement &c. 466; evidence &c. 467. [reasoning about an experiment] deduction, induction, abduction. V. experiment; essay &c. (endeavor) 675; try, try out, assay; make an experiment, make a trial of; give a trial to; put on trial, subject to trial; experiment upon; rehearse; put to the test, bring to the test, submit to the test, submit to the proof; prove, verify, test, touch, practice upon, try one's strength; road-test, test drive, take for a spin; test fly. grope; feel one's way, grope for one's way; fumble, ttonner, aller ttons[Fr], put out a feeler, throw out a feeler; send up a trial balloon, send up a pilot balloon; see how the land lies, get the lay of the land, test the waters, feel out, sound out, take the pulse, see, check, check out[coll.], see how the wind blows; consult the barometer; feel the pulse; fish for, bob for; cast for, beat about for; angle, trawl, cast one's net, beat the bushes. try one's fortune &c. (adventure) 675; explore &c. (inquire) 461. Adj. experimental, empirical. probative, probatory[obs3], probationary, provisional; analytic, docimastic[obs3]; tentative;unverified, unproven, speculative, untested. Adv. on trial, under examination, on probation, under probation, on one's trial, on approval. Phr. check it out, give it a try, see how it goes; "Run it up the flagpole and see who salutes."

#464. Comparison. — N. comparison, collation, contrast; identification; comparative estimate, relative estimate, relativity.
simile, similitude, analogy (similarity) 17; allegory &c. (metaphor) 521.
matching, pattern-matching.
[quantitative comparison] ratio, proportion (number) 84.
[results of comparison] discrimination 465; indiscrimination 465a[obs3]; identification 465b.
V. compare to, compare with; collate, confront; place side by side, juxtapose &c. (near) 197; set against one another, pit against one another; contrast, balance.
identify, draw a parallel, parallel.
compare notes; institute a comparison; parva componere magnis[Lat]..
Adj. comparative; metaphorical &c. 521.
compared with &c. v.; comparable; judged by comparison.
Adv. relatively &c. (relation) 9; as compared with &c. v.
Phr. comparisons are odious; "comparisons are odorous" [Much Ado about Nothing].
#464a. Incomparability [Lack of comparison] — N. incomparability; incommensurability; indistinguishablility &c. 465a.
Adj. incommensurable, incommensurate; incomparable; different &c.15.
Phr. like apples and oranges; no basis for comparison; no standard for comparison.
#465. [results of comparison. 1] Discrimination. — N. discrimination, distinction, differentiation, diagnosis, diorism[obs3]; nice perception; perception of difference, appreciation of difference; estimation &c. 466; nicety, refinement; taste &c. 850; critique, judgment; tact; discernment &c. (intelligence) 498; acuteness, penetration; nuances. dope*, past performances. V. discriminate, distinguish, severalize[obs3]; recognize, match, identify; separate; draw the line, sift; separate the chaff from the wheat, winnow the chaff from the wheat; separate the men from the boys; split hairs, draw a fine line, nitpick, quibble. estimate &c. (measure) 466; know which is which, know what is what, know "a hawk from a handsaw" [Hamlet]. take into account, take into consideration; give due weight to, allow due weight to; weigh carefully. Adj. discriminating &c. v.; dioristic[obs3], discriminative, distinctive; nice. Phr. il y a fagots et fagots; rem acu tetigisti[Lat][obs3]; la critique est aisee et l'art est difficile [Fr]; miles apart; a distinction without a difference.

#465a. [results of comparison. 2] Indiscrimination. — N. indiscrimination[obs3], indistinguishability; indistinctness, indistinction[obs3]; uncertainty &c. (doubt) 475; incomparability &c. 464a.
V. not discriminate &c. 465; overlook &c. (neglect) 460 a distinction: confound, confuse.
Adj. indiscriminate; undistinguishedl!, indistinguishable, undistinguishable[obs3]; unmeasured; promiscuous, undiscriminating.
Phr. valeat quantum valere potest[Lat.].
<— p. 133 —>

#465b. [results of comparison. 3] Identification. — N. identification, recognition, diagnosis, match; apperception, assimilation; dereplication; classification; memory &c. 505; interpretation &c. 522; cognizance (knowledge) 490. V. identify, recognize, match, match up; classify; recall, remember &c. (memory) 505; find similarity (similarity) 17; put in its proper place, put in its proper niche, place in order (arrangement) 60.

#466. Measurement. — N. measurement, admeasurement[obs3], mensuration, survey, valuation, appraisement, assessment, assize; estimate, estimation; dead reckoning, reckoning &c. (numeration) 85; gauging &c. v.; horse power. metrology, weights and measures, compound arithmetic. measure, yard measure, standard, rule, foot rule, compass, calipers; gage, gauge; meter, line, rod, check; dividers; velo[obs3]. flood mark, high water mark; Plimsoll line; index &c. 550. scale; graduation, graduated scale; nonius[obs3]; vernier &c. (minuteness) 193. [instruments for measuring] bathometer, galvanometer, heliometer, interferometer, odometer, ombrometer[obs3], pantometer[obs3], pluviometer[obs3], pneumatometer[obs3], pneumometer[obs3], radiometer, refractometer, respirometer, rheometer, spirometer[obs3], telemeter, udometer[obs3], vacuometer[obs3], variometer[obs3], viameter[obs3], thermometer, thermistor (heat &c. 382), barometer (air &c. 338), anemometer (wind 349), dynamometer, goniometer (angle 244) meter; landmark &c. (limit) 233; balance, scale &c. (weight) 319; marigraph[obs3], pneumatograph[obs3], stethograph[obs3]; rain gauge, rain gage; voltmeter(volts), ammeter(amps); spectrophotometer (light absorbance); mass spectrophotometer(molecular mass); geiger counter, scintillation counter(radioactivity); pycnometer (liquid density); graduated cylinder, volumetric flask (volume); radar gun (velocity); radar (distance); side-looking radar (shape, topography); sonar (depth in water); light meter (light intensity); clock, watch, stopwatch, chronometer (time); anemometer (wind velocity); densitometer (color intensity). measurability, computability, determinability[obs3]. coordinates, ordinate and abscissa, polar coordinates, latitude and longitude, declination and right ascension, altitude and azimuth. geometry, stereometry[obs3], hypsometry[obs3]; metage[obs3]; surveying, land surveying; geodesy, geodetics[obs3], geodesia[obs3]; orthometry[obs3], altimetry[obs3]; cadastre[Fr]. astrolabe, armillary sphere[obs3]. land surveyor; geometer. V. measure, mete; determine, assay; evaluate, value, assess, rate, appraise, estimate, form an estimate, set a value on; appreciate; standardize. span, pace step; apply the compass &c. n.; gauge, plumb, probe, sound, fathom; heave the log, heave the lead; survey. weigh. take an average &c. 29; graduate. Adj. measuring &c. v.; metric, metrical; measurable, perceptible, noticeable, detectable, appreciable, ponderable, determinable, fathomable; geodetical, topographic, topographical, cartographic, cartographical.

% Section III. MATERIALS FOR REASONING %

#467. Evidence [On one side.] — N. evidence; facts, premises, data, praecognita[Lat], grounds. indication &c. 550; criterion &c. (test) 463. testimony, testification[obs3], expert testimony; attestation; deposition &c. (affirmation) 535; examination. admission &c. (assent) 488; authority, warrant, credential, diploma, voucher, certificate, doquet[obs3], docket; testamur[obs3]; record &c. 551; document; pi ce justificative[obs3]; deed, warranty &c. (security) 771; signature, seal &c. (identification) 550; exhibit, material evidence, objective evidence. witness, indicator, hostile witness; eyewitness, earwitness, material witness, state's evidence; deponent; sponsor; cojuror[obs3]. oral evidence, documentary evidence, hearsay evidence, external evidence, extrinsic evidence, internal evidence, intrinsic evidence, circumstantial evidence, cumulative evidence, ex parte evidence[Lat], presumptive evidence, collateral evidence, constructive evidence; proof &c. (demonstration) 478; evidence in chief. secondary evidence; confirmation, corroboration, support; ratification &c. (assent) 488; authentication; compurgation[obs3], wager of law, comprobationl. citation, reference; legal research, literature search (experiment) 463.

V. be evidence &c. n.; evince, show, betoken, tell of; indicate &c. (denote) 550; imply, involve, argue, bespeak, breathe. have weight, carry weight; tell, speak volumes; speak for itself &c. (manifest) 525. rest upon, depend upon; repose on. bear witness &c. n.; give evidence &c. n.; testify, depose, witness, vouch for; sign, seal, undersign[obs3], set one's hand and seal, sign and seal, deliver as one's act and deed, certify, attest; acknowledge &c. (assent) 488. [provide conclusive evidence] make absolute, confirm, prove (demonstrate) 478. [add further evidence] indorse, countersign, corroborate, support, ratify, bear out, uphold, warrant. adduce, attest, cite, quote; refer to, appeal to; call, call to witness; bring forward, bring into court; allege, plead; produce witnesses, confront witnesses. place into evidence, mark into evidence. [obtain evidence] collect evidence, bring together evidence, rake up evidence; experiment &c. 463. have a case, make out a case; establish, authenticate, substantiate, verify, make good, quote chapter and verse; bring home to, bring to book. Adj. showing &c. v.; indicative, indicatory; deducible &c. 478; grounded on, founded on, based on; corroborative, confirmatory. Adv. by inference; according to, witness, a fortiori; still more, still less; raison de plus[Fr]; in corroboration &c. n. of; valeat quantum[Lat]; under seal, under one's hand and seal. Phr. dictum de dicto[Lat]; mise en evidence[Fr.].

<— p. 134 —>

#468. [Evidence on the other side, on the other hand.] Counter Evidence. — N. counter evidence; evidence on the other side, evidence on the other hand; conflicting evidence, contradictory evidence, opposing evidence; disproof, refutation &c. 479; negation &c. 536. plea &c. 617; vindication &c. 937 counter protest; "tu quoque" argument; other side of the shield, other side of the coin, reverse of the shield. V. countervail, oppose; mitigate against; rebut &c. (refute) 479; subvert &c. (destroy) 162; cheek, weaken; contravene; contradict &c. (deny) 536; tell the other side of the story, tell another story, turn the scale, alter the case; turn the tables; cut both ways; prove a negative. audire alteram partem[Lat]. Adj. countervailing &c. v.; contradictory. unattested, unauthenticated, unsupported by evidence; supposititious. Adv. on the contrary, per contra.

#469. Qualification. — N. qualification, limitation, modification, coloring.

allowance, grains of allowance, consideration, extenuating circumstances; mitigation.

condition, proviso, prerequisite, contingency, stipulation, provision, specification, sine qua non[Lat]; catch, string, strings attached; exemption; exception, escape clause, salvo, saving clause; discount &c. 813; restriction; fine print.

V. qualify, limit, modify, leaven, give a color to, introduce new conditions, narrow, temper.

waffle, quibble, hem and haw (be uncertain) 475; equivocate (sophistry) 477.

depend, depend on, be contingent on (effect) 154.

allow for, make allowance for; admit exceptions, take into account; modulate.

moderate, temper, season, leaven.

take exception.

Adj. qualifying &c. v.; qualified, conditioned, restricted, hedged; conditional; exceptional &c. (unconformable) 83.

hypothetical &c. (supposed) 514; contingent &c. (uncertain) 475.

Adv. provided, provided that, provided always; if, unless, but, yet; according as; conditionally, admitting, supposing; on the supposition of &c. (theoretically) 514; with the understanding, even, although, though, for all that, after all, at all events.

approximately &c. 197, 17; in a limited degree (smallness) 32; somewhat, sort of, something like that, to a certain extent, to a degree, in a sense, so to speak.

with grains of allowance, cum grano salis[Latin: with a grain of salt]; exceptis excipiendis[Lat]; wind and weather permitting; if possible &c. 470.

subject to, conditioned upon; with this proviso &c. n.

Phr. "if the good lord is willing and the creeks don't rise"; catch-22.
% Degrees of Evidence %

#470. Possibility. — N. possibility, potentiality; what may be, what is possible &c. adj.; compatibility &c. (agreement) 23.

practicability, feasibility; practicableness &c. adj. contingency, chance &c. 156.

V. be possible &c. adj.; stand a chance; admit of, bear.

render possible &c. adj.; put in the way of.

Adj. possible; in the cards, on the dice; in posse, within the bounds of possibility, conceivable, credible; compatible &c. 23; likely.

practicable, feasible, performable, achievable; within reach, within measurable distance; accessible, superable[obs3], surmountable; attainable, obtainable; contingent &c. (doubtful) 475, (effect) 154.

barely possible, marginally possible, just possible; possible but improbably, (improbable) 473; theoretically possible.

Adv. possibly, by possibility; perhaps, perchance, peradventure; maybe, may be, haply, mayhap.

if possible, wind and weather permitting, God willing, Deo volente[Lat], D. V.; as luck may have it.

Phr. misericordia Domini inter pontem et fontent[Lat]; "the glories of the Possible are ours" [B. Taylor]; anything is possible; in theory possible, but in practise unlikely.
<— p. 135 —>

#471. Impossibility. — N. impossibility &c. adj.; what cannot, what can never be; sour grapes; hopelessness &c. 859.

V. be impossible &c. adj.; have no chance whatever. attempt impossibilities; square the circle, wash a blackamoor white; skin a flint; make a silk purse out of a sow's ear, make bricks without straw; have nothing to go upon; weave a rope of sand, build castles in the air, prendre la lune avec les dents[Fr], extract sunbeams from cucumbers, set the Thames on fire, milk a he-goat into a sieve, catch a weasel asleep, rompre l'anguille au genou[Fr], be in two places at once. Adj. impossible; not possible &c. 470; absurd, contrary to reason; unlikely; unreasonable &c. 477; incredible &c. 485; beyond the bounds of reason, beyond the bounds of possibility, beyond the realm of possibility; from which reason recoils; visionary; inconceivable &c. (improbable) 473; prodigious &c. (wonderful) 870; unimaginable, inimaginable[obs3]; unthinkable. impracticable unachievable; unfeasible, infeasible; insuperable; unsurmountable[obs3], insurmountable; unattainable, unobtainable; out of reach, out of the question; not to be had, not to be thought of; beyond control; desperate &c. (hopeless) 859; incompatible &c. 24; inaccessible, uncomeatable[obs3], impassable, impervious, innavigable[obs3], inextricable; self-contradictory. out of one's power, beyond one's power, beyond one's depth, beyond one's reach, beyond one's grasp; too much for; ultra crepidam[Lat]. Phr. the grapes are sour; non possumus[Lat]; non nostrum tantas componere lites [Lat][Vergil]; look for a needle in a haystack, chercher une aiguille dans une botte de foin [obs3][Fr.]; il a le mer boire[obs3].

#472. Probability. — N. probability, likelihood; credibleness[obs3]; likeliness &c. adj.; vraisemblance[Fr], verisimili-tude, plausibility; color, semblance, show of; presumption; presumptive evidence, circumstantial evidence; credibility. reasonable chance, fair chance, good chance, favorable chance, reasonable prospect, fair prospect, good prospect, favorable prospect; prospect, wellgrounded hope; chance &c. 156. V. be probable &c. adj.; give color to, lend color to; point to; imply &c. (evidence) 467; bid fair &c. (promise) 511; stand fair for; stand a good chance, run a good chance. think likely, dare say, flatter oneself; expect &c. 507; count upon &c. (believe) 484. Adj. probable, likely, hopeful, to be expected, in a fair way. plausible, specious, ostensible, colorable, ben trovato[It], well- founded, reasonable, credible, easy of belief, presumable, presumptive, apparent. Adv. probably &c. adj.; belike[obs3]; in all probability, in all likelihood; very likely, most likely; like enough; odds on, odds in favor, ten &c. to one; apparently, seemingly, according to every reasonable expectation; prim facie[Lat]; to all appearance &c. (to the eye) 448. Phr. the chances, the odds are; appearances are in favor of, chances are in favor of; there is reason to believe, there is reason to think, there is reason to expect; I dare say; all Lombard Street to a China orange.

#473. Improbability. — N. improbability, unlikelihood; unfavorable chance, bad chance, ghost of a chance, little chance, small chance, poor chance, scarcely any chance, no chance; bare possibility; long odds; incredibility &c. 485. V. be improbable &c. adj.; have a small chance &c. n. Adj. improbable, unlikely, contrary to all reasonable expectation; wild, far out, out of sight, outtasight, heavy [all coll.]. rare &c. (infrequent) 137; unheard of, inconceiv-able; unimaginable, inimaginable[obs3]; incredible &c. 485; more than doubtful; strange, bizarre (uncomformable) 83. Phr. the chances are against; aquila non capit muscas[Lat]; pedir peras pal olmo[Lat].

#474. Certainty. — N. certainty; necessity &c. 601; certitude, surety, assurance; dead certainty, moral certainty; infallibleness &c. adj.; infallibility, reliability; indubitableness, inevitableness, unquestionableness[obs3]. gospel, scripture, church, pope, court of final appeal; res judicata[Lat], ultimatum positiveness; dogmatism, dogmatist, dogmatizer; doctrinaire, bigot, opinionist[obs3], Sir Oracle; ipse dixit[Lat]. fact; positive fact, matter of fact; fait accompli[Fr]. V. be certain &c. adj.; stand to reason. render certain &c. adj.; insure, ensure, assure; clinch, make sure; determine, decide, set at rest, "make assurance double sure" [Macbeth]; know &c. (believe) 484. dogmatize, lay down the law. Adj. certain, sure, assured &c. v.; solid, well-founded. unqualified, absolute, positive, determinate, definite, clear, unequivocal, categorical, unmistakable, decisive, decided, ascertained. inevitable, unavoidable, avoidless[obs3]; ineluctable. unerring, infallible; unchangeable &c. 150; to be depended on, trustworthy, reliable, bound. unimpeachable, undeniable, unquestionable; indisputable, incontestable, incontrovertible, indubitable; irrefutable &c. (proven) 478; conclusive, without power of appeal. indubious[obs3]; without doubt, beyond a doubt, without a shade or shadow of doubt, without question, beyond question; past dispute; clear as day; beyond all question, beyond all dispute; undoubted, uncontested, unquestioned, undisputed; questionless[obs3], doubtless. authoritative, authentic, official. sure as fate, sure as death and taxes, sure as a gun. evident, self-evident, axiomat-ic; clear, clear as day, clear as the sun at noonday. Adv. certainly &c. adj.; for certain, certes[Lat], sure, no doubt, doubtless, and no mistake, flagrante delicto[Lat], sure enough, to be sure, of course, as a matter of course, a coup sur, to a certainty; in truth &c. (truly) 494; at any rate, at all events; without fail; coute que coute[Fr], coute qu'il coute[Fr]; whatever may happen, if the worst come to the worst; come what may, happen what may, come what will; sink or swim; rain or shine. Phr. cela va sans dire[Fr]; there is -no question, - not a shadow of doubt; the die is cast &c. (necessity) 601; "facts are stubborn things" [Smollett].

<— p. 136 —>

#475. Uncertainty. — N. uncertainty, incertitude, doubt; doubtfulness &c. adj.; dubiety, dubitation[obs3], dubitancyl, dubitousness[obs3]. hesitation, suspense; perplexity, embarrassment, dilemma, bewilderment; timidity &c. (fear) 860; vacillation &c. 605; diaporesis[obs3], indetermination. vagueness &c. adj.; haze, fog; obscurity &c. (darkness) 421; ambiguity &c. (double meaning) 520; contingency, dependence, dependency, double contingency, possibility upon a possibility; open question &c. (question) 461; onus probandi[Lat]; blind bargain, pig in a poke, leap in the dark, something or other; needle in a haystack, needle in a bottle of hay; roving commission. precariousness &c. adj.; fallibility. V. be uncertain &c. adj.; wonder whether. lose the clue, lose the clew, scent; miss one's way. not know what to make of &c. (unintelligibility) 519, not know which way to turn, not know whether one stands on one's head or one's heels; float in a sea of doubt,hesitate, flounder; lose oneself, lose one's head; muddle one's brains. render uncertain &c. adj.; put out, pose, puzzle, perplex, embarrass; confuse, confound; bewilder, bother, molder, addle the wits, throw off the scent, ambiguas in vulgus spargere voces[Lat]; keep in suspense. doubt &c. (disbelieve) 485; hang in the balance, tremble in the balance; depend. Adj. uncertain; casual; random &c. (aimless) 621; changeable &c. 149. doubtful, dubious; indecisive; unsettled, undecided, undetermined; in suspense, open to discussion; controvertible; in question &c. (inquiry) 461. vague; indeterminate, indefinite; ambiguous, equivocal; undefined, undefinable; confused &c. (indistinct) 447; mystic, oracular; dazed. perplexing &c. v.; enigmatic, paradoxical, apocryphal, problematical, hypothetical; experimental &c. 463. unpredictable, unforeseeable (unknowable) 519. fallible, questionable, precarious, slippery, ticklish, debatable, disputable; unreliable, untrustworthy. contingent, contingent on, dependent on; subject to; dependent on circumstances; occasional; provisional. unauthentic, unau- thenticated, unauthoritative; unascertained, unconfirmed; undemonstrated; untold, uncounted. in a state of uncer- tainty, in a cloud, in a maze; bushed, off the track; ignorant.&c. 491; afraid to say; out of one's reckoning, astray, adrift; at sea, at fault, at a loss, at one's wit's end, at a nonplus; puzzled &c. v.; lost, abroad, dsorient; distracted, distraught. Adv. pendente lite[Lat]; sub spe rati[Lat]. Phr. Heaven knows; who can tell? who shall decide when doctors disagree? ambiguas in vulgum spargere voces[Lat].

<— p. 137 —>

% Section IV. REASONING PROCESSES %

#476. Reasoning, — N. {ant. 477} reasoning, ratiocination, rationalism; dialectics, induction, generalization. discus- sion, comment; ventilation; inquiry &c. 461. argumentation, controversy, debate; polemics, wrangling; contention &c. 720 logomachy[obs3]; disputation, disceptation[obs3]; paper war. art of reasoning, logic. process of reasoning, train of reasoning, chain of reasoning; deduction, induction, abduction; synthesis, analysis. argument; case, plaidoyer[obs3], opening; lemma, proposition, terms, premises, postulate, data, starting point, principle; inference &c. (judgment) 480. prosyllogism[obs3], syllogism; enthymeme[obs3], sorites[obs3], dilemma, perilepsis[obs3], a priori reasoning, reductio ad absurdum, horns of a dilemma, argumentum ad hominem [Lat.], comprehensive argument; empirema[obs3], epagoge[obs3]. [person who reasons] reasoner, logician, dialectician; disputant; controversialist, controvertist[obs3]; wrangler, arguer, debater polemic, casuist, rationalist; scientist; eristic[obs3]. logical sequence; good case; correct just reasoning, sound reasoning, valid reasoning, cogent reasoning, logical reasoning, forcible reasoning, persuasive reasoning, persuasory reasoning[obs3], consectary reasoningl, conclusive &c. 478; subtle reasoning; force of argument, strong point, strong argument, persuasive argument. arguments, reasons, pros and cons. V. reason, argue, discuss, debate, dispute, wrangle- argufy[obs3], bandy words, bandy arguments; chop logic; hold an argument, carry on an argument; controvert &c. (deny) 536; canvass; comment upon, moralize upon; spiritualize; consider &c. (examine) 461. open a discussion, open a case; try conclusions; join issue, be at issue; moot; come to the point; stir a question, agitate a question, ventilate a question, torture a ques- tion; take up a side, take up a case. contend, take one's stand upon, insist, lay stress on; infer &c. 480. follow from &c. (demonstration) 478. Adj. reasoning &c. v.; rationalistic; argumentative, controversial, dialectic, polemical; discursory[obs3], discursive; disputatious; Aristotelian[obs3], eristic[obs3], eristical[obs3]. debatable, controvertible. logical; relevant &c. 23. Adv. for, because, hence, whence, seeing that, since, sith[obs3], then thence so; for that reason, for this reason, for which reason; for as, inasmuch as; whereas, ex concesso[Lat], considering, in considera- tion of; therefore, wherefore; consequently, ergo, thus, accordingly; a fortiori. in conclusion, in fine; finally, after all, au bout du compt[Fr], on the whole, taking one thing with another. Phr. ab actu ad posse valet consecutio [Lat]; per troppo dibatter la verita si perde [It]; troppo disputare la verita fa errare [It].

#477. [The absence of reasoning.] Intuition. [False or vicious reasoning; show of reason.] Sophistry. — N. intuition, instinct, association, hunch, gut feeling; presentiment, premonition; rule of thumb; superstition; astrology[obs3]; faith (supposition) 514. sophistry, paralogy[obs3], perversion, casuistry, jesuitry, equivocation, evasion; chicane, chican- ery; quiddet[obs3], quiddity; mystification; special pleading; speciousness &c. adj.; nonsense &c. 497; word sense, tongue sense. false reasoning, vicious reasoning, circular reasoning; petitio principii[Lat], ignoratio elenchi[Lat]; post hoc ergo propter hoc[Lat]; non sequitur, ignotum per ignotius[Lat]. misjudgment &c. 481; false teaching &c. 538. sophism, solecism, paralogism[obs3]; quibble, quirk, elenchus[obs3], elench[obs3], fallacy, quodlibet, subterfuge, subtlety, quillet[obs3]; inconsistency, antilogy[obs3]; "a delusion, a mockery, and a snare" [Denman]; claptrap, cant, mere words; "lame and impotent conclusion" [Othello]. meshes of sophistry, cobwebs of sophistry; flaw in an argument; weak point, bad case. overrefinement[obs3]; hairsplitting &c. v. V. judge intuitively, judge by intuition; hazard a proposition, hazard a guess, talk at random. reason ill, falsely &c. adj.; misjudge &c. 481; paralogize[obs3]. take on faith, take as a given; assume (supposition) 514. pervert, quibble; equivocate, mystify, evade, elude; gloss over, varnish; misteach &c. 538[obs3]; mislead &c. (error) 495; cavil, refine, subtilize[obs3], split hairs; misrepresent &c. (lie) 544. beg the question, reason in a circle, reason in circles, assume the conclusion. cut blocks with a razor, beat about the bush, play fast and loose, play fast and loose with the facts, blow hot and cold, prove that black is white and white black, travel out of the record, parler a tort et a travers[Fr][obs3], put oneself out of court, not have a leg to stand on. judge hastily, shoot from the hip, jump to conclusions (misjudgment) 481. Adj. intuitive, instinctive, impulsive; independent of reason, anterior to reason; gratuitous, hazarded; unconnected. unreasonable, illogical, false, unsound, invalid; unwarranted, not following; inconsequent, inconsequential; inconsistent; absonousl, absonant[obs3]; unscientific; untenable, inconclusive, incorrect; fallacious, fallible; groundless, unproved; non sequitur[Latin: it does not follow]. deceptive, sophistical, jesuitical; illusive, illusory; specious, hollow, plausible, ad captandum[Lat], evasive; irrelevant &c. 10. weak, feeble, poor, flimsy, loose, vague. irrational; nonsensical &c. (absurd) 497. foolish &c. (imbecile) 499; frivolous, pettifogging, quibbling; finespun[obs3], overrefined[obs3]. at the end of one's tether, au bout de son latin. Adv. intuitively &c. adj.; by intuition; illogically &c. adj. Phr. non constat[Lat]; that goes for nothing.

<— p. 138 —>

#478. Demonstration. — N. {ant. 479} demonstration, proof, rigorous proof; conclusiveness &c. adj.; apodeixis[obs3], apodixis[obs3], probation, comprobationl.
    logic of facts &c. (evidence) 467; experimentum crucis &c. (test) 463[Lat]; argument &c. 476; rigorous establishment, absolute establishment.
    conviction, cogency, (persuasion) 484.
    V. demonstrate, prove, establish; make good; show, evince, manifest &c. (be evidence of) 467; confirm, corroborate, substantiate, verify &c. 467 settle the question, reduce to demonstration, set the question at rest.
    make out, make out a case; prove one's point, have the best of the argument; draw a conclusion &c. (judge) 480.
    follow, follow of course, follow as a matter of course, follow necessarily; stand to reason; hold good, hold water.
    convince, persuade (belief) 484.
    Adj. demonstrating &c. v., demonstrative, demonstrable; probative, unanswerable, conclusive; apodictic[obs3], apodeictic[obs3], apodeictical[obs3]; irresistible, irrefutable, irrefragable; necessary.
    categorical, decisive, crucial.
    demonstrated &c. v.; proven; unconfuted[obs3], unanswered, unrefuted[obs3]; evident &c. 474.
    deducible, consequential, consectary[obs3], inferential, following.
    [demonstrated to one's satisfaction] convincing, cogent, persuasive (believable) 484.
    Adv. of course, in consequence, consequently, as a matter of course; necessarily, of necessity.
    Phr. probatum est[Lat]; there is nothing more to be said; quod est demonstrandum[Lat], Q.E.D.; it must follow; exitus acta probat[Lat].
#479. Confutation. — N. {ant 478} confutation, refutation; answer, complete answer; disproof, conviction, redargution[obs3], invalidation; exposure, exposition; clincher; retort; reductio ad absurdum; knock down argument, tu quoque argument[Lat]; sockdolager * [obs3][U. S.]. correction &c. 527a; dissuasion &c. 616. V. confute, refute, disprove; parry, negative, controvert, rebut, confound, disconfirm, redargue[obs3], expose, show the fallacy of, defeat; demolish, break &c. (destroy) 162; overthrow, overturn scatter to the winds, explode, invalidate; silence; put to silence, reduce to silence; clinch an argument, clinch a question; give one a setdown[obs3], stop the mouth, shut up; have, have on the hip. not leave a leg to stand on, cut the ground from under one's feet. be confuted &c.; fail; expose one's weak point, show one's weak point. counter evidence &c. 468. Adj. confuting, confuted, &c. v.; capable

of refutation; refutable, confutable[obs3], defeasible. contravene (counter evidence) 468. condemned on one's own showing,condemned out of one's own mouth. Phr. the argument falls to the ground, cadit quaestio[Lat], it does not hold water, "suo sibi gladio hunc jugulo" [Terence]; his argument was demolished by new evidence.

<— p. 139 —>

% Section V. RESULTS OF REASONING %

#480. Judgment. [Conclusion.] — N. result, conclusion, upshot; deduction, inference, ergotism[Med]; illation; corollary, porism[obs3]; moral. estimation, valuation, appreciation, judication[obs3]; dijudication[obs3], adjudication; arbitrament, arbitrement[obs3], arbitration; assessment, ponderation[obs3]; valorization. award, estimate; review, criticism, critique, notice, report. decision, determination, judgment, finding, verdict, sentence, decree; findings of fact; findings of law; res judicata[Lat]. plebiscite, voice, casting vote; vote &c. (choice) 609; opinion &c. (belief) 484; good judgment &c. (wisdom) 498. judge, umpire; arbiter, arbitrator; asessor, referee. censor, reviewer, critic; connoisseur; commentator &c. 524; inspector, inspecting officer. twenty-twenty hindsight[judgment after the fact]; armchair general, monday morning quarterback. V. judge, conclude; come to a conclusion, draw a conclusion, arrive at a conclusion; ascertain, determine, make up one's mind. deduce, derive, gather, collect, draw an inference, make a deduction, weetl, ween[obs3]. form an estimate, estimate, appreciate, value, count, assess, rate, rank, account; regard, consider, think of; look upon &c. (believe) 484; review; size up *. settle; pass an opinion, give an opinion; decide, try, pronounce, rule; pass judgment, pass sentence; sentence, doom; find; give judgment, deliver judgment; adjudge, adjudicate; arbitrate, award, report; bring in a verdict; make absolute, set a question at rest; confirm &c. (assent) 488. comment, criticize, kibitz; pass under review &c. (examine) 457; investigate &c. (inquire) 461. hold the scales, sit in judgment; try judgment, hear a cause. Adj. judging &c. v.; judicious &c. (wise) 498; determinate, conclusive. Adv. on the whole, all things considered. Phr. "a Daniel come to judgment" [Merchant of Venice]; "and stand a critic, hated yet caress'd" [Byron]; "it is much easier to be critical than to be correct" [Disraeli]; la critique est aisee et l'art est difficile[Fr]; "nothing if not critical" [Othello]; "O most lame and impotent conclusion" [Othello].

#480a. [Result of search or inquiry.] Discovery. — N. discovery, detection, disenchantment; ascertainment[obs3], disclosure, find, revelation. trover &c.(recovery) 775[Law]. V. discover, find, determine, evolve, learn &c. 539; fix upon; pick up; find out, trace out, make out, hunt out, fish out, worm out, ferret out, root out; fathom; bring out, draw out; educe, elicit, bring to light; dig out, grub up, fish up; unearth, disinter. solve, resolve, elucidate; unriddle, unravel, unlock, crack, crack open; pick up, open the lock; find a clue, find clew a to, find the key to the riddle; interpret &c. 522; disclose &c. 529. trace, get at; hit it, have it; lay one's finger, lay one's hands upon; spot; get at the truth, arrive at the truth &c. 494; put the saddle on the right horse, hit the right nail on the head. be near the truth, be warm, get warmer, burn; smoke, scent, sniff, catch a whiff of, smell a rat. open the eyes to; see through, see daylight, see in its true colors, see the cloven foot; detect; catch, catch tripping. pitch upon, fall upon, light upon, hit upon, stumble upon, pop upon; come across, come onto; meet with, meet up with, fall in with. recognize, realize; verify, make certain of, identify. Int. eureka! aha[obs3]! I've got it!

#481. Misjudgment. — N. misjudgment, obliquity of judgment; miscalculation, miscomputation, misconception &c. (error) 495; hasty conclusion. [causes of misjudgment. 1] prejudgment, prejudication[obs3], prejudice; foregone conclusion; prenotion[obs3], prevention, preconception, predilection, prepossession, preapprehension[obs3], presumption, assumption, presentiment; fixed idea, preconceived idea; ide fixe; mentis gratissimus error[Lat]; fool's paradise. [causes of misjudgment.2] esprit de corps, party spirit, partisanship, clannishness, prestige. [causes of misjudgment. 3] bias, bigotry, warp, twist; hobby, fad, quirk, crotchet, partiality, infatuation, blind side, mote in the eye. [causes of misjudgment. 4] one-sided views, one-track mind, partial views, narrow views, confined views, superficial views, one-sided ideas, partial ideas, narrow ideas, confined ideas, superficial ideas, one-sided conceptions, partial conceptions, narrow conceptions, confined conceptions, superficial conceptions, one-sided notions, partial notions, narrow notions, confined notions, superficial notions; narrow mind; bigotry &c. (obstinacy) 606; odium theologicum[Lat]; pedantry; hypercriticism. doctrinaire &c. (positive) 474. [causes of misjudgment. 5] overestimation &c. 482; underestimation &c. 483. [causes of misjudgment. 6] ignorance &c. 491. erroneous assumptions, erroneous data, mistaken assumptions, incorrect assumptions (error) 495. V. misjudge, misestimate, misthink[obs3], misconjecture[obs3], misconceive &c. (error) 495; fly in the face of facts; miscalculate, misreckon, miscompute. overestimate &c. 482; underestimate &c. 483. prejudge, forejudge; presuppose, presume, prejudicate[obs3]; dogmatize; have a bias &c. n.; have only one idea; jurare in verba magistri[Lat], run away with the notion; jump to a conclusion, rush to a conclusion, leap to a conclusion, judge hastily, shoot from the hip, jump to conclusions; look only at one side of the shield; view with jaundiced eye, view through distorting spectacles; not see beyond one's nose; dare pondus fumo[Lat]; get the wrong sow by the ear &c. (blunder) 699. give a bias, give a twist; bias, warp, twist; prejudice, prepossess. Adj. misjudging &c. v.; ill-judging, wrong-headed; prejudiced &c. v.; jaundiced; short-sighted, purblind; partial, one-sided, superficial. narrow-minded, narrow-souled[obs3]; mean-spirited; confined, illiberal, intolerant, besotted, infatuated, fanatical, entete[Fr], positive, dogmatic, conceited; opinative, opiniative[obs3]; opinioned, opinionate, opinionative, opinionated; self-opinioned, wedded to an opinion, opinitre; bigoted &c. (obstinate) 606; crotchety, fussy, impracticable; unreasonable, stupid &c. 499; credulous &c 486; warped. misjudged &c. v. Adv. ex parte[Lat]. Phr. nothing like leather; the wish the father to the thought; wishful thinking; unshakable conviction; "my mind is made up - don't bother me with the facts".

<— p. 140 —>

#482. Overestimation. — N. overestimation &c. v.; exaggeration &c. 549; vanity &c. 880; optimism, pessimism, pessimist. much cry and little wool, much ado about nothing; storm in a teacup, tempest in a teacup; fine talking. V. overestimate, overrate, overvalue, overprize, overweigh, overreckon[obs3], overstrain, overpraise; eulogize; estimate too highly, attach too much importance to, make mountains of molehills, catch at straws; strain, magnify; exaggerate &c. 549; set too high a value upon; think much of, make much of, think too much of, make too much of; outreckon[obs3]; panegyrize[obs3]. extol, extol to the skies; make the most of, make the best of, make the worst of; make two bites of a cherry. have too high an opinion of oneself &c. (vanity) 880. Adj. overestimated &c. v.; oversensitive &c. (sensibility) 822. Phr. all his geese are swans; parturiunt montes[Lat].

#483. Underestimation. — N. underestimation; depreciation &c. (detraction) 934; pessimism, pessimist; undervaluing &c. v.; modesty &c. 881. V. underrate, underestimate, undervalue, underreckon[obs3]; depreciate; disparage &c. (detract) 934; not do justice to; misprize, disprize; ridicule &c. 856; slight &c. (despise) 930; neglect &c. 460; slur over. make light of, make little of, make nothing of, make no account of; belittle; minimize, think nothing of; set no store by, set at naught; shake off as dewdrops from the lion's mane. Adj. depreciating, depreciated &c. v.; unvalued, unprized[obs3].

#484. Belief. — N. belief; credence; credit; assurance; faith, trust, troth, confidence, presumption, sanguine expectation &c. (hope) 858; dependence on, reliance on. persuasion, conviction, convincement[obs3], plerophory[obs3], self- conviction; certainty &c. 474; opinion, mind, view; conception, thinking; impression &c. (idea) 453; surmise &c. 514; conclusion &c. (judgment) 480. tenet, dogma, principle, way of thinking; popular belief &c. (assent) 488. firm belief, implicit belief, settled belief, fixed rooted deep-rooted belief, staunch belief, unshaken belief, steadfast belief, inveterate belief, calm belief, sober belief, dispassionate belief, impartial belief, well-founded belief, firm opinion, implicit opinion, settled opinion, fixed rooted deep-rooted opinion, staunch opinion, unshaken opinion, steadfast opinion, inveterate opinion, calm opinion, sober opinion, dispassionate opinion, impartial opinion, well-founded opinion &c.; uberrima fides[Lat][obs3]. system of opinions, school, doctrine, articles, canons; article of faith, declaration of faith, profession of faith; tenets, credenda[obs3], creed; thirty-nine articles &c. (orthodoxy) 983a; catechism; assent &c. 488; propaganda &c. (teaching) 537. credibility &c. (probability) 472. V. believe, credit; give faith to, give credit to, credence to; see, realize; assume, receive; set down for, take for; have it, take it; consider, esteem, presume. count upon, depend upon, calculate upon, pin one's faith upon, reckon upon, lean upon, build upon, rely upon, rest upon; lay one's account for; make sure of. make oneself easy about, on that score; take on trust, take on credit; take for granted, take for gospel; allow some weight to, attach some weight to. know, know for certain; have know, make no doubt; doubt not; be, rest assured &c. adj.; persuade oneself, assure oneself, satisfy oneself; make up one's mind. give one credit for; confide in, believe in, put one's trust in; place in, repose in, implicit confidence in; take one's word for, at one's word; place reliance on, rely upon, swear by, regard to. think, hold; take, take it; opine, be of opinion, conceive, trow[obs3], ween[obs3], fancy, apprehend; have it, hold a belief, possess, entertain a belief, adopt a belief, imbibe a belief, embrace a belief, get hold of a belief, hazard, foster, nurture a belief, cherish a belief, have an opinion, hold an opinion, possess, entertain an opinion, adopt an opinion, imbibe an opinion, embrace an opinion, get hold of an opinion, hazard an opinion, foster an opinion, nurture an opinion, cherish an opinion &c. n. view as, consider as, take as, hold as, conceive as, regard as, esteem as, deem as, look upon as, account as, set down as; surmise &c. 514. get it into one's head, take it into one's head; come round to an opinion; swallow &c. (credulity) 486. cause to be believed &c. v.; satisfy, persuade, have the ear of, gain the confidence of, assure; convince, convict!!, convert; wean, bring round; bring over, win over; indoctrinate &c. (teach) 537; cram down the throat; produce conviction, carry conviction; bring home to, drive home to. go down, find credence, pass current; be received &c. v., be current &c. adj.; possess, take hold of, take possession of the mind. Adj. believing &c. v.; certain, sure, assured, positive, cocksure, satisfied, confident, unhesitating, convinced, secure. under the impression; impressed with, imbued with, penetrated with. confiding, suspectless[obs3]; unsuspecting, unsuspicious; void of suspicion; credulous &c. 486; wedded to. believed &c. v.; accredited, putative; unsuspected. worthy of, deserving of, commanding belief; credible, reliable, trustworthy, to be depended on; satisfactory; probably &c. 472; fiducial[obs3], fiduciary; persuasive, impressive. relating to belief, doctrinal. Adv. in the opinion of, in the eyes of; me judice[Lat]; meseems[obs3], methinks; to the best of one's belief; I dare say, I doubt not, I have no doubt, I am sure; sure enough &c. (certainty) 474; depend upon, rely upon it; be assured, rest assured; I'll warrant you &c. (affirmation) 535. Phr. experto crede [Lat][Vergil]; fata viam invenient [Lat]; Justitiae soror incorrupta Fides[Lat]; "live to explain thy doctrine by thy life" [Prior]; "stands not within the prospect of belief" [Macbeth]; tarde quae credita laedunt credimus [Lat][Ovid]; vide et crede [Lat].

<— p. 141 —>

#485. Unbelief. Doubt.— N. unbelief, disbelief, misbelief; discredit, miscreance[obs3]; infidelity &c. (irreligion) 989[obs3]; dissent &c. 489; change of opinion &c. 484; retraction &c. 607. doubt &c. (uncertainty) 475; skepticism, scepticism, misgiving, demure; distrust, mistrust, cynicism; misdoubt[obs3], suspicion, jealousy, scruple, qualm; onus probandi[Lat]. incredibility, incredibleness; incredulity. [person who doubts] doubter, skeptic, cynic.; unbeliever &c. 487. V. disbelieve, discredit; not believe &c. 484; misbelieve[obs3]; refuse to admit &c. (dissent) 489; refuse to believe &c. (incredulity) 487. doubt; be doubtful &c. (uncertain) 475; doubt the truth of; be skeptical as to &c. adj.; diffidel; distrust, mistrust; suspect, smoke, scent, smell a rat; have doubts, harbor doubts, entertain doubts, suspicions; have one's doubts. demure, stick at, pause, hesitate, scruple; stop to consider, waver. hang in suspense, hang in doubt. throw doubt upon, raise a question; bring in, call in question; question, challenge, dispute; deny &c. 536; cavil; cause a doubt, raise a doubt, start a doubt, suggest a doubt, awake a doubt, make suspicion; ergotize[obs3]. startle, stagger; shake one's faith, shake one's belief, stagger one's faith, stagger one's belief. Adj. unbelieving; skeptical, sceptical. [transitive] incredulous as to, skeptical as to; distrustful as to, shy as to, suspicious of; doubting &c. v. doubtful &c. (uncertain) 475; disputable; unworthy of, undeserving of belief &c. 484; questionable; suspect, suspicious; open to suspicion, open to doubt; staggering, hard to believe, incredible, unbelievable, not to be believed, inconceivable; impossible &c. 471. fallible &c. (uncertain) 475; undemonstrable; controvertible &c. (untrue) 495. Adv. cum grano salis[Latin: with a grain of salt]; with grains of allowance. Phr. fronti nulla fides[Lat]; nimium ne crede colori [Lat][Vergil]; "timeo Danaos et dona ferentes" [Latin: I fear the Greeks even when bearing gifts][Vergil], beware of Greeks bearing gifts; credat Judaeus Apella [Lat][Horace]; let those believe who may; ad tristem partem stenua est suspicio [Lat][Syrus].

#486. Credulity. — N. credulity, credulousness &c. adj.; cullibilityl, gullibility; gross credulity, infatuation; self delusion, self deception; superstition; one's blind side; bigotry &c. (obstinacy) 606; hyperorthodoxy &c. 984[obs3]; misjudgment &c. 481. credulous person &c (dupe) 547. V. be credulous &c. adj.; jurare in verba magistri[Lat]; follow implicitly; swallow, gulp down; take on trust; take for granted, take for gospel; run away with a notion, run away with an idea; jump to a conclusion, rush to a conclusion; think the moon is made of green cheese; take for granted, grasp the shadow for the substance; catch at straws, grasp at straws. impose upon &c. (deceive) 545. Adj. credulous, gullible; easily deceived &c. 545; simple, green, soft, childish, silly, stupid; easily convinced; over-credulous, over confident, over trustful; infatuated, superstitious; confiding &c. (believing) 484. Phr. the wish the father to the thought; credo quia impossibile [Lat][Tertullian]; all is not gold that glitters; no es oro todo lo que reluce[Sp]; omne ignotum pro magnifico[Lat].

<— p. 142 —>

#487. Incredulity.— N. incredulousness[obs3], incredulity; skepticism, pyrrhonisml!; want of faith &c. (irreligion) 989[obs3].
suspiciousness &c. adj.; scrupulosity; suspicion &c. (unbelief) 485.
mistrust, cynicism.
unbeliever, skeptic, cynic; misbeliever.1, pyrrhonist; heretic &c. (heterodox) 984.
V. be incredulous &c. adj.; distrust &c. (disbelieve) 485; refuse to believe; shut one's eyes to, shut one's ears to; turn a deaf ear to; hold aloof, ignore, nullis jurare in verba magistri[Lat].
Adj. incredulous, skeptical, unbelieving, inconvincible[obs3]; hard of belief, shy of belief, disposed to doubt, indisposed to believe; suspicious, scrupulous, distrustful, cynical.
1The word miscreant, which originally meant simply misbeliever, has now quite another meaning (949). See Trench, On the Study of Words, p. 71.

#488. Assent. — N. assent, assentment[obs3]; acquiescence, admission; nod; accord, concord, concordance;

agreement &c. 23; affirmance, affirmation; recognition, acknowledgment, avowal; confession of faith. unanimity, common consent, consensus, acclamation, chorus, vox populi; popular belief, current belief, current opinion; public opinion; concurrence &c. (of causes) 178; cooperation &c. (voluntary) 709. ratification, confirmation, corroboration, approval, acceptance, visa; indorsement &c. (record) 551[obs3]. consent &c. (compliance) 762. pressure to conform, herd instinct, peer pressure. V. assent; give assent, yield assent, nod assent; acquiesce; agree &c. 23; receive, accept, accede, accord, concur, lend oneself to, consent, coincide, reciprocate, go with; be at one with &c. adj.; go along with, chime in with, strike in with, close in with; echo, enter into one's views, agree in opinion; vote, give one's voice for; recognize; subscribe to, conform to, defer to; say yes to, say ditto, amen to, say aye to. acknowledge, own, admit, allow, avow, confess; concede &c. (yield) 762; come round to; abide by; permit &c. 760. arrive at an under-standing, come to an understanding, come to terms, come to an agreement. confirm, affirm; ratify, approve, indorse, countersign; corroborate &c. 467. go with the stream, swim with the stream, go with the flow, blow with the wind; be in fashion, join in the chorus, join the crowd, be one of the guys, be part of the group, go with the crowd, don't make waves; be in every mouth. Adj. assenting &c. v; of one accord, of one mind; of the same mind, at one with, agreed, acquiescent, content; willing &c. 602. uncontradicted, unchallenged, unquestioned, uncontroverted. carried, agreed, nem[abbr]. con. &c. adv[abbr: nemine contradicente].; unanimous; agreed on all hands, carried by acclamation. affirmative &c. 535. Adv. yes, yea, ay, aye, true; good; well; very well, very true; well and good; granted; even so, just so; to be sure, "thou hast said", you said it, you said a mouthful; truly, exactly, precisely, that's just it, indeed, certainly, you bet, certes[Lat], ex concesso[Lat]; of course, unquestionably, assuredly, no doubt, doubtless; naturally, natch. be it so; so be it, so let it be; amen; willingly &c. 602. affirmatively, in the affirmative. OK, all right, might as well, why not? with one consent, with one voice, with one accord; unanimously, una voce, by common consent, in chorus, to a man; nem[abbr]. con.[abbr: nemine contradicente], nemine dissentiente[Lat]; without a dissentient voice; as one man, one and all, on all hands. Phr. avec plaisir[Fr]; chi tace accousente[It][obs3]; "the public mind is the creation of the Master-Writers" [Disraeli]; you bet your sweet ass it is; what are we waiting for? whenever you're ready; anytime you're ready.

#489. Dissent. — N. dissent; discordance &c. (disagreement) 24; difference diversity of opinion.

nonconformity &c. (heterodoxy) 984; protestantism, recusancy, schism; disaffection; secession &c. 624; recantation &c. 607.

dissension &c (discord) 713; discontent &c. 832; cavilling.

protest; contradiction &c (denial) 536; noncompliance &c (rejection) 764.

dissentient, dissenter; non-juror, non-content, nonconformist; sectary, separatist, recusant, schismatic, protestant, heretic.

refusal &c. 764.

V. dissent, demur; call in question &c. (doubt) 485; differ in opinion, disagree; say no &c. 536; refuse assent, refuse to admit; cavil, protest, raise one's voice against, repudiate; contradict &c. (deny) 536.

have no notion of, differ toto caelo[Lat]; revolt at, revolt from the idea.

shake the head, shrug the shoulders; look askance, look askant[obs3].

secede; recant &c. 607.

Adj. dissenting &c. v; negative &c. 536; dissident, dissentient; unconsenting &c. (refusing) 764; non-content, nonjuring[obs3]; protestant, recusant; unconvinced, unconverted.

unavowed, unacknowledged; out of the question.

discontented &c. 832; unwilling &c. 603; extorted.

sectarian, denominational, schismatic; heterodox; intolerant.

Adv. no &c. 536; at variance, at issue with; under protest.

Int. God forbid! not for the world; I'll be hanged if; never tell me; your humble servant, pardon me.

Phr. many men many minds; quot homines tot sententiae [Lat][Terence]; tant s'en faut[Fr]; il s'en faut bien[Fr];no way; by no means; count me out.

<— p. 143 —>

#490. Knowledge. — N. knowledge; cognizance, cognition, cognoscencel; acquaintance, experience, ken, privity[obs3], insight, familiarity; comprehension, apprehension; recognition; appreciation &c. (judgment) 480;

intuition; conscience, consciousness; perception, precognition; acroamaticsl!. light, enlightenment; glimpse, inkling; glimmer, glimmering; dawn; scent, suspicion; impression &c. (idea) 453; discovery &c. 480a. system of knowledge, body of knowledge; science, philosophy, pansophy[obs3]; acroamal!; theory, aetiology[obs3], etiology; circle of the sciences; pandect[obs3], doctrine, body of doctrine; cyclopedia, encyclopedia; school &c. (system of opinions) 484. tree of knowledge; republic of letters &c. (language) 560. erudition, learning, lore, scholarship, reading, letters; literature; book madness; book learning, bookishness; bibliomania[obs3], bibliolatry[obs3]; information, general information; store of knowledge &c.; education &c. (teaching) 537; culture, menticulture[obs3], attainments; acquirements, acquisitions; accomplishments; proficiency; practical knowledge &c. (skill) 698; liberal education; dilettantism; rudiments &c (beginning) 66. deep knowledge, profound knowledge, solid knowledge, accurate knowledge, acroatic knowledge[obs3], acroamatic knowledge[obs3], vast knowledge, extensive knowledge, encyclopedic knowledge, encyclopedic learning; omniscience, pantology[obs3]. march of intellect; progress of science, advance of science, advance of learning; schoolmaster abroad. [person who knows much] scholar &c. 492. V. know, ken, scan, wot[obs3]; wot aware[obs3], be aware &c. adj.- of; ween[obs3], weet[obs3], trow[obs3], have, possess. conceive; apprehend, comprehend; take, realize, understand, savvy* [U.S.], appreciate; fathom, make out; recognize, discern, perceive, see, get a sight-of, experience. know full well; have some knowledge of, possess some knowledge of; be au courant &c. adj.; have in one's head, have at one' fingers ends; know by heart, know by rote; be master of; connaitre le dessous des cartes[Fr], know what's what &c. 698. see one's way; discover &c. 480a. come to one's knowledge &c. (information) 527. Adj. knowing &c. v.; cognitive; acroamatic[obs3]. aware of, cognizant of, conscious of; acquainted with, made acquainted with; privy to, no stranger to; au -fait, au courant; in the secret; up to, alive to; behind the scenes, behind the curtain; let into; apprized of, informed of; undeceived. proficient with, versed with, read with, forward with, strong with, at home in; conversant with, familiar with. erudite, instructed, leaned, lettered, educated; well conned, well informed, well read, well grounded, well educated; enlightened, shrewd, savant, blue, bookish, scholastic, solid, profound, deep-read, book- learned; accomplished &c (skillful) 698; omniscient; self-taught. known &c. v.; ascertained, well-known, recognized, received, notorious, noted; proverbial; familiar, familiar as household words, familiar to every schoolboy; hackneyed, trite, trivial, commonplace. cognoscible[obs3], cognizable. Adv. to one's knowledge, to the best of one's knowledge. Phr. one's eyes being opened &c. (disclosure) 529; ompredre tout c'est tout pardonner[French: to know all is to pardon all]; empta dolore docet experientia[Lat];<gr/ gnothi seauton/gr>[Grk]; "half our knowledge we must snatch not take" [Pope]; Jahre lehren mehr als Bucher[German: years teach more than books]; "knowledge comes but wisdom lingers"[Tennyson]; "knowledge is power" [Bacon]; les affaires font les hommes [Fr]; nec scire fas est omnia [Lat][Horace]; "the amassed thought and experience of innumerable minds" [Emerson]; was ich nicht weiss macht mich nicht heiss[Ger].

<— p. 144 —>

#491. Ignorance. — N. ignorance, nescience, tabula rasa[Lat], crass ignorance, ignorance crasse[Fr]; unfamiliarity, unacquaintance[obs3]; unconsciousness &c. adj.; darkness, blindness; incomprehension, inexperience, simplicity. unknown quantities, x, y, z. sealed book, terra incognita, virgin soil, unexplored ground; dark ages. [Imperfect knowledge] smattering, sciolism[obs3], glimmering, dilettantism; bewilderment &c. (uncertainty) 475; incapacity. [Affectation of knowledge] pedantry; charlatanry, charlatism[obs3]; Philister[obs3], Philistine. V. be ignorant &c. adj.; not know &c. 490; know not, know not what, know nothing of; have no idea, have no notion, have no conception; not have the remotest idea; not know chalk from cheese. ignore, be blind to; keep in ignorance &c. (conceal) 528. see through a glass darkly; have a film over the eyes, have a glimmering &c. n.; wonder whether; not know what to make of &c. (unintelligibility) 519; not pretend to take upon, not take upon one self to say. Adj. ignorant; nescient; unknowing, unaware, unacquainted, unapprised, unapprized[obs3], unwitting, unweetingl, unconscious; witless, weetless[obs3]; a stranger to; unconversant[obs3]. uninformed, uncultivated, unversed, uninstructed, untaught, uninitiated, untutored, unschooled, misguided, unenlightened; Philistine; behind the age. shallow, superficial, green, rude, empty, half-learned, illiterate; unread, uninformed, uneducated, unlearned, unlettered, unbookish; empty-headed, dizzy, wooly-headed; pedantic; in the dark; benighted, belated; blinded, blindfolded; hoodwinked; misinformed; au bout de son latin, at the end of his tether, at fault; at sea &c. (uncertain) 475; caught tripping. unknown, unapprehended, unexplained, unascertained, uninvestigated[obs3], unexplored, unheard of, not perceived; concealed &c. 528; novel. Adv. ignorantly &c. adj.; unawares; for anything, for aught one knows; not that one knows. Int. God knows, Heaven knows, the Lord knows, who knows, nobody knows. Phr. "ignorance never settles a question" [Disraeli]; quantum animis erroris inest[Lat]! [Ovid]; "small Latin and less Greek" [B. Jonson]; "that unlettered small-knowing soul" [Love's Labor's Lost]; "there is no darkness but ignorance" [Twelfth NIght].

#492. Scholar.— N. scholar, connoisseur, savant, pundit, schoolman[obs3], professor, graduate, wrangler; academician, academist[obs3]; master of arts, doctor, licentitate, gownsman; philosopher, master of math; scientist, clerk; sophist, sophister[obs3]; linguist; glossolinguist, philologist; philologer[obs3]; lexicographer, glossographer; grammarian; litterateur[Fr], literati, dilettanti, illuminati, cogniscenti[It]; fellow, Hebraist, lexicologist, mullah, munshi[obs3], Sanskritish; sinologist, sinologue[obs3]; Mezzofanti[obs3], admirable Crichton, Mecaenas. bookworm, helluo librorum[Lat]; bibliophile, bibliomaniac[obs3]; bluestocking, bas-bleu[Fr]; bigwig, learned Theban, don; Artium Baccalaureus[Lat][obs3], Artium Magister[Lat]. learned man, literary man; homo multarum literarum[Lat]; man of learning, man of letters, man of education, man of genius. antiquarian, antiquary; archaeologist. sage &c. (wise man) 500. pedant, doctrinaire; pedagogue, Dr. Pangloss; pantologist[obs3], criminologist. schoolboy &c. (learner) 541. Adj. learned &c. 490; brought up at the feet of Gamaliel. Phr. "he was a scholar and a ripe and good one" [Henry VIII]; "the manifold linguist" [All's Well That Ends Well].

#493. Ignoramus.— N. ignoramus, dunce; wooden spoon; no scholar.
[insulting terms for ignorant person: see also imbecility 499, folly
501] moron, imbecile, idiot; fool, jerk, nincompoop, asshole [vulgar].
[person with superficial knowledge] dilettante, sciolist[obs3],
smatterer, dabbler, half scholar; charlatan; wiseacre.
greenhorn, amateur &c (dupe) 547; novice, tyro &c (learner) 541;
numskull.
lubber &c (bungler) 701; fool &c. 501; pedant &c 492.
Adj. bookless[obs3], shallow; ignorant &c. 491.
Phr. "a wit with dunces and a dunce with wits" [Pope].

<— p. 145 —>

#494. [Object of knowledge.] Truth. — N. fact, reality &c. (existence) 1; plain fact, plain matter of fact; nature &c. (principle) 5; truth, verity; gospel, gospel truth, God's honest truth; orthodoxy &c. 983a; authenticity; veracity &c. 543; correctness, correctitude[obs3]. accuracy, exactitude; exactness, preciseness &c. adj.; precision, delicacy; rigor, mathematical precision, punctuality; clockwork precision &c. (regularity) 80; conformity to rule; nicety. orthology[obs3]; ipsissima verba[Lat]; realism. plain truth, honest truth, sober truth, naked truth, unalloyed truth, unqualified truth, stern truth, exact truth, intrinsic truth; nuda veritas[Lat]; the very thing; not an -illusion &c 495; real Simon Pure; unvarnished tale, unvarnished truth; the truth the whole truth and nothing but the truth; just the thing. V. be true &c. adj., be the case; sand the test; have the true ring; hold good, hold true, hold water. render true, prove true &c. adj.; substantiate &c. (evidence) 467. get at the truth &c. (discover) 480a. Adj. real, actual &c. (existing) 1; veritable, true; right, correct; certain &c. 474; substantially true, categorically true, definitively true &c; true to the letter, true as gospel; unimpeachable; veracious &c. 543; unreconfuted[obs3], unconfuted[obs3], unideal[obs3], unimagined; realistic. exact, accurate, definite, precise, well-defined, just, just so, so; strict, severe; close &c. (similar) 17; literal; rigid, rigorous; scrupulous &c. (conscientious) 939; religiously exact, punctual, mathematical, scientific; faithful, constant, unerring; curious, particular, nice, delicate, fine; clean-cut, clear-cut. verified, empirically true, experimentally verified, substantiated, proven (demonstrated) 478. rigorously true, unquestionably true. true by definition. genuine, authentic, legitimate; orthodox &c. 983a; official, ex officio. pure, natural, sound, sterling; unsophisticated, unadulterated, unvarnished, unalloyed, uncolored; in its true colors; pukka[obs3]. well-grounded, well founded; solid, substantial, tangible, valid; undistortcd, undisguised; unaffected, unexaggerated, unromantic, unflattering. Adv. truly &c. adj.; verily, indeed, really, in reality; with truth &c. (veracity) 543; certainly &c. (certain) 474; actually &c. (existence) 1; in effect &c (intrinsically) 5. exactly &c. adj.; ad amussim[Lat]; verbatim, verbatim et literatim [Lat]; word for word, literally, literatim[Lat], totidem vervis[Lat], sic, to the letter, chapter and verse, ipsissimis verbis[Lat]; ad unguem[Lat]; to an inch; to a nicety, to a hair, to a tittle, to a turn, to a T; au pied de la lettre [Fr]; neither more nor less; in every respect, in all respects; sous tous les rapports[Fr]; at any rate, at all events; strictly speaking. Phr. the truth is, the fact is; rem acu tetigisti[obs3][Lat]; en suivant la verite [Fr]; ex facto jus oritur [Lat]; la verita e figlia del empo [It]; locos y ninos dicen la verdad [Spanish: crazy people and children tell the truth]; nihil est veritatis luce dulcius [Lat][Cicero]; veritas nunquam perit [Lat][Seneca]; veritatem dies aperit [Lat][Seneca]; "the truth, the whole truth, and nothing but the truth"; "just the facts, ma'am, just the facts." [Dragnet].

#495. Error. — N. error, fallacy; misconception, misapprehension, misstanding[obs3], misunderstanding; inexactness &c. adj.; laxity; misconstruction &c. (misinterpretation) 523; miscomputation &c. (misjudgment) 481; non sequitur &c. 477; mis-statement, mis-report; mumpsimus[obs3]. mistake; miss, fault, blunder, quiproquo, cross purposes, oversight, misprint, erratum, corrigendum, slip, blot, flaw, loose thread; trip, stumble &c. (failure) 732; botchery &c. (want of skill) 699[obs3]; slip of the tongue, slip of the lip, Freudian slip; slip of the pen; lapsus linguae[Lat], clerical error; bull &c. (absurdity) 497; haplography[obs3]. illusion, delusion; snare; false impression, false idea; bubble; self- decit, self-deception; mists of error. heresy &c. (heterodoxy) 984; hallucination &c. (insanity) 503; false light &c. (fallacy of vision) 443; dream &c. (fancy) 515; fable &c. (untruth) 546; bias &c. (misjudgment) 481; misleading &c. v. V. be erroneous &c. adj. cause error; mislead, misguide; lead astray, lead into error; beguile, misinform &c. (misteach) 538[obs3]; delude; give a false impression, give a false idea; falsify, misstate; deceive &c. 545; lie &c. 544. err; be -in error &c. adj., be mistaken &c. v.; be deceived &c. (duped) 547; mistake, receive a false impression, deceive oneself; fall into error, lie under error, labor under an error &c. n.; be in the wrong, blunder; misapprehend, misconceive, misunderstand, misreckon, miscount, miscalculate &c. (misjudge) 481. play at cross purposes, be at cross purposes &c. (misinterpret) 523. trip, stumble; lose oneself &c. (uncertainty) 475; go astray; fail &c. 732; be in the wrong box; take the wrong sow by the ear &c. (mismanage) 699; put the saddle on the wrong horse; reckon without one's host; take the shadow for the substance &c (credulity) 486; dream &c (imagine) 515. Adj. erroneous, untrue, false, devoid of truth, fallacious, apocryphal, unreal, ungrounded, groundless; unsubstantial &c. 4; heretical &c. (heterodox) 984; unsound; illogical &c. 477. inexact, unexact inaccurate[obs3], incorrect; indefinite &c. (uncertain) 475. illusive, illusory; delusive; mock, ideal &c (imaginary) 515; spurious &c. 545; deceitful &c. 544; perverted. controvertible, unsustainable; unauthenticated, untrustworthy. exploded, refuted; discarded. in error, under an error &c. n.; mistaken &c. v.; tripping &c. v.; out, out in one's reckoning; aberrant; beside the mark, wide of the mark, wide of the truth, way off, far off; astray &c (at fault) 475; on a false scent, on the wrong scent; in the wrong box, outside the ballpark; at cross purposes, all in the wrong; all out. Adv. more or less. Phr. errare est humanum[Lat]; mentis gratissimus error [Lat][Horace]; "on the dubious waves of error tost" [Cowper]; "to err is human, to forgive divine" [Pope]; "you lie — under a mistake" [Shelley].

<— p. 146 —>

#496. Maxim.— N. maxim, aphorism; apothegm, apophthegm[obs3]; dictum, saying, adage, saw, proverb; sentence, mot[Fr], motto, word, byword, moral, phylactery, protasis[obs3].
axiom, theorem, scholium[obs3], truism, postulate.
first principles, a priori fact, assumption (supposition) 514.
reflection &c (idea) 453; conclusion &c (judgment) 480; golden rule &c. (precept) 697; principle, principia[Lat]; profession of faith &c. (belief) 484; settled principle, accepted principle, formula.
accepted fact.
received truth, wise maxim, sage maxim, received maxim, admitted maxim, recognized maxim &c; true saying, common saying, hackneyed saying, trite saying, commonplace saying &c.
Adj. aphoristic, proverbial, phylacteric[obs3]; axiomatic, gnomic.
Adv. as the saying goes, as the saying is, as they say.
#497. Absurdity. — N. absurdity, absurdness &c. adj.; imbecility &c. 499; alogy[l], nonsense, utter nonsense; paradox, inconsistency; stultiloquy[obs3], stultiloquence[obs3]; nugacity[obs3]. blunder, muddle, bull; Irishism[l]!, Hibernicism[l]!; slipslop[obs3]; anticlimax, bathos; sophism &c. 477. farce, galimathias[obs3], amphigouri[obs3], rhapsody; farrago &c (disorder) 59; betise[Fr]; extravagance, romance; sciamachy[obs3]. sell, pun, verbal quibble, macaronic[obs3]. jargon, fustian, twaddle, gibberish &c (no meaning) 517; exaggeration &c 549; moonshine, stuff; mare's nest, quibble, self-delusion. vagary, tomfoolery, poppycock, mummery, monkey trick, boutade[Fr], escapade. V. play the fool &c. 499; talk nonsense, parler a tort et a travess[Fr]; battre la campagne[Fr][obs3]; <gr/ hanemolia bazein/gr>; be - absurd &c. adj. Adj. absurd, nonsensical, preposterous, egregious, senseless, inconsistent, ridiculous, extravagant, quibbling; self-annulling, self- contradictory; macaronic[obs3], punning. foolish &c. 499; sophistical &c. 477; unmeaning &c. 517; without rhyme or reason; fantastic. Int. fiddlededee! pish! pho[obs3]! "in the name of the Prophet—figs!" [Horace Smith]. Phr. credat Judaeus Apella [Lat][Horace]; tell it to the marines.

<— p. 147 —>

#498. Intelligence. Wisdom. — N. intelligence, capacity, comprehension, understanding; cuteness, sabe * [obs3] [U.S.], savvy * [U.S.]; intellect &c. 450; nous[Fr], parts, sagacity, mother wit, wit, esprit, gumption, quick parts, grasp of intellect; acuteness &c adj.; acumen, subtlety, penetration, perspicacy[obs3], perspicacity; discernment, due sense of, good judgment; discrimination &c 465; cunning &c. 702; refinement &c (taste) 850. head, brains, head-piece, upper story, long head; eagle eye, eagle- glance; eye of a lynx, eye of a hawk. wisdom, sapience, sense; good sense, common sense, horse sense [U.S.], plain sense; rationality, reason; reasonableness &c. adj; judgment; solidity, depth, profundity, caliber; enlarged views; reach of thought, compass of thought; enlargement of mind. genius, inspiration, geist[Ger], fire of genius, heaven-born genius, soul; talent &c. (aptitude) 698. [Wisdom in action] prudence &c. 864; vigilance &c. 459; tact &c 698; foresight &c 510; sobriety, self-possession, aplomb, ballast. a bright thought, not a bad idea. Solomon-like wisdom. V. be -intelligent &c. adj.; have all one's wits about one; understand &c. (intelligible) 518; catch an idea, take in an idea; take a joke, take a hint. see through, see at a glance, see with half an eye, see far into, see through a millstone; penetrate; discern &c (descry) 441; foresee &c 510. discriminate &c. 465; know what's what &c. 698; listen to reason. Adj. intelligent[Applied to persons], quick of apprehension, keen, acute, alive, brainy, awake, bright, quick, sharp; quick witted, keen witted, clear witted, sharp-eyed, sharp sighted, sharp witted; wide-awake; canny, shrewd, astute; clear-headed; farsighted &c 510; discerning, perspicacious, penetrating, piercing; argute[obs3]; quick-witted, nimble- witted, needle-witted; sharp as a needle, sharp as a tack; alive to &c (cognizant) 490; clever &c. (apt) 698; arch &c (cunning) 702; pas si bete[Fr]; acute &c 682. wise, sage, sapient, sagacious, reasonable, rational, sound, in one's right mind, sensible, abnormis sapiens[Lat], judicious, strong-minded. unprejudiced, unbiased, unbigoted[obs3], unprepossessed[obs3]; undazzled[obs3], unperplexed[obs3]; unwarped judgment[obs3], impartial, equitable, fair. cool; cool-headed, long-headed, hardheaded, strong-headed; long- sighted, calculating, thoughtful, reflecting; solid, deep, profound. oracular; heaven-directed, heaven-born. prudent &c (cautious) 864; sober, stand, solid; considerate, politic, wise in one's generation; watchful &c. 459; provident &c (prepared) 673; in advance of one' age; wise as a serpent, wise as Solomon, wise as Solon. [Applied to actions] wise, sensible, reasonable, judicious; well- thought-out, well-planned, well-judged, well-advised; prudent, politic; expedient &c. 646. Phr. aut regem aut fatuum nasci oportet[Lat]; "but with the morning cool reflection came" [Scott]; flosculi sententiarum[Lat]; les affaires font les hommes[Fr]; mas vale saber que haber[Sp]; mas vale ser necio que profiadol nemo solus sapit [Lat][Plautus]; nosce te[Lat]; <gr/gnothi seauton/gr>[Grk]; nullum magnum ingenium sine mixtura dementiae fuit [Lat][Seneca, from Aristotle]; sapere aude [Lat] [Horace]; victrix fortunae sapientia [Lat][Juvenal].

#499. Imbecility. Folly — N. want of -intelligence &c. 498, want of - intellect &c. 450; shadowness[obs3], silliness, foolishness &c. adj.; imbecility, incapacity, vacancy of mind, poverty of intellect, weakness of intellect, clouded perception, poor head, apartments to let; stupidity, stolidity; hebetude[obs3], dull understanding, meanest capacity, shortsightedness; incompetence &c (unskillfulness) 699. one's weak side, not one's strong point; bias &c 481; infatuation &c. (insanity) 503. simplicity, puerility, babyhood; dotage, anility[obs3], second childishness, fatuity; idiocy, idiotism[obs3]; driveling. folly, frivolity, irrationality, trifling, ineptitude, nugacity[obs3], inconsistency, lip wisdom, conceit; sophistry &c. 477; giddiness &c (inattention) 458; eccentricity &c. 503; extravagance &c (absurdity) 497; rashness &c. 863. act of folly &c. 699. b. be - imbecile &c adj.; have no -brains, have no sense &c. 498. trifle, drivel, radoter[obs3], dote; ramble &c (madness) 503; play the fool, play the monkey, monkey around, fool around; take leave of one's senses (insanity) 503; not see an inch beyond one's nose; stultify oneself &c. 699; talk nonsense &c. 497. Adj. unintelligent[Applied to persons], unintellectual, unreasoning; mindless, witless, reasoningless[obs3], brainless; halfbaked; having no head &c. 498; not -bright &c. 498; inapprehensible[obs3]. weak headed, addle headed, puzzle headed, blunder headed, muddle headed, muddy headed, pig headed, beetle headed, buffle headed[obs3], chuckle headed, mutton headed, maggoty headed, grossheaded[obs3]; beef headed, fat witted, fat-headed. weak-minded, feeble-minded; dull minded, shallow minded, lack-brained; rattle-brained, rattle headed; half witted, lean witted, short witted, dull witted, blunt-witted, shallow-pated[obs3], clod-pated[obs3], addle-pated[obs3]; dim-sighted, short-sighted; thick-skulled; weak in the upper story. shallow, borne, weak, wanting, soft, sappy, spoony; dull, dull as a beetle; stupid, heavy, insulse[obs3], obtuse, blunt, stolid, doltish; asinine; inapt &c. 699; prosaic &c. 843; hebetudinous[obs3]. childish, child-like; infantine[obs3], infantile, babyish, babish[obs3]; puerile, anile; simple &c. (credulous) 486; old-womanish. fatuous, idiotic, imbecile, driveling; blatant, babbling; vacant; sottish; bewildered &c.475. blockish[obs3], unteachable Boeotian, Boeotic; bovine; ungifted, undiscerning[obs3], unenlightened, unwise, unphilosophical[obs3]; apish; simious[obs3]. foolish, silly, senseless, irrational, insensate, nonsensical, inept; maudlin. narrow-minded &c. 481; bigoted &c. (obstinate) 606; giddy &c. (thoughtless) 458; rash &c. 863; eccentric &c. (crazed) 503. [Applied to actions] foolish, unwise, injudicious, improper, unreasonable, without reason, ridiculous, absurd, idiotic, silly, stupid, asinine; ill-imagined, ill-advised, ill-judged, ill-devised; mal entendu[Fr]; inconsistent, irrational, unphilosophical[obs3]; extravagant &c (nonsensical) 497; sleeveless, idle; pointless, useless &c. 645; inexpedient &c. 647; frivolous &c. (trivial) 643. Phr. Davus sum non [Lat] [Oedipus]; "a fool's bolt is soon shot" clitellae bovi sunt impositae [obs3][Henry V.][Lat][Cicero]; "fools rush in where angels fear to tread" [Pope]; il n' a ni bouche ni eperon [Fr]; "the bookful blockhead, ignorantly read" [Pope]; "to varnish nonsense with the charms of sound" [Churchill].

<— p. 148 —>

#500. Sage — N. sage, wise man; genius; master mind, master spirit of the age; longhead[obs3], thinker; intellectual, longhair.
    authority, oracle, luminary, shining light, esprit fort, magnus Apollo[Lat][obs3], Solon, Solomon, Nestor, Magi, "second Daniel."
    man of learning &c. 492; expert &c. 700; wizard &c. 994.
    [Ironically] wiseacre, bigwig, know-it-all; poor man's Einstein.

Adj. venerable, reverenced, emeritus.

Phr. barba tenus sapientes[Lat].

#501. Fool. — N. fool, idiot, tomfool, wiseacre, simpleton, witling[obs3], dizzard[obs3], donkey, ass; ninny, ninnyhammer[obs3]; chowderhead[obs3], chucklehead[obs3]; dolt, booby, Tom Noddy, looby[obs3], hoddy-doddy[obs3], noddy, nonny, noodle, nizy[obs3], owl; goose, goosecap[obs3]; imbecile; gaby[obs3]; radoteur[obs3], nincompoop, badaud[obs3], zany; trifler, babbler; pretty fellow; natural, niais[obs3]. child, baby, infant, innocent, milksop, sop. oaf, lout, loon, lown[obs3], dullard, doodle, calf, colt, buzzard, block, put, stick, stock, numps[obs3], tony. bull head, dunderhead, addlehead[obs3], blockhead, dullhead[obs3], loggerhead, jolthead[obs3], jolterhead[obs3], beetlehead[obs3], beetlebrain, grosshead[obs3], muttonhead, noodlehead, giddyhead[obs3]; numbskull, thickskull[obs3]; lackbrain[obs3], shallowbrain[obs3]; dimwit, halfwit, lackwit[obs3]; dunderpate[obs3]; lunkhead sawney[obs3][U.S.], gowk[obs3]; clod, clod-hopper; clod-poll, clot- poll, clot-pate; bull calf; gawk, Gotham-ite, lummox, rube [U.S.]; men of Boeotia, wise men of Gotham. un sot a triple etage[Fr], sot; jobbernowl[obs3], changeling, mooncalf, gobemouche[obs3]. dotard, driveler; old fogey, old woman, crock; crone, grandmother; cotquean[obs3], henhussy[obs3]. incompetent (insanity) 503. greenhorn &c (dupe) 547; dunce &c (ignoramus) 493; lubber &c (bungler) 701; madman &c 504. one who will not set the Thames on fire; one who did not invent gunpow-der, qui n'a pas invente' la poudre [Fr]; no conjuror. Phr. fortuna favet fatuis[Lat]; les fous font les festinas et les sages les mangent [Fr]; nomina stultorum parietibus harrent [Lat]; stultorum plena sunt omnia [Lat][Cicero].

#502. Sanity. — N. sanity; soundness &c. adj.; rationality, sobriety, lucidity, lucid interval; senses, sober senses, right mind, sound mind, mens sana[Lat].

V. be sane &c. adj.; retain one's senses, retain one's reason.

become sane &c. adj.; come to one's senses, sober down.

render sane &c. adj; bring to one's senses, sober.

Adj. sane, rational, reasonable, compos mentis, of sound mind; sound, sound-minded; lucid.

self-possessed; sober, sober-minded.

in one's sober senses, in one's right mind; in possession of one's faculties.

Adv. sanely &c.adj.

<— p. 149 —>

#503. Insanity. — N. disordered reason, disordered intellect; diseased mind, unsound mind, abnormal mind; derangement, unsoundness; psychosis; neurosis; cognitive disorder; affective disorder[obs3]. insanity, lunacy; madness &c. adj.; mania, rabies, furor, mental alienation, aberration; paranoia, schizophrenia; dementation[obs3], dementia, demency[obs3]; phrenitis[obs3], phrensy[obs3], frenzy, raving, incoherence, wandering, delirium, calen-ture of the brain[obs3]; delusion, hallucination; lycanthropy[obs3]; brain storml!. vertigo, dizziness, swimming; sunstroke, coup de soleil[Fr], siriasis[obs3]. fanaticism, infatuation, craze; oddity, eccentricity, twist, monomania (caprice) 608; kleptodipsomania[obs3]; hypochondriasis &c. (low spirits) 837[Med]; melancholia, depression, clinical depression, severe depression; hysteria; amentia[obs3]. screw loose, tile loose, slate loose; bee in one's bonnet, rats in the upper story. dotage &c. (imbecility) 499. V. be insane &c. adj. become insane &c. adj; lose one's senses, lose one's reason, lose one's faculties, lose one's wits; go mad, run mad, lose one's marbles [coll.], go crazy, go bonkers [coll.], flip one's wig [coll.], flip one's lid[coll.], flip out[coll.], flip one's bush [coll.]. rave, dote, ramble, wander; drivel &c. (be imbecile) 499; have a screw loose &c. n., have a devil; avoir le diable au corps[Fr]; lose one's head &c. (be uncertain) 475. render mad, drive mad &c adj.; madden, dementate[obs3], addle the wits, addle the brain, derange the head, infatuate, befool[obs3]; turn the brain, turn one's head; drive one nuts [coll.]. Adj. insane, mad, lunatic, loony[coll.]; crazy, crazed, aliene[obs3], non compos mentis; not right, cracked, touched; bereft of reason; all possessed, unhinged, unsettled in one's mind; insensate, reasonless, beside oneself, demented, daft; phrenzied[obs3], frenzied, frenetic; possessed, possessed with a devil; deranged, maddened, moonstruck; shatterpated[obs3]; mad-brained, scatter brained, shatter brained, crackbrained; touched, tetched [dialect]; off one's head. [behavior suggesting insanity] maniacal; delirious, lightheaded, incoherent, rambling, doting, wandering; frantic, raving, stark staring mad, stark raving mad, wild-eyed, berserk; delusional, hallucinatory. [behavior somewhat resembling insanity] corybantic[obs3], dithyrambic; rabid, giddy, vertiginous, wild; haggard, mazed; flighty; distracted, distraught; depressed; agitated, hyped up; bewildered &c. (uncertain) 475. mad as a March hare, mad as a hatter; of unsound mind &c. n.; touched in one's head, wrong in one's head, not right in one's head, not in one's right mind, not right in one's wits, upper story; out of one's mind, out of one's wits, out of one's skull [coll.], far gone, out of one's senses, out of one's wits; not in one's right mind. fanatical, infatuated, odd, eccentric; hypped[obs3], hyppish[obs3]; spaced out [coll.]. imbecile, silly, &c. 499. Adv. like one possessed. Phr. the mind having lost its balance; the reason under a cloud; tet exaltee[French], tet montee[French]; ira furor brevis est[Latin]; omnes stultos insanire [Latin] [Horace].

#504. Madman. — N. madman, lunatic, maniac, bedlamite[obs3], candidate for Bedlam, raver[obs3], madcap, crazy; energumen[obs3]; automaniac[obs3], monomaniac, dipsomaniac, kleptomaniac; hypochondriac &c. (low spirits); crank, Tom o'Bedlam. dreamer &c. 515; rhapsodist, seer, highflier[obs3], enthusiast, fanatic, fanatico[Sp]; exalte[French]; knight errant, Don Quixote. idiot &c. 501.

<— p. 150 —> % SECTION VI EXTENSION OF THOUGHT

1. To the Past %

#505. Memory.— N. memory, remembrance; retention, retentiveness; tenacity; veteris vestigia flammae[Lat]; tablets of the memory; readiness. reminiscence, recognition, recollection, rememoration[obs3]; recurrence, flashback; retrospect, retrospection. afterthought, post script, PS. suggestion &c. (information) 527; prompting &c. v.; hint, reminder; remembrancer[obs3], flapper; memorial &c. (record) 551; commemoration &c. (celebration) 883. [written reminder] note, memo, memorandum; things to be remembered, token of remembrance, memento, souvenir, keepsake, relic, memorabilia. art of memory, artificial memory; memoria technica[Lat]; mnemonics, mnemotechnics[obs3]; phrenotypics[obs3]; Mnemosyne. prompt-book; crib sheet, cheat sheet. retentive memory, tenacious memory, photographic memory, green memory!!, trustworthy memory, capacious memory, faithful memory, correct memory, exact memory, ready memory, prompt memory, accurate recollection; perfect memory, total recall. celebrity, fame, renown, reputation &c. (repute) 873. V. remember, mind; retain the memory of, retain the remembrance of; keep in view. recognize, recollect, bethink oneself, recall, call up, retrace; look back, trace back, trace backwards; think back, look back upon; review; call upon, recall upon, bring to mind, bring to remembrance; carry one's thoughts back; rake up the past. have in the thoughts, hold in the thoughts, bear in the thoughts, carry in the thoughts, keep in the thoughts, retain in the thoughts, have in the memory, hold in the memory, bear in the memory, carry in the memory, keep in the memory, retain in the memory, have in the mind, hold in the mind, bear in the mind, carry in the mind, keep in the mind, retain in the mind, hold in remembrance; be in one's thoughts, live in one's thoughts, remain in one's thoughts, dwell in one's thoughts, haunt one's thoughts, impress one's thoughts, be in one's mind, live in one's mind, remain in one's mind, dwell in one's mind, haunt one's mind, impress one's mind, dwell in one's memory. sink in the mind; run in the head; not be able to get out of one's head; be deeply impressed with; rankle &c. (revenge) 919. recur to the mind; flash on the mind, flash across the memory. [cause to remember] remind; suggest &c. (inform) 527; prompt; put in mind, keep in mind, bring to mind; fan the embers; call up, summon up, rip up; renew; infandum renovare dolorem [Lat]; jog the memory, flap the memory, refresh the memory, rub up the memory, awaken the memory; pull by the sleeve; bring back to the memory, put in remembrance, memorialize. task the memory, tax the memory. get at one's fingers' ends, have at one's fingers', learn at one's fingers', know one's lesson, say one's lesson, repeat by heart, repeat by rote; say one's lesson; repeat, repeat as a parrot; have at one's fingers' ends. [transitive] commit to memory, memorize; con over, con; fix in the memory, rivet in the memory, imprint in the memory, impress in the memory, stamp in the memory, grave in the memory, engrave in the memory, store in the memory, treasure up in the memory, bottle up in the memory, embalm in the memory, enshrine in the memory; load the memory with, store the memory with, stuff the memory with, burden the memory with. redeem from oblivion; keep the memory alive, keep the wound green, pour salt in the wound, reopen old wounds'; tangere ulcus[obs3][Lat]; keep up the memory of; commemorate &c. (celebrate) 883. make a note of, jot a note, pen a memorandum &c. (record) 551. Adj. remembering, remembered &c. v.; mindful, reminiscential[obs3]; retained in the memory &c. v.; pent up in one's memory; fresh; green, green in remembrance; unforgotten, present to the mind; within one's memory &c. n.; indelible; uppermost in one's thoughts; memorable &c. (important) 642. Adv. by heart, by rote; without book, memoriter[obs3]. in memory of; in memoriam; memoria in aeterna[Lat]; suggestive. Phr. manet alta mente repostum [Lat][Vergil]; forsan et haec olim meminisse juvabit [Lat][Vergil]; absens haeres non erit [Lat]; beatae memoriae [Lat]; "briefly thyself remember" [Lear]; mendacem memorem esse oportet [Lat][Quintilian]; "memory the warder of the brain" [Macbeth]; parsque est meminisse doloris [Lat][Ovid]; "to live in hearts we leave behind is not to die" [Campbell]; vox audita peril littera scripta manet [Lat]; out of sight, out of mind.

#506. Oblivion.— N. oblivion, obliviousness, lethe; forgetfulness &c. adj.; amnesia; obliteration &c. 552 of, insensibility &c. 823 to the past. short memory, treacherous memory, poor memory, loose memory, slippery memory, failing memory; decay of memory, failure of memory, lapse of memory; waters of Lethe, waters of oblivion. amnesty, general pardon. [deliberate or unconscious forgetting] repressed memory. V. forget; be forgetful &c. adj.; fall into oblivion, sink into oblivion; have a short memory &c. n., have no head. forget one's own name, have on the tip of one's tongue, come in one ear and go out the other. slip memory, escape memory, fade from memory, die away from the memory; lose, lose sight of. fail to recall, not be able to recall. [cause oneself to forget: transitive] unlearn; efface &c. 552, discharge from the memory; consign to oblivion, consign to the tomb of the Capulets; think no more of &c. (turn the attention from) 458; cast behind one's back, wean one's thoughts from; let bygones be bygones &c. (forgive) 918. Adj. forgotten &c. v.; unremembered, past recollection, bygone, out of mind; buried in oblivion, sunk in oblivion; clean forgotten; gone out of one's head, gone out of one's recollection. forgetful, oblivious, mindless, Lethean; insensible &c. 823 to the past; heedless. Phr. non mi ricordo[It]; the memory failing, the memory deserting one, being at (or in) fault.

<— p. 151 —>

#507. Expectation. — N. expectation, expectance, expectancy; anticipation, reckoning, calculation; foresight &c. 510. contemplation, prospection[obs3], lookout; prospect, perspective, horizon, vista; destiny &c. 152. suspense, waiting, abeyance; curiosity &c. 455; anxious expectation, ardent expectation, eager expectation, breathless expectation, sanguine expectation; torment of Tantalus. hope &c. 858; trust &c. (belief) 484; auspices &c. (prediction) 511; assurance, confidence, presumption, reliance. V. expect; look for, look out for, look forward to; hope for; anticipate; have in prospect, have in contemplation; keep in view; contemplate, promise oneself; not wonder &c. 870 at, not wonder if. wait for, tarry for, lie in wait for, watch for, bargain for; keep a good lookout for, keep a sharp lookout for; await; stand at "attention," abide, bide one's time, watch. foresee &c. 510; prepare for &c. 673; forestall &c. (be early) 132; count upon &c. (believe in) 484; think likely &c. (probability) 472. lead one to expect &c. (predict) 511; have in store for &c. (destiny) 152. prick up one's ears, hold one's breath. Adj. expectant; expecting &c. v.; in expectation &c. n.; on the watch &c. (vigilant) 459; open-eyed, open-mouthed, in wide-eyed anticipation; agape, gaping, all agog; on tenterhooks, on tiptoe, on the tiptoe of expectation; aux aguets[obs3]; ready; curious &c. 455; looking forward to. expected &c. v.; long expected, foreseen; in prospect &c. n.; prospective; in one's eye, in one's view, in the horizon, on the horizon, just over the horizon, just around the corner, around the corner; impending &c. (destiny) 152. Adv. on the watch &c. adj.; with breathless expectation &c. n.; with bated breath, with rapt anticipation; arrectis auribus[Lat]. Phr. we shall see; nous verrons[Fr]; "expectation whirls me round" [Troilus and Cressida]; the light at the end of the tunnel.

#508. Inexpectation. — N. inexpectation[obs3], non-expectation; false expectation &c. (disappointment) 509; miscalculation &c. 481. surprise, sudden burst, thunderclap, blow, shock, start; bolt out of the blue; wonder &c. 870; eye opener. unpleasant surprise, pleasant surprise. V. not expect &c. 507; be taken by surprise; start; miscalculate &c. 481; not bargain for; come upon, fall upon. be unexpected &c. adj.; come unawares &c. adv.; turn up, pop, drop from the clouds; come upon one, burst upon one, flash upon one, bounce upon one, steal upon one, creep upon one; come like a thunder clap, burst like a thunderclap, thunder bolt; take by surprise, catch by surprise, catch unawares, catch napping; yach [obs3][S. Africa]. pounce upon, spring a mine upon. surprise, startle, take aback, electrify, stun, stagger, take away one's breath, throw off one's guard; astonish, dumbfound &c. (strike with wonder) 870. Adj. nonexpectant[obs3]; surprised &c. v.; unwarned, unaware; off one's guard; inattentive 458. unexpected, unanticipated, unpredicted[obs3], unlooked for, unforeseen, unhoped for; dropped from the clouds; beyond expectation, contrary to expectation, against expectation, against all expectation; out of one's reckoning; unheard of &c. (exceptional) 83; startling, surprising; sudden &c. (instantaneous) 113. unpredictable, unforeseeable (unknowable) 519. Adv. abruptly, unexpectedly, surprisingly; plump, pop, a l'improviste[Fr], unawares; without notice, without warning, without a "by your leave"; like a thief in the night, like a thunderbolt; in an unguarded moment; suddenly &c. (instantaneously) 113. Int. heydey[obs3]! &c. (wonder) 870. Phr. little did one think, little did one expect; nobody would ever suppose, nobody would ever think, nobody would ever expect; who would have thought? it beats the Dutch!!.

#509. [Failure of expectation.] Disappointment. — N. disappointment; blighted hope, balk; blow; anticlimax; slip 'twixt cup and lip; nonfulfillment of one's hopes; sad disappointment, bitter disappointment; trick of fortune; afterclap; false expectation, vain expectation; miscalculation &c. 481; fool's paradise; much cry and little wool. V. be disappointed; look blank, look blue; look aghast, stand aghast &c. (wonder) 870; find to one's cost; laugh on the wrong side of one's mouth; find one a false prophet. not realize one's hope, not realize one's expectation. [cause to be disappointed] disappoint; frustrate, discomfit, crush, defeat (failure) 732; crush one's hope, dash one's hope, balk one's hope, disappoint one's hope, blight one's hope, falsify one's hope, defeat one's hope, discourage; balk, jilt, bilk; play one false, play a trick; dash the cup from the lips, tantalize; dumfound, dumbfound, dumbfounder, dumfounder (astonish) 870. Adj. disappointed &c. v.; disconcerted, aghast; disgruntled; out of one's reckoning. Phr. the mountain labored and brought forth a mouse; parturiunt montes[Lat]; nascitur ridiculus mus [Lat][Horace]; diis aliter visum[Lat][obs3], the bubble burst; one's countenance falling.

<— p. 152 —>

#510. Foresight. — N. foresight, prospicience[obs3], prevision, long- sightedness; anticipation; providence &c. (preparation) 673. forethought, forecast; predeliberation[obs3], presurmise[obs3]; foregone conclusion &c. (prejudgment) 481; prudence &c. (caution) 864. foreknowledge; prognosis; precognition, prescience, prenotion[obs3], presentiment; second sight; sagacity &c. (intelligence) 498; antepast[obs3], prelibation[obs3], prophasis[obs3]. prospect &c. (expectation) 507; foretaste; prospectus &c. (plan) 626. V. foresee; look forwards to, look ahead, look beyond; scent from afar; look into the future, pry into the future, peer into the future. see one's way; see how the land lies, get the lay of the land, see how the wind blows, test the waters, see how the cat jumps. anticipate; expect &c. 507; be beforehand &c. (early) 132; predict &c. 511; foreknow, forejudge, forecast; presurmise[obs3]; have an eye to the future, have an eye to the main chance; respicere finem[Lat]; keep a sharp lookout &c. (vigilance) 459; forewarn &c. 668. Adj. foreseeing &c. v.; prescient; farseeing, farsighted; sagacious &c. (intelligent) 498; weatherwise[obs3]; provident &c. (prepared) 673; prospective &c. 507. Adv. against the time when. Phr. cernit omnia Deus vindex[Lat]; mihi cura futuri[Lat]; run it up the flagpole and see who salutes.

#511. Prediction.— N. prediction, announcement; program, programme &c. (plan) 626[Brit]; premonition &c. (warning) 668; prognosis, prophecy, vaticination, mantology[obs3], prognostication, premonstrationl; augury, augurationl; ariolationl; hariolationl; foreboding, abodingl[obs3]; bodement[obs3], abodement[obs3]; omniationl, omniousness[obs3]; auspices, forecast; omen &c. 512; horoscope, nativity; sooth[obs3], soothsaying; fortune telling, crystal gazing; divination; necromancy &c. 992. [Divination by the stars] astrology[obs3], horoscopy[obs3], judicial astrology1[obs3]. [obs3] adytum[Place of prediction]. prefiguration[obs3], prefigurement; prototype, type. [person who predicts] oracle &c. 513. V. predict, prognosticate, prophesy, vaticinate, divine, foretell, soothsay, augurate[obs3], tell fortunes; cast a horoscope, cast a nativity; advise; forewarn &c. 668. presage, augur, bode; abode, forebode; foretoken, betoken; prefigure, preshow[obs3]; portend; foreshow[obs3], foreshadow; shadow forth, typify, pretypify[obs3], ominate[obs3], signify, point to. usher in, herald, premise, announce; lower. hold out expectation, raise expectation, excite expectation, excite hope; bid fair, promise, lead one to expect; be the precursor &c 64. [predict by mathematical or statistical means from past experience] extrapolate, project. Adj. predicting &cv.; predictive, prophetic; fatidic[obs3], fatidical[obs3]; vaticinal, oracular, fatiloquent[obs3], haruspical, Sibylline; weatherwise[obs3]. ominous, portentous, augurous[obs3], augurial, augural; auspicial[obs3], auspicious; prescious[obs3], monitory, extispicious[obs3], premonitory, significant of, pregnant with, bit with the fate of. Phr. "coming events cast their shadows before" [Campbell]; dicamus bona verba[Lat]; "there buds the promise of celestial worth" [Young].

[1] The following terms, expressive of different forms of divination, have been collected from various sources, and are here given as a curious illustration of bygone superstitions:- Divination by oracles, Theomancy[obs3]; by the Bible, Bibliomancy; by ghosts, Psychomancy[obs3]; by crystal gazing, Crystallomancy[obs3]; by shadows or manes, Sciomancy; by appearances in the air, Aeromancy[obs3], Chaomancy[obs3]; by the stars at birth, Genethliacs; by meteors, Meteoromancy[obs3]; by winds, Austromancy[obs3]; by sacrificial appearances, Aruspicy (or Haruspicy) [obs3], Hieromancy[obs3], Hieroscopy[obs3]; by the entrails of animals sacrificed, Extispicy[obs3], Hieromancy[obs3]; by the entrails of a human sacrifice, Anthropomancy[obs3]; by the entrails of fishes, Ichthyomancy[obs3]; by sacrificial fire, Pyromancy[obs3]; by red-hot iron, Sideromancy[obs3]; by smoke from the altar, Capnomancy[obs3]; by mice, Myomancy[obs3]; by birds, Orniscopy[obs3], Ornithomancy[obs3]; by a cock picking up grains, Alectryomancy (or Alectromancy)[obs3]; by fishes, Ophiomancy[obs3]; by herbs, Botanomancy[obs3]; by water, Hydromancy[obs3]; by fountains, Pegomancy[obs3]; by a wand, Rhabdomancy; by dough of cakes, Crithomancy[obs3]; by meal, Aleuromancy[obs3], Alphitomancy[obs3]; by salt, Halomancy[obs3]; by dice, Cleromancy[obs3]; by arrows, Belomancy[obs3]; by a balanced hatchet, Axinomancy[obs3]; by a balanced sieve, Coscinomancy[obs3]; by a suspended ring, Dactyliomancy[obs3]; by dots made at random on paper, Geomancy[obs3]; by precious stones, Lithomancy[obs3]; by pebbles, Pessomancy[obs3]; by pebbles drawn from a heap, Psephomancy[obs3]; by mirrors, Catoptromancy[obs3]; by writings in ashes, Tephramancy[obs3]; by dreams, Oneiromancy[obs3]; by the hand, Palmistry, Chiromancy; by nails reflecting the sun's rays, Onychomancy[obs3]; by finger rings, Dactylomancy[obs3]; by numbers, Arithmancy[obs3]; by drawing lots, Sortilege[obs3]; by passages in books, Stichomancy[obs3]; by the letters forming the name of the person, Onomancy[obs3], Nomancy; by the features, Anthroposcopy[obs3]; by the mode of laughing, Geloscopy[obs3]; by ventriloquism, Gastromancy[obs3]; by walking in a circle, Gyromancy[obs3]; by dropping melted wax into water, Ceromancy[obs3]; by currents, Bletonism; by the color and peculiarities of wine, Oenomancy[obs3].

<— p. 153 —>

#512. Omen.— N. omen, portent, presage, prognostic, augury, auspice;
sign &c. (indication) 550; harbinger &c. (precursor) 64; yule candlel!.

bird of ill omen; signs of the times; gathering clouds; warning &c.
668.

prefigurement &c. 511.

Adj. ill-boding.

Phr. auspicium melioris aevi[Lat][obs3].

#513. Oracle.— N. oracle; prophet, prophesier, seer, soothsayer, augur, fortune teller, crystal gazer[obs3], witch, geomancer[obs3], aruspex[obs3]; aruspice[obs3], haruspice[obs3]; haruspex; astrologer, star gazer[obs3]; Sibyl; Python, Pythoness[obs3]; Pythia; Pythian oracle, Delphian oracle; Monitor, Sphinx, Tiresias, Cassandra[obs3], Sibylline leaves; Zadkiel, Old Moore; sorcerer &c. 994; interpreter &c. 524. [person who predicts by non-mystical (natural) means] predictor, prognosticator, forecaster; weather forecaster, weatherman. Phr. a prophet is without honor in his own country; "you don't need a weatherman to know which way the wind blows" [Bob Dylan].

% SECTION VII. CREATIVE THOUGHT %

#514. Supposition.— N. supposition, assumption, assumed position, postulation, condition, presupposition, hypothesis, blue sky hypothesis, postulate, postulatum[Lat], theory; thesis, theorem; data; proposition, position; proposal &c. (plan) 626; presumption &c. (belief) 484; divination. conjecture; guess, guesswork, speculation; rough guess, shot, shot in the dark [coll.]; conjecturality[obs3]; surmise, suspicion, sneaking suspicion; estimate, approximation (nearness) 197. inkling, suggestion, hint, intimation, notion, impression; bare supposition, vague supposition, loose supposition, loose suggestion. association of ideas, (analogy) 514a; metonym[Gram], metonymy[Gram], simile (metaphor) 521. conceit, idea, thought; original idea, invention (imagination) 515. V. suppose, conjecture, surmise, suspect, guess, divine; theorize; presume, presurmise[obs3], presuppose; assume, fancy, wis[obs3], take it; give a guess, speculate, believe, dare say, take it into one's head, take for granted; imagine &c. 515. put forth; propound, propose; start, put a case, submit, move, make a motion; hazard out, throw out a suggestion, put forward a suggestion, put forward conjecture. allude to, suggest, hint, put it into one's head. suggest itself &c. (thought) 451; run in the head &c. (memory) 505; marvel if, wonder if, wonder whether. Adj. supposing &c. v.; given, mooted, postulatory[obs3]; assumed &c. v.; supposititious, suppositive[obs3], suppositious; gratuitous, speculative, conjectural, hypothetical, theoretical, academic, supposable, presumptive, putative; suppositional. suggestive, allusive. Adv. if, if so be; an; on the supposition &c. n.;ex hypothesi[Lat]; in the case, in the event of; quasi, as if, provided; perhaps &c. (by possibility) 470; for aught one knows.

<— p. 154 —>
<— under creative thought we should include a separate section on analogy,
metaphor, association etc. distinct from 521?? —>

#514a. Analogy — N. analogy, association, association of ideas.

metaphor &c. 521.

analogical thinking; free association; train of thought.

Adj. analogical.

#515. Imagination. — N. imagination; originality; invention; fancy; inspiration; verve. warm imagination, heated imagination, excited imagination, sanguine imagination, ardent imagination, fiery imagination, boiling imagination, wild imagination, bold imagination, daring imagination, playful imagination, lively imagination, fertile imagination, fancy. "mind's eye"; "such stuff as dreams are made of" [Tempest]. ideality, idealism; romanticism, utopianism, castle-building. dreaming; phrensy[obs3], frenzy; ecstasy, extasy[obs3]; calenture &c. (delirium) 503[obs3]; reverie, trance; day dream, golden dream; somnambulism. conception, Vorstellung[Ger], excogitation[obs3], "a fine frenzy"; cloudland[obs3], dreamland; flight of fancy, fumes of fancy; "thick coming fancies" [Macbeth]; creation of the brain, coinage of the brain; imagery. conceit, maggot, figment, myth, dream, vision, shadow, chimera; phantasm, phantasy; fantasy, fancy; whim, whimsey[obs3], whimsy; vagary, rhapsody, romance, gest[obs3], geste[obs3], extravaganza; air drawn dagger, bugbear, nightmare. flying Dutchman, great sea serpent, man in the moon, castle in the air, pipe dream, pie-in-the-sky, chateau en Espagne[Fr]; Utopia, Atlantis[obs3], happy valley, millennium, fairyland; land of Prester John, kingdom of Micomicon; work of fiction &c. (novel) 594; Arabian nights[obs3]; le pot au lait[Fr]; dream of Alnashar &c. (hope) 858[obs3]. illusion &c. (error) 495; phantom &c. (fallacy of vision) 443; Fata Morgana &c. (ignis fatuus) 423[Lat]; vapor &c. (cloud) 353; stretch of the imagination &c. (exaggeration) 549; mythogenesis[obs3]. idealist, romanticist, visionary; mopus[obs3]; romancer, dreamer; somnambulist; rhapsodist &c. (fanatic) 504; castle-builder, fanciful projector. V. imagine, fancy, conceive; idealize, realize; dream, dream of, dream up; "give to airy nothing a local habitation and a name" [Midsummer Night's Dream]. create, originate, devise, invent, coin, fabricate; improvise, strike out something new. set one's wits to work; strain one's invention, crack one's invention;

rack one's brains, ransack one's brains, cudgel one's brains; excogitate[obs3]; brainstorm. give play, give the reins, give a loose to the imagination, give fancy; indulge in reverie. visualize, envision, conjure up a vision; fancy oneself, represent oneself, picture, picture-oneself, figure to oneself; vorstellen[Ger]. float in the mind; suggest itself &c. (thought) 451. Adj. imagined &c. v.; ben trovato[It]; air drawn, airbuilt[obs3]. imagining &cv. v, imaginative; original, inventive, creative, fertile. romantic, high flown, flighty, extravagant, fanatic, enthusiastic, unrealistic, Utopian, Quixotic. ideal, unreal; in the clouds, in nubibus[Lat]; unsubsantial[obs3] &c. 4; illusory &c. (fallacious) 495. fabulous, legendary; mythical, mythic, mythological; chimerical; imaginary, visionary; notional; fancy, fanciful, fantastic, fantastical[obs3]; whimsical; fairy, fairy-like; gestic[obs3]. Phr. "a change came o'er the spirit of my dream" [Byron]; aegri somnia vana[Lat][obs3]; dolphinum appingit sylvis in fluctibus aprum [obs3][Latin][Horace]; "fancy light from fancy caught" [Tennyson]; "imagination rules the world" [Napoleon]; l'imagination gallope[Fr], le jugement ne va que le pas[French]; musaeo contingens cuncta lepore [Latin][Lucretius]; tous songes sont mensonges[French]; Wahrheil und Dichtung[German].

% DIVISION (II) COMMUNICATION OF IDEAS

SECTION I. NATURE OF IDEAS COMMUNICATED. %

#516. [Idea to be conveyed.] Meaning. [Thing signified.] — N. meaning; signification, significance; sense, expression; import, purport; force; drift, tenor, spirit, bearing, coloring; scope. [important part of the meaning] substance; gist, essence, marrow, spirit &c. 5. matter; subject, subject matter; argument, text, sum and substance. general meaning, broad meaning, substantial meaning, colloquial meaning, literal meaning, plain meaning, simple meaning, natural meaning, unstrained meaning, true &c. (exact) 494 meaning, honest &c. 543 meaning, prima facie &c. (manifest) 525 meaning[Lat]; letter of the law. literally; after acceptation. synonym; implication, allusion &c. (latency) 526; suggestion &c. (information) 527; figure of speech &c. 521; acceptation &c. (interpretation) 522. V. mean, signify, express; import, purport; convey, imply, breathe, indicate, bespeak, bear a sense; tell of, speak of; touch on; point to, allude to; drive at; involve &c. (latency) 526; declare &c. (affirm) 535. understand by &c. (interpret) 522. Adj. meaning &c. v.; expressive, suggestive, allusive; significant, significative[obs3], significatory[obs3]; pithy; full of meaning, pregnant with meaning. declaratory &c. 535; intelligible &c. 518; literal; synonymous; tantamount &c. (equivalent) 27; implied &c. (latent) 526; explicit &c. 525. Adv. to that effect; that is to say &c. (being interpreted) 522.

<— p. 155 —>

#517. [Absence of meaning.] Unmeaningness. — N. meaninglessness, unmeaningness &c. adj[obs3].; scrabble. empty sound, dead letter, vox et praeterea nihil[Lat]; "a tale told by an idiot, full of sound and fury, signifying nothing"; "sounding brass and a tinkling cymbal." nonsense, utter nonsense, gibberish; jargon, jabber, mere words, hocus-pocus, fustian, rant, bombast, balderdash, palaver, flummery, verbiage, babble, baverdage, baragouin[obs3], platitude, niaiserie[obs3]; inanity; flap-doodle; rigmarole, rodomontade; truism; nugae canorae[Lat]; twaddle, twattle, fudge, trash, garbage, humbug; poppy-cock [U.S.]; stuff, stuff and nonsense; bosh, rubbish, moonshine, wish-wash, fiddle-faddle; absurdity &c. 497; vagueness &c. (unintelligibility) 519. [routine or reflexive statements without substantive thought, esp. legal] boilerplate. V. mean nothing; be unmeaning &c. adj.; twaddle, quibble, scrabble. Adj. unmeaning; meaningless, senseless; nonsensical; void of sense &c. 516. inexpressive, unexpressive; vacant; not significant &c. 516; insignificant. trashy, washy, trumpery, trivial, fiddle-faddle, twaddling, quibbling. unmeant, not expressed; tacit &c. (latent) 526. inexpressible, undefinable, incommunicable.

#518. Intelligibility. — N. intelligibility; clearness, explicitness &c. adj.; lucidity, comprehensibility, perspicuity; legibility, plain speaking &c. (manifestation) 525; precision &c. 494; <gr/phonanta synetoisy/gr>[Grk][Grk]; a word to the wise.

V. be intelligible &c. adj.; speak for itself, speak volumes; tell its own tale, lie on the surface.

render intelligible &c. adj.; popularize, simplify, clear up; elucidate &c. (explain) 522.

understand, comprehend, take, take in; catch, grasp, follow, collect, master, make out; see with half an eye, see daylight, see one's way; enter into the ideas of; come to an understanding.

Adj. intelligible; clear, clear as day, clear as noonday; lucid; perspicuous, transpicuous[obs3]; luminous, transparent.

easily understood, easy to understand, for the million, intelligible to the meanest capacity, popularized.

plain, distinct, explicit; positive; definite &c. (precise) 494.

graphic; expressive &c. (meaning) 516; illustrative &c. (explanatory) 522.

unambiguous, unequivocal, unmistakable &c. (manifest) 525; unconfused; legible, recognizable; obvious &c. 525.

Adv. in plain terms, in plain words, in plain English.

Phr. he that runs may read &c. (manifest) 525.

#519. Unintelligibility.— N. unintelligibility; incomprehensibility, imperspicuity[obs3]; inconceivableness, vagueness &c. adj.; obscurity; ambiguity &c. 520; doubtful meaning; uncertainty &c. 475; perplexity &c. (confusion) 59; spinosity[obs3]; obscurum per obscurius[Lat]; mystification &c. (concealment) 528; latency &c. 526; transcendentalism. paradox, oxymoron; riddle, enigma, puzzle &c. (secret) 533; diagnus vindice nodus[Lat]; sealed book; steganography[obs3], freemasonry. pons asinorum[Lat], asses' bridge; high Dutch, Greek, Hebrew; jargon &c. (unmeaning) 517. V. be unintelligible &c. adj.; require explanation &c. 522; have a doubtful meaning, pass comprehension. render unintelligible &c. adj.; conceal &c 528; darken &c. 421; confuse &c. (derange) 61; perplex &c. (bewilder) 475. not understand &c. 518; lose, lose the clue; miss; not know what to make of, be able to make nothing of, give it up; not be able to account for, not be able to make either head or tail of; be at sea &c. (uncertain) 475; wonder &c. 870; see through a glass darkly &c. (ignorance) 491. not understand one another; play at cross purposes &c. (misinterpret) 523. Adj. unintelligible, unaccountable, undecipherable, undiscoverable, unknowable, unfathomable; incognizable[obs3], inexplicable, inscrutable; inapprehensible[obs3], incomprehensible; insolvable[obs3], insoluble; impenetrable. illegible, as Greek to one, unexplained, paradoxical; enigmatic, enigmatical, puzzling (secret) 533; indecipherable. obscure, dark, muddy, clear as mud, seen through a mist, dim, nebulous, shrouded in mystery; opaque, dense; undiscernible &c. (invisible) 447[obs3]; misty &c. (opaque) 426; hidden &c 528; latent &c 526. indefinite, garbled &c (indistinct) 447; perplexed &c. (confused) 59; undetermined, vague, loose, ambiguous; mysterious; mystic, mystical; acroamatic[obs3], acroamatical[obs3]; metempirical; transcendental; occult, recondite, abstruse, crabbed. inconceivable, inconceptible[obs3]; searchless[obs3]; above comprehension, beyond comprehension, past comprehension; beyond one's depth; unconceived. inexpressible, undefinable, incommunicable. unpredictable, unforeseeable. Phr. it's Greek to me. <— p. 156 —>

#520. [Having a double sense] Equivocalness.— N. equivocalness &c adj.; double meaning &c. 516; ambiguity, double entente, double entendre[Fr], pun, paragram[obs3], calembour[obs3], quibble, equivoque[Fr], anagram; conundrum &c (riddle) 533; play on words, word play &c. (wit) 842; homonym, homonymy[Gram]; amphiboly[obs3], amphibology[obs3]; ambilogy[obs3], ambiloquyl. Sphinx, Delphic oracle. equivocation &c. (duplicity) 544; white lie, mental reservation &c. (concealment) 528; paltering. V. be -equivocal &c. adj.; have two meanings &c. 516; equivocate &c. (alter) 544. Adj. equivocal, ambiguous, amphibolous[obs3], homonymous[obs3]; double-tongued &c. (lying) 544; enigmatical, indeterminate. Phr. on the one hand, on the other hand.

#521. Metaphor.— N. figure of speech; facon de parler [French], way of speaking, colloquialism.

phrase &c. 566; figure, trope, metaphor, enallage[obs3], catachresis[obs3]; metonymy[Gram], synecdoche[Semant]; autonomasia!, irony, figurativeness &c. adj.; image, imagery; metalepsis[obs3], type, anagoge[obs3], simile, personification, prosopopoeia[obs3], allegory, apologue[obs3], parable, fable; allusion, adumbration; application.

exaggeration, hyperbole &c. 549.

association, association of ideas (analogy) 514a

V. employ -metaphor &c. n.; personify, allegorize, adumbrate, shadow forth, apply, allude to.

Adj. metaphorical, figurative, catachrestical[obs3], typical, tralatitious[obs3], parabolic, allegorical, allusive, anagogical[obs3]; ironical; colloquial; tropical.

Adv. so to speak, so to say, so to express oneself; as it were.

Phr. mutato nomine de te fabula narratur [Lat][Horace].

#522. Interpretation. — N. interpretation, definition; explanation, explication; solution, answer; rationale; plain interpretation, simple interpretation, strict interpretation; meaning &c. 516. translation; rendering, rendition; redition[obs3]; literal translation, free translation; key; secret; clew &c. (indication) 550; clavis[obs3], crib, pony, trot [U.S.]. exegesis; expounding, exposition; hermeneutics; comment, commentary; inference &c. (deduction) 480; illustration, exemplification; gloss, annotation, scholium[obs3], note; elucidation, dilucidationl; eclaircissement[Fr], mot d'enigme[Fr]. [methods of interpreting - list] symptomatology[Med], semiology, semeiology[obs3], semiotics; metoposcopy[obs3], physiognomy; paleography &c. (philology) 560; oneirology acception[obs3], acceptation, acceptance; light, reading, lection, construction, version. equivalent, equivalent meaning &c. 516; synonym; paraphrase, metaphrase[obs3]; convertible terms, apposition; dictionary &c. 562; polyglot. V. interpret, explain, define, construe, translate, render; do into, turn into; transfuse the sense of. find out &c. 480a the meaning &c. 516 of; read; spell out, make out; decipher, unravel, disentangle; find the key of, enucleate, resolve, solve; read between the lines. account for; find the cause, tell the cause &c. 153 of; throw light upon, shed light upon, shed new light upon, shed fresh light upon; clear up, clarify, elucidate. illustrate, exemplify; unfold, expound, comment upon, annotate; popularize &c. (render intelligible) 518. take in a particular sense, understand in a particular sense, receive in a particular sense, accept in a particular sense; understand by, put a construction on, be given to understand. Adj. explanatory, expository; explicative, explicatory; exegetical[obs3]; construable. polyglot; literal; paraphrastic, metaphrastic[obs3]; consignificative[obs3], synonymous; equivalent &c. 27. Adv. in explanation &c. n.; that is to say, id est, videlicet, to wit, namely, in other words. literally, strictly speaking; in plain, in plainer terms, in plainer words, in plainer English; more simply.

<— p. 157 —>

#523. Misinterpretation. — N. misinterpretation, misapprehension, misunderstanding, misacceptationl, misconstruction, misapplication; catachresis[obs3]; eisegesis[obs3]; cross-reading, cross-purposes; mistake &c. 495. misrepresentation, perversion, exaggeration &c. 549; false coloring, false construction; abuse of terms; parody, travesty; falsification &c. (lying) 544. V. misinterpret, misapprehend, misunderstand, misconceive, misspell, mistranslate, misconstrue, misapply; mistake &c. 495. misrepresent, pervert; explain wrongly, misstate; garble &c. (falsify) 544; distort, detortl; travesty, play upon words; stretch the sense, strain the sense, stretch the meaning, strain the meaning, wrest the sense, wrest the meaning; explain away; put a bad construction on, put a false construction on; give a false coloring. be at cross purposes, play at cross purposes. Adj. misinterpreted &c. v.; untranslated, untranslatable.

#524. Interpreter.— N. interpreter; expositor, expounder, exponent, explainer; demonstrator.
scholiast, commentator, annotator; metaphrast[obs3], paraphrast[obs3]; glossarist[obs3], prolocutor.
spokesman, speaker, mouthpiece.
dragoman, courier, valet de place, cicerone, showman; oneirocritic[obs3]; (Edipus; oracle &c. 513)

% SECTION II. MODES OF COMMUNICATION %

#525. Manifestation.— N. {ant. 526} manifestation; plainness &c. adj.; plain speaking; expression; showing &c. v.; exposition, demonstration; exhibition, production; display, show; showing off; premonstrationl. exhibit[Thing shown]. indication &c. (calling attention to) 457. publicity &c. 531; disclosure &c. 529; openness &c. (honesty) 543, (artlessness) 703; panchement. evidence &c. 467. V. make manifest, render manifest &c. adj.; bring forth, bring forward, bring to the front, bring into view; give notice; express; represent, set forth, exhibit; show, show up; expose; produce; hold up to view, expose to view; set before one, place before one, lay before one, one's eyes; tell to one's face; trot out, put through one's paces, bring to light, display, demonstrate, unroll; lay open; draw out, bring out; bring out in strong relief; call into notice, bring into notice; hold up the mirror; wear one's heart upon his sleeve; show one's face, show one's colors; manifest oneself; speak out; make no mystery, make no secret of; unfurl the flag; proclaim &c. (publish) 531. indicate &c. (direct attention to) 457; disclose &c. 529; elicit &c. 480a. be manifest &c. adj.; appear &c. (be visible) 446; transpire &c. (be disclosed) 529; speak for itself, stand to reason; stare one in the face, rear its head; give token, give sign, give indication of; tell its own tale &c. (intelligible) 518. Adj. manifest, apparent; salient, striking, demonstrative, prominent, in the foreground, notable, pronounced. flagrant; notorious &c. (public) 531; arrant; stark staring; unshaded, glaring. defined, definite. distinct, conspicuous &c. (visible) 446; obvious, evident, unmistakable, indubitable, not to be mistaken, palpable, self-evident, autoptical[obs3]; intelligible &c. 518. plain, clear, clear as day, clear as daylight, clear as noonday; plain as a pike staff, plain as the sun at noon-day, plain as the nose on one's face, plain as the way to parish church. explicit, overt, patent, express; ostensible; open, open as day; naked, bare, literal, downright, undisguised, exoteric. unreserved, frank, plain-spoken &c. (artless) 703; candid (veracious) 543; barefaced. manifested &c. v.; disclosed &c. 529; capable of being shown, producible; inconcealable[obs3], unconcealable; no secret. Adv. manifestly, openly &c. adj.; before one's eyes, under one's nose, to one's face, face to face, above board, cartes sur table, on the stage, in open court, in the open streets; in market overt; in the face of day, face of heaven; in broad daylight, in open daylight; without reserve; at first blush, prima facie[Lat], on the face of; in set terms. Phr. cela saute aux yeux[French]; he that runs may read; you can see it with half an eye; it needs no ghost to tell us [Hamlet]; the meaning lies on the surface; cela va sans dire[Fr]; res ipsa loquitur[Lat]; "clothing the palpable and familiar" [Coleridge]; fari quae sentiat[Lat]; volto sciolto i pensieri stretti [It]; "you don't need a weatherman to know which way the wind blows" [Bob Dylan].

<— p. 158 —>

#526. Latency. Implication. — N. {ant. 525} latency, inexpression[obs3]; hidden meaning, occult meaning; occultness, mystery, cabala[obs3], anagoge[obs3]; silence &c (taciturnity) 585; concealment &c. 528; more than meets the eye, more than meets the ear; Delphic oracle; le dessous des cartes[Fr], undercurrent. implication, logical implication; logical consequence; entailment. allusion, insinuation; innuendo &c. 527; adumbration; "something rotten in the state of Denmark" [Hamlet]. snake in the grass &c. (pitfall) 667; secret &c. 533. darkness, invisibility, imperceptibility. V. be latent &c. adj.; lurk, smolder, underlie, make no sign; escape observation, escape detection, escape recognition; lie hid &c. 528. laugh in one's sleeve; keep back &c. (conceal) 528. involve, imply, understand, allude to, infer, leave an inference; entail; whisper &c. (conceal) 528. [understand the implication] read between the lines. Adj. latent; lurking &c.v.; secret &c. 528; occult; implied &c. v.; dormant; abeyant. unapparent, unknown, unseen &c. 441; in the background; invisible &c. 447; indiscoverable[obs3], dark; impenetrable &c. (unintelligible) 519; unspied[obs3], unsuspected. unsaid, unwritten, unpublished, unbreathed[obs3], untalked of[obs3], untold &c. 527, unsung, unexposed, unproclaimed[obs3], undisclosed &c. 529, unexpressed; not expressed, tacit. undeveloped, solved, unexplained, untraced[obs3], undiscovered &c. 480a, untracked, unexplored, uninvented[obs3]. indirect, crooked, inferential; by inference, by implication; implicit; constructive; allusive, covert, muffled; steganographic[obs3]; understood, underhand, underground; delitescent[obs3], concealed &c. 528. Adv. by a side wind; sub silentio[Lat]; in the background; behind the scenes, behind one's back; on the tip of one's tongue; secretly &c. 528; between the lines. Phr. "thereby hangs a tale" [As You Like It]; tacitum vivit sub pectore vulnus [Lat][Vergil]; where there's smoke, there's fire.

#527. Information.— N. information, enlightenment, acquaintance, knowledge &c. 490; publicity &c. 531; data &c. 467. communication, intimation; notice, notification; enunciation, annunciation; announcement; communiqu; representation, round robin, presentment. case, estimate, specification, report, advice, monition; news &c. 532; return &c. (record) 551; account &c. (description) 594; statement &c. (affirmation) 535. mention; acquainting &c. v; instruction &c. (teaching) 537; outpouring; intercommunication, communicativeness. informant, authority, teller, intelligencer[obs3], reporter, exponent, mouthpiece; informer, eavesdropper, delator, detective; sleuth; mouchard[obs3], spy, newsmonger; messenger &c. 534; amicus curiae[Lat]. valet de place, cicerone, pilot, guide; guid, handbook; vade mecum[Latin]; manual; map, plan, chart, gazetteer; itinerary &c. (journey) 266. hint, suggestion, innuendo, inkling, whisper, passing word, word in the ear, subaudition[obs3], cue, byplay; gesture &c. (indication) 550; gentle hint, broad hint; verbum sapienti [Latin: a word to the wise]; insinuation &c. (latency) 526. information theory. [units of information] bit, byte, word, doubleword[Comp], quad word, paragraph, segment. [information storage media] magnetic media, paper medium, optical media; random access memory, RAM; read-only memory, ROM; write once read mostly memory, WORM. V. tell; inform, inform of; acquaint, acquaint with; impart, impart to; make acquaintance with, apprise, advise, enlighten, awaken; transmit. let fall, mention, express, intimate, represent, communicate, make known; publish &c. 531; notify, signify, specify, convey the knowledge of. let one know, have one to know; give one to understand; give notice; set before, lay before, put before; point out, put into one's head; put one in possession of; instruct &c. (teach) 537; direct the attention to &c. 457. announce, annunciate; report, report progress; bringword[obs3], send word, leave word, write word; telegraph, telephone; wire; retail, render an account; give an account &c. (describe) 594; state &c (affirm) 535. [disclose inadvertently or reluctantly] let slip, blurt out, spill the beans, unburden oneself of, let off one's chest; disclose &c. 529. show cause; explain &c. (interpret) 522. hint; given an inkling of; give a hint, drop a hint, throw out a hint; insinuate; allude to, make allusion to; glance at; tip the wink &c. (indicate) 550; suggest, prompt, give the cue, breathe; whisper, whisper in the ear. give a bit of one's mind; tell one plainly, tell once for all; speak volumes. undeceive[obs3], unbeguile[obs3]; set right, correct, open the eyes of, disabuse, disillusion one of. be informed of &c.; know &c 490; learn &c. 539; get scent of, get wind of, gather from; awaken to, open one's eyes to; become alive, become awake to; hear, overhear, understand. come to one's ears, come to one's knowledge; reach one's ears. Adj. informed &c. v.; communique; reported &c. v.; published &c. 531. expressive &c. 516; explicit &c. (open) 525, (clear) 518; plain spoken &c, (artless) 703. nuncupative, nuncupatoryl; declaratory, expository; enunciative[obs3]; communicative, communicatory[obs3]. Adv. from information received. Phr. a little bird told me; I heard it through the grapevine.

#527a. Correction. [Correct an error of information; distinguish from correcting a flaw or misbehavior] — N. correction.

disillusionment &c. 616.

V. correct, set right, set straight, put straight; undeceive[obs3]; enlighten.

show one one's error; point out an error, point out a fallacy; pick out an error, pick out the fallacy; open one's eyes.

pick apart an argument, confutation &c. 479; reasoning &c. 476.

Adj. corrective.

Phr. I stand corrected.

<— p. 159 —>

#528. Concealment.— N. concealment; hiding &c. v.; occultation, mystification. seal of secrecy; screen &c. 530; disguise &c. 530; masquerade; masked battery; hiding place &c. 530; cryptography, steganography[obs3]; freemasonry. stealth, stealthiness, sneakiness; obreptionl; slyness &c. (cunning) 702. latitancy[obs3], latitation[obs3]; seclusion &c. 893; privacy, secrecy, secretness[obs3]; incognita. reticence; reserve; mental reserve, reservation; arriere pensee[Fr], suppression, evasion, white lie, misprision; silence &c. (taciturnity) 585; suppression of truth &c. 544; underhand dealing; closeness, secretiveness &c. adj.; mystery. latency &c. 526; snake in the grass; secret &c. 533; stowaway. V. conceal, hide, secrete, put out of sight; lock up, seal up, bottle up. encrypt, encode, cipher. cover, screen, cloak, veil, shroud; cover up one's tracks; screen from sight, screen from observation; drawing the veil; draw the curtain, close the curtain; curtain, shade, eclipse, throw a view over; becloud, bemask; mask, disguise; ensconce, muffle, smother; befog; whisper. keep from; keep back, keep to oneself; keep snug, keep close, keep secret, keep dark; bury; sink, suppress; keep from, keep from out of view, keep from out of sight; keep in the shade, throw into the shade, throw into background; stifle, hush up, smother, withhold, reserve; fence with a question; ignore &c. 460. keep a secret, keep one's own counsel; hold one's tongue &c. (silence) 585; make no sign, not let it go further; not breathe a word, not breathe a syllable about; not let the right hand know what the left is doing; hide one's light under a bushel, bury one's talent in a napkin. keep in the dark, leave in the dark, keep in the ignorance; blind, blind the eyes; blindfold, hoodwink, mystify; puzzle &c. (render uncertain) 475; bamboozle &c. (deceive) 545. be concealed &c. v.; suffer an eclipse; retire from sight, couch; hide oneself; lie hid, lie in perdu[Fr], lie in close; lie in ambush (ambush) 530; seclude oneself &c. 893; lurk, sneak, skulk, slink, prowl; steal into, steal out of, steal by, steal along; play at bopeep[obs3], play at hide and seek; hide in holes and corners; still hunt. Adj. concealed &c. v.; hidden; secret, recondite, mystic, cabalistic, occult, dark; cryptic, cryptical[obs3]; private, privy, in petto, auricular, clandestine, close, inviolate; tortuous. behind a screen &c. 530; undercover, under an eclipse; in ambush, in hiding, in disguise; in a cloud, in a fog, in a mist, in a haze, in a dark corner; in the shade, in the dark; clouded, wrapped in clouds, wrapt in clouds[obs3]; invisible &c.447; buried, underground, perdu[Fr]; secluded &c. 893. undisclosed &c. 529, untold &c. 527; covert &c. (latent) 526; untraceable; mysterious &c. (unintelligible) 519. irrevealable[obs3], inviolable; confidential; esoteric; not to be spoken of; unmentionable. obreptitious[obs3], furtive, stealthy, feline; skulking &c. v.; surreptitious, underhand, hole and corner; sly &c. (cunning). 702; secretive, evasive; reserved, reticent, uncommunicative, buttoned up; close, close as wax; taciturn &c. 585. Adv. secretly &c. adj.; in secret, in private, in one's sleeve, in holes and corners; in the dark &c. adj. januis clausis[Lat], with closed doors, a huis clos[Fr]; hugger mugger, a la derobee[Fr]; under the cloak of, under the rose, under the table; sub rosa[Lat], en tapinois[Fr], in the background, aside, on the sly, with bated breath, sotto voce[Lat], in a whisper, without beat of drum, a la sourdine[obs3]. behind the veil; beyond mortal ken, beyond the grave, beyond the veil; hid from mortal vision; into the eternal secret, into the realms supersensible[obs3], into the supreme mystery. in confidence, in strict confidence, in strictest confidence; confidentially &c. adj.; between ourselves, between you and me; between you and me and the bedpost; entre nous[Fr], inter nos, under the seal of secrecy; a couvert[Fr]. underhand, by stealth, like a thief in the night; stealthily &c. adj.; behind the scenes, behind the curtain, behind one's back, behind a screen &c. 530; incognito; in camera. Phr. it must go no further, it will go no further; don't tell a soul;"tell it not in Gath,"nobody the wiser; alitur vitium vivitque tegendo[Lat][obs3]; "let it be tenable in your silence still"[Hamlet]. [confidential disclosure to news reporters] background information, deep background information, deep background; background session, backgrounder; not for attribution

<— p. 160 —>

#529. Disclosure — N. disclosure; retectionl; unveiling &c.v.; deterration[obs3], revealment, revelation; exposition, exposure; expose; whole truth; telltale &c (news) 532. acknowledgment, avowal; confession, confessional; shrift. bursting of a bubble; denouement. [person who discloses a secret] tattletale, snitch, fink, stool pigeon, canary. V. disclose, discover, dismaskl; draw the veil, draw aside the veil, lift the veil, raise the veil, lift up the veil, remove the veil, tear aside the veil, tear the curtain; unmask, unveil, unfold, uncover, unseal, unkennel; take off the seal, break the seal; lay open, lay bare; expose; open, open up; bare, bring to light. divulge, reveal, break; squeal, tattle, sing, rat, snitch [all coll.]; let into the secret; reveal the secrets of the prison house; tell &c (inform) 527; breathe, utter, blab, peach; let out, let fall, let drop, let slip, spill the beans, let the cat out of the bag; betray; tell tales, come out of school; come out with; give vent, give utterance to; open the lips, blurt out, vent, whisper about; speak out &c (make manifest) 525; make public &c 531; unriddle &c (find out) 480a; split. acknowledge, allow, concede, grant, admit, own, own up to, confess, avow, throw off all disguise, turn inside out, make a clean breast; show one's hand, show one's cards; unburden one's mind, disburden one's mind, disburden one's conscience, disburden one's heart; open one's mind, lay bare one's mind, tell a piece of one's mind[Fr]; unbosom oneself, own to the soft impeachment; say the truth, speak the truth; turn King's (or Queen's) evidence; acknowledge the corn* [U.S.]. raise the mask, drop the mask, lift the mask, remove the mask, throw off the mask; expose; lay open; undeceive[obs3], unbeguile[obs3]; disabuse, set right, correct, open the eyes of; dsillusionner. be disclosed &c.; transpire, come to light; come in sight &c. (be visible) 446; become known, escape the lips; come out, ooze out, creep out, leak out, peep out, crop-out; show its face, show its colors; discover &c. itself; break through the clouds, flash on the mind. Adj. disclosed &c.v.; open, public &c. 525. Int.out with it! Phr. the murder is out; a light breaks in upon one; the scales fall from one's eyes; the eyes are opened.

#530. Ambush [Means of concealment]. — N. camouflage; mimicry; hiding place; secret place, secret drawer; recess, hold, holes and corners; closet, crypt, adytum[obs3], abditory[obs3], oubliette.
    ambush, ambuscade; stalking horse; lurking hole, lurking place; secret path, back stairs; retreat &c. (refuge) 666.
    screen, cover, shade, blinker; veil, curtain, blind, cloak, cloud.
    mask, visor, vizor[obs3], disguise, masquerade dress, domino.
    pitfall &c. (source of danger) 667; trap &c. (snare) 545.
    V. blend in, blend into the background.
    lie in ambush &c (hide oneself) 528; lie in wait for, lurk; set a trap for &c (deceive) 545; ambuscade, ambush.
    [transitive] camouflage.
    Adj. camouflaged, hidden, concealed.
    Adv. aux aguets[obs3].
<— p. 161 —>

#531. Publication.— N. publication; public announcement &c 527; promulgation, propagation, proclamation, pronun-ziamento [Italian]; circulation, indiction[obs3], edition; hue and cry. publicity, notoriety, currency, flagrancy, cry, bruit, hype; vox populi; report &c (news) 532. the Press, public press, newspaper, journal, gazette, daily; telegraphy; publisher &c v.; imprint. circular, circular letter; manifesto, advertisement, ad., placard, bill, affiche[obs3], broadside, poster; notice &c. 527. V. publish; make public, make known &c (information) 527; speak of, talk of; broach, utter; put forward; circulate, propagate, promulgate; spread, spread abroad; rumor, diffuse, disseminate, evulugate; put forth, give forth, send forth; emit, edit, get out; issue; bring before the public, lay before the public, drag before the public; give out, give to the world; put about, bandy about, hawk about, buzz about, whisper about, bruit about, blaze about; drag into the open day; voice. proclaim, herald, blazon; blaze abroad, noise abroad; sound a trumpet; trumpet forth, thunder forth; give tongue; announce with beat of drum, announce with flourish of trumpets; proclaim from the housetops, proclaim at Charing Cross. advertise, placard; post, post up afficher[obs3], publish in the Gazette, send round the crier. raise a cry, raise a hue and cry, raise a report; set news afloat. be published &c; be public, become public &c adj.; come out; go about, fly about, buzz about, blow about; get about, get abroad, get afloat, get wind; find vent; see the light; go forth, take air, acquire currency, pass current; go the rounds, go the round of the newspapers, go through the length and breadth of the land; virum volitare per ora[Lat]; pass from mouth to mouth; spread; run like wildfire, spread like wildfire. Adj. published &c.v.; current &c. (news) 532; in circulation, public; notorious; flagrant, arrant; open &c 525; trumpet-tongued; encyclical, encyclic[obs3], promulgatory[obs3]; exoteric. Adv. publicly &c. adj.; in open court, with open doors. Int. Oyez! O yes! notice! Phr. notice is hereby given; this is to give, these are to give notice; nomina stultorum parietibus haerent[Lat]; semel emissum volat irrevocabile verbum[Lat]..

#532. News.— N. news; information &c 527; piece of news[Fr], budget of news, budget of information; intelligence, tidings. word, advice, aviso[Sp], message; dispatch, despatch; telegram, cable, marconigram[obs3], wire, communi-cation, errand, embassy. report, rumor, hearsay, on dit[Fr], flying rumor, news stirring, cry, buzz, bruit, fame; talk, oui dire[Fr], scandal, eavesdropping; town tattle, table talk; tittle tattle; canard, topic of the day, idea afloat. bulletin, fresh news, stirring news; glad tidings; flash, news just in; on-the-spot coverage; live coverage. old story, old news, stale news, stale story; chestnut*. narrator &c (describe) 594; newsmonger, scandalmonger; talebearer, telltale, gossip, tattler. [study of news reporting] journalism. [methods of conveying news] media, news media, the press, the information industry; newspaper, magazine, tract, journal, gazette, publication &c. 531; radio, television, ticker
143

(electronic information transmission). [organizations producing news reports] United Press International, UPI; Associated Press, AP; The Dow Jones News Service, DJ; The New York Times News Service, NYT[abbr]; Reuters [England]; TASS [Soviet Union]; The Nikkei [Japan]. [person reporting news as a profession] newscaster, newsman, newswoman, reporter, journalist, correspondent, foreign correspondent, special correspondent, war correspondent, news team, news department; anchorman, anchorwoman[obs3]; sportscaster; weatherman. [officials providing news for an organization] press secretary, public relations department, public relations man. V. transpire &c (be disclosed) 529; rumor &c (publish) 531. Adj. many-tongued; rumored; publicly rumored, currently rumored, currently reported; rife, current, floating, afloat, going about, in circulation, in every one's mouth, all over the town. in progress; live; on the spot; in person. Adv. as the story goes, as the story runs; as they say, it is said; by telegraph, by wireless. Phr. "airy tongues that syllable men's names" [Milton]; what's up?; what's the latest?; what's new?; what's the latest poop?.

#533. Secret.— N. secret; dead secret, profound secret; arcanum[obs3], mystery; latency &c 526; Asian mystery[obs3]; sealed book, secrets of the prison house; le desous des cartes [Fr].
   enigma, riddle, puzzle, nut to crack, conundrum, charade, rebus, logogriph[obs3]; monogram, anagram; Sphinx; crux criticorum[Lat].
   maze, labyrinth, Hyrcynian wood; intricacy, meander.
   problem &c (question) 461; paradox &c (difficulty) 704; unintelligibility &c. 519; terra incognita &c. (ignorance) 491.
   Adj. secret &c. (concealed) 528; involved &c, 248; labyrinthine, labyrinthian[obs3], mazy.
   confidential; top secret.

<— p. 162 —>

#534. Messenger.— N. messenger, envoy, emissary, legate; nuncio, internuncio[obs3]; ambassador &c (diplomatist) 758. marshal, flag bearer, herald, crier, trumpeter, bellman[obs3], pursuivant[obs3], parlementaire[Fr], apparitor[obs3]. courier, runner; dak[obs3], estafette[obs3]; Mercury, Iris, Ariel[obs3]. commissionaire[Fr]; errand boy, chore boy; newsboy. mail, overnight mail, express mail, next-day delivery; post, post office; letter bag; delivery service; United Parcel Service, UPS; Federal Express, Fedex. telegraph, telephone; cable, wire (electronic information transmission); carrier pigeon. [person reporting news: see news &c. 532] reporter, gentleman of the press, representative of the press; penny-a-liner; special correspondent, own correspondent; spy, scout; informer &c. 527.

#535. Affirmation.— N. affirmance, affirmation; statement, allegation, assertion, predication, declaration, word, averment; confirmation. asseveration, adjuration, swearing, oath, affidavit; deposition &c (record) 551; avouchment; assurance; protest, protestation; profession; acknowledgment &c. (assent) 488; legal pledge, pronouncement; solemn averment, solemn avowal, solemn declaration. remark, observation; position &c. (proposition) 514, saying, dictum, sentence, ipse dixit[Lat]. emphasis; weight; dogmatism &c. (certainty) 474; dogmatics &c 887. V. assert; make an assertion &c n.; have one's say; say, affirm, predicate, declare, state; protest, profess. put forth, put forward; advance, allege, propose, propound, enunciate, broach, set forth, hold out, maintain, contend, pronounce, pretend. depose, depone, aver, avow, avouch, asseverate, swear; make oath, take one's oath; make an affidavit, swear an affidavit, put in an affidavit; take one's Bible oath, kiss the book, vow, vitam impendere vero[Lat]; swear till one is black in the face, swear till one is blue in the face, swear till all's blue; be sworn, call Heaven to witness; vouch, warrant, certify, assure, swear by bell book and candle. swear by &c (believe) 484; insist upon, take one's stand upon; emphasize, lay stress on; assert roundly, assert positively; lay down, lay down the law; raise one's voice, dogmatize, have the last word; rap out; repeat; reassert, reaffirm. announce &c (information) 527; acknowledge &c (assent) 488; attest &c (evidence) 467; adjure &c (put to one's oath) 768. Adj. asserting &c.v.; declaratory, predicatory[obs3], pronunciative[obs3], affirmative, soi-disant[Fr]; positive; certain &c 474; express, explicit &c (patent) 525; absolute, emphatic, flat, broad, round, pointed, marked, distinct, decided, confident, trenchant, dogmatic, definitive, formal, solemn, categorical, peremptory; unretracted[obs3]; predicable. Adv. affirmatively &c adj.; in the affirmative. with emphasis, ex-cathedra, without fear of contradiction. as God is my witness, I must say, indeed, i' faith, let me tell you, why, give me leave to say, marry, you may be sure, I'd have you to know; upon my word, upon my honor; by my troth, egad, I assure you; by jingo, by Jove, by George, &c.; troth, seriously, sadly; in sadness, in sober sadness, in truth, in earnest; of a truth, truly, perdy[obs3], in all conscience, upon oath; be assured &c (belief) 484; yes &c (assent) 488; I'll warrant, I'll warrant you, I'll engage, I'll answer for it, I'll be bound, I'll venture to say, I'll take my oath; in fact, forsooth, joking apart; so help me God; not to mince the matter. Phr. quoth he; dixi[Lat].

#536. Negation. — N. negation, abnegation; denial; disavowal, disclaimer; abjuration; contradiction, contravention; recusation[obs3][Law], protest; recusancy &c (dissent) 489; flat contradiction, emphatic contradiction, emphatic denial, dementi[Lat]. qualification &c 469; repudiation &c 610; retraction &c 607; confutation &c 479; refusal &c 764; prohibition &c 761. V. deny; contradict, contravene; controvert, give denial to, gainsay, negative, shake the head. disown, disaffirm, disclaim, disavow; recant &c 607; revoke &c (abrogate) 756. dispute; impugn, traverse, rebut, join issue upon; bring in question, call in question &c. (doubt) 485; give (one) the lie in his throat. deny flatly, deny peremptorily, deny emphatically, deny absolutely, deny wholly, deny entirely; give the lie to, belie. repudiate &c 610; set aside, ignore &c 460; rebut &c. (confute) 479; qualify &c 469; refuse &c 764. recuse[Law]. Adj. denying &c.v.; denied &c.v.; contradictory; negative, negatory; recusant &c (dissenting) 489; at issue upon. Adv. no, nay, not, nowise; not a bit, not a whit, not a jot; not at all, nohow, not in the least, not so; negative, negatory; no way [coll.]; no such thing; nothing of the kind, nothing of the sort; quite the contrary, tout au contraire[Fr]; far from it; tant s'en faut[Fr]; on no account, in no respect; by no, by no manner of means; negatively. [negative with respect to time] never, never in a million years; at no time. Phr. there never was a greater mistake; I know better; non haec in faedera[Lat]; a thousand times no.

<— p. 163 —>

#537. Teaching. — N. teaching &c.v.; instruction; edification; education; tuition; tutorage, tutelage; direction, guidance; opsimathy[obs3]. qualification, preparation; training, schooling &c. v.; discipline; excitation. drill, practice; book exercise. persuasion, proselytism, propagandism[obs3], propaganda; indoctrination, inculcation, inoculation; advise &c. 695. explanation &c (interpretation) 522; lesson, lecture, sermon; apologue[obs3], parable; discourse, prolection[obs3], preachment; chalk talk; Chautauqua [U.S.]. exercise, task; curriculum; course, course of study; grammar, three R's, initiation, A.B.C. &c (beginning) 66. elementary education, primary education, secondary education, technical education, college education, collegiate education, military education, university education, liberal education, classical education, religious education, denominational education, moral education, secular education; propaedeutics[obs3], moral tuition. gymnastics, calisthenics; physical drill, physical education; sloyd[obs3]. [methods of teaching] phonics; rote, rote memorization, brute memory; cooperative learning; Montessori method, ungraded classes. [measuring degree of learning of pupils] test, examination, exam; final exam, mid-term exam grade[result of measurement of learning], score, marks; A,B,C,D,E,F; gentleman's C; pass, fail, incomplete. homework; take-home lesson; exercise for the student; theme, project. V. teach, instruct, educate, edify, school, tutor; cram, prime, coach; enlighten &c (inform) 527. inculcate, indoctrinate, inoculate, infuse, instill, infix, ingraft[obs3], infiltrate; imbue, impregnate, implant; graft, sow the seeds of, disseminate. given an idea of; put up to, put in the way of; set right. sharpen the wits, enlarge the mind; give new ideas, open the eyes, bring forward, "teach the young idea how to shoot" [Thomson]; improve &c. 658. expound &c (interpret) 522; lecture; read a lesson, give a lesson, give a lecture, give a sermon, give a discourse; incept[obs3]; hold forth, preach; sermonize, moralize; point a moral. train, discipline; bring up, bring up to; form, ground, prepare, qualify; drill, exercise, practice, habituate, familiarize with, nurture, drynurse[obs3], breed, rear, take in hand; break, break in; tame; preinstruct[obs3]; initiate; inure &c (habituate) 613. put to nurse, send to school. direct, guide; direct attention to &c. (attention) 457; impress upon the mind, impress upon the memory; beat into, beat into the head; convince &c (belief) 484. [instructional materials] book, workbook, exercise book. [unnecessary teaching] preach to the wise, teach one's grandmother to suck eggs, teach granny to suck eggs; preach to the converted. Adj. teaching &c.v; taught &c.v.; educational; scholastic, academic, doctrinal; disciplinal[obs3]; instructive, instructional, didactic; propaedeutic[obs3], propaedeutical[obs3]. Phr. the schoolmaster abroad; a bovi majori disscit arare minor[Lat]; adeo in teneris consuecere multum est [Lat][Vergil]; docendo discimus[Lat]; quaenocent docent[Lat]; qui docet discit[Latin]; "sermons in stones and good in everything" [As You Like It].

#538. Misteaching. — N. misteaching[obs3], misinformaton, misintelligence[obs3], misguidance, misdirection, mispersuasion[obs3], misinstruction[obs3], misleading &c.v.; perversion, false teaching; sophistry &c 477; college of Laputa; the blind leading the blind.
[misteaching by government agents] propaganda, disinformation, agitprop; indoctrination.
V. misinform, misteach[obs3], misdescribe[obs3], misinstruct[obs3], miscorrect[obs3]; misdirect, misguide; pervert; put on a false scent, throw off the scent, throw off the trail; deceive &c 545; mislead &c (error) 495; misrepresent; lie &c 544; ambiguas in vulgum spargere voces [Lat][Vergil].
propagandize, disinform.
render unintelligible &c 519; bewilder &c (uncertainty) 475; mystify

&c. (conceal) 528; unteach.

 [person or government agent who misteaches] propagandist.

 Adj. misteaching &c.v[obs3]; unedifying.

 Phr. piscem natare doces [Lat]; the blind leading the blind.

<— p. 164 —>

#539. Learning — N. learning; acquisition of knowledge &c 490, acquisition of skill &c 698; acquirement, attainment; edification, scholarship, erudition; acquired knowledge, lore, wide information; self- instruction; study, reading, perusal; inquiry &c 451. apprenticeship, prenticeship[obs3]; pupilage, pupilarity[obs3]; tutelage, novitiate, matriculation. docility &c (willingness) 602; aptitude &c 698. V. learn; acquire knowledge, gain knowledge, receive knowledge, take in knowledge, drink in knowledge, imbibe knowledge, pick up knowledge, gather knowledge, get knowledge, obtain knowledge, collect knowledge, glean knowledge, glean information, glean learning. acquaint oneself with, master; make oneself master of, make oneself acquainted with; grind, cram; get up, coach up; learn by heart, learn by rote. read, spell, peruse; con over, pore over, thumb over; wade through; dip into; run the eye over, run the eye through; turn over the leaves. study; be studious &c adj. [study intensely] burn the midnight oil, consume the midnight oil, mind one's book; cram. go to school, go to college, go to the university; matriculate; serve an (or one's) apprenticeship, serve one's time; learn one's trade; be informed &c 527; be taught &c 537. [stop going to school voluntarily (intransitive)] drop out, leave school, quit school; graduate; transfer; take a leave. [cause to stop going to school (transitive)] dismiss, expel, kick out of school. [stop going to school involuntarily] flunk out; be dismissed &c. Adj. studious; scholastic, scholarly; teachable; docile &c (willing) 602; apt &c 698, industrious &c 682. Adv. at one's books; in statu pupillari &c (learner) 541[Lat]. Phr. "a lumber-house of books in every head" [Pope]; ancora imparo[Lat][obs3]! "hold high converse with the mighty dead" [Thomson]; "lash'd into Latin by the tingling rod" [Gay].

#540. Teacher. — N. teacher, trainer, instructor, institutor, master, tutor, director, Corypheus, dry nurse, coach, grinder, crammer, don; governor, bear leader; governess, duenna[Sp]; disciplinarian.

 professor, lecturer, reader, prelector[obs3], prolocutor, preacher; chalk talker, khoja[obs3]; pastor &c (clergy) 996; schoolmaster, dominie[Fr], usher, pedagogue, abecedarian; schoolmistress, dame, monitor, pupil teacher.

 expositor &c 524; preceptor, guide; guru; mentor &c (adviser) 695; pioneer, apostle, missionary, propagandist, munshi[obs3], example &c (model for imitation) 22.

 professorship &c (school) 542.

 tutelage &c (teaching) 537.

 Adj. professorial.

 Phr. qui doet discet[Lat].

#541. Learner. — N. learner, scholar, student, pupil; apprentice, prentice[obs3], journeyman; articled clerk; beginner, tyro, amateur, rank amateur; abecedarian, alphabetarian[obs3]; alumnus, eleve[Fr].

 recruit, raw recruit, novice, neophyte, inceptor[obs3], catechumen, probationer; seminarian, chela, fellow-commoner; debutant.

 [apprentice medical doctors] intern; resident.

 schoolboy; fresh, freshman, frosh; junior soph[obs3], junior; senior soph[obs3], senior; sophister[obs3], sophomore; questionist[obs3].

 [college and university students] undergraduate; graduate student; law student; medical student; pre-med; post-doctoral student, post-doc; matriculated student; part-time student, night student, auditor.

 [group of learners] class, grade, seminar, form, remove; pupilage &c (learning) 539.

 disciple, follower, apostle, proselyte; fellow-student, condisciple[obs3].

 [place of learning] school &c. 542.

 V. learn; practise.

 Adj. in statu pupillari[Lat], in leading strings.

 Phr. practise makes perfect.

#542. School. — N. school, academy, university, alma mater, college, seminary, Lyceum; institute, institution; palaestra, Gymnasium, class, seminar. day school, boarding school, preparatory school, primary school, infant school, dame's school, grammar school, middle class school, Board school, denominational school, National school, British and Foreign school, collegiate school, art school, continuation school, convent school, County Council school, government school, grant-in-aid school, high school, higher grade school, military school, missionary school, naval school, naval academy, state-aided school, technical school, voluntary school, school; school of art; kindergarten, nursery, creche, reformatory. pulpit, lectern, soap box desk, reading desk, ambo[obs3], lecture room, theater, auditorium, amphitheater, forum, state, rostrum, platform, hustings, tribune. school book, horn book, text book; grammar, primer, abecedary[obs3], rudiments, manual, vade mecum; encyclopedia, cyclopedia; Lindley Murray, Cocker; dictionary, lexicon. professorship, lectureship, readership, fellowship, tutorship; chair. School Board Council of Education; Board of Education; Board of Studies, Prefect of Studies; Textbook Committee; propaganda. Adj. scholastic, academic, collegiate; educational. Adv. ex cathedra[Lat].

<— p. 165 —>

#543. Veracity.— N. veracity; truthfulness, frankness, &c. adj.; truth, sincerity, candor, unreserve!!, honesty, fidelity; plain dealing, bona fides[Lat]; love of truth; probity &c. 939; ingenuousness &c (artlessness) 703. the truth the whole truth and nothing but the truth; honest truth, sober truth &c (fact) 494; unvarnished tale; light of truth. V. speak the truth, tell the truth; speak by the card; paint in its true colors, show oneself in one's true colors; make a clean breast &c (disclose) 529; speak one's mind &c. (be blunt) 703; not lie &c 544, not deceive &c. 545. Adj. truthful, true; veracious, veridical; scrupulous &c (honorable) 939; sincere, candid, frank, open, straightforward, unreserved; open hearted, true hearted, simple-hearted; honest, trustworthy; undissembling &c (dissemble &c 544)[obs3]; guileless, pure; truth-loving; unperjured[obs3]; true blue, as good as one's word; unaffected, unfeigned, bona fide; outspoken, ingenuous &c (artless) 703; undisguised &c (real) 494. uncontrived. Adv. truly &c (really) 494; in plain words &c 703; in truth, with truth, of a truth, in good truth; as the dial to the sun, as the needle to the pole; honor bright; troth; in good sooth[obs3], in good earnest; unfeignedly, with no nonsense, in sooth[obs3], sooth to say[obs3], bona fide, in foro conscientiae[Lat]; without equivocation; cartes sur table, from the bottom of one's heart; by my troth &c (affirmation) 535. Phr. di il vero a affronterai il diavolo[It][obs3]; Dichtung und Wahrheit[Ger]; esto quod esse videris[Lat]; magna est veritas et praevalet[Lat]; "that golden key that opes the palace of eternity" [Milton]; veritas odium parit[Lat]; veritatis simplex oratio est[Lat]; verite sans peur[Fr].

<— should clarify distinction between untruth generally (objectively false) and untruth in communication (lie, deception) —> #544. Falsehood. — N. falsehood, falseness; falsity, falsification; deception &c. 545; untruth &c 546; guile; lying &c. 454; untruth &c 546; guile; lying &c. v. misrepresentation; mendacity, perjury, false swearing; forgery, invention, fabrication; subreption[obs3]; covin[obs3]. perversion of truth, suppression of truth; suppressio veri[Lat]; perversion, distortion, false coloring; exaggeration &c 549; prevarication, equivocation, shuffling, fencing, evasion, fraud; suggestio falsi &c (lie) 546[Lat]; mystification &c (concealment) 528; simulation &c (imitation) 19; dissimulation, dissembling; deceit; blague[obs3]. sham; pretense, pretending, malingering. lip homage, lip service; mouth honor; hollowness; mere show, mere outside; duplicity, double dealing, insincerity, hypocrisy, cant, humbug; jesuitism, jesuitry; pharisaism; Machiavelism, "organized hypocrisy"; crocodile tears, mealy-mouthedness[obs3], quackery; charlatanism[obs3], charlatanry; gammon; bun-kum[obs3], bumcombe, flam; bam*[obs3], flimflam, cajolery, flattery; Judas kiss; perfidy &c (bad faith) 940; il volto sciolto i pensieri stretti[It]. unfairness &c (dishonesty) 940; artfulness &c (cunning) 702; misstatement &c (error) 495. V. be false &c adj., be a liar &c 548; speak falsely &c adv.; tell a lie &c. 546; lie, fib; lie like a trooper; swear false, forswear, perjure oneself, bear false witness. misstate, misquote, miscite[obs3], misreport, misrepresent; belie, falsify, pervert, distort; put a false construction upon &c. (misinterpret) prevaricate, equivocate, quibble; palter, palter to the understanding; repondre en Normand[Fr]; trim, shuffle, fence, mince the truth, beat about the bush, blow hot and cold, play fast and loose. garble, gloss over, disguise, give a color to; give a gloss, put a gloss, put false coloring upon; color, varnish, cook, dress up, embroider; varnish right and puzzle wrong; exaggerate &c 549; blague[obs3]. invent, fabricate; trump up, get up; force, fake, hatch, concoct; romance &c (imagine) 515; cry "wolf!" dissemble, dissimulate; feign, assume, put on, pretend, make believe; play possum; play false, play a double game; coquet; act a part, play a part; affect &c. 855; simulate, pass off for; counterfeit, sham, make a show of; malinger; say the grapes are sour. cant, play the hypocrite, sham Abraham, faire pattes de velours, put on the mask, clean the outside of the platter, lie like a conjuror; hand out false colors, hold out false colors, sail under false colors; "commend the poisoned chalice to the lips" [Macbeth]; ambiguas in vulgum spargere voces [Lat]; deceive &c 545. Adj. false, deceitful, mendacious, unveracious, fraudulent, dishonest, faithless, truthless, trothless; unfair, uncandid; hollow-hearted; evasive; uningenuous, disingenuous; hollow, sincere, Parthis mendacior; forsworn. artificial, contrived; canting; hypocritical, jesuitical, pharisaical; tartuffish; Machiavelian; double, double tongued, double faced, double handed, double minded, double hearted, double dealing; Janus faced; smooth- faced, smooth spoken, smooth tongued; plausible; mealy-mouthed; affected &c 855. collusive, collusory; artful &c. (cunning) 702; perfidious &c 940; spurious &c (deceptive) 545; untrue &c 546; falsified

&c v.; covinous. Adv. falsely &c adj.; a la tartufe, with a double tongue; silly &c (cunning) 702. Phr. blandae mendacia lingua[Lat]; falsus in uno falsus in omnibus[Lat]; "I give him joy that's awkward at a lie" [Young]; la mentira tiene las piernas cortas [Sp]; "O what a goodly outside falsehood hath" [Merchant of Venice].

<— p. 166 —>

#545. Deception. — N. deception; falseness &c 544; untruth &c 546; imposition, imposture; fraud, deceit, guile; fraudulence, fraudulency[obs3]; covin[obs3]; knavery &c. (cunning) 702; misrepresentation &c (falsehood) 544; bluff; straw-bail, straw bid [U.S.]; spoof*. delusion, gullery[obs3]; juggling, jugglery[obs3]; slight of hand, legerdemain; prestigiationl, prestidigitation; magic &c 992; conjuring, conjuration; hocus-pocus, escamoterie[obs3], jockeyship[obs3]; trickery, coggeryl, chicanery; supercherie[obs3], cozenage[obs3], circumvention, ingannationl, collusion; treachery &c 940; practical joke. trick, cheat, wile, blind, feint, plant, bubble, fetch, catch, chicane, juggle, reach, hocus, bite; card sharping, stacked deck, loaded dice, quick shuffle, double dealing, dealing seconds, dealing from the bottom of the deck; artful dodge, swindle; tricks upon travelers; stratagem &c (artifice) 702; confidence trick, fake, hoax; theft &c. 791; ballot-box stuffing barney*[obs3][U.S.], brace* game, bunko game, drop* game, gum* game, panel game[U.S.]; shell game, thimblerig; skin* game [U.S.]. snare, trap, pitfall, decoy, gin; springe[obs3], springel; noose, hoot; bait, decoy-duck, tub to the whale, baited trap, guet-a-pens; cobweb, net, meshes, toils, mouse trap, birdlime; dionaea[obs3], Venus's flytrap[obs3]; ambush &c 530; trapdoor, sliding panel, false bottom; spring-net, spring net, spring gun, mask, masked battery; mine; flytrap[obs3]; green goods [U.S.]; panel house. Cornish hug; wolf in sheep's clothing &c (deceiver) 548; disguise, disguisement[obs3]; false colors, masquerade, mummery, borrowed plumes; pattes de velours[Fr]. mockery &c (imitation) 19; copy &c 21; counterfeit, sham, make- believe, forgery, fraud; lie &c 546; "a delusion a mockery and a snare" [Denman], hollow mockery. whited sepulcher, painted sepulcher; tinsel; paste, junk jewelry, costume jewelry, false jewelry, synthetic jewels; scagliola[obs3], ormolu, German silver, albata[obs3], paktong[obs3], white metal, Britannia metal, paint; veneer; jerry building; man of straw. illusion &c (error) 495; ignis fatuus &c 423[Lat]; mirage &c 443. V. deceive, take in; defraud, cheat, jockey, do, cozen, diddle, nab, chouse, play one false, bilk, cully[obs3], jilt, bite, pluck, swindle, victimize; abuse; mystify; blind one's eyes; blindfold, hoodwink; throw dust into the eyes; dupe, gull, hoax, fool, befool[obs3], bamboozle, flimflam, hornswoggle; trick. impose upon, practice upon, play upon, put upon, palm off on, palm upon, foist upon; snatch a verdict; bluff off, bluff; bunko, four flush*, gum* [U.S.], spoof*, stuff (a ballot box) [U.S.]. circum-vent, overreach; outreach, out wit, out maneuver; steal a march upon, give the go-by, to leave in the lurch decoy, waylay, lure, beguile, delude, inveigle; entrap, intrap[obs3], ensnare; nick, springe[obs3]; set a trap, lay a trap, lay a snare for; bait the hook, forelay[obs3], spread the toils, lime; trapan[obs3], trepan; kidnap; let in, hook in; nousle[obs3], nousel[obs3]; blind a trail; enmesh, immesh[obs3]; shanghai; catch, catch in a trap; sniggle, entangle, illaqueate[obs3], hocus, escamoter[obs3], practice on one's credulity; hum, humbug; gammon, stuff up*, sell; play a trick upon one, play a practical joke upon one, put something over on one, put one over on; balk, trip up, throw a tub to a whale; fool to the top of one's bent, send on a fool's errand; make game, make a fool of, make an April fool of[obs3], make an ass of; trifle with, cajole, flatter; come over &c (influence) 615; gild the pill, make things pleasant, divert, put a good face upon; dissemble &c 544. cog, cog the dice, load the dice, stack the deck; live by one's wits, play at hide and seek; obtain money under false pretenses &c (steal) 791; conjure, juggle, practice chicanery; deacon [U.S.]. play off, palm off, foist off, fob- off. lie &c 544; misinform &c 538; mislead &c (error) 495; betray &c 940; be deceived &c 547. Adj. deceived &c v.; deceiving &c; cunning &c 702; prestigiousl, prestigiatoryl; deceptive, deceptious[obs3]; deceitful, covinous[obs3]; delusive, delusory; illusive, illusory; elusive, insidious, ad captandum vulgus[Lat]. untrue &c 546; mock, sham, make-believe, counterfeit, snide*, pseudo, spurious, supposititious, so-called, pretended, feigned, trumped up, bogus, scamped, fraudulent, tricky, factitious;bastard; surreptitious, illegitimate, contraband, adulterated, sophisticated; unsound, rotten at the core; colorable; disguised; meretricious, tinsel, pinchbeck, plated; catchpenny; Brummagem. artificial, synthetic, ersatz[&German]; simulated &c 544. Adv. under false colors, under the garb of, under cover of; over the left. Phr. "keep the word of promise to the ear and break it to the hope" [Macbeth]; fronti nulla fides[Lat]; "ah that deceit should steal such gentle shapes" [Richard III]; "a quicksand of deceit" [Henry VI]; decipimur specie recti [Lat][Horace]; falsi crimen[Lat]; fraus est celare fraudem[Lat]; lupus in fabula[Lat]; "so smooth, he daubed his vice with show of virtue" [Richard III].

<— p. 167 —>

#546. Untruth.— N. untruth, falsehood, lie, story, thing that is not, fib, bounce, crammer, taradiddle[obs3], whopper; jhuth[obs3]. forgery, fabrication, invention; misstatement, misrepresentation; perversion, falsification, gloss, sugges-tio falsi[Lat]; exaggeration &c 549. invention, fabrication, fiction; fable, nursery tale; romance &c (imagination) 515; absurd story, untrue story, false story, trumped up story, trumped up statement; thing devised by the enemy; canard; shave, sell, hum, traveler's tale, Canterbury tale, cock and bull story, fairy tale, fake; claptrap. press agent's yarn;

puff, puffery (exaggeration) 549. myth, moonshine, bosh, all my eye and Betty Martin, mare's nest, farce. irony; half truth, white lie, pious fraud; mental reservation &c (concealment) 528. pretense, pretext; false plea &c 617; subterfuge, evasion, shift, shuffle, make-believe; sham &c (deception) 545. profession, empty words; Judas kiss &c (hypocrisy) 544; disguise &c (mask) 530. V. have a false meaning. Adj. untrue, false, phony, trumped up; void of foundation, without- foundation; fictive, far from the truth, false as dicer's oaths; unfounded, ben trovato[It], invented, fabulous, fabricated, forged; fictitious, factitious, supposititious, surreptitious; elusory[obs3], illusory; ironical; soi-disant &c (misnamed) 565[Fr]. Phr. se non e vero e ben trovato[It]; "where none is meant that meets the ear"[Milton].

<— p. 168 —>

#547. Dupe.— N. dupe, gull, gudgeon, gobemouche[obs3], cull*, cully[obs3], victim, pigeon, April fool[obs3]; jay*, sucker*; laughingstock &c 857; Cyclops, simple Simon, flat; greenhorn; fool &c 501; puppet, cat's paw. V. be deceived &c 545, be the dupe of; fall into a trap; swallow the bait, nibble at the bait; bite, catch a Tartar. Adj. credulous &c 486; mistaken &c. (error) 495.

#548. Deceiver.— N. deceiver &c (deceive &c 545); dissembler, hypocrite; sophist, Pharisee, Jesuit, Mawworm[obs3], Pecksniff, Joseph Surface, Tartufe[obs3], Janus; serpent, snake in the grass, cockatrice, Judas, wolf in sheep's clothing; jilt; shuffler!!, stool pigeon. liar &c (lie &c 544); story-teller, perjurer, false witness, menteur a triple etage[Fr], Scapin[obs3]; bunko steerer* [U.S.], carpetbagger* [U.S.], capper* [U.S.], faker, fraud, four flusher*, horse coper[obs3], ringer*, spieler[obs3], straw bidder [U.S.]. imposter, pretender, soi-disant[Fr], humbug; adventurer; Cagliostro, Fernam Mendez Pinto; ass in lion's skin &c (bungler) 701; actor &c (stage player) 599. quack, charlatan, mountebank, saltimbanco[obs3], saltimbanque[obs3], empiric, quacksalver, medicaster[obs3], Rosicrucian, gypsy; man of straw. conjuror, juggler, trickster, prestidigitator, jockey; crimp, decoy, decoy duck; rogue, knave, cheat; swindler &c (thief) 792; jobber. Phr. "saint abroad and a devil at home" [Bunyan].

#549. Exaggeration.— N. exaggeration; expansion &c 194; hyperbole, stretch, strain, coloring; high coloring, caricature, caricatura[obs3]; extravagance &c. (nonsense) 497; Baron Munchausen; men in buckram, yarn, fringe, embroidery, traveler's tale; fish story, gooseberry* storm in a teacup; much ado about nothing &c (overestimation) 482; puff, puffery &c (boasting) 884; rant &c (turgescence) 577[obs3]. figure of speech, facon de parler[Fr]; stretch of fancy, stretch of the imagination; flight of fancy &c (imagination) 515. false coloring &c (falsehood) 544; aggravation &c. 835. V. exaggerate, magnify, pile up, aggravate; amplify &c (expand) 194; overestimate &c 482; hyperbolize; overcharge, overstate, overdraw, overlay, overshoot the mark, overpraise; make over much, over the most of; strain, strain over a point; stretch, stretch a point; go great lengths; spin a long yarn; draw with a longbow, shoot with a longbow; deal in the marvelous. out-Herod Herod, run riot, talk at random. heighten, overcolor[obs3]; color highly, color too highly; broder[obs3]; flourish; color &c. (misrepresent) 544; puff &c (boast) 884. Adj. exaggerated &c. v.; overwrought; bombastic &c. (grandiloquent) 577; hyperbolical[obs3], on stilts; fabulous, extravagant, preposterous, egregious, outre[Fr], highflying[obs3]. Adv. hyperbolically &c adj. Phr. excitabat enim fluctus in simpulo [Lat][Cicero].

<— p. 169 —>

% Section III. MEANS OF COMMUNICATING IDEAS 1. Natural Means % <— recognition of something by its features must be broken out into a separate entry. Include the terms recognition, identification, dereplication, classification; note memory 505, identification (comparison, 464, discovery 480a) distinguish recognition and recall in technical sense —>

#550. Indication — N. indication; symbolism, symbolization; semiology, semiotics, semeiology[obs3], semeiotics[obs3]; Zeitgeist. [means of recognition: property] characteristic, diagnostic; lineament, feature, trait; fingerprint, voiceprint, footprint, noseprint [for animals]; cloven hoof; footfall; recognition (memory) 505. [means of recognition: tool] diagnostic, divining rod; detector. sign, symbol; index, indicel, indicator; point, pointer; exponent, note, token, symptom; dollar sign, dollar mark. type, figure, emblem, cipher, device; representation &c. 554; epigraph, motto, posy. gesture, gesticulation; pantomime; wink, glance, leer; nod, shrug, beck; touch, nudge; dactylology[obs3], dactylonomy[obs3]; freemasonry, telegraphy, chirology[Med], byplay, dumb show; cue; hint &c. 527; clue, clew, key, scent. signal, signal post; rocket, blue light; watch fire, watch tower; telegraph, semaphore, flagstaff; cresset[obs3], fiery cross; calumet; heliograph; guidon; headlight. [sign (evidence) on physobj of contact with another physobj] mark, scratch, line, stroke, dash, score, stripe, streak, tick, dot, point, notch, nick. print; imprint, impress, impression. [symbols accompanying written text to signify modified interpretation] keyboard symbols, printing symbols; red letter[for emphasis], italics, sublineation[obs3], underlining, bold font; jotting; note, annotation, reference; blaze, cedilla, guillemets[obs3], hachure[Topography]; quotation marks, double quotes,""; parentheses, brackets, braces, curly brackets, arrows, slashes; left parenthesis[list], "("; right parenthesis, ")"; opening bracket, "["; closing bracket, "]"; left curly brace, "{"; right curly brace, "}"; left arrow, "<"; right arrow, ">"; forward slash, "/"; backward slash, "\"; exclamation point, "!"; commercial at, "@"; pound sign, "#"; percent sign, "%"; carat, ""; ampersand, "&"; asterisk, "*"; hyphen, "-"; dash, "-", "_"; em dash, "—"; plus sign, "+"; equals sign, "="; question mark, "?"; period, "."; semicolon, ";"; colon, ":"; comma, ","; apostrophe, ""; single quote, ""; tilde, "~". [For identification: general] badge, criterion; countercheck[obs3], countermark[obs3], countersign, counterfoil; duplicate, tally; label, ticket, billet, letter, counter, check, chip, chop; dib[obs3]; totem; tessera[obs3], card, bill; witness, voucher; stamp; cacher[Fr]; trade mark, Hall mark. [For identification of people, on a document] signature, mark, autograph, autography; attestation; hand, hand writing, sign manual; cipher; seal, sigil[Lat], signet, hand and seal [Law]; paraph[obs3], brand; superscription; indorsement[obs3], endorsement. [For identification of people, to gain access to restricted (locations or information)] password, watchword, catchword; security card, pass, passkey; credentials &c. (evidence) 467; open sesame; timbrology[obs3]; mot de passe[Fr], mot du guet[Fr]; pass-parole; shibboleth. title, heading, docket. address card, visiting card; carte de visite[Fr]. insignia; banner, banneret[obs3], bannerol[obs3]; bandrol[obs3]; flag, colors, streamer, standard, eagle, labarum[obs3], oriflamb[obs3], oriflamme; figurehead; ensign; pennon, pennant, pendant; burgee[obs3], blue Peter, jack, ancient, gonfalon, union jack; banderole, "old glory" [U.S.], quarantine flag; vexillum[obs3]; yellow-flag, yellow jack; tricolor, stars and stripes; bunting. heraldry, crest; coat of arms, arms; armorial bearings, hatchment[obs3]; escutcheon, scutcheon; shield, supporters; livery, uniform; cockade, epaulet, chevron; garland, love knot, favor. [Of locality] beacon, cairn, post, staff, flagstaff, hand, pointer, vane, cock, weathercock; guidepost, handpost[obs3], fingerpost[obs3], directing post, signpost; pillars of Hercules, pharos; bale-fire, beacon- fire; l'etoile du Nord[Fr]; landmark, seamark; lighthouse, balize[obs3]; polestar, loadstar[obs3], lodestar; cynosure, guide; address, direction, name; sign, signboard. [Of the future] warning &c. 668; omen &c. 512; prefigurement &c. 511. trace[Of the past], record &c. 551. warning &c. 668[Of danger]; alarm &c. 669. scepter &c. 747[Of authority]. trophy &c. 733[Of triumph]. gauge &c. 466[Of quantity]. milestone[Of distance], milepost. brand[Of disgrace], fool's cap. check[For detection], telltale; test &c. (experiment) 463; mileage ticket; milliary[obs3]. notification &c. (information) 527; advertisement &c. (publication) 531. word of command, call; bugle call, trumpet call; bell, alarum, cry; battle cry, rallying cry; angelus[obs3]; reveille; sacring bell[obs3], sanctus bell[Lat]. exposition &c. (explanation) 522, proof &c. (evidence) 463; pattern &c. (prototype) 22. V. indicate; be the sign &c. n. of; denote, betoken; argue, testify &c. (evidence) 467; bear the impress &c. n. of; connote, connotate[obs3]. represent, stand for; typify &c. (prefigure) 511; symbolize. put an indication, put a mark &c. n.; note, mark, stamp, earmark; blaze; label, ticket, docket; dot, spot, score, dash, trace, chalk; print; imprint, impress; engrave, stereotype. make a sign &c. n. signalize; underscore; give a signal, hang out a signal; beckon; nod; wink, glance, leer, nudge, shrug, tip the wink; gesticulate; raise the finger, hold up the finger, raise the hand, hold up the hand; saw the air, "suit the action to the word" [Hamlet]. wave a banner, unfurl a banner, hoist a banner, hang out a banner &c. n.; wave the hand, wave a kerchief; give the cue &c. (inform) 527; show one's colors; give an alarm, sound an alarm; beat the drum, sound the trumpets, raise a cry. sign, seal, attest &c. (evidence) 467; underline &c. (give importance to) 642; call attention to &c. (attention) 457; give notice &c. (inform) 527. Adj. indicating &c. v., indicative, indicatory; denotative, connotative; diacritical, representative, typical, symbolic, pantomimic, pathognomonic[obs3], symptomatic, characteristic, demonstrative, diagnostic, exponential, emblematic, armorial; individual &c. (special) 79. known by, recognizable by; indicated &c. v.; pointed, marked. [Capable of being denoted] denotable[obs3]; indelible. Adv. in token of; symbolically &c. adj.; in dumb show. Phr. ecce signum[Lat]; ex ungue leonem[Lat], ex pede Herculem[Lat]; vide ut supra; vultus ariete fortior[Lat][obs3].

<— p. 170 —>

#551. Record. — N. trace, vestige, relic, remains; scar, cicatrix; footstep, footmark[obs3], footprint; pug; track mark, wake, trail, scent, piste[obs3]. monument, hatchment[obs3], slab, tablet, trophy, achievement; obelisk, pillar, column, monolith; memorial; memento &c. (memory) 505; testimonial, medal; commemoration &c. (celebration) 883. record, note, minute; register, registry; roll &c. (list) 86; cartulary, diptych, Domesday book; catalogue raisonne[Fr]; entry, memorandum, indorsement[obs3], inscription, copy, duplicate, docket; notch &c. (mark) 550; muniment[obs3], deed &c. (security) 771; document; deposition, proces verbal[Fr]; affidavit; certificate &c. (evidence) 467. not, memorandum book, memo book, pocketbook, commonplace book; portfolio; pigeonholes, excerpta[obs3], adversaria[Lat], jottings, dottings[obs3]. gazette, gazetteer; newspaper, daily, magazine; almanac, almanack[obs3]; calendar, ephemeris, diary, log, journal, daybook, ledger; cashbook[obs3], petty cashbook[obs3]; professional journal, scientific literature, the literature, primary literature, secondary literature, article, review article. archive, scroll, state paper, return, blue book; statistics &c. 86; compte rendu[Fr]; Acts of, Transactions of, Proceedings of; Hansard's Debates; chronicle,annals, legend; history, biography &c. 594; Congressional Records. registration; registry; enrollment, inrollment[obs3]; tabulation; entry, booking; signature &c (identification) 550; recorder &c. 553; journalism. [analog recording media] recording, tape recording, videotape. [digital recording media] compact disk; floppy disk, diskette; hard disk, Winchester disk; read-only memory, ROM; write once read mostly memory, WORM. V. record; put on record, place on record; chronicle, calendar, hand down to posterity; keep up the memory &c. (remember) 505; commemorate &c. (celebrate) 883; report &c. (inform) 527; write, commit to writing, reduce to writing; put in writing, set down in writing, writing in black and white; put down, jot down, take down, write down, note down, set down; note, minute, put on paper; take note, make a note, take minute, take memorandum; make a return. mark &c. (indicate) 550; sign &c. (attest) 467. enter, book; post, post up, insert, make an entry of; mark off, tick off; register, enroll, inscroll[obs3]; file &c. (store) 636. burn into memory; carve in stone. Adv. on record. Phr. exegi monumentum aere perennium [Lat][obs3][Horace]; "read their history in a nation's eyes" [Gray]; "records that defy the tooth of time" [Young].

#552. [Suppression of sign.] Obliteration. — N. obliteration; erasure, rasure[obs3]; cancel, cancellation; circumduction[obs3]; deletion, blot; tabula rasa[Lat]; effacement, extinction.
V. efface, obliterate, erase, razel!, rase[obs3], expunge, cancel; blot out, take out, rub out, scratch out, strike out, wipe out, wash out, sponge out; wipe off, rub off; wipe away; deface, render illegible; draw the pen through, apply the sponge.
be effaced &c.; leave no trace &c. 550; "leave not a rack behind."
Adj. obliterated &c. v.; out of print; printless[obs3]; leaving no trace; intestate; unrecorded, unregistered, unwritten.
Int. dele; out with it!
Phr. delenda est Carthago [Lat][Cato].
#553. Recorder. — N. recorder, notary, clerk; registrar, registrary[obs3], register; prothonotary[Law]; amanuensis, secretary, scribe, babu[obs3], remembrancer[obs3], bookkeeper, custos rotulorum[Lat], Master of the Rolls. annalist; historian, historiographer; chronicler, journalist; biographer &c. (narrator) 594; antiquary &c. (antiquity) 122; memorialist[obs3]; interviewer.

#554. Representation. — N. representation, representment[obs3]; imitation &c. 19; illustration, delineation, depictment[obs3]; imagery, portraiture, iconography; design, designing; art, fine arts; painting &c. 556; sculpture &c. 557; engraving &c. 558; photography, cinematography; radiography, autoradiography[Bioch], fluorography[Chem], sciagraphy[obs3]. personation, personification; impersonation; drama &c. 599. picture, photo, photograph, daguerre-otype, snapshot; X-ray photo; movie film, movie; tracing, scan, TV image, video image, image file, graphics, computer graphics, televideo, closed-circuit TV. copy &c. 21; drawing, sketch, draught, draft; plot, chart, figure, scheme. image, likeness, icon, portrait, striking likeness, speaking likeness; very image; effigy, facsimile. figure, figure head; puppet, doll, figurine, aglet[obs3], manikin, lay-figure, model, mammet[obs3], marionette, fantoccini[obs3], waxwork, bust; statue, statuette. ideograph, hieroglyphic, anaglyph [obs3],kanji[Jap]; diagram, monogram. map, plan, chart, ground plan, projection, elevation (plan) 626. ichnography[obs3], cartography; atlas; outline, scheme; view &c. (painting) 556; radiograph, scotograph[obs3], sciagraph[obs3]; spectrogram, heliogram[obs3]. V. represent, delineate; depict, depicture[obs3]; portray; take a likeness, catch a likeness &c. n.; hit off, photograph, daguerreotype; snapshot; figure, shadow forth, shadow out; adumbrate; body forth; describe &c. 594; trace, copy; mold. dress up; illustrate, symbolize. paint &c. 556; carve &c. 557; engrave &c. 558. personate, personify; impersonate; assume a character; pose as; act; play &c. (drama) 599; mimic &c. (imitate) 19; hold the mirror up to nature. Adj. represent, representing &c. v., representative; *illustrative; represented &c. v.; imitative, figurative; iconic. like &c. 17; graphic &c. (descriptive) 594; cinquecento quattrocento[Fr][obs3], trecento[obs3].

<— p. 171 —>

#555. Misrepresentation. — N. misrepresentation, distortion, caricatural, exaggeration; daubing &c. v.; bad likeness, daub, sign painting; scratch, caricature; anamorphosis[obs3]; burlesque, falsification, misstatement; parody, lampoon, take-off, travesty. V. misrepresent, distort, overdraw, exaggerate, caricature, daub; burlesque, parody, travesty. Adj. misrepresented &c. v.

<— photography should be separated from painting —>

#556. Painting. — N. painting; depicting; drawing &c. v.; design; perspective, sciagraphy[obs3], skiagraphy[obs3]; chiaroscuro &c. (light) 420 composition; treatment. historical painting, portrait painting, miniature painting; landscape painting, marine painting; still life, flower painting, scene painting; scenography[obs3]. school, style; the grand style, high art, genre, portraiture; ornamental art &c. 847. monochrome, polychrome; grisaille[Fr]. pallet, palette; easel; brush, pencil, stump; black lead, charcoal, crayons, chalk, pastel; paint &c. (coloring matter) 428; watercolor, body color, oil color; oils, oil paint; varnish &c. 356a, priming; gouache, tempera, distemper, fresco, water glass; enamel; encaustic painting; mosaic; tapestry. photography, heliography, color photography; sun painting; graphics, computer graphics. picture, painting, piece[Fr], tableau, canvas; oil painting &c.; fresco, cartoon; easel picture, cabinet picture, draught, draft; pencil &c. drawing, water color drawing, etching, charcoal, pen-and-ink; sketch, outline, study. photograph, color photograph, black-and-white photograph, holograph, heliograph; daguerreotype, talbotype[obs3], calotype[obs3], heliotype[obs3]; negative, positive; print, glossy print, matte print; enlargement, reduction, life-size print; instant photo, Polaroid photo. technicolor, Kodachrome, Ektachrome; Polaroid. portrait &c. (representation) 554; whole length, full length, half length; kitcat, head; miniature; shade, silhouette; profile. landscape, seapiece[obs3]; view, scene, prospect; panorama, diorama; still life. picture gallery, exhibit; studio, atelier; pinacotheca[obs3]. V. paint, design, limn draw, sketch, pencil, scratch, shade, stipple, hatch, dash off, chalk out, square up; color, dead color, wash, varnish; draw in pencil &c. n.; paint in oils &c. n.; stencil; depict &c. (represent) 554. Adj. painted &c. v.; pictorial, graphic, picturesque. pencil, oil &c. n. Adv. in pencil &c. n. Phr. fecit[Lat], delineavit[Lat]; mutum est pictura poema[Lat].

#557. Sculpture. — N. sculpture, insculpturel [obs3]; carving &c. v.; statuary.

high relief, low relief, bas relief[Fr]; relief; relieve; bassorilievo[obs3], altorilievo[obs3], mezzorilievo[obs3]; intaglio, anaglyph[obs3]; medal, medallion; cameo.

marble, bronze, terra cotta[Sp], papier-mache; ceramic ware, pottery, porcelain, china, earthenware; cloisonne, enamel, faience, Laocoon, satsuma.

statue.&c. (image) 554; cast &c (copy) 21; glyptotheca[obs3].

V. sculpture, carve, cut, chisel, model, mold; *cast.

Adj. sculptured &c, v. in relief, anaglyptic[obs3], ceroplastic[obs3], ceramic; parian[obs3]; marble &c. n.; xanthian[obs3].

<— p. 172 —>

#558. Engraving. — N. engraving, chalcography[obs3]; line engraving, mezzotint engraving, stipple engraving, chalk engraving; dry point, bur; etching, aquatinta[obs3]; chiseling; plate engraving, copperplate engraving, steel engraving, wood engraving; xylography, lignography[obs3], glyptography[obs3], cerography[obs3], lithography, chromolithography[obs3], photolithography, zincography[obs3], glyphography, xylograph, lignograph[obs3], glyptograph[obs3], cerograph[obs3], lithograph, chromolithograph, photolithograph, zincograph[obs3], glyphograph[obs3], holograph. impression, print, engraving, plate; steelplate, copperplate; etching; mezzotint, aquatint, lithotint[obs3]; cut, woodcut; stereotype, graphotype[obs3], autotype[obs3], heliotype[obs3]. graver, burin[obs3], etching point, style; plate, stone, wood block, negative; die, punch, stamp. printing; plate printing, copperplate printing, anastatic printing[obs3], color printing, lithographic printing; type printing &c. 591; three-color process. illustration, illumination; half tone; photogravure; vignette, initial letter, cul de lampe[Fr], tailpiece. [person who inscribes on stone] lapidary, lapidarian. V. engrave, grave, stipple, scrape, etch; bite, bite in; lithograph &c., n.; print. Adj. insculptured[obs3]; engraved &c. v.. [of inscriptions on stone] lapidary. Phr. sculpsit[Lat], imprimit[Lat].

#559. Artist. — N. artist; painter, limner, drawer, sketcher, designer, engraver; master, old master; draftsman, draughtsman; copyist, dauber, hack; enamel, enameler, enamelist; caricaturist. historical painter, landscape painter, marine painter, flower painter, portrait painter, miniature painter, miniaturist, scene painter, sign painter, coach painter; engraver; Apelles[obs3]; sculptor, carver, chaser, modeler, figuriste[obs3], statuary; Phidias, Praxiteles; Royal Academician. photographer, cinematographer, lensman, cameraman, camera technician, camera buff; wildlife photographer. Phr. photo safari; "with gun and camera"

% 2. Conventional Means Language generally %

#560. Language. — N. language; phraseology &c. 569; speech &c. 582; tongue, lingo, vernacular; mother tongue, vulgar tongue, native tongue; household words; King's English, Queen's English; dialect &c. 563. confusion of tongues, Babel, pasigraphie[obs3]; pantomime &c. (signs) 550; onomatopoeia; betacism[obs3], mimmation, myatism[obs3], nunnation[obs3]; pasigraphy[obs3]. lexicology, philology, glossology[obs3], glottology[obs3]; linguistics, chrestomathy[obs3]; paleology[obs3], paleography; comparative grammar. literature, letters, polite literature, belles lettres[Fr], muses, humanities, literae humaniores[Lat], republic of letters, dead languages, classics; genius of language; scholarship &c. (scholar) 492. V. express by words &c. 566. Adj. lingual, linguistic; dialectic; vernacular, current; bilingual; diglot[obs3], hexaglot[obs3], polyglot; literary. Phr. "syllables govern the world" [Selden].

#561. Letter. — N. letter; character; hieroglyphic &c. (writing) 590; type &c. (printing) 591; capitals; digraph, trigraph; ideogram, ideograph; majuscule, minuscule; majuscule, minuscule; alphabet, ABC[obs3], abecedary[obs3], christ-cross-row. consonant, vowel; diphthong, triphthong[Gram]; mute, liquid, labial, dental, guttural. syllable; monosyllable, dissyllable[obs3], polysyllable; affix, suffix. spelling, orthograph[obs3]; phonography[obs3], phonetic spelling; anagrammatism[obs3], metagrammatism[obs3]. cipher, monogram, anagram; doubleacrostic[obs3]. V. spell. Adj. literal; alphabetical, abecedarian; syllabic; majuscular[obs3], minuscular[obs3]; uncial &c. (writing) 590.

#562. Word. — N. word, term, vocable; name &c. 564; phrase &c. 566; root, etymon; derivative; part of speech &c. (grammar) 567; ideophone[obs3].

dictionary, vocabulary, lexicon, glossary; index, concordance; thesaurus; gradus[Lat], delectus[Lat].

etymology, derivation; glossology[obs3], terminology orismology[obs3]; paleology &c. (philology) 560[obs3].

lexicography; glossographer &c. (scholar) 492; lexicologist, verbarian[obs3].

Adj. verbal, literal; titular, nominal. conjugate[Similarly derived], paronymous[obs3]; derivative.

Adv. verbally &c. adj.; verbatim &c. (exactly) 494.

Phr. "the artillery of words" [Swift].

<— p. 173 —>

#563. Neologism. — N. neology, neologism; newfangled expression, nonce expression; back-formation; caconym[obs3]; barbarism.

archaism, black letter, monkish Latin.

corruption, missaying[obs3], malapropism, antiphrasis[obs3].

pun, paranomasia[obs3], play upon words; word play &c. (wit) 842; double-entendre &c. (ambiguity) 520[Fr]; palindrome, paragram[obs3], anagram, clinch; abuse of language, abuse of terms.

dialect, brogue, idiom, accent, patois; provincialism, regionalism, localism; broken English, lingua franca; Anglicism, Briticism, Gallicism, Scotticism, Hibernicism; Americanism[obs3]; Gypsy lingo, Romany; pidgin, pidgin English, pigeon English; Volapuk, Chinook, Esperanto, Hindustani, kitchen Kaffir.

dog Latin, macaronics[obs3], gibberish; confusion of tongues, Babel; babu English[obs3], chi-chi.

figure of speech &c. (metaphor) 521; byword.

colloquialism, informal speech, informal language.

substandard language, vernacular.

vulgar language, obscene language, obscenity, vulgarity.

jargon, technical terms, technicality, lingo, slang, cant, argot; St. Gile's Greek, thieves' Latin, peddler's French, flash tongue, Billingsgate, Wall Street slang.

pseudology[obs3].

pseudonym &c. (misnomer) 565; Mr. So-and-so; wha d'ye call 'em[obs3], whatchacallim, what's his name; thingummy[obs3], thingumbob; je ne sais quoi[Fr].

neologist[obs3], coiner of words.

V. coin words, coin a term; backform; Americanize, Anglicize.

Adj. neologic[obs3], neological[obs3]; archaic; obsolete &c. (old) 124; colloquial; Anglice[obs3].

#564. Nomenclature. — N. nomenclature; naming &c. v.; nuncupationl, nomination, baptism; orismology[obs3]; onomatopoeia; antonomasia[obs3]. name; appellation[obs3], appelative[obs3]; designation, title; heading, rubric; caption; denomination; by-name, epithet. style, proper name; praenomen[Lat], agnomen[obs3], cognomen; patro-nymic, surname; cognomination[obs3]; eponym; compellation[obs3], description, antonym; empty title, empty name;

handle to one's name; namesake. term, expression, noun; byword; convertible terms &c. 522; technical term; cant &c. 563. V. name, call, term, denominate designate, style, entitle, clepe[obs3], dub, christen, baptize, characterize, specify, define, distinguish by the name of; label &c. (mark) 550. be -called &c v.; take the name of, bean the name of, go by the name of, be known by the name of, go under the name of, pass under the name of, rejoice in the name of. Adj. named &c. v.; hight[obs3], ycleped, known as; what one may well, call fairly, call properly, call fitly. nuncupatory[obs3], nuncupative; cognominal[obs3], titular, nominal, orismological[obs3]. Phr. "beggar'd all description" [Antony and Cleopatra].

#565. Misnomer. — N. misnomer; lucus a non lucendo[Lat]; Mrs. Malaprop; what d'ye call 'em &c. (neologism) 563[obs3]; Hoosier.

nickname, sobriquet, by-name; assumed name, assumed title; alias; nom de course, nom de theatre, nom de guerre[Fr], nom de plume; pseudonym, pseudonymy.

V. misname, miscall, misterm[obs3]; nickname; assume a name.

Adj. misnamed &c. v.; pseudonymous; soi-disant[Fr]; self called, self styled, self christened; so-called.

nameless, anonymous; without a having no name; innominate, unnamed; unacknowledged.

Adv. in no sense.

#566. Phrase. — N. phrase, expression, set phrase; sentence, paragraph; figure of speech &c. 521; idiom, idiotism[obs3]; turn of expression; style. paraphrase &c. (synonym) 522; periphrase &c. (circumlocution) 573 motto &c. (proverb) 496[obs3]. phraseology &c. 569. V. express, phrase; word, word it; give words to, give expression to; voice; arrange in words, clothe in words, put into words, express by words; couch in terms; find words to express; speak by the card; call, denominate, designate, dub. Adj. expressed &c. v.; idiomatic. Adv. in round terms, in set terms, in good set terms, set terms; in set phrases.

<— p. 174 —>

#567. Grammar. — N. grammar, accidence, syntax, praxis, punctuation; parts of speech; jussive[obs3]; syllabication; inflection, case, declension, conjugation; us et norma loquendi[Lat]; Lindley Murray &c. (schoolbook) 542; correct style, philology &c. (language) 560. V. parse, punctuate, syllabicate[obs3].

#568. Solecism. — N. solecism; bad grammar, false grammar, faulty grammar; slip of the pen, slip of the tongue; lapsus linguae[Lat]; slipslop[obs3]; bull; barbarism, impropriety. V. use bad grammar, faulty grammar; solecize[obs3], commit a solecism; murder the King's English, murder the Queen's English, break Priscian's head. Adj. ungrammatical; incorrect, inaccurate; faulty; improper, incongruous; solecistic, solecistical[obs3].

#569. Style. — N. style, diction, phraseology, wording; manner, strain; composition; mode of expression, choice of words; mode of speech, literary power, ready pen, pen of a ready writer; command of language &c. (eloquence) 582; authorship; la morgue litteraire[Fr].. V. express by words &c. 566; write. Phr. le style c'est de l'homme [Fr][Buffon]; "style is the dress of thoughts" [Chesterfield].

Various Qualities of Style

#570. Perspicuity. — N. perspicuity, perspicuousness &c. (intelligibility) 518; plain speaking &c. (manifestation) 525; definiteness, definition; exactness &c. 494; explicitness, lucidness. Adj. lucid &c. (intelligible) 518; explicit &c. (manifest) 525; exact &c. 494.

#571. Obscurity. — N. obscurity &c. (unintelligibility) 519; involution; hard words; ambiguity &c. 520; unintelligible-ness; vagueness &c. 475, inexactness &c. 495; what d'ye call 'em &c. (neologism) 563[obs3]; darkness of meaning. Adj. obscure &c. n.; crabbed, involved, confused.

#572. Conciseness. — N. conciseness &c. adj.; brevity, "the soul of wit", laconism[obs3]; Tacitus; ellipsis; syncope; abridgment &c. (shortening) 201; compression &c. 195; epitome &c. 596; monostich[obs3]; brunch word, portmanteau word. V. be concise &c. adj.; condense &c. 195; abridge &c. 201; abstract &c. 596; come to the point. Adj. concise, brief, short, terse, close; to the point, exact; neat, compact; compressed, condensed, pointed; laconic, curt, pithy, trenchant, summary; pregnant; compendious &c. (compendium) 596; succinct; elliptical, epigrammatic, quaint, crisp; sententious. Adv. concisely &c. adj.; briefly, summarily; in brief, in short, in a word, in a few words; for shortness sake; to come to the point, to make a long story short, to cut the matter short, to be brief; it comes to this, the long and the short of it is. Phr. brevis esse laboro obscurus fio [Lat][Horace].

#573. Diffuseness. — N. diffuseness &c. adj.; amplification &c. v.; dilating &c. v.; verbosity, verbiage, cloud of words, copia verborum[Lat]; flow of words &c. (loquacity) 584; looseness. Polylogy[obs3], tautology, battology[obs3], perissologyl; pleonasm, exuberance, redundancy; thrice-told tale; prolixity; circumlocution, ambages [obs3]; periphrase[obs3], periphrasis; roundabout phrases; episode; expletive; pennya-lining; richness &c. 577. V. be diffuse &c. adj.; run out on, descant, expatiate, enlarge, dilate, amplify, expand, inflate; launch out, branch out; rant. maunder, prose; harp upon &c. (repeat) 104; dwell on, insist upon. digress, ramble, battre la campagne[Fr][obs3], beat about the bush, perorate, spin a long yarn, protract; spin out, swell out, draw out; battologize[obs3]. Adj. diffuse, profuse; wordy, verbose, largiloquentl, copious, exuberant, pleonastic, lengthy; longsome[obs3], long-winded, longspun[obs3], long drawn out; spun out, protracted, prolix, prosing, maundering; circumlocutory, periphrastic, ambagious[obs3], roundabout; digressive; discursive, excursive; loose; rambling episodic; flatulent, frothy. Adv. diffusely &c. adj.; at large, in extenso[Lat]; about it and about it.

<— p. 175 —>

#574. Vigor. — N. vigor, power, force; boldness, raciness &c. adj.; intellectual, force; spirit, point, antithesis, piquance, piquancy; verve, glow, fire, warmth; strong language; gravity, sententiousness; elevation, loftiness, sublimity.

eloquence; command of words, command of language.

Adj. vigorous, nervous, powerful, forcible, trenchant, incisive, impressive; sensational.

spirited, lively, glowing, sparkling, racy, bold, slashing; pungent, piquant, full of point, pointed, pithy, antithetical; sententious.

lofty, elevated, sublime; eloquent; vehement, petulant, impassioned; poetic.

Adv. in glowing terms, in good set terms, in no measured terms.

Phr. "thoughts that breath and words that burn" [Gray].

#575. Feebleness. — N. feebleness &c. adj. Adj. feeble, bald, tame, meager, jejune, vapid, bland, trashy, lukewarm, cold, frigid, poor, dull, dry, languid; colorless, enervated; proposing, prosy, prosaic; unvaried, monotonous, weak, washy, wishy-washy; sketchy, slight. careless, slovenly, loose, lax (negligent) 460; slipshod, slipslop[obs3]; inexact; puerile, childish; flatulent; rambling &c. (diffuse) 573.

#576. Plainness. — N. plainness &c. adj.; simplicity, severity; plain terms, plain English; Saxon English; household words

V. call a spade "a spade"; plunge in medias res; come to the point.

Adj. plain, simple; unornamented, unadorned, unvarnished; homely, homespun; neat; severe, chaste, pure, Saxon; commonplace, matter-of-fact, natural, prosaic.

dry, unvaried,monotonous &c. 575.

Adv. in plain terms, in plain words, in plain English, in plain common parlance; point-blank.

#577. Ornament. — N. ornament; floridness c[obs3]. adj. turgidity, turgescence[obs3]; altiloquence &c. adj[obs3].; declamation, teratologyl!; well-rounded periods; elegance &c. 578; orotundity. inversion, antithesis, alliteration, paronomasia; figurativeness &c. (metaphor) 521. flourish; flowers of speech, flowers of rhetoric; frills of style, euphuism[obs3], euphemism. big-sounding words, high-sounding words; macrology[obs3], sesquipedalia verba[Lat], Alexandrine; inflation, pretension; rant, bombast, fustian, prose run mad; fine writing; sesquipedality[obs3]; Minerva press. phrasemonger; euphuist[obs3], euphemist. V. ornament, overlay with ornament, overcharge; smell of the lamp. Adj. ornament &c. v.; beautified &c. 847; ornate, florid, rich, flowery; euphuistic[obs3], euphemistic; sonorous; high-sounding, big- sounding; inflated, swelling, tumid; turgid, turgescent; pedantic, pompous, stilted; orotund; high flown, high flowing; sententious, rhetorical, declamatory; grandiose; grandiloquent, magniloquent, altiloquent[obs3]; sesquipedal[obs3], sesquipedalian; Johnsonian, mouthy; bombastic; fustian; frothy, flashy, flaming. antithetical, alliterative; figurative &c. 521; artificial &c. (inelegant) 579. Adv. ore rutundo[Lat].

#578. Elegance. — N. elegance, purity, grace, ease; gracefulness, readiness &c. adj.; concinnity[obs3], euphony, numerosity[obs3];

155

Atticism[obs3], classicalism[obs3], classicism.

well rounded periods, well turned periods, flowing periods; the right word in the right place; antithesis &c. 577.

*purist.

V. point an antithesis, round a period.

Adj. elegant, polished, classical, Attic, correct, Ciceronian, artistic; chaste, pure, Saxon, academical[obs3].

graceful, easy, readable, fluent, flowing, tripping; unaffected, natural, unlabored[obs3]; mellifluous; euphonious, euphemism, euphemistic; numerosel, rhythmical.

felicitous, happy, neat; well put, neatly put, well expressed, neatly expressed

<— p. 176 —>

#579. Inelegance. — N. inelegance; stiffness &c. adj.; "unlettered Muse" [Gray]; barbarism; slang &c. 563; solecism &c. 568; mannerism &c. (affectation) 855; euphuism[obs3]; fustian &c. 577; cacophony; words that break the teeth, words that dislocate the jaw; marinism[obs3]. V. be inelegant &c. adj. Adj. inelegant, graceless, ungraceful; harsh, abrupt; dry, stiff, cramped, formal, guinde[Fr]; forced, labored; artificial, mannered, ponderous; awkward, uncourtly[obs3], unpolished; turgid &c. 577; affected, euphuistic[obs3]; barbarous, uncouth, grotesque, rude, crude, halting; offensive to ears polite.

% Spoken Language %

#580. Voice. — N. voice; vocality[obs3]; organ, lungs, bellows; good voice, fine voice, powerful voice &c. (loud) 404; musical voice &c. 413; intonation; tone of voice &c. (sound) 402. vocalization; cry &c. 411; strain, utterance, prolation[obs3]; exclamation, ejaculation, vociferation, ecphonesis[obs3]; enunciation, articulation; articulate sound, distinctness; clearness, of articulation; stage whisper; delivery. accent, accentuation; emphasis, stress; broad accent, strong accent, pure accent, native accent, foreign accent; pronunciation. [Word similarly pronounced] homonym. orthoepy[obs3]; cacoepy[obs3]; euphony &c. (melody) 413. gastriloquism[obs3], ventriloquism; ventrilo-quist; polyphonism[obs3], polyphonist[obs3]. [Science of voice] phonology &c. (sound) 402. V. utter, breathe; give utterance, give tongue; cry &c. (shout) 411; ejaculate, rap out; vocalize, prolatel, articulate, enunciate, pronounce, accentuate, aspirate, deliver, mouth; whisper in the ear. Adj. vocal, phonetic, oral; ejaculatory, articulate, distinct, stertorous; euphonious &c. (melodious) 413. Phr. "how sweetly sounds the voice of a good woman" [Massinger]; "the organ of the soul" [Longfellow]; "thy voice is a celestial melody" [Longfellow].

#581. Aphony. — N. aphony[obs3], aphonia[obs3]; dumbness &c. adj.; obmutescence[obs3]; absence of voice, want of voice; dysphony[obs3]; cacoepy[obs3]; silence &c. (taciturnity) 585; raucity[obs3]; harsh voice &c. 410, unmusical voice &c. 414; falsetto, "childish treble mute"; dummy. V. keep silence &c. 585; speak low, speak softly; whisper &c. (faintness) 405. silence; render mute, render silent; muzzle, muffle, suppress, smother, gag, strike dumb, dumfound-er; drown the voice, put to silence, stop one's mouth, cut one short. stick in the throat. Adj. aphonous[obs3], dumb, mute; deafmute, deaf and dumb; mum; tongue- tied; breathless, tongueless, voiceless, speechless, wordless; mute as a fish, mute as a stockfish[obs3], mute as a mackerel; silent &c. (taciturn) 585; muzzled; inarticulate, inaudible. croaking, raucous, hoarse, husky, dry, hollow, sepulchral, hoarse as a raven; rough. Adv. with bated breath, with the finger on the lips; sotto voce[Lat]; in a low tone, in a cracked voice, in a broken voice. Phr. vox faucibus haesit [Lat] [Vergil].

#582. Speech. — N. speech, faculty of speech; locution, talk, parlance, verbal intercourse, prolation[obs3], oral communication, word of mouth, parole, palaver, prattle; effusion. oration, recitation, delivery, say, speech, lecture, harangue, sermon, tirade, formal speech, peroration; speechifying; soliloquy &c. 589; allocution &c. 586; conversa-tion &c. 588; salutatory; screed; valedictory [U.S.][U.S.]. oratory; elocution, eloquence; rhetoric, declamation; grandiloquence, multiloquence[obs3]; burst of eloquence; facundity[obs3]; flow of words, command of words, command of language; copia verborum[Lat]; power of speech, gift of the gab; usus loquendi[Lat]. speaker &c. v.; spokesman; prolocutor, interlocutor; mouthpiece, Hermes; orator, oratrix[obs3], oratress[obs3]; Demosthenes, Cicero; rhetorician; stump orator, platform orator; speechmaker, patterer[obs3], improvisatore[obs3]. V. speak of; say, utter, pronounce, deliver, give utterance to; utter forth, pour forth; breathe, let fall, come out with; rap out, blurt out have on one's lips; have at the end of one's tongue, have at the tip of one's tongue. break silence; open one's lips, open one's mouth; lift one's voice, raise one's voice; give the tongue, wag the tongue; talk, outspeak[obs3]; put in a word or two. hold forth; make a speech,.deliver a speech &c. n.; speechify, harangue, declaim, stump, flourish, recite, lecture, sermonize, discourse, be on one's legs; have one's say, say one's say; spout, rant, rave, vent one's fury, vent one's rage; expatiate &c. (speak at length) 573; speak one's mind, go on the stump, take the stump [U. S.]. soliloquize &c. 589; tell &c. (inform) 527; speak to &c. 586; talk together &c. 588. be eloquent &c. adj; have a tongue in one's head, have the gift of the gab &c. n. pass one's lips, escape one's lips; fall from the lips, fall from the mouth. Adj. speaking &c., spoken &c. v.; oral, lingual, phonetic, not written, unwritten, outspoken; eloquent, elocutionary; oratorical, rhetorical; declamatory; grandiloquent &c. 577; talkative &c. 584; Ciceronian, nuncupative, Tullian. Adv. orally &c. adj.; by word of mouth, viva voce, from the lips of. Phr. quoth he, said he &c.; "action is eloquence" [Coriolanus]; "pour the full tide of eloquence along" [Pope]; "she speaks poignards and every word stabs" [Much Ado About Nothing]; "speech is but broken light upon the depth of the unspoken [G. Eliot]; "to try thy eloquence now 'tis time [Antony and Cleopatra].

<— p. 177 —>

#583. [Imperfect Speech.] Stammering. — N. inarticulateness; stammering &c. v.; hesitation &c. v.; impediment in one's speech; titubancy[obs3], traulisml; whisper &c. (faint sound) 405; lisp, drawl, tardiloquence[obs3]; nasal tone, nasal accent; twang; falsetto &c. (want of voice) 581; broken voice, broken accents, broken sentences. brogue &c. 563; slip of the tongue, lapsus linouae [Lat]. V. stammer, stutter, hesitate, falter, hammer; balbutiatel, balbucinatel, haw, hum and haw, be unable to put two words together. mumble, mutter; maudl, mauder[obs3]; whisper &c. 405; mince, lisp; jabber, gibber; sputter, splutter; muffle, mump[obs3]; drawl, mouth; croak; speak thick, speak through the nose; snuffle, clip one's words; murder the language, murder the King's English, murder the Queen's English; mispronounce, missay[obs3]. Adj. stammering &c. v.; inarticulate, guttural, nasal; tremulous; affected. Adv. sotto voce &c. (faintly) 405[Lat].

#584. Loquacity. — N. loquacity, loquaciousness; talkativeness &c. adj.; garrulity; multiloquence[obs3], much speaking. jaw; gabble; jabber, chatter; prate, prattle, cackle, clack; twaddle, twattle, rattle; caquet[obs3], caquetterie[Fr]; blabber, bavardage[obs3], bibble-babble[obs3], gibble-gabble[obs3]; small talk &c. (converse) 588. fluency, flippancy, volubility, flowing, tongue; flow of words; flux de bouche[Fr], flux de mots[Fr], copia verborum[Lat], cacoethes loquendi[Lat]; furor loquendi[Lat]; verbosity &c. (diffuseness) 573; gift of the gab &c. (eloquence) 582. talker; chatterer, chatterbox; babbler &c. v.; rattle; ranter; sermonizer, proser[obs3], driveler; blatherskite [U. S.]; gossip &c. (converse) 588; magpie, jay, parrot, poll, Babel; moulin a paroles[Fr].. V. be loquacious &c. adj.; talk glibly, pour forth, patter; prate, palaver, prose, chatter, prattle, clack, jabber, jaw; blather, blatter[obs3], blether[obs3]; rattle, rattle on; twaddle, twattle; babble, gabble; outtalk; talk oneself out of breath, talk oneself hoarse; expatiate &c. (speak at length) 573; gossip &c. (converse) 588; din in the ears &c. (repeat) 104; talk at random, talk nonsense &c. 497; be hoarse with talking. Adj. loquacious, talkative, garrulous, linguaciousl, multiloquous[obs3]; largiloquentl; chattering &c. v.; chatty &c. (sociable) 892; declamatory &c. 582; open-mouthed. fluent, voluble, glib, flippant; long tongued, long winded &c. (diffuse) 573. Adv. trippingly on the tongue; glibly &c. adj.; off the reel. Phr. the tongue running fast, the tongue running loose, the tongue running on wheels; all talk and no cider; "foul whisperings are abroad" [Macbeth]; "what a spendthrift is he of his tongue!" [Tempest].

<— p. 178 —>

#585. Taciturnity. — N. silence, muteness, obmutescence[obs3]; taciturnity, pauciloquy[obs3], costivenessl, curtness; reserve, reticence &c. (concealment) 528. man of few words. V. be silent &c. adj.; keep silence, keep mum; hold one's tongue, hold one's peace, hold one's jaw; not speak. &c. 582; say nothing, keep one's counsel; seal the lips, close the lips, button the lips, zipper the lips, put a padlock on the lips, put a padlock on the mouth; put a bridle on one's tongue; bite one's tongue, keep one's tongue between one's teeth; make no sign, not let a word escape one; keep a secret &c. 528; not have a word to say; hush up, hush, lay the finger on the lips, place the finger on the lips; render mute &c. 581. stick in one's throat. Adj. silent, mute, mum; silent as a post, silent as a stone, silent as the grave &c. (still) 403; dumb &c. 581; unconversable[obs3]. taciturn, sparing of words; closetongued; costivel, inconversablel, curt; reserved; reticent &c. (concealing) 528. Int. shush! tush! silence! mum! hush! chut[obs3]! hist! tut! chup[obs3]! mum's the word; keep your mouth shut![vulgar]. Phr. cave quid dicis quando et cui[Lat]; volto sciolto i pensieri stretti[It].

    #586. Allocution. — N. allocution, alloquyl, address; speech &c. 582;
apostrophe, interpellation, appeal, invocation, salutation; word in the
ear.
    [Feigned dialogue] dialogism[obs3].
    platform &c. 542; plank; audience &c. (interview) 588.

V. speak to, address, accost, make up to, apostrophize, appeal to, invoke; ball, salute; call to, halloo.

take aside, take by the button; talk to in private.

lecture &c. (make a speech) 582.

Int. soho[obs3]! halloo! hey! hist!

#587. Response — N. &c., see Answer 462.

#588. Conversation. — N. conversation, interlocution; collocution[obs3], colloquy, converse, confabulation, talk, discourse, verbal intercourse; oral communication, commerce; dialogue, duologue, trialogue. causerie, chat, chitchat; small talk, table talk, teatable talk[obs3], town talk, village talk, idle talk; tattle, gossip, tittle-tattle; babble, babblement[obs3]; tripotage[obs3], cackle, prittle-prattle[obs3], cancan, on dit[Fr]; talk of the town, talk of the village. conference, parley, interview, audience, pourparler; tete-a-tete; reception, conversazione[It]; congress &c. (council) 696; powwow [U. S.]. hall of audience, durbar[obs3]. palaver, debate, logomachy[obs3], war of words. gossip, tattler; Paul Pry; tabby; chatterer &c. (loquacity) 584; interlocutor &c. (spokesman) 582; conversationist[obs3], dialogist[obs3]. "the feast of reason and the flow of soul" [Pope]; mollia tempora fandi[Lat][obs3]. V. talk together, converse, confabulate; hold on a conversation, carry on a conversation, join in a conversation, engage in a conversation; put in a word; shine in conversation; bandy words; parley; palaver; chat, gossip, tattle; prate &c. (loquacity) 584; powwow [U.S.].. discourse with, confer with, commune with, commerce with; hold converse, hold conference, hold intercourse; talk it over; be closeted with; talk with one in private, tete-a-tete. Adj. conversing &c. v.; interlocutory; conversational, conversable[obs3]; discursive, discoursive[obs3]; chatty &c. (sociable) 892; colloquial. Phr. "with thee conversing I forget all time" [Paradise Lost].

#589. Soliloquy. — N. soliloquy, monologue, apostrophe; monology[obs3].

V. Soliloquize; say to oneself, talk to oneself; say aside, think aloud, apostrophize.

Adj. soliloquizing &c. v.

Adv. aside.

<— p. 179 —> % Written Language %

#590. Writing. — N. writing &c. v.; chirography, stelography[obs3], cerography[obs3]; penmanship, craftmanship[obs3]; quill driving; typewriting. writing, manuscript, MS., literae scriptae[Lat]; these presents. stroke of the pen, dash of the pen; coupe de plume; line; headline; pen and ink. letter &c. 561; uncial writing, cuneiform character, arrowhead, Ogham, Runes, hieroglyphic; contraction; Brahmi[obs3], Devanagari, Nagari; script. shorthand; stenography, brachygraphy[obs3], tachygraphy[obs3]; secret writing, writing in cipher; cryptography, stenography[obs3]; phonography[obs3], pasigraphy[obs3], Polygraphy[obs3], logography[obs3]. copy; transcript, rescript; rough copy, fair copy; handwriting; signature, sign manual; autograph, monograph, holograph; hand, fist. calligraphy; good hand, running hand, flowing hand, cursive hand, legible hand, bold hand. cacography[obs3], griffonage[obs3], barbouillage[obs3]; bad hand, cramped hand, crabbed hand, illegible hand; scribble &c. v.; pattes de mouche[Fr]; ill-formed letters; pothooks and hangers. stationery; pen, quill, goose quill; pencil, style; paper, foolscap, parchment, vellum, papyrus, tablet, slate, marble, pillar, table; blackboard; ink bottle, ink horn, ink pot, ink stand, ink well; typewriter. transcription &c. (copy) 21; inscription &c. (record) 551; superscription &c. (indication) 550; graphology. composition, authorship; cacoethes scribendi[Lat]; graphoidea[obs3], graphomania[obs3]; phrenoia[obs3]. writer, scribe, amanuensis, scrivener, secretary, clerk, penman, copyist, transcriber, quill driver; stenographer, typewriter, typist; writer for the press &c. (author) 593. V. write, pen; copy, engross; write out, write out fair; transcribe; scribble, scrawl, scrabble, scratch; interline; stain paper; write down &c. (record) 551; sign &c. (attest) 467; enface[obs3]. compose, indite, draw up, draft, formulate; dictate; inscribe, throw on paper, dash off; manifold. take up the pen, take pen in hand; shed ink, spill ink, dip one's pen in ink. Adj. writing &c. v.; written &c. v.; in writing, in black and white; under one's hand. uncial, Runic, cuneiform, hieroglyphical[obs3]. Adv. currente calamo[Sp]; pen in hand. Phr. audacter et sincere[Lat]; le style est l'homme meme [Fr]; "nature's noblest gift - my gray goose quill" [Byron]; scribendi recte sapere et principium et fons [Lat][Horace]; "that mighty instrument of little men" [Byron]; "the pen became a clarion" [Longfellow].

#591. Printing. — N. printing; block printing, type- printing; plate printing &c. 558[engraving]; the press &c. (publication) 531; composition. print, letterpress, text; context, note, page, column. typography; stereotype, electrotype, aprotype[obs3]; type, black letter, font, fount; pi, pie; capitals &c. (letters) 561; brevier[obs3], bourgeois, pica &c. boldface, capitals, caps., catchword; composing-frame, composing room, composing rule, composing stand, composing stick; italics, justification, linotype, live matter, logotype, lower case, upper case; make-up, matrix, matter, monotype[obs3], point system: 4-1/2, 5, 5-1/2, 6, 7, 8 point, etc.; press room, press work; reglet[obs3], roman; running head, running title; scale, serif, shank, sheet work, shoulder, signature, slug, underlay. folio &c. (book) 593; copy, impression, pull, proof, revise; author's proof, galley proof, press proof; press revise. printer, compositor, reader; printer's devil copyholder. V. print; compose; put to press, go to press; pass through the press, see through the press; publish &c. 531; bring out; appear in print, rush into print; distribute, makeup, mortise, offset, overrun, rout. Adj. printed &c. v.; in type; typographical &c. n.; solid in galleys.

<— p. 180 —>

#592. Correspondence. — N. correspondence, letter, epistle, note, billet, post card, missive, circular, favor, billet-doux; chit, chitty[obs3], letter card, picture post card; postal [U.S.], card; despatch; dispatch; bulletin, these presents; rescript, rescription[obs3]; post &c. (messenger) 534. V. correspond with; write to, send a letter to; keep up a correspondence. Adj. epistolary. Phr. furor scribendi[Lat].

<— Book, periodical should be separated —>

#593. Book. — N. booklet; writing, work, volume, tome, opuscule[obs3]; tract, tractate[obs3]; livret[obs3]; brochure, libretto, handbook, codex, manual, pamphlet, enchiridion[obs3], circular, publication; chap book. part, issue, number livraison[Fr]; album, portfolio; periodical, serial, magazine, ephemeris, annual, journal. paper, bill, sheet, broadsheet[obs3]; leaf, leaflet; fly leaf, page; quire, ream [subdivisions of a book] chapter, section, head, article, paragraph, passage, clause; endpapers, frontispiece; cover, binding. folio, quarto, octavo; duodecimo[obs3], sextodecimo[obs3], octodecimo[obs3]. encyclopedia; encompilation[obs3]. [collection of books] library, bibliotheca[obs3]. press &c. (publication) 531. [complete description] definitive work, treatise, comprehensive treatise (dissertation) 595. [person who writes a book] writer, author, litterateur[Fr], essayist, journalism; pen, scribbler, the scribbling race; literary hack, Grub-street writer; writer for the press, gentleman of the press, representative of the press; adjective jerker[obs3], diaskeaust[obs3], ghost, hack writer, ink slinger; publicist; reporter, penny a liner; editor, subeditor[obs3]; playwright &c. 599; poet &c. 597. bookseller, publisher; bibliopole[obs3], bibliopolist[obs3]; librarian; bookstore, bookshop, bookseller's shop. knowledge of books, bibliography; book learning &c. (knowledge) 490. Phr. "among the giant fossils of my past" [E. B. Browning]; craignez tout d'un auteur en courroux[Fr]; "for authors nobler palms remain" [Pope]; "I lived to write and wrote to live" [Rogers]; "look in thy heart and write" [Sidney]; "there is no Past so long as Books shall live" [Bulwer Lytton]; "the public mind is the creation of the Master-Writers" [Disraeli]; "volumes that I prize above my dukedom" [Tempest].

#594. Description. — N. description, account, statement, report; expose &c. (disclosure) 529 specification, particu-lars; state of facts, summary of facts; brief &c. (abstract) 596; return &c. (record) 551; catalogue raisonne &c. (list) 86[Fr]; guid &c. (information) 527. delineation &c (representation) 554; sketch; monograph; minute account, detailed particular account, circumstantial account, graphic account; narration, recital, rehearsal, relation. historiography[obs3], chronography[obs3]; historic Muse, Clio; history; biography, autobiography; necrology, obituary. narrative, history; memoir, memorials; annals &c. (chronicle) 551; saga; tradition, legend, story, tale, historiette[obs3]; personal narrative, journal, life, adventures, fortunes, experiences, confessions; anecdote, ana[obs3], trait. work of fiction, novel, romance, Minerva press; fairy tale, nursery tale; fable, parable, apologue[obs3]; dime novel, penny dreadful, shilling shocker relator &c. v.; raconteur, historian &c. (recorder) 553; biographer, fabulist[obs3], novelist. V. describe; set forth &c. (state) 535; draw a picture, picture; portray &c. (repre-sent) 554; characterize, particularize; narrate, relate, recite, recount, sum up, run over, recapitulate, rehearse, fight one's battles over again. unfold a tale &c. (disclose) 529; tell; give an account of, render an account of; report, make a report, draw up a statement. detail; enter into particulars, enter into details, descend to particulars, descend to details; itemize. Adj. descriptive, graphic, narrative, epic, suggestive, well-drawn; historic; traditional, traditionary; legendary; anecdotic[obs3], storied; described &c. v. Phr. furor scribendi[Lat].

#595. Dissertation. — N. dissertation, treatise, essay; thesis, theme; monograph, tract, tractate[obs3], tractation[obs3]; discourse, memoir, disquisition, lecture, sermon, homily, pandect[obs3]; excursus. commentary, review, critique, criticism, article; leader, leading article; editorial; running commentary. investigation &c. (inquiry) 461; study &c. (consideration) 451; discussion &c. (reasoning) 476; exposition &c. (explanation) 522. commentator, critic, essayist, pamphleteer. V. expound upon a subject, dissert upon a subject[obs3], descant upon a subject, write upon a subject, touch upon a subject; treat a subject, treat a subject thoroughly, treat of a subject, take up a subject, ventilate a subject, discuss a subject, deal with a subject, go into a subject, go into a subject at length, canvass a subject, handle a subject, do justice to a subject. hold forth[oral dissertation], discourse, delve into. Adj. discursive, discoursive[obs3]; disquisitionary[obs3]; expository.

<— p. 181 —>

#596. Compendium. — N. compend, compendium; abstract, precis, epitome, multum in parvo[Lat], analysis, pandect[obs3], digest, sum and substance, brief, abridgment, summary, apercu, draft, minute, note; excerpt; synopsis, textbook, conspectus, outlines, syllabus, contents, heads, prospectus. album; scrap book, note book, memorandum book, commonplace book; extracts, excerpta[obs3], cuttings; fugitive pieces, fugitive writing; spicilegium[obs3], flowers, anthology, collectanea[obs3], analecta[obs3]; compilation. recapitulation, resume, review. abbreviation, abbreviature[obs3]; contraction; shortening &c. 201; compression &c. 195. V. abridge, abstract, epitomize, summarize; make an abstract, prepare an abstract, draw an abstract, compile an abstract &c. n. recapitulate, review, skim, run over, sum up. abbreviate &c. (shorten) 201; condense &c. (compress) 195; compile &c. (collect) 72. Adj. compendious, synoptic, analectic[obs3]; abrege[Fr], abridged &c. v.; variorum[obs3]. Adv. in short, in epitome, in substance, in few words. Phr. it lies in a nutshell.

#597. Poetry. — N. poetry, poetics, poesy, Muse, Calliope, tuneful Nine, Parnassus, Helicon[obs3], Pierides, Pierian spring. versification, rhyming, making verses; prosody, orthometry[obs3]. poem; epic, epic poem; epopee[obs3], epopoea, ode, epode[obs3], idyl, lyric, eclogue, pastoral, bucolic, dithyramb, anacreontic[obs3], sonnet, roundelay, rondeau[Fr], rondo, madrigal, canzonet[obs3], cento[obs3], *monody, elegy; amoebaeum, ghazal[obs3], palinode. dramatic poetry, lyric poetry; opera; posy, anthology; disjecta membra poetae song[Lat], ballad, lay; love song, drinking song, war song, sea song; lullaby; music &c. 415; nursery rhymes. [Bad poetry] doggerel, Hudibrastic verse[obs3], prose run mad; macaronics[obs3]; macaronic verse[obs3], leonine verse; runes. canto, stanza, distich, verse, line, couplet, triplet, quatrain; strophe, antistrophe[obs3]. verse, rhyme, assonance, crambo[obs3], meter, measure, foot, numbers, strain, rhythm; accentuation &c. (voice) 580; dactyl, spondee, trochee, anapest &c.; hexameter, pentameter; Alexandrine; anacrusis[obs3], antispast[obs3], blank verse, ictus. elegiacs &c. adj.; elegiac verse, elegaic meter, elegaic poetry. poet, poet laureate; laureate; bard, lyrist[obs3], scald, skald[obs3], troubadour, trouvere[Fr]; minstrel; minnesinger, meistersinger[Ger]; improvisatore[obs3]; versifier, sonneteer; rhymer, rhymist[obs3], rhymester; ballad monger, runer[obs3]; poetaster; genus irritabile vatum [Latin]. V. poetize, sing, versify, make verses, rhyme, scan. Adj. poetic, poetical; lyric, lyrical, tuneful, epic, dithyrambic &c. n.; metrical; a catalectin[obs3]; elegiac, iambic, trochaic, anapestic[obs3]; amoebaeic, Melibean, skaldic[obs3]; Ionic, Sapphic, Alcaic[obs3], Pindaric. Phr. "a poem round and perfect as a star" [Alex. Smith]; Dichtung und Wahrheit [Ger]; furor poeticus[Lat]; "his virtues formed the magic of his song" [Hayley]; "I do but sing because I must" [Tennyson]; "I learnt life from the poets" [de Stael]; licentia vatum[Lat]; mutum est pictura poema[Lat]; "O for a muse of fire!" [Henry V]; "sweet food of sweetly uttered knowledge" [Sidney]; "the true poem is the poet's mind" [Emerson]; Volk der Dichter und Denker[Ger]; "wisdom married to immortal verse" [Wordsworth].

#598. Prose. — N. prose, prose writer. prosaicism[obs3], prosaism[obs3], prosaist[obs3], proser[obs3].
V. prose.
write prose, write in prose.
Adj. prosal[obs3],prosy, prosaic; unpoetic, unpoetical[obs3].
rhymeless[obs3], unrhymed, in prose, not in verse.

<— p. 182 —>

#599. The Drama. — N. the drama, the stage, the theater, the play; film the film, movies, motion pictures, cinema, cinematography; theatricals, dramaturgy, histrionic art, buskin, sock, cothurnus[obs3], Melpomene and Thalia, Thespis. play, drama, stage play, piece[Fr], five-act play, tragedy, comedy, opera, vaudeville, comedietta[obs3], lever de rideau[Fr], interlude, afterpiece[obs3], exode[obs3], farce, divertissement, extravaganza, burletta[obs3], harlequinade[obs3], pantomime, burlesque, opera bouffe[Fr], ballet, spectacle, masque, drame comedie drame[Fr]; melodrama, melodrame[obs3]; comidie larmoyante[Fr], sensation drama; tragicomedy, farcical-comedy; monodrame monologue[obs3];duologue trilogy; charade, proverbs; mystery, miracle play; musical, musical comedy. [movies] western, horse opera; flick [coll.]; spy film, love story, adventure film, documentary, nature film; pornographic film, smoker, skin flick, X-rated film. act, scene, tableau; induction, introduction; prologue, epilogue; libretto. performance, representation, mise en scene[French], stagery[obs3], jeu de theatre[French]; acting; gesture &c. 550; impersonation &c. 554; stage business, gag, buffoonery. light comedy, genteel comedy, low comedy. theater; playhouse, opera house; house; music hall; amphitheater, circus, hippodrome, theater in the round; puppet show, fantoccini[obs3]; marionettes, Punch and Judy. auditory, auditorium, front of the house, stalls, boxes, pit, gallery, parquet; greenroom, coulisses[Fr]. flat; drop, drop scene; wing, screen, side scene; transformation scene, curtain, act drop; proscenium. stage, scene, scenery, the boards; trap, mezzanine floor; flies; floats, footlights; offstage; orchestra. theatrical costume, theatrical properties. movie studio, back lot, on location. part, role, character, dramatis personae[Lat]; repertoire. actor, thespian, player; method actor; stage player, strolling player; stager, performer; mime, mimer[obs3]; artists; comedian, tragedian; tragedienne, Roscius; star, movie star, star of stage and screen, superstar, idol, sex symbol; supporting actor, supporting cast; ham, hamfatter *[obs3]; masker[obs3]. pantomimist, clown harlequin, buffo[obs3], buffoon, farceur, grimacer, pantaloon, columbine; punchinello[obs3]; pulcinello[obs3]; pulcinella[obs3]; extra, bit-player, walk-on role, cameo appearance; mute, figurante[obs3], general utility; super, supernumerary. company; first tragedian, prima donna[Sp], protagonist; jeune premier[French]; debutant, debutante[French]; light comedian, genteel comedian, low comedian; walking gentleman, amoroso[obs3], heavy father, ingenue[French], jeune veuve[French]. mummer, guiser[obs3], guisard[obs3], gysart I, masque. mountebank, Jack Pudding; tumbler, posture master, acrobat; contortionist; ballet dancer, ballet girl; chorus singer; coryphee danseuse[Fr]. property man, costumier, machinist; prompter, call boy; manager; director, stage manager, acting manager. producer, entrepreneur, impresario; backer, investor, angel[fig]. dramatic author, dramatic writer; play writer, playwright; dramatist, mimographer[obs3]. V. act, play, perform; put on the stage; personate &c. 554; mimic &c. (imitate) 19; enact; play a part, act a part, go through a part, perform a part; rehearse, spout, gag, rant; "strut and fret one's hour upon a stage"; tread the boards, tread the stage; come out; star it. Adj. dramatic; theatric, theatrical; scenic, histrionic, comic, tragic, buskined[obs3], farcical, tragicomic, melodramatic, operatic; stagy. Adv. on the stage, on the boards; on film; before the floats, before an audience; behind the scenes. Phr. fere totus mundus exercet histrionem [Lat] [Petronius Arbiter]; "suit the action to the word, the word to the action" [Hamlet]; "the play's the thing" [Hamlet]; "to wake the soul by tender strokes of art" [Pope].

<— p. 183 —>
%
CLASS V
WORDS RELATING TO THE VOLUNTARY POWERS
Division (I) INDIVIDUAL VOLITION

Section I. VOLITION IN GENERAL

1. Acts of Volition %

#600. Will. — N. will, volition, conation[obs3], velleity; liberum arbitrium[Lat]; will and pleasure, free will; freedom &c. 748; discretion; option &c. (choice) 609; voluntariness[obs3]; spontaneity, spontaneousness; originality. pleasure, wish, mind; desire; frame of mind &c. (inclination) 602; intention &c. 620; predetermination &c. 611; selfcontrol &c. determination &c. (resolution) 604; force of will. V. will, list; see fit, think fit; determine &c. (resolve) 604; enjoin; settle &c. (choose) 609; volunteer. have a will of one's own; do what one chooses &c. (freedom) 748; have it all one's own way; have one's will, have one's own way. use one's discretion, exercise one's discretion; take upon oneself, take one's own course, take the law into one's own hands; do of one's own accord, do upon one's own authority; originate &c. (cause) 153. Adj. voluntary, volitional, willful; free &c. 748; optional; discretional, discretionary; volitient[obs3], volitive[obs3]. minded &c. (willing) 602; prepense &c. (predetermined) 611[obs3]; intended &c. 620; autocratic; unbidden &c. (bid &c. 741); spontaneous; original &c. (casual) 153; unconstrained. Adv. voluntarily &c. adj.; at will, at pleasure; a volonte[Fr], a discretion; al piacere[It]; ad libitum, ad arbitrium[Lat]; as one thinks proper, as it seems good to; a beneplacito[It]. of one's won accord, of one's own free will; proprio motu[Lat], suo motu[Lat], ex meromotu[Lat]; out of one's own head; by choice &c. 609; purposely &c. (intentionally) 620; deliberately &c. 611. Phr. stet pro ratione voluntas[Lat]; sic volo sic jubeo[Lat]; a vostro beneplacito[It]; beneficium accipere libertatem est vendere[Lat]; Deus vult[Lat]; was man nicht kann meiden muss man willig leiden[Ger].

#601. Necessity. — N. involuntariness; instinct, blind impulse; inborn proclivity, innate proclivity; native tendency, natural tendency; natural impulse, predetermination. necessity, necessitation; obligation; compulsion &c. 744; subjection &c. 749; stern necessity, hard necessity, dire necessity, imperious necessity, inexorable necessity, iron necessity, adverse necessity; fate; what must be. destiny, destination; fatality, fate, kismet, doom, foredoom, election, predestination; preordination, foreordination; lot fortune; fatalism; inevitableness &c. adj.; spell &c. 993. star, stars; planet, planets; astral influence; sky, Fates, Parcae, Sisters three, book of fate; God's will, will of Heaven; wheel of Fortune, Ides of March, Hobson's choice. last shift, last resort; dernier ressort[Fr]; pis aller &c. (substitute) 147[Fr]; necessaries &c. (requirement) 630. necessarian[obs3], necessitarian[obs3]; fatalist; automaton. V. lie under a necessity; befated[obs3], be doomed, be destined &c. in for, under the necessity of; have no choice, have no alternative; be one's fate &c. n. to be pushed to the wall to be driven into a corner, to be unable to help. destine, doom, foredoom, devote; predestine, preordain; cast a spell &c. 992; necessitate; compel &c. 744. Adj. necessary, needful &c (requisite) 630. fated; destined &c. v.; elect; spellbound, compulsory &c. (compel) 744; uncontrollable, inevitable, unavoidable, irresistible, irrevocable, inexorable; avoidless[obs3], resistless. involuntary, instinctive, automatic, blind, mechanical; unconscious, unwitting, unthinking; unintentional &c. (undesigned) 621; impulsive &c. 612. Adv. necessarily &c. adv.; of necessity, of course; ex necessitate rei[Lat]; needs must; perforce &c. 744; nolens volens[Lat]; will he nil he, willy nilly, bon gre mal gre[Fr], willing or unwilling, coute que coute[Fr]. faute de mieux[Fr]; by stress of; if need be. Phr. it cannot be helped; there is no help for, there is no helping it; it will be, it must be, it needs to be, it must be so, it will have its way; the die is cast; jacta est alea[obs3][Lat]; che sara sara[French]; "it is written"; one's days are numbered, one's fate is sealed; Fata obstant[Latin]; diis aliter visum[obs3][Latin]; actum me invito factus[Latin], non est meus actus[Latin]; aujord'hui roi demain rien[French]; quisque suos patimur manes [Latin][Vergil];"The moving finger writes and having writ moves on. Nor all your piety and wit can bring it back to cancel half a line, nor all your tears wash out a word of it."[Rubayyat of Omar Khayyam].

<— p. 184 —>

#602. Willingness. — N. willingness, voluntariness &c. adj[obs3].; willing mind, heart. disposition, inclination, leaning, animus; frame of mind, humor, mood, vein; bent &c. (turn of mind) 820; penchant &c. (desire) 865; aptitude &c. 698. docility, docibleness[obs3]; persuasibleness[obs3], persuasibility[obs3]; pliability &c. (softness) 324. geniality, cordiality; goodwill; alacrity, readiness, earnestness, forwardness; eagerness &c. (desire) 865. asset &c. 488; compliance &c. 762; pleasure &c. (will) 600; gratuitous service. labor of love; volunteer, volunteering. V. be willing &c. adj.; incline, lean to, mind, propend; had as lief; lend a willing ear, give a willing ear, turn a willing ear; have a half a mind to, have a great mind to; hold to, cling to; desire &c. 865. see fit, think good, think proper; acquiesce &c (assent) 488; comply with &c. 762. swallow the bait, nibble at the bait; gorge the hook; have no scruple of, make no scruple of; make no bones of; jump at, catch at; meet halfway; volunteer. Adj. willing, minded, fain, disposed, inclined, favorable; favorably- minded, favorably inclined, favorably disposed; nothing loth; in the vein, in the mood, in the humor, in the mind. ready, forward, earnest, eager; bent upon &c. (desirous) 865; predisposed, propense[obs3]. docile; persuadable, persuasible; suasible[obs3], easily persuaded, facile, easy-going; tractable &c. (pliant) 324; genial, gracious, cordial, cheering, hearty; content &c. (assenting) 488. voluntary, gratuitous, spontaneous; unasked &c. (ask &c. 765); unforced &c. (free) 748. Adv. willingly &c. adj.; fain, freely, as lief, heart and soul; with pleasure, with all one's heart, with open arms; with good will, with right will; de bonne volonte[Fr], ex animo[Lat]; con amore[It], heart in hand, nothing loth, without reluctance, of one's own accord, graciously, with a good grace. a la bonne heure[Fr]; by all means, by all manner of means; to one's heart's content; yes &c. (assent) 488.

#603. Unwillingness. — N. unwillingness &c. adj.; indisposition, indisposedness[obs3]; disinclination, aversation[obs3]; nolleity[obs3], nolition[obs3]; renitence[obs3], renitency; reluctance; indifference &c. 866; backwardness &c. adj.; slowness &c. 275; want of alacrity, want of readiness; indocility &c. (obstinacy) 606[obs3]. scrupulousness, scrupulosity; qualms of conscience, twinge of conscience; delicacy, demur, scruple, qualm, shrinking, recoil; hesitation &c. (irresolution) 605; fastidiousness &c. 868. averseness &c. (dislike) 867[obs3]; dissent &c. 489; refusal &c. 764. V. be unwilling &c. adj.; nill; dislike &c. 867; grudge, begrudge; not be able to find it in one's heart to, not have the stomach to. demur, stick at, scruple, stickle; hang fire, run rusty; recoil, shrink, swerve; hesitate &c. 605; avoid &c. 623. oppose &c. 708; dissent &c. 489; refuse &c. 764. Adj. unwilling; not in the vein, loth, loath, shy of, disinclined, indisposed, averse, reluctant, not content; adverse &c. (opposed) 708; laggard, backward, remiss, slack, slow to; indifferent &c. 866; scrupulous; squeamish &c. (fastidious) 868; repugnant &c. (dislike) 867; restiffl, restive; demurring &c. v.; unconsenting &c. (refusing) 764; involuntary &c. 601. Adv. unwillingly &c. adj.; grudgingly, with a heavy heart; with a bad, with an ill grace; against one's wishes, against one's will, against the grain, sore against one's wishes, sore against one's will, sore against one's grain; invita Minerva[Lat]; a contre caeur[Fr]; malgre soi[Fr]; in spite of one's teeth, in spite of oneself; nolens volens &c. (necessity) 601[Lat]; perforce &c. 744; under protest; no &c. 536; not for the world, far be it from me.

<— p. 185 —>

#604. Resolution. — N. determination, will; iron will, unconquerable will; will of one's own, decision, resolution; backbone; clear grit, true grit, grit [U. S. &can.]; sand, strength of mind, strength of will; resolve &c. (intent) 620; firmness &c. (stability) 150; energy, manliness, vigor; game, pluck; resoluteness &c. (courage) 861; zeal &c. 682; aplomb; desperation; devotion, devotedness. mastery over self; self control, self command, self possession, self reliance, self government, self restraint, self conquest, self denial; moral courage, moral strength; perseverance &c. 604a; tenacity; obstinacy &c. 606; bulldog; British lion. V. have determination &c. n.; know one's own mind; be resolved &c. adj.; make up one's mind, will, resolve, determine; decide &c. (judgment) 480; form a determination, come to a determination, come to a resolution, come to a resolve; conclude, fix, seal, determine once for all, bring to a crisis, drive matters to an extremity; take a decisive step &c. (choice) 609; take upon oneself &c. (undertake) 676.

devote oneself to, give oneself up to; throw away the scabbard, kick down the ladder, nail one's colors to the mast, set one's back against the wall, set one's teeth, put one's foot down, take one's stand; stand firm &c. (stability) 150; steel oneself; stand no nonsense, not listen to the voice of the charmer. buckle to; buckle oneself put one's shoulder to the wheel, lay one's shoulder to the wheel, set one's shoulder to the wheel; put one's heart into; run the gauntlet, make a dash at, take the bull by the horns; rush in medias res, plunge in medias res; go in for; insist upon, make a point of; set one's heart upon, set one's mind upon. stick at nothing, stop at nothing; make short work of &c. (activity) 682; not stick at trifles; go all lengths, go the limit *, go the whole hog; persist &c. (persevere) 604a; go through fire and water, ride the tiger, ride in the whirlwind and direct the storm. Adj. resolved &c. v.; determined; strong-willed, strong-minded; resolute &c. (brave) 861; self-possessed; decided, definitive, peremptory, tranchant[obs3]; unhesitating, unflinching, unshrinking[obs3]; firm, iron, gritty [U.S.], indomitable, game to the backbone; inexorable, relentless, not to be shaken, not to be put down; tenax propositi[Lat]; inflexible &c. (hard) 323; obstinate &c. 606; steady &c. (persevering) 604a. earnest, serious; set upon, bent upon, intent upon. steel against, proof against; in utrumque paratus[Lat]. Adv. resolutely &c. adj.; in earnest, in good earnest; seriously, joking apart, earnestly, heart and soul; on one's mettle; manfully, like a man, with a high hand; with a strong hand &c. (exertion) 686. at any rate, at any risk, at any hazard at any price, at any cost, at any sacrifice; at all hazards, at all risks, at all events; a bis ou a blanc[Fr] [obs3]; cost what it may; coute[Fr]; a tort et a travers[obs3]; once for all; neck or nothing; rain or shine. Phr. spes sibi quisque[Lat]; celui qui veut celui-la peut[Fr]; chi non s'arrischia non guadagna[Fr][obs3]; frangas non flectes[Lat]; manu forti[Lat]; tentanda via est[Lat].

#604a. Perseverance. — N. perseverance; continuance &c. (inaction) 143; permanence &c. (absence of change) 141; firmness &c. (stability) 150. constancy, steadiness; singleness of purpose, tenacity of purpose; persistence, plodding, patience; sedulity &c. (industry) 682; pertinacyl, pertinacity, pertinaciousness; iteration &c. 104 bottom, game, pluck, stamina, backbone, grit; indefatigability, indefatigableness; bulldog courage. V. persevere, persist; hold on, hold out; die in the last ditch, be in at the death; stick to, cling to, adhere to; stick to one's text, keep on; keep to one's course, keep to one's ground, maintain one's course, maintain one's ground; go all lengths, go through fire and water; bear up, keep up, hold up; plod; stick to work &c. (work) 686; continue &c. 143; follow up; die in harness, die at one's post. Adj. persevering, constant; steady, steadfast; undeviating, unwavering, unfaltering, unswerving, unflinching, unsleeping[obs3], unflagging, undrooping[obs3]; steady as time; unrelenting, unintermitting[obs3], unremitting; plodding; industrious &c. 682; strenuous &c. 686; pertinacious; persisting, persistent. solid, sturdy, staunch, stanch, true to oneself; unchangeable &c. 150; unconquerable &c. (strong) 159; indomitable, game to the last, indefatigable, untiring, unwearied, never tiring. Adv. through evil report and good report, through thick and thin, through fire and water; per fas et nefas[Lat]; without fail, sink or swim, at any price, vogue la galere[Fr].. Phr. never say die; give it the old college try; vestigia nulla retrorsum[Lat]; aut vincer aut mori[Lat]; la garde meurt et ne se rend pas[Fr]; tout vient a temps pour qui sait attendre[Fr].

<— p. 186 —>

#605. Irresolution. — N. irresolution, infirmity of purpose, indecision; indetermination, undeterminationl!; unsettlement; uncertainty &c. 475; demur, suspense; hesitating &c. v., hesitation, hesitancy; vacillation; changeableness &c. 149; fluctuation; alternation &c. (oscillation) 314; caprice &c. 608. fickleness, levity, legerete[Fr]; pliancy &c. (softness) 324; weakness; timidity &c. 860; cowardice &c. 862; half measures. waverer, ass between two bundles of hay; shuttlecock, butterfly, wimp; doughface [obs3][U. S.]. V. be irresolute &c. adj.; hang in suspense, keep in suspense; leave "ad referendum"; think twice about, pause; dawdle &c. (inactivity) 683; remain neuter; dillydally, hesitate, boggle, hover, dacker[obs3], hum and haw, demur, not know one's own mind; debate, balance; dally with, coquet with; will and will not, chaser-balancer[obs3]; go halfway, compromise, make a compromise; be thrown off one's balance, stagger like a drunken man; be afraid &c. 860; "let 'I dare not' wait upon 'I would'" [Macbeth]; falter, waver vacillate &c. 149; change &c. 140; retract &c. 607; fluctuate; pendulate[obs3]; alternate &c. (oscillate) 314; keep off and on, play fast and loose; blow hot and cold &c. (caprice) 608. shuffle, palter, blink; trim. Adj. irresolute, infirm of purpose, double-minded, half-hearted; undecided, unresolved, undetermined; shilly-shally; fidgety, tremulous; hesitating &c. v.; off one's balance; at a loss &c. (uncertain) 475. vacillating &c. v.; unsteady &c. (changeable) 149; unsteadfast[obs3], fickle, without ballast; capricious &c. 608; volatile, frothy; light, lightsome, light-minded; giddy; fast and loose. weak, feeble-minded, frail; timid, wimpish, wimpy &c. 860; cowardly &c. 862; dough-faced [U.S.]; facile; pliant &c. (soft) 324; unable to say "no", easy-going, revocable, reversible. Adv. irresolutely &c. adj.; irresolved[obs3], irresolvedly[obs3]; in faltering accents; off and on; from pillar to post; seesaw &c. 314. Int. "how happy could I be with either!" [Gay].

#606. Obstinacy. — N. obstinateness &c. adj.; obstinacy, tenacity; cussedness [U. S.]; perseverance &c. 604a; immovability; old school; inflexibility &c. (hardness) 323; obduracy, obduration[obs3]; dogged resolution; resolution

&c. 604; ruling passion; blind side. self-will, contumacy, perversity; pervicacyl, pervicacity[obs3]; indocility[obs3]. bigotry, intolerance, dogmatism; opiniatryl, opiniativeness; fixed idea &c. (prejudgment) 481; fanaticism, zealotry, infatuation, monomania; opinionatedness opinionativeness[obs3]. mule; opinionistl, opinionatist[obs3], opiniatorl, opinatorl; stickler, dogmatist; bigot; zealot, enthusiast, fanatic. V. be obstinate &c. adj.; stickle, take no denial, fly in the face of facts; opinionate, be wedded to an opinion, hug a belief; have one's own way &c. (will) 600; persist &c. (persevere) 604a; have the last word, insist on having the last word. die hard, fight against destiny, not yield an inch, stand out. Adj. obstinate, tenacious, stubborn, obdurate, casehardened; inflexible &c. (hard) 323; balky; immovable, unshakable, not to be moved; inert &c. 172; unchangeable &c. 150; inexorable &c. (determined) 604; mulish, obstinate as a mule, pig-headed. dogged; sullen, sulky; unmoved, uninfluenced, unaffected. willful, self-willed, perverse; resty[obs3], restive, restiffl; pervicacious[obs3], wayward, refractory, unruly; heady, headstrong; entete[Fr]; contumacious; crossgrained[obs3]. arbitrary, dogmatic, positive, bigoted; prejudiced &c. 481; creed- bound; prepossessed, infatuated; stiff-backed, stiff necked, stiff hearted; hard-mouthed, hidebound; unyielding; impervious, impracticable, inpersuasible[obs3]; unpersuadable; intractable, untractable[obs3]; incorrigible, deaf to advice, impervious to reason; crotchety &c. 608. Adv. obstinately &c. adj. Phr. non possumus[Lat]; no surrender; ils n'ont rien appris ne rien oublie[Fr].

<— p. 187 —>

#607. Tergiversation. — N. change of mind, change of intention, change of purpose; afterthought. tergiversation, recantation; palinode, palinody[obs3]; renunciation; abjuration,abjurement[obs3]; defection &c. (relinquishment) 624; going over &c. v.; apostasy; retraction, retractation[obs3]; withdrawal; disavowal &c. (negation) 536; revocation, revokement[obs3]; reversal; repentance &c. 950- redintegratio amoris[Lat]. coquetry; vacillation &c. 605; backsliding; volte-face[Fr]. turn coat, turn tippetl; rat, apostate, renegade; convert, pervert; proselyte, deserter; backslider; blackleg, crawfish [U. S.], scab*, mugwump [U. S.], recidivist. time server, time pleaser[obs3]; timistl, Vicar of Bray, trimmer, ambidexter[obs3]; weathercock &c. (changeable) 149; Janus. V. change one's mind, change one's intention, change one's purpose, change one's note; abjure, renounce; withdraw from &c. (relinquish) 624; waver, vacillate; wheel round, turn round, veer round; turn a pirouette; go over from one side to another, pass from one side to another, change from one side to another, skip from one side to another; go to the rightabout; box the compass, shift one's ground, go upon another tack. apostatize, change sides, go over, rat; recant, retract; revoke; rescind &c. (abrogate) 756; recall; forswear, unsay; come over, come round to an opinion; crawfish *[U. S.], crawl* [U. S.]. draw in one's horns, eat one's words; eat the leek, swallow the leek; swerve, flinch, back out of, retrace one's steps, think better of it; come back return to one's first love; turn over a new leaf &c. (repent) 950. trim, shuffle, play fast and loose, blow hot and cold, coquet, be on the fence, straddle, bold with the hare but run with the hounds; nager entre deux eaux[Fr]; wait to see how the cat jumps, wait to see how the wind blows. Adj. changeful &c. 149; irresolute &c. 605; ductile, slippery as an eel, trimming, ambidextrous, timeserving[obs3]; coquetting &c. v. revocatory[obs3], reactionary. Phr. "a change came o'er the spirit of my dream" [Byron].

#608. Caprice. — N. caprice, fancy, humor; whim, whimsy, whimsey[obs3], whimwham[obs3]; crotchet, capriccio, quirk, freak, maggot, fad, vagary, prank, fit, flimflam, escapade, boutade[Fr], wild-goose chase; capriciousness &c. adj.; kink. V. be capricious &c. adj.; have a maggot in the brain; take it into one's head, strain at a gnat and swallow a camel; blow hot and cold; play fast and loose, play fantastic tricks; tourner casaque[Fr]. Adj. capricious; erratic, eccentric, fitful, hysterical; full of whims &c. n.; maggoty; inconsistent, fanciful, fantastic, whimsical, crotchety, kinky [U. S.], particular, humorsome[obs3], freakish, skittish, wanton, wayward; contrary; captious; arbitrary; unconformable &c. 83; penny wise and pound foolish; fickle &c. (irresolute) 605; frivolous, sleeveless, giddy, volatile. Adv. by fits and starts, without rhyme or reason. Phr. nil fuit unquain sic inipar sibi[Lat]; the deuce is in him.

<— p. 188 —>

#609. Choice. — N. choice, option; discretion &c. (volition) 600; preoption[obs3]; alternative; dilemma, embarras de choix[Fr]; adoption, cooptation[obs3]; novation[obs3]; decision &c. (judgment) 480. election; political election (politics) 737a. selection, excerption, gleaning, eclecticism; excerpta[obs3], gleanings, cuttings, scissors and paste; pick &c. (best) 650. preference, prelation[obs3], opinion poll, survey; predilection &c. (desire) 865. V. offers one's choice, set before; hold out the alternative, present the alternative, offer the alternative; put to the vote. use option, use discretion, exercise option, exercise discretion, one's option; adopt, take up, embrace, espouse; choose, elect, opt for; take one's choice, make one's choice; make choice of, fix upon. vote, poll, hold up one's hand; divide. settle; decide &c. (adjudge) 480; list &c. (will) 600; make up one's mind &c. (resolve) 604. select; pick and choose; pick out, single out; cull, glean, winnow; sift the chaff from the wheat, separate the chaff from the wheat, winnow the chaff from the wheat; pick up, pitch upon; pick one's way; indulge one's fancy. set apart, mark out for; mark &c. 550.

prefer; have rather, have as lief; fancy &c. (desire) 865; be persuaded &c. 615. take a decided step, take a decisive step; commit oneself to a course; pass the Rubicon, cross the Rubicon; cast in one's lot with; take for better or for worse. Adj. optional; discretional &c. (voluntary) 600. eclectic; choosing &c. v.; preferential; chosen &c. v.; choice &c. (good) 648. Adv. optionally &c. adj.; at pleasure &c. (will) 600; either the one or the other; or at the option of; whether or not; once and for all; for one's money. by choice, by preference; in preference; rather, before.

#609a. Absence of Choice. — N. no choice, Hobson's choice; first come first served, random selection; necessity &c. 601; not a pin to choose &c. (equality) 27; any, the first that comes; that or nothing.

neutrality, indifference; indecision &c. (irresolution) 605; arbitrariness.

coercion (compulsion) 744.

V. be neutral &c. adj.; have no choice, have no election; waive, not vote; abstain from voting, refrain from voting; leave undecided; "make a virtue of necessity" [Two Gentlemen].

Adj. neutral, neuter; indifferent, uninterested; undecided &c. (irresolute) 605.

Adv. either &c. (choice) 609.

Phr. who cares? what difference does it make? "There's not a dime's worth of difference between them." [George Wallace].

#610. Rejection. — N. rejection, repudiation, exclusion; refusal &c. 764; declination V. reject; set aside, lay aside; give up; decline &c. (refuse) 764; exclude, except; pluck, spin; cast. repudiate, scout, set at naught; fling to the winds, fling to the dogs, fling overboard, fling away, cast to the winds, cast to the dogs, cast overboard, cast away, throw to the winds, throw to the dogs, throw overboard, throw away, toss to the winds, toss to the dogs, toss overboard, toss away; send to the right about; disclaim &c. (deny) 536; discard &c. (eject) 297, (have done with) 678. Adj. rejected &c. v.; reject, rejectaneousl, rejectiousl; not chosen &c. 609, to be thought of, out of the question Adv. neither, neither the one nor the other; no &c 536. Phr. non haec in faedera[Lat].

#611. Predetermination. — N. predestination, preordination, premeditation, predeliberation[obs3], predetermination; foregone conclusion, fait accompli[Fr]; parti pris[Fr]; resolve, propendencyl; intention &c. 620; project &c. 626; fate, foredoom, necessity. V. predestine, preordain, predetermine, premeditate, resolve, concert; resolve beforehand, predesignate. Adj. prepense[obs3], premeditated &c. v., predesignated, predesigned[obs3]; advised, studied, designed, calculated; aforethought; intended &c. 620; foregone. well-laid, well-devised, well-weighed; maturely considered; cunning. Adv. advisedly &c. adj.; with premeditation, deliberately, all things considered, with eyes open, in cold blood; intentionally &c. 620.

#612. Impulse. — N. impulse, sudden thought; impromptu, improvisation; inspiration, flash, spurt. improvisatore[obs3]; creature of impulse. V. flash on the mind. say what comes uppermost; improvise, extemporize. Adj. extemporaneous, impulsive, indeliberate[obs3]; snap; improvised, improvisate[obs3], improvisatory[obs3]; unpremeditated, unmeditated; improvise; unprompted, unguided; natural, unguarded; spontaneous &c. (voluntary) 600; instinctive &c. 601. Adv. extempore, extemporaneously; offhand, impromptu, a limproviste[Fr]; improviso[obs3]; on the spur of the moment, on the spur of the occasion.

<— p. 189 —>

#613. Habit. [includes commonness due to frequency of occurrence] — N. habit, habitude; assuetudel, assuefactionl, wont; run, way. common state of things, general state of things, natural state of things, ordinary state of things, ordinary course of things, ordinary run of things; matter of course; beaten path, beaten track, beaten ground. prescription, custom, use, usage, immemorial usage, practice; prevalence, observance; conventionalism, conventionality; mode, fashion, vogue; etiquette &c. (gentility) 852; order of the day, cry; conformity &c. 82; consuetude,. dustoor[obs3]. one's old way, old school, veteris vestigia flammae[Lat]; laudator temporis acti[Lat]. rule, standing order, precedent, routine; red-tape, red-tapism[obs3]; pipe clay; rut, groove. cacoethes[Lat]; bad habit, confirmed habit, inveterate habit, intrinsic habit &c.; addiction, trick. training &c. (education) 537; seasoning, second nature, acclimatization; knack &c. V. be wont &c. adj. fall into a rut, fall into a custom &c. (conform to) 82; tread the beaten track, follow the beaten track, tread the beaten path, follow the beaten; stare super antiquas vias[Lat][obs3]; move in a rut, run on in a groove, go round like a horse in a mill, go on in the old jog trot way. habituate, inure, harden, season, caseharden; accustom, familiarize; naturalize, acclimatize; keep one's hand in; train &c. (educate) 537. get into the way, get into the knack of; learn &c. 539; cling to, adhere to; repeat &c. 104; acquire a habit, contract a habit, fall into a habit, acquire a trick, contract a trick, fall into a trick; addict oneself to, take to, get into. be habitual &c. adj.; prevail; come into use, become a habit, take root; gain upon one, grow upon one. Adj. habitual; accustomary[obs3]; prescriptive, accustomed &c. v.; of daily occurrence, of everyday occurrence; consuetudinary[obs3]; wonted, usual, general, ordinary, common, frequent, everyday, household, garden variety, jog, trot; well-trodden, well-known; familiar, vernacular, trite, commonplace, conventional, regular, set, stock, established, stereotyped; prevailing, prevalent; current, received, acknowledged, recognized, accredited; of course, admitted, understood. conformable. &c. 82; according to use, according to custom, according to routine; in vogue, in fashion, in, with it; fashionable &c. (genteel) 852. wont; used to, given to, addicted to, attuned to, habituated &c. v.; in the habit of; habitue; at home in &c. (skillful) 698; seasoned; imbued with; devoted to, wedded to. hackneyed, fixed, rooted, deep-rooted, ingrafted[obs3], permanent, inveterate, besetting; naturalized; ingrained &c. (intrinsic) 5. Adv. habitually &c. adj.; always &c. (uniformly) 16. as usual, as is one's wont, as things go, as the world goes, as the sparks fly upwards; more suo, more solito[Lat]; ex more. as a rule, for the most part; usually, generally, typically &c. adj.; most often, most frequently. Phr. cela s'entend[Fr]; abeunt studia in mores[Lat]; adeo in teneris consuescere multum est[Lat]; consuetudo quasi altera natura [Lat][Cicero]; hoc erat in more majorum[Lat]; "How use doth breed a habit in a man!" [Two Gentlemen]; magna est vis consuetudinis[Lat]; morent fecerat usus [Lat][Ovid].

#614. Desuetude. — N. desuetude, disusage[obs3]; obsolescence, disuse &c. 678; want of habit, want of practice; inusitation[obs3]; newness to; new brooms. infraction of usage &c. (unconformity) 83; nonprevalence[obs3]; "a custom more honored in the breach than the observance" [Hamlet]. V. be -unaccustomed &c. adj.; leave off a habit, cast off a habit, break off a habit, wean oneself of a habit, violate a habit, break through a habit, infringe a habit, leave off a custom, cast off a custom, break off a custom, wean oneself of a custom, violate a custom, break through a custom, infringe a custom, leave off a usage, cast off a usage, break off a usage, wean oneself of a usage, violate a usage, break through a usage, infringe a usage; disuse &c. 678; wear off. Adj. unaccustomed, unused, unwonted, unseasoned, uninured[obs3], unhabituated[obs3], untrained; new; green &c. (unskilled) 699; unhackneyed. unusual &c. (unconformable) 83; nonobservant[obs3]; disused &c. 678.

<— p. 190 —> % 2. Causes of Volition %

#615. Motive. — N. motive, springs of action, wellsprings of action. reason, ground, call, principle; by end, by purpose; mainspring, primum mobile[Lat], keystone; the why and the wherefore; pro and con, reason why; secret motive, arriere pensee[Fr]; intention &c. 620. inducement, consideration; attraction; loadstone; magnet, magnetism, magnetic force; allectationl, allectivel; temptation, enticement, agacerie[obs3], allurement, witchery; bewitchment, bewitchery; charm; spell &c. 993; fascination, blandishment, cajolery; seduction, seducement; honeyed words, voice of the tempter, song of the Sirens forbidden fruit, golden apple. persuasibility[obs3], persuasibleness[obs3]; attractability[obs3]; impressibility, susceptibility; softness; persuasiveness, attractiveness; tantalization[obs3]. influence, prompting, dictate, instance; impulse, impulsion; incitement, incitation; press, instigation; provocation &c. (excitation of feeling) 824; inspiration; persuasion, suasion; encouragement, advocacy; exhortation; advice &c. 695; solicitation &c. (request) 765; lobbyism; pull*. incentive, stimulus, spur, fillip, whip, goad, ankus[obs3], rowel, provocative, whet, dram. bribe, lure; decoy, decoy duck; bait, trail of a red herring; bribery and corruption; sop, sop for Cerberus. prompter, tempter; seducer, seductor[obs3]; instigator, firebrand, incendiary; Siren, Circe; agent provocateur; lobbyist. V. induce, move; draw, draw on; bring in its train, give an impulse &c. n.; to; inspire; put up to, prompt, call up; attract, beckon. stimulate &c. (excite) 824; spirit up, inspirit; rouse, arouse; animate, incite, foment, provoke, instigate, set on, actuate; act upon, work upon, operate upon; encourage; pat on the back, pat on the shoulder, clap on the back, clap on the shoulder. influence, weigh with, bias, sway, incline, dispose, predispose, turn the scale, inoculate; lead by the nose; have influence with, have influence over, have influence upon, exercise influence with, exercise influence over, exercise influence upon; go round, come round one; turn the head, magnetize; lobby. persuade; prevail with, prevail upon; overcome, carry; bring round to one's senses, bring to one's senses; draw over, win over, gain over, come over, talk over; procure, enlist, engage; invite, court. tempt, seduce, overpersuade[obs3], entice, allure, captivate, fascinate, bewitch, carry away, charm, conciliate, wheedle, coax, lure; inveigle; tantalize; cajole &c. (deceive) 545. tamper with, bribe, suborn, grease the palm, bait with a silver hook, gild the pill, make things pleasant, put a sop into the pan, throw a sop to, bait the hook. enforce, force; impel &c. (push) 276; propel &c. 284; whip, lash, goad, spur, prick, urge; egg on, hound, hurry on; drag &c. 285; exhort; advise &c. 695; call upon &c. press &c. (request) 765; advocate. set an example, set the fashion; keep in countenance. be persuaded &c.; yield to temptation, come round; concede &c. (consent) 762; obey a call; follow advice, follow the bent,.follow the dictates of; act on principle. Adj. impulsive, motive; suasive, suasory[obs3], persuasive, persuasory[obs3], hortative, hortatory; protrepticall; inviting, tempting, &c. v.; suasive, suasory[obs3]; seductive, attractive; fascinating &c. (pleasing) 829; provocative &c. (exciting) 824. induced &c. v.; disposed; persuadable &c. (docile) 602; spellbound; instinct with, smitten with, infatuated; inspired &c. v.; by. Adv. because, therefore &c.

(cause) 155; from this motive, from that motive; for this reason, for that reason; for; by reason of, for the sake of, count of; out of, from, as, forasmuch as. for all the world; on principle. Phr. fax mentis incendium gloriae[Lat]; "temptation hath a music for all ears" "to beguile many and be beguiled by one" [Willis][Othello].

#615a. Absence of Motive. — N. absence of motive, aimlessness; caprice &c. 608; chance &c. (absence of design) 621.
V. have no motive; scruple &c. (be unwilling) 603.
Adj. without rhyme or reason; aimless, capricious, whimsical &c. (chance) 621.
Adv. out of mere caprice.

<— p. 191 —>

#616. Dissuasion. — N. dissuasion, dehortation[obs3], expostulation, remonstrance; deprecation &c. 766. discouragement, damper, wet blanket; disillusionment, disenchantment. cohibition &c. (restraint) 751[obs3]; curb &c. (means of restraint) 752; check &c. (hindrance) 706. reluctance &c. (unwillingness) 603; contraindication. V. dissuade, dehort[obs3], cry out against, remonstrate, expostulate, warn, contraindicate. disincline, indispose, shake, stagger; dispirit; discourage, dishearten; deter; repress, hold back, keep back &c. (restrain) 751; render averse &c. 603; repel; turn aside &c. (deviation) 279; wean from; act as a drag &c. (hinder) 706; throw cold water on, damp, cool, chill, blunt, calm, quiet, quench; deprecate &c. 766. disenchant, disillusion, deflate, take down a peg, pop one's balloon, prick one's balloon, burst one's bubble; disabuse (correction) 527a. Adj. dissuading &c. v.; dissuasive; dehortatory[obs3], expostulatory[obs3]; monitivel, monitory. dissuaded &c. v.; admonitory; uninduced &c. (induce &c. 615); unpersuadable &c. (obstinate) 606; averse &c. (unwilling) 603; repugnant &c. (dislike) 867. repressed.

#617. [Ostensible motive, ground, or reason assigned.] Pretext. — N. pretext, pretense, pretension, pleal; allegation, advocation; ostensible motive, ostensible ground, ostensible reason, phony reason; excuse &c. (vindication) 937; subterfuge; color; gloss, guise, cover. loop hole, starting hole; how to creep out of, salvo, come off; way of escape. handle, peg to hang on, room locus standi[Lat]; stalking-horse, cheval de bataille[Fr], cue. pretense &c. (untruth) 546; put off, dust thrown in the eyes; blind; moonshine; mere pretext, shallow pretext; lame excuse, lame apology; tub to a whale; false plea, sour grapes; makeshift, shift, white lie; special pleading &c. (sophistry) 477; soft sawder &c. (flattery) 933[obs3]. V. pretend, plead, allege; shelter oneself under the plea of; excuse &c. (vindicate) 937; lend a color to; furnish a handle &c. n.; make a pretext of, make a handle of; use as a plea &c. n.; take one's stand upon, make capital out of, pretend &c. (lie) 544. Adj. ostensibly &c. (manifest) 525; alleged, apologetic; pretended &c. 545. Adv. ostensibly; under color; under the plea, under the pretense of, under the guise of.

% 3. Objects of Volition %

#618. Good. — N. good, benefit, advantage; improvement &c. 658; greatest good, supreme good; interest, service, behoof, behalf; weal; main chance, summum bonum[Lat], common weal; "consummation devoutly to be wished"; gain, boot; profit, harvest. boon &c. (gift) 784; good turn; blessing; world of good; piece of good luck[Fr], piece of good fortune[Fr]; nuts, prize, windfall, godsend, waif, treasure-trove. good fortune &c. (prosperity) 734; happiness &c. 827. [Source of good] goodness &c. 648; utility &c. 644; remedy &c. 662; pleasure giving &c. 829. Adj. commendable &c. 931; useful &c. 644; good &c., beneficial &c. 648. Adv. well, aright, satisfactorily, favorably, not amis[Fr]; all for the best; to one's advantage &c. n.; in one's favor, in one's interest &c. n. Phr. so far so good; magnum bonum[Lat].

#619. Evil. — N. evil, ill, harm, hurt., mischief, nuisance; machinations of the devil, Pandora's box, ills that flesh is heir to.
blow, buffet, stroke, scratch, bruise, wound, gash, mutilation; mortal blow, wound; immedicabile vulnus[Lat]; damage, loss &c. (deterioration) 659.
disadvantage, prejudice, drawback.
disaster, accident, casualty; mishap &c. (misfortune) 735; bad job, devil to pay; calamity, bale, catastrophe, tragedy; ruin &c. (destruction) 162; adversity &c. 735.
mental suffering &c. 828. * demon &v[Evil spirit]. 980. bane &c. 663[Cause of evil]. badness &c. 649[Production of evil]; painfulness &c. 830; evil doer &c. 913.
outrage, wrong, injury, foul play; bad turn, ill turn; disservice,

spoliation &c. 791; grievance, crying evil.

    V. be in trouble &c. (adversity) 735.

    Adj. disastrous, bad &c. 649; awry, out of joint; disadvantageous.

    Adv. amis[Fr], wrong, ill, to one's cost

    Phr. "moving accidents by flood and field" [Othello].

<— p. 192 —> % Section II. Prospective Volition 1. Conceptional Volition %

#620. Intention. — N. intent, intention, intentionality; purpose; quo animo[Lat]; project &c. 626; undertaking &c. 676; predetermination &c. 611; design, ambition. contemplation, mind, animus, view, purview, proposal; study; look out. final cause; raison d'etre[Fr]; cui bono[Lat]; object, aim, end; "the be all and the end all"; drift &c. (meaning) 516; tendency &c. 176; destination, mark, point, butt, goal, target, bull's-eye, quintain[obs3][medeival]; prey, quarry, game. decision, determination, resolve; fixed set purpose, settled purpose; ultimatum; resolution &c. 604; wish &c. 865; arriere pensee[Fr]; motive &c. 615. [Study of final causes] teleology. V. intend, purpose, design, mean; have to; propose to oneself; harbor a design; have in view, have in contemplation, have in one's eye, have in- petto; have an eye to. bid for, labor for; be after, aspire after, endeavor after; be at, aim at, drive at, point at, level at, aspire at; take aim; set before oneself; study to. take upon oneself &c. (undertake) 676; take into one's head; meditate, contemplate of, think of, dream of, talk of; premeditate &c. 611; compass, calculate; destine, destinate[obs3]; propose. project &c. (plan) 626; have a mind to &c. (be willing) 602; desire &c. 865; pursue &c. 622. Adj. intended &c. v.; intentional, advised, express, determinate; prepense &c. 611[obs3]; bound for; intending &c. v.; minded; bent upon &c. (earnest) 604; at stake; on the anvil, on the tapis[obs3]; in view, in prospect, in the breast of; in petto; teleological Adv. intentionally &c. adj.; advisedly, wittingly, knowingly, designedly, purposely, on purpose, by design, studiously, pointedly; with intent &c. n.; deliberately &c. (with premeditation) 611; with one's eyes open, in cold blood. for; with a view, with an eye to; in order to, in order that; to the end that, with the intent that; for the purpose of, with the view of, in contemplation of, on account of. in pursuance of, pursuant to; quo animo[Lat]; to all intents and purposes. Phr. "The road to hell is paved with good intentions" [Johnson]; sublimi feriam sidera vertice [Lat][Horace].

<— p. 193 —>

#621. [Absence of purpose in the succession of events] Chance. 2 — N. chance &c. 156; lot, fate &c. (necessity) 601; luck; good luck &c. (good) 618; mascot. speculation, venture, stake, game of chance; mere shot, random shot; blind bargain, leap in the dark; pig in a poke &c. (uncertainty) 475; fluke, potluck; faro bank; flyer*; limit. uncertainty; uncertainty principle, Heisenberg's uncertainty principle. drawing lots; sortilegy[obs3], sortitionl; sortes[obs3], sortes Virgilianae[obs3]; rouge et noir[Fr], hazard, ante, chuck-a-luck, crack-loo [obs3][U.S.], craps, faro, roulette, pitch and toss, chuck, farthing, cup tossing, heads or tails cross and pile, poker-dice; wager; bet, betting; gambling; the turf. gaming house, gambling house, betting house; bucket shop; gambling joint; totalizator, totalizer; hell; betting ring; dice, dice box. [person who takes chances] gambler, gamester; man of the turf; adventurer; dicerl!. V. chance &c. (hap) 156; stand a chance &c. (be possible) 470. toss up; cast lots, draw lots; leave to chance, trust to chance, leave to the chapter of accidents, trust to the chapter of accidents; tempt fortune; chance it, take one's chance, take a shot at it (attempt) 675; run the risk, run the chance, incur the risk, incur the chance, encounter the risk, encounter the chance; stand the hazard of the die. speculate, try one's luck, set on a cast, raffle, put into a lottery, buy a pig in a poke, shuffle the cards. risk, venture, hazard, stake; ante; lay, lay a wager; make a bet, wager, bet, gamble, game, play for; play at chuck farthing. Adj. fortuitous &c. 156; unintentional, unintended; accidental; not meant; undesigned, purposed; unpremeditated &c. 612; unforeseen, uncontemplated, never thought of. random, indiscriminate, promiscuous; undirected; aimless, driftless[obs3], designless[obs3], purposeless, causeless; without purpose. possible &c. 470. unforeseeable, unpredictable, chancy, risky, speculative, dicey. Adv. randomly, by chance, fortuitously; unpredictably, unforeseeably; casually &c. 156; unintentionally &c. adj.; unwittingly. en passant[Fr], by the way, incidentally; as it may happen; at random, at a venture, at haphazard. Phr. acierta errando[Lat]; dextro tempore[Lat]; "fearful concatenation of circumstances" [D. Webster]; "fortuitous combination of circumstances" [Dickens]; le jeu est le fils d'avarice et le pere du desespoir[Fr]; "the happy combination of fortuitous circumstances" [Scott]; "the fortuitous or casual concourse of atoms" [Bentley]; "God does not play dice with the universe" [A. Einstein].

#622. [Purpose in action.] Pursuit — N. pursuit; pursuing &c. v.; prosecution; pursuance; enterprise &c. (undertaking) 676; business &c. 625; adventure &c. (essay) 675; quest &c. (search) 461; scramble, hue and cry, game; hobby; still-hunt. chase, hunt, battue[obs3], race, steeple chase, hunting, coursing, venation, venery; fox chase; sport, sporting; shooting, angling, fishing, hawking; shikar[Geogloc:India]. pursuer; hunter, huntsman; shikari[Geogloc:India], sportsman, Nimrod; hound &c. 366. V. pursue, prosecute, follow; run after, make after, be after, hunt after, prowl after; shadow; carry on &c. (do) 680; engage in &c. (undertake) 676; set about &c. (begin) 66; endeavor &c. 675; court &c. (request) 765 seek &c. (search) 461; aim at &c. (intention) 620; follow the trail &c. (trace) 461; fish for &c.

(experiment) 463; press on &c. (haste) 684; run a race &c. (velocity) 274. chase, give chase, course, dog, hunt, hound; tread on the heels, follow on the heels of, &c. (sequence) 281. rush upon; rush headlong &c. (violence) 173 ride full tilt at, run full tilt at; make a leap at, jump at, snatch at run down; start game. tread a path; take a course, hold- a course; shape one's steps, direct one's steps, bend one's steps, course; play a game; fight one's way, elbow one's way; follow up; take to, take up; go in for; ride one's hobby. Adj. pursuing &c. v.; in quest of &c. (inquiry) 461 in pursuit, in full cry, in hot pursuit; on the scent. Adv. in pursuance of &c. (intention) 620; after. Int. tallyho! yoicks! soho[obs3]!

#623. [Absence of pursuit.] Avoidance. — N. abstention, abstinence; for bearance[obs3]; refraining &c. v.; inaction &c. 681; neutrality. avoidance, evasion, elusion; seclusion &c. 893. avolationl, flight; escape &c. 671; retreat &c. 287; recoil &c. 277; departure &c. 293; rejection &c. 610. shirker &c. v.; truant; fugitive, refugee; runaway, runagate; maroon. V. abstain, refrain, spare, not attempt; not do &c. 681; maintain the even tenor of one's way. eschew, keep from, let alone, have nothing to do with; keep aloof keep off, stand aloof, stand off, hold aloof, hold off; take no part in, have no hand in. avoid, shun; steer clear of, keep clear of; fight shy of; keep one's distance, keep at a respectful distance; keep out of the way, get out of the way; evade, elude, turn away from; set one's face against &c. (oppose) 708; deny oneself. shrink back; hang back, hold back, draw back; recoil &c. 277; retire &c. (recede) 287; flinch, blink, blench, shy, shirk, dodge, parry, make way for, give place to. beat a retreat; turn tail, turn one's back; take to one's heels; runaway, run for one's life; cut and run; be off like a shot; fly, flee; fly away, flee away, run away from; take flight, take to flight; desert, elope; make off, scamper off, sneak off, shuffle off, sheer off; break away, tear oneself away, slip away, slink away, steel away, make away from, scamper away from, sneak away from, shuffle away from, sheer away from; slip cable, part company, turn one's heel; sneak out of, play truant, give one the go by, give leg bail, take French leave, slope, decamp, flit, bolt, abscond, levant, skedaddle, absquatulate [obs3][U.S.], cut one's stick, walk one's chalks, show a light pair of heels, make oneself scarce; escape &c. 671; go away &c. (depart) 293; abandon &c. 624; reject &c. 610. lead one a dance, lead one a pretty dance; throw off the scent, play at hide and seek. Adj. unsought, unattempted; avoiding &c. v.; neutral, shy of &c. (unwilling) 603; elusive, evasive, fugitive, runaway; shy, wild. Adj. lest, in order to avoid. Int. forbear! keep off, hands off! sauve qui peut[Fr]! [French: every man for himself]; devil take the hindmost! Phr. "things unattempted yet in prose or rhyme" [Paradise Lost].

<— p. 194 —>

#624. Relinquishment. — N. relinquishment, abandonment; desertion, defection, secession, withdrawal; cave of Adullam[obs3]; nolle prosequi[Lat]. discontinuance &c. (cessation) 142; renunciation &c. (recantation) 607; abrogation &c. 756; resignation &c. (retirement) 757; desuetude &c. 614; cession &c. (of property) 782. V. relinquish, give up, abandon, desert, forsake, leave in the lurch; go back on; depart from, secede from, withdraw from; back out of; leave, quit, take leave of, bid a long farewell; vacate &c. (resign) 757. renounce &c (abjure) 607; forego, have done with, drop; disuse &c. 678; discard &c. 782; wash one's hands of; drop all idea of. break off, leave off; desist; stop &c. (cease) 142; hold one's hand, stay one's hand; quit one's hold; give over, shut up shop. throw up the game, throw up the cards; give up the point, give up the argument; pass to the order of the day, move to the previous question. Adj. unpursued[obs3]; relinquished &c. v.; relinquishing &c. v. Int. avast! &c. (stop) 142. Phr. aufgeschoben ist nicht aufgehoben[Ger]; entbehre gern was du nicht hast[Ger].

#625. Business. — N. business, occupation, employment; pursuit &c. 622; what one is doing, what one is about; affair, concern, matter, case. matter in hand, irons in the fire; thing to do, agendum, task, work, job, chore [U.S.], errand, commission, mission, charge, care; duty &c. 926. part, role, cue; province, function, lookout, department, capacity, sphere, orb, field, line; walk, walk of life; beat, round, routine; race, career. office, place, post, chargeship[obs3], incumbency, living; situation, berth, employ; service &c. (servitude) 749; engagement; undertaking &c. 676. vocation, calling, profession, cloth, faculty; industry, art; industrial arts; craft, mystery, handicraft; trade &c. (commerce) 794. exercise; work &c. (action) 680; avocation; press of business &c. (activity) 682. V. pass one's time in, employ one's time in, spend one's time in; employ oneself in, employ oneself upon; occupy oneself with, concern oneself with; make it one's business &c. n.; undertake &c. 676; enter a profession; betake oneself to, turn one's hand to; have to do with &c. (do) 680. office, place, post, chargeship[obs3], incumbency, living; situation, berth, employ; service &c. (servitude) 749; engagement; undertaking &c. 676. drive a trade; carry on a trade, do a trade, transact a trade, carry on business, do business, transact business &c. n.; keep a shop; ply one's task, ply one's trade; labor in one's vocation; pursue the even tenor of one's way; attend to business, attend to one's work. officiate, serve, act; act one's part, play one's part; do duty; serve the office of, discharge the office of, perform the office of, perform the duties of, perform the functions of; hold an office, fill an office, fill a place, fill a situation; hold a portfolio, hold a place, hold a situation. be about, be doing, be engaged in, be employed in, be occupied with, be at work on; have one's hands in, have in hand; have on one's hands, have on one's shoulders; bear the burden; have one's hands full &c. (activity) 682. be in the hands of, be on the stocks, be on the anvil; pass through one's hands. Adj. businesslike; workaday; professional; official, functional; busy &c. (actively employed) 682; on hand, in hand, in one's hands; afoot; on foot, on the anvil; going on; acting. Adv. in the course of business, all in one's day's work; professionally &c. Adj. Phr. "a business with an income at its heels" [Cowper]; amoto quaeramus seria ludo [Lat] [Horace]; par negotiis neque supra [Lat][Tacitus].

<— p. 195 —>

#626. Plan. — N. plan, scheme, design, project; proposal, proposition, suggestion; resolution, motion; precaution &c. (provision) 673; deep-laid plan &c. (premeditated) 611; system &c. (order) 58; organization &c. (arrangement) 60; germ &c. (cause) 153. sketch, skeleton, outline, draught, draft, ebauche[Fr], brouillon[Fr]; rough cast, rough draft, draught copy; copy; proof, revise. drawing, scheme, schematic, graphic, chart, flow chart (representation) 554. forecast, program(me), prospectus; carte du pays[Fr]; card; bill, protocol; order of the day, list of agenda; bill of fare &c. (food) 298; base of operations; platform, plank, slate [U. S.], ticket [U. S.]. role; policy &c. (line of conduct) 692. contrivance, invention, expedient, receipt, nostrum, artifice, device; pipelaying [U. S.]; stratagem &c. (cunning) 702; trick &c. (deception) 545; alternative, loophole; shift &c. (substitute) 147; last shift &c. (necessity) 601. measure, step; stroke, stroke of policy; master stroke; trump card, court card; cheval de bataille[Fr], great gun; coup, coup d'etat[Fr]; clever stroke, bold stroke, good move, good hit, good stroke; bright thought, bright idea. intrigue, cabal, plot, conspiracy, complot[obs3], machination; subplot, underplot[obs3], counterplot. schemer, schemist[obs3], schematistl; strategist, machinator; projector, artist, promoter, designer &c. v.; conspirator; intrigant &c. (cunning) 702[obs3]. V. plan,,scheme, design, frame, contrive, project, forecast, sketch; devise, invent &c. (imagine) 515; set one's wits to work &c. 515; spring a project; fall upon, hit upon; strike out, chalk out, cut out, lay out, map out; lay down a plan; shape out a course, mark out a course; predetermine &c. 611; concert, preconcert, preestablish; prepare &c. 673; hatch, hatch a plot concoct; take steps, take measures. cast, recast, systematize, organize; arrange &c. 60; digest, mature. plot; counter-plot, counter-mine; dig a mine; lay a train; intrigue &c. (cunning) 702. Adj. planned &c. v.; strategic, strategical; planning &c. v.; prepared, in course of preparation &c. 673; under consideration; on the tapis[obs3], on the carpet, on the floor.

#627. Method. [Path.] — N. method, way, manner, wise, gait, form, mode, fashion, tone, guise; modus operandi, MO; procedure &c. (line of conduct) 692. path, road, route, course; line of way, line of road; trajectory, orbit, track, beat, tack. steps; stair, staircase; flight of stairs, ladder, stile; perron[obs3]. bridge, footbridge, viaduct, pontoon, steppingstone, plank, gangway; drawbridge; pass, ford, ferry, tunnel; pipe &c. 260. door; gateway &c. (opening) 260; channel, passage, avenue, means of access, approach, adit[obs3]; artery, lane, alley, aisle, lobby, corridor; backdoor, back-stairs; secret passage; covert way; vennel[obs3]. roadway, pathway, stairway; express; thoroughfare; highway; turnpike, freeway, royal road, coach road; broad highway, King's highway, Queen's highway; beaten track, beaten path; horse road, bridle road, bridle track, bridle path; walk, trottoir[obs3], footpath, pavement, flags, sidewalk; crossroad, byroad, bypath, byway; cut; short cut &c. (mid-course) 628; carrefour[obs3]; private road, occupation road; highways and byways; railroad, railway, tram road, tramway; towpath; causeway; canal &c. (conduit) 350; street &c. (abode) 189; speedway. adv. how; in what way, in what manner; by what mode; so, in this way, after this fashion. one way or another, anyhow; somehow or other &c. (instrumentality) 631; by way of; via; in transitu &c. 270[Lat]; on the high road to. Phr. hae tibi erunt artes[Lat].

<— p. 196 —>

#628. Mid-course. — N. middle course, midcourse; mean &c. 29 middle &c. 68; juste milieu[Fr], mezzo termine[It], golden mean, <gr/ariston metron/gr>[obs3][Grk], aurea mediocritas[Lat].
straight &c. (direct) 278 straight course, straight path; short cut, cross cut; great circle sailing.
neutrality; half measure, half and half measures; compromise.
V. keep in a middle course, preserve a middle course, preserve an even course, go straight &c. (direct) 278.
go halfway, compromise, make a compromise.
Adj. straight &c. (direct) 278.
Phr. medium tenuere beati[Lat].
#629. Circuit. — N. circuit, roundabout way, digression, detour, circumbendibus, ambages[obs3], loop; winding &c. (circuition) 311[obs3]; zigzag &c. (deviation) 279.

V. perform a circuit; go round about, go out of one's way; make a detour; meander &c. (deviate) 279.

lead a pretty dance; beat about the bush; make two bites of a cherry.

Adj. circuitous, indirect, roundabout; zigzag &c. (deviating) 279; backhanded.

Adv. by a side wind, by an indirect course; in a roundabout way; from pillar to post.

#630. Requirement. — N. requirement, need, wants, necessities; necessaries, necessaries of life; stress, exigency, pinch, sine qua non, matter of necessity; case of need, case of life or death.

needfulness, essentiality, necessity, indispensability, urgency.

requisition &c. (request) 765, (exaction) 741; run upon; demand, call for.

charge, claim, command, injunction, mandate, order, precept.

desideratum &c. (desire) 865; want &c. (deficiency) 640.

V. require, need, want, have occasion for; not be able to do without, not be able to dispense with; prerequire[obs3].

render necessary, necessitate, create a, necessity for, call for, put in requisition; make a requisition &c. (ask for) 765, (demand) 741.

stand in need of; lack &c. 640; desiderate[obs3]; desire &c. 865; be necessary &c. Adj.

Adj. required &c. v.; requisite, needful, necessary, imperative, essential, indispensable, prerequisite; called for; in demand, in request.

urgent, exigent, pressing, instant, crying, absorbing.

in want of; destitute of &c. 640.

Adv. ex necessitate rei &c. (necessarily) 601[Lat]; of necessity.

Phr. there is no time to lose; it cannot be spared, it cannot be dispensed with; mendacem memorem esse oportet [Lat][Quintilian]; necessitas non habet legem[Lat]; nec tecum possum trivere nec sine te [Lat][Martial].
%
2. Subservience to Ends
Actual Subservience %

#631. Instrumentality. — N. instrumentality; aid &c. 707; subservience, subserviency; mediation, intervention, medium, intermedium[obs3], vehicle, hand; agency &c. 170. minister, handmaid; midwife, accoucheur[Fr], accoucheuse[Fr], obstetrician; gobetween; cat's-paw; stepping-stone. opener &c. 260; key; master key, passkey, latchkey; "open sesame"; passport, passe-partout, safe-conduct, password. instrument &c. 633; expedient &c. (plan) 626; means &c. 632. V. subserve, minister, mediate, intervene; be instrumental &c. adj.; pander to; officiate; tend.
Adj. instrumental; useful &c. 644; ministerial, subservient, mediatorial[obs3]; intermediate, intervening; conducive.
Adv. through, by, per; whereby, thereby, hereby; by the agency of &c. 170; by dint of; by virtue of, in virtue of; through the medium of &c. n.; along with; on the shoulders of; by means of &c. 632; by the aid of, with the aid of &c. (assistance) 707.

<— p. 197 —>

per fas et nefas[Lat], by fair means or foul; somehow, somehow or other; by hook or by crook.

#632. Means. — N. means, resources, wherewithal, ways and means; capital &c. (money) 800; revenue; stock in trade &c. 636; provision &c. 637; a shot in the locker; appliances &c. (machinery) 633; means and appliances; conveniences; cards to play; expedients &c. (measures) 626; two strings to one's bow; sheet anchor &c. (safety) 666; aid &c. 707; medium &c. 631. V. find means, have means, possess means &c. n. Adj. instrumental &c. 631; mechanical &c. 633. Adv. by means of, with; by what means, by all means, by any means, by some means; where-with, herewith, therewith; wherewithal. how &c. (in what manner) 627; through &c. (by the instrumentality of) 631; with the aid of, by the aid of &c. (assistance) 707; by the agency of &c. 170

#633. Instrument. — N. machinery, mechanism, engineering. instrument, organ, tool, implement, utensil, machine, engine, lathe, gin, mill; air engine, caloric engine, heat engine. gear; tackle, tackling, rig, rigging, apparatus, appliances; plant, materiel; harness, trappings, fittings, accouterments; barde[obs3]; equipment, equipmentage[obs3];

appointments, furniture, upholstery; chattels; paraphernalia &c. (belongings) 780. mechanical powers; lever, leverage; mechanical advantage; crow, crowbar; handspike[obs3], gavelock[obs3], jemmy[obs3], jimmy, arm, limb, wing; oar, paddle; pulley; wheel and axle; wheelwork, clockwork; wheels within wheels; pinion, crank, winch; cam; pedal; capstan &c. (lift) 307; wheel &c. (rotation) 312; inclined plane; wedge; screw; spring, mainspring; can hook, glut, heald[obs3], heddle[obs3], jenny, parbuckle[obs3], sprag[obs3], water wheel. handle, hilt, haft, shaft, heft, shank, blade, trigger, tiller, helm, treadle, key; turnscrew, screwdriver; knocker. hammer &c. (impulse) 276; edge tool &c. (cut) 253; borer &c. 262; vice, teeth, &c. (hold) 781; nail, rope &c. (join) 45; peg &c. (hang) 214; support &c. 215; spoon &c. (vehicle) 272; arms &c. 727; oar &c. (navigation) 267; cardiograph, recapper[obs3], snowplow, tenpenny[obs3], votograph[obs3]. Adj. instrumental &c. 631; mechanical, machinal[obs3]; brachial[Med].

#634. Substitute. — N. substitute &c. 147; deputy &c. 759; badli[obs3].

#635. Materials. — N. material, raw material, stuff, stock, staple; adobe, brown stone; chinking; clapboard; daubing; puncheon; shake; shingle, bricks and mortar; metal; stone; clay, brick crockery &c. 384; compo, composition; concrete; reinforced concrete, cement; wood, ore, timber. materials; supplies, munition, fuel, grist, household stuff pabulum &c. (food) 298; ammunition &c. (arms) 727; contingents; relay, reinforcement, reenforcement[obs3]; baggage &c. (personal property) 780; means &c. 632; calico, cambric, cashmere. Adj. raw &c. (unprepared) 674; wooden &c. n.; adobe.

#636. Store. — N. stock, fund, mine, vein, lode, quarry; spring; fount, fountain; well, wellspring; milch cow. stock in trade, supply; heap &c. (collection) 72; treasure; reserve, corps de reserve, reserved fund, nest egg, savings, bonne bouche[Fr]. crop, harvest, mow, vintage. store, accumulation, hoard, rick, stack; lumber; relay &c. (provision) 637. storehouse, storeroom, storecloset[obs3]; depository, depot, cache, repository, reservatory[obs3], repertory; repertorium[obs3]; promptuary[obs3], warehouse, entrepot[Fr], magazine; buttery, larder, spence[obs3]; garner, granary; cannery, safe-deposit vault, stillroom[obs3]; thesaurus; bank &c. (treasury) 802; armory; arsenal; dock; gallery, museum, conservatory; menagery[obs3], menagerie.

<— p. 198 —>

reservoir, cistern, aljibar[obs3], tank, pond, mill pond; gasometer[obs3].
budget, quiver, bandolier, portfolio; coffer &c. (receptacle) 191.
conservation; storing &c. v.; storage.
V. store; put by, lay by, set by; stow away; set apart, lay apart; store treasure, hoard treasure, lay up, heap up, put up, garner up, save up; bank; cache; accumulate, amass, hoard, fund, garner, save.
reserve; keep back, hold back; husband, husband one's resources.
deposit; stow, stack, load; harvest; heap, collect &c. 72; lay in store &c.
Adj.; keep, file [papers]; lay in &c. (provide) 637; preserve &c. 670.
Adj. stored &c. v.; in store, in reserve, in ordinary; spare, supernumerary.
Phr. adde parvum parvo magnus acervus erit[Lat].
#637. Provision. — N. provision, supply; grist, grist for the mill; subvention &c. (aid) 707; resources &c. (means) 632; groceries, grocery.
providing &c. v.; purveyance; reinforcement, reenforcement[obs3]; commissariat.
provender &c. (food) 298; ensilage; viaticum.
caterer, purveyor, commissary, quartermaster, maniple[obs3], feeder, batman, victualer, grocer, comprador[Sp], restaurateur; jackal, pelican; sutler &c. (merchant) 797[obs3].
grocery shop [U. S.], grocery store.
V. provide; make provision, make due provision for; lay in, lay in a stock, lay in a store.
supply, suppeditate!; furnish; find, find one in; arm.
cater, victual, provision, purvey, forage; beat up for; stock, stock with; make good, replenish; fill, fill up; recruit, feed.
have in store, have in reserve; keep, keep by one, keep on foot, keep

on hand; have to fall back upon; store &c. 636; provide against a rainy day &c. (economy) 817.

#638. Waste. — N. consumption, expenditure, exhaustion; dispersion &c. 73; ebb; leakage &c. (exudation) 295; loss &c. 776; wear and tear; waste; prodigality &c. 818; misuse &c. 679; wasting &c. v.; rubbish &c. (useless) 645. mountain in labor. V. spend, expend, use, consume, swallow up, exhaust; impoverish; spill, drain, empty; disperse &c. 73. cast away, fool away, muddle away, throw away, fling away, fritter away; burn the candle at both ends, waste; squander &c. 818. "waste its sweetness on the desert air" [Gray]; cast one's bread upon the waters, cast pearls before swine; employ a steam engine to crack a nut, waste powder and shot, break a butterfly on a wheel; labor in vain &c. (useless) 645; cut blocks with a razor, pour water into a sieve. leak &c. (run out) 295; run to waste; ebb; melt away, run dry, dry up. Adj. wasted &c. v.; at a low ebb. wasteful &c. (prodigal) 818; penny wise and pound foolish. Phr. magno conatu magnas nugas[Lat]; le jeu ne vaut pas la chandelle[Fr]; "idly busy rolls their world away" [Goldsmith].

#639. Sufficiency. — N. sufficiency, adequacy, enough, withal, satisfaction, competence; no less; quantum sufficit[Lat], Q.S.. mediocrity &c. (average) 29. fill; fullness &c. (completeness) 52; plenitude, plenty; abundance; copiousness &c. Adj.; amplitude, galore, lots, profusion; full measure; "good measure pressed down and running, over." luxuriance &c. (fertility) 168; affluence &c. (wealth) 803; fat of the land; "a land flowing with milk and honey"; cornucopia; horn of plenty, horn of Amalthaea; mine &c. (stock) 636. outpouring; flood &c. (great quantity) 31; tide &c. (river) 348; repletion &c. (redundancy) 641; satiety &c. 869. V. be sufficient &c. Adj.; suffice, do, just do, satisfy, pass muster; have enough &c. n.; eat. one's fill, drink one's fill, have one's fill; roll in, swim in, wallow in &c. (supera-bundance) 641; wanton. abound, exuberate, teem, flow, stream, rain, shower down; pour, pour in; swarm; bristle with; superabound. render sufficient &c. Adj.; replenish &c. (fill) 52. Adj. sufficient, enough, adequate, up to the mark, commensurate, competent, satisfactory, valid, tangible. measured; moderate &c. (temperate) 953. full.&c. (complete) 52; ample; plenty, plentiful, plenteous; plenty as blackberries; copious, abundant; abounding &c. v.; replete, enough and to spare, flush; choke-full, chock-full; well-stocked, well-provided; liberal; unstinted, unstinting; stintless[obs3]; without stint; unsparing, unmeasured; lavish &c. 641; wholesale. rich; luxuriant &c. (fertile) 168; affluent &c. (wealthy) 803; wantless[obs3]; big with &c. (pregnant) 161. unexhausted[obs3], unwasted[obs3]; exhaustless, inexhaustible. Adv. sufficiently, amply &c. Adj.; full; in abundance &c. n. with no sparing hand; to one's heart's content, ad libitum, without stint. Phr. "cut and come again" [Crabbe]; das Beste ist gut genug[Ger].

#640. Insufficiency. — N. insufficiency; inadequacy, inadequateness; incompetence &c. (impotence) 158; deficiency &c. (incompleteness) 53; imperfection &c. 651; shortcoming &c. 304; paucity; stint; scantiness &c. (smallness) 32; none to spare, bare subsistence. scarcity, dearth; want, need, lack, poverty, exigency; inanition, starvation, famine, drought. dole, mite, pittance; short allowance, short commons; half rations; banyan day. emptiness, poorness &c. Adj.; depletion, vacancy, flaccidity; ebb tide; low water; "a beggarly account of empty boxes" [Romeo and Jul.]; indigence &c. 804; insolvency &c. (nonpayment) 808. V. be insufficient &c. Adj.; not suffice &c. 639; come short of &c. 304 run dry. want, lack, need, require; caret; be in want &c. (poor) 804, live from hand to mouth. render insuf-ficient &c. Adj.; drain of resources, impoverish &c. (waste) 638; stint &c. (begrudge) 819; put on short allowance. do insufficiently &c. adv.; scotch the snake. Adj. insufficient, inadequate; too little &c. 32; not enough &c. 639; unequal to; incompetent &c. (impotent) 158; "weighed in the balance and found wanting"; perfunctory &c. (neglect) 460; deficient &c. (incomplete) 53; wanting, &c. v.; imperfect &c. 651; ill-furnished, ill-provided, ill- stored, ill-off. slack, at a low ebb; empty, vacant, bare; short of, out of, destitute of, devoid of, bereft of &c. 789; denuded of; dry, drained. unprovided, unsupplied[obs3], unfurnished; unreplenished, unfed[obs3]; unstored[obs3], untreasured[obs3]; empty-handed. meager, poor, thin, scrimp, sparing, spare, stinted; starved, starving; halfstarved, famine-stricken, famished; jejune. scant &c. (small) 32; scarce; not to be had, not to be had for love or money, not to be had at any price; scurvy; stingy &c. 819; at the end of one's tether; without resources &c. 632; in want &c. (poor) 804; in debt &c. 806. Adv. insufficiently &c. Adj.; in default of, for want of; failing. Phr. semper avarus eget [Lat][Horace].

<— p. 199 —>

#641. Redundancy. — N. redundancy, redundance[obs3]; too much, too many; superabundance, superfluity, superfluencel; saturation; nimiety[obs3], transcendency, exuberance, profuseness; profusion &c. (plenty) 639; repletion, enough in all conscience, satis superque[Lat], lion's share; more than enough &c. 639; plethora, engorge-ment, congestion, load, surfeit, sickener[obs3]; turgescence &c. (expansion) 194[obs3]; overdose, overmeasure[obs3], oversupply, overflow; inundation &c. (water) 348; avalanche. accumulation &c. (store) 636; heap &c. 72; drug, drug in the market; glut; crowd; burden. excess; surplus, overplus[obs3]; epact[obs3]; margin; remainder &c. 40; duplicate; surplusage[obs3], expletive; work of supererogation; bonus, bonanza. luxury; intemper-ance &c. 954; extravagance &c. (prodigality) 818; exorbitance, lavishment[obs3]. pleonasm &c. (diffuseness) 573;

too many irons in the fire; embarras de richesses[Fr]. V. superabound, overabound[obs3]; know no bounds, swarm; meet one at every turn; creep with, crawl with, bristle with; overflow; run over, flow over, well over, brim over; run riot; overrun, overstock, overlay, overcharge, overdose, overfeed, overburden, overload, overdo, overwhelm, overshoot the mark &c. (go beyond) 303; surcharge, supersaturate, gorge, glut, load, drench, whelm, inundate, deluge, flood; drug, drug the market; hepatize[obs3].

<— p. 200 —>

choke, cloy, accloy[obs3], suffocate; pile up, lay on thick; impregnate with; lavish &c. (squander) 818. send coals to Newcastle, carry coals to Newcastle, carry owls to Athens[obs3]; teach one's grandmother to suck eggs; pisces natare docere[Lat]; kill the slain, "gild refined gold", "gild the lily", butter one's bread on both sides, put butter upon bacon; employ a steam engine to crack a nut &c. (waste) 638. exaggerate &c. 549; wallow in roll in &c. (plenty) 639 remain on one's hands, hang heavy on hand, go a begging. Adj. redundant; too much, too many; exuberant, inordinate, superabundant, excessive, overmuch, replete, profuse, lavish; prodigal &c. 818; exorbitant; overweening; extravagant; overcharged &c. v.; supersaturated, drenched, overflowing; running over, running to waste, running down. crammed to overflowing, filled to overflowing; gorged, ready to burst; dropsical, turgid, plethoric; obese &c. 194. superfluous, unnecessary, needless, supervacaneousl, uncalled for, to spare, in excess; over and above &c. (remainder) 40; de trop[Fr]; adscititious &c. (additional) 37; supernumerary &c. (reserve) 636; on one's hands, spare, duplicate, supererogatory, expletive; un peu fort[Fr]. Adv. over, too, over and above; overmuch, too much; too far; without measure, beyond measure, out of measure; with . . . to spare; over head and ears; up to one's eyes, up to one's ears; extra; beyond the mark &c. (transcursion) 303; acervatim [Lat]. Phr. it never rains but it pours; fortuna multis dat nimium nulli satis [Lat].

#642. Importance. — N. importance, consequence, moment, prominence, consideration, mark, materialness. import, significance, concern; emphasis, interest. greatness &c. 31; superiority &c. 33; notability &c. (repute) 873; weight &c. (influence) 175; value &c. (goodness) 648; usefulness &c. 644. gravity, seriousness, solemnity; no joke, no laughing matter; pressure, urgency, stress; matter of life and death. memorabilia, notabilia[obs3], great doings; red-letter day. great thing, great point; main chance, "the be all and the end all" [Macbeth]; cardinal point; substance, gist &c. (essence) 5; sum and substance, gravamen, head and front; important part, principal part, prominent part, essential part; half the battle; sine qua non; breath of one's nostrils &c. (life) 359;cream, salt, core, kernel, heart, nucleus; keynote, keystone; corner stone; trump card &c. (device) 626; salient points. top sawyer, first fiddle, prima donna[Sp], chief; triton among the minnows; "it" [U.S.]. V. be important &c. adj., be somebody, be something; import, signify, matter, boot, be an object; carry weight &c. (influence) 175; make a figure &c. (repute) 873; be in the ascendant, come to the front, lead the way, take the lead, play first fiddle, throw all else into the shade; lie at the root of; deserve notice, merit notice, be worthy of notice, be worthy of regard, be worthy of consideration. attach importance to, ascribe importance to, give importance to &c. n.; value, care for, set store upon, set store by; mark &c. 550; mark with a white stone, underline; write in italics, put in italics, print in italics, print in capitals, print in large letters, put in large type, put in letters. of gold; accentuate, emphasize, lay stress on. make a fuss about, make a fuss over, make a stir about, make a piece of work about[Fr], make much ado about; make much ado of, make much of. Adj. important; of importance &c. n.; momentous, material; to the point; not to be overlooked, not to be despised, not to be sneezed at; egregious; weighty &c. (influential) 175; of note &c. (repute) 873; notable, prominent, salient, signal; memorable, remarkable; unforgettable; worthy of remark, worthy of notice; never to be forgotten; stirring, eventful. grave, serious, earnest, noble, grand, solemn, impressive, commanding, imposing. urgent, pressing, critical, instant. paramount, essential, vital, all-absorbing, radical, cardinal, chief, main, prime, primary, principal, leading, capital, foremost, overruling; of vital &c. importance. in the front rank, first-rate; superior &c. 33; considerable &c. (great) 31; marked &c. v.; rare &c. 137. significant, telling, trenchant, emphatic, pregnant; tanti[Lat]. Adv. materially &c. adj.; in the main; above all, <gr/kat' exochin/gr>, par excellence, to crown all, to beat all. Phr. expende Hannibalem![Lat] [Juvenal].

#643. Unimportance. — N. unimportance, insignificance, nothingness, immateriality. triviality, levity, frivolity; paltriness &c. Adj.; poverty; smallness &c. 32; vanity &c. (uselessness) 645; matter of indifference &c. 866; no object. nothing, nothing to signify,, nothing worth speaking of, nothing particular, nothing to boast of, nothing to speak of; small matter, no great matter, trifling matter &c. Adj.; mere joke, mere nothing; hardly anything; scarcely anything; nonentity, small beer, cipher; no great shakes, peu de chose[Fr]; child's play, kinderspiel. toy, plaything, popgun, paper pellet, gimcrack, gewgaw, bauble, trinket, bagatelle, Rickshaw, knickknack, whim-wham, trifle, "trifles light as air"; yankee notions [U. S.]. trumpery, trash, rubbish, stuff, fatras[obs3], frippery; "leather or prunello"; chaff, drug, froth bubble smoke, cobweb; weed; refuse &c. (inutility) 645; scum &c. (dirt) 653. joke, jest, snap of the fingers; fudge &c. (unmeaning) 517; fiddlestick[obs3], fiddlestick end[obs3]; pack of nonsense, mere farce. straw, pin, fig, button, rush; bulrush, feather, halfpenny, farthing, brass farthing, doit[obs3], peppercorn, jot, rap, pinch of snuff, old son; cent, mill, picayune, pistareen[obs3], red cent [U.S.].

<— p. 201 —>

minutiae, details, minor details, small fry; dust in the balance, feather in the scale, drop in the ocean, flea-bite, molehill. nine days' wonder, ridiculus mus[Lat]; flash in the pan &c. (impotence) 158; much ado about nothing &c. (overestimation) 482. V. be unimportant &c. Adj.; not matter &c. 642; go for nothing, matter nothing, signify nothing, matter little, matter little or nothing; not matter a straw &c. n. make light of &c. (underestimate) 483; catch at straws &c. (overestimate) 482. Adj. unimportant; of little account, of small account, of no account, of little importance, of no importance &c. 642; immaterial; unessential, nonessential; indifferent. subordinate &c. (inferior) 34; mediocre &c. (average) 29; passable, fair, respectable, tolerable, commonplace; uneventful, mere, common; ordinary &c. (habitual) 613; inconsiderable, so-so, insignificant, inappreciable. trifling, trivial; slight, slender, light, flimsy, frothy, idle; puerile &c. (foolish) 499; airy, shallow; weak &c. 160; powerless &c. 158; frivolous, petty, niggling; piddling, peddling; fribble[obs3], inane, ridiculous, farcical; finical, finikin[obs3]; fiddle-faddle, fingle- fangle[obs3], namby-pamby, wishy-washy, milk and water. poor, paltry, pitiful; contemptible &c. (contempt) 930; sorry, mean, meager, shabby, miserable, wretched, vile, scrubby, scrannel[obs3], weedy, niggardly, scurvy, putid[obs3], beggarly, worthless, twopennyhalfpenny, cheap, trashy, catchpenny, gimcrack, trumpery; one-horse [U. S.]. not worth the pains, not worth while, not worth mentioning, not worth speaking of, not worth a thought, not worth a curse, not worth a straw &c. n.;1 beneath notice, unworthy of notice, beneath regard, unworthy of regard, beneath consideration, unworthy of consideration; de lana caprina[It][obs3]; vain &c. (useless) 645.

Adv. slightly &c. adj.; rather, somewhat, pretty well, tolerably. for aught one cares. Int. no matter! pish! tush! tut! pshaw! pugh! pooh, pooh-pooh! fudge! bosh! humbug! fiddlestick[obs3], fiddlestick end[obs3]! fiddlededee! never mind! n'importe[Fr]! what signifies it, what boots it, what of it, what of that, what matter, what's the odds, a fig for' stuff and nonsense, stuff! nonsense! Phr. magno conatu magnas nugas[Lat]; le jeu ne vaut pas la chandelle[Fr]; it matters not, it does not signify; it is of no consequence, it is of no importance; elephantus non capit murem[Lat]; tempete dans un verre d'eau[Fr].

<— p. 202 —>

#644. Utility. — N. utility; usefulness &c. adj.; efficacy, efficiency, adequacy; service, use, stead, avail; help &c. (aid) 707; applicability &c. adj.; subservience &c. (instrumentality) 631; function &c. (business) 625; value; worth &c. (goodness) 648; money's worth; productiveness &c. 168; cui bono &c. (intention) 620[Lat]; utilization &c. (use) 677 step in the right direction. common weal; commonwealth public good, public interest; utilitarianism &c. (philanthropy) 910. V. be useful &c. adj.; avail, serve; subserve &c. (be instrumental to) 631; conduce &c. (tend) 176; answer, serve one's turn, answer a purpose, serve a purpose. act a part &c. (action) 680; perform a function, discharge a function &c.; render a service, render good service, render yeoman's service; bestead[obs3], stand one in good stead be the making of; help &c. 707. bear fruit &c. (produce) 161; bring grist to the mill; profit, remunerate; benefit &c. (do good) 648. find one's account in, find one's advantage in; reap the benefit of &c. (be better for) 658. render useful &c. (use) 677. Adj. useful; of use &c. n.; serviceable, proficuousl, good for; subservient &c. (instrumental) 631.; conducive &c. (tending) 176; subsidiary &c. (helping) 707. advantageous &c. (beneficial) 648; profitable, gainful, remunerative, worth one's salt; valuable; prolific &c. (productive) 168. adequate; efficient, efficacious; effective, effectual; expedient &c. 646. applicable, available, ready, handy, at hand, tangible; commodious, adaptable; of all work. Adv. usefully &c. adj.; pro bono publico[Lat].

<— p. 203 —>

#645. Inutility. — N. inutility; uselessness &c. adj.; inefficacy[obs3], futility; ineptitude, inaptitude; unsubservience[obs3]; inadequacy &c. (insufficiency) 640; inefficiency.&c. (incompetence) 158; unskillfulness &c. 699; disservice; unfruitfulness &c.(unproductiveness). 169; labor in vain, labor lost, labor of Sisyphus; lost trouble, lost labor; work of Penelope; sleeveless errand, wild goose chase, mere farce. tautology &c. (repetition) 104; supererogation &c. (redundancy) 641. vanitas vanitatum[Lat], vanity, inanity, worthlessness, nugacity[obs3]; triviality &c. (unimportance) 643. caput mortuum[Lat][obs3], waste paper, dead letter; blunt tool. litter, rubbish, junk, lumber, odds and ends, cast-off clothes; button top; shoddy; rags, orts[obs3], trash, refuse, sweepings, scourings, offscourings[obs3], waste, rubble, debris, detritus; stubble, leavings; broken meat; dregs &c. (dirt) 653, weeds, tares; rubbish heap, dust hole; rudera[obs3], deads[obs3]. fruges consumere natus &c. (drone) 683[Lat][Horace]. V. be useless &c. Adj.; go a begging &c. (redundant) 641; fail &c. 732. seek after impossibilities, strive after impossibilities;

175

use vain efforts, labor in vain, roll the stone of Sisyphus, beat the air, lash the waves, battre l'eau avec un baton[Fr], donner un coup d'epee dans l'eau[Fr], fish in the air, milk the ram, drop a bucket into an empty well, sow the sand; bay the moon; preach to the winds, speak to the winds; whistle jigs to a milestone; kick against the pricks, se battre contre des moulins[Fr]; lock the stable door when the steed is stolen, lock the barn door after the horse is stolen &c. (too late) 135; hold a farthing candle to the sun; cast pearls before swine &c. (waste) 638; carry coals to Newcastle &c. (redundancy) 641; wash a blackamoor white &c. (impossible) 471. render useless &c. adj.; dismantle, dismast, dismount, disqualify, disable; unrig; cripple, lame &c. (injure) 659; spike guns, clip the wings; put out of gear. Adj. useless, inutile, inefficacious, futile, unavailing, bootless; inoperative &c. 158; inadequate &c. (insufficient) 640; inserventl, unsubservient; inept, inefficient &c. (impotent) 158; of no avail &c. (use) 644; ineffectual &c. (failure) 732; incompetent &c. (unskillful) 699; "stale, flat and unprofitable"; superfluous &c. (redundant) 641; dispensable; thrown away &c. (wasted) 638; abortive &c. (immature) 674. worthless, valueless, priceless; unsalable; not worth a straw &c. (trifling) 643 dear at any price. vain, empty, inane; gainless[obs3], profitless, fruitless; unserviceable, unprofitable; ill-spent; unproductive &c. 169; hors de combat[Fr]; effete, past work &c. (impaired) 659; obsolete &c. (old) 124; fit for the dust hole; good for nothing; of no earthly use; not worth having, not worth powder and shot; leading to no end, uncalled for; unnecessary, unneeded. Adv. uselessly &c. adj.; to little purpose, to no purpose, to little or no purpose. Int. cui bono?[Lat]; what's the good! Phr. actum ne agas[Lat][obs3]; chercher une aiguille dans une botte de foin[obs3][Fr]; tanto buon che val niente[It].

#646. [Specific subservience.] Expedience. — N. expedience, expediency; desirableness, desirability &c. adj.; fitness &c. (agreement) 23; utility &c. 644; propriety; opportunism; advantage. high time &c. (occasion) 134. V. be expedient &c. Adj.; suit &c. (agree) 23; befit; suit the time, befit the time, suit the season, befit the season, suit the occasion, befit the occasion. conform &c. 82. Adj. expedient; desirable, advisable, acceptable; convenient; worth while, meet; fit, fitting; due, proper, eligible, seemly, becoming; befitting &c. v.; opportune &c. (in season) 134; in loco; suitable &c. (accordant) 23; applicable &c. (useful) 644. Adv. in the right place; conveniently &c. adj. Phr. operae pretium est[Lat].

#647. Inexpedience. — N. inexpedience, inexpediency; undesirableness, undesirability &c. Adj.; discommodity[obs3], impropriety; unfitness &c. (disagreement) 24; inutility &c. 645; disadvantage. V. be inexpedient &c. Adj.; come amiss &c. (disagree) 24; embarrass &c. (hinder) 706; put to inconvenience; pay too dear for one's whistle. Adj. inexpedient, undesirable; unadvisable, inadvisable; objectionable; inapt, ineligible, inadmissible, inconvenient; incommodious, discommodious[obs3]; disadvantageous; inappropriate, unfit &c. (inconsonant) 24. ill-contrived, ill-advised; unsatisfactory; unprofitable &c., unsubservient &c. (useless) 645; inopportune &c. (unseasonable) 135; out of place, in the wrong place; improper, unseemly. clumsy, awkward; cumbrous, cumbersome; lumbering, unwieldy, hulky[obs3]; unmanageable &c. (impracticable) 704; impedient &c. (in the way) 706[obs3]. unnecessary &c. (redundant) 641. Phr. it will never do.

#648. [Capability of producing good. Good qualities.] Goodness. — N. goodness &c. adj.; excellence, merit; virtue &c. 944; value, worth, price. super-excellence, supereminence; superiority &c. 33; perfection &c. 650; coup de maitre[Fr]; masterpiece, chef d'ouvre[Fr], prime, flower, cream, elite, pick, A1, nonesuch, nonpareil, creme de la creme, flower of the flock, cock of the roost, salt of the earth; champion; prodigy. tidbit; gem, gem of the first water; bijou, precious stone, jewel, pearl, diamond, ruby, brilliant, treasure; good thing; rara avis[Lat], one in a thousand. beneficence &c. 906; good man &c. 948. V. be beneficial &c. Adj.; produce good, do good &c. 618; profit &c. (be of use) 644; benefit; confer a benefit &c. 618. be the making of, do a world of good, make a man of. produce a good effect; do a good turn, confer an obligation; improve &c. 658. do no harm, break no bones. be good &c. adj.; excel, transcend &c. (be superior) 33; bear away the bell. stand the proof, stand the test; pass muster, pass an examination. challenge comparison, vie, emulate, rival. Adj. harmless, hurtless[obs3]; unobnoxious[obs3], innocuous, innocent, inoffensive. beneficial, valuable, of value; serviceable &c. (useful) 644; advantageous, edifying, profitable; salutary &c. (healthful) 656. favorable; propitious &c. (hope-giving) 858; fair. good, good as gold; excellent; better; superior &c. 33; above par; nice, fine; genuine &c. (true) 494. best, choice, select, picked, elect, recherche, rare, priceless; unparagoned[obs3], unparalleled &c. (supreme) 33; superlatively &c. 33; good; bully*, crackajack*[obs3], giltedged; superfine, superexcellent[obs3]; of the first water; first-rate, first-class; high- wrought, exquisite, very best, crack, prime, tiptop, capital, cardinal; standard &c. (perfect) 650; inimitable. admirable, estimable; praiseworthy &c. (approve) 931; pleasing &c. 829; couleur de rose[Fr], precious, of great price; costly &c. (dear) 814; worth its weight in gold, worth a Jew's eye; priceless, invaluable, inestimable, precious as the apple of the eye. tolerable &c. (not very good) 651; up to the mark, unexceptionable, unobjectionable; satisfactory, tidy. in good condition, in fair condition; fresh; sound &c. (perfect) 650. Adv. beneficially &c. adj.; well &c. 618. Phr. "Jewels five words long" [Tennyson]; "long may such goodness live!" [Rogers]; "the luxury of doing good" [Goldsmith].

<– p. 204 –>

#649. [Capability of producing evil. Bad qualities.] Badness. — N. hurtfulness &c. Adj[obs3].; virulence. evil doer &c. 913; bane &c. 663; plague spot &c. (insalubrity) 657; evil star, ill wind; hoodoo; Jonah; snake in the grass, skeleton in the closet; amari aliquid[Lat][obs3], thorn in the side. malignity; malevolence &c. 907; tender mercies [ironically]. ill-treatment, annoyance, molestation, abuse, oppression, persecution, outrage; misusage &c. 679; injury &c. (damage) 659; knockout drops [U. S.]. badness &c. adj.; peccancy[obs3], abomination; painfulness &c. 830; pestilence &c. (disease) 655; guilt &c. 947; depravity &c. 945. V. be hurtful &c. adj.; cause evil, produce evil, inflict evil, work evil, do evil &c. 619; damnify[obs3], endamage[obs3], hurt, harm; injure &c. (damage) 659; pain &c. 830. wrong, aggrieve, oppress, persecute; trample upon, tread upon, bear hard upon, put upon; overburden; weigh down, weigh heavy on; victimize; run down; molest &c. 830. maltreat, abuse; ill-use, ill-treat; buffet, bruise, scratch, maul; smite &c. (scourge) 972; do violence, do harm, do a mischief; stab, pierce, outrage. do mischief, make mischief; bring into trouble. destroy &c. 162. Adj. hurtful, harmful, scathful[obs3], baneful, baleful; injurious, deleterious, detrimental, noxious, pernicious, mischievous, full of mischief, mischief-making, malefic, malignant, nocuous, noisome; prejudicial; disserviceable[obs3], disadvantageous; wide-wasting. unlucky, sinister; obnoxious; untoward, disastrous. oppressive, burdensome, onerous; malign &c. (malevolent) 907. corrupting &c. (corrupt &c. 659); virulent, venomous, envenomed, corrosive; poisonous &c. (morbific) 657[obs3]; deadly &c. (killing) 361; destructive &c. (destroying) 162; inauspicious &c. 859. bad, ill, arrant, as bad as bad can be, dreadful; horrid, horrible; dire; rank, peccant, foul, fulsome; rotten, rotten at the core. vile, base, villainous; mean &c. (paltry) 643; injured &c. deteriorated &c. 659; unsatisfactory, exceptionable, indifferent; below par &c. (imperfect) 651; illcontrived, ill-conditioned; wretched, sad, grievous, deplorable, lamentable; pitiful, pitiable, woeful &c. (painful) 830. evil, wrong; depraved &c. 945; shocking; reprehensible &c. (disapprove) 932. hateful, hateful as a toad; abominable, detestable, execrable, cursed, accursed, confounded; damned, damnable; infernal; diabolic &c. (malevolent) 907. unadvisable &c. (inexpedient) 647; unprofitable &c. (useless) 645; incompetent &c. (unskillful) 699; irremediable &c. (hopeless) 859.

Adv. badly &c. Adj.; wrong, ill; to one's cost; where the shoe pinches.

Phr. bad is the best; the worst come to the worst; herba mala presto cresco [Lat]; "wrongs unredressed or insults unavenged" [Wordsworth].

#650. Perfection. — N. perfection; perfectness &c. adj.; indefectibility[obs3]; impeccancy[obs3], impeccability. pink, beau ideal, phenix, paragon; pink of perfection, acme of perfection; ne plus ultra[Lat]; summit &c. 210. cygne noir[Fr]; philosopher's stone; chrysolite, Koh-i-noor. model, standard, pattern, mirror, admirable Crichton; trump, very prince of. masterpiece, superexcellence &c. (goodness) 648[obs3]; transcendence &c. (superiority) 33. V. be perfect &c. adj.; transcend &c. (be supreme) 33. bring to perfection, perfect, ripen, mature; complete &,,c. 729; put in trim &c. (prepare) 673; maturate. Adj. perfect, faultless; indefective[obs3], indeficient[obs3], indefectible; immaculate, spotless, impeccable; free from imperfection &c. 651; unblemished, uninjured &c. 659; sound, sound as a roach; in perfect condition; scathless[obs3], intact, harmless; seaworthy &c. (safe) 644; right as a trivet; in seipso totus teres atque rotundus [Lat][Horace]; consummate &c. (complete) 52; finished &c. 729. best &c. (good) 648; model, standard; inimitable, unparagoned[obs3], unparalleled &c. (supreme) 33; superhuman, divine; beyond all praise &c. (approbation) 931; sans peur et sans reproche[Fr]. adv. to perfection; perfectly &c. adj.; ad unguem[Lat]; clean, - as a whistle. phr. "let us go on unto perfection" [Hebrews vi, 1]; "the perfection of art is to conceal art" [Quintilian].

<– p. 205 –>

#651. Imperfection. — N. imperfection; imperfectness &c. Adj.; deficiency; inadequacy &c. (insufficiency) 640; peccancy &c. (badness) 649[obs3]; immaturity &c. 674. fault, defect, weak point; screw loose; flaw &c. (break) 70; gap &c. 198; twist &c. 243; taint, attainder; bar sinister, hole in one's coat; blemish &c. 848; weakness &c. 160; half blood; shortcoming &c. 304; drawback; seamy side. mediocrity; no great shakes, no great catch; not much to boast of; one-horse shay. V. be imperfect &c. adj.; have a defect &c. n.; lie under a disadvantage; spring a leak. not pass muster, barely pass muster; fall short &c. 304. Adj. imperfect; not perfect &c. 650; deficient, defective; faulty, unsound, tainted; out of order, out of tune; cracked, leaky; sprung; warped &c. (distort) 243; lame; injured &c. (deteriorated) 659; peccant &c. (bad) 649; frail &c. (weak) 160; inadequate &c. (insufficient) 640; crude &c. (unprepared) 674; incomplete &c. 53; found wanting; below par; short- handed; below its full strength, under its full strength, below its full complement. indifferent, middling, ordinary, mediocre; average &c. 29; so-so; coucicouci, milk and water; tolerable, fair, passable; pretty well, pretty good; rather good, moderately good; good; good enough, well enough, adequate; decent; not bad, not amiss; inobjectionable[obs3], unobjectionable, admissible, bearable, only better than nothing. secondary, inferior; second-rate, second-best; one-horse [U.S.]. Adv. almost &c.; to a limited extent, rather &c. 32; pretty, moderately, passing; only, considering, all things considered, enough. Phr. surgit amari aliquid[Lat].

#652. Cleanness. — N. cleanness, cleanliness &c. adj.; purity; cleaning &c. v.; purification, defecation &c. v.; purgation, lustration[obs3]; detersion[obs3], abstersion[obs3]; epuration[obs3], mundationl; ablution, lavation[obs3], colaturel; disinfection &c. v.; drainage, sewerage. lavatory, laundry, washhouse[obs3]; washerwoman, laundress, dhobi[obs3], laundryman, washerman[obs3]; scavenger, dustman[obs3], sweep; white wings brush[Local U. S.]; broom, besom[obs3], mop, rake, shovel, sieve, riddle, screen, filter; blotter. napkin, cloth, maukinl, malkinl, handkerchief, towel, sudary[obs3]; doyley[obs3], doily, duster, sponge, mop, swab. cover, drugget[obs3]. wash, lotion, detergent, cathartic, purgative; purifier &c. v.; disinfectant; aperient[obs3]; benzene, benzine benzol, benolin[obs3]; bleaching powder, chloride of lime, dentifrice, deobstruent[obs3], laxative. V. be clean, render clean &c. Adj. clean, cleanse; mundifyl, rinse, wring, flush, full, wipe, mop, sponge, scour, swab, scrub, brush up. wash, lave, launder, buck; abstergel, deterge[obs3]; decrassify[obs3]; clear, purify; depurate[obs3], despumate[obs3], defecate; purge, expurgate, elutriate[Chem], lixiviate[obs3], edulcorate[obs3], clarify, refine, rack; filter, filtrate; drain, strain. disinfect, fumigate, ventilate, deodorize; whitewash; castrate, emasculate. sift, winnow, pick, weed, comb, rake, brush, sweep. rout out, clear out, sweep out &c.; make a clean sweep of. Adj. clean, cleanly; pure; immaculate; spotless, stainless, taintless; trig; without a stain, unstained, unspotted, unsoiled, unsullied, untainted, uninfected; sweet, sweet as a nut. neat, spruce, tidy, trim, gimp, clean as a new penny, like a cat in pattens; cleaned &c. v.; kempt[obs3]. abstergent[obs3], cathartic, cleansing, purifying. Adv. neatly &c. adj.; clean as a whistle.

<— p. 206 —>

#653. Uncleanness. — N. uncleanness &c. Adj.; impurity; immundity[obs3], immundicity[obs3]; impurity &c. 961[of mind]. defilement, contamination &c. v.; defoedationl; soilure[obs3], soilinessl; abomination; leaven; taint, tainturel; fetor &c. 401[obs3]. decay; putrescence, putrefaction; corruption; mold, must, mildew, dry rot, mucor, rubigol. slovenry[obs3]; slovenliness &c. Adj. squalor. dowdy, drab, slut, malkin[obs3], slattern, sloven, slammerkinl, slammock[obs3], slummock[obs3], scrub, draggle-tail, mudlark[obs3], dust- man, sweep; beast. dirt, filth, soil, slop; dust, cobweb, flue; smoke, soot, smudge, smut, grit, grime, raff[obs3]; sossle[obs3], sozzle[obs3]. sordes[obs3], dregs, grounds, lees; argol[obs3]; sediment, settlement heeltap[obs3]; dross, drossiness[obs3]; motherl, precipitate, scoriae, ashes, cinders. recrement[obs3], slag; scum, froth. hogwash; ditchwater[obs3], dishwater, bilgewater[obs3]; rinsings, cheeseparings; sweepings &c. (useless refuse) 645; offscourings[obs3], outscourings[obs3]; off scum; caput mortuum[Lat][obs3], residuum, sprue, fecula[Lat], clinker, draff[obs3]; scurf, scurfiness[obs3]; exuviae[Lat], morphea; fur, furfur[obs3]; dandruff, tartar. riffraff; vermin, louse, flea, bug, chinch[obs3]. mud, mire, quagmire, alluvium, silt, sludge, slime, slush, slosh, sposh [obs3][U. S.]. spawn, offal, gurry [obs3][U. S.]; lientery[obs3]; garbage, carrion; excreta &c. 299; slough, peccant humor, pus, matter, suppuration, lienteria[obs3]; faeces, feces, excrement, ordure, dung, crap[vulgar], shit[vulgar]; sewage, sewerage; muck; coprolite; guano, manure, compost. dunghill, colluvies[obs3], mixen[obs3], midden, bog, laystall[obs3], sink, privy, jakes; toilet, john, head; cess[obs3], cesspool; sump, sough, cloaca, latrines, drain, sewer, common sewer; Cloacina; dust hole. sty, pigsty, lair, den, Augean stable[obs3], sink of corruption; slum, rookery. V. be unclean, become unclean &c. Adj.; rot, putrefy, ferment, fester, rankle, reek; stink &c. 401; mold, molder; go bad &c. adj. render unclean &c. adj.; dirt, dirty; daub, blot, blur, smudge, smutch[obs3], soil, smoke, tarnish, slaver, spot, smear; smirch; begrease[obs3]; dabble, drabble[obs3], draggle, daggle[obs3]; spatter, slubber; besmear &c., bemire, beslime[obs3], begrime, befoul; splash, stain, distain[obs3], maculate, sully, pollute, defile, debase, contaminate, taint, leaven; corrupt &c. (injure) 659; cover with dust &c. n.; drabble in the mud[obs3]; roil. wallow in the mire; slobber, slabber[obs3]. Adj. dirty, filthy, grimy; unclean, impure; soiled &c. v.; not to be handled with kid gloves; dusty, snuffy[obs3], smutty, sooty, smoky; thick, turbid, dreggy; slimy; mussy [U.S.]. slovenly, untidy, messy, uncleanly. [of people] unkempt, sluttish, dowdy, draggle-tailed; uncombed. unscoured[obs3], unswept, unwiped[obs3], unwashed, unstrained, unpurified[obs3]; squalid; lutose[obs3], slammocky[obs3], slummocky[obs3], sozzly[obs3]. nasty, coarse, foul, offensive, abominable, beastly, reeky, reechy[obs3]; fetid &c. 401. [of rotting living matter] decayed, moldy, musty, mildewed, rusty, moth-eaten, mucid[obs3], rancid, weak, bad, gone bad, etercoral[obs3], lentiginous[obs3], touched, fusty, effete, reasty[obs3], rotten, corrupt, tainted, high, flyblown, maggoty; putrid, putrefactive, putrescent, putrefied; saprogenic, saprogenous[obs3]; purulent, carious, peccant; fecal, feculent; stercoraceous[obs3], excrementitious[obs3]; scurfy, scurvy, impetiginous[obs3]; gory, bloody; rotting &c. v.; rotten as a pear, rotten as cheese. crapulous &c. (intemperate) 954[obs3]; gross &c. (impure in mind) 961; fimetarious[obs3], fimicolous[obs3]. Phr. "they that touch pitch will be defiled" [Much Ado About Nothing].

<— p. 207 —>

#654. Health. — N. health, sanity; soundness &c. adj.; vigor; good health, perfect health, excellent health, rude health, robust health; bloom. mens sana in corpore sano[Lat]; Hygeia[obs3]; incorruption, incorruptibility; good state of health, clean bill of health; eupepsia[obs3]; euphoria, euphory[obs3]; St. Anthony's fire[obs3]. V. be in health &c. adj. bloom, flourish. keep body and soul together, keep on one's legs; enjoy good health, enjoy a good state of health; have a clean bill of health. return to health; recover &c. 660; get better &c. (improve) 658; take a new lease of life, fresh lease of life; recruit; restore to health; cure &c. (restore) 660; tinker. Adj. healthy, healthful; in health &c. n.; well, sound, hearty, hale, fresh, green, whole; florid, flush, hardy, stanch, staunch, brave, robust, vigorous, weather-proof. unscathed, uninjured, unmaimed[obs3], unmarred, untainted; sound of wind and limb, safe and sound. on one's legs; sound as a roach, sound as a bell; fresh as a daisy, fresh as a rose, fresh as April[obs3]; hearty as a buck; in fine feather, in high feather; in good case, in full bloom; pretty bobbish[obs3], tolerably well, as well as can be expected. sanitary &c. (health-giving) 656; sanatory &c. (remedial) 662[obs3]. Phr. "health that snuffs the morning air" [Grainger]; non est vivere sed valere vita [Lat][Martial].

#655. Disease. — N. disease; illness, sickness &c. adj.; ailing &c. "all the ills that flesh is heir to" [Hamlet]; morbidity, morbosityl; infirmity, ailment, indisposition; complaint, disorder, malady; distemper, distemperature[obs3]. visitation, attack, seizure, stroke, fit. delicacy, loss of health, invalidation, cachexy[obs3]; cachexia[Med], atrophy, marasmus[obs3]; indigestion, dyspepsia; decay &c. (deterioration) 659; decline, consumption, palsy, paralysis, prostration. taint, pollution, infection, sepsis, septicity[obs3], infestation; epidemic, pandemic, endemic, epizootic; murrain, plague, pestilence, pox. sore, ulcer, abscess, fester, boil; pimple, wen &c. (swelling) 250; carbuncle, gathering, imposthume[obs3], peccant humor, issue; rot, canker, cold sore, fever sore; cancer, carcinoma, leukemia, neoplastic disease, malignancy, tumor; caries, mortification, corruption, gangrene, sphacelus[obs3], sphacelation[obs3], leprosy; eruption, rash, breaking out. fever, temperature, calenture[obs3]; inflammation. ague, angina pectoris[Lat], appendicitis; Asiatic cholera[obs3], spasmodic cholera; biliary calculus, kidney stone, black death, bubonic plague, pneumonic plague; blennorrhagia[obs3], blennorrhoea[obs3]; blood poisoning, bloodstroke[obs3], bloody flux, brash; breakbone fever[obs3], dengue fever, malarial fever, Q-fever; heart attack, cardiac arrest, cardiomyopathy[Med]; hardening of the arteries, arteriosclerosis, atherosclerosis; bronchocele[Med], canker rash, cardialgia[Med], carditis[Med], endocarditis[Med]; cholera, asphyxia; chlorosis, chorea, cynanche[obs3]; dartre[Fr]; enanthem[obs3], enanthema[obs3]; erysipelas; exanthem[obs3], exanthema; gallstone, goiter, gonorrhea, green sickness; grip, grippe, influenza, flu; hay fever, heartburn, heaves, rupture, hernia, hemorrhoids, piles, herpes, itch, king's evil, lockjaw; measles, mumps[obs3], polio; necrosis, pertussis, phthisis[obs3], pneumonia, psora[obs3], pyaemia[obs3], pyrosis[Med], quinsy, rachitis[obs3], ringworm, rubeola, St. Vitus's dance, scabies, scarlatina, scarlet fever, scrofula, seasickness, struma[obs3], syntexis[obs3], tetanus, tetter[obs3], tonsillitis, tonsilitis[obs3], tracheocele[Med], trachoma, trismus[Med], varicella[Med], varicosis[Med], variola[Med], water qualm, whooping cough; yellow fever, yellow jack. fatal disease &c. (hopeless) 859; dangerous illness, galloping consumption, churchyard cough; general breaking up, break up of the system. [Disease of mind] idiocy &c. 499; insanity &c. 503. martyr to disease; cripple; "the halt the lame and the blind"; valetudinary[obs3], valetudinarian; invalid, patient, case; sickroom, sick- chamber. [Science of disease] pathology, etiology, nosology[obs3]. [Veterinary] anthrax, bighead; blackleg, blackquarter[obs3]; cattle plague, glanders[obs3], mange, scrapie, milk sickness; heartworm, feline leukemia, roundworms; quarter-evil, quarter-ill; rinderpest. [disease-causing agents] virus, bacterium, bacteria. [types of viruses] DNA virus; RNA virus. [RNA viruses] rhinovirus; rhabdovirus; picornavirus. [DNA viruses] herpesvirus; cytomegalovirus, CMV; human immunodefficiency virus, HIV. V. be ill &c. adj.; ail, suffer, labor under, be affected with, complain of, have; droop, flag, languish, halt; sicken, peak, pine; gasp. keep one's bed; feign sickness &c. (falsehood) 544. lay by, lay up; take a disease, catch a disease &c. n., catch an infection; break out. Adj. diseased; ailing &c. v.; ill, ill of; taken ill, seized with; indisposed, unwell, sick, squeamish, poorly, seedy; affected with illness, afflicted with illness; laid up, confined, bedridden, invalided, in hospital, on the sick list; out of health, out of sorts; under the weather [U. S.]; valetudinary[obs3]. unsound, unhealthy; sickly, morbid, morbose[obs3], healthless[obs3], infirm, chlorotic[Med], unbraced[obs3]. drooping, flagging, lame, crippled, halting. morbid, tainted, vitiated, peccant, contaminated, poisoned, tabid[obs3], mangy, leprous, cankered; rotten, rotten to the core, rotten at the core; withered, palsied, paralytic; dyspeptic; luetic[obs3], pneumonic, pulmonic[Med], phthisic[obs3], rachitic; syntectic[obs3], syntectical[obs3]; tabetic[obs3], varicose. touched in the wind, broken-winded, spavined, gasping; hors de combat &c. (useless) 645[Fr]. weakly, weakened &c. (weak) 160; decrepit; decayed &c. (deteriorated) 659; incurable &c. (hopeless) 859; in declining health; cranky; in a bad way, in danger, prostrate; moribund &c. (death) 360. morbific &c. 657[obs3]; epidemic, endemic; zymotic[obs3].

<— p. 208 —>

#656. Salubrity. — N. salubrity; healthiness &c. Adj.
fine air, fine climate; eudiometer[obs3].

[Preservation of health] hygiene; valetudinarian, valetudinarianism; sanitarian; sanitarium, sanitorium.

V. be salubrious &c. Adj.; agree with; assimilate &c. 23.

Adj. salubrious, salutary, salutiferous[obs3]; wholesome; healthy, healthful; sanitary, prophYlactic, benign, bracing, tonic, invigorating, good for, nutritious; hygeian[obs3], hygienic.

innoxious[obs3], innocuous, innocent; harmless, uninjurious, uninfectious.

sanative &c. (remedial) 662; restorative &c. (reinstate) 660; useful &c. 644.

#657. Insalubrity. — N. insalubrity; unhealthiness &c. Adj.; nonnaturals[obs3]; plague spot; malaria &c. (poison) 663; death in the pot, contagion; toxicity. Adj. insalubrious; unhealthy, unwholesome; noxious, noisome, morbific[obs3], morbiferous[obs3]; mephitic, septic, azotic[obs3], deleterious; pestilent, pestiferous, pestilential; virulent, venomous, envenomed; poisonous, toxic, toxiferous[obs3], teratogenic; narcotic. contagious, infectious, catching, taking, epidemic, zymotic[obs3]; epizootic. innutritious[obs3], indigestible, ungenial; uncongenial &c. (disagreeing) 24. deadly &c. (killing) 361.

#658. Improvement. — N. improvement; amelioration, melioration; betterment; mend, amendment, emendation; mending &c. v.; advancement; advance &c. (progress) 282; ascent &c. 305; promotion, preferment; elevation &c. 307; increase &c. 35; cultivation, civilization; culture, march of intellect; menticulture[obs3]; race-culture, eugenics.

reform, reformation; revision, radical reform; second thoughts, correction, limoe labor[Lat], refinement, elaboration; purification &c. 652; oxidation; repair &c. (restoration) 660; recovery &c. 660.

revise, new edition.

reformer, radical.

V. improve; be better, become better, get better; mend, amend.

advance &c. (progress) 282; ascend &c. 305; increase &c. 35; fructify, ripen, mature; pick up, come about, rally, take a favorable turn; turn over a new leaf, turn the corner; raise one's head, sow one's wild oats; recover &c. 660.

be better &c. adj., be improved by; turn to right account, turn to good account, turn to best account; profit by, reap the benefit of; make good use of, make capital out of; place to good account.

render better, improve, mend, amend, better; ameliorate, meliorate; correct; decrassify[obs3].

improve upon, refine upon; rectify; enrich, mellow, elaborate, fatten.

promote, cultivate, advance, forward, enhance; bring forward, bring on; foster &c. 707; invigorate &c. (strengthen) 159.

touch up, rub up, brush up, furbish up, bolster up, vamp up, brighten up, warm up; polish, cook, make the most of, set off to advantage; prune; repair &c. (restore) 660; put in order &c. (arrange) 60.

review, revise; make corrections, make improvements &c. n.; doctor &c. (remedy) 662; purify,&c. 652.

relieve, refresh, infuse new blood into, recruit.

reform, remodel, reorganize; new model.

view in a new light, think better of, appeal from Philip drunk to Philip sober.

palliate, mitigate; lessen an evil &c. 36.

Adj. improving &c. v.; progressive, improved &c. v.; better, better off, better for; all the better for; better advised.

reformatory, emendatory[obs3]; reparatory &c. (restorative) 660[obs3]; remedial &c. 662.

corrigible, improvable; accultural[obs3].

adv. on consideration, on reconsideration, on second thoughts, on better advice; ad melius inquirendum[Lat].

phr. urbent latericiam invenit marmoream reliquit[Lat].

<— p. 209 —>

#659. Deterioration. — N. deterioration, debasement; wane, ebb; recession &c. 287; retrogradation &c. 283[obs3]; decrease &c. 36. degeneracy, degeneration, degenerateness; degradation; depravation, depravement; devolution; depravity &c. 945; demoralization, retrogression; masochism. impairment, inquinationl, injury, damage, loss, detriment, delacerationl, outrage, havoc, inroad, ravage, scath[obs3]; perversion, prostitution, vitiation, discoloration, oxidation, pollution, defoedationl, poisoning, venenationl, leaven, contamination, canker, corruption, adulteration, alloy. decline, declension, declination; decadence, decadency[obs3]; falling off &c. v.; caducity[obs3], decrepitude. decay, dilapidation, ravages of time, wear and tear; corrosion, erosion; moldiness, rottenness; moth and rust, dry rot, blight, marasmus[obs3], atrophy, collapse; disorganization; delabrement &c. (destruction)[Fr]. 162; aphid, Aphis, plant louse, puceron[obs3]; vinefretter[obs3], vinegrub[obs3]. wreck, mere wreck, honeycomb, magni nominis umbra[Lat]; jade, plug, rackabones [obs3][U. S.], skate [U. S.]; tackey[obs3], tacky [U. S.]. V. be worse, be deterio-rated, become worse, become deteriorated &c. Adj.; have seen better days, deteriorate, degenerate, fall off; wane &c. (decrease) 36; ebb; retrograde &c. 283- decline, droop; go down &c. (sink) 306; go downhill, go from bad to worse, go farther and fare worse; jump out of the frying pan into the fire. run to seed, go to seed, run to waste swalel, sweall; lapse, be the worse for; sphacelate; break[obs3], break down; spring a leak, crack, start; shrivel &c. (contract) 195; fade, go off, wither, molder, rot, rankle, decay, go bad; go to decay, fall into decay; "fall into the sear and yellow leaf", rust, crumble, shake; totter, totter to its fall; perish &c. 162; die &c. 360. [Render less good] deterio-rate; weaken &c. 160; put back, set back; taint, infect, contaminate, poison, empoison[obs3], envenom, canker, corrupt, exulceratel, pollute, vitiate, inquinatel; debase, embasel; denaturalize, denature, leaven; deflower, debauch, defile, deprave, degrade; ulcerate; stain &c. (dirt) 653; discolor; alloy, adulterate, sophisticate, tamper with, preju-dice. pervert, prostitute, demoralize, brutalize; render vicious &c. 945. embitter, acerbate, exacerbate, aggravate. injure, impair, labefy[obs3], damage, harm, hurt, shendl, scathl, scathe, spoil, mar, despoil, dilapidate, waste; overrun; ravage; pillage &c. 791. wound, stab, pierce, maim, lame, surbatel, cripple, hough[obs3], hamstring, hit between wind and water, scotch, mangle, mutilate, disfigure, blemish, deface, warp. blight, rot; corrode, erode; wear away, wear out; gnaw, gnaw at the root of; sap, mine, undermine, shake, sap the foundations of, break up; disorgan-ize, dismantle, dismast; destroy &c. 162. damnify &c. (aggrieve) 649[obs3]; do one's worst; knock down; deal a blow to; play havoc with, play sad havoc with, play the mischief with, play the deuce with, play the very devil with, play havoc among, play sad havoc among, play the mischief among, play the deuce among, play the very devil among; decimate. Adj. unimproved &c. (improve &c. 658); deteriorated &c. v.; altered, altered for the worse; injured &c. v.; sprung; withering, spoiling &c. v.; on the wane, on the decline; tabid[obs3]; degenerate; marescent[obs3]; worse; the worse for, all the worse for; out of repair, out of tune; imperfect &c. 651; the worse for wear; battered; weathered, weather-beaten; stale, passe, shaken, dilapidated, frayed, faded, wilted, shabby, secondhand, threadbare; worn, worn to a thread, worn to a shadow, worn to the stump, worn to rags; reduced, reduced to a skeleton; far gone; tacky [U. S.*]. decayed &c. v.; moth-eaten, worm-eaten; mildewed, rusty, moldy, spotted, seedy, time-worn, moss-grown; discolored; effete, wasted, crumbling, moldering, rotten, cankered, blighted, tainted; depraved &c. (vicious) 945; decrepid[obs3], decrepit; broke, busted, broken, out of commission, hors de combat[Fr], out of action, broken down; done, done for, done up; worn out, used up, finished; beyond saving, fit for the dust hole, fit for the wastepaper basket, past work &c. (useless) 645. at a low ebb, in a bad way, on one's last legs; undermined, deciduous; nodding to its fall &c. (destruction) 162; tottering &c,. (dangerous) 665: past cure &c. (hopeless) 859; fatigued &c. 688; retrograde &c. (retrogressive) 283; deleterious &c. 649. Phr. out of the frying pan into the fire; agrescit medendo[Latin]; "what a falling off was there!" [Hamlet].

<— p. 210 —>

#660. Restoration. — N. restoration, restoral; reinstatement, replacement, rehabilitation, reestablishment, reconstitu-tion, reconstruction; reproduction &c. 163; renovation, renewal; revival, revivessence[obs3], reviviscence[obs3]; refreshment &c. 689; resuscitation, reanimation, revivification, revictionl; Phenix; reorganization. renaissance, second youth, rejuvenescence[obs3],. new birth; regeneration, regeneracy[obs3], regenerateness[obs3]; palingenesis[obs3], reconversion. redress, retrieval, reclamation, recovery; convalescence; resumption, resumption; sanativeness[obs3]. recurrence &c. (repetition) 104; rechauffe[Fr], rifacimento[It]. cure, recurel, sanationl; healing &c. v.; redintegration[obs3]; rectification; instauration[obs3]. repair, reparation, remanufacture; recruiting &c. v.; cicatrization; disinfection; tinkering. reaction; redemption &c. (deliverance) 672; restitution &c. 790; relief &c. 834. tinker, cobbler; vis medicatrix &c. (remedy) 662[obs3]. curableness. V. return to the original state; recover, rally, revive; come come to, come round, come to oneself; pull through, weather the storm, be oneself again; get well ,get round, get the better of, get over, get about; rise from one's ashes, rise from the grave; survive &c. (outlive) 110; resume, reappear; come to, come to life again; live again, rise again. heal, skin over, cicatrize; right itself. restore, put back, place in statu quo[Lat]; reinstate, replace, reseat, rehabilitate, reestablish, reestate[obs3], reinstall.

reconstruct, rebuild, reorganize, reconstitute; reconvert; renew, renovate; regenerate; rejuvenate. redeem, reclaim, recover, retrieve; rescue &c. (deliver) 672. redress, recure[obs3]; cure, heal, remedy, doctor, physic, medicate; break of; bring round, set on one's legs. resuscitate, revive, reanimate, revivify, recall to life; reproduce &c. 163; warm up; reinvigorate, refresh &c. 689. make whole, redintegrate[obs3]; recoup &c. 790; make good, make all square; rectify, correct; put right, put to rights, set right, set to rights, set straight; set up; put in order &c. (arrange) 60; refit, recruit; fill up, fill up the ranks; reinforce. repair; put in repair, remanufacture, put in thorough repair, put in complete repair; retouch, refashion, botchl, vamp, tinker, cobble; do up, patch up, touch up, plaster up, vamp up; darn, finedraw[obs3], heelpiece[obs3]; stop a gap, stanch, staunch, caulk, calk, careen, splice, bind up wounds. Adj. restored &c. v.; redivivus[Lat], convalescent; in a fair way; none the worse; rejuvenated. restoring &c. v.; restorative, recuperative; sanative, reparative, sanatory[obs3], reparatory[obs3]; curative, remedial. restorable, recoverable, sanable[obs3], remediable, retrievable, curable. Adv. in statu quo[Lat]; as you were. phr. revenons a nos moutons[Fr]; medecin[Fr], gueris-toi toi-meme[Fr]; vestigia nulla retrorsum [Lat][Horace].

   #661. Relapse. — N. relapse, lapse; falling back &c. v.;
retrogradation &c. (retrogression) 283[obs3]; deterioration &c. 659.
   [Return to, or recurrence of a bad state] backsliding, recidivation l;
recidivism, recidivity[obs3]; recrudescence.
   V. relapse, lapse; fall back, slide back, sink back; return;
retrograde &c. 283; recidivate; fall off again &c. 659.
<— p. 211 —>

<— remedy = medicine; needs to be greatly expanded —> #662. Remedy. — N. remedy, help, cure, redress; medicine, medicament; diagnosis, medical examination; medical treatment; surgery; preventive medicine. [medical devices] clinical thermometer, stethoscope, X-ray machine. anthelmintic[Med]; antidote, antifebrile[Med], antipoison[obs3], counterpoison[obs3], antitoxin, antispasmodic; bracer, faith cure, placebo; helminthagogue[obs3], lithagogue[obs3], pick-meup, stimulant, tonic; vermifuge, prophylactic, corrective, restorative; sedative &c. 174; palliative; febrifuge; alterant[obs3], alterative; specific; antiseptic, emetic, analgesic, pain-killer, antitussive[Med], antiinflammatory[Med], antibiotic, antiviral[Med], antifungal[Med], carminative; Nepenthe, Mithridate. cure, treatment, regimen; radical cure, perfect cure, certain cure; sovereign remedy. examination, diagnosis, diagnostics; analysis, urinalysis, biopsy, radiology. medicine, physic, Galenicals[obs3], simples, drug, pharmaceutical, prescription, potion, draught, dose, pill, bolus, injection, infusion, drip, suppository, electuary[obs3]; linctus[obs3], lincture[obs3]; medica- ment; pharmacon[obs3]. nostrum, receipt, recipe, prescription; catholicon[obs3], panacea, elixir, elixir vitae, philoso- pher's stone; balm, balsam, cordial, theriac[obs3], ptisan[obs3]. agueweed[obs3], arnica, benzoin, bitartrate of potash, boneset[obs3], calomel, catnip, cinchona, cream of tartar, Epsom salts[Chem]; feverroot[obs3], feverwort; friar's balsam, Indian sage; ipecac, ipecacuanha; jonquil, mercurous chloride, Peruvian bark; quinine, quinquina[obs3]; sassafras, yarrow. salve, ointment, cerate, oil, lenitive, lotion, cosmetic; plaster; epithem[obs3], embrocation[obs3], liniment, cataplasm[obs3], sinapism[obs3], arquebusade[obs3], traumatic, vulnerary, pepastic[obs3], poultice, collyrium[obs3], depilatory; emplastrum[obs3]; eyewater[obs3], vesicant, vesicatory[Med]. compress, pledget[obs3]; bandage &c. (support) 215. treatment, medical treatment, regimen; dietary, dietetics; vis medicatrix[obs3], vis medicatrix naturae[Lat][obs3]; medecine expectante[Fr]; bloodletting, bleeding, venesection[Med], phlebotomy, cupping, sanguisae, leeches; operation, surgical operation; transfusion, infusion, intravenous infusion, catheter, feeding tube; prevention, preventative medicine, immunization, inoculation, vaccina- tion, vaccine, shot, booster, gamma globulin. pharmacy, pharmacology, pharmaceutics; pharmacopoeia, formulary; acology[obs3], Materia Medica[Lat], therapeutics, posology[obs3]; homeopathy, allopathy[obs3], heteropathy[Med], osteopathy, hydropathy[Med]; cold water cure; dietetics; surgery, chirurgery[Med], chirurgy[obs3]; healing art, leechcraft[obs3]; orthopedics, orthopedy[obs3], orthopraxy[obs3]; pediatrics; dentistry, midwifery, obstetrics, gynecol- ogy; tocology[obs3]; sarcology[obs3]. hospital, infirmary; pesthouse[obs3], lazarhouse[obs3]; lazaretto; lock hospital; maison de sante[Fr]; ambulance. dispensary; dispensatory[obs3], drug store, pharmacy, apothecary, druggist, chemist. Hotel des Invalides; sanatorium, spa, pump room, well; hospice; Red Cross. doctor, physician, surgeon; medical practitioner, general practitioner, specialist; medical attendant, apothecary, druggist; leech; osteopath, osteopathist[obs3]; optometrist, ophthalmologist; internist, oncologist, gastroenterologist; epidemiologist[Med], public health specialist; dermatologist; podiatrist; witch doctor, shaman, faith healer, quack, exorcist; Aesculapius[obs3], Hippocrates, Galen; accoucheur[Fr], accoucheuse[Fr], midwife, oculist, aurist[obs3]; operator; nurse, registered nurse, practical nurse, monthly nurse, sister; nurse's aide, candystriper; dresser; bonesetter; pharmaceutist[obs3], pharmacist, druggist, chemist, pharmacopolist[obs3]. V. apply a remedy &c. n.; doctor, dose, physic, nurse, minister to, attend, dress the wounds, plaster; drain; prevent &c. 706; relieve &c. 834; palliate &c. 658; restore &c. 660; drench with physic; bleed, cup, let blood; manicure. operate, excise, cut out; incise. Adj. remedial; restorative &c. 660; corrective, palliative, healing; sanatory[obs3], sanative; prophylactic, preventative, immunizing; salutiferous &c.
182

(salutary) 656[obs3]; medical, medicinal; therapeutic, chirurgical[Med], epuloticl, paregoric, tonic, corroborant, analeptic[obs3], balsamic, anodyne, hypnotic, neurotic, narcotic, sedative, lenitive, demulcentl, emollient; depuratory[obs3]; detersive[obs3], detergent; abstersive[obs3], disinfectant, febrifugal[obs3], alterative; traumatic, vulnerary. allopathic[obs3], heteropathic[obs3], homeopathic, hydropathic[Med]; anthelmintic[Med]; antifebrile[Med], antiluetic[obs3]; aperient[obs3], chalybeate[obs3], deobstruent[obs3], depurative[obs3], laxative, roborant[obs3]. dietetic, alimentary; nutritious, nutritive; peptic; alexipharmic[obs3], alexiteric[obs3]; remediable, curable. phr. aux grands maux les grands remedes[Fr]; Dios que da la llaga da la medicina[Sp]; para todo hay remedio sino para la muerte[Sp]; temporis ars medicina fere est [Lat][Ovid]; "the remedy is worse than the disease" [Dryden]; "throw physic to the dogs, I'll none of it" [Macbeth].

<— p. 212 —>

#663. Bane. — N. bane, curse; evil &c. 619; hurtfulness &c. (badness) 649[obs3]; painfulness &c. (cause of pain) 830; scourge &c. (punishment) 975; damnosa hereditas[Lat]; white elephant. sting, fang, thorn, tang, bramble, brier, nettle. poison, toxin; teratogen; leaven, virus venom; arsenic; antimony, tartar emetic; strychnine, nicotine; miasma, miasm[obs3], mephitis[obs3], malaria, azote[obs3], sewer gas; pest. [poisonous substances, examples] Albany hemp[obs3], arsenious oxide, arsenious acid; bichloride of mercury; carbonic acid, carbonic gas; choke damp, corrosive sublimate, fire damp; hydrocyanic acid, cyanide, Prussic acid[ISA:chemsubcfp], hydrogen cyanide; marsh gas, nux vomica[Lat], ratsbane[obs3]. [poisonous plants] hemlock, hellebore, nightshade, belladonna, henbane, aconite; banewort[obs3], bhang, ganja[obs3], hashish; Upas tree. [list of poisonous substances(on-line)] Toxline. rust, worm, helminth[Med], moth, moth and rust, fungus, mildew; dry rot; canker, cankerworm; cancer; torpedo; viper &c. (evil doer) 913; demon &c. 980. [Science of poisons] toxicology. Adj. baneful &c. (bad) 649; poisonous &c. (unwholesome) 657. phr. bibere venenum in auro[Lat].

% Contingent Subservience %

#664. Safety. — N. safety, security, surety, impregnability; invulnerability, invulnerableness &c. Adj.; danger past, danger over; storm blown over; coast clear; escape &c. 671; means of escape; blow valve, safety valve, release valve, sniffing valve; safeguard, palladium. guardianship, wardship, wardenship; tutelage, custody, safekeeping; preservation &c. 670; protection, auspices. safe-conduct, escort, convoy; guard, shield &c. (defense) 717; guardian angel; tutelary god, tutelary deity, tutelary saint; genius loci. protector, guardian; warden, warder; preserver, custodian, duenna[Sp], chaperon, third person. watchdog, bandog[obs3]; Cerberus; watchman, patrolman, policeman; cop, dick, fuzz, smokey, peelerl, zarpl[all slang]; sentinel, sentry, scout &c. (warning) 668; garrison; guardship[obs3]. [Means of safety] refuge &c. anchor &c. 666; precaution &c. (preparation) 673; quarantine, cordon sanitaire[Fr]. confidence &c. 858[Sense of security]. V. be safe &c. Adj.; keep one's head above water, tide over, save one's bacon; ride out the storm, weather the storm; light upon one's feet, land on one's feet; bear a charmed life; escape &c. 671. make safe, render safe &c. Adj.; protect; take care of &c. (care) 459; preserve &c. 670; cover, screen, shelter, shroud, flank, ward; guard &c. (defend) 717; secure &c. (restrain) 751; entrench, intrench[obs3], fence round &c. (circumscribe) 229; house, nestle, ensconce; take charge of. escort, convoy; garrison; watch, mount guard, patrol. make assurance doubly sure &c. (caution) 864; take up a loose thread; take precautions &c. (prepare for) 673; double reef topsails. seek safety; take shelter, find shelter &c. 666. Adj. safe, secure, sure; in safety, in security; on the safe side; under the shield of, under the shade of, under the wing of, under the shadow of one's wing; under cover, under lock and key; out of danger, out of the woods, out of the meshes, out of harm's way; unharmed, unscathed; on sure ground, at anchor, high and dry, above water; unthreatened[obs3], unmolested; protected &c. v.; cavendo tutus[Lat]; panoplied &c. (defended) 717[obs3]. snug, seaworthy; weatherproof, waterproof, fireproof. defensible, tenable, proof against, invulnerable; unassailable, unattackable, impenetrable; impregnable, imperdiblel; inexpugnable; Achillean[obs3]. safe and sound &c. (preserved) 670;scathless &c. (perfect) 650[obs3]; unhazarded[obs3]; not dangerous &c. 665. unthreatening, harmless; friendly (cooperative) 709. protecting, protective &c. v.; guardian, tutelary; preservative &c. 670; trustworthy &c 939. adv. ex abundanti cautela[Lat][obs3]; with impunity. phr. all's well; salva res est[Lat]; suave mari magno[Lat]; a couvert[Fr]; e terra alterius spectare laborem [Lat][Lucretius]; Dieu vous garde[Fr].

<— p. 213 —>

#665. Danger. — N. danger, peril, insecurity, jeopardy, risk, hazard, venture, precariousness, slipperiness; instability &c. 149; defenselessness &c. Adj. exposure &c. (liability) 177; vulnerability; vulnerable point, heel of Achilles[obs3]; forlorn hope &c. (hopelessness) 859. [Dangerous course] leap in the dark &c. (rashness) 863; road to ruin, faciles descensus Averni [Lat][Vergil], hairbreadth escape. cause for alarm; source of danger &c. 667. rock ahead[Approach of danger], breakers ahead; storm brewing; clouds in the horizon, clouds gathering; warning &c. 668; alarm &c. 669. [Sense of danger] apprehension &c. 860. V. be in danger &c. Adj.; be exposed to danger, run into danger, incur danger, encounter danger &c. n.; run a risk; lay oneself open to &c. (liability) 177; lean on a broken reed, trust to a broken reed; feel the ground sliding from under one, have to run for it; have the chances against one, have the odds against one, face long odds; be in deep trouble, be between a rock and a hard place. hang by a thread, totter; sleep on a volcano, stand on a volcano; sit on a barrel of gunpowder, live in a glass house. bring in danger, place in danger, put in danger, place in jeopardy, put in jeopardy &c. n.; endanger, expose to danger, imperil; jeopard[obs3], jeopardize; compromise; sail too near the wind &c. (rash) 863. adventure, risk, hazard, venture, stake, set at hazard; run the gauntlet &c. (dare) 861; engage in a forlorn hope. threaten danger &c. 909; run one hard; lay a trap for &c. (deceive) 545. Adj. in danger &c. n.; endangered &c. v.; fraught with danger; dangerous, hazardous, perilous, parlous, periculousl; unsafe, unprotected &c. (safe, protect &c. 664);insecure, untrustworthy; built upon sand, on a sandy basis; wildcat. defenseless, fenceless, guardless[obs3], harborless; unshielded; vulnerable, expugnable[obs3], exposed; open to &c. (liable) 177. aux abois[Fr], at bay; on the wrong side of the wall, on a lee shore, on the rocks. at stake, in question; precarious, critical, ticklish; slippery, slippy; hanging by a thread &c. v.; with a halter round one's neck; between the hammer and the anvil, between Scylla and Charybdis, between a rock and a hard place, between the devil and the deep blue sea, between two fires; on the edge of a precipice, on the brink of a precipice, on the verge of a precipice, on the edge of a volcano; in the lion's den, on slippery ground, under fire; not out of the wood. unwarned, unadmonished, unadvised, unprepared &c. 674; off one's guard &c. (inexpectant) 508[obs3]. tottering; unstable, unsteady; shaky, top-heavy, tumbledown, ramshackle, crumbling, waterlogged; helpless, guideless[obs3]; in a bad way; reduced to the last extremity, at the last extremity; trembling in the balance; nodding to its fall &c. (destruction) 162. threatening &c. 909; ominous, illomened; alarming &c. (fear) 860; explosive. adventurous &c. (rash) 863, (bold) 861. Phr. incidit in Scyllam qui vult vitare Charybdim[Lat]; nam tua res agitur paries dum proximus ardet[Lat].

#666. [Means of safety.] Refuge. — N. refuge, sanctuary, retreat, fastness; acropolis; keep, last resort; ward; prison &c. 752; asylum, ark, home, refuge for the destitute; almshouse[obs3]; hiding place &c. (ambush) 530; sanctum sanctorum &c. (privacy) 893[Lat]. roadstead, anchorage; breakwater, mole, port, haven; harbor, harbor of refuge; seaport; pier, jetty, embankment, quay. covert, cover, shelter, screen, lee wall, wing, shield, umbrella; barrier; dashboard, dasher [U.S.]. wall &c. (inclosure) 232; fort &c. (defense) 717. anchor, kedge; grapnel, grappling iron; sheet anchor, killick[obs3]; mainstay; support &c. 215; cheek &c. 706; ballast. jury mast; vent-peg; safety valve, blow-off valve; safety lamp; lightning rod, lightning conductor; safety belt, airbag, seat belt; antilock brakes, antiskid tires, snow tires. means of escape &c. (escape) 671 lifeboat, lifejacket, life buoy, swimming belt, cork jacket; parachute, plank, steppingstone; emergency landing. safeguard &c. (protection) 664. V. seek refuge, take refuge, find refuge &c. n.; seek safety, find safety &c. 664; throw oneself into the arms of; break for taller timber [U. S.]. create a diversion. Phr. any port in a storm; bibere venenum in auro[Lat]; valet anchora virtus[obs3].

<— pitfall is related to deceiver and danger —>

#667. [Source of danger.] Pitfall. — N. rocks, reefs, coral reef, sunken rocks, snags; sands, quicksands; syrtl, syrtisl; Goodwin sands, sandy foundation; slippery ground; breakers, shoals, shallows, bank, shelf, flat, lee shore, iron-bound coast; rock ahead, breakers ahead. precipice; maelstrom, volcano; ambush &c. 530; pitfall, trapdoor; trap &c. (snare) 545. sword of Damocles; wolf at the door, snake in the grass, death in the pot; latency &c. 526. ugly customer, dangerous person, le chat qui dort[Fr]; firebrand, hornet's nest. Phr. latet anquis in herba [Lat][Vergil]; proximus ardet Ucalegon [Lat][Vergil].

<— p. 214 —>

#668. Warning. — N. warning, early warning, caution, caveat; notice &c. (information) 527; premonition, premonishment[obs3]; prediction &c. 511; contraindication, lesson, dehortation[obs3]; admonition, monition; alarm &c. 669. handwriting on the wall, mene mene tekel upharsin, red flag, yellow flag; fog-signal, foghorn; siren; monitor, warning voice, Cassandra[obs3], signs of the times, Mother Cary's chickens[obs3], stormy petrel, bird of ill omen, gathering clouds, clouds in the horizon, death watch. watchtower, beacon, signal post; lighthouse &c. (indication of locality) 550. sentinel, sentry; watch, watchman; watch and ward; watchdog, bandog[obs3], housedog[obs3]; patrol, patrolman, vedette[obs3], picket, bivouac, scout, spy, spiall; undercover agent, mole, plainclothesman; advanced guard, rear guard; lookout. cautiousness &c. 864. monitor, guard camera, radar, AWACS, spy satellite, spy-in-the-sky, U2 plane, spy plane. V. warn, caution; forewarn, prewarn[obs3]; admonish, premonish[obs3]; give notice, give warning, dehort[obs3]; menace &c. (threaten) 909; put on one's guard; sound the alarm &c. 669; croak. beware, ware; take warning, take heed at one's peril; keep watch and ward &c. (care) 459. Adj. warning &c. v.; premonitory,

monitory, cautionary; admonitory, admonitive[obs3]; sematic[Biol]. warned, forewarned &c. v.; on one's guard &c. (careful) 459, (cautious) 864. Adv. in terrorem[Lat] &c. (threat) 909. Int. beware! ware! take care! look out! fore![golf], mind what you are about!, take care what you are about! mind! Phr. ne reveillez pas le chat qui dort [French: don't wake a sleeping cat]; foenum habet in cornu[Lat]; caveat actor; le silence du people est la legon des rois[Fr]; verbum sat sapienti [Latin: a word to the wise is sufficient]; un averti en vaut deux[Fr].

#669. [Indication of danger.] Alarm. — N. alarm; alarum, larum[obs3], alarm bell, tocsin, alerts, beat of drum, sound of trumpet, note of alarm, hue and cry, fire cross, signal of distress; blue lights; war-cry, war- whoop; warning &c. 668; fogsignal, foghorn; yellow flag; danger signal; red light, red flag; fire bell; police whistle. false alarm, cry of wolf; bug-bear, bugaboo. V. give the alarm, raise the alarm, sound the alarm, turn in the alarm, beat the alarm, give an alarm, raise an alarm, sound an alarm, turn in an alarm, beat an alarm &c. n.; alarm; warn &c. 668; ring the tocsin; battre la generale[Fr]; cry wolf. Adj. alarming &c. v. Int. sauve qui peut[Fr]! [French: every man for himself]; qui vive? [Fr].

#670. Preservation. — N. preservation; safe-keeping; conservation &c. (storage) 636; maintenance, support, susteritation[obs3], conservatism; vis conservatrix[obs3]; salvation &c. (deliverance) 672. [Means of preservation] prophylaxis; preserver, preservative, additive; antibiotics, antifungals[Med], biocide; hygiastics[obs3], hygiantics[obs3]; cover, drugget[obs3]; cordon sanitaire[Fr]; canning; ensilage; tinned goods, canned goods. [Superstitious remedies] snake oil, spider webs, cure-all; laetrile; charm &c. 993. V. preserve, maintain, keep, sustain, support, hold; keep up, keep alive; refrigerate, keep on ice; not willingly let die; bank up; nurse; save, rescue; be safe, make safe &c. 664; take care of &c. (care) 459; guard &c. (defend) 717. stare super antiquas vias [Lat][Bacon]; hold one's own; hold one's ground, stand one's ground &c. (resist) 719. embalm, cure, salt, pickle, season, kyanizel, bottle, pot, tin, can; sterilize, pasteurize, radiate; dry, lyophilize[Chem], freeze-dry, concentrate, evaporate; freeze, quick-freeze, deep-freeze; husband &c. (store) 636. Adj. preserving &c. v.; conservative; prophy-lactic; preservatory[obs3], preservative; hygienic. preserved &c. v.; unimpaired, unbroken, uninjured, unhurt, unsinged[obs3], unmarred; safe, safe and sound; intact, with a whole skin. Phr. nolumus leges Angliae mutari[Lat] [obs3].

#671. Escape. — N. escape, scape; avolationl, elopement, flight; evasion &c. (avoidance) 623; retreat; narrow escape, hairbreadth escape; close call; come off, impunity. [Means of escape] loophole &c. (opening) 260; path &c. 627; refuse &c. 666; vent, vent peg; safety valve; drawbridge, fire escape. reprieve &c. (deliverance) 672; liberation &c. 750. refugee &c. (fugitive) 623. V. escape, scape; make one's escape, effect one's escape, make good one's escape; break jail; get off, get clear off, get well out of; echapper belle[Fr], save one's bacon, save one's skin; weather the storm &c. (safe) 664; escape scot-free. elude &c., make off &c. (avoid) 623; march off &c. (go away) 293; give one the slip; slip through the hands, slip through the fingers; slip the collar, wriggle out of prison, break out, break loose, break loose from prison; break away, slip away, get away; find vent, find a hole to creep out of. disap-pear, vanish. Adj..escaping, escaped &c. v. stolen away, fled. Phr. the bird has flown the coop.

<— p. 215 —>

#672. Deliverance. — N. deliverance, extrication, rescue; reprieve, reprieval[obs3]; respite; liberation &c. 750; emancipation; redemption, salvation; riddance; gaol delivery; redeemableness[obs3]. V. deliver, extricate, rescue, save, emancipate, redeem, ransom; bring off, bring through; tirer d'affaire[Fr], get the wheel out of the rut, snatch from the jaws of death, come to the rescue; rid; retrieve &c. (restore) 660; be rid of, get rid of. Adj. saved &c. v. extricable, redeemable, rescuable. Int. to the rescue!

% 3. Precursory Measures %

#673. Preparation. — N. preparation; providing &c. v.; provision, providence; anticipation &c. (foresight) 510; precaution, preconcertation[obs3], predisposition; forecast &c. (plan) 626; rehearsal, note of preparation. [Putting in order] arrangement &c. 60; clearance; adjustment &c. 23; tuning; equipment, outfit, accouterment, armament, array. ripening &c. v.; maturation, evolution; elaboration, concoction, digestion; gestation, batching, incubation, sitting. groundwork, first stone, cradle, stepping-stone; foundation, scaffold &c. (support) 215; scaffolding, echafaudage[Fr]. [Preparation of men] training &c. (education) 537; inurement &c. (habit) 613; novitiate; cooking[Preparation of food], cookery; brewing, culinary art; tilling[Preparation of the soil], plowing, sowing; semination[obs3], cultivation. [State of being prepared] preparedness, readiness, ripeness, mellowness; maturity; un impromptu fait a loisir[Fr]. [Preparer] preparer, trainer; pioneer, trailblazer; avant- courrier[Fr], avant-coureur[Fr]; voortrekker[Afrikaans]; sappers and miners, pavior[obs3], navvy[obs3]; packer, stevedore; warming pan. V. prepare; get ready, make ready; make preparations, settle preliminaries, get up, sound the note of preparation. set in order, put in order &c. (arrange) 60; forecast &c. (plan) 626 prepare the ground, plow the ground, dress the ground; till the soil, cultivate the soil; predispose, sow the seed, lay a train, dig a mine; lay the groundwork, fix the groundwork, lay the basis, fix the basis, lay the foundations, fix the foundations; dig the foundations, erect the scaffolding; lay the first stone &c. (begin) 66. roughhew; cut out work; block out, hammer out; lick into shape &c. (form) 240. elaborate, mature, ripen, mellow, season, bring to maturity; nurture &c. (aid) 707; hatch, cook, brew; temper, anneal, smelt; barbecue; infumatel; maturate. equip, arm, man; fit-out, fit up; furnish, rig, dress, garnish, betrim[obs3], accouter, array, fettle, fledge; dress up, furbish up, brush up, vamp up; refurbish; sharpen one's tools, trim one's foils, set, prime, attune; whet the knife, whet the sword; wind up, screw up; adjust &c. (fit) 27; put in trim, put in train, put in gear, put in working order, put in tune, put in a groove for, put in harness; pack. train &c. (teach) 537; inure &c. (habituate) 613; breed; prepare &c. for; rehearse; make provision for; take steps, take measures, take precautions; provide, provide against; beat up for recruits; open the door to &c. (facilitate) 705. set one's house in order, make all snug; clear the decks, clear for action; close one's ranks; shuffle the cards. prepare oneself; serve an apprenticeship &c. (learn) 539; lay oneself out for, get into harness, gird up one's loins, buckle on one's armor, reculer pour mieux sauter[Fr], prime and load, shoulder arms, get the steam up, put the horses to. guard against, make sure against; forearm, make sure, prepare for the evil day, have a rod in pickle, provide against a rainy day, feather one's nest; lay in provisions &c. 637; make investments; keep on foot. be prepared, be ready &c. Adj.; hold oneself in readiness, keep one's powder dry; lie in wait for &c. (expect) 507; anticipate &c. (foresee) 510; principiis obstare[Lat]; veniente occurrere morbo[Lat].

Adj. preparing &c. v.; in preparation, in course of preparation, in agitation, in embryo, in hand, in train; afoot, afloat; on foot, on the stocks, on the anvil; under consideration &c. (plan) 626; brewing, batching, forthcoming, brooding; in store for, in reserve. precautionary, provident; preparative, preparatory; provisional, inchoate, under revision; preliminary &c. (precedent) 62. prepared &c. v.; in readiness; ready, ready to one's band, ready made, ready cut and dried; made to one's hand, handy, on the table; in gear; in working order, in working gear; snug; in practice. ripe, mature, mellow; pukka[obs3]; practiced &c. (skilled) 698; labored, elaborate, highly-wrought, smelling of the lamp, worked up. in full feather, in best bib and tucker; in harness, at harness; in the saddle, in arms, in battle array, in war paint; up in arms; armed at all points, armed to the teeth, armed cap a pie; sword in hand; booted and spurred. in utrumque paratus[Lat], semper paratus[Lat]; on the alert &c. (vigilant) 459; at one's post. Adv. in preparation, in anticipation of; against, for; abroach[obs3]. Phr. a bove majori discit arare minor[Lat]; "looking before and after" [Hamlet], si vis pacem para bellum[Lat].

<- p. 216 ->

#674. Nonpreparation. — N. non-preparation, absence of preparation, want of preparation; inculturel, inconcoctionl, improvidence. immaturity, crudity; rawness &c. Adj.; abortion; disqualification. [Absence of art] nature, state of nature; virgin soil, unweeded garden; neglect &c. 460. rough copy &c. (plan) 626; germ &c. 153; raw material &c. 635. improvisation &c. (impulse) 612. V. be unprepared &c. Adj.; want preparation, lack preparation; lie fallow; s'embarquer sans biscuits[Fr]; live from hand to mouth. [Render unprepared] dismantle &c. (render useless) 645; undress &c. 226. extemporize, improvise, ad lib. Adj. unprepared &c. [prepare &c. 673]; without preparation &c. 673; incomplete &c. 53; rudimental, embryonic, abortive; immature, unripe, kachcha[obs3], raw, green, crude; coarse; rough cast, rough hewn; in the rough; unhewn[obs3], unformed, unfashioned[obs3], unwrought, unlabored[obs3], unblown, uncooked, unboiled, unconcocted, unpolished. unhatched, unfledged, unnurtured[obs3], unlicked[obs3], untaught, uneducated, uncultivated,. untrained, untutored, undrilled, unexercised; deckle-edged[obs3]; precocious, premature; undigested, indigested[obs3]; unmellowed[obs3], unseasoned, unleavened. unrehearsed, unscripted, extemporaneous, improvised, spontaneous, ad lib, ad libitem [Latin]. fallow; unsown, untilled; natural, in a state of nature; undressed; in dishabille, en deshabille[Fr]. unqualified, disqualified; unfitted; ill-digested; unbegun, unready, unarranged[obs3], unorganized, unfurnished, unprovided, unequipped, untrimmed; out of gear, out of order; dismantled &c. v. shiftless, improvident, unthrifty, thriftless, thoughtless, unguarded; happy-go-lucky; caught napping &c. (inexpectant) 508[obs3]; unpremeditated &c. 612. Adv. extempore &c. 612.

#675. Essay. — N. essay, trial, endeavor, attempt; aim, struggle, venture, adventure, speculation, coup d'essai[Fr], debut; probation &c. (experiment) 463. V. try, essay; experiment &c. 463; endeavor, strive; tempt, attempt, make an attempt; venture, adventure, speculate, take one's chance, tempt fortune; try one's fortune, try one's luck, try one's hand; use one's endeavor; feel one's way, grope one's way, pick one's way. try hard, push, make a bold push, use one's best endeavor; do one's best &c. (exertion) 686. Adj. essaying &c. v.; experimental &c. 463; tentative, empirical, probationary. Adv. experimentally &c. Adj.; on trial, at a venture; by rule of thumb. if one may be so bold. Phr. aut non tentaris aut perfice [Lat][Ovid]; chi non s'arrischia non guadagna[Fr][obs3].

<— p. 217 —>

#676. Undertaking. — N. undertaking; compact &c. 769; adventure, venture; engagement &c. (promise) 768; enterprise, emprise[obs3]; pilgrimage; matter in hand &c. (business) 625; move; first move &c. (beginning) 66. V. undertake; engage in, embark in; launch into, plunge into; volunteer; apprentice oneself to; engage &c. (promise) 768; contract &c. 769; take upon oneself, take upon one's shoulders; devote oneself to &c. (determination) 604. take up, take in hand; tackle; set about, go about; set to, fall to, set to work; launch forth; set up shop; put in hand, put in execution; set forward; break the neck of a business, be in, for; put one's hand to, put one's foot in; betake oneself to, turn one's hand to, go to do; begin &c. 66; broach, institute &c. one's (originate) 153; put one's hand to the plow, lay one's hand to the plow, put one's shoulder to the wheel. have in hand &c. (business) 625; have many irons in the fire &c. (activity) 682. Adj. undertaking &c. v.; on the anvil &c. 625. Int. here goes!

#677. Use. — N. use; employ, employment; exercise, exercitation[obs3]; application, appliance; adhibition[obs3], disposal; consumption; agency &c. (physical) 170; usufruct; usefulness &c. 644; benefit; recourse, resort, avail. [Conversion to use] utilization, service, wear. [Way of using] usage. V. use,.make use of, employ, put to use; put in action, put in operation, put in practice; set in motion, set to work. ply, work, wield, handle, manipulate; play, play off; exert, exercise, practice, avail oneself of, profit by, resort to, have recourse to, recur to, take betake oneself to; take up with, take advantage of; lay one's hands on, try. render useful &c. 644; mold; turn to account, turn to use; convert to use, utilize; work up; call into play, bring into play; put into requisition; call forth, draw forth; press into service, enlist into the service; bring to bear upon, devote, dedicate, consecrate, apply, adhibit[obs3], dispose of; make a handle of, make a cat's-paw of. fall back upon, make a shift with; make the most of, make the best of. use up, swallow up; consume, absorb, expend; tax, task, wear, put to task. Adj. in use; used &c. v.; well-worn, well-trodden. useful &c. 644; subservient &c. (instrumental) 631.

#678. Disuse. — N. forbearance, abstinence; disuse; relinquishment &c. 782; desuetude &c. (want of habit) 614; disusage[obs3]. V. not use; do without, dispense with, let alone, not touch, forbear, abstain, spare, waive, neglect; keep back, reserve. lay up, lay by, lay on the shelf, keep on the shelf, lay up in ordinary; lay up in a napkin; shelve; set aside, put aside, lay aside; disuse, leave off, have done with; supersede; discard &c. (eject) 297; dismiss, give warning. throw aside &c. (relinquish) 782; make away with &c. (destroy) 162; cast overboard, heave overboard, throw overboard; cast to the dogs, cast to the winds; dismantle &c. (Render useless) 645. lie unemployed, remain unemployed &c. Adj. Adj. not used &c. v.; unemployed, unapplied, undisposed of, unspent, unexercised, untouched, untrodden, unessayed[obs3], ungathered[obs3], unculled; uncalled for, not required. disused &c. v.; done with.

#679. Misuse. — N. misuse, misusage, misemployment[obs3], misapplication, misappropriation.
abuse, profanation, prostitution, desecration; waste &c. 638.
V. misuse, misemploy, misapply, misappropriate.
desecrate, abuse, profane, prostitute; waste &c. 638; overtask, overtax, overwork; squander &c. 818.
cut blocks with a razor, employ a steam engine to crack a nut; catch at a straw.
Adj. misused &c. v.
Phr. ludere cum sacris[Lat].
<— p. 218 —> % Section III. VOLUNTARY ACTION

1. Simple voluntary Action %

#680. Action. — N. action, performance; doing, &c. v.; perpetration; exercise, excitation; movement, operation, evolution, work; labor &c. (exertion) 686; praxis, execution; procedure &c. (conduct) 692; handicraft; business &c. 625; agency &c. (power at work) 170. deed, act, overt act, stitch, touch, gest transaction[obs3], job, doings, dealings, proceeding, measure, step, maneuver, bout, passage, move, stroke, blow; coup, coup de main, coup d'etat[Fr]; tour de force &c. (display) 882; feat, exploit; achievement &c. (completion) 729; handiwork, workmanship; manufacture; stroke of policy &c. (plan) 626. actor &c. (doer) 690. V. do, perform, execute; achieve &c. (complete) 729; transact, enact; commit, perpetrate, inflict; exercise, prosecute, carry on, work, practice, play. employ oneself, ply one's task; officiate, have in hand &c. (business) 625; labor &c. 686; be at work; pursue a course; shape one's course &c. (conduct) 692. act, operate; take action, take steps; strike a blow, lift a finger, stretch forth one's hand; take in hand &c. (undertake) 676; put oneself in motion; put in practice; carry into execution &c. (complete) 729; act upon. be an actor &c. 690; take a part in, act a part in, play a part in, perform a part in; participate in; have a hand in, have a finger in the pie; have to do with; be a party to, be a participator in; bear a hand, lend a hand; pull an oar, run in a race; mix oneself up with &c. (meddle) 682. be in action; come into operation &c. (power at work) 170. Adj. doing &c. v.; acting; in action; in harness; on duty; in operation &c. 170. Adv. in the act, in the midst of, in the thick of; red-handed, in flagrante delicto[Lat]; while one's hand is in. Phr. "action is eloquence" [Coriolanus]; actions speak louder than words; actum aiunt ne agas [obs3][Lat][Terence]; "awake, arise, or be forever fall'n" [Paradise Lost]; dii pia facta vident [Lat][Ovid]; faire sans dire[Fr]; fare fac[It]; fronte capillata post est occasio calva[Lat]; "our deeds are sometimes better than our thoughts" [Bailey]; "the great end of life is not knowledge but action" [Huxley]; "thought is the soul of act" [R. Browning]; vivre-ce nest pas respirer c'est agir[Fr][obs3]; "we live in deeds not years" [Bailey].

#681. Inaction. — N. inaction, passiveness, abstinence from action; noninterference, nonintervention; Fabian policy, conservative policy; neglect &c. 460. inactivity &c. 683; rest &c. (repose) 687; quiescence &c. 265; want of occupation, inoccupation[obs3]; idle hours, time hanging on one's hands, dolce far niente[It]; sinecure, featherbed, feather-bedding, cushy job, no- show job; soft snap, soft thing. V. not do, not act, not attempt; be inactive &c. 683; abstain from doing, do nothing, hold, spare; not stir, not move, not lift a finger, not lift a foot, not lift a peg; fold one's arms, fold one's hands; leave alone, let alone; let be, let pass, let things take their course, let it have its way, let well alone, let well enough alone; quieta non movere[Lat]; stare super antiquas vias[Lat][obs3]; rest and be thankful, live and let live; lie rest upon one's oars; laisser aller[Fr], faire[Fr]; stand aloof; refrain &c. (avoid) 623 keep oneself from doing; remit one's efforts, relax one's efforts; desist &c. (relinquish) 624; stop &c. (cease) 142; pause &c. (be quiet) 265. wait, lie in wait, bide one's time, take time, tide it over. cool one's heels, kick one's heels; while away the time, while away tedious hours; pass the time, fill up the time, beguile the time; talk against time; let the grass grow under one's feet; waste time &c. (inactive) 683. lie by, lie on the shelf, lie in ordinary, lie idle, lie to, lie fallow; keep quiet, slug; have nothing to do, whistle for want of thought. undo, do away with; take down, take to pieces; destroy &c. 162. Adj. not doing &c. v.; not done &c. v.; undone; passive; unoccupied, unemployed; out of employ, out of work; fallow; desaeuvre[Fr]. Adv. re infecta[Lat], at a stand, les bras croisis[Fr], with folded arms; with the hands in the pockets, with the hands behind one's back; pour passer le temps[Fr]. Int. so let it be! stop! &c. 142; hands off! Phr. cunctando restituit rem "If it ain't broke don't fix it" [Lat][Bert Lance]; stare decisis [Latin: (Law) let the decision stand].

<— p. 219 —>

#682. Activity. — N. activity; briskness, liveliness &c. adj.; animation, life, vivacity, spirit, dash, energy; snap, vim. nimbleness, agility; smartness, quickness &c. adj.; velocity, &c. 274; alacrity, promptitude; despatch, dispatch; expedition; haste &c. 684; punctuality &c. (early) 132. eagerness, zeal, ardor, perfervidum aingenium[Lat][obs3], empressement[Fr], earnestness, intentness; abandon; vigor &c. (physical energy) 171; devotion &c. (resolution) 604; exertion &c. 686. industry, assiduity; assiduousness &c. adj.; sedulity; laboriousness; drudgery &c. (labor) 686; painstaking, diligence; perseverance &c. 604a; indefatigationl; habits of business. vigilance &c. 459; wakefulness; sleeplessness, restlessness; insomnia; pervigilium[obs3], insomnium[obs3]; racketing. movement, bustle, stir, fuss, ado, bother, pottering, fidget, fidgetiness; flurry &c. (haste) 684. officiousness; dabbling, meddling; interference, interposition, intermeddling; tampering with, intrigue. press of business, no sinecure, plenty to do, many irons in the fire, great doings, busy hum of men, battle of life, thick of the action. housewife, busy bee; new brooms; sharp fellow, sharp blade; devotee, enthusiast, zealot, meddler, intermeddler, intriguer, busybody, pickthank[obs3]; hummer, hustler, live man [U.S.], rustler * [U. S.]. V. be active &c. adj.; busy oneself in; stir, stir about, stir one's stumps; bestir oneself, rouse oneself; speed, hasten, peg away, lay about one, bustle, fuss; raise up, kick up a dust; push; make a push, make a fuss, make a stir; go ahead, push forward; fight one's way, elbow one's way; make progress &c. 282; toll &c. (labor) 686; plod, persist &c. (persevere) 604a; keep up the ball, keep the pot boiling. look sharp; have all one's eyes about one &c. (vigilance) 459; rise, arouse oneself, hustle, get up early, be about, keep moving, steal a march, kill two birds with one stone; seize the opportunity &c. 134 lose no time, not lose a moment, make the most of one's time, not suffer the grass to grow under one's feet, improve the shining hour, make short work of; dash off; make haste &c. 684; do one's best take pains &c. (exert oneself) 686; do wonders, work wonders. have many irons in the fire, have one's hands full, have much on one's hands; have other things to do, have other fish to fry; be busy; not have a moment to spare, not have a moment that one can call one's own. have one's fling, run the round of; go all lengths, stick at nothing, run riot. outdo; overdo, overact, overlay, overshoot the mark; make a toil of a pleasure. have a hand in &c. (act in) 680; take an active part, put in one's oar, have a finger in the pie, mix oneself up with, trouble, one's head about, intrigue; agitate. tamper with, meddle, moil; intermeddle, interfere, interpose; obtrude; poke one's nose in, thrust one's nose in. Adj. active, brisk, brisk as a lark, brisk as a bee; lively, animated, vivacious; alive, alive and kicking; frisky, spirited, stirring. nimble, nimble as a squirrel; agile; light-footed, nimble-footed; featly[obs3], tripping. quick, prompt, yare[obs3], instant, ready, alert, spry, sharp, smart; fast &c. (swift) 274; quick as a lamplighter, expeditious; awake, broad awake; go-ahead, live wide-awake &c. (intelligent) 498[U.S.]. forward, eager, strenuous, zealous, enterprising, in earnest; resolute &c. 604. industrious, assiduous, diligent, sedulous, notable, painstaking; intent &c. (attention) 457; indefatigable &c. (persevering) 604a; unwearied; unsleeping[obs3], never tired; plodding, hard-working &c. 686; businesslike, workaday. bustling; restless, restless as a hyena; fussy, fidgety, pottering; busy, busy as hen with one chicken. working, at work, on duty, in harness; up in arms; on one's legs, at call; up and doing, up and stirring. busy, occupied; hard at work, hard at it; up to one's ears in, full of business, busy as a bee, busy as a one-armed paperhanger. meddling &c. v.; meddlesome, pushing, officious, overofficious[obs3], intrigant[obs3]. astir, stirring; agoing[obs3], afoot; on foot; in full swing; eventful; on the alert, &c. (vigilant) 459. Adv. actively &c. adj.; with life and spirit, with might and main &c. 686,with haste &c. 684, with wings; full tilt, in mediis rebus[Lat]. Int. be alive, look alive, look sharp! move on, push on! keep moving! go ahead! stir your stumps! age quod agis[Lat]! jaldi[obs3]! karo[obs3]! step lively! Phr. carpe diem &c. (opportunity) 134[Latin: seize the day]; nulla dies sine linea [Latin][Pliny]; nec mora nec requies [Latin][Vergil]; the plot thickens; No sooner said than done &c. (early) 132; "veni vidi vici" [Lat][Suetonius]; catch a weasel asleep; abends wird der Faule fleissig [obs3][German]; dictum ac factum [Lat][Terence]; schwere Arbeit in der Jugend ist sanfte Ruhe im Alter[German: hard work in youth means soft rest in age]; "the busy hum of men" [Milton].

<— p. 220 —>

#683. Inactivity. — N. inactivity; inaction &c. 681; inertness &c. 172; obstinacy &c. 606. lull &c. (cessation) 142; quiescence &c. 265; rust, rustiness. idleness, remissness &c. adj.; sloth, indolence, indiligence[obs3]; dawdling &c. v. ergophobia[obs3], otiosity[obs3]. dullness &c. adj.; languor; segnityl, segnitudel; lentor[obs3]; sluggishness &c. (slowness) 275; procrastination &c. (delay) 133; torpor, torpidity, torpescence[obs3]; stupor &c. (insensibility) 823; somnolence; drowsiness &c. adj.; nodding &c. v.; oscitation[obs3], oscitancy[obs3]; pandiculation[obs3], hypnotism, lethargy; statuvolence heaviness[obs3], heavy eyelids. sleep, slumber; sound sleep, heavy sleep, balmy sleep; Morpheus; Somnus; coma, trance, ecstasis[obs3], dream, hibernation, nap, doze, snooze, siesta, wink of sleep, forty winks, snore; hypnology[obs3]. dull work; pottering; relaxation &c. (loosening) 47; Castle of Indolence. [Cause of inactivity] lullaby, sedative, tranquilizer, hypnotic, sleeping pill, relaxant, anaesthetic, general anaesthetic &c. 174; torpedo. [person who is inactive] idler, drone, droil[obs3], dawdle, mopus[obs3]; do-little faineant[Fr], dummy, sleeping partner; afternoon farmer; truant &c. (runaway) 623: bummerl!, loafer, goldbrick, goldbicker, lounger, lazzarone[It]; lubber, lubbard[obs3]; slow coach &c. (slow.) 275; opium eater, lotus eater; slug, lagl!, sluggard, slugabed; slumberer, dormouse, marmot; waiter on Providence, fruges consumere natus[Lat]. V. be inactive &c. adj.; do nothing &c. 681; move slowly &c. 275; let the grass grow under one's feet; take one's time, dawdle, drawl, droil[obs3], lag, hang back, slouch; loll, lollop[obs3]; lounge, poke, loaf, loiter; go to sleep over; sleep at one's post, ne battre que d'une aile[Fr][obs3]. take it easy, take things as they come; lead an easy life, vegetate, swim with the stream, eat the bread of idleness; loll in the lap of luxury, loll in the lap of indolence; waste time, consume time, kill time, lose time; burn daylight, waste the precious hours. idle away time, trifle away time, fritter away time, fool away time; spend time in, take time in; peddle, piddle; potter, pudder[obs3], dabble, faddle fribble[obs3], fiddle-faddle; dally, dilly-dally. sleep, slumber, be asleep; hibernate; oversleep; sleep like a top, sleep like a log, sleep like a dormouse; sleep soundly, heavily; doze, drowze[obs3], snooze, nap; take a nap &c. n.; dream; snore one's best; settle to sleep, go to sleep, go off to sleep; doze off, drop off; fall asleep; drop asleep; close the eyes, seal up the eyes, seal up eyelids; weigh down the eyelids; get sleep, nod, yawn; go to bed, turn; get some z's, stack z's [coll.]. languish, expend itself, flag, hang fire; relax. render idle &c. adj.; sluggardize[obs3]; mitigate &c. 174. Adj. inactive; motionless &c. 265; unoccupied &c. (doing nothing) 681 unbusied[obs3]. indolent, lazy, slothful, idle, lusk[obs3], remiss, slack, inert, torpid, sluggish, otiose, languid, supine, heavy, dull, leaden, lumpish[obs3]; exanimate[obs3], soulless; listless; drony[obs3], dronish[obs3]; lazy as Ludlam's dog. dilatory, laggard; lagging &c. v.; slow &c. 275; rusty, flagging; lackadaisical, maudlin, fiddle-faddle; pottering &c. v.;shilly-shally &c. (irresolute) 605. sleeping, &c. v.; asleep; fast asleep, dead asleep, sound asleep; in a sound sleep; sound as a top, dormant, comatose; in the arms of Morpheus, in the lap of Morpheus. sleepy, sleepful[obs3]; dozy[obs3], drowsy, somnolent, torpescent[obs3], lethargic, lethargical[obs3]; somnifacient[obs3]; statuvolent[obs3], statuvolic[obs3]; heavy, heavy with sleep; napping; somnific[obs3], somniferous; soporous[obs3], soporific, soporiferous[obs3]; hypnotic; balmy, dreamy; unawakened, unawakened. sedative &c. 174. Adv. inactively &c. adj.; at leisure &c. 685. Phr. the eyes begin to draw straws; "bankrupt of life yet prodigal of ease" [Dryden]; "better 50 years of Europe than a cycle of Cathay" [Tennyson]; "idly busy rolls their world away" [Goldsmith]; "the mystery of folded sleep" [Tennyson]; "the timely dew of sleep" [Milton]; "thou driftest gently down the tides of sleep" [Longfellow]; "tired Nature's sweet restorer, balmy sleep" [Young].

<— p. 221 —>

#684. Haste. — N. haste, urgency; despatch, dispatch; acceleration, spurt, spirt[obs3], forced march, rush, dash; speed, velocity &c. 274; precipitancy, precipitation, precipitousness &c. adj.; impetuosity; brusquerie[obs3]; hurry, drive, scramble, bustle, fuss, fidget, flurry, flutter, splutter. V. haste, hasten; make haste, make a dash &c. n.; hurry

189

on, dash on, whip on, push on, press on, press forward; hurry, skurry[obs3], scuttle along, barrel along, bundle on, dart to and fro, bustle, flutter, scramble; plunge, plunge headlong; dash off; rush &c. (violence) 173; express. bestir oneself &c. (be active) 682; lose no time, lose not a moment, lose not an instant; make short work of; make the best of one's time, make the best of one's way. be precipitate &c. adj.; jump at, be in haste, be in a hurry &c. n.; have no time, have not a moment to lose, have not a moment to spare; work against time. quicken &c. 274; accelerate, expedite, put on, precipitate, urge, whip; railroad. Adj. hasty, hurried, brusque; scrambling, cursory, precipitate, headlong, furious, boisterous, impetuous, hotheaded; feverish, fussy; pushing. in haste, in a hurry &c. n.; in hot haste, in all haste; breathless, pressed for time, hard pressed, urgent. Adv. with haste, with all haste, with breathless speed; in haste &c. adj.; apace &c. (swiftly) 274; amain[obs3]; all at once &c. (instantaneously) 113; at short notice &c., immediately &c. (early) 132; posthaste; by cable, by express, by telegraph, by forced marches. hastily, precipitately &c. adj.; helter-skelter, hurry-skurry[obs3], holus-bolus; slapdash, slap-bang; full-tilt, full drive; heels over head, head and shoulders, headlong, a corps perdu[Fr]. by fits and starts, by spurts; hop skip and jump. Phr. sauve qui peut[French: every man for himself][panic], devil take the hindmost, no time to be lost; no sooner said than done &c. (early) 132; a word and a blow; haste makes waste, maggiore fretta minore atto [Italian]; ohne Hast aber ohne Rast [German][Goethe's motto]; "stand not upon the order of your going but go at once" [Macbeth]; "swift, swift, you dragons of the night" [Cymbeline].

#685. Leisure. — N. leisure; convenience; spare time, spare hours, spare moments; vacant hour; time, time to spare, time on one's hands; holiday, relaxation &c. (rest) 687; otium cum dignitate [Lat][obs3][Cic.], ease.

no hurry; no big rush; no deadline.

V. have leisure &c. n.; take one's time, take one's leisure, take one's ease; repose &c. 687; move slowly &c. 275; while away the time &c. (inaction) 681; be master of one's time, be an idle man.

Adj. leisure, leisurely; slow &c. 275; deliberate, quiet, calm, undisturbed; at leisure, at one's ease, at loose ends, at a loose end.

Adv. unhurriedly, deliberately, without undue haste; anytime.

Phr. time hanging heavy on one's hands; eile mit Weile[Ger].

#686. Exertion. — N. exertion, effort, strain, tug, pull, stress, throw, stretch, struggle, spell, spurt, spirt[obs3]; stroke of work, stitch of work. "a strong pull a long pull and a pull all together"; dead lift; heft; gymnastics; exercise, exercitation[obs3]; wear and tear; ado; toil and trouble; uphill work, hard work, warm work; harvest time. labor, work, toil, travail, manual labor, sweat of one's brow, swink[obs3], drudgery, slavery, fagging[obs3], hammering; limae labor[Lat]; industry, industriousness, operoseness[obs3], operosity[obs3]. trouble, pains, duty; resolution &c. 604; energy &c. (physical) 171. V. exert oneself; exert one's energies, tax one's energies; use exertion. labor, work, toil, moil, sweat, fag, drudge, slave, drag a lengthened chain, wade through, strive, stretch a long arm; pull, tug, ply; ply the oar, tug at the oar; do the work; take the laboring oar bestir oneself (be active) 682; take trouble, trouble oneself. work hard; rough it; put forth one's strength, put forth a strong arm; fall to work, bend the bow; buckle to, set one's shoulder to the wheel &c. (resolution) 604; work like a horse, work like a cart horse, work like a galley slave, work like a coal heaver; labor day and night, work day and night; redouble one's efforts; do double duty; work double hours, work double tides; sit up, burn the candle at both ends; stick to &c. (persevere) 604a; work one's way, fight one's way; lay about one, hammer at. take pains; do one's best, do one's level best, do one's utmost; give one hundred percent, do the best one can, do all one can, do all in one's power, do as much as in one lies, do what lies in one's power; use one's best endeavor, use one's utmost endeavor; try one's best, try one's utmost; play one's best card; put one's best leg foremost, put one's right leg foremost; have one's whole soul in his work, put all one's strength into, strain every nerve; spare no efforts, spare no pains; go all lengths; go through fire and water &c. (resolution) 604; move heaven and earth, leave no stone unturned. Adj. laboring &c. v. laborious, operose[obs3], elaborate; strained; toilsome, troublesome, wearisome; uphill; herculean, gymnastic, palestric[obs3]. hard-working, painstaking; strenuous, energetic. hard at work, on the stretch. Adv. laboriously &c. adj.; lustily; pugnis et calcibus[Lat]; with might and main, with all one's might, with a strong hand, with a sledge hammer, with much ado; to the best of one's abilities, totis viribus[Lat], vi et armis[Lat], manibus pedibusque[Lat], tooth and nail, unguibus et rostro[Lat], hammer and tongs, heart and soul; through thick and thin &c. (perseverance) 604a. by the sweat of one's brow, suo Marte. Phr. aide-toi le ciel t'aidera[Fr]; "and still be doing, never done" [Butler]; buen principio la mitad es hecha [Sp]; cosa ben fatta e' fatta due volie [It];"it is better to wear out than to rust out" [Bp. Hornel]; labor omnia vincit "labor, wide as the earth, has its summit in Heaven" [Lat][Vergil][Carlyle]; le travail du corps delivre des peines de l'esprit [Fr][fr]; manu forti[Lat]; ora et labora[Lat].

#687. Repose. — N. repose, rest, silken repose; sleep &c. 683.

relaxation, breathing time; halt, stay, pause &c. (cessation) 142; respite.

day of rest, dies non, Sabbath, Lord's day, holiday, red-letter day, vacation, recess.

V. repose; rest, rest and be thankful; take a rest, take one's ease, take it easy.

relax, unbend, slacken; take breath &c. (refresh) 689; rest upon one's oars; pause &c. (cease) 142; stay one's hand.

lie down; recline, recline on a bed of down, recline on an easy chair; go to rest, go to bed, go to sleep &c. 683.

take a holiday, shut up shop; lie fallow &c. (inaction) 681.

Adj. reposing &c. v[of people].; relaxed &c. v.; unstrained. [of materials and people] unstressed.

Adv. at rest.

Phr."the best of men have ever loved repose" [Thompson]; "to repair our nature with comforting repose" [Henry VIII].

<— p. 222 —>

#688. Fatigue. — N. fatigue; weariness &c. 841; yawning, drowsiness &c. 683; lassitude, tiredness, fatigationl, exhaustion; sweat; dyspnoea. anhelation, shortness of breath; faintness; collapse, prostration, swoon, fainting, deliquium[Lat], syncope, lipothymy[obs3]; goneness[obs3]. V. be fatigued &c. adj.; yawn &c. (get sleepy) 683; droop, sink, flag; lose breath, lose wind; gasp, pant, puff, blow, drop, swoon, faint, succumb. fatigue, tire, weary, irk, flag, jade, harass, exhaust, knock up, wear out, prostrate. tax, task, strain; overtask, overwork, overburden, overtax, overstrain. Adj. fatigued, tired &c. v.; weary &c. 841; drowsy &c. 683; drooping &c. v.; haggard; toilworn[obs3], wayworn; footsore, surbatedl, weather- beaten; faint; done up, used up, knocked up; bushed * [U.S.]; exhausted, prostrate, spent; overtired, overspent, overfatigued; unrefreshed[obs3], unrestored. worn, worn out; battered, shattered, pulled down, seedy, altered. breathless, windless; short of breath, out of breath, short of wind; blown, puffing and blowing; short-breathed; anhelose[obs3]; broken winded, short-winded; dyspnaeal[obs3], dyspnaeic[obs3]. ready to drop, all in, more dead than alive, dog-weary, walked off one's legs, tired to death, on one's last legs, played out, hors de combat[Fr]. fatiguing &c v.; tiresome, irksome, wearisome; weary, trying.

#689. Refreshment. — N. bracing &c. v.; recovery of strength, recuperation &c. 159; restoration, revival &c. 660; repair, refection, refocillationl, refreshment, regalement[obs3], bait; relief &c. 834. break, spell. refreshment stand; refreshments; ice cream[list], cold soda, soda pop, hot dogs (food). V. brace &c. (strengthen) 159; reinvigorate; air, freshen up, refresh, recruit; repair &c. (restore) 660; fan, refocillatel; refresh the inner man. breathe, respire; drink in the ozone; take a break, take a breather, take five, draw breath, take a deep breath, take breath, gather breath, take a long breath, regain breath, recover breath; get better, raise one's head; recover one's strength, regain one's strength, renew one's strength &c. 159; perk up, get one's second wind. come to oneself &c. (revive) 660; feel refreshed, feel like a giant refreshed. Adj. refreshing &c v.; recuperative &c. 660. refreshed &c. v.; untired[obs3], unwearied.

<— p. 223 —>

#690. Agent.— N. doer, actor, agent, performer, perpetrator, operator; executor, executrix; practitioner, worker, stager. bee, ant, working bee, termite, white ant; laboring oar, servant of all work, factotum. workman, artisan; craftsman, handicraftsman; mechanic, operative; working man; laboring man; demiurgus, hewers of wood and drawers of water, laborer, navvy[obs3]; hand, man, day laborer, journeyman, charwoman, hack; mere tool &c. 633; beast of burden, drudge, fag; lumper[obs3], roustabout. maker, artificer, artist, wright, manufacturer, architect, builder, mason, bricklayer, smith, forger, Vulcan; carpenter; ganger, platelayer; blacksmith, locksmith, sailmaker, wheelwright. machinist, mechanician, engineer. sempstress[obs3], semstress[obs3], seamstress; needlewoman[obs3], workwoman; tailor, cordwainer[obs3]. minister &c. (instrument) 631; servant &c. 746; repre- sentative &c. (commissioner) 758, (deputy) 759. coworker, party to, participator in, particeps criminis[Lat], dramatis personae[Lat]; personnel. Phr. quorum pars magna fui [Lat][Vergil]; faber est quisque fortunae suae [Lat].

#691. Workshop. — N. workshop, workhouse, workplace, shop, place of business; manufactory, mill, plant, works, factory; cabinet, studio; office, branch office bureau, atelier. hive[specific types of workplace: list], hive of industry; nursery; hothouse, hotbed; kitchen; mint, forge, loom; dock, dockyard; alveary[obs3]; armory; laboratory, lab, research institute; refinery; cannery; power plant; beauty parlor; beehive, bindery, forcing pit, nailery[obs3], usine[obs3], slip, yard, wharf; foundry, foundery[obs3]; furnace; vineyard. crucible, alembic, caldron, matrix. Adj. at work, at the office, at the shop; working.

% 2. Complex Voluntary Action %

#692. Conduct. — N. conduct[actions of an individual agent]; behavior; deportment, comportment; carriage, maintien[obs3], demeanor, guise, bearing, manner, observance. dealing, transaction &c. (action) 680; business &c. 625. tactics, game, game plan, policy, polity; generalship, statesmanship, seamanship; strategy, strategics[obs3]; plan &c. 626. management; husbandry; housekeeping, housewifery; stewardship; menage; regime; economy, economics; political economy; government &c. (direction) 693. execution, manipulation, treatment, campaign, career, life, course, walk, race, record. course of conduct, line of conduct, line of action, line of proceeding; role; process, ways, practice, procedure, modus operandi, MO, method of operating; method &c., path &c. 627. V. transact[cause to occur], execute; despatch, dispatch; proceed with, discharge; carry on, carry through, carry out, carry into effect, put into effect; work out; go through, get through; enact; put into practice; do &c. 680; officiate &c. 625. bear oneself, behave oneself, comport oneself, demean oneself, carry oneself, conduct oneself, acquit oneself. run a race, lead a life, play a game; take a course, adopt a course; steer one's course, shape one's course; play one's paint, play one's cards, shift for oneself; paddle one's own canoe; bail one's own boat. conduct; manage, supervise &c. (direct) 693. participate &c. 680. deal with, have to do with; treat, handle a case; take steps, take measures. Adj. conducting &c. v. strategical, businesslike, practical, executive.

<— p. 224 —>

#693. Direction. — N. direction; management, managery[obs3]; government, gubernation[obs3], conduct, legislation, regulation, guidance; bossism [U.S.]; legislature; steerage, pilotage; reins, reins of government; helm, rudder, needle, compass; guiding star, load star, lode star, pole star; cynosure. supervision, superintendence; surveillance, oversight; eye of the master; control, charge; board of control &c. (council) 696; command &c. (authority) 737. premiership, senatorship; director &c. 694; chair, portfolio. statesmanship; statecraft, kingcraft[obs3], queencraft[obs3]. ministry, ministration; administration; stewardship, proctorship[obs3]; agency. [person who directs] director &c. 694. V. direct, manage, govern, conduct; order, prescribe, cut out work for; bead, lead; lead the way, show the way; take the lead, lead on; regulate, guide, steer, pilot; tackle [intransitive] take the helm, be at the helm; have the reins, handle the reins, hold the reins, take the reins; drive, tool. superintend, supervise; overlook, control, keep in order, look after, see to, legislate for; administer, ministrate[obs3]; matronize[obs3]; have the care of, have the charge of; be in charge of, have charge of, take the direction; boss, boss one around; pull the strings, pull the wires; rule &c. (command) 737; have the direction, hold office, hold the portfolio; preside, preside at the board; take the chair, occupy the chair, be in the chair; pull the stroke oar. Adj. directing &c. v.; hegemonic. Adv. at the helm, at the head of.

#694. Director. — N. director, manager, governor, rector, comptroller. superintendent, supervisor, straw boss. intendant; overseer, overlooker[obs3]; supercargo[obs3], husband, inspector, visitor, ranger, surveyor, aedile[obs3]; moderator, monitor, taskmaster; master &c. 745; leader, ringleader, demagogue, corypheus, conductor, fugleman[obs3], precentor[obs3], bellwether, agitator; caporal[obs3], choregus[obs3], collector, file leader, flugelman[obs3], linkboy[obs3]. guiding star &c. (guidance) 693; adviser &c. 695; guide &c. (information) 527; pilot; helmsman; steersman, steermate[obs3]; wire- puller. driver, whip, Jehu, charioteer; coachman, carman, cabman; postilion, vetturino[obs3], muleteer, arriero[obs3], teamster; whipper in. head, head man, head center, boss; principal, president, speaker; chair, chairman, chairwoman, chairperson; captain &c. (master) 745; superior; mayor &c. (civil authority) 745; vice president, prime minister, premier, vizier, grand vizier, eparch[obs3]. officer, functionary, minister, official, red-tapist[obs3], bureaucrat; man in office, Jack in office; office bearer; person in authority &c. 745. statesman, strategist, legislator, lawgiver, politician, statistl!, statemonger[obs3]; Minos, Draco; arbiter &c. (judge) 967; boss [U.S.], political dictator. board &c. (council) 696. secretary, secretary of state; Reis Effendi; vicar &c. (deputy) 759; steward, factor; agent &c. 758; bailiff, middleman; foreman, clerk of works; landreeve[obs3]; factotum, major-domo[obs3], seneschal, housekeeper, shepherd, croupier; proctor, procurator. Adv. ex officio.

#695. Advice. — N. advice, counsel, adhortationl; word to the wise;
suggestion, submonitionl, recommendation, advocacy; advisement.
exhortation &c. (persuasion) 615; expostulation &c. (dissuasion) 616;
admonition &c. (warning) 668; guidance &c. (direction) 693.
instruction, charge, injunction, obtestation[obs3]; Governor's
message, President's message; King's message, Queen's speech; message,

speech from the throne.

adviser, prompter; counsel, counselor; monitor, mentor, Nestor, magnus Apollo[Lat][obs3], senator; teacher &c. 540.

guide, manual, chart &c. (information) 527.

physician, doctor, leechl!, archiater[obs3].

arbiter &c. (judge) 967.

reference, referment[obs3]; consultation, conference, pourparler.

V. advise, counsel; give advice, give counsel, give a piece of advice[Fr]; suggest, prompt, submonish[obs3], recommend, prescribe, advocate; exhort &c. (persuade) 615.

enjoin, enforce, charge, instruct, call; call upon &c. (request) 765; dictate.

expostulate &c. (dissuade) 616; admonish &c. (warn) 668.

advise with; lay heads together, consult together; compare notes; hold a council, deliberate, be closeted with.

confer, consult, refer to, call in; take advice, follow advice; be advised by, have at one's elbow, take one's cue from.

Adj. recommendatory; hortative &c. (persuasive) 615; dehortatory &c. (dissuasive) 616[obs3]; admonitory &c. (warning) 668.

Int. go to!

Phr. "give every man thine ear but few thy voice" [Hamlet]; "I pray thee cease thy counsel" [Much Ado About Nothing]; "my guide, philosopher, and friend" [Pope]; "'twas good advice and meant, my son be good" [Crabbe]; verbum sat sapienti [Latin: a word to the wise is sufficient]; vive memor leti[Lat]; "we, ask advice but we mean approbation" [Colton].
<— p. 225 —>

#696. Council. — N. council, committee, subcommittee, comitia[Lat], court, chamber, cabinet, board, bench, staff. senate, senatus[Lat], parliament, chamber of deputies, directory, reichsrath[Ger], rigsdag, cortes[Sp], storthing[obs3], witenagemote[obs3], junta, divan, musnud[obs3], sanhedrim; classis[obs3]; Amphictyonic council[obs3]; duma[Russ], house of representatives; legislative assembly, legislative council; riksdag[obs3], volksraad[Ger], witan[obs3], caput[obs3], consistory, chapter, syndicate; court of appeal &c. (tribunal) 966; board of control, board of works; vestry; county council, local board. audience chamber, council chamber, state chamber. cabinet council, privy council; cockpit, convocation, synod, congress, convention, diet, states-general. [formal gathering of members of a council: script] assembly, caucus, conclave, clique, conventicle; meeting, sitting, seance, conference, convention, exhibition, session, palaver, pourparler, durbar[obs3], house; quorum; council fire [N.Am.], powwow [U.S.], primary [U.S.]. meeting, assemblage &c. 72. [person who is member of a council] member; senator; member of parliament, M.P.; councilor, representative of the people; assemblyman, congressman; councilman, councilwoman, alderman, freeholder. V. assemble, gather together, meet (assemblage) 72; confer, caucus, hold council; huddle [coll.]. Adj. senatorial, curule[obs3]; congressional, parliamentary; legislative, law-making; regulatory; deliberative.

#697. Precept. — N. precept, direction, instruction, charge; prescript, prescription; recipe, receipt; golden rule; maxim &c. 496.

rule, canon, law, code, corpus juris[Lat], lex scripta[Lat], act, statute, rubric, stage direction, regulation; form, formula, formulary; technicality; canon law; norm.

order &c. (command) 741.

#698. Skill. — N. skill, skillfulness, address; dexterity, dexterousness; adroitness, expertness &c. adj.; proficiency, competence, technical competence, craft, callidity[obs3], facility, knack, trick, sleight; mastery, mastership, excellence, panurgy[obs3]; ambidexterity, ambidextrousness[obs3]; sleight of hand &c. (deception) 545. seamanship, airmanship, marksmanship, horsemanship; rope-dancing. accomplishment, acquirement, attainment; art, science; technicality, technology; practical knowledge, technical knowledge. knowledge of the world, world wisdom, savoir faire[Fr]; tact; mother wit &c. (sagacity) 498; discretion &c. *(caution) 864; finesse; craftiness &c. (cunning) 702; management &c. (conduct) 692; self-help. cleverness, talent, ability, ingenuity, capacity, parts, talents, faculty, endowment, forte, turn, gift, genius; intelligence &c. 498; sharpness, readiness &c. (activity) 682; invention &c. 515; aptness, aptitude; turn for, capacity for, genius for; felicity, capability, curiosa felicitas[Lat], qualification, habilitation. proficient &c. 700. masterpiece, coup de maitre[Fr], chef d'euvre[Fr], tour de force; good stroke &c. (plan) 626. V. be skillful &c. adj.; excel in, be master of; have a turn for &c. n. know what's what, know a hawk from a handsaw, know what one is about, know on which side one's bread is buttered, know what's o'clock; have cut one's eye teeth, have cut one's wisdom teeth. see one's way, see where the wind lies, see which way the wind blows; have all one's wits about one, have one's hand in; savoir vivre[Fr]; scire quid valeant humeri quid ferre recusent[Lat][obs3]. look after the main chance; cut one's coat according to one's cloth; live by one's wits; exercise one's discretion, feather the oar, sail near the wind; stoop to conquer &c. (cunning) 702; play one's cards well, play one's best card; hit the right nail on the head, put the saddle on the right horse. take advantage of, make the most of; profit by &e. (use) 677; make a hit &c. (succeed) 731; make a virtue of necessity; make hay while the sun shines &c. (occasion) 134. Adj. skillful, dexterous, adroit, expert, apt, handy, quick, deft, ready, gain; slick, smart &c. (active) 682; proficient, good at, up to, at home in, master of, a good hand at, au fait, thoroughbred, masterly, crack, accomplished; conversant &c. (knowing) 490. experienced, practiced, skilled, hackneyed; up in, well up in; in practice, in proper cue; competent, efficient, qualified, capable, fitted, fit for, up to the mark, trained, initiated, prepared, primed, finished. clever, cute, able, ingenious, felicitous, gifted, talented, endowed; inventive &c. 515; shrewd, sharp, on the ball &c. (intelligent) 498; cunning &c. 702; alive to, up to snuff, not to be caught with chaff; discreet. neat-handed, fine-fingered, nimble-fingered, ambidextrous, sure- footed; cut out for, fitted for. technical, artistic, scientific, daedalian[obs3], shipshape; workman- like, business-like, statesman-like. Adv. skillfully &c. adj.; well &c. 618; artistically; with skill, with consummate skill; secundum artem[Lat], suo Marte; to the best of one's abilities &c. (exertion) 686. Phr. ars celare artem[Lat]; artes honorabit[Lat]; celui qui veut celui-la peut[Fr]; c'est une grande habilite que de savoir cacher sonhabilite[Fr]; expertus metuit [Lat][Horace]; es bildet ein Talent sich in der Stille sich ein Charakter in dem Strom der Welt[Ger]; "heart to conceive the understanding to direct, or the hand to execute" [Junius]; if you have lemons, make lemonade.

<— p. 226 —>

#699. Unskillfulness. — N. unskillfulness &c. adj.; want of skill &c. 698; incompetence, incompentency[obs3]; inability, infelicity, indexterity[obs3], inexperience; disqualification, unproficiency[obs3]; quackery. folly, stupidity &c. 499; indiscretion &c. (rashness) 863; thoughtlessness &c. (inattention) 458 (neglect) 460; sabotage. mismanagement, misconduct; impolicy[obs3]; maladministration; misrule, misgovernment, misapplication, misdirection, misfeasance; petticoat government. absence of rule, rule of thumb; bungling &c. v.; failure &c. 732; screw loose; too many cooks. blunder &c. (mistake) 495; etourderie gaucherie[Fr], act of folly, balourdise[obs3]; botch, botchery[obs3]; bad job, sad work. sprat sent out to catch a whale, much ado about nothing, wild-goose chase. bungler &c. 701; fool &c. 501. V. be unskillful &c. adj.; not see an inch beyond one's nose; blunder, bungle, boggle, fumble, botch, bitch, flounder, stumble, trip; hobble &c. 275; put one's foot in it; make a mess of, make hash of, make sad work of; overshoot the mark. play tricks with, play Puck, mismanage, misconduct, misdirect, misapply, missend. stultify oneself, make a fool of oneself, commit oneself; act foolishly; play the fool; put oneself out of court; lose control, lose control of oneself, lose one's head, lose one's cunning. begin at the wrong end; do things by halves &c. (not complete) 730; make two bites of a cherry; play at cross purposes; strain at a gnat and swallow a camel &c. (caprice) 608; put the cart before the horse; lock the stable door when the horse is stolen &c. (too late) 135. not know what one is about, not know one's own interest, not know on which side one's bread is buttered; stand in one's own light, quarrel with one's bread and butter, throw a stone in one's own garden, kill the goose which lays the golden eggs, pay dear for one's whistle, cut one's own throat, bum one's fingers; knock one's head against a stone wall, beat one's head against a stone wall; fall into a trap, catch a Tartar, bring the house about one's ears; have too many eggs in one basket (imprudent) 863, have too many irons in the fire. mistake &c. 495; take the shadow for the substance &c. (credulity) 486; bark up the wrong tree; be in the wrong box, aim at a pigeon and kill a crow; take the wrong pig by the tail, get the wrong pig by the tail, get the wrong sow by the ear, get the dirty end of the stick; put the saddle on the wrong horse, put a square peg into a round hole, put new wine into old bottles. cut blocks with a razor; hold a farthing candle to the sun &c. (useless) 645; fight with a shadow, grasp at a shadow; catch at straws, lean on a broken reed, reckon without one's host, pursue a wild goose chase; go on a fool's goose chase, sleeveless errand; go further and fare worse; lose one's way, miss one's way; fail &c. 732. Adj. unskillful &c. 698; inexpert; bungling &c.v.; awkward, clumsy, unhandy, lubberly, gauche, maladroit; left-handed, heavy-handed; slovenly, slatternly; gawky. adrift, at fault. inapt, unapt; inhabile[Fr]; untractable[obs3], unteachable; giddy &c. (inattentive) 458; inconsiderate &c. (neglectful) 460; stupid &c. 499; inactive &c. 683; incompetent; unqualified, disqualified, ill-qualified; unfit; quackish; raw, green, inexperienced, rusty, out of practice. unaccustomed, unused, untrained &c. 537, uninitiated, unconversant &c. (ignorant) 491[obs3]; shiftless; unstatesmanlike. unadvised; ill-advised, misadvised; ill-devised, ill-imagined, ill- judged, ill-contrived, ill-conducted; unguided, misguided; misconducted, foolish, wild; infelicitous; penny wise and pound foolish &c. (inconsistent) 608. Phr. one's fingers being all thumbs; the right hand forgets its cunning; il se noyerait dans une goutte d'eau[Fr]; incidit in Scyllam qui vult vitare Charybdim[Lat]; out of the frying pan into the fire; non omnia possumus omnes [Lat][Vergil].

<— p. 227 —>

#700. Proficient. — N. proficient, expert, adept, dab; dabster[obs3], crackerjack; connoisseur &c. (scholar) 492; master, master hand; prima donna[Sp], first fiddle, top gun, chef de cuisine, top sawyer; protagonist; past master; mahatma. picked man; medallist, prizeman[obs3]. veteran; old stager, old campaigner, old soldier, old file, old hand; man of business, man of the world. nice hand, good hand, clean hand; practiced hand, experienced eye, experienced hand; marksman; good shot, dead shot, crack shot; ropedancer, funambulist[obs3], acrobat; cunning man; conjuror &c. (deceiver) 548; wizard &c. 994. genius; mastermind, master head, master spirit. cunning blade, sharp blade, sharp fellow; jobber; cracksman &c. (thief) 792[obs3]; politician, tactician, strategist. pantologist[obs3], admirable Crichton, Jack of all trades; prodigy of learning.

#701. Bungler. — N. bungler; blunderer, blunderhead[obs3]; marplot, fumbler, lubber, duffer, dauber, stick; bad hand, poor hand, poor shot; butterfingers[obs3]. no conjurer, flat, muff, slow coach, looby[obs3], lubber, swab; clod, yokel, awkward squad, blanc-bec; galoot[obs3]. land lubber; fresh water sailor, fair weather sailor; horse marine; fish out of water, ass in lion's skin, jackdaw in peacock's feathers; quack &c. (deceiver) 548; lord of misrule. sloven, slattern, trapes[obs3]. amateur, novice, greenhorn (learner) 541. Phr. il n'a pas invente' la poudre[Fr]; he will never set the Thames on fire; acierta errando[Lat]; aliquis in omnibus nullus in singulis[Lat][obs3].

#702. Cunning. — N. cunning, craft; cunningness[obs3], craftiness &c. adj.; subtlety, artificiality; maneuvering &c. v.; temporization; circumvention. chicane, chicanery; sharp practice, knavery, jugglery[obs3]; concealment &c. 528; guile, doubling, duplicity &c. (falsehood) 544; foul play. diplomacy, politics; Machiavelism; jobbery, backstairs influence. art, artifice; device, machination; plot &c. (plan) 626; maneuver, stratagem, dodge, sidestep, artful dodge, wile; trick, trickery &c. (deception) 545; ruse, ruse de guerre[Fr]; finesse, side blow, thin end of the wedge, shift, go by, subterfuge, evasion; white lie &c (untruth) 546; juggle, tour de force; tricks of the trade, tricks upon travelers; espieglerie[Fr]; net, trap &c. 545. Ulysses, Machiavel, sly boots, fox, reynard; Scotchman; Jew, Yankee; intriguer, intrigant[obs3]; floater [U.S.], Indian giver [U.S.], keener [U.S.], repeater [U.S. politics]. V. be cunning &c. adj.; have cut one's eyeteeth; contrive &c (plan) 626; live by one's wits; maneuver; intrigue, gerrymander, finesse, double, temporize, stoop to conquer, reculer pour mieux sauter[Fr], circumvent, steal a march upon; overreach &c. 545; throw off one's guard; surprise &c. 508; snatch a verdict; waylay, undermine, introduce the thin end of the wedge; play a deep game, play tricks with; ambiguas in vulgum spargere voces[Lat]; flatter, make things pleasant; have an ax to grind. dodge, sidestep, bob and weave. Adj. cunning, crafty, artful; skillful &c. 698; subtle, feline, vulpine; cunning as a fox, cunning as a serpent; deep, deep laid; profound; designing, contriving; intriguing &c.v.; strategic, diplomatic, politic, Machiavelian, timeserving[obs3]; artificial; tricky, tricksy[obs3]; wily, sly, slim, insidious, stealthy; underhand &c (hidden) 528; subdolous[obs3]; deceitful &c. 545; slippery as an eel, evasive &c. 623; crooked; arch, pawky[obs3], shrewd, acute; sharp, sharp as a tack, sharp as a needle!; canny, astute, leery, knowing, up to snuff, too clever by half, not to be caught with chaff. tactful, diplomatic, politic; polite &c. 894. Adv. cunningly &c. adj.; slyly, slily[obs3], on the sly, by a side wind. Phr. diamond cut diamond; a' bis ou a blanc[Fr][obs3]; fin contre fin[Fr]; "something is rotten in the state of Denmark" [Hamlet].

<— p. 228 —>

#703. Artlessness. — N. artlessness &c. adj; nature, simplicity; innocence &c. 946; bonhomie, naivete, abandon, candor, sincerity; singleness of purpose, singleness of heart; honesty &c 939; plain speaking; epanchement[Fr]. rough diamond, matter of fact man; le palais de verite[Fr]; enfant terrible[Fr]. V. be artless &c. adj; look one in the face; wear one's heart upon his sleeves for daws to peck at[obs3]; think aloud; speak out, speak one's mind; be free with one, call a spade a spade. Adj. artless, natural, pure, native, confiding, simple, lain, inartificial[obs3], untutored, unsophisticated, ingenu[obs3], unaffected, naive; sincere, frank; open, open as day; candid, ingenuous, guileless; unsuspicious, honest &c. 939; innocent &c. 946; Arcadian[obs3]; undesigning, straightforward, unreserved, above-board; simple-minded, single-minded; frank-hearted, open-hearted, single-hearted, simple-hearted. free-spoken, plain-spoken, outspoken; blunt, downright, direct, matter of fact, unpoetical[obs3]; unflattering. Adv. in plain words, in plain English; without mincing the matter; not to mince the matter &c. (affirmation) 535. Phr. Davus sum non Oedipus [Terence]; liberavi animam meam[Lat]; "as frank as rain on cherry blossoms" [E.B. Browning].

% Section IV. ANTAGONISM

1. Conditional Antagonism %

#704. Difficulty. — N. difficulty; hardness &c. adj.; impracticability &c. (impossibility) 471; tough work, hard work, uphill work; hard task, Herculean task, Augean task[obs3]; task of Sisyphus, Sisyphean labor, tough job, teaser, rasper[obs3], dead lift. dilemma, embarrassment; deadlock; perplexity &c. (uncertainty) 475; intricacy; entanglement, complexity &c. 59; cross fire; awkwardness, delicacy, ticklish card to play, knot, Gordian knot, dignus vindice nodus[Lat], net, meshes, maze; coil &c. (convolution) 248; crooked path; involvement. nice point, delicate point, subtle point, knotty point; vexed question, vexata quaestio[Lat], poser; puzzle &c. (riddle) 533; paradox; hard nut to crack, nut to crack; bone to pick, crux, pons asinorum[Lat], where the shoe pinches. nonplus, quandary, strait, pass, pinch, pretty pass, stress, brunt; critical situation, crisis; trial, rub, emergency, exigency, scramble. scrape, hobble, slough, quagmire, hot water, hornet's nest; sea of troubles, peck of troubles; pretty kettle of fish; pickle, stew, imbroglio, mess, ado; false position. set fast, stand, standstill; deadlock, dead set. fix, horns of a dilemma, cul de sac[Fr]; hitch; stumbling block &c (hindrance) 706. [difficult person] crab; curmudgeon. V. be difficult &c. adj.; run one hard, go against the grain, try one's patience, put one out; put to one's shifts, put to one's wit's end; go hard with one, try one; pose, perplex &c. (uncertain) 475; bother, nonplus, gravel, bring to a deadlock; be impossible &c. 471; be in the way of &c (hinder) 706. meet with difficulties; labor under difficulties; get into difficulties; plunge into difficulties; struggle with difficulties; contend with difficulties; grapple with difficulties; labor under a disadvantage; be in difficulty &c. adj. fish in troubled waters, buffet the waves, swim against the stream, scud under bare poles. Have much ado with, have a hard time of it; come to the push, come to the pinch; bear the brunt. grope in the dark, lose one's way, weave a tangled web, walk among eggs. get into a scrape &c. n.; bring a hornet's nest about one's ears; be put to one's shifts; flounder, boggle, struggle; not know which way to turn &c. (uncertain) 475; perdre son Latin[Fr]; stick at, stick in the mud, stick fast; come to a stand, come to a standstill, come to a deadlock; hold the wolf by the ears, hold the tiger by the tail. render difficult &c. adj.; enmesh, encumber, embarrass, ravel, entangle; put a spoke in the wheel &c. (hinder) 706; lead a pretty dance. Adj. difficult, not easy, hard, tough; troublesome, toilsome, irksome; operose[obs3], laborious, onerous, arduous, Herculean, formidable; sooner said than done; more easily said than done, easier said than done. [pertaining to person's disposition sensu 802] difficult to deal with, hard to deal with; ill-conditioned, crabbed, crabby; not to be handled with kid gloves, not made with rose water. awkward, unwieldy, unmanageable; intractable, stubborn &c. (obstinate) 606; perverse, refractory, plaguy[obs3], trying, thorny, rugged; knotted, knotty; inviousl; pathless, trackless; labyrinthine &c (convoluted) 248; intricate, complicated &c (tangled) 59; impracticable &c. (impossible) 471; not feasible &c. 470; desperate &c. (hopeless) 859. embarrassing, perplexing &c. (uncertain) 475; delicate, ticklish, critical; beset with difficulties, full of difficulties, surrounded by difficulties, entangled by difficulties, encompassed with difficulties. under a difficulty; in a box; in difficulty, in hot water, in the suds, in a cleft stick, in a fix, in the wrong box, in a scrape &c.n., in deep water, in a fine pickle; in extremis; between two stools, between Scylla and Charybdis; surrounded by shoals, surrounded by breakers, surrounded by quicksands; at cross purposes; not out of the wood. reduced to straits; hard pressed, sorely pressed; run hard; pinched, put to it, straitened; hard up, hard put to it, hard set; put to one's shifts; puzzled, at a loss, &c (uncertain) 475; at the end of one's tether, at the end of one's rope, at one's wit's end, at a nonplus, at a standstill; graveled, nonplused, nonplussed, stranded, aground; stuck fast, set fast; up a tree, at bay, aux abois[Fr], driven into a corner, driven from pillar to post, driven to extremity, driven to one's wit's end, driven to the wall; au bout de son Latin; out of one's depth; thrown out. accomplished with difficulty; hard-fought, hard-earned. Adv. with difficulty, with much ado; barely, hardly &c. adj.; uphill; against the stream, against the grain; d rebours[Fr]; Invita Minerva[Lat]; in the teeth of; at a pinch, upon a pinch; at long odds, against long odds. Phr. "ay there's the rub" [Hamlet]; hic labor hoc opus [Lat][Vergil]; things are come to a pretty pass, ab inconvenienti[Lat]; ad astra per aspera[Lat]; acun chemin de fleurs ne conduit a la gloire[Fr].

<— p. 229 —>

#705. Facility. — N. facility, ease; easiness &c. adj.; capability; feasibility &c. (practicability) 470; flexibility, pliancy &c. 324; smoothness &c. 255. plain sailing, smooth sailing, straight sailing; mere child's play, holiday task; cinch [U.S.]. smooth water, fair wind; smooth royal road; clear coast, clear stage; tabula rasa[Lat]; full play &c. (freedom) 748. disencumbrance[obs3], disentanglement; deoppilationl!; permission &c. 760. simplicity, lack of complication. V. be easy &c. adj.; go on smoothly, run smoothly; have full play &c. n.; go on all fours, run on all fours; obey the helm, work well. flow with the stream, swim with the stream, drift with the stream, go with the stream, flow with the tide, drift with the tide; see one's way; have all one's own way, have the game in one's own hands; walk over the course, win at a canter; make light of, make nothing of, make no bones of. be at home in, make it look easy, do it with one's eyes closed, do it in one's sleep &c. (skillful) 698. render easy &c. adj.; facilitate, smooth, ease; popularize; lighten, lighten the labor; free, clear; disencumber, disembarrass, disentangle, disengage; deobstruct[obs3], unclog, extricate, unravel; untie the knot, cut the knot; disburden, unload, exonerate, emancipate, free from, deoppilatel!; humor &c. (aid) 707; lubricate &c. 332; relieve &c. 834. leave a hole to creep out of, leave a loophole, leave the matter open; give the reins to, give full play, give full swing; make way for; open the door to, open the way, prepare the ground, smooth the ground, clear the ground, open the way, open the path, open the road; pave the way, bridge over; permit &c. 760. Adj. easy, facile; feasible &c (practicable) 470; easily managed, easily accomplished; within reach, accessible, easy of access, for the million, open to. manageable, wieldy; towardly[obs3], tractable; submissive; yielding, ductile; suant[obs3]; pliant &c. (soft) 324; glib, slippery; smooth &c. 255; on friction wheels, on velvet. unembarrassed, disburdened, unburdened, disencumbered, unencumbered, disembarrassed; exonerated; unloaded, unobstructed, untrammeled; unrestrained &c. (free) 748; at ease, light. [able to do easily] at home with; quite at home; in one's element, in smooth water; skillful &c. 698;accustomed &c. 613. Adv. easily &c. adj.; readily, smoothly, swimmingly, on easy terms, single-handed. Phr. touch and go.

<— p. 230 —>

#706. Hindrance. — N. prevention, preclusion, obstruction, stoppage; embolus, embolism [medical]; infarct [medical]; interruption, interception, interclusionl; hindrance, impeditionl; retardment[obs3], retardation; embarrassment, oppilationll; coarctation[obs3], stricture, restriction; restraint &c. 751; inhibition &c. 761; blockade &c. (closure) 261. interference, interposition; obtrusion; discouragement, discountenance. impediment, let, obstacle, obstruction, knot, knag[obs3]; check, hitch, contretemps, screw loose, grit in the oil. bar, stile, barrier; [barrier to vehicles] turnstile, turnpike; gate, portcullis. beaver dam; trocha[obs3]; barricade &c. (defense) 717; wall, dead wall, sea wall, levee breakwater, groyne[obs3]; bulkhead, block, buffer; stopper &c. 263; boom, dam, weir, burrock[obs3]. drawback, objection; stumbling-block, stumbling-stone; lion in the path, snag; snags and sawyers. encumbrance, incumbrance[obs3]; clog, skid, shoe, spoke; drag, drag chain, drag weight; stay, stop; preventive, prophylactic; load, burden, fardel[obs3], onus, millstone round one's neck, impedimenta; dead weight; lumber, pack; nightmare, Ephialtes[obs3], incubus, old man of the sea; remora. difficulty &c. 704; insuperable &c. 471; obstacle; estoppel [Law]; ill wind; head wind &c. (opposition) 708; trammel, tether &c. (means of restraint) 752; hold back, counterpoise. [person who hinders] damper, wet blanket, hinderer, marplot, killjoy; party pooper[coll]; party crasher, interloper. trail of a red herring; opponent &c. 710. V. hinder, impede, filibuster [U.S.], impedite[obs3], embarrass. keep off, stave off, ward off; obviate; avert, antevertl; turn aside, draw off, prevent, forefend, nip in the bud; retard, slacken, check, let; counteract, countercheck[obs3]; preclude, debar, foreclose, estop[Law]; inhibit &c. 761; shackle &c. (restrain) 751; restrict. obstruct, stop, stay, bar, bolt, lock; block, block up; choke off; belay, barricade; block the way, bar the way, stop the way; forelay[obs3]; dam up &c. (close) 261; put on the brake &c. n.; scotch the wheel, lock the wheel, put a spoke in the wheel; put a stop to &c. 142; traverse, contravene; interrupt, intercept; oppose &c. 708; hedge in, hedge round; cut off; includel. interpose, interfere, intermeddle &c. 682. cramp, hamper; clog, clog the wheels; cumber; encumber, incumber; handicap; choke; saddle with, load with; overload, lay; lumber, trammel, tie one's hands, put to inconvenience; incommode, discommode; discompose; hustle, corner, drive into a corner. run foul of, fall foul of; cross the path of, break in upon. thwart, frustrate, disconcert, balk, foil; faze, feaze[obs3], feeze [obs3][U.S.]; baffle, snub, override, circumvent; defeat &c. 731; spike guns &c. (render useless) 645; spoil, mar, clip the wings of; cripple &c. (injure) 659; put an extinguisher on; damp; dishearten &c (dissuade) 616; discountenance, throw cold water on, spoil sport; lay a wet blanket, throw a wet blanket on; cut the ground from under one, take the wind out of one's sails, undermine; be in the way of, stand in the way of; act as a drag; hang like a millstone round one's neck. Adj. hindering &c. v.; obstructive, obstruent[obs3]; impeditive[obs3], impedient[obs3]; intercipientl; prophylactic &c. (remedial) 662; impedimentary. in the way of, unfavorable; onerous, burdensome; cumbrous, cumbersome; obtrusive. hindered &c v.; windbound[obs3], waterlogged, heavy laden; hard pressed. unassisted &c. (see assist &c. 707); single-handed, alone; deserted &c. 624. Phr. occurrent nubes[Lat].

<— p. 231 —>

#707. Aid. — N. aid, aidance[obs3]; assistance, help, opitulationl, succor; support, lift, advance, furtherance, promotion; coadjuvancy &c. (cooperation) 709[obs3]. patronage, championship, countenance, favor, interest, advocacy. sustentation, subvention, alimentation, nutrition, nourishment; eutrophy; manna in the wilderness; food &c. 298; means &c. 632. ministry, ministration; subministration[obs3]; accommodation. relief, rescue; help at a dead lift; supernatural aid; deus ex machina[Lat]. supplies, reinforcements, reenforcements[obs3], succors, contingents, recruits; support &c. (physical) 215; adjunct, ally &c. (helper) 711. V. aid, assist, help, succor, lend one's aid; come to the aid &c. n. of; contribute, subscribe to; bring aid, give aid, furnish aid, afford aid, supply aid &c. n.; give a helping hand, stretch a hand, lend a helping hand, lend a hand, bear a helping hand, hold out a hand, hold out a helping hand; give one a life, give one a cast, give one a turn; take by the hand, take in tow; help a lame dog over a stile, lend wings to. relieve, rescue; set up, set agoing[obs3], set on one's legs; bear through, pull through; give new life to, be the making of; reinforce, reenforce, recruit; set forward, put forward, push forward; give a lift, give a shove, give an impulse to; promote, further, forward, advance expedite, speed, quicken, hasten. support, sustain, uphold, prop, hold up, bolster. cradle, nourish; nurture, nurse, dry nurse, suckle, put out to nurse; manure, cultivate, force;

foster, cherish, foment; feed the flame, fan the flame. serve; do service to, tender to, pander to; administer to, subminister to[obs3], minister to; tend, attend, wait on; take care of &c. 459; entertain; smooth the bed of death. oblige, accommodate, consult the wishes of; humor, cheer, encourage. second, stand by; back, back up; pay the piper, abet; work for, make interest for, stick up for, take up the cudgels for; take up the cause of, espouse the cause of, adopt the cause of; advocate, beat up for recruits, press into the service; squire, give moral support to, keep in countenance, countenance, patronize; lend oneself to, lend one's countenance to; smile upon, shine upon; favor, befriend, take in hand, enlist under the banners of; side with &c. (cooperate) 709. be of use to; subserve &c. (instrument) 631; benefit &c. 648; render a service &c. (utility) 644; conduce &c. (tend) 176. Adj. aiding &c. v.; auxiliary, adjuvant, helpful; coadjuvant &c. 709[obs3]; subservient, ministrant, ancillary, accessory, subsidiary. at one's beck, at one's beck and call; friendly, amicable, favorable, propitious, well-disposed; neighborly; obliging &c. (benevolent) 906. Adv. with the aid, by the aid &c. of; on behalf of, in behalf of; in aid of, in the service of, in the name of, in favor of, in furtherance of; on account of; for the sake of, on the part of; non obstante[Lat]. Int. help! save us! to the rescue! Phr. alterum alterius auxilio eget [Lat][Sallust]; "God befriend us as our cause is just" [Henry IV]; at your service.

<— p. 232 —>

#708. Opposition. — N.. opposition, antagonism; oppugnancy[obs3], oppugnation[obs3]; impugnation!!; contrariety; contravention; counteraction &c. 179; counterplot. cross fire, undercurrent, head wind. clashing, collision, conflict. competition, two of a trade, rivalry, emulation, race. absence of aid &c. 708; resistance &c. 719; restraint &c. 751; hindrance &c. 706. V. oppose, counteract, run counter to; withstand &c. (resist) 719; control &c. (restrain) 751; hinder &c. 706; antagonize, oppugn, fly in the face of, go dead against, kick against, fall afoul of, run afoul of; set against, pit against; face, confront, cope with; make a stand, make a dead set against; set oneself against, set one's face against; protest against, vote against, raise one's voice against; disfavor, turn one's back upon; set at naught, slap in the face, slam the door in one's face. be at cross purposes; play at cross purposes; counterwork[obs3], countermine; thwart, overthwart[obs3]; work against, undermine. stem, breast, encounter; stem the tide, breast the tide, stem the current, stem the flood; buffet the waves; beat up against, make head against; grapple with; kick against the pricks &c. (resist) 719; contend &c. 720; do battle &c. (warfare) 722 -with, do battle against. contradict, contravene; belie; go against, run against, beat against, militate against; come in conflict with. emulate &c. (compete) 720; rival, spoil one's trade. Adj. opposing, opposed &c.v.; adverse, antagonistic; contrary &c. 14; at variance &c. 24; at issue, at war with. unfavorable, unfriendly; hostile, inimical, cross, unpropitious. in hostile array, front to front, with crossed bayonets, at daggers drawn; up in arms; resistant &c. 719. competitive, emulous. Adv. against, versus, counter to, in conflict with, at cross purposes. against the grain, against the current, against the stream, against the wind, against the tide; with a headwind; with the wind ahead, with the wind in one's teeth. in spite, in despite, in defiance; in the way, in the teeth of, in the face of; across; athwart, overthwart[obs3]; where the shoe pinches; in spite of one's teeth. though &c. 30; even; quand meme[Fr]; per contra. Phr. nitor in adversum[Lat].

#709. Cooperation. — N. cooperation; coadjuvancy[obs3], coadjutancy[obs3]; coagency[obs3], coefficiency[obs3]; concert, concurrence, complicity, participation; union &c. 43; additivity, combination &c. 48; collusion. association, alliance, colleagueship[obs3], joint stock, copartnership[obs3]; cartel; confederation &c. (party) 712; coalition, fusion; a long pull a strong pull and a pull all together; logrolling, freemasonry. unanimity &c. (assent) 488; esprit de corps, party spirit; clanship[obs3], partisanship; concord &c 714. synergy, coaction[obs3]. V. cooperate, concur; coact[obs3], synergize. conduce &c. 178; combine, unite one's efforts; keep together, draw together, pull together, club together, hand together, hold together, league together, band together, be banded together; pool; stand shoulder to shoulder, put shoulder to shoulder; act in concert, join forces, fraternize, cling to one another, conspire, concert, lay one's heads together; confederate, be in league with; collude, understand one another, play into the hands of, hunt in couples. side with, take side with, go along with, go hand in hand with, join hands with, make common cause with, strike in with, unite with, join with, mix oneself up with, take part with, cast in one's lot with; join partnership, enter into partnership with; rally round, follow the lead of; come to, pass over to, come into the views of; be in the same boat, row in the same boat; sail in the same boat; sail on the same tack. be a party to, lend oneself to; chip in; participate; have a hand in, have a finger in the pie; take part in, bear part in; second &c. (aid) 707; take the part of, play the game of; espouse a cause, espouse a quarrel. Adj. cooperating &c. v.; in cooperation &c.n., in league &c. (party) 712; coadjuvant[obs3], coadjutant[obs3]; dyed in the wool; cooperative; additive; participative; coactive[obs3], synergetic, synergistic. favorable &c. 707 to; unopposed &c. 708. Adv. as one &c. (unanimously) 488; shoulder to shoulder; synergistically; cooperatively. Phr. due teste valgono piu che una sola [It].

<— p. 233 —>

#710. Opponent. — N. opponent, antagonist, adversary; adverse party, opposition; enemy &c. 891; the other side; assailant.

oppositionist, obstructive; brawler, wrangler, brangler[obs3], disputant; filibuster [U.S.], obstructionist.

malcontent; Jacobin, Fenian; demagogue, reactionist[obs3].

rival, competitor.

bete noir[Fr].

#711. Auxiliary. — N. auxiliary; recruit; assistant; adjuvant, adjutant; ayudante[obs3], coaid[obs3]; adjunct; help, helper, help mate, helping hand; midwife; colleague, partner, mate, confrere, cooperator; coadjutor, coadjutrix[obs3]; collaborator. ally; friend &c. 890, confidant, fidus Achates[Lat][obs3], pal, buddy, alter ego. [criminal law] confederate; accomplice; complice; accessory, accessory after the fact; particeps criminis[Lat]; socius criminis[Lat]. aide-de-camp, secretary, clerk, associate, marshal; right-hand, right- hand man, Friday, girl Friday, man Friday, gopher, gofer; candle-holder, bottle-holder; handmaid; servant &c. 746; puppet, cat's-paw, jackall!. tool, dupe, stooge, ame damnee[Fr]; satellite, adherent. votary; sectarian, secretary; seconder, backer, upholder, abettor, advocate, partisan, champion, patron, friend at court, mediator; angel [theater, entertainment]. friend in need, Jack at a pinch, deus ex machina[Lat], guardian angel, tutelary genius.

#712. Party. — N. party, faction, side, denomination, communion, set, crew, band. horde, posse, phalanx; family, clan, &c. 166; team; tong. council &c. 696. community, body, fellowship, sodality, solidarity; confraternity; familistere[obs3], familistery[obs3]; brotherhood, sisterhood. knot, gang, clique, ring, circle, group, crowd, in-crowd; coterie, club, casino!!; machine; Tammany, Tammany Hall [U.S.]. corporation, corporate body, guild; establishment, company; copartnership[obs3], partnership; firm, house; joint concern, joint-stock company; cahoot, combine [U.S.], trust. society, association; institute, institution; union; trades union; league, syndicate, alliance, Verein[Ger], Bund[Ger], Zollverein[Ger], combination; Turnverein[Ger]; league offensive and defensive, alliance offensive and defensive; coalition; federation; confederation, confederacy; junto, cabal, camarilla[obs3], camorra[obs3], briguel; freemasonry; party spirit &c. (cooperation) 709. Confederates, Conservatives, Democrats, Federalists, Federals, Freemason, Knight Templar; Kuklux, Kuklux Klan, KKK; Liberals, Luddites, Republicans, Socialists, Tories, Whigs &c. staff; dramatis personae[Lat]. V. unite, join; club together &c. (cooperate) 709; cement a party, form a party &c. n.; associate &c. (assemble) 72; enleague[obs3], federalize, go cahoots. Adj. in league, in partnership, in alliance &c. n. bonded together, banded together, linked &c. (joined) 43- together; embattled; confederated, federative, joint. Adv. hand in hand, side by side, shoulder to shoulder, en masse, in the same boat.

#713. Discord. — N. disagreement &c. 24; discord, disaccord[obs3], dissidence, dissonance; jar, clash, shock; jarring, jostling &c. v.; screw loose. variance, difference, dissension, misunderstanding, cross purposes, odds, brouillerie[Fr]; division, split, rupture, disruption, division in the camp, house divided against itself, disunion, breach; schism &c. (dissent) 489; feud, faction. quarrel, dispute, tiff, tracasserie[obs3], squabble, altercation, barney *[obs3], demel, snarl, spat, towrow[obs3], words, high words; wrangling &c. v.; jangle, brabble[obs3], cross questions and crooked answers, snip-snap; family jars. polemics; litigation; strife &c. (contention) 720; warfare &c. 722; outbreak, open rupture, declaration of war. broil, brawl, row, racket, hubbub, rixation!; embroilment, embranglement[obs3], imbroglio, fracas, breach of the peace, piece of work[Fr], scrimmage, rumpus; breeze, squall; riot, disturbance &c (disorder) 59; commotion &c. (agitation) 315; bear garden, Donnybrook, Donnybrook Fair. subject of dispute, ground of quarrel, battle ground, disputed point; bone of contention, bone to pick; apple of discord, casus belli[Lat]; question at issue &c. (subject of inquiry) 461; vexed question, vexata quaestio[Lat], brand of discord. troublous times[obs3]; cat-and-dog life; contentiousness &c. adj.; enmity &c. 889; hate &c. 898; Kilkenny cats; disputant &c. 710; strange bedfellows. V. be discordant &c. adj.; disagree, come amiss &c. 24; clash, jar, jostle, pull different ways, conflict, have no measures with, misunderstand one another; live like cat and dog; differ; dissent &c. 489; have a bone to pick, have a crow to pluck with. fall out, quarrel, dispute; litigate; controvert &c. (deny) 536; squabble, wrangle, jangle, brangle[obs3], bicker, nag; spar &c. (contend) 720; have words &c. n. with; fall foul of. split; break with, break squares with, part company with; declare war, try conclusions; join issue, put in issue; pick a quarrel, fasten a quarrel on; sow dissension, stir up dissension &c. n.; embroil, entangle, disunite, widen the breach; set at odds, set together by the ears; set against, pit against. get into hot water, fish in troubled waters, brawl; kick up a row, kick up a dust; turn the house out of window. Adj. discordant; disagreeing &c. v.; out of tune, ajar, on bad terms, dissentient &c. 489; unreconciled, unpacified; contentious &c. 720. quarrelsome, unpacific[obs3]; gladiatorial, controversial, polemic, disputatious; factious; litigious, litigant; pettifogging. at odds, at loggerheads, at daggers drawn, at variance, at issue, at cross purposes, at sixes and sevens, at feud, at high words; up in arms, together by the ears, in hot water, embroiled. torn, disunited. Phr. quot homines tot sententiae [Lat][Terence]; no love lost between them, non nostrum tantas componere lites [Lat][Vergil]; Mars gravior sub pace latet [Lat][Claudius].

<— p. 234 —>

#714. Concord. — N. concord, accord, harmony, symphony; homologue; agreement &c. 23; sympathy, empathy &c. (love) 897; response; union, unison, unity; bonds of harmony; peace &c. 721; unanimity &c. (assent) 488; league &c. 712; happy family. rapprochement; reunion; amity &c. (friendship) 888; alliance, entente cordiale[Fr], good understanding, conciliation, peacemaker; intercessor, mediator. V. agree &c. 23; accord, harmonize with; fraternize; be-concordant &c. adj.; go hand in hand; run parallel &c. (concur) 178; understand one another, pull together &c. (cooperate) 709; put up one's horses together, sing in chorus. side with, sympathize with, go with, chime in with, fall in with; come round; be pacified &c. 723; assent &c. 488; empathize with, enter into the ideas of, enter into the feelings of; reciprocate. hurler avec les loups[Fr]; go with the stream, swim with the stream. keep in good humor, render accordant, put in tune; come to an understanding, meet halfway; keep the peace, remain at peace. Adj. concordant, congenial; agreeing &c.v.; in accord &c. n.; harmonious, united, cemented; banded together &c. 712; allied; friendly &c. 888; fraternal; conciliatory; at one with; of one mind &c. (assent) 488. at peace, in still water; tranquil &c. (pacific) 721. Adv. with one voice &c. (assent) 488; in concert with, hand in hand; on one's side. Phr. commune periculum concordiam parit[Lat][obs3].

#715. Defiance. — N. defiance; daring &. v.; dare; challenge, cartell!; threat &c. 909; war cry, war whoop.

chest-beating, chest-thumping; saber rattling.

V. defy, dare, beard; brave &c. (courage) 861; bid defiance to; set at defiance, set at naught; hurl defiance at; dance the war dance, beat the war drums; snap the fingers at, laugh to scorn; disobey &c. 742.

show fight, show one's teeth, show a bold front; bluster, look big, stand akimbo, beat one's chest; double the fist, shake the fist; threaten &c. 909.

challenge, call out; throw down the gauntlet, fling down the gauntlet, fling down the gage, fling down the glove, throw down the glove.

Adj. defiant; defying &c. v.;"with arms akimbo".

Adv. in defiance of, in the teeth of; under one's very nose.

Int. do your worst! come if you dare! come on! marry come up! hoity toity!!

Phr. noli me tangere[Lat]; nemo me impune lacessit[Lat]; don't tread on me; don't you dare; don't even think of it; "Go ahead, make my day!" [Dirty Harry].

<— p. 235 —>

#716. Attack. — N. attack; assault, assault and battery; onset, onslaught, charge. aggression, offense; incursion, inroad, invasion; irruption; outbreak; estrapade[obs3], ruade[obs3]; coupe de main, sally, sortie, camisade[obs3], raid, foray; run at, run against; dead set at. storm, storming; boarding, escalade[obs3]; siege, investment, obsession!!, bombardment, cannonade. fire, volley; platoon fire, file fire; fusillade; sharpshooting, broadside; raking fire, cross fire; volley of grapeshot, whiff of the grape, feu d'enfer [Fr]. cut, thrust, lunge, pass, passado[obs3], carte and tierce[Fr][obs3], home thrust; coupe de bec[Fr]; kick, punch &c. (impulse) 276. battue[obs3], razzia[obs3], Jacquerie, dragonnade[obs3]; devastation &c. 162; eboulement[Fr]. assailant, aggressor, invader. base of operations, point of attack; echelon. V. attack, assault, assail; invade; set upon, fall upon; charge, impugn, break a lance with, enter the lists. assume the offensive, take the offensive; be the aggressor, become the aggressor; strike the first blow, draw first blood, throw the first stone at; lift a hand against, draw the sword against; take up the cudgels; advance against, march against; march upon, harry; come on, show fight. strike at, poke at, thrust at; aim a blow at, deal a blow at; give one a blow, fetch one a blow, fetch one a kick, give one a kick; have a cut at, have a shot at, take a cut at, take a shot at, have a fling at, have a shy at; be down upon, pounce upon; fall foul of, pitch into, launch out against; bait, slap on the face; make a thrust at, make a pass at, make a set at, make a dead set at; bear down upon. close with, come to close quarters; bring to bay. ride full tilt against; attack tooth and nail, go at hammer and tongs. let fly at, dash at, run a tilt at, rush at, tilt at, run at, fly at, hawk at, have at, let out at; make a dash, make a rush at; strike home; drive one hard; press one hard; be hard upon, run down, strike at the root of. lay about one, run amuck. aim at, draw a bead on [U.S.]. fire upon, fire at, fire a shot at; shoot at, pop at, level at, let off a gun at; open fire, pepper, bombard, shell, pour a broadside into; fire a volley, fire red-hot shot; spring a mine. throw a stone, throw stones at; stone, lapidate[obs3], pelt; hurl at, hurl against, hurl at the head of; rock beset[U.S.], besiege, beleaguer; lay siege to, invest, open the trenches, plant a battery, sap, mine; storm, board, scale the walls. cut and thrust, bayonet, butt; kick, strike &c. (impulse) 276; whip &c. (punish) 972. [attack verbally] assail, impugn; malign (detract) 934. bomb, rocket, blast. Adj. attacking &c.v.; aggressive, offensive, obsidional[obs3]. up in arms. Adv. on the offensive. Int. "up and at them!" Phr. "the din of arms, the yell of savage rage, the shriek of agony, the groan of death" [Southey]; "their fatal hands no second stroke intend" [Paradise Lost]; "thirst for glory quells the love of life" [Addison].

#717. Defense — N. defense, protection, guard, ward; shielding &c.v.; propugnationl, preservation &c. 670; guardianship. area defense; site defense. self-defense, self-preservation; resistance &c. 719. safeguard &c. (safety) 664; balistraria[obs3]; bunker, screen &c. (shelter) 666; camouflage &c. (concealment) 530; fortification; munition, muniment[obs3]; trench, foxhole; bulwark, fosse[obs3], moat, ditch, entrenchment, intrenchment[obs3]; kila[obs3]; dike, dyke; parapet, sunk fence, embankment, mound, mole, bank, sandbag, revetment; earth work, field-work; fence, wall dead wall, contravallation[obs3]; paling &c. (inclosure) 232; palisade, haha, stockade, stoccado[obs3], laager[obs3], sangar[obs3]; barrier, barricade; boom; portcullis, chevaux de frise[Fr]; abatis, abattis[obs3], abbatis[obs3]; vallum[obs3], circumvallation[obs3], battlement, rampart, scarp; escarp[obs3], counter-scarp; glacis, casemate[obs3]; vallation[obs3], vanfos[obs3]. buttress, abutment; shore &c. (support) 215. breastwork, banquette, curtain, mantlet[obs3], bastion, redan[obs3], ravelin[obs3]; vauntmure[obs3]; advance work, horn work, outwork; barbacan[obs3], barbican; redoubt; fort-elage[Fr], fort-alice; lines. loophole, machicolation[obs3]; sally port. hold, stronghold, fastness; asylum &c. (refuge) 666; keep, donjon, dungeon, fortress, citadel, capitol, castle; tower of strength, tower of strength; fort, barracoon[obs3], pah[obs3], sconce, martello tower[obs3], peelhouse[obs3], blockhouse, rath[obs3]; wooden walls. [body armor] bulletproof vest, armored vest, buffer, corner stone, fender, apron, mask, gauntlet, thimble, carapace, armor, shield, buckler, aegis, breastplate, backplate[obs3], cowcatcher, face guard, scutum[obs3], cuirass, habergeon[obs3], mail, coat of mail, brigandine[obs3], hauberk, lorication[obs3], helmet, helm, bassinet, salade[obs3], heaume[obs3], morion[obs3], murrion[obs3], armet[obs3], cabaset[obs3], vizor[obs3], casquetel[obs3], siege cap, headpiece, casque, pickelhaube, vambrace[obs3], shako &c. (dress) 225. bearskin; panoply; truncheon &c. (weapon) 727. garrison, picket, piquet; defender, protector; guardian &c. (safety) 664; bodyguard, champion; knight-errant, Paladin; propugner[obs3]. bulletproof window. hardened site. V. defend, forfend, fend; shield, screen, shroud; engarrison[obs3]; fend round &c. (circumscribe) 229; fence, entrench, intrench[obs3]; guard &c. (keep safe) 664; guard against; take care of &c. (vigilance) 459; bear harmless; fend off, keep off, ward off, beat off, beat back; hinder &c. 706. parry, repel, propugn[obs3], put to flight; give a warm reception to [ironical]; hold at bay, keep at bay, keep arm's length. stand on the defensive, act on the defensive; show fight; maintain one's ground, stand one's ground; stand by; hold one's own; bear the brunt, stand the brunt; fall back upon, hold, stand in the gap. Adj. defending &c.v.; defensive; murall!; armed, armed at all points, armed cap-a-pie, armed to the teeth; panoplied[obs3]; iron-plated, ironclad; loopholed, castellated, machicolated[obs3]; casemated[obs3]; defended &c.v.; proof against. armored, ballproofl!, bulletproof; hardened. Adv. defensively; on the defense, on the defensive; in defense; at bay, pro aris et focis[obs3][Lat]. Int. no surrender! Phr. defense not defiance; Dieu defend le droit [Fr]; fidei defensor [Lat: defender of the faith].

<— p. 236 —>

#718. Retaliation. — N. retaliation, reprisal, retort, payback; counter-stroke, counter-blast, counterplot, counter-project; retribution, lex talionis[Lat]; reciprocation &c. (reciprocity) 12. tit for tat, give and take, blow for blow, quid pro quo, a Roland for an Oliver, measure for measure, diamond cut diamond, the biter bit, a game at which two can play; reproof valiant, retort courteous. recrimination &c. (accusation) 938; revenge &c. 919; compensation &c. 30; reaction &c. (recoil) 277. V. retaliate, retort, turn upon; pay, pay off, pay back; pay in one's own coin, pay in the same coin; cap; reciprocate &c. 148; turn the tables upon, return the compliment; give a quid pro quo &c. n., give as much as one takes, give as good as one gets; give and take, exchange fisticuffs; be quits, be even with; pay off old scores. serve one right, be hoist on one's own petard, throw a stone in one's own garden, catch a Tartar. Adj. retaliating &c. v.; retaliatory, retaliative; talionic[obs3]. Adv. in retaliation; en revanche. Phr. mutato nomine de te fabula narratur [Lat][Horace]; par pari refero [Lat][Terence]; tu quoque[Lat: you too]; you're another; suo sibi gladio hunc jugulo [Lat]; a beau jeu beau retour[Fr]; litem [Lat]. . . lite resolvit [Lat][Horace].

#719. Resistance. — N. resistance, stand, front, oppugnation[obs3]; oppugnancy[obs3]; opposition &c. 708; renitence[obs3], renitency; reluctation[obs3], recalcitration[obs3]; kicking &c. v. repulse, rebuff. insurrection &c. (disobedience) 742; strike; turn out, lock out, barring out; levee en masse[Fr], Jacquerie; riot &c. (disorder) 59. V. resist; not submit &c. 725; repugn[obs3], reluct, reluctate[obs3], withstand; stand up against, strive against, bear up under, bear up against, be proof against, make head against; stand, stand firm, stand one's ground, stand the brunt of, stand out; hold one's grounds, hold one's own, hold out, hold firm. breast the wave, breast the current; stem the tide, stem the torrent; face, confront, grapple with; show a bold front &c. (courage) 861; present a front; make a stand, take one's stand. kick, kick against; recalcitrate[obs3], kick against the pricks; oppose &c. 708; fly in the face of; lift the hand against &c. (attack) 716; rise up in arms &c. (war) 722; strike, turn out; draw up a round robin &c.

(remonstrate) 932; revolt &c. (disobey) 742; make a riot. prendre le mors aux dents [French: take the bit between the teeth]; sell one's life dearly, die hard, keep at bay; repel, repulse. Adj. resisting &c.v.; resistive, resistant; refractory &c. (disobedient) 742; recalcitrant, renitent; up in arms. repulsive, repellant. proof against; unconquerable &c. (strong) 159; stubborn, unconquered; indomitable &c. (persevering) 604a; unyielding &c. (obstinate) 606. Int. hands off! keep off!

<— p. 237 —>

#720. Contention. — N. contention, strife; contest, contestation[obs3]; struggle; belligerency; opposition &c. 708. controversy, polemics; debate &c. (discussion) 476; war of words, logomachy[obs3], litigation; paper war; high words &c. (quarrel) 713; sparring &c. v. competition, rivalry; corrivalry[obs3], corrivalship[obs3], agonisml, concours[obs3], match, race, horse racing, heat, steeple chase, handicap; regatta; field day; sham fight, Derby day; turf, sporting, bullfight, tauromachy[obs3], gymkhana[obs3]; boat race, torpids[obs3]. wrestling, greco-roman wrestling; pugilism, boxing, fisticuffs, the manly art of self-defense; spar, mill, set-to, round, bout, event, prize fighting; quarterstaff, single stick; gladiatorship[obs3], gymnastics; jiujitsu, jujutsu, kooshti[obs3], sumo; athletics, athletic sports; games of skill &c. 840. shindy[obs3]; fracas &c. (discord) 713; clash of arms; tussle, scuffle, broil, fray; affray, affraymentl; velita-tionl; colluctationl, luctation[obs3]; brabble[obs3], briguel, scramble, melee, scrimmage, stramash[obs3], bushfighting[obs3]. free fight, stand up fight, hand to hand, running fight. conflict, skirmish; rencounter[obs3], encounter; rencontre[obs3], collision, affair, brush, fight; battle, battle royal; combat, action, engagement, joust, tournament; tilt, tilting [medieval times]; tournay[obs3], list; pitched battle. death struggle, struggle for life or death, life or death struggle, Armageddon[obs3]. hard knocks, sharp contest, tug of war. naval engagement, naumachia[obs3], sea fight. duel, duello[It]; single combat, monomachy[obs3], satisfaction, passage d'armes[Fr], passage of arms, affair of honor; triangular duel; hostile meeting, digladiation[obs3]; deeds of arms, feats of arms; appeal to arms &c. (warfare) 722. pugnacity; combativeness &c. adj.; bone of contention &c. 713. V. contend; contest, strive, struggle, scramble, wrestle; spar, square; exchange blows, exchange fisticuffs; fibl!, justle[obs3], tussle, tilt, box, stave, fence; skirmish; pickeer[obs3]; fight &c. (war) 722; wrangle &c. (quarrel) 713. contend &c. with, grapple with, engage with, close with, buckle with, bandy with, try conclusions with, have a brush &c. n. with, tilt with; encounter, fall foul of, pitch into, clapperclaw[obs3], run a tilt at; oppose &c. 708; reluct. join issue, come to blows, go to loggerheads, set to, come to the scratch, exchange shots, measure swords, meet hand to hand; take up the cudgels, take up the glove, take up the gauntlet; enter the lists; couch one's lance; give satisfaction; appeal to arms &c. (warfare) 722. lay about one; break the peace. compete with, cope with, vie with, race with; outvie[obs3], emulate, rival; run a race; contend &c. for, stipulate for, stickle for; insist upon, make a point of. Adj. contending &c. v.; together by the ears, at loggerheads at war at issue. competitive, rival; belligerent; contentious, combative, bellicose, unpeaceful[obs3]; warlike &c. 722; quarrelsome &c. 901; pugnacious; pugilistic, gladiatorial; palestric[obs3], palestrical[obs3]. Phr. a verbis ad verbera[Lat]; a word and a blow; "a very pretty quarrel as it stands" [Sheridan]; commune periculum concordiam parit[Lat]; lis litem generat[Lat].

#721. Peace. — N. peace; amity &c. (friendship) 888; harmony &c. (concord) 714; tranquility, calm &c. (quiescence) 265; truce, peace treaty, accord &c. (pacification) 723; peace pipe, pipe of peace, calumet of peace.
piping time of peace, quiet life; neutrality.
[symbol of peace] dove of peace, white dove.
[person who favors peace] dove.
pax Romana[Lat]; Pax Americana[Lat][obs3].
V. be at peace; keep the peace &c. (concord) 714.
make peace &c. 723.
Adj. pacific; peaceable, peaceful; calm, tranquil, untroubled, halcyon; bloodless; neutral.
dovish
Phr. the storm blown over; the lion lies down with the lamb; "all quiet on the Potomac"; paritur pax bello [Lat][Nepos]; "peace hath her victories no less renowned than war" [Milton]; "they make a desert and they call it peace".

<— p. 238 —>

#722. Warfare. — N. warfare; fighting &c.v.; hostilities; war, arms, the sword; Mars, Bellona, grim visaged war, horrida bella[Lat]; bloodshed. appeal to arms, appeal to the sword; ordeal of battle; wager of battle; ultima ratio regum[Lat], arbitrament of the sword. battle array, campaign, crusade, expedition, operations; mobilization; state of siege; battlefield, theater of operations &c. (arena) 728; warpath. art of war, tactics, strategy, castrametation[obs3]; generalship; soldiership; logistics; military evolutions, ballistics, gunnery; chivalry. gunpowder, shot. battle, tug of war &c. (contention) 720; service, campaigning, active service, tented field; kriegspiel[Ger], Kriegsspiel[Ger]; fire cross, trumpet, clarion, bugle, pibroch[obs3], slogan; war-cry, war-whoop; battle cry, beat of drum, rappel, tom-tom; calumet of war; word of command; password, watchword; passage d-armes[Fr]. war to the death, war to the knife; guerre a mort[Fr], guerre a outrance[Fr][obs3]; open war, internecine war, civil war. V. arm; raise troops, mobilize troops; raise up in arms; take up the cudgels &c. 720; take up arms, fly to arms, appeal to arms, fly to the sword; draw the sword, unsheathe the sword; dig up the hatchet, dig up the tomahawk; go to war, wage war, 'let slip the dogs of war' [Julius Caesar]; cry havoc; kindle the torch of war, light the torch of war; raise one's banner, raise the fire cross; hoist the black flag; throw away, fling away the scabbard; enroll, enlist; take the field; take the law into one's own hands; do battle, give battle, join battle, engage in battle, go to battle; flesh one's sword; set to, fall to, engage, measure swords with, draw the trigger, cross swords; come to blows, come to close quarters; fight; combat; contend &c. 720; battle with, break a lance with. [pirates engage in battle] raise the jolly roger, run up the jolly roger. serve; see service, be on service, be on active service; campaign; wield the sword, shoulder a musket, smell powder, be under fire; spill blood, imbrue the hands in blood; on the warpath. carry on war, carry on hostilities; keep the field; fight the good fight; fight it out, fight like devils, fight one's way, fight hand to hand; sell one's life dearly; pay the ferryman's fee. Adj. contending, contentious &c. 720; armed, armed to the teeth, armed cap-a-pie; sword in hand; in arms, under arms, up in arms; at war with; bristling with arms; in battle array, in open arms, in the field; embattled; battled. unpacific[obs3], unpeaceful[obs3]; belligerent, combative, armigerous[obs3], bellicose, martial, warlike; military, militant; soldier- like, soldierly. chivalrous; strategical, internecine. Adv. flagrante bello[Lat], in the thick of the fray, in the cannon's mouth; at the sword's point, at the point of the bayonet. Int. vae victis[Lat]! to arms! to your tents O Israel! Phr. the battle rages; a la guerre comme a la guerre[Fr]; bis peccare in bello non licet[Lat][obs3]; jus gladii[Lat]; "my voice is still for war" [Addison]; "'tis well that war is so terrible, otherwise we might grow fond of it" [Robert E. Lee]; "my sentence is for open war" [Milton]; "pride, pomp, and circumstance of glorious war" [Othello]; "the cannons have their bowels full of wrath" [King John]; "the cannons . . .spit forth their iron indignation" [King John]; "the fire-eyed maid of smoky war" [Henry IV]; silent leges inter arma [Lat][Cicero]; si vis pacem para bellum[Lat].

#723. Pacification. — N. pacification, conciliation; reconciliation, reconcilement; shaking of hands, accommodation, arrangement, adjustment; terms, compromise; amnesty, deed of release. peace offering; olive branch; calumet of peace, preliminaries of peace. truce, armistice; suspension of arms, suspension of hostilities, stand-down; breathing time; convention; modus vivendi[Lat]; flag of truce, white flag, parlementaire[Fr], cartell!. hollow truce, pax in bello[Lat]; drawn battle. V. pacify, tranquilize, compose; allay &c. (moderate) 174; reconcile, propitiate, placate, conciliate, meet halfway, hold out the olive branch, heal the breach, make peace, restore harmony, bring to terms. settle matters, arrange matters, accommodate matters, accommodate differences; set straight; make up a quarrel, tantas componere lites[Lat]; come to an understanding, come to terms; bridge over, hush up; make it, make matters up; shake hands; mend one's fences [U.S.]. raise a siege, lift a siege; put up the sword, sheathe the sword; bury the hatchet, lay down one's arms, turn swords into plowshares; smoke the calumet of peace, close the temple of Janus; keep the peace &c. (concord) 714; be pacified &c.; come round. Adj. conciliatory; composing &c.v.; pacified &c.v. Phr. requiescat in pace[Lat].

<— p. 239 —>

#724. Mediation. — N. mediation, mediatorship[obs3], mediatization[obs3]; intervention, interposition, interference, intermeddling, intercession; arbitration; flag of truce &c. 723; good offices, peace offering; parley, negotiation; diplomatics[obs3], diplomacy; compromise &c. 774. [person who mediates] mediator, arbitrator, intercessor, peace-maker, makepeace[obs3], negotiator, go-between; diplomatist &c. (consignee) 758; moderator; propitiator; umpire. V. mediate, mediatize[obs3]; intercede, interpose, interfere, intervene; step in, negotiate; meet halfway; arbitrate; magnas componere lites[Lat]. bargain &c. 794 Adj. mediatory.

#725. Submission. — N. submission, yielding; nonresistance; obedience &c. 743. surrender, cession, capitulation, resignation; backdown[obs3]. obeisance, homage, kneeling, genuflexion[obs3], courtesy, curtsy, kowtow, prostration. V. succumb, submit, yeild, bend, resign, defer to. lay down one's arms, deliver up one's arms; lower colors, haul down colors, strike one's flag, strike colors. surrender, surrender at discretion; cede, capitulate, come to terms, retreat, beat a retreat; draw in one's horns &c. (humility) 879; give way, give round, give in, give up; cave in; suffer judgment by default; bend, bend to one's yoke, bend before the storm; reel back; bend down, knuckle down, knuckle to, knuckle under; knock under. eat dirt, eat the leek, eat humble pie; bite the dust, lick the dust; be at one's feet, fall at one's feet; craven; crouch before, throw oneself at the feet of; swallow the leek, swallow the pill; kiss the rod; turn the other cheek; avaler les couleuvres[Fr], gulp down. obey &c. 743; kneel to, bow to, pay homage to, cringe to, truckle to; bend the neck, bend the knee; kneel, fall on one's knees, bow submission, courtesy, curtsy, kowtow. pocket the affront; make the best of, make a virtue of necessity; grin and abide, grin and bear it, shrug the shoulders, resign oneself; submit with a good grace &c. (bear with) 826. Adj. surrendering &c. v.; submissive, resigned, crouching; downtrodden; down on one's marrow bones; on one's bended knee; unresistant, unresisting, nonresisting; pliant &c. (soft) 324; undefended. untenable, indefensible; humble &c. 879. Phr. have it your own way; it can't be helped; amen &c. (assent) 488; da locum melioribus[Lat]; tempori parendum[Lat].

#726. Combatant. — N. combatant; disputant, controversialist, polemic, litigant, belligerent; competitor, rival, corrival[obs3]; fighter, assailant; champion, Paladin; mosstrooper[obs3], swashbuckler fire eater, duelist, bully, bludgeon man, rough. prize fighter, pugilist, boxer, bruiser, the fancy, gladiator, athlete, wrestler; fighting-cock, game-cock; warrior, soldier, fighting man, Amazon, man at arms, armigerent[obs3]; campaigner, veteran; swords- man, sabreur[obs3], redcoat, military man, Rajput. armed force, troops, soldiery, military forces, sabaoth[obs3], the army, standing army, regulars, the line, troops of the line, militia, yeomanry, volunteers, trainband, fencible[obs3]; auxiliary, bersagliere[obs3], brave; garde-nationale, garde-royale[Fr]; minuteman [Am. Hist.]; auxiliary forces, reserve forces; reserves, posse comitatus[Lat], national guard, gendarme, beefeater; guards, guardsman; yeomen of the guard, life guards, household troops. janissary; myrmidon; Mama, Mameluke; spahee[obs3], spahi[obs3], Cossack, Croat, Pandoz. irregular, guerilla, partisan, condottiere[obs3]; franctireur[Fr], tirailleur[obs3], bashi-bazouk; vietminh[guerilla organization names: list], vietcong; shining path; contras; huk, hukbalahap. mercenary, soldier of fortune; hired gun, gunfighter, gunslinger; bushwhacker, free lance, companion; Hessian. hit man[criminals special- izing in violence: see bad man], torpedo, soldier. levy, draught; Landwehr[Ger], Landsturm[Ger]; conscript, recruit, cadet, raw levies. infantry, infantryman, private, private soldier, foot soldier; Tommy Atkins[obs3], rank and file, peon, trooper, sepoy[obs3], legionnaire, legionary, cannon fodder, food for powder; officer &c. (commander) 745; subal- tern, ensign, standard bearer; spearman, pikeman[obs3]; spear bearer; halberdier[obs3], lancer; musketeer, carabineer[obs3], rifleman, jager[Ger], sharpshooter, yager[obs3], skirmisher; grenadier, fusileer[obs3]; archer, bowman. horse and foot; horse soldier; cavalry, horse, artillery, horse artillery, light horse, voltigeur[Fr], uhlan, mounted rifles, dragoon, hussar; light dragoon, heavy dragoon, heavy; cuirassier[Fr]; Foot Guards, Horse Guards. gunner, cannoneer, bombardier, artilleryman[obs3], matross[obs3]; sapper, sapper and miner; engineer; light infantry, rifles,chasseur[Fr], zouave; military train, coolie. army, corps d'armee[Fr], host, division, battalia[obs3], column, wing, detachment, garrison, flying column, brigade, regiment, corps, battalion, sotnia[obs3], squadron, company, platoon, battery, subdivision, section, squad; piquet, picket, guard, rank, file; legion, phalanx, cohort; cloud of skirmishers. war horse, charger, destrier. marine, man-of-war's man &c. (sailor) 269; navy, wooden walls, naval forces, fleet, flotilla, armada, squadron. [ships of war] man-of-war; destroyer; submarine; minesweeper; torpedo- boat, torpedo-destroyer; patrol torpedo boat, PT boat; torpedo-catcher, war castle, H.M.S.; battleship, battle wagon, dreadnought, line of battle ship, ship of the line; aircraft carrier, carrier. flattop[coll.]; helicopter carrier; missile platform, missile boat; ironclad, turret ship, ram, monitor, floating battery; first-rate, frigate, sloop of war, corvette, gunboat, bomb vessel; flagship, guard ship, cruiser; armored cruiser, protected cruiser; privateer. [supporting ships] tender; store ship, troop ship; transport, catamaran; merchant marine.

<— p. 240 —>

#727. Arms. — N. arm, arms; weapon, deadly weapon; armament, armaments, armature; panoply, stand of arms; armor &c. (defense) 717; armory &c. (store) 636; apparatus belli[Lat]. ammunition; powder, powder and shot; cartridge; ball cartridge, cartouche, fireball; "villainous saltpeter" [Hen. IV]; dumdum bullet. explosive; gunpowder, guncotton; mercury fulminate; picrates; pentaerythritol tetranitrate[ISA:chemsub][Chemsub], PETN. high explosive; trinitrotoluene, TNT; dynamite, melinite[obs3], cordite, lyddite, plastic explosive, plastique; pyroxyline[obs3]. [knives and swords: list] sword, saber, broadsword, cutlass, falchion[obs3], scimitar, cimeter[obs3], brand, whinyard, bilbo, glaive[obs3], glave[obs3], rapier, skean, Toledo, Ferrara, tuck, claymore, adaga[obs3], baselard[obs3], Lochaber ax, skean dhu[obs3], creese[obs3], kris, dagger, dirk, banger[obs3], poniard, stiletto, stylet[obs3], dudgeon, bayonet; sword-bayonet, sword-stick; side arms, foil, blade, steel; ax, bill; pole-ax, battle-ax; gisarme[obs3], halberd, partisan, tomahawk, bowie knife[obs3]; ataghan[obs3], attaghan[obs3], yataghan[obs3]; yatacban[obs3]; assagai, assegai[obs3]; good sword, trusty sword, naked sword; cold steel. club, mace, truncheon, staff, bludgeon, cudgel, life preserver, shillelah, sprig; hand staff, quarter staff; bat, cane, stick, knuckle duster; billy, blackjack, sandbag, waddy[obs3]. gun, piece[Fr]; firearms; artillery, ordnance; siege train, battering train; park, battery; cannon, gun of position, heavy gun, field piece[Fr], mortar, howitzer, carronade[obs3], culverin[obs3], basilisk; falconet, jingal[obs3], swivel, pederero[obs3], bouche a feu[Fr]; petard, torpedo; mitrailleur[Fr], mitrailleuse[Fr]; infernal machine; smooth bore, rifled cannon, Armstrong gun[obs3], Lancaster gun, Paixhan gun, Whitworth gun, Parrott gun, Krupp gun, Gatling gun, Maxim gun, machine gun; pompom[obs3]; ten pounder. small arms; musket, musketry, firelock[obs3], fowling piece[Fr], rifle, fusil[obs3], caliver[obs3], carbine, blunderbuss, musketoon[obs3], Brown Bess, matchlock, harquebuss[obs3], arquebus, haguebut[obs3]; pistol, postolet[obs3]; petronel; small bore; breach-loader, muzzle-loader; revolver, repeater; Minis rifle, Enfield rifle, Flobert rifle, Westley Richards rifle, Snider rifle, Martini-Henry rifle, Lee-Metford rifle, Lee- Enfield rifle, Mauser rifle, magazine rifle; needle gun, chassepot[obs3]; wind gun, air gun; automatic gun, automatic pistol; escopet[obs3], escopette[obs3], gunflint, gun-lock; hackbut[obs3], shooter, shooting iron * [U.S.], six-shooter [U.S.], shotgun; Uzzi, assault rifle, Kalashnikov. bow, crossbow, balister[obs3], catapult, sling; battering ram &c. (impulse) 276; gunnery; ballistics &c. (propulsion) 284. missile, bolt, projectile, shot, ball; grape; grape shot, canister shot, bar shot, cannon shot, langrel shot[obs3], langrage shot[obs3], round shot, chain shot; balista[obs3], ballista[obs3], slung shot, trebucbet[obs3], trebucket[obs3]; bullet, slug, stone, brickbat, grenade, shell, bomb, carcass, rocket; congreve[obs3], congreve rocket[obs3]; shrapnel, mitraille[Fr]; levin bolt[obs3], levin brand[obs3]; thunderbolt. pike, lance, spear, spontoon[obs3], javelin, dart, jereed[obs3], jerid[obs3], arrow, reed, shaft, bolt, boomerang, harpoon, gaff; eelspear[obs3], oxgoad[obs3], weet-weet, wommerah[obs3]; cattle prod; chemical mace. Phr. en flute; nervos belli pecuniam infinitam[Lat].

<− p. 241 −>

#728. Arena. — N. arena, field, platform; scene of action, theater; walk, course; hustings; stare, boards &c. (play-house) 599; amphitheater; Coliseum, Colosseum; Flavian amphitheater, hippodrome, circus, race course, corso[Sp], turf, cockpit, bear garden, playground, gymnasium, palestra, ring, lists; tiltyard[obs3], tilting ground; Campus Martins, Champ de Allars[obs3]; campus [U.S.]. boxing ring, canvas. theater of war, seat of war; battle-field, battle-ground; field of battle, field of slaughter; Aceldama[obs3], camp; the enemy's camp; trusting place &c. (place of meeting) 74.

% Section V. RESULTS OF VOLUNTARY ACTION %

#729. Completion. — N. completion, accomplishment, achievement, fulfillment; performance, execution; despatch, dispatch; consummation, culmination; finish, conclusion; close &c. (end) 67; terminus &c. (arrival) 292; winding up; finale, denouement, catastrophe, issue, upshot, result; final touch, last touch, crowning touch, finishing touch, finishing stroke; last finish, coup de grace; crowning of the edifice; coping-stone, keystone; missing link &c. 53; superstructure, ne plus ultra[Lat], work done, fait accompli[Fr]. elaboration; finality; completeness &c. 52. V. effect[transitive], effectuate; accomplish, achieve, compass, consummate, hammer out; bring to maturity, bring to perfection; perfect, complete; elaborate. do, execute, make; go through, get through; work out, enact; bring about, bring to bear, bring to pass, bring through, bring to a head. despatch, dispatch; knock off, finish off, polish off; make short work of; dispose of, set at rest; perform, discharge, fulfill, realize; put in practice, put in force; carry out, carry into effect, carry into execution; make good; be as good as one's word. do thoroughly, not do by halves, go the whole hog; drive home; be in at the death &c. (persevere) 604a; carry through, play out, exhaust; fill the bill [U.S.]. finish, bring to a close &c. (end) 67; wind up, stamp, clinch, seal, set the seal on, put the seal; give the final touch &c.n. to; put the last, put the finishing hand to, put the finishing touches on; crown, crown all; cap. [intransitive] ripen, culminate; come to a head, come to a crisis; come to its end; die a natural death, die of old age; run its course, run one's race; touch the goal, reach the goal, attain the goal; reach &c. (arrive) 292; get in the harvest. Adj. completing, final; concluding, conclusive; crowning &c. v.; exhaustive. done, completed &c. v.; done for, sped, wrought out; highly wrought &c. (preparation) 673; thorough &c. 52; ripe &c. (ready) 673. Adv. completely &c.(thoroughly) 52; to crown all, out of hand. Phr. the race is run; actum est[Lat]; finis coronat opus[Lat]; consummatum est[Lat]; c'en est fait[Fr]; it is all over; the game is played out, the bubble has burst; aussitot dit aussitot fait[Fr]; aut non tentaris aut perfice [Lat] [Ovid].

#730. Noncompletion. — N. noncompletion, nonfulfillment; shortcoming &c. 304; incompleteness &c. 53; drawn battle, drawn game; work of Penelope.

nonperformance, inexecution[obs3]; neglect &c. 460.

V. not complete &c. 729; leave unfinished &c. adj., leave undone, drop, put down; neglect &c. 460; let alone, let slip; lose sight of (forget) 506.

fall short of &c. 304; do things by halves, parboil, scotch the snake not lull it; hang fire; be slow to; collapse &c. 304.

drop out.

Adj. not completed &c. v.; incomplete &c. 53; uncompleted, unfinished, unaccomplished, unperformed, unexecuted; sketchy, addle.

in progress, in hand; ongoing, going on, proceeding; on one's hands; on the anvil; in the fire, in the oven.

parboiled, half-baked.

Adv. re infecta[Lat].

<— p. 242 —>

#731. Success. — N. success, successfulness; speed; advance &c. (progress) 282. trump card; hit, stroke, score; lucky hit, fortunate hit, good hit, good stroke; direct hit, bull's eye; goal, point, touchdown; home run, homer, hole-in-one, grand slam; killing[make money], windfall bold stroke, master stroke; ten strike [U.S.]; coup de maitre[Fr], checkmate; half the battle, prize; profit &c. (acquisition) 775. continued success; good fortune &c. (prosperity) 734; time well spent. advantage over; upper hand, whip hand; ascendancy, mastery; expugnationl, conquest, victory, subdual[obs3]; subjugation &c. (subjection) 749. triumph &c. (exultation) 884; proficiency &c. (skill) 698. conqueror, victor, winner; master of the situation, master of the position, top of the heap, king of the hill; achiever, success, success story. V. succeed; be successful &c. adj.; gain one's end, gain one's ends; crown with success. gain a point, attain a point, carry a point, secure a point, win a point, win an object; get there *[U.S.]; manage to, contrive to; accomplish &c. (effect, complete) 729; do wonders, work wonders; make a go of it. come off well, come off successful, come off with flying colors; make short work of; take by storm, carry by storm; bear away the bell; win one's wings, win one's spurs, win the battle; win the day, carry the day, gain the day, gain the prize, gain the palm; have the best of it, have it all one's own way, have the game in one's owns hands, have the ball at one's feet, have one on the hop; walk over the course; carry all before one, remain in possession of the field; score a success. speed; make progress &c. (advance) 282; win one's way, make one's way, work one's way, find one's way; strive to some purpose; prosper &c. 734; drive a roaring trade; make profit &c. (acquire) 775; reap the fruits, gather the fruits, reap the benefit of, reap the harvest; strike oil * [U.S.], gain a windfall; make one's fortune, get in the harvest, turn to good account; turn to account &c. (use) 677. triumph, be triumphant; gain a victory, obtain a victory, gain an advantage; chain victory to one's car; nail a coonskin to the wall. surmount a difficulty, overcome a difficulty, get over a difficulty, get over an obstacle &c. 706; se tirer d'affaire[Fr]; make head against; stem the torrent, stem the tide, stem the current; weather the storm, weather a point; turn a corner, keep one's head above water, tide over; master; get the better of, have the better of, gain the better of, gain the best of, gain the upper hand, gain the ascendancy, gain the whip hand, gain the start of; distance; surpass &c. (superiority) 33. defeat, conquer, vanquish, discomfit; euchre; overcome, overthrow, overpower, overmaster, overmatch, overset[obs3], override, overreach; outwit, outdo, outflank, outmaneuver, outgeneral, outvote; take the wind out of one's adversary's sails; beat, beat hollow; rout, lick, drub, floor, worst; put down, put to flight, put to the rout, put hors de combat[Fr], put out of court. silence, quell, nonsuit[obs3], checkmate, upset, confound, nonplus, stalemate, trump; baffle &c. (hinder) 706; circumvent, elude; trip up, trip up the heels of; drive into a corner, drive to the wall; run hard, put one's nose out of joint. settle, do for; break the neck of, break the back of; capsize, sink, shipwreck, drown, swamp; subdue; subjugate &c. (subject) 749; reduce; make the enemy bite the dust; victimize, roll in the dust, trample under foot, put an extinguisher upon. answer, answer the purpose; avail, prevail, take effect, do, turn out well, work well, take, tell, bear fruit; hit it, hit the mark, hit the right nail on the head; nick it; turn up trumps, make a hit; find one's account in. Adj. succeeding &c. v.; successful; prosperous &c. 734; triumphant; flushed with success, crowned with success; victorious, on top; set up; in the ascendant; unbeaten &c. (see beat &c. v.); well-spent; felicitous, effective, in full swing. Adv. successfully &c. adj.; well flying colors, in triumph, swimmingly; a merveille[Fr], beyond all hope; to some purpose, to good purpose; to one's heart's content. Phr. veni vidi vici[Lat], the day being one's own, one's star in the ascendant; omne tulit punctum[Lat]. bis vincit qui se vincit in victoria[obs3][Lat]; cede repugnanti cedendo victor abibis [Lat][Ovid]; chacun est l'artisan de sa fortune[Fr]; dies faustus[Lat]; l'art de vaincre est celui de mepriser la mort[Fr]; omnia vincit amor [Lat: love conquers all]; "peace hath her victories no less renowned than war" [Milton]; "the race by vigor not by vaunts is won" [Pope]; vincit qui patitur[Lat]; vincit qui se vincit[Lat]; "The race is not always to the swift, nor the battle to the strong, but that's the way to bet" [Mark Twain].

<— p. 243 —>

#732. Failure. — N. failure; nonsuccess[obs3], nonfulfillment; dead failure, successlessness[obs3]; abortion, miscarriage; brutum fulmen &c. 158[Lat]; labor in vain &c. (inutility) 645; no go; inefficacy[obs3]; inefficaciousness &c. adj.; vain attempt, ineffectual attempt, abortive attempt, abortive efforts; flash in the pan, "lame and impotent conclusion" [Othello]; frustration; slip 'twixt cup and lip &c. (disappointment) 509. blunder &c. (mistake) 495; fault, omission, miss, oversight, slip, trip, stumble, claudicationl, footfall; false step, wrong step; faux pas[Fr], titubation[obs3], bvue[Fr], faute[Fr], lurch; botchery &c. (want of skill) 699[obs3]; scrape, mess, fiasco, breakdown; flunk [U.S.]. mishap &c. (misfortune) 735; split, collapse, smash, blow, explosion. repulse, rebuff, defeat, rout, overthrow, discomfiture; beating, drubbing; quietus, nonsuit[obs3], subjugation; checkmate, stalemate, fool's mate. fall, downfall, ruin, perdition; wreck &c. (destruction) 162; deathblow; bankruptcy &c. (nonpayment) 808. losing game, affaire flambe. victim; bankrupt; flunker[obs3], flunky [U.S.]. V. fail; be unsuccessful &c. adj.; not succeed &c.

731; make vain efforts &c.n.; do in vain, labor in vain, toil in vain; flunk [U.S.]; lose one's labor, take nothing by one's motion; bring to naught, make nothing of; wash a blackamoor white &c. (impossible) 471; roll the stones of Sisyphus &c. (useless) 645; do by halves &c. (not complete) 730; lose ground &c. (recede) 282; fall short of &c. 304. miss, miss one's aim, miss the mark, miss one's footing, miss stays; slip, trip, stumble; make a slip &c., n. blunder &c. 495, make a mess of, make a botch of; bitch itl, miscarry, abort, go up like a rocket and come down like the stick, come down in flames, get shot down, reckon without one's host; get the wrong pig by the tail, get the wrong sow by the ear &c. (blunder, mismanage) 699. limp, halt, hobble, titubate[obs3]; fall, tumble; lose one's balance; fall to the ground, fall between two stools; flounder, falter, stick in the mud, run aground, split upon a rock; beat one's head against a stone wall, run one's head against a stone wall, knock one's head against a stone wall, dash one's head against a stone wall; break one's back; break down, sink, drown, founder, have the ground cut from under one; get into trouble, get into a mess, get into a scrape; come to grief &c. (adversity) 735; go to the wall, go to the dogs, go to pot; lick the dust, bite the dust; be defeated &c. 731; have the worst of it, lose the day, come off second best, lose; fall a prey to; succumb &c. (submit) 725; not have a leg to stand on. come to nothing, end in smoke; flat out l; fall to the ground, fall through, fall dead, fall stillborn, fall flat; slip through one's fingers; hang fire, miss fire; flash in the pan, collapse; topple down &c. (descent) 305; go to wrack and ruin &c. (destruction) 162. go amiss, go wrong, go cross, go hard with, go on a wrong tack; go on ill, come off ill, turn out ill, work ill; take a wrong term, take an ugly term; take an ugly turn, take a turn for the worse. be all over with, be all up with; explode; dash one's hopes &c. (disappoint) 509; defeat the purpose; sow the wind and reap the whirlwind, jump out of the frying pan into the fire, go from the frying pan into the fire. Adj. unsuccessful, successless[obs3]; failing, tripping &c.v.; at fault; unfortunate &c. 735. abortive, addle, stillborn; fruitless, bootless; ineffectual, ineffective, inconsequential, trifling, nugatory; inefficient &c. (impotent) 158; insufficient &c. 640; unavailing &c. (useless) 645; of no effect. aground, grounded, swamped, stranded, cast away, wrecked, foundered, capsized, shipwrecked, nonsuited[obs3]; foiled; defeated &c. 731; struck down, borne down, broken down; downtrodden; overborne, overwhelmed; all up with; ploughed, plowed, plucked. lost, undone, ruined, broken; bankrupt &c. (not paying) 808; played out; done up, done for; dead beat, ruined root and branch, flambe[obs3], knocked on the head; destroyed &c. 162. frustrated, crossed, unhinged, disconcerted dashed; thrown off one's balance, thrown on one's back, thrown on one's beam endsl; unhorsed, in a sorry plight; hard hit. stultified, befooled[obs3], dished, hoist on one's own petard; victimized, sacrificed. wide of the mark &c. (error) 495; out of one's reckoning &c. (inexpectation) 508[obs3]; left in the lurch; thrown away &c. (wasted) 638; unattained; uncompleted &c. 730. Adv. unsuccessfully &c. adj.; to little or no purpose, in vain, re infecta[Lat]. Phr. the bubble has burst, "the jig is up", "the game is up" [Cymbeline]; all is lost; the devil to pay; parturiunt montes &c. (disappointment) 509[Lat]; dies infaustus[Lat]; tout est perdu hors l'honneur[Fr].

#733. Trophy. — N. trophy; medal, prize, palm, award; laurel, laurels; bays, crown, chaplet, wreath, civic crown; insignia &c. 550; feather in one's cap &c. (honor) 873; decoration &c. 877; garland, triumphal arch, Victoria Cross, Iron Cross.
    triumph &c. (celebration) 883; flying colors &c. (show) 882.
    monumentum aere perennius [Lat][obs3][Hor.].
    Phr. "for valor."
<— p. 244 —>

<— break out luck from prosperity —> #734. Prosperity. — N. prosperity, welfare, well-being; affluence &c. (wealth) 803; success &c. 731; thrift, roaring trade; good fortune, smiles of fortune; blessings, godsend. luck; good luck, run of luck; sunshine; fair weather, fair wind; palmy days, bright days, halcyon days; piping times, tide, flood, high tide. Saturnia regna[Lat], Saturnian age; golden time, golden age; bed of roses, fat city [coll.]; fat of the land, milk and honey, loaves and fishes. made man, lucky dog, enfant gate[Fr], spoiled child of fortune. upstart, parvenu, skipjack[obs3], mushroom. V. prosper, thrive, flourish; be prosperous &c adj.; drive a roaring trade, do a booming business; go on well, go on smoothly, go on swimmingly; sail before the wind, swim with the tide; run smooth, run smoothly, run on all fours. rise in the world, get on in the world; work one's way, make one's way; look up; lift one's head, raise one's head, make one's fortune, feather one's nest, make one's pile. flower, blow, blossom, bloom, fructify, bear fruit, fatten. keep oneself afloat; keep one's head above water, hold one's head above water; land on one's feet, light on one's feet, light on one's legs, fall on one's legs, fall on one's feet; drop into a good thing; bear a charmed life; bask in the sunshine; have a good time of it, have a fine time of it; have a run of luck; have the good fortune &c. n. to; take a favorable turn; live on the fat of the land, live off the fat of the land, live in clover. Adj. prosperous; thriving &c. v.; in a fair way, buoyant; well off, well to do, well to do in the world; set up, at one's ease; rich &c. 803; in good case; in full, in high feather; fortunate, lucky, in luck; born with a silver spoon in one's mouth, born under a lucky star; on the sunny side of the hedge. auspicious, propitious, providential. palmy, halcyon; agreeable &c. 829; couleur de rose[Fr]. Adv. prosperously &c. adj.; swimmingly; as good luck would have it; beyond

all hope. Phr. one's star in the ascendant, all for the best, one's course runs smooth. chacun est l'artisan de sa fortune[Fr]; donec eris felix multos numerabis amicos [Lat][Ovid]; felicitas multos habet amicos[Lat]; felix se nescit amari [Lat][Lucan]; 'good luck go with thee' [Henry V]; nulli est homini perpetuum bonum [Lat][Plautus].

#735. Adversity. — N. adversity, evil &c. 619; failure &c. 732; bad luck, ill luck, evil luck, adverse luck, hard fortune, hard hap, hard luck, hard lot; frowns of fortune; evil dispensation, evil star, evil geniusl; vicissitudes of life, ups and downs of life, broken fortunes; hard case, hard lines, hard life; sea of troubles; peck of troubles; hell upon earth; slough of despond. trouble, hardship, curse, blight, blast, load, pressure. pressure of the times, iron age, evil day, time out of joint; hard times, bad times, sad times; rainy day, cloud, dark cloud, gathering clouds, ill wind; visitation, infliction; affliction &c. (painfulness) 830; bitter pill; care, trial; the sport of fortune. mishap, mischance, misadventure, misfortune; disaster, calamity, catastrophe; accident, casualty, cross, reverse, check, contretemps, rub; backset[obs3], comedown, setback [U.S.]. losing game; falling &c. v.; fall, downfall; ruination, ruinousness; undoing; extremity; ruin &c. (destruction) 162. V. be ill off &c. adj.; go hard with; fall on evil, fall on evil days; go on ill; not prosper &c. 734. go downhill, go to rack and ruin &c. (destruction) 162, go to the dogs; fall, fall from one's high estate; decay, sink, decline, go down in the world; have seen better days; bring down one's gray hairs with sorrow to the grave; come to grief; be all over, be up with; bring a wasp's nest about one's ears, bring a hornet's nest about one's ears. Adj. unfortunate, unblest[obs3], unhappy, unlucky; improsperous[obs3], unprosperous; hoodooed [U.S.]; luckless, hapless; out of luck; in trouble, in a bad way, in an evil plight; under a cloud; clouded; ill off, badly off; in adverse circumstances; poor &c. 804; behindhand, down in the world, decayed, undone; on the road to ruin, on its last legs, on the wane; in one's utmost need. planet-struck, devoted; born under an evil star, born with a wooden ladle in one's mouth; ill-fated, ill-starred, ill-omened. adverse, untoward; disastrous, calamitous, ruinous, dire, deplorable.

#736. Mediocrity. — N. moderate circumstances, average circumstances; respectability; middle classes; mediocrity; golden mean &c. (mid-course) 628, (moderation) 174. V. jog on; go fairly, go quietly, go peaceably, go tolerably, go respectably, get on fairly, get on quietly, get on peaceably, get on tolerably, get on respectably.

<— p. 245 —> % DIVISION (II) INTERSOCIAL VOLITION

SECTION I. GENERAL INTERSOCIAL VOLITION % <— Implying the action of the will of one mind over the will of another. —>

#737. Authority. — N. authority; influence, patronage, power, preponderance, credit, prestige, prerogative, jurisdiction; right &c. (title) 924; direction &c. 693; government &c. 737a. divine right, dynastic rights, authoritativeness; absoluteness, absolutism; despotism; jus nocendi[Lat]; jus divinum[Lat]. mastery, mastership, masterdom[obs3]; dictation, control. hold, grasp; grip, gripe; reach; iron sway &c. (severity) 739; fangs, clutches, talons; rod of empire &c. (scepter) 747. [Vicarious authority] commission &c. 755; deputy &c.759; permission &c. 760. V. authorize &c. (permit) 760; warrant &c. (right) 924; dictate &c. (order) 741. be at the head of &c. adj.; hold office, be in office, fill an office; hold master, occupy master, a post master, be master &c. 745. have the upper hand, get the upper hand, have the whip, get the whip; gain a hold upon, preponderate, dominate, rule the roost; boss [U.S.]; override, overrule, overawe; lord it over, hold in hand, keep under, make a puppet of, lead by the nose, turn round one's little finger, bend to one's will, hold one's own, wear the breeches; have the ball at one's feet, have it all one's own way, have the game in one's own hand, have on the hip, have under one's thumb; be master of the situation; take the lead, play first fiddle, set the fashion; give the law to; carry with a high hand; lay down the law; "ride in the whirlwind and direct the storm" [Addison]; rule with a rod of iron &c. (severity) 739. Adj. at the head, dominant, paramount, supreme, predominant, preponderant, in the ascendant, influential; arbitrary; compulsory &c. 744: stringent. at one's command; in one's power, in one's grasp; under control. Adv. in the name of, by the authority of, de par le Roi[Fr], in virtue of; under the auspices of, in the hands of. at one's pleasure; by a dash if the pen, by a stroke of the pen; ex mero motu[Lat]; ex cathedra[Lat: from the chair]. Phr. the gray mare the better horse; "every inch a king" [Lear].

<— in 4e sections 741 to 748 deal with government and politics. Lots of words and concepts are new since 1911! Here we make a start with one heading Yet to do: take political subdivisions from territory 181 and 780, put them all here. —> #737a. Government. — N. government, legal authority, soveriegn, sovereign authority; authority &c. 737; master &c. 745; direction &c. 693. [nations] national government, nation, state, country, nation-state, dominion, republic, empire, union, democratic republic; kingdom, principality. [subdivisions of nations] state government[U.S terminology], state; shire[England]; province[Canada]; county[Ireland]; canton[Switzerland]; territory [Australia]; duchy, archduchy, archdukedom[obs3]; woiwodshaft; commonwealth; region &c. 181; property &c. 780. [smaller subdivisions] county, parish[Louisiana]; city, domain, tract, arrondissement[Fr], mofussil[obs3], commune; wappen-

take, hundred, riding, lathe, garth[obs3], soke[obs3], tithing; ward, precinct, bailiwick. command, empire, sway, rule; dominion, domination; sovereignty, supremacy, suzerainty; lordship, headship[obs3]; chiefdom[obs3]; seigniory, seigniority[obs3]. rule, sway, command, control, administer; govern &c. (direct) 693; lead, preside over, reign, possess the throne, be seated on the throne, occupy the throne; sway the scepter, wield the scepter; wear the crown. state, realm, body politic, posse comitatus[Lat]. [person in the governing authority] judicature &c. 965; cabinet &c. (council) 696; seat of government, seat of authority; headquarters. [Acquisition of authority] accession; installation &c. 755; politics &c. 737a. reign, regime, dynasty; directorship, dictatorship; protectorate, protectorship; caliphate, pashalic[obs3], electorate; presidency, presidentship[obs3]; administration; proconsul, consulship; prefecture; seneschalship; magistrature[obs3], magistracy. monarchy; kinghood[obs3], kingship; royalty, regality; aristarchy[obs3], aristocracy; oligarchy, democracy, theocracy, demagogy; commonwealth; dominion; heteronomy; republic, republicanism; socialism; collectivism; mob law, mobocracy[obs3], ochlocracy[obs3]; vox populi, imperium in imperio[Lat]; bureaucracy; beadledom[obs3], bumbledom[obs3]; stratocracy; military power, military government, junta; feodality[obs3], feudal system, feudalism. thearchy[obs3], theocracy, dinarchy[obs3]; duarchy[obs3], triarchy, heterarchy[obs3]; duumvirate; triumvirate; autocracy, autonomy; limited monarchy; constitutional government, constitutional monarchy; home rule; representative government; monocracy[obs3], pantisocracy[obs3]. gynarchy[obs3], gynocracy[obs3], gynaeocracy[obs3]; petticoat government. [government functions] legislature, judiciary, administration. [Government agencies and institutions] office of the president, office of the prime minister, cabinet; senate, house of representatives, parliament; council &c. 696; courts, supreme court; state[U.S. national government departments (list)], interior, labor, health and human services, defense, education, agriculture, justice, commerce, treasury; Federal Bureau of Investigation, FBI; Central Intelligence Agency, CIA; National Institutes of Health, NIH; Postal Service, Post Office; Federal Aviation Administration, FAA. [national government officials] president, vice president, cabinet member, prime minister, minister; senator, representatative, president pro tem[Lat], speaker of the house; department head, section head, section chief; federal judge, justice, justice of the supreme court, chief justice; treasurer, secretary of the treasury; director of the FBI. [state government officials] governor, state cabinet member; state senator, assemblyman, assemblywoman. V. govern, rule, have authority, hold authority, possess authority, exercise authority, exert authority, wield authority &c. n.; reign, be sovereign. [acquire authority] ascend the throne, mount the throne; take the reins, take the reins into one's hand; assume authority &c. n., assume the reins of government; take command, assume command. [contend for authority] politics &c. 737a. be governed by, be in the power of, be a subject of, be a citizen of. Adj. regal, sovereign, governing; royal, royalist; monarchical, kingly; imperial, imperiatorial[obs3]; princely; feudal; aristocratic, autocratic; oligarchic &c. n.; republican, dynastic. ruling &c. v.; regnant, gubernatorial; imperious; authoritative, executive, administrative, clothed with authority, official, departmental, ex officio, imperative, peremptory, overruling, absolute; hegemonic, hegemonical[obs3]; authorized &c. (due) 924. [pertaining to property owned by government] government, public; national, federal; his majesty's[Great Britain], her majesty's; state, county, city, &c. n. Phr[cf. nations, subdivisions of nations, smaller subdivisions]. "a dog's obeyed in office" [Lear]; cada uno tiene su alguazil[obs3][Sp]; le Roi le veut[Fr]; regibus esse manus en nescio longas[obs3][Lat]; regnant populi[Lat]; "the demigod Authority" [Measure for Measure]; "the right divine of kings to govern wrong" [Pope]; "uneasy lies the head that wears a crown" [Henry IV].

#737b. Politics. [contention for governmental authority or influence]. — N. politics; political science; candidacy, campaign, campaigning, electioneering; partisanship, ideology, factionalism. election, poll, ballot, vote, referendum, recall, initiative, voice, suffrage, plumper, cumulative vote, plebiscitum[Lat], plebiscite, vox populi; electioneering; voting &c. v.; elective franchise; straight ticket [U.S.]; opinion poll, popularity poll. issue; opinion, stand, position; program, platform; party line. [ideologies] democracy, republicanism; communism, statism, state socialism; socialism; conservatism, toryism; liberalism, whigism; theocracy; constitutional monarchy. [political parties] party &c. 712; Democratic Party[U.S: list], Republican Party, Socialist Party, Communist Party; Federalist Party[U.S. defunct parties: list], Bull Moose Party, Abolitionist Party; Christian Democratic Party[Germany: list], Social Democratic Party; National Socialist Worker's Party[Germany, 1930-1945], Nazi Party; Liberal Party[Great Britain:list], Labor Party, Conservative Party. ticket, slate. [person active in politics] politician[general], activist; candidate[specific politicians: list], aspirant, hopeful, office-seeker, front-runner, dark horse, long shot, shoo-in; supporter, backer, political worker, campaign worker; lobbyist, contributor; party hack, ward heeler; regional candidate, favorite son; running mate, stalking horse; perpetual candidate, political animal. political contribution, campaign contribution; political action committee, PAC. political district, electoral division, electoral district, bailiwick. electorate, constituents. get-out-the-vote campaign, political education. negative campaigning, dirty politics, smear campaign. [unsuccessful candidate] also-ran, loser; has-been. [successful candidate] office holder, official, occupant of a position; public servant, incumbent; winner. V. run for office, stand for office; campaign, stump; throw one's hat in the ring; announce one's candidacy. Adj. political, partisan. Phr. "Money is the mother's milk of politics" [Tip O'Neill].

<— p. 246 —>

#738. [Absence of authority] Laxity.— N. laxity; laxness, looseness, slackness; toleration &c. (lenity) 740; freedom &c. 748. anarchy, interregnum; relaxation; loosening &c. v.; remission; dead letter, brutum fulmen[Lat], misrule; license, licentiousness; insubordination &c. (disobedience) 742; lynch law &c. (illegality) 964; nihilism, reign of violence. [Deprivation of power] dethronement, deposition, usurpation, abdication. V. be -lax &c. adj.; laisser faire[Fr], laisser aller[Fr]; hold a loose rein; give the reins to, give rope enough, give a loose to; tolerate; relax; misrule. go beyond the length of one's tether; have one's swing, have one's fling; act without instructions, act without authority, act outside of one's authority; act on one's own responsibility, usurp authority. dethrone, depose; abdicate. Adj. lax, loose; slack; remiss &c. (careless) 460; weak. relaxed; licensed; reinless[obs3], unbridled; anarchical; unauthorized &c. (unwarranted) 925; adespotic[obs3].

#739. Severity.— N. severity; strictness, harshness &c. adj.; rigor, stringency, austerity; inclemency &c. (pitilessness) 914a; arrogance &c. 885; precisianism[obs3]. arbitrary power; absolutism, despotism; dictatorship, autocracy, tyranny, domineering, oppression; assumption, usurpation; inquisition, reign of terror, martial law; iron heel, iron rule, iron hand, iron sway; tight grasp; brute force, brute strength; coercion &c. 744; strong hand, tight hand. hard lines, hard measure; tender mercies [ironical]; sharp practice; pipe-clay, officialism. tyrant, disciplinarian, precisian[obs3], martinet, stickler, bashaw[obs3], despot, hard master, Draco, oppressor, inquisitor, extortioner, harpy, vulture; accipitres[obs3], birds of prey, raptorials[obs3], raptors[obs3]. V. be -severe &c. adj. assume, usurp, arrogate, take liberties; domineer, bully &c. 885; tyrannize, inflict, wreak, stretch a point, put on the screw; be hard upon; bear a heavy hand on, lay a heavy hand on; be down upon, come down upon; ill treat; deal hardly with, deal hard measure to; rule with a rod of iron, chastise with scorpions; dye with blood; oppress, override; trample under foot; tread under foot, tread upon, trample upon, tread down upon, trample down upon; crush under an iron heel, ride roughshod over; rivet the yoke; hold a tight hand, keep a tight hand; force down the throat; coerce &c. 744; give no quarter &c. (pitiless) 914a. Adj. severe; strict, hard, harsh, dour, rigid, stiff, stern, rigorous, uncompromising, exacting, exigent, exigeant[obs3], inexorable, inflexible, obdurate, austere, hard-headed, hard-nosed, hard-shell [U.S.], relentless, Spartan, Draconian, stringent, strait-laced, searching, unsparing, iron- handed, peremptory, absolute, positive, arbitrary, imperative; coercive &c. 744; tyrannical, extortionate, grinding, withering, oppressive, inquisitorial; inclem- ent &c. (ruthless) 914a; cruel &c. (malevolent) 907; haughty, arrogant &c. 885; precisian[obs3]. Adv. severely &c. adj.; with a high hand, with a strong hand, with a tight hand, with a heavy hand. at the point of the sword, at the point of the bayonet. Phr. Delirant reges plectuntur Achivi[Lat]; manu forti[Lat]; ogni debole ha sempre il suo tiranno[It].

<— p. 247 —>

#740. Lenity.— N. lenity, lenience, leniency; moderation &c. 174; tolerance, toleration; mildness, gentleness; favor, indulgence, indulgency[obs3]; clemency, mercy, forbearance, quarter; compassion &c. 914. V. be -lenient &c. adj.; tolerate, bear with; parcere subjectis[Lat], give quarter. indulge, allow one to have his own way, spoil. Adj. lenient; mild, mild as milk; gentle, soft; tolerant, indulgent, easy-going; clement &c. (compassionate) 914; forbearing; long-suffering.

#741. Command.— N. command, order, ordinance, act, fiat, hukm[obs3], bidding, dictum, hest[obs3], behest, call, beck, nod. despatch, dispatch; message, direction, injunction, charge, instructions; appointment, fixture. demand, exaction, imposition, requisition, claim, reclamation, revendication[obs3]; ultimatum &c. (terms) 770; request &c. 765; requirement. dictation; dictate, mandate; caveat, decree, senatus consultum[Lat]; precept; prescript, rescript; writ, ordination, bull, ex cathedra pronouncement[Lat], edict, decretal[obs3], dispensation, prescription, brevet, placit[obs3], ukase, ukaz [Russian], firman, hatti-sherif[obs3], warrant, passport, mittimus[Law@crim], mandamus, summons, subpoena, nisi prius[Lat], interpellation, citation; word, word of command; mot d'ordre[Fr]; bugle call, trumpet call; beat of drum, tattoo; order of the day; enactment &c. (law) 963; plebiscite &c. (choice) 609. V. com- mand, order, decree, enact, ordain, dictate, direct, give orders. prescribe, set, appoint, mark out; set a task, pre- scribe a task, impose a task; set to work, put in requisition. bid, enjoin, charge, call upon, instruct; require at the hands of; exact, impose, tax, task; demand; insist on &c. (compel) 744. claim, lay claim to, revendicate[obs3], reclaim. cite, summon; call for, send for; subpoena; beckon. issue a command; make a requisition, issue a requisi- tion, promulgate a requisition, make a decree, issue a decree, promulgate a decree, make an order, issue an order, promulgate an order &c. n.; give the word of command, give the word, give the signal; call to order; give the law, lay down the law; assume the command &c. (authority) 737; remand. be -ordered &c.; receive an order &c. n. Adj. commanding &c. v.; authoritative &c. 737; decretory[obs3], decretive[obs3], decretal[obs3]; callable, jussive[obs3]. Adv. in a commanding tone; by a stroke of the pen, by a dash of the pen; by order, at beat of drum, on the first summons. Phr. the decree is gone forth; sic volo sic jubeo[Lat]; le Roi le veut[Fr]; boutez en avant[Fr].

<– p. 248 –>

#742. Disobedience.— N. disobedience, insubordination, contumacy; infraction, infringement; violation, noncompli- ance; nonobservance &c. 773. revolt, rebellion, mutiny, outbreak, rising, uprising, insurrection, emeute[Fr]; riot, tumult &c. (disorder) 59; strike &c.(resistance) 719; barring out; defiance &c. 715. mutinousness &c. adj.; mutineering[obs3]; sedition, treason; high treason, petty treason, misprision of treason; premunire[Lat]; lese majeste[Fr]; violation of law &c. 964; defection, secession. insurgent, mutineer, rebel, revolter, revolutionary, rioter, traitor, quisling, carbonaro[obs3], sansculottes[Fr], red republican, bonnet rouge, communist, Fenian, frondeur; seceder, secessionist, runagate, renegade, brawler, anarchist, demagogue; Spartacus, Masaniello, Wat Tyler, Jack Cade; ringleader. V. disobey, violate, infringe; shirk; set at defiance &c. (defy) 715; set authority at naught, run riot, fly in the face of; take the law into one's own hands; kick over the traces. turn restive, run restive; champ the bit; strike &c. (resist) 719; rise, rise in arms; secede; mutiny, rebel. Adj. disobedient; uncomplying, uncompliant; unsubmissive[obs3], unruly, ungovernable; breachy[obs3], insubordinate, impatient of control, incorrigible; restiffl, restive; refractory, contumacious, recusant &c. (refuse) 764; recalcitrant; resisting &c. 719; lawless, mutinous, seditions, insurgent, riotous. unobeyed[obs3]; unbidden. Phr. seditiosissimus quisque ignavus [Lat][Tacitus]; "unthread the rude eye of rebellion" [King John].

#743. Obedience.— N. obedience; observance &c. 772; compliance; submission &c. 725; subjection &c. 749; nonresistance; passiveness, resignation. allegiance, loyalty, fealty, homage, deference, devotion; constancy, fidelity. submissness[obs3], submissiveness; ductility &c. (softness) 324; obsequiousness &c. (servility) 886. V. be -obedient &c. adj.; obey, bear obedience to; submit &c. 725; comply, answer the helm, come at one's call; do one's bidding, do what one is told, do suit and service; attend to orders, serve faithfully. follow the lead of, follow to the world's end; serve &c. 746; play second fiddle. Adj. obedient; complying, compliant; loyal, faithful, devoted; at one's call, at one's command, at one's orders, at one's beck and call; under beck and call, under control. restrainable; resigned, passive; submissive &c. 725; henpecked; pliant &c. (soft) 324. unresisted[obs3]. Adv. obediently &c. adj.; in compli- ance with, in obedience to. Phr. to hear is to obey; as you please, if you please; your wish is my command; as you wish; no sooner said than done.

#744. Compulsion.— N. compulsion, coercion, coaction[obs3], constraint, duress, enforcement, press, conscription. force; brute force, main force, physical force; the sword, ultima ratio[Lat]; club law, lynch law, mob law, arguementum baculinum[obs3], le droit du plus fort[Fr], martial law. restraint &c. 751; necessity &c. 601; force majeure[Fr]; Hob- son's choice. V. compel, force, make, drive, coerce, constrain, enforce, necessitate, oblige. force upon, press; cram down the throat, thrust down the throat, force down the throat; say it must be done, make a point of, insist upon, take no denial; put down, dragoon. extort, wring from; squeeze, put on the squeeze; put on the screws, turn on the screw; drag into; bind, bind over; pin down, tie down; require, tax, put in force; commandeer; restrain &c. 751. Adj. compel- ling &c. v.; coercive, coactive[obs3]; inexorable &c. 739; compulsory, compulsatory[obs3]; obligatory, stringent, peremptory. forcible, not to be trifled with; irresistible &c. 601; compelled &c. v.; fain to. Adv. by force &c. n., by force of arms; on compulsion, perforce; vi et armis[Lat], under the lash; at the point of the sword, at the point of the bayonet; forcibly; by a strong arm. under protest, in spite of one's teeth; against one's will &c. 603; nolens volens &c. (of necessity) 601[Lat]; by stress of circumstances, by stress of weather; under press of; de rigueur. with a gun to one's head. Phr. I'll make him an offer he can't refuse.

<– p. 249 –>

#745. Master.— N. master, padrone; lord, lord paramount; commander, commandant; captain; chief, chieftain; sirdar[obs3], sachem, sheik, head, senior, governor, ruler, dictator; leader &c. (director) 694; boss, cockarouse[obs3], sagamore[ISA:chief@algonquin], werowance[obs3]. lord of the ascendant; cock of the walk, cock of the roost; gray mare; mistress. potentate; liege, liege lord; suzerain, sovereign, monarch, autocrat, despot, tyrant, oligarch. crowned head, emperor, king, anointed king, majesty, imperator[Lat], protector, president, stadholder[obs3], judge. ceasar, kaiser, czar, tsar, sultan, soldanl, grand Turk, caliph, imaum[obs3], shah, padishah[obs3], sophi[obs3], mogul, great mogul, khan, lama, tycoon, mikado, tenno[Jap], inca, cazique[obs3]; voivode[obs3]; landamman[obs3]; seyyid[obs3]; Abuna[obs3], cacique[obs3], czarowitz[obs3], grand seignior. prince, duke &c. (nobility) 875; archduke, doge, elector; seignior; marland[obs3], margrave; rajah, emir, wali, sheik nizam[obs3], nawab. empress, queen, sultana, czarina, princess, infanta, duchess, margravine[obs3]; czarevna[obs3], czarita[obs3]; maharani, rani, rectrix[obs3]. regent, viceroy, exarch[obs3], palatine, khedive, hospodar[obs3], beglerbeg[obs3], three-tailed bashaw[obs3], pasha, bashaw[obs3], bey, beg, dey[obs3], scherif[obs3], tetrarch, satrap, mandarin, subahdar[obs3], nabob, maharajah; burgrave[obs3]; laird &c. (proprietor) 779; collector, commissioner, deputy commissioner, woon[obs3]. the authorities, the powers that be, the government; staff, etat major[Fr], aga[obs3], official, man in office, person in authority; sircar[obs3], sirkar[obs3], Sublime Porte. [Military authorities] marshal, field marshal, marechal[obs3]; general, generalissimo; commander in chief, seraskier[obs3], hetman[obs3]; lieutenant general, major general; colonel, lieutenant colonel, major, captain, centurion, skipper, lieutenant, first lieutenant, second lieutenant, sublieutenant, officer, staff officer, aide-de-camp, brigadier, brigade major, adjutant, jemidar[obs3], ensign, cornet, cadet, subaltern, noncommissioned officer, warrant officer; sergeant, sergeant major; color sergeant; corporal, corporal major; lance corporal, acting corporal; drum major; captain general, dizdar[obs3], knight marshal, naik[obs3], pendragon. [Civil authorities] mayor, mayoralty; prefect, chancellor, archon, provost, magistrate, syndic; alcalde[obs3], alcaid[obs3]; burgomaster, corregidor[obs3], seneschal, alderman, councilman, committeeman, councilwoman, warden, constable, portreeve[obs3]; lord mayor; officer &c. (executive) 965; dewan[obs3], fonctionnaire[Fr]. [Naval authorities] admiral, admiralty; rear admiral, vice admiral, port admiral; commodore, captain, commander, lieutenant, ensign, skipper, mate, master, officer of the day, OD; navarch[obs3]. Phr. da locum melioribus[Lat]; der Furst ist der erste Diener seines Staats [German: the prince is the first servant of his state]; "lord of thy presence and no land beside" [King John].

#746. Servant. — N. subject, liegeman[obs3]; servant, retainer, follower, henchman, servitor, domestic, menial, help, lady help, employe, attache; official. retinue, suite, cortege, staff, court. attendant, squire, usher, page, donzel[obs3], footboy[obs3]; train bearer, cup bearer; waiter, lapster[obs3], butler, livery servant, lackey, footman, flunky, flunkey, valet, valet de chambre[Fr]; equerry, groom; jockey, hostler, ostler[obs3], tiger, orderly, messenger, cad, gillie[obs3], herdsman, swineherd; barkeeper, bartender; bell boy, boots, boy, counterjumper[obs3]; khansamah[obs3], khansaman[obs3]; khitmutgar[obs3]; yardman. bailiff, castellan[obs3], seneschal, chamberlain, major-domo[obs3], groom of the chambers. secretary; under secretary, assistant secretary; clerk; subsidiary; agent &c. 758; subaltern; underling, understrapper; man. maid, maidservant; handmaid; confidente[Fr], lady's maid, abigail, soubrette; amah[obs3], biddy, nurse, bonne[Fr], ayah[obs3]; nursemaid, nursery maid, house maid, parlor maid, waiting maid, chamber maid, kitchen maid, scullery maid; femme de chambre[Fr], femme fille[Fr]; camarista[obs3]; chef de cuisine,cordon bleu[Fr], cook, scullion, Cinderella; potwalloper[obs3]; maid of all work, servant of all work; laundress, bedmaker[obs3]; journeyman, charwoman &c. (worker) 690; bearer, chokra[obs3], gyp [Cambridge], hamal[obs3], scout [Oxford]. serf, vassal, slave, negro, helot; bondsman, bondswoman[obs3]; bondslave[obs3]; ame damnee[Fr], odalisque, ryot[obs3], adscriptus gleboe[Lat]; villian[obs3], villein; beadsman[obs3], bedesman[obs3]; sizar[obs3]; pensioner, pensionary[obs3]; client; dependant, dependent; hanger on, satellite; parasite &c. (servility) 886; led captain; protege[Fr], ward, hireling, mercenary, puppet, tool, creature. badge of slavery; bonds &c. 752. V. serve; wait upon, attend upon, dance attendance upon, pin oneself upon; squire, tend, hang on the sleeve of; chore [U.S.]. Adj. in the train of; in one's pay, in one's employ; at one's call &c. (obedient) 743; in bonds.

#747. [Insignia of authority.] Scepter. — N. scepter, regalia, caduceus; Mercury's rod, Mercury's staff, Mercury's wand; rod of empire, mace, fasces[obs3], wand; staff, staff of office; baton, truncheon; flag &c. (insignia) 550; ensign of authority, emblem of authority, badge of authority, insignia of authority. throne, chair, musnud[obs3], divan, dais, woolsack[obs3]. toga, pall, mantle, robes of state, ermine, purple. crown, coronet, diadem, tiara, cap of maintenance; decoration; title &c. 877; portfolio. key, signet, seals, talisman; helm; reins &c. (means of restraint) 752.

<— p. 250 —>

#748. Freedom. — N. freedom, liberty, independence; license &c. (permission) 760; facility &c. 705.

scope, range, latitude, play; free play, full play, free scope, full scope; free stage and no favor; swing, full swing, elbowroom, margin, rope, wide berth; Liberty Hall.

franchise, denization[obs3]; free man, freed man, livery man; denizen.

autonomy, self-government, liberalism, free trade; noninterference &c. 706; Monroe Doctrine [U.S.].

immunity, exemption; emancipation &c. (liberation) 750; enfranchisement, affranchisement[obs3].

free land, freehold; allodium[obs3]; frankalmoigne[Fr], mortmain[Fr].

bushwhacker; freelance, free thinker, free trader; independent.

V. be free &c. adj.; have scope &c. n., have the run of, have one's own way, have a will of one's own, have one's fling; do what one likes, do what one wishes, do what one pleases, do what one chooses; go at large, feel at home, paddle one's own canoe; stand on one's legs, stand on one's rights; shift for oneself.

take a liberty; make free with, make oneself quite at home; use a freedom; take leave, take French leave.

set free &c. (liberate) 750; give a loose to &c. (permit) 760; allow scope &c. n. to, give scope &c. n. to; give a horse his head.

make free of; give the freedom of, give the franchise; enfranchise, affranchise[obs3].

laisser faire[Fr], laisser aller[Fr]; live and let live; leave to oneself; leave alone, let alone.

Adj. free, free as air; out of harness, independent, at large, loose, scot-free; left alone, left to oneself.

in full swing; uncaught, unconstrained, unbuttoned, unconfined, unrestrained, unchecked, unprevented[obs3], unhindered, unobstructed, unbound, uncontrolled, untrammeled.

unsubject[obs3], ungoverned, unenslaved[obs3], unenthralled[obs3], unchained, unshackled, unfettered, unreined[obs3], unbridled, uncurbed, unmuzzled.

unrestricted, unlimited, unmitigated, unconditional; absolute; discretionary &c. (optional) 600.

unassailed, unforced, uncompelled.

unbiassed[obs3], spontaneous.

free and easy; at ease, at one's ease; degage[Fr], quite at home; wanton, rampant, irrepressible, unvanquished[obs3].

exempt; freed &c. 750; freeborn; autonomous, freehold, allodial[obs3]; gratis &c. 815; eleutherian[obs3].

unclaimed, going a begging.

Adv. freely &c. adj.; ad libitum &c. (at will) 600.

Phr. ubi libertas ibi patria[Lat]; free white and twenty-one.

#749. Subjection.— N. subjection; dependence, dependency; subordination; thrall, thralldom, thraldom, enthrallment, subjugation, bondage, serfdom; feudalism, feudality[obs3]; vassalage, villenage; slavery, enslavement, involuntary servitude; conquest. service; servitude, servitorship[obs3]; tendence[obs3], employ, tutelage, clientship[obs3]; liability &c. 177; constraint &c.751; oppression &c. (severity) 739; yoke &c. (means of restraint) 752; submission &c. 725; obedience &c. 743. V. be subject &c. adj.; be at the mercy of, lie at the mercy of; depend upon, lean upon, hang upon; fall a prey to, fall under; play second fiddle. be a mere machine, be a puppet, be a football; not dare to say one's soul is his own; drag a chain. serve &c. 746; obey &c. 743; submit &c. 725. break in, tame; subject, subjugate; master &c. 731; tread down, tread under foot; weigh down; drag at one's chariot wheels; reduce to subjection, reduce to slavery; enthrall, inthrall[obs3], bethrall[obs3]; enslave, lead captive; take into custody &c. (restrain) 751; rule &c. 737; drive into a corner, hold at the sword's point; keep under; hold in bondage, hold in leading strings, hold in swaddling clothes. Adj. subject, dependent, subordinate; feudal, feudatory; in subjection to, under control; in leading strings, in harness; subjected, enslaved &c. v.; constrained &c. 751; downtrodden; overborne, overwhelmed; under the lash, on the hip, led by the nose, henpecked; the puppet of, the sport of, the plaything of; under one's orders, under one's command, under one's thumb; a slave to; at the mercy of; in the power of, in the hands of, in the clutches of; at the feet of; at one's beck and call &c. (obedient) 743; liable &c. 177; parasitical; stipendiary. Adv. under. Phr. "slaves - in a land of light and law" [Whittier].

<— p. 251 —>

#750. Liberation.— N. liberation, disengagement, release, enlargement, emancipation; disenthrallment[obs3], disenthralment[obs3]; affranchisement[obs3], enfranchisement; manumission; discharge, dismissal. deliverance &c. 672; redemption, extrication, acquittance, absolution; acquittal &c. 970; escape &c.671. V. liberate, free; set free, set clear, set at liberty; render free, emancipate, release; enfranchise, affranchise[obs3]; manumit; enlarge; disband, discharge, disenthrall, disenthral, dismiss; let go, let loose, loose, let out, let slip; cast adrift, turn adrift; deliver &c. 672; absolve &c. (acquit) 970. unfetter &c. 751, untie &c. 43; loose &c. (disjoin) 44; loosen, relax; unbolt, unbar, unclose, uncork, unclog, unhand, unbind, unchain, unharness, unleash; disengage, disentangle; clear, extricate, unloose. gain one's liberty, obtain one's liberty, acquire one's liberty &c. 748; get rid of, get clear of; deliver oneself from; shake off the yoke, slip the collar; break loose, break prison; tear asunder one's bonds, cast off trammels; escape &c. 671. Adj. liberated &c. v.; out of harness &c. (free) 748. Int. unhand me! let me go!

#751. Restraint.— N. restraint; hindrance &c. 706; coercion &c. (compulsion) 744; cohibition[obs3], constraint, repression, suppression; discipline, control. confinement; durance, duress; imprisonment; incarceration, coarctationl, entombment, mancipation[obs3], durance vile, limbo, captivity; blockade. arrest, arrestation[obs3]; custody, keep, care, charge, ward, restringency[obs3]. curb &c. (means of restraint) 752; lettres de cachet[Fr]. limitation, restriction, protection, monopoly; prohibition &c. 761. prisoner &c. 754; repressionist[obs3]. V. restrain, check; put under restraint, lay under restraint; enthral, enthrall, inthral[obs3], inthrall[obs3], bethral[obs3], bethrall[obs3]; restrict; debar &c. (hinder) 706; constrain; coerce &c. (compel) 744; curb, control; hold back, hold from, hold in, hold in check, hold within bounds, keep back, keep from, keep in, keep in check, keep within bounds; hold in leash, hold in leading strings; withhold. keep under; repress, suppress; smother; pull in, rein in; hold, hold fast; keep a tight hand on; prohibit &c. 761; inhibit, cohibit[obs3]. enchain; fasten &c. (join) 43; fetter, shackle; entrammel[obs3]; bridle, muzzle, hopple[obs3], gag, pinion, manacle, handcuff, tie one's hands, hobble, bind hand and foot; swathe, swaddle; pin down, tether; picket; tie down, tie up; secure; forge fetters; disable, hamstring (incapacitate) 158. confine; shut up, shut in; clap up, lock up, box up, mew up, bottle up, cork up, seal up, button up; hem in, bolt in, wall in, rail in; impound, pen, coop; inclose &c. (circumscribe) 229; cage; incage[obs3], encage[obs3]; close the door upon, cloister; imprison, immure; incarcerate, entomb; clap under hatches, lay under hatches; put in irons, put in a strait-waistcoat; throw into prison, cast into prison; put into bilboes. arrest; take up, take charge of, take into custody; take prisoner, take captive, make prisoner, make captive; captivate; lead captive, lead into captivity; send to prison, commit to prison; commit; give in charge, give in custody; subjugate &c. 749. Adj. restrained, constrained; imprisoned &c.v.; pent up; jammed in, wedged in; under lock and key, under restraint, under hatches; in swaddling clothes; on parole; in custody, doing time &c. (prisoner) 754; cohibitive[obs3]; coactive &c. (compulsory) 744[obs3]. stiff, restringent[obs3], strait-laced, hidebound, barkbound[obs3]. ice bound, wind bound, weather bound; "cabined cribbed confined" [Macbeth]; in Lob's pound, laid by the heels.

<— p. 252 —>

#752. [Means of restraint.] Prison.— N. prison, prison house; jail, gaol, cage, coop, den, cell; stronghold, fortress, keep, donjon, dungeon, Bastille, oubliette, bridewell[obs3], house of correction, hulks, tollbooth, panopticon[obs3], penitentiary, guardroom, lockup, hold; round house, watch house, station house, sponging house; station; house of detention, black hole, pen, fold, pound; inclosure &c. 232; isolation (exclusion) 893; penal settlement, penal colony; bilboes, stocks, limbo, quod*[Lat]; calaboose, chauki[obs3], choky[obs3], thana[obs3]; workhouse [U.S.]. Newgate, Fleet, Marshalsea; King's (or Queen's) Bench. bond; bandage; irons, pinion, gyve, fetter, shackle, trammel, manacle, handcuff, straight jacket, strait jacket, strait-jacket, strait-waistcoat, hopples[obs3]; vice, vise. yoke, collar, halter, harness; muzzle, gag, bit, brake, curb, snaffle, bridle; rein, reins; bearing rein; martingale; leading string; tether, picket, band, guy, chain; cord &c. (fastening) 45; cavesson[obs3], hackamore [obs3][U.S.], headstall, jaquima [obs3] [U.S.], lines, ribbons. bolt, deadbolt, bar, lock, police lock, combination lock, padlock, rail, wall, stone wall; paling, palisade; fence, picket fence, barbed wire fence, Cyclone fence, stockade fence, chain-link fence; barrier, barricade. drag &c. (hindrance) 706.

#753. Keeper.— N. keeper, custodian, custos[Lat], ranger, warder, jailer, gaoler, turnkey, castellan[obs3], guard; watchdog, watchman; Charley; chokidar[obs3], durwan[obs3], hayward[obs3]; sentry, sentinel, watch and ward; concierge, coast guard, guarda costa[Sp], game keeper. escort, bodyguard. protector, governor, duenna[Sp]; guardian; governess &c. (teacher) 540; nurse, nanny, babysitter, catsitter, dogsitter, bonne[Fr], ayah[obs3].

#754. Prisoner.— N. prisoner, prisoner of war, POW, captive, inmate, detainee, hostage, abductee[obs3], detenu[Fr], close prisoner.
jail bird, ticket of leave man, chevronne[Fr].
V. stand committed; be imprisoned &c. 751.
take prisoner, take hostage (capture) 789.
Adj. imprisoned &c. 751; in prison, in quod*[Lat], in durance vile, in limbo, in custody, doing time, in charge, in chains; under lock and key, under hatches; on parole.
#755. [Vicarious authority.] Commission.— N. commission, delegation; consignment, assignment; procuration[obs3]; deputation, legation, mission, embassy; agency, agentship[obs3]; power of attorney; clerkship; surrogacy.
errand, charge, brevet, diploma, exequatur[Lat], permit &c. (permission) 760.
appointment, nomination, designation, return; charter; ordination; installation, inauguration, investiture, swearing-in; accession, coronation, enthronement.

vicegerency; regency, regentship.

viceroy &c. 745; consignee &c. 758; deputy &c. 759.

[person who receives a commission] agent, delegate, consignee &c. 758.

V. commission, delegate, depute; consign, assign; charge; intrust, entrust; commit, commit to the hands of; authorize &c. (permit) 760.

put in commission, accredit, engage, hire, bespeak, appoint, name, nominate, return, ordain; install, induct, inaugurate, swear in, invest, crown; enroll, enlist; give power of attorney to.

employ, empower; set over, place over; send out.

be commissioned, be accredited; represent, stand for; stand in the stead of, stand in the place of, stand in the shoes of.

Adj. commissioned &c. v.

Adv. per procurationem[Lat].

#756. Abrogation.— N. abrogation, annulment, nullification, recision; vacatur[Lat]; canceling &c. v.; cancel; revocation, revokement[obs3]; repeal, rescission, defeasance. dismissal, conge[Fr], demissionl; bounce* [U.S.]; deposal, deposition; dethronement; disestablishment, disendowment[obs3]; deconsecration; sack*, walking papers, pink slip, walking ticket; yellow cover*. abolition, abolishment; dissolution. counter order, countermand; repudiation, retraction, retractation[obs3]; recantation &c. (tergiversation) 607; abolitionist. V. abrogate, annul, cancel; destroy &c. 162; abolish; revoke, repeal, rescind, reverse, retract, recall; abolitionize[obs3]; overrule, override; set aside; disannul, dissolve, quash, nullify, declare null and void; disestablish, disendow[obs3]; deconsecrate. disclaim &c. (deny) 536; ignore, repudiate; recant &c. 607; divest oneself, break off. countermand, counter order; do away with; sweep away, brush away; throw overboard, throw to the dogs; scatter to the winds, cast behind. dismiss, discard; cast off, turn off, cast out, cast adrift, cast out of doors, cast aside, cast away; send off, send away, send packing, send about one's business; discharge, get rid of &c. (eject) 297; bounce* [U.S.]; fire*, fire out*; sack*. cashier; break; oust; unseat, unsaddle; unthrone[obs3], dethrone, disenthrone[obs3]; depose, uncrown[obs3]; unfrock, strike off the roll; disbar, disbench[obs3]. be abrogated &c.; receive its quietus; walk the plank. Adj. abrogated &c. v.; functus officio[Lat]. Int. get along with you! begone! go about your business! away with!

<— p. 253 —>

#757. Resignation.— N. resignation, retirement, abdication, renunciation, abjuration; abandonment, relinquishment.

V. resign; give up, throw up; lay down, throw up the cards, wash one's hands of, abjure, renounce, forego, disclaim, retract; deny &c. 536.

abrogate &c. 756; desert &c. (relinquish) 624; get rid of &c. 782.

abdicate; vacate, vacate one's seat; accept the stewardship of the Chiltern Hundreds; retire; tender one's resignation.

Adj. abdicant[obs3].

Phr. "Othello's occupation's gone" [Othello].

#758. Consignee.— N. consignee, trustee, nominee, committee. agent, delegate; commissary, commissioner; emissary, envoy, commissionaire[Fr]; messenger &c. 534. diplomatist, diplomat(e), corps diplomatique[Fr], embassy; ambassador, embassador[obs3]; representative, resident, consul, legate, nuncio, internuncio[obs3], charge d'affaires[Fr], attache. vicegerent &c. (deputy) 759; plenipotentiary. functionary, placeman[obs3], curator; treasurer &c. 801; factor, bailiff, clerk, secretary, attorney, advocate, solicitor, proctor, broker, underwriter, commission agent, auctioneer, one's man of business; factotum &c. (director) 694; caretaker; dalal[obs3], dubash[obs3], garnishee, gomashta[obs3]. negotiator, go-between; middleman; under agent, employe; servant &c. 746; referee, arbitrator &c.. (judge) 967. traveler, bagman, commis-voyageur[Fr], touter[obs3], commercial traveler, drummer [U.S.], traveling man. newspaper correspondent, own correspondent, special correspondent.

#759. Deputy.— N. deputy, substitute, vice, proxy, locum tenens, badli[obs3], delegate, representative, next friend, surrogate, secondary.

regent, viceregent[obs3], vizier, minister, vicar; premier &c. (director) 694; chancellor, prefect, provost, warden, lieutenant, archon, consul, proconsul; viceroy &c. (governor) 745; commissioner &c. 758; Tsung-li Yamen, Wai Wu Pu; plenipotentiary, alter ego.

team, eight, eleven; champion.

V. be deputy &c. n.; stand for, appear for, hold a brief for, answer for; represent; stand in the shoes of, walk in the shoes of; stand in the

215

stead of.

ablegate[obs3], accredit.

Adj. acting, vice, vice regal; accredited to.

Adv. in behalf of.

<— p. 254 —> % Section II. SPECIAL INTERSOCIAL VOLITION %

#760. Permission.— N. permission, leave; allowance, sufferance; tolerance, toleration; liberty, law, license, conces-
sion, grace; indulgence &c. (lenity) 740; favor, dispensation, exemption, release; connivance; vouchsafement[obs3].
authorization, warranty, accordance, admission. permit, warrant, brevet, precept, sanction, authority, firman;
hukm[obs3]; pass, passport; furlough, license, carte blanche[Fr], ticket of leave; grant, charter; patent, letters patent.
V. permit; give permission &c. n., give power; let, allow, admit; suffer, bear with, tolerate, recognize; concede &c.
762; accord, vouchsafe, favor, humor, gratify, indulge, stretch a point; wink at, connive at; shut one's eyes to. grant,
empower, charter, enfranchise, privilege, confer a privilege, license, authorize, warrant; sanction; intrust &c. (commission) 755. give carte blanche[Fr], give the reins to, give scope to &c. (freedom) 748; leave alone, leave it to one,
leave the door open; open the door to, open the flood gates; give a loose to. let off; absolve &c. (acquit) 970;
release, exonerate, dispense with. ask permission, beg permission, request permission, ask leave, beg leave,
request leave. Adj. permitting &c. v.; permissive, indulgent; permitted &c. v.; patent, chartered, permissible, allowable, lawful, legitimate, legal; legalized &c. (law) 963; licit; unforbid[obs3], unforbidden[obs3]; unconditional. Adv. by
leave, with leave, on leave &c. n.; speciali gratia[It]; under favor of; pace; ad libitum &c. (freely) 748, (at will) 600; by
all means &c. (willingly) 602; yes &c. (assent) 488. Phr. avec permissin[Fr]; brevet d'invention [Fr].

#761. Prohibition.— N. prohibition, inhibition; veto, disallowance; interdict, interdiction; injunction, estoppel[Law];
embargo, ban, taboo, proscription; index expurgatorius[Lat]; restriction &c. (restraint) 751; hindrance &c.706;
forbidden fruit; Maine law [U.S.]. V. prohibit, inhibit; forbid, put one's veto upon, disallow, enjoin, ban, outlaw, taboo,
proscribe, estop[Law]; bar; debar &c. (hinder) 706, forefend. keep in, keep within bounds; restrain &c. 751;
cohibit[obs3], withhold, limit, circumscribe, clip the wings of, restrict; interdict, taboo; put under an interdiction, place
under an interdiction; put under the ban, place under the ban; proscribe; exclude, shut out; shut the door, bolt the
door, show the door; warn off; dash the cup from one's lips; forbid the banns. Adj. prohibitive, prohibitory; proscrip-
tive; restrictive, exclusive; forbidding &c. v. prohibited &c. v.; not permitted &c. 760; unlicensed, contraband, imper-
missible, under the ban of; illegal &c. 964; unauthorized, not to be thought of, uncountenanced, unthinkable, beyond
the pale. Adv. on no account &c. (no) 536. Int. forbid it heaven! &c. (deprecation) 766. hands off! keep off! hold! stop!
desist! cease and desist! avast! Phr. that will never do; don't you dare; forget it; don't even think about doing it;"go
ahead; make my day [ironical, threatening]" [Dirty Harry].

#762. Consent.— N. consent; assent &c. 488; acquiescence; approval &c. 931; compliance, agreement, concession;
yieldancel, yieldingness[obs3]; accession, acknowledgment, acceptance, agnitionl. settlement, ratification, confirmation, adjustment. permit &c. (permission) 760; promise &c. 768. V. consent; assent &c. 488; yield assent, admit,
allow, concede, grant, yield; come round, come over; give into, acknowledge, agnize[obs3], give consent, comply
with, acquiesce, agree to, fall in with, accede, accept, embrace an offer, close with, take at one's word, have no
objection. satisfy, meet one's wishes, settle, come to terms &c. 488; not refuse &c. 764; turn a willing ear &c.
(willingness) 602; jump at; deign, vouchsafe; promise &c. 768. Adj. consenting &c. v.; squeezable; agreed &c.
(assent) 488; unconditional. Adv. OK, yes &c. (assent) 488; by all means &c. (willingly) 602; no problem; if you
please, as you please; be it so, so be it, well and good, of course; please do; don't hesitate. Phr. chi tace
accousente[It][obs3].

#763. Offer.— N. offer, proffer, presentation, tender, bid, overture; proposal, proposition; motion, invitation; candida-
ture; offering &c. (gift) 784. V. offer, proffer, present, tender; bid; propose, move; make a motion, make advances;
start; invite, hold out, place in one's way, put forward. hawk about; offer for sale &c. 796; press &c. (request) 765; lay
at one's feet. offer oneself, present oneself; volunteer, come forward, be a candidate; stand for, bid for; seek; be at
one's service; go a begging; bribe &c. (give) 784. Adj. offering, offered &c. v.; in the market, for sale, to let, disen-
gaged, on hire.

<— p. 255 —>

#764. Refusal.— N. refusal, rejection; noncompliance, incompliance[obs3]; denial; declining &c. v.; declension;
declinature[obs3]; peremptory refusal, flat refusal, point blank refusal; repulse, rebuff; discountenance. recusancy,
abnegation, protest, disclaimer; dissent &c. 489; revocation &c. 756. V. refuse, reject, deny, decline, turn down; nill,
negative; refuse one's assent, withhold one's assent; shake the head; close the hand, close the purse; grudge,

216

begrudge, be slow to, hang fire; pass [at cards]. be deaf to; dismiss, turn a deaf ear to, turn one's back upon; set one's face against, discountenance, not hear of, have nothing to do with, wash one's hands of, stand aloof, forswear, set aside, cast behind one; not yield an inch &c. (obstinacy) 606. resist, cross; not grant &c. 762; repel, repulse, shut the door in one's face, slam the door in one's face; rebuff; send back, send to the right about, send away with a flea in the ear; deny oneself, not be at home to; discard, spurn, &c. (repudiate) 610; rescind &c. (revoke) 756; disclaim, protest; dissent &c. 489. Adj. refusing &c. v.; restive, restiffl; recusant; uncomplying, unconsenting; not willing to hear of, deaf to. refused &c. v.; ungranted, out of the question, not to be thought of, impossible. Adv. no &c. 536; on no account, not for the world; no thank you, thanks but no thanks. Phr. non possumus[Lat]; your humble servant[ironically]; bien oblige[Fr]; not on your life [U.S.]; no way; not even if you beg on your knees.

#765. Request. — N. request, requisition; claim &c. (demand) 741; petition, suit, prayer; begging letter, round robin. motion, overture, application, canvass, address, appeal, apostrophe; imprecation; rogation; proposal, proposition. orison &c. (worship) 990; incantation &c. (spell) 993. mendicancy; asking, begging &c. v.; postulation, solicitation, invitation, entreaty, importunity, supplication, instance, impetration[obs3], imploration[obs3], obsecration[obs3], obtestation[obs3], invocation, interpellation. V. request, ask; beg, crave, sue, pray, petition, solicit, invite, pop the question, make bold to ask; beg leave, beg a boon; apply to, call to, put to; call upon, call for; make a request, address a request, prefer a request, put up a request, make a prayer, address a prayer, prefer a prayer, put up a prayer, make a petition, address a petition, prefer a petition, put up a petition; make application, make a requisition; ask trouble, ask one for; claim &c. (demand) 741; offer up prayers &c. (worship) 990; whistle for. beg hard, entreat, beseech, plead, supplicate, implore; conjure, adjure; obtest[obs3]; cry to, kneel to, appeal to; invoke, evoke; impetrate[obs3], imprecate, ply, press, urge, beset, importune, dun, tax, clamor for; cry aloud, cry for help; fall on one's knees; throw oneself at the feet of; come down on one's marrowbones. beg from door to door, send the hat round, go a begging; mendicate[obs3], mump[obs3], cadge, beg one's bread. dance attendance on, besiege, knock at the door. bespeak, canvass, tout, make interest, court; seek, bid for &c. (offer) 763; publish the banns. Adj. requesting &c. v.; precatory[obs3]; suppliant, supplicant, supplicatory; postulant; obsecratory[obs3]. importunate, clamorous, urgent; cap in hand; on one's knees, on one's bended knees, on one's marrowbones. Adv. prithee, do, please, pray; be so good as, be good enough; have the goodness, vouchsafe, will you, I pray thee, if you please. Int. for God's sake! for heaven's sake! for goodness' sake! for mercy's sake! Phr. Dieu vous garde[Fr]; dirigenos Domine[Lat]; would you be so kind as to.

#766. [Negative request.] Deprecation. — N. deprecation, expostulation; intercession, mediation, protest, remonstrance.
    V. deprecate, protest, expostulate, enter a protest, intercede for; remonstrate.
    Adj. deprecatory, expostulatory[obs3], intercessory, mediatorial[obs3].
    deprecated, protested.
    unsought, unbesought[obs3]; unasked &c. (see ask &c. 765).
    Int. cry you mercy! God forbid! forbid it Heaven! Heaven forefend, Heaven forbid! far be it from! hands off! &c. (prohibition) 761; please don't.

<— p. 256 —>

#767. Petitioner. — N. petitioner, solicitor, applicant; suppliant, supplicant; suitor, candidate, claimant, postulant, aspirant, competitor, bidder; place hunter, pot hunter; prizer[obs3]; seeker. beggar, mendicant, moocher, panhandler, freeloader, sponger, mumper[obs3], sturdy beggar, cadger; hotel runner, runner, steerer [U.S.], tout, touter[obs3]. [poor person] pauper, homeless person, hobo, bum, tramp, bindle stiff, bo, knight of the road (poverty) 804; hippie, flower child; hard core unemployed; welfare client, welfare case. canvasser, bagman &c.758; salesman.

% Section III. CONDITIONAL INTERSOCIAL VOLITION %

#768. Promise. — N. promise, undertaking, word, troth, plight, pledge, parole, word of honor, vow; oath &c. (affirmation) 535; profession, assurance, warranty, guarantee, insurance, obligation; contract &c. 769; stipulation. engagement, preengagement; affiance; betroth, betrothal, betrothment. V. promise; give a promise &c. n.; undertake, engage; make an engagement, form an engagement; enter into an engagement, enter on an engagement; bind oneself, tie oneself, pledge oneself, commit oneself, take upon oneself; vow; swear &c. (affirm) 535, give one's word, pass one's word, pledge one's word, plight one's word, give one's honor, pass one's honor, pledge one's honor, plight one's honor, give credit, pass credit, pledge credit, plight credit, give troth, pass troth, pledge troth, plight troth; betroth, plight faith. assure, warrant, guarantee; covenant &c. 769; attest &c. (bear witness) 467. hold out an expectation; contract an obligation; become bound to, become sponsor for; answer for, be answerable for; secure; give security &c. 771; underwrite. adjure, administer an oath, put to one's oath, swear a witness. Adj. promising &c. v.; promissory; votive; under hand and seal, upon oath. promised &c. v.; affianced, pledged, bound; committed, compromised; in for it. Adv. as one's head shall answer for. Phr. in for a penny in for a pound; ex voto[Lat]; gage d'amour.

#768a. Release from engagement.— N. release &c. (liberation) 750.
Adj. absolute; unconditional &c. (free) 748.
#769. Compact.— N. compact, contract, agreement, bargain; affidation[obs3]; pact, paction[obs3]; bond, covenant, indenture; bundobast[obs3], deal.
stipulation, settlement, convention; compromise, cartel.
Protocol, treaty, concordat, Zollverein[Ger], Sonderbund[Ger], charter, Magna Charta[Lat], Progmatic Sanction, customs union, free trade region; General Agreement on Tariffs and Trade, GATT; most favored nation status.
negotiation &c. (bargaining) 794; diplomacy &c. (mediation) 724; negotiator &c. (agent) 758.
ratification, completion, signature, seal, sigil[Lat], signet.
V. contract, covenant, agree for; engage &c. (promise) 768.
treat, negotiate, stipulate, make terms; bargain &c. (barter) 794.
make a bargain, strike a bargain; come to terms, come to an understanding; compromise &c. 774; set at rest; close, close with; conclude, complete, settle; confirm, ratify, clench, subscribe, underwrite; endorse, indorse; put the seal to; sign, seal &c. (attest) 467; indent.
take one at one's word, bargain by inch of candle.
Adj. agreed &c. v.; conventional; under hand and seal.
Phr. caveat emptor.
#770. Conditions.— N. conditions, terms; articles, articles of agreement; memorandum.
clauses, provisions; proviso &c. (qualification) 469; covenant, stipulation, obligation, ultimatum, sine qua non; casus foederris[Lat].
V. make terms, come to terms &c. (contract) 769; make it a condition, stipulate, insist upon, make a point of; bind, tie up.
Adj. conditional, provisional, guarded, fenced, hedged in.
Adv. conditionally &c. (with qualification) 469; provisionally, pro re nata[Lat]; on condition; with a string to it.
<— p. 257 —>

#771. Security.— N. security; guaranty, guarantee; gage, warranty, bond, tie, pledge, plight, mortgage, collateral, debenture, hypothecation, bill of sale, lien, pawn, pignoration[obs3]; real security; vadium[obs3].
stake, deposit, earnest, handsel, caution.
promissory note; bill, bill of exchange; I.O.U.; personal security, covenant, specialty; parole &c. (promise) 768.
acceptance, indorsement[obs3], signature, execution, stamp, seal.
sponsor, cosponsor, sponsion[obs3], sponsorship; surety, bail; mainpernor[obs3], hostage; godchild, godfather, godmother.
recognizance; deed of indemnity, covenant of indemnity.
authentication, verification, warrant, certificate, voucher, docket, doquet[obs3]; record &c. 551; probate, attested copy.
receipt; acquittance, quittance; discharge, release.
muniment[obs3], title deed, instrument; deed, deed poll; assurance, indenture; charter &c. (compact) 769; charter poll; paper, parchment, settlement, will, testament, last will and testament, codicil.
V. give security, give bail, give substantial bail; go bail; pawn, impawn[obs3], spout, mortgage, hypothecate, impignorate[obs3].

guarantee, warrant, warrantee, assure; accept, indorse, underwrite, insure;cosign, countersign, sponsor, cosponsor.

execute, stamp; sign, seal &c. (evidence) 467.

let, sett[obs3]; grant a lease, take a lease, hold a lease; hold in pledge; lend on security &c. 787.

Phr. bonis avibus[Lat]; "gone where the woodbine twineth".

#772. Observance.— N. observance, performance, compliance, acquiescence, concurrence; obedience &c. 743; fulfillment, satisfaction, discharge; acquittance, acquittal. adhesion, acknowledgment; fidelity &c. (probity) 939; exact &c. 494 - observance. V. observe, comply with, respect, acknowledge, abide by; cling to, adhere to, be faithful to, act up to; meet, fulfill; carry out, carry into execution; execute, perform, keep, satisfy, discharge; do one's office. perform an obligation, fulfill an obligation, discharge an obligation, acquit oneself of an obligation; make good; make good one's word, make good one's promise, keep one's word, keep one's promise; redeem one's pledge; keep faith with, stand to one's engagement. Adj. observant, faithful, true, loyal; honorable &c. 939; true as the dial to the sun, true as the needle to the pole; punctual, punctilious; literal &c. (exact) 494; as good as one's word. Adv. faithfully &c. adj. Phr. ignoscito saepe alteri nunquam tibi[Lat]; tempori parendum[Lat]; "to God, thy country, and thy friend be true" [Vaughan].

#773. Nonobservance.— N. nonobservance &c. 772; evasion, inobservance, failure, omission, neglect, laches[Law], laxity, informality.

infringement, infraction; violation, transgression; piracy.

retraction, retractation[obs3], repudiation, nullification; protest; forfeiture.

lawlessness; disobedience &c. 742; bad faith &c. 940.

V. fail, neglect, omit, elude, evade, give the go-by to, set aside, ignore; shut one's eyes to, close one's eyes to.

infringe, transgress, violate, pirate, break, trample under foot, do violence to, drive a coach and six through.

discard, protest, repudiate, fling to the winds, set at naught, nullify, declare null and void; cancel &c. (wipe off) 552.

retract, go back from, be off, forfeit, go from one's word, palter; stretch a point, strain a point.

Adj. violating &c. v.; lawless, transgressive; elusive, evasive.

unfulfilled &c. (see fulfill &c. 772).

<— p. 258 —>

#774. Compromise.— N. compromise, commutation, composition; middle term, mezzo termine[It]; compensation &c. 30; abatement of differences, adjustment, mutual concession. V. compromise, commute, compound; take the mean; split the difference, meet one halfway, give and take; come to terms &c. (contract) 769; submit to arbitration, abide by arbitration; patch up, bridge over, arrange; straighten out, adjust, differences, agree; make the best of, make a virtue of necessity; take the will for the deed.

% Section IV. POSSESSIVE RELATIONS % <— That is, relations which concern property. —> % 1. Property in general %

#775. Acquisition.— N. acquisition; gaining &c. v.; obtainment; procuration[obs3], procurement; purchase, descent, inheritance; gift &c. 784. recovery, retrieval, revendication[obs3], replevin[Law], restitution &c. 790; redemption, salvage, trover[Law]. find, trouvaille[obs3], foundling. gain, thrift; money-making, money grubbing; lucre, filthy lucre, pelf; loaves and fishes, the main chance; emolument &c. (remuneration) 973. profit, earnings, winnings, innings, pickings, net profit; avails; income &c. (receipt) 810; proceeds, produce, product; outcome, output; return, fruit, crop, harvest; second crop, aftermath; benefit &c. (good) 618. sweepstakes, trick, prize, pool; pot; wealth &c. 803. subreption[obs3][Fraudulent acquisition]; obreption[obs3]; stealing &c. 791. V. acquire, get, gain, win, earn, obtain, procure, gather; collect &c. (assemble) 72; pick, pickup; glean.

find; come upon, pitch upon, light upon; scrape up, scrape together; get in, reap and carry, net, bag, sack, bring home, secure; derive, draw, get in the harvest. profit; make profit, draw profit, turn a quick profit; turn to profit, turn to account; make capital out of, make money by; obtain a return, reap the fruits of; reap an advantage, gain an advantage; turn a penny, turn an honest penny; make the pot boil, bring grist to the mill; make money, coin money, raise money; raise funds, raise the wind; fill one's pocket &c. (wealth) 803. treasure up &c. (store) 636; realize, clear;

produce &c. 161; take &c. 789. get back, recover, regain, retrieve, revendicate[obs3], replevy[Law], redeem, come by one's own. come by, come in for; receive &c. 785; inherit; step into a fortune, step into the shoes of; succeed to. get hold of, get between one's finger and thumb, get into one's hand, get at; take possession, come into possession, enter into possession. be profitable &c. adj.; pay, answer. accrue &c. (be received) 785. Adj. acquiring, acquired &c. v.; profitable, advantageous, gainful, remunerative, paying, lucrative. Phr. lucri causa[Lat].

#776. Loss.— N. loss; deperdition[obs3], perdition; forfeiture, lapse.

privation, bereavement; deprivation &c. (dispossession) 789; riddance; damage, squandering, waste.

V. lose; incur a loss, experience a loss, meet with a loss; miss; mislay, let slip, allow to slip through the fingers; be without &c. (exempt) 777a; forfeit.

get rid of &c. 782; waste &c. 638.

be lost; lapse.

Adj. losing &c. v.; not having &c. 777a.

shorn of, deprived of; denuded, bereaved, bereft, minus, cut off; dispossessed &c. 789; rid of, quit of; out of pocket.

lost &c. v.; long lost; irretrievable &c. (hopeless) 859; off one's hands.

Int. farewell to! adieu to.
<— p. 259 —>

<— emphasize the abstract meaning of possession - legal possession, as a distinct entity from physical possession, stewardship —>

#777. Possession.— N. possession, seizin[Law], seisin[Law]; ownership &c. 780; occupancy; hold, holding; tenure, tenancy, feodality[obs3], dependency; villenage, villeinage[obs3]; socage[obs3], chivalry, knight service. exclusive possession, impropriation[obs3], monopoly, retention &c.781; prepossession, preoccupancy[obs3]; nine points of the law; corner, usucaption[obs3]. future possession, heritage, inheritance, heirship, reversion, fee, seigniority[obs3]; primogeniture, ultimogeniture[obs3]. futures contract[right of future possession; financial instruments], warrant, put, call, option; right of first refusal. bird in hand, uti possidetis[Lat], chose in possession. V. possess, have, hold, occupy, enjoy; be possessed of &c. adj.; have in hand &c. adj.; own &c. 780; command. inherit; come to, come in for. engross, monopolize, forestall, regrate[obs3], impropriate[obs3], have all to oneself; corner; have a firmhold of &c. (retain) 781[obs3]; get into one's hand &c. (acquire) 775. belong to, appertain to, pertain to; be in one's possession &c. adj.; vest in. Adj. possessing &c. v.; worth; possessed of, seized of, master of, in possession of; usucapient[obs3]; endowed with, blest with, instinct with, fraught with, laden with, charged with. possessed &c. v.; on hand, by one; in hand, in store, in stock; in one's hands, in one's grasp, in one's possession; at one's command, at one's disposal; one's own &c. (property) 780. unsold, unshared. Phr. entbehre gern was du nicht hast[Ger]; meum et tuum[Lat]; tuum est[Lat].

#777a. Exemption.— N. exemption; absence &c. 187; exception, immunity, privilege, release.

V. not have &c. 777; be without &c. adj.; excuse.

Adj. exempt from, devoid of, without, unpossessed of[obs3], unblest with[obs3]; immune from.

not having &c. 777; unpossessed[obs3]; untenanted &c. (vacant) 187; without an owner.

unobtained[obs3], unacquired.

#778. [Joint possession.] Participation.— N. participation; cotenancy[obs3], joint tenancy; occupancy in common, possession in common, tenancy in common; joint stock, common stock; co-partnership, partnership; communion; community of possessions, community of goods; communism, socialism; cooperation &c. 709.

snacks, coportionl, picnic, hotchpot[obs3]; co-heirship, co-parceny[obs3], co-parcenary; gavelkind[obs3].

participator, sharer; co-partner, partner; shareholder; co-tenant, joint tenant; tenants in common; co-heir, co-parcener[obs3].

communist, socialist.

V. participate, partake; share, share in; come in for a share; go shares, go snacks, go halves; share and share alike.

have in common, possess in common, be seized in common, have as joint tenants, possess as joint tenants, be seized as joint tenants &c. n.

join in; have a hand in &c. (cooperate) 709.

Adj. partaking &c. v.; communistic.

Adv. share and share alike.

#779. Possessor. — N. possessor, holder; occupant, occupier; tenant; person in possession, man in possession &c.777; renter, lodger, lessee, underlessee[obs3]; zemindar[obs3], ryot[obs3]; tenant on sufferance, tenant at will, tenant from year to year, tenant for years, tenant for life.

owner; proprietor, proprietress, proprietary; impropriator[obs3], master, mistress, lord.

land holder, land owner, landlord, land lady, slumlord; lord of the manor, lord paramount; heritor, laird, vavasour[obs3], landed gentry, mesne lord[obs3]; planter.

cestui-que-trust[Fr], beneficiary, mortgagor.

grantee, feoffee[obs3], releasee[Law], relessee[obs3], devisee; legatee, legatary[obs3].

trustee; holder &c. of the legal estate; mortgagee.

right owner, rightful owner.

[Future possessor] heir presumptive, heir apparent; heiress; inheritor, inheritress, inheritrix; reversioner[obs3], remainderman[obs3].

<— p. 260 —>

#780. Property. — N. property, possession, suum cuique[Lat], meum et tuum[Lat]. ownership, proprietorship, lordship; seignority[obs3]; empire &c. (dominion) 737. interest, stake, estate, right, title, claim, demand, holding; tenure &c. (possession) 777; vested interest, contingent interest, beneficial interest, equitable interest; use, trust, benefit; legal estate, equitable estate; seizin[Law], seisin[Law]. absolute interest, paramount estate, freehold; fee tail, fee simple; estate in fee, estate in tail, estate tail; estate in tail male, estate in tail female, estate in tail general. limitation, term, lease, settlement, strict settlement, particular estate; estate for life, estate for years, estate pur autre vie[Fr]; remainder, reversion, expectancy, possibility. dower, dowry, jointure[obs3], appanage, inheritance, heritage, patrimony, alimony; legacy &c. (gift) 784; Falcidian law, paternal estate, thirds. assets, belongings, means, resources, circumstances; wealth &c. 803; money &c. 800; what one is worth, what one will cut up for; estate and effects. landed property, landed real estate property; realty; land, lands; tenements; hereditaments; corporeal hereditaments, incorporeal hereditaments; acres; ground &c. (earth) 342; acquest[obs3], messuage, toft[obs3]. territory, state, kingdom, principality, realm, empire, protectorate, sphere of influence. manor, honor, domain, demesne; farm, plantation, hacienda; allodium &c. (free) 748[obs3]; fief, fieff[obs3], feoff[obs3], feud, zemindary[obs3], dependency; arado[obs3], merestead[obs3], ranch. free lease-holds, copy lease-holds; folkland[obs3]; chattels real; fixtures, plant, heirloom; easement; right of common, right of user. personal property, personal estate, personal effects; personalty, chattels, goods, effects, movables; stock, stock in trade; things, traps, rattletraps, paraphernalia; equipage &c. 633. parcels, appurtenances. impedimenta; luggage, baggage; bag and baggage; pelf; cargo, lading. rent roll; income &c. (receipts) 810; maul and wedges [U.S.]. patent, copyright; chose in action; credit &c. 805; debt &c.806. V. possess &c. 777; be the possessor &c. 779 of; own; have for one's own, have for one's very own; come in for, inherit. savor of the realty. be one's property &c. n.; belong to; appertain to, pertain to. Adj. one's own; landed, predial[obs3], manorial, allodial[obs3]; free lease-hold, copy lease-hold; feudal, feodal[obs3]. Adv. to one's credit, to one's account; to the good. to one and his heirs for ever, to one and the heirs of his body, to one and his heirs and assigns, to one and his executors administrators and assigns.

#781. Retention. — N. retention; retaining &c. v.; keep, detention, custody; tenacity, firm hold, grasp, gripe, grip, iron grip.

fangs, teeth, claws, talons, nail, unguis, hook, tentacle, tenaculum; bond &c. (vinculum) 45.

clutches, tongs, forceps, pincers, nippers, pliers, vice.

paw, hand, finger, wrist, fist, neaf[obs3], neif[obs3].

bird in hand; captive &c.754.

V. retain, keep; hold fast one's own, hold tight one's own, hold fast one's ground, hold tight one's ground; clinch, clench, clutch, grasp, gripe, hug, have a firm hold of.

secure, withhold, detain; hold back, keep back; keep close; husband &c. (store) 636; reserve; have in stock, have on hand, keep in stock &c. (possess) 777; entail, tie up, settle.

Adj. retaining &c. v.; retentive, tenacious.

unforfeited[obs3], undeprived, undisposed, uncommunicated.

incommunicable, inalienable; in mortmain[Fr]; in strict settlement.

Phr. uti possidetis[Lat].

<— p. 261 —>

#782. Relinquishment.— N. relinquishment, abandonment &c. (of a course) 624; renunciation, expropriationll!, dereliction; cession, surrender, dispensation; quitclaim deed; resignation &c.757; riddance. derelict &c. adj.; foundling; jetsam, waif. discards, culls, rejects; garbage, refuse, rubbish. V. relinquish, give up, surrender, yield, cede; let go, let slip; spare, drop, resign, forego, renounce, abandon, expropriatel!, give away, dispose of, part with; lay aside, lay apart, lay down, lay on the shelf &c. (disuse) 678; set aside, put aside, put away; make away with, cast behind; maroon. give notice to quit, give warning; supersede; be rid of, get rid of, be quit of, get quit of; eject &c. 297. rid oneself of, disburden oneself of, divest oneself of, dispossess oneself of; wash one's hands of. discard, cast off, dismiss; cast away, throw away, pitch away, fling away, cast aside, cast overboard, cast to the dogs, throw aside, throw overboard, throw to the dogs, pitch aside, pitch overboard, pitch to the dogs, fling aside, fling overboard, fling to the dogs; cast to the winds, throw to the winds, sweep to the winds; put away, turn away, sweep away; jettison; reject. quit one's hold, quitclaim. Adj. relinquished &c. v.; cast off, derelict; unowned, unappropriated, unculled; left &c. (residuary) 40. Int. away with!

% 2. Transfer of Property %

#783. Transfer.— N. transfer, conveyance, assignment, alienation, abalienation[obs3]; demise, limitation; conveyancing[obs3]; transmission &c. (transference) 270; enfeoffment[obs3], bargain and sale, lease and release; exchange &c. (interchange) 148; barter &c. 794; substitution &c. 147.

succession, reversion; shifting use, shifting trust; devolution.

V. transfer, convey; alienate, alien; assign; grant &c. (confer) 784; consign; make over, hand over; pass, hand, transmit, negotiate; hand down; exchange &c.(interchange) 148.

change hands, change hands from one to another; devolve, succeed; come into possession &c. (acquire) 775.

abalienate[obs3]; disinherit; dispossess &c. 789; substitute &c. 147.

Adj. alienable, negotiable.

Phr. estate coming into possession.

#784. Giving.— N. giving &c. v.; bestowal, bestowment[obs3], donation; presentation, presentment; accordance; concession; delivery, consignment, dispensation, communication, endowment; investment, investiture; award.

almsgiving[obs3], charity, liberality, generosity.

[Thing given] gift, donation, present, cadeau[obs3]; fairing; free gift, boon, favor, benefaction, grant, offering, oblation, sacrifice, immolation; lagniappe [U.S.], pilon [obs3][U.S.].

grace, act of grace, bonus.

allowance, contribution, subscription, subsidy, tribute, subvention.

bequest, legacy, devise, will, dotation[obs3], dot, appanage; voluntary settlement, voluntary conveyance &c. 783; amortization.

alms, largess, bounty, dole, sportulel, donative[obs3], help, oblation, offertory, honorarium, gratuity, Peter pence, sportula[obs3], Christmas box, Easter offering, vail[obs3], douceur[Fr], drink money, pourboire, trinkgeld[Ger], bakshish[obs3]; fee &c. (recompense) 973; consideration.

bribe, bait, ground bait; peace offering, handsel; boodle*, graft, grease*;blat[Russian].

giver, grantor &c. v.; donor, feoffer[obs3], settlor.

V. deliver, hand, pass, put into the hands of; hand over, make over, deliver over, pass over, turn over; assign dower.

present, give away, dispense, dispose of; give out, deal out, dole out, mete out, fork out, squeeze out.

pay &c. 807; render, impart, communicate.

concede, cede, yield, part with, shed, cast; spend &c. 809.

give, bestow, confer, grant, accord, award, assign.

intrust, consign, vest in.

make a present; allow, contribute, subscribe, furnish its quota.

invest, endow, settle upon; bequeath, leave, devise.

furnish, supply, help; administer to; afford, spare; accommodate with, indulge with, favor with; shower down upon; lavish, pour on, thrust upon.

tip, bribe; tickle the palm, grease the palm; offer &c. 763; sacrifice, immolate.

Adj. giving &c. v.; given &c. v.; allowed, allowable; concessional[obs3]; communicable; charitable, eleemosynary, sportularyl, tributary; gratis &c. 815; donative[obs3].

Phr. auctor pretiosa facit[Lat]; ex dono[Lat]; res est ingeniosa dare [Lat][Ovid].
<— p. 262 —>

#785. Receiving.— N. receiving &c. v.; acquisition &c. 775; reception &c. (introduction) 296; suscipiencyl!, acceptance, admission.

recipient, accipient[obs3]; assignee, devisee; legatee, legatary[obs3]; grantee, feoffee[obs3], donee[Fr], releasee[Law], relessee[obs3], lessee; receiver.

sportularyl, stipendiary; beneficiary; pensioner, pensionary[obs3]; almsman[obs3].

income &c. (receipt) 810.

V. receive; take &c. 789; acquire &c. 775; admit.

take in, catch, touch; pocket; put into one's pocket, put into one's purse; accept; take off one's hands.

be received; come in, come to hand; pass into one's hand, fall into one's hand; go into one's pocket; fall to one's lot, fall to one's share; come to one, fall to one; accrue; have given &c. 784 to one.

Adj. receiving &c. v.; recipient, suscipientl!.

received &c. v.; given &c. 784; secondhand.

not given, unbestowed &c. (see give, bestow &c. 784).

#786. Apportionment.— N. apportionment, allotment, consignment, assignment, appointment; appropriation; dispensation, distribution; division, deal; repartition, partition; administration.

dividend, portion, contingent, share, allotment, fair share, allocation, lot, measure, dose; dole, meed, pittance; quantum, ration; ratio, proportion, quota, modicum, mess, allowance; suerte[obs3].

V. apportion, divide; distribute, administer, dispense; billet, allot, detail, cast, share, mete; portion out, parcel out, dole out; deal, carve.

allocate, ration, ration out; assign; separate &c. 44.

partition, assign, appropriate, appoint.

come in for one's share &c. (participate) 778.

Adj. apportioning &c. v.; respective.

Adv. respectively, each to each.

#787. Lending.— N. lending &c. v.; loan, advance, accommodation, fenerationl; mortgage, second mortgage, home loan &c. (security) 771; investment; note, bond, commercial paper.

mont de piete[Fr], pawnshop, my uncle's.

lender, pawnbroker, money lender; usurer, loan shark.

loaner

V[item loaned][coll.]. lend, advance, accommodate with; lend on security; loan; pawn &c. (security) 771.

intrust, invest; place out to interest, put out to interest.

let, demise, lease, sett[obs3], underlet.

Adj. lending &c. v.; lent &c. v.; unborrowed &c. (see borrowed &c. 788)[obs3].

Adv. in advance; on loan, on security.

#788. Borrowing. — N. borrowing, pledging.

borrowed plumes; plagiarism &c. (thieving) 791.

replevin[Law].

V. borrow, desumel.

hire, rent, farm; take a lease, take a demise; take by the hour, take by the mile, take by the year &c., hire by the hour, hire by the mile, hire by the year &c.; adopt, apply, appropriate, imitate, make use of, take.

raise money, take up money; raise the wind; fly a kite, borrow from Peter to pay Paul; run into debt &c. (debt) 806.

replevy[Law].

<— p. 263 —>

#789. Taking. — N. taking &c. v.; reception &c. (taking in) 296; deglutition &c. (taking food) 298; appropriation, prehension, prensationl; capture, caption; apprehension, deprehensionl; abreptionl, seizure, expropriation, abduction, ablation; subtraction, withdrawal &c. 38; abstraction, ademption[obs3]; adrolepsyl!. dispossession; deprivation, deprivement[obs3]; bereavement; divestment; disherison[obs3]; distraint, distress; sequestration, confiscation; eviction &c. 297. rapacity, rapaciousness, extortion, vampirism; theft &c.791. resumption; reprise, reprisal; recovery &c. 775. clutch, swoop, wrench; grip &c. (retention) 781; haul, take, catch; scramble. taker, captor. [Geol: descent of one of the earth's crustal plates under another plate] subduction. V. take, catch, hook, nab, bag, sack, pocket, put into one's pocket; receive; accept. reap, crop, cull, pluck; gather &c. (get) 775; draw. appropriate, expropriate, impropriate[obs3]; assume, possess oneself of; take possession of; commandeer; lay one's hands on, clap one's hands on; help oneself to; make free with, dip one's hands into, lay under contribution; intercept; scramble for; deprive of. take away, carry away, bear away, take off, carry off, bear off; adeeml!; abstract; hurry off with, run away with; abduct; steal &c. 791; ravish; seize; pounce upon, spring upon; swoop to, swoop down upon; take by storm, take by assault; snatch, reave[obs3]. snap up, nip up, whip up, catch up; kidnap, crimp, capture, lay violent hands on. get hold of, lay hold of, take hold of, catch hold of, lay fast hold of, take firm hold of; lay by the heels, take prisoner; fasten upon, grip, grapple, embrace, gripe, clasp, grab, clutch, collar, throttle, take by the throat, claw, clinch, clench, make sure of. catch at, jump at, make a grab at, snap at, snatch at; reach, make a long arm, stretch forth one's hand. take from, take away from; disseize[obs3]; deduct &c. 38; retrench &c. (curtail) 201; dispossess, ease one of, snatch from one's grasp; tear from, tear away from, wrench from, wrest from, wring from; extort; deprive of, bereave; disinherit, cut off with a shilling. oust &c. (eject) 297; divest; levy, distrain, confiscate; sequester, sequestrate; accroach[obs3]; usurp; despoil, strip, fleece, shear, displume[obs3], impoverish, eat out of house and home; drain, drain to the dregs; gut, dry, exhaust, swallow up; absorb &c. (suck in) 296; draw off; suck the blood of, suck like a leech. retake, resume; recover &c. 775. Adj. taking &c.v.; privative[obs3], prehensile; predaceous, predal[obs3], predatory, predatorial[obs3]; lupine, rapacious, raptorial; ravenous; parasitic. bereft &c. 776. Adv. at one fell swoop. Phr. give an inch and take an ell.

#790. Restitution. — N. restitution, return; rendition, reddition[obs3]; restoration; reinvestment, recuperation; rehabilitation &c. (reconstruction) 660; reparation, atonement; compensation, indemnification.

release, replevin[Law], redemption; recovery &c. (getting back) 775; remitter, reversion.

V. return, restore; give back, carry back, bring back; render, render up; give up; let go, unclutch; disgorge, regorge[obs3]; regurgitate; recoup, reimburse, compensate, indemnify; remit, rehabilitate; repair &c. (make good) 660.

[transitive] reinvest, revest, reinstate.

redeem, recover &c. (get back) 775; take back again.

[intransitive] revest, revert.

Adj. restoring &c. v.; recuperative &c. 660.
Phr. suum cuique[Lat].

<— p. 264 —>

#791. Stealing. — N. stealing &c. v.; theft, thievery, latrocinyl, direption[obs3]; abstraction, appropriation; plagiary, plagiarism; autoplagiarism[obs3]; latrocinium[obs3].

spoliation, plunder, pillage; sack, sackage[obs3]; rapine, brigandage, foray, razzia[obs3], rape, depredation, raid; blackmail.

piracy, privateering, buccaneering; license to plunder, letters of marque, letters of mark and reprisal.

filibustering, filibusterism[obs3]; burglary; housebreaking; badger game*.

robbery, highway robbery, hold-up* [U.S.], mugging.

peculation, embezzlement; fraud &c. 545; larceny, petty larceny, grand larceny, shoplifting.

thievishness, rapacity, kleptomania, Alsatia[obs3], den of Cacus, den of thieves.

blackmail, extortion, shakedown, Black Hand [U.S.].

[person who commits theft] thief &c. 792.

V. steal, thieve, rob, mug, purloin, pilfer, filch, prig, bag, niml, crib, cabbage, palm; abstract; appropriate, plagiarize.

convey away, carry off, abduct, kidnap, crimp; make off with, walk off with, run off with; run away with; spirit away, seize &c. (lay violent hands on) 789.

plunder, pillage, rifle, sack, loot, ransack, spoil, spoliate[obs3], despoil, strip, sweep, gut, forage, levy blackmail, pirate, pickeerl, maraud, lift cattle, poach; smuggle, run; badger*; bail up, hold up, stick up; bunco, bunko, filibuster.

swindle, peculate, embezzle; sponge, mulct, rook, bilk, pluck, pigeon, fleece; defraud &c.545; obtain under false pretenses; live by one's wits.

rob Peter to pay Paul, borrow of Peter to pay Paul; set a thief to catch a thief.

disregard the distinction between meum and tuum[Lat].

[receive stolen goods] fence, launder, launder money.

Adj. thieving &c. v.; thievish, light-fingered; furacious[obs3], furtive; piratical; predaceous, predal[obs3], predatory, predatorial[obs3]; raptorial &c. (rapacious) 789.

stolen &c. v.

Phr. sic vos non vobis[Lat].

#792. Thief. — N. thief, robber, homo triumliterarum[obs3][Lat], pilferer, rifler, filcher[obs3], plagiarist. spoiler, depredator, pillager, marauder; harpy, shark*, land shark, falcon, mosstrooper[obs3], bushranger[obs3], Bedouinl!, brigand, freebooter, bandit, thug, dacoit[obs3]; pirate, corsair, viking, Paul Jonesl!, buccaneer, buccanierl!; piqueererl, pickeererl; rover, ranger, privateer, filibuster; rapparee[obs3], wrecker, picaroon[obs3]; smuggler, poacher; abductor, badger*, bunko man, cattle thief, chor[obs3], contrabandist[obs3], crook, hawk, holdup man, hold-up* [U.S.], jackleg* [obs3][U.S.], kidnaper, rustler, cattle rustler, sandbagger, sea king, skin*, sneak thief, spieler[obs3], strong-arm man [U.S.]. highwayman, Dick Turpin, Claude Duval, Macheath, footpad, sturdy beggar. cut purse, pick purse; pickpocket, light-fingered gentry; sharper; card sharper, skittle sharper; thimblerigger; rook*, Greek, blackleg, leg, welsher*; defaulter; Autolycus[obs3], Jeremy Diddler[obs3], Robert Macaire, artful dodger, trickster; swell mob*, chevalier d'industrie [Fr]; shoplifter. swindler, peculator; forger, coiner; fence, receiver of stolen goods, duffer; smasher. burglar, housebreaker; cracksman[obs3], magsman*[obs3]; Bill Sikes, Jack Sheppard, Jonathan Wild. gang[group of thieves], gang of thieves, theft ring; organized crime, mafia, the Sicilian Mafia, the mob, la cosa nostra [Italian]. Dillinger[famous thieves], Al Capone; Robin Hood.

#793. Booty. — N. booty, spoil, plunder, prize, loot, swag*, pickings; spolia opima[Lat], prey; blackmail; stolen goods.
Adj. manubiall.

% 3. Interchange of Property %

#794. Barter.— N. barter, exchange, scorsel, truck system; interchange &c. 148.

a Roland for an Oliver; quid pro quo; commutation, composition; Indian gift [U.S.].

trade, commerce, mercaturel, buying and selling, bargain and sale; traffic, business, nundinationl, custom, shopping; commercial enterprise, speculation, jobbing, stockjobbing[obs3], agiotage[obs3], brokery[obs3].

deal, dealing, transaction, negotiation, bargain.

free trade.

V. barter, exchange, swap, swop[obs3], truck, scorsel; interchange &c. 148; commutate &c.(substitute) 147; compound for.

trade, traffic, buy and sell, give and take, nundinatel; carry on a trade, ply a trade, drive a trade; be in business, be in the city; keep a shop, deal in, employ one's capital in.

trade with, deal with, have dealings with; transact business with, do business with; open an account with, keep an account with.

bargain; drive a bargain, make a bargain; negotiate, bid for; haggle, higgle[obs3]; dicker [U.S.]; chaffer, huckster, cheapen, beat down; stickle, stickle for; out bid, under bid; ask, charge; strike a bargain &c. (contract) 769.

speculate, give a sprat to catch a herring; buy in the cheapest and sell in the dearest market, buy low and sell high; corner the market; rig the market, stag the market.

Adj. commercial, mercantile, trading; interchangeable, marketable, staple, in the market, for sale.

wholesale, retail.

Adv. across the counter.

Phr. cambio non e furto[It].

<— p. 265 —>

#795. Purchase.— N. purchase, emption[obs3]; buying, purchasing, shopping; preemption, refusal.

coemption[obs3], bribery; slave trade.

buyer, purchaser, emptor, vendee; patron, employer, client, customer, clientele.

V. buy, purchase, invest in, procure; rent &c. (hire) 788; repurchase, buy in.

keep in one's pay, bribe, suborn; pay &c.807; spend &c.809.

make a purchase, complete a purchase; buy over the counter.

shop, market, go shopping.

Adj. purchased &c. v.

Phr. caveat emptor; the customer is always right.

#796. Sale.— N. sale, vent, disposal; auction, roup, Dutch auction; outcry, vendue[obs3]; custom &c. (traffic) 794.

vendibility, vendibleness[obs3].

seller; vender, vendor; merchant &c. 797; auctioneer.

V. sell, vend, dispose of, effect a sale; sell over the counter, sell by auction &c. n.; dispense, retail; deal in &c. 794; sell off, sell out; turn into money, realize; bring to the hammer, bring under the hammer, put up to auction, put up for auction; offer for sale, put up for sale; hawk, bring to market; offer &c. 763; undersell.

let; mortgage &c.(security) 771.

Adj. under the hammer, on the market, for sale.

salable, marketable, vendible; unsalable &c., unpurchased[obs3], unbought; on one's hands.

Phr. chose qui plait est a demi vendue[obs3][Fr].

#797. Merchant.— N. merchant, trader, dealer, monger, chandler, salesman; changer; regrater[obs3]; shopkeeper,

226

shopman[obs3]; tradesman, tradespeople, tradesfolk. retailer; chapman, hawker, huckster, higgler[obs3]; pedlar, colporteur, cadger, Autolycus[obs3]; sutler[obs3], vivandiere[obs3]; costerman[obs3], costermonger[obs3]; tallyman; camelot; faker; vintner. money broker, money changer, money lender; cambist[obs3], usurer, moneyer[obs3], banker. jobber; broker &c. (agent) 758; buyer &c. 795; seller &c.796; bear, bull. concern; firm &c. (partnership) 712.

#798. Merchandise.— N. merchandise, ware, commodity, effects, goods, article, stock, product, produce, staple commodity; stock in trade &c. (store) 636; cargo &c. (contents) 190.

#799. Mart.— N. mart; market, marketplace; fair, bazaar, staple, exchange, change, bourse, hall, guildhall; tollbooth, customhouse; Tattersall's. stall, booth, stand, newsstand; cart, wagon. wharf; office, chambers, countinghouse, bureau; counter, compter[Fr]. shop, emporium, establishment; store &c.636; department store, general store, five and ten, variety store, co-op, finding store [U.S.], grindery warehouse[obs3]. [food stores: list] grocery, supermarket, candy store, sweet shop, confectionery, bakery, greengrocer, delicatessen, bakeshop, butcher shop, fish store, farmers' market, mom and pop store, dairy, health food store. [specialized stores: list] tobacco shop, tobacco store, tobacconists, cigar store, hardware store, jewelry shop, bookstore, liquor store, gun shop, rod and reel shop, furniture store, drugstore, chemist's [British], florist, flower shop, shoe store, stationer, stationer's, electronics shop, telephone store, music store, record shop, fur store, sporting goods store, video store, video rental store; lumber store, lumber yard, home improvements store, home improvement center; gas station, auto repair shop, auto dealer, used car dealer. mall, suburban mall, commons, pedestrian mall; shopping street. surplus store, army-navy surplus store. [locations where used articles are sold] auction; flea market; yard sale, garage sale; pawn shop; antiques store; second-hand store, second time around shop, thrift shop. warehouse, wareroom[obs3]; depot, interposit[obs3], entrepot[Fr]. market-overt. real-estate broker. vending machine.

<— here add entry for stock market (financial instruments market) and securities —> #799a. Stock Market [special-ized markets for financial instruments] — N. stock market, stock exchange, securities exchange; bourse, board; the big board, the New York Stock Exchange; the market, the open market; over- the-counter market; privately traded issues. commodities exchange, futures exchange, futures market. the pit, the floor. ticker, stock ticker, quotation; stock index, market index, the Dow Jones Index, the Dow Industrials, the transportation index, utilities, the utilities index; the New York Stock Exchange index, the Nikkei index [Japan]; the Financial Times index, the FTI [England], the over-the-counter index, NASDAQ index. [person or firm trading securities] broker, stockbroker, jobber, stock dealer, odd-lot dealer; specialist. [person who buys or sells stocks] investor, speculator, operator; bull, buyer; bear, short seller; scalper, arbitrager[obs3], arbitrageur[obs3]; stockholder, share-holder, stockholder of record; bond holder, coupon-clipper [derogatory]. investment; speculation. V. speculate, invest, trade, trade stocks, play the market; buy long, sell short, take a position, straddle; take a plunge, plunge in, take a flier [coll.].

#799b. Securities. — N. securities, stocks, common stock, preferred stock, bonds, puts, calls, options, option contract, warrants, commercial paper, bearer bond, tax-exempt bond, callable bond, convertable bond[obs3].
share, stock certificate; coupon, bond coupon.
liquid assets.
<— p. 266 —> % 4. Monetary Relations %

#800. Money.— N. money, legal tender; money matters, money market; finance; accounts &c. 811; funds, treasure; capital, stock; assets &c.(property) 780; wealth &c. 803; supplies, ways and means, wherewithal, sinews of war, almighty dollar, needful, cash; mammon. [colloquial terms for money] dough, cabbage. money-like instruments, M1, M2. sum, amount; balance, balance sheet; sum total; proceeds &c.(receipts) 810. currency, circulating medium, specie, coin, piece[Fr], hard cash, cold cash; dollar, sterling coin; pounds shillings and pence; Ls.d.; pocket, breech-es pocket, purse; money in hand, cash at hand; ready money, ready cash; slug [U.S.], wad* wad of bills[U.S.], wad of money, thick wad of bills, roll of dough[coll]; rhinol!, bluntl!, dustl!, mopusl!, tinl!, saltl!, chinkl!; argent comptant[Lat]; bottom dollar, buzzard dollarl!; checks, dibs*[obs3]. [specific types of currency] double eagle, eagle; Federal currency, fractional currency, postal currency; Federal Reserve Note, United States Note, silver certificate [obsolete], gold certificate [obsolete]; long bit, short bit [U.S.]; moss, nickel, pile*, pin money, quarter [U.S.], red cent, roanoke[obs3], rock*; seawan[obs3], seawant[obs3]; thousand dollars, grand[coll.]. [types of paper currency, U.S.] single, one-dollar bill; two-dollar bill; five-dollar bill, fiver[coll.], fin [coll.], Lincoln; ten-dollar bill, sawbuck; twenty-dollar bill, Jackson, double sawbuck; fifty-dollar bill; hundred-dollar bill, C-note. [types of U.S. coins: list] penny, cent, Lincoln cent, indian head penny, copper[1700 -1900]; two-cent piece three-cent piece [Fr][obsolete][obsolete], half-dime[obsolete], nickel, buffalo nickel, V nickel [obsolete], dime, dismel!, mercury dime[obsolete], quarter, two bits, half dollar, dollar, silver dollar, Eisenhower dollar, Susan B. Anthony dollar[obs3]. precious metals, gold, silver, copper, bullion, ingot, nugget. petty cash, pocket money, change, small change, small coin, doit[obs3], stiver[obs3], rap, mite, farthing, sou, penny, shilling, tester, groat, guinea; rouleau[obs3]; wampum; good sum, round sum, lump sum; power of money, plum, lac of rupees. major coin, crown; minor coin. monetarist, monetary theory. [Science of coins] numismatics, chrysology[obs3]. [coin scholar or collector] numismatist. paper money, greenback; major denomination, minor denomination; money order, postal money order, Post Office order; bank note; bond; bill, bill of exchange; order, warrant, coupon, debenture, exchequer bill, assignat[obs3]; blueback [obs3][U.S.], hundi[obs3], shinplaster* [U.S.]. note, note of hand; promissory note, I O U; draft, check, cheque, back-dated check; negotiable order of withdrawal, NOW. remittance &c.(payment) 807; credit &c.805; liability &c.806. drawer, drawee[obs3]; obligor[obs3], obligee[obs3]; moneyer[obs3], coiner. false money, bad money; base coin, flash note, slip!, kite*; fancy stocks; Bank of Elegance. argumentum ad crumenam[Lat]. letter of credit. circulation, multiplier effect. [variation in the value of currency] inflation, double-digit inflation, hyperinflation, erosion of the currency, debasement of the currency; deflation; stagflation. [relative value of two currencies] exchange rate, rate of exchange, floating exchange rates, fixed rates. [place to exchange currencies] currency counter, currency exchange, bureau de change [French]. gold-backed currency, gold standard, silver standard. bank account, savings account, checking account, money market account, NOW account, time deposit, deposit, demand deposit, super NOW account; certificate of deposit, CD. [money symbols] $, U.S. $, A$. [authorities controlling currency, U.S] Federal Reserve Bank, central bank; Federal Reserve Board, board of governors of the Federal Reserve; Treasury Department; Secret Service. [place where money is manufactured] mint, bureau of engraving. [government profit in manufacturing money] seigniorage. [false money] counterfeit, funny money, bogus money, (see falsehood) 545. [cost of money] interest, interest rate, discount rate. V. amount to, come to, mount up to; touch the pocket; draw, draw upon; indorse &c. (security) 771; issue, utter; discount &c. 813; back; demonetize, remonetize; fiscalize[obs3], monetize. circulate, be in circulation; be out of circulation. [manufacture currency] mint[coins], coin; print[paper currency]. [vary the value of money] inflate, deflate; debase; devalue, revalue. [vary the amount of money] circulate, put in circulation; withdraw from circulation. [change the type of currency] exchange currencies, change money. charge interest; pay interest; lose interest. Adj. monetary, pecuniary, crumenall, fiscal, financial, sumptuary, numismatic, numismatical[obs3]; sterling; nummary[obs3]. Phr. barbarus ipse placet dummodo sit dives [Lat][Ovid]; "but the jingling of the guinea helps the hurt that honor feels" [Tennyson]; Gelt regiert die Welt [German: money rules the world], money makes the world go round; nervos belli pecuniam infinitam [Lat][Cicero]; redet Geld so schweigt die Welt [German]; "money is the mother's milk of politics" [Tip O'Neill]; money is the root of all evil; money isn't everything; "as phony as a three-dollar bill"; "don't take any wooden nickels".

#801. Treasurer.— N. treasurer; bursar, bursary; purser, purse bearer; cash keeper, banker; depositary; questor[obs3], receiver, steward, trustee, accountant, Accountant General, almoner, liquidator, paymaster, cashier, teller; cambist[obs3]; money changer &c. (merchant) 797. financier. Secretary of the Treasury; Chancellor of the Exchequer, minister of finance.

#802. Treasury.— N. treasury, bank, exchequer, fisc, hanaper[obs3]; cash register, kutcherry[obs3], bursary; strong box, strong hold, strong room; coffer; chest &c.(receptacle) 191; safe; bank vault; depository &c. 636; till, tiller; purse; money bag, money box; porte-monnaie[Fr]. purse strings; pocket, breeches pocket. sinking fund; stocks; public stocks, public funds, public securities, parliamentary stocks, parliamentary funds, parliamentary securities; Consols, credit mobilier[Fr]; bonds.

#803. Wealth.— N. wealth, riches, fortune, handsome fortune, opulence, affluence; good circumstances, easy circumstances; independence; competence &c. (sufficiency) 639; solvency. provision, livelihood, maintenance; alimony, dowry; means, resources, substance; property &c. 780; command of money. income &c. 810; capital, money; round sum &c. (treasure) 800; mint of money, mine of wealth, El Dorado[Sp], bonanza, Pacatolus, Golconda, Potosi. long purse, full purse, well lined purse, heavy purse, deep pockets; purse of Fortunatus[Lat]; embarras de richesses[Fr]. pelf, Mammon, lucre, filthy lucre; loaves and fishes!. rich man, moneyed man, warm man; man of substance; capitalist, millionaire, tippybob*[obs3], Nabob, Croesus, idas, Plutus, Dives, Timon of Athens[obs3]; Timocracy, Plutocracy; Danae. V. be rich &c. adj.; roll in wealth, roll in riches, wallow in wealth, wallow in riches. afford, well afford; command money, command a sum; make both ends meet, hold one's head above water. become rich &c. adj.; strike it rich; come into a sum of money, receive a windfall, receive an inheritance, hit the jackpot, win the lottery; fill one's pocket &c. (treasury) 802; feather one's nest, make a fortune; make money &c. (acquire) 775. [transitive] enrich, imburse[obs3]. worship the golden calf, worship Mammon. Adj. wealthy, rich, affluent, opulent, moneyed, monied, worth much; well to do, well off; warm; comfortable, well, well provided for. made of money; rich as Croesus, filthy rich, rich as a Jew!; rolling in riches, rolling in wealth. flush, flush of cash, flush of money, flush of tin*; in funds, in cash, in full feather; solvent, pecunious[obs3], out of debt, in the black, all straight. Phr. one's ship coming in. amour fait beaucoup mais argent fait tout [French: love does much but money does everything]; aurea rumpunt tecta quietem [Lat][Seneca]; magna servitus ist magna fortuna[Latin]; "mammon, the least erected spirit that fell from Heaven" [Paradise Lost]; opum furiata cupido [Lat][Ovid]; vera prosperita e non aver necessita [It]; wie gewonnen so zerronnen [German].

<— p. 267 —>

#804. Poverty.— N. poverty, indigence, penury, pauperism, destitution, want; need, neediness; lack, necessity, privation, distress, difficulties, wolf at the door. bad circumstances, poor circumstances, need circumstances, embarrassed circumstances, reduced circumstances, straightened circumstances; slender means, narrow means; straits; hand to mouth existence, res angusta domi[obs3][Lat], low water, impecuniosity. beggary; mendicancy, mendicity[obs3]; broken fortune, loss of fortune; insolvency &c. (nonpayment) 808. empty pocket, empty purse; light purse; beggarly account of empty boxes. [poor people] poor man, pauper, mendicant, mumper[obs3], beggar, starveling; pauvre diable[Fr]; fakirl!, schnorrerl!; homeless person. V. be poor &c. adj.; want, lack, starve, live from hand to mouth, have seen better days, go down in the world, come upon the parish; go to the dogs, go to wrack and ruin; not have a penny &c. (money) 800, not have a shot in one's locker; beg one's bread; tirer le diable par la queue[Fr]; run into debt &c. (debt) 806. render poor &c. adj.; impoverish; reduce, reduce to poverty; pauperize, fleece, ruin, bring to the parish. Adj. poor, indigent; poverty-stricken; badly off, poorly off, ill off; poor as a rat, poor as a church mouse, poor as a Job; fortuneless[obs3], dowerless[obs3], moneyless[obs3], penniless; unportioned[obs3], unmoneyed[obs3]; impecunious; out of money, out of cash, short of money, short of cash; without a rap, not worth a rap &c.(money) 800; qui n'a pas le sou[Fr], out of pocket, hard up; out at elbows, out at heels; seedy, bare-footed; beggarly, beggared; destitute; fleeced, stripped; bereft, bereaved; reduced; homeless. in want &c. n.; needy, necessitous, distressed, pinched, straitened; put to one's shifts, put to one's last shifts; unable to keep the wolf from the door, unable to make both ends meet; embarrassed, under hatches; involved &c. (in debt) 806; insolvent &c. (not paying) 808. Adv. in forma pauperis[Lat]. Phr. zonam perdidit[Lat]; "a penniless lass wi' a lang pedigree" [Lady Nairne]; a pobreza no hay verguenza[Sp]; "he that is down can fall no lower" [Butler]; poca roba poco pensiero[It]; "steeped . . . in poverty to the very lips" [Othello]; "the short and simple annals of the poor" [Gray].

#805. Credit.— N. credit, trust, tick, score, tally, account.
letter of credit, circular note; duplicate; mortgage, lien, debenture, paper credit, floating capital; draft, lettre de creance[Fr][obs3], securities.
creditor, lender, lessor, mortgagee; dun; usurer.
credit account, line of credit, open line of credit.
credit card.
V. keep an account with, run up an account with; intrust, credit, accredit.
place to one's credit, credit to one's account, place to one's accountl!; give credit, take credit; fly a kitel!.
Adj. crediting, credited; accredited.
Adv. on credit &c. n.; on account; to the account of, to the credit of; a compte[Fr].
#806. Debt.— N. debt, obligation, liability, indebtment[obs3], debit, score.
bill; check; account (credit) 805.
arrears, deferred payment, deficit, default, insolvency &c. (nonpayment) 808; bad debt.
interest; premium; usance[obs3], usury; floating debt, floating capital.
debtor, debitor[obs3]; mortgagor; defaulter &c. 808; borrower.
V. be in debt &c. adj.; owe; incur a debt, contract a debt &c. n.; run up a bill, run up a score, run up an account; go on tick; borrow &c. 788; run into debt, get into debt, outrun the constable; run up debts, run up bills (spend) 809..
answer for, go bail for.
[notify a person of his indebtedness: ISA:written_communication] bill, charge.
Adj. indebted; liable, chargeable, answerable for.
in debt, in embarrassed circumstances, in difficulties; incumbered,

involved; involved in debt, plunged in debt, deep in debt, over one's head in debt, over head and ears in debt; deeply involved; fast tied up;

insolvent &c. (not paying) 808; minus, out of pocket.

unpaid; unrequited, unrewarded; owing, due, in arrear[obs3], outstanding; past due.

Phr. aes alienum debitorem leve gravius inimicum facit [obs3][Latin]; "neither a borrower nor a lender be" [Hamlet].

<— p. 268 —>

<— make salary separate —> #807. Payment.— N. payment, defrayment[obs3]; discharge; acquittance, quittance; settlement, clearance, liquidation, satisfaction, reckoning, arrangement. acknowledgment, release; receipt, receipt in full, receipt in full of all demands; voucher. salary, compensation, remuneration (reward) 973. repayment, reimbursement, retribution; pay &c.(reward) 973; money paid &c. (expenditure) 809. ready money &c. (cash) 800; stake, remittance, installment. payer, liquidator &c. 801. pay cash, pay cash on the barrelhead. V. pay, defray, make payment; paydown, pay on the nail, pay ready money, pay at sight, pay in advance; cash, honor a bill, acknowledge; redeem; pay in kind. pay one's way, pay one's shot, pay one's footing; pay the piper, pay sauce for all, pay costs; do the needful; shell out, fork out; cough up [coll.], fork over; come down with, come down with the dust; tickle the palm, grease the palm; expend &c. 809; put down, lay down. discharge, settle, quit, acquit oneself of; foot the bill; account with, reckon with, settle with, be even with, be quits with; strike a balance; settle accounts with, balance accounts with, square accounts with; quit scores; wipe off old scores, clear off old scores; satisfy; pay in full; satisfy all demands, pay in full of all demands; clear, liquidate; pay up, pay old debts. disgorge, make repayment; repay, refund, reimburse, retribute[obs3]; make compensation &c.30. pay by credit card, put it on the plastic. Adj. paying &c. paid &c. v.; owing nothing, out of debt, all straight; unowed[obs3], never indebted. Adv. to the tune of; on the nail, money down.

#808. Nonpayment — N. nonpayment; default, defalcation; protest, repudiation; application of the sponge!!; whitewashing.

insolvency, bankruptcy, failure; insufficiency &c. 640; run upon a bank; overdrawn account.

waste paper bonds; dishonored bills, protested bills; bogus check, bogus cheque, rubber check.

bankrupt, insolvent, debtor, lame duck, man of straw, welsher, stag, defaulter, levanter!!.

V. not pay &c. 807; fail, break, stop payment; become insolvent, become bankrupt; be gazetted.

protest, dishonor, repudiate, nullify, refuse payment.

pay under protest; button up one's pockets, draw the purse strings; apply the sponge; pay over the left shoulder, get whitewashed; swindle &c. 791; run up bills, fly kites.

Adj. not paying, non-paying, non-performing; in debt &c. 806; behindhand, in arrear[obs3], behind in payments, in arrears; beggared &c. (poor) 804; unable to make both ends meet, minus; worse than nothing; worthless.

insolvent, bankrupt, in the gazette, gazetted.

unpaid &c. (outstanding) 806; gratis &c. 815; unremunerated.

#809. Expenditure.— N. expenditure, money going out; out goings, out lay; expenses, disbursement; prime cost &c. (price) 812; circulation; run upon a bank.

payment &c.807[Money paid]; pay &c. (remuneration) 973; bribe &c. 973; fee, footing, garnish; subsidy; tribute; contingent, quota; donation &c.784.

pay in advance, earnest, handsel, deposit, installment.

investment; purchase &c. 795.

V. expend, spend; run through, get through; pay, disburse; ante, ante up; pony up* [U.S.]; open the purse strings, loose the purse strings, untie the purse strings; lay out, shell out*, fork out*, fork over; bleed; make up a sum, invest, sink money.

run up debts, run up bills (debt) 806.

fee &c. (reward) 973; pay one's way &c. (pay) 807; subscribe &c.
(give) 784; subsidize.
 Adj. expending, expended &c. v.; sumptuary.
 Phr. vectigalia nervos esse reipublicae [Lat][Cicero].
 #810. Receipt.— N. receipt, value received, money coming in; income,
incomings, innings, revenue, return, proceeds; gross receipts, net profit;
earnings &c. (gain) 775; accepta[obs3], avails.
 rent, rent roll; rental, rentage[obs3]; rack-rent.
 premium, bonus; sweepstakes, tontine.
 pension, annuity; jointure &c.(property) 780[obs3]; alimony, palimony
[coll.], pittance; emolument &c. (remuneration) 973.
 V. receive &c. 785; take money; draw from, derive from; acquire &c.
775; take &c. 789.
 bring in, yield, afford, pay, return; accrue &c. (be received from)
785.
 Adj. receiving, received &c. v.; profitable &c. (gainful) 775.
<— p. 269 —>

#811. Accounts.— N. accounts, accompts!!; commercial arithmetic, monetary arithmetic; statistics &c. (numeration)
85; money matters, finance, budget, bill, score, reckoning, account. books, account book, ledger; day book, cash
book, pass book; journal; debtor and creditor account, cash account, running account; account current; balance,
balance sheet; compte rendu[Fr], account settled, acquit, assets, expenditure, liabilities, outstanding accounts; profit
and loss account, profit and loss statement, receipts. bookkeeping, accounting, double entry bookkeeping, reckoning. audit. [person who keeps accounts] accountant, auditor, actuary, bookkeeper, bean counter [derogatory];
financier &c. 801; accounting party; chartered accountant, certified accountant; accounting firm, auditing firm. V.
keep accounts, enter, post, book, credit, debit, carry over; take stock; balance accounts, make up accounts, square
accounts, settle accounts, wind up accounts, cast up accounts; make accounts square, square accounts. bring to
book, tax, surcharge and falsify. audit, field audit; check the books, verify accounts. falsify an account, garble an
account, cook an account, cook the books, doctor an account. Adj. monetary &c.800; accountable, accounting.

<— tax, value and cost should have separate entries —> #812. Price.— N. price, amount, cost, expense, prime
cost, charge, figure; demand, damage; fare, hire, wages &c. (remuneration) 973; value &c. 812a. dues, duty, toll,
tax, impost, cess[obs3], sess[obs3], tallage[obs3], levy; abkari[obs3]; capitation tax, poll tax; doomage [obs3][U.S.],
likin[obs3]; gabel[obs3], gabelle[obs3]; gavel, octroi[obs3], custom, excise, assessment, benevolence, tithe, tenths,
exactment[obs3], ransom, salvage, tariff; brokerage, wharfage, freightage. bill &c. (account) 811; shot. V. bear a
price, set a price, fix a price; appraise, assess, doom [U.S.], price, charge, demand, ask, require, exact, run up;
distrain; run up a bill &c. (debt) 806; have one's price; liquidate. amount to, come to, mount up to; stand one in.
fetch, sell for, cost, bring in, yield, afford. Adj. priced &c. v.; to the tune of, ad valorem; dutiable; mercenary, venal.
Phr. no penny no paternoster[Lat]; point d'argent point de Suisse[Fr], no longer pipe no longer dance, no song no
supper, if you dance you have to pay the piper, you get what you pay for, there's no such thing as a free lunch. one
may have it for; a bon marche[Fr].

 #812a. Value [intrinsic worth] — N. {ant. to 812b} worth, rate,
value, intrinsic value, quality; par value.
 [estimated value] valuation, appraisal, assessment, appraisement.
 [value as estimated in a market] price current, market price,
quotation; fair price, going price; what it will fetch &c. v.; what the
market will bear.
 money's worth; penny &c. worth.
 cost (price) 812.
 V. value[transitive], esteem; appreciate.
 [estimate value] appraise, evaluate, assess.
 Adj. valuable, estimable; worthwhile; worthy, full of worth.
 precious (expensive) 814.
 Phr. worth the price; worth a king's ransom; accountants who know the
price of everything and the value of nothing.
 #812b. Worthlessness — N. {ant. to 812a} worthlessness,
valuelessness[obs3]; lack of value; uselessness.

[low value] cheapness, shoddiness; low quality, poor quality.

[worthless item] trash, garbage.

Adj. worthless, valueless; useless.

[of low value] cheap, shoddy; slapdash.

inexpensive &c. 815.

Phr. not worth the paper it's printed on, not worth a sou.

#813. Discount.— N. discount, abatement, concession, reduction, depreciation, allowance; qualification, set-off, drawback, poundage, agio[obs3], percentage; rebate, rebatement[obs3]; backwardation, contango[obs3]; salvage; tare and tret[obs3].

sale, bargain; half price; price war.

wholesale, wholesale price; dealer's price; trade price.

coupon, discount coupon, cents-off coupon; store coupon, manufacturer's coupon; double coupon discount, triple coupon discount.

V. discount, bate; abate, rebate; reduce, price down, mark down take off, allow, give, make allowance; tax.

Adj. discounting &c. v.

Adv. at a discount, below par; at wholesale; have a friend in the business.

#814. Dearness.— N. dearness &c. adj.; high price, famine price, fancy price; overcharge; extravagance; exorbitance, extortion; heavy pull upon the purse.

V. be dear &c. adj.; cost much, cost a pretty penny; rise in price, look up.

[demand a price in excess of value] overcharge, bleed, fleece, extort.

[pay a price in excess of value] pay too much, pay through the nose, pay too dear for one's whistle, pay top dollar.

Adj. dear; high, high priced; of great price, expensive, costly, precious; worth a Jew's eye!, dear bought.

at a premium.

not to be had, not to be had for love or money; beyond price, above price, priceless, of priceless value.

[priced in excess of value] unreasonable, extravagant, exorbitant, extortionate; overpriced, more than it's woth.

Adv. dear, dearly; at great cost, heavy cost; a grands frais[Fr].

Phr. prices looking up; le jeu ne vaut pas la chandelle[French]; le cout en ote le gout[Fr]; vel prece vel pretio[Lat][obs3]; too high a price to pay, not worth it.

<— p. 270 —>

#815. Cheapness.— N. cheapness, low price; depreciation; bargain; good penny &c. worth; snap [U.S.].

[Absence of charge] gratuity; free quarters, free seats, free admission, pass, free pass, free warren, give-away, freebee [coll.]; run of one's teeth; nominal price, peppercorn rent; labor of love.

drug in the market; deadhead[obs3].

V. be cheap &c. adj.; cost little; come down in price, fall in price.

buy for a mere nothing, buy for an old song; have one's money's worth.

Adj. cheap; low, low priced; moderate, reasonable; inexpensive, unexpensive[obs3]; well worth the money, worth the money; magnifique et pas cher[French]; good at the price, cheap at the price; dirt cheap, dog cheap; cheap, cheap as dirt, cheap and nasty; catchpenny; discounted &c. 813.

half-price, depreciated, unsalable.

gratuitous, gratis, free, for nothing; costless, expenseless[obs3]; without charge, not charged, untaxed; scotfree, shotfree[obs3], rent-free; free of cost, free of expense; honorary, unbought, unpaid.

Adv. for a mere song, for a song; at cost, at cost price, at prime cost, at a reduction; a bon marche[Fr].

#816. Liberality.— N. liberality, generosity, munificence; bounty, bounteousness, bountifulness; hospitality; charity &c. (beneficence) 906. V. be liberal &c.adj.; spend freely, bleed freely; shower down upon; open one's purse strings &c. (disburse) 809; spare no expense, give carte blanche[Fr]. Adj. liberal, free, generous; charitable &c. (beneficent) 906; hospitable; bountiful, bounteous; handsome; unsparing, ungrudging; unselfish; open handed, free handed, full handed; open hearted, large hearted, free hearted; munificent, princely. overpaid. Phr. "handsome is that handsome does" [Goldsmith].

#817. Economy.— N. economy, frugality; thrift, thriftiness; care, husbandry, good housewifery, savingness[obs3], retrenchment.

savings; prevention of waste, save-all; cheese parings and candle ends; parsimony &c. 819.

cost-cutting, cost control.

V. be economical &c. adj.; practice economy; economize, save; retrench, cut back expenses, cut expenses; cut one's coat according to one's cloth, make both ends meet, keep within compass, meet one's expenses, pay one's way, pay as you go; husband &c. (lay by) 636.

save money, invest money; put out to interest; provide for a rainy day, save for a rainy day, provide against a rainy day, save against a rainy day; feather one's nest; look after the main chance.

cut costs.

Adj. economical, frugal, careful, thrifty, saving, chary, spare, sparing; parsimonious &c.819.

underpaid.

Adv. sparingly &c. adj.; ne quid nimis[Lat].

Phr. adde parvum parvo magnus acervus erit[Latin]; magnum est vectigal parsimonia [Latin][Cicero].

#817a. Greed [excessive desire] — N. covetousness, ravenousness &c. adj.; venality, avidity, cupidity; acquisitiveness (acquisition) 775; desire &c. 865.

[greed for money or material things] greed, greediness, avarice, avidity, rapacity, extortion.

selfishness &c.943; auri sacra fames[Lat].

grasping, craving, canine appetite, rapacity.

V. covet, crave (desire) 865; grasp; exact, extort.

Adj. greedy, avaricious, covetous, acquisitive, grasping; rapacious; lickerish[obs3].

greedy as a hog; overeager; voracious; ravenous, ravenous as a wolf; openmouthed, extortionate, exacting, sordid!!, alieni appetens[Lat]; insatiable, insatiate; unquenchable, quenchless; omnivorous.

#818. Prodigality.— N. prodigality, prodigence!; unthriftiness[obs3], waste; profusion, profuseness; extravagance; squandering &c. v.; malversation. prodigal; spendthrift, waste thrift; losel[obs3], squanderer[obs3], locust; high roller* [U.S.]. V. be prodigal &c. adj.; squander, lavish, sow broadcast; pour forth like water; blow, blow in*; pay through the nose &c. (dear) 814; spill, waste, dissipate, exhaust, drain, eat out of house and home, overdraw, outrun the constable; run out, run through; misspend; throw good money after bad, throw the helve after the hatchet[obs3]; burn the candle at both ends; make ducks and drakes of one's money; fool away one's money, potter away one's money, muddle away one's money, fritter away one's money, throw away one's money, run through one's money; pour water into a sieve, kill the goose that lays the golden eggs; manger son ble en herbe[Fr]. Adj. prodigal, profuse, thriftless, unthrifty, improvident, wasteful, losel[obs3], extravagant, lavish, dissipated, overliberal; full-handed &c. (liberal) 816. penny wise and pound foolish. Adv. with an unsparing hand; money burning a hole in one's pocket. Phr. amor nummi [Latin]; facile largiri de alieno[Lat]; wie gewonnen so zerronnen [German]; les fous font les festins et les sages les mangent [French]; "spendthrift alike of money and of wit" [Cowper]; "squandering wealth was his peculiar art" [Dryden].

<— p. 271 —> <— separate greed, acquisitiveness => 817a from parsimony, frugality —>

#819. Parsimony.— N. parsimony, parcityl; parsimoniousness[obs3], stinginess &c. adj.; stint; illiberality, tenacity. avarice, greed &c. 817a. miser, niggard, churl, screw, skinflint, crib, codger, muckworm[obs3], scrimp, lickpenny[obs3], hunks, curmudgeon, Harpagon, harpy, extortioner, Jew, usurer; Hessian [U.S.]; pinch fist, pinch penny. V. be parsimonious &c. adj.; grudge, begrudge, stint, pinch, gripe, screw, dole out, hold back, withhold, starve, famish, live upon nothing, skin a flint. drive a bargain, drive a hard bargain; cheapen, beat down; stop one hole in a sieve; have an itching palm, grasp, grab. Adj. parsimonious, penurious, stingy, miserly, mean, shabby, peddling, scrubby, penny wise, near, niggardly, close; fast handed, close handed, strait handed; close fisted, hard fisted, tight fisted; tight, sparing; chary; grudging, griping &c. v.; illiberal, ungenerous, churlish, hidebound, sordid, mercenary, venal, covetous, usurious, avaricious, greedy, extortionate, rapacious. Adv. with a sparing hand. Phr. desunt inopioe multa avaritiae omnia [Latin][Syrus]; "hoards after hoards his rising raptures fill" [Goldsmith]; "the unsunn'd heaps of miser's treasures" [Milton].

<— p. 272 —>

%
CLASS VI
WORDS RELATION TO THE SENTIMENT AND MORAL POWERS
Section I. Affections in General %

#820. Affections. — N. affections, affect; character, qualities, disposition, nature, spirit, tone; temper, temperament; diathesis[obs3], idiosyncrasy; cast of mind, cast of soul, habit of mind, habit of soul, frame of mind, frame of soul; predilection, turn, natural turn of mind; bent, bias, predisposition, proneness, proclivity, propensity, propenseness[obs3], propension[obs3], propendencyl; vein, humor, mood, grain, mettle; sympathy &c. (love) 897. soul, heart, breast, bosom, inner man; heart's core, heart's strings, heart's blood; heart of hearts, bottom of one's heart, penetralia mentis[Lat]; secret and inmost recesses of the heart, cockles of one's heart; inmost heart, inmost soul; backbone. passion, pervading spirit; ruling passion, master passion; furore[obs3]; fullness of the heart, heyday of the blood, flesh and blood, flow of soul. energy, fervor, fire, force. V. have affections, possess affections &c. n.; be of a character &c. n.; be affected &c. adj.; breathe. Adj. affected, characterized, formed, molded, cast; attempered[obs3], tempered; framed; predisposed; prone, inclined; having a bias &c. n.; tinctured with, imbued with, penetrated with, eaten up with. inborn, inbred, ingrained; deep-rooted, ineffaceable, inveterate; pathoscopicl!; congenital, dyed in the wool, implanted by nature, inherent, in the grain. affective [obs3][med. and general]. Adv. in one's heart &c. n.; at heart; heart and soul &c. 821. Phr. "affection is a coal that must be cool'd else suffer'd it will set the heart on fire" [Venus and Adonis].

#821. Feeling. — N. feeling; suffering &c. v.; endurance, tolerance, sufferance, supportance[obs3], experience, response; sympathy &c. (love) 897; impression, inspiration, affection, sensation, emotion, pathos, deep sense. warmth, glow, unction, gusto, vehemence; fervor, fervency; heartiness, cordiality; earnestness, eagerness; empressement[Fr], gush, ardor, zeal, passion, enthusiasm, verve, furore[obs3], fanaticism; excitation of feeling &c. 824; fullness of the heart &c. (disposition) 820; passion &c. (state of excitability) 825; ecstasy &c. (pleasure) 827. blush, suffusion, flush; hectic; tingling, thrill, turn, shock; agitation &c. (irregular motion) 315; quiver, heaving, flutter, flurry, fluster, twitter, tremor; throb, throbbing; pulsation, palpitation, panting; trepidation, perturbation; ruffle, hurry of spirits, pother, stew, ferment; state of excitement. V. feel; receive an impression &c. n.; be impressed with &c. adj., entertain feeling, harbor feeling, cherish feeling &c. n. respond; catch the flame, catch the infection; enter the spirit of. bear, suffer, support, sustain, endure, thole [obs3][Scottish], aby[obs3]; abide &c. (be composed) 826; experience &c. (meet with) 151; taste, prove; labor under, smart under; bear the brunt of, brave, stand. swell, glow, warm, flush, blush, change color, mantle; turn color, turn pale, turn red, turn black in the face; tingle, thrill, heave, pant, throb, palpitate, go pitapat, tremble, quiver, flutter, twitter; shake &c. 315; be agitated, be excited &c. 824; look blue, look black; wince; draw a deep breath. impress &c. (excite the feelings) 824. Adj. feeling &c. v.; sentient; sensuous; sensorial, sensory; emotive, emotional; of feeling, with feeling &c. n. warm, quick, lively, smart, strong, sharp, acute, cutting, piercing, incisive; keen, keen as a razor; trenchant, pungent, racy, piquant, poignant, caustic. impressive, deep, profound, indelible; deep felt, home felt, heartfelt; swelling, soul-stirring, deep-mouthed, heart-expanding, electric, thrilling, rapturous, ecstatic. earnest, wistful, eager, breathless; fervent; fervid; gushing, passionate, warm-hearted, hearty, cordial, sincere, zealous, enthusiastic, glowing, ardent, burning, red-hot, fiery, flaming; boiling over. pervading, penetrating, absorbing; rabid, raving, feverish, fanatical, hysterical; impetuous &c. (excitable) 825. impressed with, moved with, touched with, affected with, penetrated with, seized with, imbued with &c. 82; devoured by; wrought up &c. (excited) 824; struck all of a heap; rapt; in a quiver &c. n.; enraptured &c. 829. Adv. heart and soul, from the bottom of one's heart, ab imo pectore[Lat], at heart, con amore[It], heartily, devoutly, over head and ears, head over heels. Phr. the heart big, the heart full, the heart swelling, the heart beating, the heart pulsating, the heart throbbing, the heart thumping, the heart beating high, the heart melting, the heart overflowing, the heart bursting, the heart breaking; the heart goes out, a heart as big as all outdoors (sympathy) 897.

<— p. 273 —>

#822. Sensibility. — N. sensibility, sensibleness, sensitiveness; moral sensibility; impressibility, affectibility[obs3]; susceptibleness, susceptibility, susceptivity[obs3]; mobility; vivacity, vivaciousness; tenderness, softness; sentimental, sentimentality; sentimentalism. excitability &c. 825; fastidiousness &c. 868; physical sensibility &c. 375. sore point, sore place; where the shoe pinches. V. be sensible &c. adj.; have a tender heart, have a warm heart, have a sensitive heart. take to heart, treasure up in the heart; shrink. "die of a rose in aromatic pain" [Pope]; touch to the quick; touch on the raw, touch a raw nerve. Adj. sensible, sensitive; impressible, impressionable; susceptive, susceptible; alive to, impassionable[obs3], gushing; warm hearted, tender hearted, soft hearted; tender as a chicken; soft, sentimental, romantic; enthusiastic, highflying[obs3], spirited, mettlesome, vivacious, lively, expressive, mobile, tremblingly alive; excitable &c. 825; oversensitive, without skin, thin-skinned; fastidious &c. 868. Adv. sensibly &c. adj; to the quick, to the inmost core. Phr. mens aequa in arduis[Lat]; pour salt in the wound.

#823. Insensibility. — N. insensibility, insensibleness[obs3]; moral insensibility; inertness, inertia; vis inertiae[Lat]; impassibility, impassibleness; inappetency[obs3], apathy, phlegm, dullness, hebetude[obs3], supineness, lukewarmness[obs3]. cold fit, cold blood, cold heart; coldness, coolness; frigidity, sang froid[Fr]; stoicism, imperturbation &c. (inexcitability) 826[obs3]; nonchalance, unconcern, dry eyes; insouciance &c. (indifference) 866; recklessness &c. 863; callousness; heart of stone, stock and stone, marble, deadness. torpor, torpidity; obstupefactionl, lethargy, coma, trance, vegetative state; sleep &c. 683; suspended animation; stupor, stupefaction; paralysis, palsy; numbness &c. (physical insensibility) 376. neutrality; quietism, vegetation. V. be insensible &c. adj.; have a rhinoceros hide; show insensibility &c. n.; not mind, not care, not be affected by; have no desire for &c. 866; have no interest in, feel no interest in, take no interest in; nil admirari[Lat]; not care a straw &c. (unimportance) 643 for; disregard &c. (neglect) 460; set at naught &c. (make light of) 483; turn a deaf ear to &c. (inattention) 458; vegetate. render insensible, render callous; blunt, obtund[obs3], numb, benumb, paralyze, deaden, hebetate[obs3], stun, stupefy; brutify[obs3]; brutalize; chloroform, anaesthetize[obs3], put under; assify[obs3]. inure; harden the heart; steel, caseharden, sear. Adj. insensible, unconscious; impassive, impassible; blind to, deaf to, dead to; unsusceptible, insusceptible; unimpressionable[obs3], unimpressible[obs3]; passionless, spiritless, heartless, soulless; unfeeling, unmoral. apathetic; leuco-l, phlegmatic; dull, frigid; cold blooded, cold hearted; cold as charity; flat, maudlin, obtuse, inert, supine, sluggish, torpid, torpedinous[obs3], torporific[obs3]; sleepy &c. (inactive) 683; languid, halfhearted, tame; numbed; comatose; anaesthetic &c. 376; stupefied, chloroformed, drugged, stoned; palsy-stricken. indifferent, lukewarm; careless, mindless, regardless; inattentive &c. 458; neglectful &c. 460; disregarding. unconcerned, nonchalant, pococurante[obs3], insouciant, sans souci[Fr]; unambitious &c. 866. unaffected, unruffled, unimpressed, uninspired, unexcited, unmoved, unstirred, untouched, unshocked[obs3], unstruck[obs3]; unblushing &c. (shameless) 885; unanimated; vegetative. callous, thick-skinned, hard-nosed, pachydermatous, impervious; hardened; inured, casehardened; steeled against, proof against; imperturbable &c. (inexcitable) 826[obs3]; unfelt. Adv. insensibly &c. adj.; aequo animo[Lat]; without being moved, without being touched, without being impressed; in cold blood; with dry eyes, with withers unwrung[obs3]. Phr. never mind; macht nichts [German], it is of no consequence &c. (unimportant) 643; it cannot be helped; nothing coming amiss; it is all the same to, it is all one to.

<— p. 274 —>

#824. Excitation. — N. excitation of feeling; mental excitement; suscitation[obs3], galvanism, stimulation, piquance, piquancy, provocation, inspiration, calling forth, infection; animation, agitation, perturbation; subjugation, fascination, intoxication; enravishment[obs3]; entrancement; pressure, tension, high pressure. unction, impressiveness &c. adj. trail of temper, casus belli[Lat]; irritation &c. (anger) 900; passion &c. (state of excitability) 825; thrill &c. (feeling) 821; repression of feeling &c. 826; sensationalism, yellow journalism. V. excite, affect, touch, move, impress, strike, interest, animate, inspire, impassion, smite, infect; stir the blood, fire the blood, warm the blood; set astir; wake, awake, awaken; call forth; evoke, provoke; raise up, summon up, call up, wake up, blow up, get up, light up; raise; get up the steam, rouse, arouse, stir; fire, kindle, enkindle, apply the torch, set on fire, inflame. stimulate; exsuscitatel; inspirit; spirit up, stir up, work up, pique; infuse life into, give new life to; bring new blood, introduce new blood; quicken; sharpen, whet; work upon &c. (incite) 615; hurry on, give a fillip, put on one's mettle. fan the fire, fan the flame; blow the coals, stir the embers; fan into a flame; foster, heat, warm, foment, raise to a fever heat; keep up, keep the pot boiling; revive, rekindle; rake up, rip up. stir the feelings, play on the feelings, come home to the feelings; touch a string, touch a chord, touch the soul, touch the heart; go to one's heart, penetrate, pierce, go through one, touch to the quick; possess the soul, pervade the soul, penetrate the soul, imbrue the soul, absorb the soul, affect the soul, disturb the soul. absorb, rivet the attention; sink into the mind, sink into the heart; prey on the mind, distract; intoxicate; overwhelm, overpower; bouleverser[Fr], upset, turn one's head. fascinate; enrapture &c. (give pleasure) 829. agitate, perturb, ruffle, fluster, shake, disturb, startle, shock, stagger; give one a shock, give one a turn; strike all of a heap; stun, astound, electrify, galvanize, petrify. irritate, sting; cut to the heart, cut to the quick; try one's temper; fool to the top of one's bent, pique; infuriate, madden, make one's blood boil; lash into fury &c. (wrath) 900. be excited &c. adj.; flush up, flare up; catch the infection; thrill &c. (feel) 821; mantle; work oneself up; seethe, boil, simmer, foam, fume, flame, rage, rave; run mad &c. (passion) 825. Adj. excited &c. v.; wrought up, up the qui vive[Fr], astir, sparkling; in a quiver &c. 821, in a fever, in a ferment, in a blaze, in a state of excitement; in hysterics; black in the face, overwrought, tense, taught, on a razor's edge; hot, red-hot, flushed, feverish; all of a twitter, in a pucker; with quivering lips, with tears in one's eyes. flaming; boiling over; ebullient, seething; foaming at the mouth; fuming, raging, carried away by passion, wild, raving, frantic, mad, distracted, beside oneself, out of one's wits, ready to burst, bouleverse[obs3], demoniacal. lost, eperdu[Fr], tempest-tossed; haggard; ready to sink. stung to the quick, up, on one's high ropes. exciting, absorbing, riveting, distracting &c. v.; impressive, warm, glowing, fervid, swelling, imposing, spirit-stirring, thrilling; high- wrought; soul-stirring, soul-subduing; heart-stirring, heart-swelling, heart-thrilling; agonizing &c. (painful) 830; telling, sensational, hysterical; overpowering, overwhelming; more than flesh and blood can bear; yellow. piquant &c. (pungent) 392; spicy, appetizing, provocative, provoquant[obs3], tantalizing. eager to go, anxious to go, chafing at the bit. Adv. till one is black in the face. Phr. the heart beating high, the heart going pitapat, the heart leaping into one's mouth; the blood being up, the blood boiling in one's veins; the eye glistening - "in a fine frenzy rolling"; the head turned; "when the going gets tough, the tough get going" [Richard Nixon].

<— p. 275 —>

#825. [Excess of sensitiveness] Excitability — N. excitability, impetuosity, vehemence; boisterousness &c. adj.; turbulence; impatience, intolerance, nonendurance[obs3]; irritability &c. (irascibility) 901; itching &c. (desire) 865; wincing; disquiet, disquietude; restlessness; fidgets, fidgetiness; agitation &c. (irregular motion) 315. trepidation, perturbation, ruffle, hurry, fuss, flurry; fluster, flutter; pother, stew, ferment; whirl; buck fever; hurry-skurry[obs3], thrill &c. (feeling) 821; state of excitement, fever of excitement; transport. passion, excitement, flush, heat; fever, heat; fire, flame, fume, blood boiling; tumult; effervescence, ebullition; boiling over; whiff, gust, story, tempest; scene, breaking out, burst, fit, paroxysm, explosion; outbreak, outburst; agony. violence &c. 173; fierceness &c. adj.; rage, fury, furor, furore[obs3], desperation, madness, distraction, raving, delirium; phrensy[obs3], frenzy, hysterics; intoxication; tearing passion, raging passion; anger &c. 900. fascination, infatuation, fanaticism; Quixotism, Quixotry; tete montee[Fr]. V. be impatient &c. adj.; not able to bear &c. 826; bear ill, wince, chafe, champ a bit; be in a stew &c. n.; be out of all patience, fidget, fuss, not have a wink of sleep; toss on one's pillow. lose one's temper &c. 900; break out, burst out, fly out; go off, fly off, fly off at a tangent, fly off the handle, lose one's cool [coll.]; explode, flare up, flame up, fire up, burst into a flame, take fire, fire, burn; boil, boil over; foam, fume, rage, rave, rant, tear; go wild, run wild, run mad, go into hysterics; run riot, run amuck; battre la campagne[Fr], faire le diable a quatre[Fr], play the deuce. Adj. excitable, easily excited, in an excitable state; high-strung; irritable &c. (irascible) 901; impatient, intolerant. feverish, febrile, hysterical; delirious, mad, moody, maggoty-headed. unquiet, mercurial, electric, galvanic, hasty, hurried, restless, fidgety, fussy; chafing &c. v. startlish[obs3], mettlesome, high-mettled[obs3], skittish. vehement, demonstrative, violent, wild, furious, fierce, fiery, hot- headed, madcap. overzealous, enthusiastic, impassioned, fanatical; rabid &c. (eager) 865. rampant, clamorous, uproarious, turbulent, tempestuous, tumultuary[obs3], boisterous. impulsive, impetuous, passionate; uncontrolled, uncontrollable; ungovernable, irrepressible, stanchless[obs3], inextinguishable, burning, simmering, volcanic, ready to burst forth, volatile. excited, exciting &c. 824. Int. pish! pshaw! Phr. noli me tangere[Lat]; "filled with fury, rapt, inspir'd" [Collins]; maggiore fretta minore atto[It].

<— p. 276 —>

#826. [Absence of excitability, or of excitement.] Inexcitability. — N. inexcitability[obs3], imperturbability, inirritability[obs3]; even temper, tranquil mind, dispassion; tolerance, patience, coolth [coll.]. passiveness &c. (physical inertness) 172; hebetude[obs3], hebetation[obs3]; impassibility &c. (insensibility) 823; stupefaction. coolness, calmness &c. adj.; composure, placidity, indisturbance[obs3], imperturbation[obs3], sang froid[Fr], tranquility, serenity; quiet, quietude; peace of mind, mental calmness. staidness &c. adj.; gravity, sobriety, Quakerism[obs3]; philosophy, equanimity, stoicism, command of temper; self-possession, self-control, self-command, self-restraint, ice water in one's veins; presence of mind. submission &c. 725; resignation; sufferance, supportance[obs3], endurance, longsufferance[obs3], forbearance; longanimity[obs3]; fortitude; patience of Job, patience "on a monument" [Twelfth Night], patience "sovereign o'er transmuted ill" [Johnson]; moderation; repression of feelings, subjugation of feeling; restraint &c. 751. tranquillization &c. (moderation) 174[obs3]. V. be composed &c. adj. laisser faire[Fr], laisser aller[Fr]; take things easily, take things as they come; take it easy, rub on, live and let live; take easily, take cooly[obs3], take in good part; aequam servare mentem [Latin]. bear the brunt, bear well; go through, support, endure, brave, disregard. tolerate, suffer, stand, bide; abide, aby[obs3]; bear with, put up with, take up with, abide with; acquiesce; submit &c. (yield) 725; submit with a good grace; resign oneself to, reconcile oneself to; brook, digest, eat, swallow, pocket, stomach. make light of, make the best of, make "a virtue of necessity" [Chaucer]; put a good face on, keep one's countenance; check &c. 751 check oneself. compose, appease &c. (moderate)174; propitiate; repress &c. (restrain) 751; render insensible &c. 823; overcome one's excitability, allay one's excitability, repress one's excitability &c. 825; master one's feelings. make oneself easy; make one's mind easy; set one's mind at ease, set one's mind at rest. calm down, cool down; gentle; thaw, grow cool. be borne, be endured; go down. Adj. inexcitable[obs3], unexcitable; imperturbable; unsusceptible &c. (insensible) 823; unpassionate[obs3], dispassionate; cold-blooded, irritable; enduring &c. v.; stoical, Platonic, philosophic, staid, stayed; sober, sober minded; grave; sober as a judge, grave as a judge; sedate, demure, cool-headed. easy-going, peaceful, placid, calm; quiet as a mouse; tranquil, serene; cool as a cucumber, cool as a custard; undemonstrative. temperate &c. (moderate) 174; composed, collected; unexcited, unstirred, unruffled, undisturbed, unperturbed, unim-passioned; unoffended[obs3]; unresisting. meek, tolerant; patient, patient as Job; submissive &c. 725; tame; content, resigned, chastened, subdued, lamblike[obs3]; gentle as a lamb; suaviter in modo[Lat]; mild as mothers milk; soft as peppermint; armed with patience, bearing with, clement, long-suffering. Adv. "like patience on a monument smiling at grief" [Twelfth Night]; aequo animo[Lat], in cold blood &c. 823; more in sorrow than in anger. Int. patience! and shuffle the cards. Phr. "cool calm and collected", keep calm in the midst of a storm; "adversity's sweet milk, philoso-phy" [Romeo and Juliet]; mens aequa in arduis philosophia stemma non inspecite [Lat][Seneca]; quo me cumque rapit tempestas deferor hospes [Lat][Horace]; "they also serve who only stand and wait" [Milton].

% Section II Personal Affections

1. Passive Affections %

#827. Pleasure. — N. pleasure, gratification, enjoyment, fruition; oblectation, delectation, delection[obs3]; relish, zest; gusto &c. (physical pleasure) 377; satisfaction &c. (content) 831; complacency. well-being; good &c. 618; snugness, comfort, ease; cushion &c. 215; sans souci[French:without worry], mind at ease. joy, gladness, delight, glee, cheer, sunshine; cheerfulness &c. 836. treat, refreshment; amusement &c. 840; luxury &c. 377. mens sana in corpore sano [Latin: a sound mind in a sound body][Juvenal]. happiness, felicity, bliss; beatitude, beautification; enchantment, transport, rapture, ravishment, ecstasy; summum bonum[Lat]; paradise, elysium &c. (heaven) 981; third heavenl!, seventh heaven, cloud nine; unalloyed happiness &c.; hedonics[obs3], hedonism. honeymoon; palmy days, halcyon days; golden age, golden time; Dixie, Dixie's land; Saturnia regna[Lat], Arcadia[obs3], Shangri-La, happy valley, Agapemone[obs3]. V. be pleased &c. 829; feel pleasure, experience pleasure &c. n.; joy; enjoy oneself, hug oneself; be in clover &c. 377, be in elysium &c. 981; tread on enchanted ground; fall into raptures, go into raptures. feel at home, breathe freely, bask in the sunshine. be pleased &c. 829 with; receive pleasure, derive pleasure &c. n. from; take pleasure &c. n. in; delight in, rejoice in, indulge in, luxuriate in; gloat over &c. (physical pleasure) 377; enjoy, relish, like; love &c. 897; take to, take a fancy to; have a liking for; enter into the spirit of. take in good part. treat oneself to, solace oneself with. Adj. pleased &c. 829; not sorry; glad, gladsome; pleased as Punch. happy, blest, blessed, blissful, beatified; happy as a clam at high water [U.S.], happy as a clam, happy as a king, happy as the day is long; thrice happy, ter quaterque beatus[Lat]; enjoying &c. v.; joyful &c. (in spirits) 836; hedonic[obs3]. in a blissful state, in paradise &c. 981, in raptures, in ecstasies, in a transport of delight. comfortable &c. (physical pleasure) 377; at ease; content &c. 831; sans souci[Fr]. overjoyed, entranced, enchanted; enraptures; enravished[obs3]; transported; fascinated, captivated. with a joyful face, with sparkling eyes. pleasing &c. 829; ecstatic, beatic[obs3]; painless, unalloyed, without alloy, cloudless. Adv. happily &c. adj.; with pleasure &c. (willing-fully) 602[obs3]; with glee &c. n.. Phr. one's heart leaping with joy. "a wilderness of sweets" [P.L.]; "I wish you all the joy that you can wish" [M. of Venice]; jour de ma vie; "joy ruled the day and love the night" [Dryden]; "joys season'd high and tasting strong of guilt" [Young]; "oh happiness, our being's end and aim!" [Pope]; "there is a pleasure that is born of pain" [O Meridith]; "throned on highest bliss" [P.L.]; vedi Napoli e poi muori[It]; zwischen Freud und Leid ist die Brucke nicht weit [German: the bridge between joy and sorrow is not wide].

<— p. 277 —>

#828. Pain. — N. mental suffering, pain, dolor; suffering, sufferance; ache, smart &c. (physical pain) 378; passion. displeasure, dissatisfaction, discomfort, discomposure, disquiet; malaise; inquietude, uneasiness, vexation of spirit; taking; discontent &c. 832. dejection &c. 837; weariness &c. 841; anhedonia[obs3]. annoyance, irritation, worry, infliction, visitation; plague, bore; bother, botheration; stew, vexation, mortification, chagrin, esclandre[Fr]; mauvais quart d'heur[Fr]. care, anxiety, solicitude, trouble, trial, ordeal, fiery ordeal, shock, blow, cark[obs3], dole, fret, burden, load. concern, grief, sorrow, distress, affliction, woe, bitterness, heartache; carking cares; heavy heart, aching heart, bleeding heart, broken heart; heavy affliction, gnawing grief. unhappiness, infelicity, misery, tribulation, wretchedness, desolation; despair &c. 859; extremity, prostration, depth of misery. nightmare, ephialtes[obs3], incubus. pang, anguish, agony; torture, torment; purgatory &c. (hell) 982. hell upon earth; iron age, reign of terror; slough of despond &c. (adversity) 735; peck of troubles; "ills that flesh is heir to" &c. (evil) 619[Hamlet]; miseries of human life; "unkindest cut of all" [Julius Caesar]. sufferer, victim, prey, martyr, object of compassion, wretch, shorn lamb. V. feel pain, suffer pain, experience pain, undergo pain, bear pain, endure pain &c. n., smart, ache &c. (physical pain) 378; suffer, bleed, ail; be the victim of. labor under afflictions; bear the cross; quaff the bitter cup, have a bad time of it; fall on evil days &c. (adversity) 735; go hard with, come to grief, fall a sacrifice to, drain the cup of misery to the dregs, "sup full of horrors" [Macbeth]. sit on thorns, be on pins and needles, wince, fret, chafe, worry oneself, be in a taking, fret and fume; take on, take to heart; cark[obs3]. grieve; mourn &c. (lament) 839; yearn, repine, pine, droop, languish, sink; give way; despair &c. 859; break one's heart; weigh upon the heart &c. (inflict pain) 830. Adj. in pain, in a state of pain, full of pain &c. n.; suffering &c. v.; pained, afflicted, worried, displeased &c. 830; aching, griped, sore &c. (physical pain) 378; on the rack, in limbo; between hawk and buzzard. uncomfortable, uneasy; ill at ease; in a taking, in a way; disturbed; discontented &c. 832; out of humor &c. 901a; weary &c. 841. heavy laden, stricken, crushed, a prey to, victimized, ill-used. unfortunate &c. (hapless) 735; to be pitied, doomed, devoted, accursed, undone, lost, stranded; fey. unhappy, infelicitous, poor, wretched, miserable, woe-begone; cheerless &c. (dejected) 837; careworn. concerned, sorry; sorrowing, sorrowful; cut up, chagrined, horrified, horror-stricken; in grief, plunged in grief, a prey to grief &c. n.; in tears &c. (lamenting) 839; steeped to the lips in misery; heart-stricken, heart-broken, heart-scalded; broken-hearted; in despair &c. 859. Phr. "the iron entered into our soul"; haeret lateri lethalis arundo [Lat][Vergil]; one's heart bleeding; "down, thou climbing sorrow" [Lear]; "mirth cannot move a soul in agony" [Love's Labor's Lost]; nessun maggior dolere che ricordarsi del tempo felice nella miseria [It]; "sorrow's crown of sorrow is remembering happier things" [Tennyson]; "the Niobe of Nations" [Byron].

<— p. 278 —>

#829. [Capability of giving pleasure; cause or source of pleasure.] Pleasurableness. — N. pleasurableness, pleas-antness, agreeableness &c. adj.; pleasure giving, jucundity[obs3], delectability; amusement &c. 840. attraction &c. (motive) 615; attractiveness, attractability[obs3]; invitingness &c. adj[obs3].; harm, fascination, enchantment, witchery, seduction, winning ways, amenity, amiability; winsomeness. loveliness &c. (beauty) 845; sunny side, bright side; sweets &c. (sugar) 396; goodness &c. 648; manna in the wilderness, land flowing with milk and honey; bittersweet; fair weather. treat; regale &c. (physical pleasure) 377; dainty; titbit[obs3], tidbit; nuts, sauce piquante[Fr]. V. cause pleasure, produce pleasure, create pleasure, give pleasure, afford pleasure, procure pleasure, offer pleasure, present pleasure, yield pleasure &c. 827. please, charm, delight, becharm[obs3], imparadise[obs3]; gladden &c. (make cheerful) 836; take, captivate, fascinate; enchant, entrance, enrapture, transport, bewitch; enravish[obs3]. bless, beatify; satisfy; gratify, desire; &c. 865; slake, satiate, quench; indulge, humor, flatter, tickle; tickle the palate &c. (savory) 394; regale, refresh; enliven; treat; amuse &c. 840; take one's fancy, tickle one's fancy, hit one's fancy; meet one's wishes; win the heart, gladden the heart, rejoice the heart, warm the cockles of the heart; do one's heart good. attract, allure &c. (move) 615; stimulate &c. (excite) 824; interest. make things pleasant, popularize, gild the pill, sugar-coat the pill, , sweeten. Adj. causing pleasure &c. v.; laeticant[obs3]; pleasure-giving, pleasing, pleasant, pleasurable; agreeable; grateful, gratifying; leefl, lief, acceptable; welcome, welcome as the roses in May; welcomed; favorite; to one's taste, to one's mind, to one's liking; satisfactory &c. (good) 648. refresh-ing; comfortable; cordial; genial; glad, gladsome; sweet, delectable, nice, dainty; delicate, delicious; dulcet; luscious &c. 396; palatable &c. 394; luxurious, voluptuous; sensual &c. 377. [of people] attractive &c. 615; inviting, prepos-sessing, engaging; winning, winsome; taking, fascinating, captivating, killing; seducing, seductive; heart-robbing, alluring, enticing; appetizing &c. (exciting) 824; cheering &c. 836; bewitching; enchanting, entrancing, enravishing[obs3]. charming; delightful, felicitous, exquisite; lovely &c. (beautiful) 845; ravishing, rapturous; heartfelt, thrilling, ecstatic; beatic[obs3]; beatific; seraphic; empyrean; elysian &c. (heavenly) 981. palmy, halcyon, Saturnian. Phr. decies repetita placebit[Lat]; "charms strike the sight but merit wins the soul" [Pope]; "sweetness and light" [Swift]; beauty is only skin deep.

<— p. 279 —>

#830. [Capability of giving pain; cause or source of pain]. Painfulness. — N. painfulness &c. adj.; trouble, care &c. (pain) 828; trial; affliction, infliction; blow, stroke, burden, load, curse; bitter pill, bitter draught; waters of bitterness. annoyance, grievance, nuisance, vexation, mortification, sickener[obs3]; bore, bother, pother, hot water, "sea of troubles" [Hamlet], hornet's nest, plague, pest. cancer, ulcer, sting, thorn; canker &c. (bane) 663; scorpion &c. (evil doer) 913; dagger &c. (arms) 727; scourge &c. (instrument of punishment) 975; carking care, canker worm of care. mishap, misfortune &c. (adversity) 735; desagrement[Fr], esclandre[Fr], rub. source of irritation, source of annoyance; wound, open sore; sore subject, skeleton in the closet; thorn in the flesh, thorn in one's side; where the shoe pinches, gall and wormwood. sorry sight, heavy news, provocation; affront &c. 929; "head and front of one's offending" [Othello]. infestation, molestation; malignity &c. (malevolence) 907. V. cause pain, occasion pain, give pain, bring pain, induce pain, produce pain, create pain, inflict pain &c. 828; pain, hurt, wound. pinch, prick, gripe &c. (physical pain) 378; pierce, lancinate[obs3], cut. hurt the feelings, wound the feelings, grate upon the feelings, grate upon the nerves, jar upon the feelings; wring the heart, pierce the heart, lacerate the heart, break the heart, rend the heart; make the heart bleed; tear the heart strings, rend the heart strings; draw tears from the eyes. sadden; make unhappy &c. 828; plunge into sorrow, grieve, fash[obs3], afflict, distress; cut up, cut to the heart. displease, annoy, incommode, discompose, trouble, disquiet; faze, feaze[obs3], feeze (U[obs3].S.); disturb, cross, perplex, molest, tease, tire, irk, vex, mortify, wherretl, worry, plague, bother, pester, bore, pother, harass, harry, badger, heckle, bait, beset, infest, persecute, importune. wring, harrow, torment, torture; bullyrag; put to the rack, put to the question; break on the wheel, rack, scarify; cruciate[obs3], crucify; convulse, agonize; barb the dart; plant a dagger in the breast, plant a thorn in one's side. irritate, provoke, sting, nettle, try the patience, pique, fret, rile, tweak the nose, chafe, gall; sting to the quick, wound to the quick, cut to the quick; aggrieve, affront, enchafe[obs3], enrage, ruffle, sour the temper; give offense &c. (resentment) 900. maltreat, bite, snap at, assail; smite &c. (punish) 972. sicken, disgust, revolt, nauseate, disenchant, repel, offend, shock, stink in the nostrils; go against the stomach, turn the stomach; make one sick, set the teeth on edge, go against the grain, grate on the ear; stick in one's throat, stick in one's gizzard; rankle, gnaw, corrode, horrify, appal[obs3], appall, freeze the blood; make the flesh creep, make the hair stand on end; make the blood curdle, make the blood run cold; make one shudder. haunt the memory; weigh on the heart, prey on the heart, weigh on the mind, prey on the mind, weigh on the spirits, prey on the spirits; bring one's gray hairs with sorrow to the grave; add a nail to one's coffin. Adj. causing pain, hurting &c. v.; hurtful &c. (bad) 649; painful; dolorific[obs3], dolorous; unpleasant; unpleasing, displeasing; disagreeable, unpalatable, bitter, distasteful; uninviting; unwelcome; undesirable, undesired; obnoxious; unacceptable, unpopular, thankless. unsatisfactory, untoward, unlucky, uncomfortable. distressing; afflicting, afflictive; joyless, cheerless, comfortless; dismal, disheartening; depressing, depressive; dreary, melancholy, grievous, piteous; woeful, rueful, mournful, deplorable, pitiable, lamentable; sad, affecting, touching, pathetic. irritating, provoking, stinging, annoying, aggravating, mortifying, galling; unaccommodating, invidious, vexatious; troublesome, tiresome, irksome, wearisome; plaguing, plaguy[obs3]; awkward. importunate; teasing, pestering, bothering, harassing, worrying, tormenting, carking. intolerable, insufferable, insupportable; unbearable, unendurable; past bearing; not to be borne, not to be endured; more than flesh and blood can bear; enough to drive one mad, enough to provoke a saint, enough to make a parson swear, enough to gag a maggot. shocking, terrific, grim, appalling, crushing; dreadful, fearful, frightful; thrilling, tremendous, dire; heart-breaking, heart-rending, heart-wounding, heart-corroding, heart-sickening; harrowing, rending. odious, hateful, execrable, repulsive, repellent, abhorrent; horrid, horrible, horrific, horrifying; offensive. nauseous, nauseating; disgusting, sickening, revolting; nasty; loathsome, loathful[obs3]; fulsome; vile &c. (bad) 649; hideous &c. 846. sharp, acute, sore, severe, grave, hard, harsh, cruel, biting, caustic; cutting, corroding, consuming, racking, excruciating, searching, grinding, grating, agonizing; envenomed; catheretic[obs3], pyrotic[Med]. ruinous, disastrous, calamitous, tragical; desolating, withering; burdensome, onerous, oppressive; cumbrous, cumbersome. Adv. painfully &c. adj.; with pain &c. 828; deuced. Int. hinc illae lachrymae[Lat]! Phr. surgit amari aliquid[Lat][obs3]; the place being too hot to hold one; the iron entering into the soul; "he jests at scars that never felt a wound" [Romeo and Juliet]; "I must be cruel only to be kind" [Hamlet]; "what deep wounds ever closed without a scar?" [Byron].

<— p. 280 —>

#831. Content. — N. content, contentment, contentedness; complacency, satisfaction, entire satisfaction, ease, heart's ease, peace of mind; serenity &c. 826; cheerfulness &c. 836; ray of comfort; comfort &c. (well- being) 827. reconciliation; resignation &c. (patience) 826. [person who is contented] waiter on Providence. V. be content &c. adj.; rest satisfied, rest and be thankful; take the good the gods provide, let well alone, let well enough alone, feel oneself at home, hug oneself, lay the flattering unction to one's soul. take up with, take in good part; accept, tolerate; consent &c. 762; acquiesce, assent &c. 488; be reconciled to, make one's peace with; get over it; take heart, take comfort; put up with &c. (bear) 826. render content &c. adj.; set at ease, comfort; set one's heart at ease, set one's mind at ease, set one's heart at rest, set one's mind at rest; speak peace; conciliate, reconcile, win over, propitiate, disarm, beguile; content, satisfy; gratify &c. 829. be tolerated &c. 826; go down, go down well, go down with; do; be OK. Adj. content, contented; satisfied &c. v.; at ease, at one's ease, at home; with the mind at ease, sans souci[Fr], sine cura[Lat], easygoing, not particular; conciliatory; unrepining[obs3], of good comfort; resigned &c. (patient) 826; cheerful &c. 836. unafflicted, unvexed[obs3], unmolested, unplagued[obs3]; serene &c. 826; at rest, snug, comfortable; in one's element. satisfactory, tolerable, good enough, OK, all right, acceptable. Adv. contently[obs3], contentedly, to one's heart's content; a la bonne heure[Fr]; all for the best. Int. amen &c. (assent) 488; very well, all the better, so much the better, well and good; it will do, that will do; it cannot be helped. Phr. nothing comes amiss. "a heart with room for every joy" [Bailey]; ich habe genossen das irdische Gluck ich habe gelebt und geliebet [Ger] [Schiller]; "nor cast one longing lingering look behind" [Gray]; "shut up in measureless content" [Macbeth]; "sweet are the thoughts that savor of content" [R. Greene]; "their wants but few their wishes all confined" [Goldsmith]; might as well relax and enjoy it.

#832. Discontent. — N. discontent, discontentment; dissatisfaction; dissent &c. 489. disappointment, mortification; cold comfort; regret &c. 833; repining, taking on &c. v.; heart-burning, heart-grief; querulousness &c. (lamentation) 839; hypercriticism. inquietude, vexation of spirit, soreness; worry, concern, fear &c. 860. [person who is discontented] malcontent, grumbler, growler, croaker, dissident, dissenter, laudator temporis acti[Lat]; censurer, complainer, fault-finder, murmurer[obs3]. cave of Adullam[obs3], indignation meeting, "winter of our discontent" [Henry VI]; "with what I most enjoy contented least" [Shakespeare]. V. be discontented &c. adj.; quarrel with one's bread and butter; repine; regret &c. 833; wish one at the bottom of the Red Sea; take on, take to heart; shrug the shoulders; make a wry face, pull a long face; knit one's brows; look blue, look black, look black as thunder, look blank, look glum. take in bad part, take ill; fret, chafe, make a piece of work[Fr]; grumble, croak; lament &c. 839. cause discontent &c. n.; dissatisfy, disappoint, mortify, put out, disconcert; cut up; dishearten. Adj. discontented; dissatisfied &c. v.; unsatisfied, ungratified; dissident; dissentient &c. 489; malcontent, malcontented, exigent, exacting, hypercritical. repining &c. v.; regretful &c. 833; down in the mouth &c. (dejected) 837. in high dudgeon, in a fume, in the sulks, in the dumps, in bad humor; glum, sulky; sour as a crab; soured, sore; out of humor, out of temper. disappointing &c. v.; unsatisfactory. frustrated (failure) 732. Int. so much the worse! Phr. that won't do, that will never do, it will never do; curtae nescio quid semper abest rei [Lat][Horace]; ne Jupiter Quidem omnibus placet[Lat][obs3]; "poor in abundance, famished at a feast" [Young].

#833. Regret. — N. regret, repining; homesickness, nostalgia; mal du pays, maladie[Fr]; lamentation &c.. 839; penitence &c. 950.
  bitterness, heartburning[obs3].
  recrimination (accusation) 938.
  laudator temporis acti &c. (discontent) 832[Lat].
  V. regret, deplore; bewail &c. (lament) 839; repine, cast a longing lingering look behind; rue, rue the day; repent &c. 950; infandum renovare dolorem [Lat].
  prey on the mind, weigh on the mind, have a weight on the mind; leave an aching void.
  Adj. regretting &c. v.; regretful; homesick.
  regretted &c. v.; much to be regretted, regrettable; lamentable &c. (bad) 649.
  Adv. regrettably, unfortunately; most unfortunately.
  Int. alas!; what a pity! hang it!
  Phr. 'tis pity, 'tis too true; "sigh'd and look'd and sigh'd again" [Dryden]; "I'm sorry.".
<— p. 281 —>

#834. Relief. — N. relief; deliverance; refreshment &c. 689; easement, softening, alleviation, mitigation, palliation, soothing, lullaby.
  solace, consolation, comfort, encouragement.
  lenitive, restorative &c. (remedy) 662; cushion &c. 215; crumb of comfort, balm in Gilead.
  V. relieve, ease, alleviate, mitigate, palliate, soothe; salve; soften, soften down; foment, stupe[obs3], poultice; assuage, allay.
  cheer, comfort, console; enliven; encourage, bear up, pat on the back, give comfort, set at ease; gladden the heart, cheer the heart; inspirit, invigorate.
  remedy; cure &c. (restore) 660; refresh; pour balm into, pour oil on.
  smooth the ruffled brow of care, temper the wind to the shorn lamb, lay the flattering unction to one's soul.
  disburden &c. (free) 705; take a load off one's chest, get a load off one's chest, take off a load of care.
  be relieved; breathe more freely, draw a long breath; take comfort;

dry the tears, dry the eyes, wipe the tears, wipe the eyes.

Adj. relieving &c. v.; consolatory, soothing; assuaging, assuasive[obs3]; balmy, balsamic; lenitive, palliative; anodyne &c. (remedial) 662; curative &c. 660.

Phr. "here comes a man of comfort" [Measure for Measure].

#835. Aggravation. — N. aggravation, worsening, heightening; exacerbation; exasperation; overestimation &c. 482; exaggeration &c. 549.

V. aggravate, render worse, heighten, embitter, sour; exacerbate; exasperate, envenom; enrage, provoke, tease.

add fuel to the fire, add fuel to the flame; fan the flame &c. (excite) 824; go from bad to worse &c. (deteriorate) 659.

Adj. aggravated &c. v.; worse, unrelieved; aggravable[obs3]; aggravating &c. v.

Adv. out of the frying pan into the fire, from bad to worse, worse and worse.

Int. so much the worse!

#836. Cheerfulness. — N. cheerfulness &c. adj.; geniality, gayety, l'allegro[Fr], cheer, good humor, spirits; high spirits, animal spirits, flow of spirits; glee, high glee, light heart; sunshine of the mind, sunshine of the breast; gaiete de coeur[Fr], bon naturel[Fr]. liveliness &c. adj.; life, alacrity, vivacity, animation, allegresse[obs3]; jocundity, joviality, jollity; levity; jocularity &c. (wit) 842. mirth, merriment, hilarity, exhilaration; laughter &c. 838; merrymaking &c. (amusement) 840; heyday, rejoicing &c. 838; marriage bell. nepenthe, Euphrosyne[obs3], sweet forgetfulness. optimism &c. (hopefulness) 858; self complacency; hedonics[obs3], hedonism. V. be cheerful &c. adj.; have the mind at ease, smile, put a good face upon, keep up one's spirits; view the bright side of the picture, view things en couleur de rose[Fr]; ridentem dicere verum[Lat], cheer up, brighten up, light up, bear up; chirp, take heart, cast away care, drive dull care away, perk up. keep a stiff upper lip. rejoice &c. 838; carol, chirrup, lilt; frisk, rollick, give a loose to mirth. cheer, enliven, elate, exhilarate, gladden, inspirit, animate, raise the spirits, inspire; perk up; put in good humor; cheer the heart, rejoice the heart; delight &c. (give pleasure) 829. Adj. cheerful; happy &c. 827; cheery, cheerly[obs3]; of good cheer, smiling; blithe; in spirits, in good spirits; breezy, bully, chipper [U.S.]; in high spirits, in high feather; happy as the day is long, happy as a king; gay as a lark; allegro; debonair; light, lightsome, light hearted; buoyant, debonnaire, bright, free and easy, airy; janty[obs3], jaunty, canty[obs3]; hedonic[obs3]; riant[obs3]; sprightly, sprightful[obs3]; spry; spirited, spiritful[obs3]; lively, animated, vivacious; brisk as a bee; sparklinly as a thrush, jolly as a sandboy[obs3]; blithesome; gleeful, gleesome[obs3]; hilarious, rattling. winsome, bonny, hearty, buxom. playful, playsome[obs3]; folatre[Fr], playful as a kitten, tricksy[obs3], frisky, frolicsome; gamesome; jocose, jocular, waggish; mirth loving, laughter-loving; mirthful, rollicking. elate, elated; exulting, jubilant, flushed; rejoicing &c. 838. cock-a- hoop. cheering, inspiriting, exhilarating; cardiac, cardiacal[obs3]; pleasing &c. 829; palmy. Adv. cheerfully &c. adj. Int. never say die! come! cheer up! hurrah! &c. 838; "hence loathed melancholy!" begone dull care! away with melancholy! Phr. "a merry heart goes all the day" [A winter's Tale]; "as merry as the day is long" [Much Ado]; ride si sapis [Lat][Martial].

<— p. 282 —>

#837. Dejection. — N. dejection; dejectedness &c. adj.; depression, prosternationl; lowness of spirits, depression of spirits; weight on the spirits, oppression on the spirits, damp on the spirits; low spirits, bad spirits, drooping spirits, depressed spirits; heart sinking; heaviness of heart, failure of heart. heaviness &c. adj.; infestivity[obs3], gloom; weariness &c. 841; taedium vitae, disgust of life; mal du pays &c. (regret) 833; anhedonia[obs3]. melancholy; sadness &c. adj.; il penseroso[It], melancholia, dismals[obs3], blues, lachrymals[obs3], mumps[obs3], dumps, blue devils, doldrums; vapors, megrims, spleen, horrors, hypochondriasis[Med], pessimism; la maladie sans maladie [Fr]; despondency, slough of Despond; disconsolateness &c. adj.; hope deferred, blank despondency; voiceless woe. prostration of soul; broken heart; despair &c. 859; cave of despair, cave of Trophonius demureness &c. adj.; gravity, solemnity; long face, grave face. hypochondriac, seek sorrow, self-tormentor, heautontimorumenos[obs3], malade imaginaire[Fr], medecin tant pis[Fr]; croaker, pessimist; mope, mopus[obs3]. [Cause of dejection] affliction &c. 830; sorry sight; memento mori[Lat]; damper, wet blanket, Job's comforter. V. be dejected &c. adj.; grieve; mourn &c. (lament) 839; take on, give way, lose heart, despond, droop, sink. lower, look downcast, frown, pout; hang down the head; pull a long face, make a long face; laugh on the wrong side of the mouth; grin a ghastly smile; look blue, look like a drowned man; lay to heart, take to heart. mope, brood over; fret; sulk; pine, pine away; yearn; repine &c. (regret) 833; despair &c. 859. refrain from laughter, keep one's countenance; be grave, look grave &c. adj.; repress a smile. depress; discourage, dishearten; dispirit; damp, dull, deject, lower, sink, dash, knock down, unman, prostrate, break one's heart; frown upon; cast a gloom, cast a shade on; sadden; damp one's hopes, dash one's hopes, wither one's hopes; weigh on the mind, lie heavy on the mind, prey on the mind, weigh on the spirits, lie heavy on the spirits, prey on the spirits; damp the spirits, depress the spirits. Adj. cheerless, joyless, spiritless; uncheerful, uncheery[obs3]; unlively[obs3]; unhappy &c. 828; melancholy, dismal, somber, dark, gloomy, triste[Fr], clouded, murky, lowering, frowning, lugubrious, funereal, mournful, lamentable, dreadful. dreary, flat; dull, dull as a beetle, dull as ditchwater[obs3]; depressing &c. v. "melancholy as a gib cat"; oppressed with melancholy, a prey to melancholy; downcast, downhearted; down in the mouth, down in one's luck; heavy-hearted; in the dumps, down in the dumps, in the suds, in the sulks, in the doldrums; in doleful dumps, in bad humor; sullen; mumpish[obs3], dumpish, mopish[obs3], moping; moody, glum; sulky &c. (discontented) 832; out of sorts, out of humor, out of heart, out of spirits; ill at ease, low spirited, in low spirits, a cup too low; weary &c. 841; discouraged, disheartened; desponding; chapfallen[obs3], chopfallen[obs3], jaw fallen, crest fallen. sad, pensive, penseroso[It], tristful[obs3]; dolesome[obs3], doleful; woebegone; lacrymose, lachrymose, in tears, melancholic, hypped[obs3], hypochondriacal, bilious, jaundiced, atrabilious[obs3], saturnine, splenetic; lackadaisical. serious, sedate, staid, stayed; grave as a judge, grave as an undertaker, grave as a mustard pot; sober, sober as a judge, solemn, demure; grim; grim-faced, grim-visaged; rueful, wan, long-faced. disconsolate; unconsolable, inconsolable; forlorn, comfortless, desolate, desole[Fr], sick at heart; soul sick, heart sick; au desespoir[Fr]; in despair &c. 859; lost. overcome; broken down, borne down, bowed down; heartstricken &c (mental suffering) 828[obs3]; cut up, dashed, sunk; unnerved, unmanned; down fallen, downtrodden; broken-hearted; careworn. Adv. with a long face, with tears in one's eyes; sadly &c. adj. Phr. the countenance falling; the heart failing, the heart sinking within one; "a plague of sighing and grief" [Henry IV]; "thick-ey'd musing and curs'd melancholy" [Henry IV]; "the sickening pang of hope deferred" [Scott].

<— p. 283 —>

#838. [Expression of pleasure.] Rejoicing. — N. rejoicing, exultation, triumph, jubilation, heyday, flush, revelling; merrymaking &c. (amusement) 840; jubilee &c. (celebration) 883; paean, Te Deum &c. (thanksgiving) 990[Lat]; congratulation &c. 896.
   smile, simper, smirk, grin; broad grin, sardonic grin.
   laughter (amusement) 840.
   risibility; derision &c. 856.
   Momus; Democritus the Abderite[obs3]; rollicker[obs3].
   V. rejoice, thank one's stars, bless one's stars; congratulate oneself, hug oneself; rub one's hands, clap one's hands; smack the lips, fling up one's cap; dance, skip; sing, carol, chirrup, chirp; hurrah; cry for joy, jump for joy, leap with joy; exult &c. (boast) 884; triumph; hold jubilee &c. (celebrate) 883; make merry &c. (sport) 840.
   laugh, raise laughter &c. (amuse) 840.
   Adj. rejoicing &c. v.; jubilant, exultant, triumphant; flushed, elated, pleased, delighted, tickled pink.
   amused &c. 840; cheerful &c. 836.
   laughable &c. (ludicrous) 853.
   Int. hurrah! Huzza! aha[obs3]! hail! tolderolloll[obs3]! Heaven be praised! io triumphe[obs3]! tant mieux[Fr]! so much the better.
   Phr. the heart leaping with joy; ce n'est pas etre bien aise que de rire[Fr]; "Laughter holding both his sides" [Milton]; "le roi est mort, vive le roi"; "with his eyes in flood with laughter" [Cymbeline].
#839. [Expression of pain.] Lamentation. — N. lament, lamentation; wail, complaint, plaint, murmur, mutter, grumble, groan, moan, whine, whimper, sob, sigh, suspiration, heaving, deep sigh. cry &c. (vociferation) 411; scream, howl; outcry, wail of woe, ululation; frown, scowl. tear; weeping &c. v.; flood of tears, fit of crying, lacrimation, lachrymation[obs3], melting mood, weeping and gnashing of teeth. plaintiveness &c. adj.; languishment[obs3]; condolence &c. 915. mourning, weeds, willow, cypress, crape, deep mourning; sackcloth and ashes; lachrymatory[obs3]; knell &c. 363; deep death song, dirge, coronach[obs3], nenia[obs3], requiem, elegy, epicedium[obs3]; threne[obs3]; monody, threnody; jeremiad, jeremiadel!; ullalulla[obs3]. mourner; grumbler &c. (discontent) 832; Noobe; Heraclitus. V. lament, mourn, deplore, grieve, weep over; bewail, bemoan; condole with &c. 915; fret &c. (suffer) 828; wear mourning, go into mourning, put on mourning; wear the willow, wear sackcloth and ashes; infandum renovare dolorem &c. (regret) 833[Lat][Vergil]; give sorrow words. sigh; give a sigh, heave, fetch a sigh; "waft a sigh from Indus to the pole" [Pope]; sigh "like a furnace" [As you Like It]; wail. cry, weep, sob, greet, blubber, pipe, snivel, bibber[obs3], whimper, pule; pipe one's eye; drop tears, shed tears, drop a tear, shed a tear; melt into tears, burst into tears; fondre en larmes[Fr]; cry oneself blind, cry one's eyes out; yammer. scream &c. (cry

out) 411; mew &c. (animal sounds) 412; groan, moan, whine; roar; roar like a bull, bellow like a bull; cry out lustily, rend the air. frown, scowl, make a wry face, gnash one's teeth, wring one's hands, tear one's hair, beat one's breast, roll on the ground, burst with grief. complain, murmur, mutter, grumble, growl, clamor, make a fuss about, croak, grunt, maunder; deprecate &c. (disapprove) 932. cry out before one is hurt, complain without cause. Adj. lamenting &c. v.; in mourning, in sackcloth and ashes; sorrowing, sorrowful &c. (unhappy) 828; mournful, tearful; lachrymose; plaintive, plaintful[obs3]; querulous, querimonious[obs3]; in the melting mood; threnetic[obs3]. in tears, with tears in one's eyes; with moistened eyes, with watery eyes; bathed in tears, dissolved in tears; "like Niobe all tears" [Hamlet]. elegiac, epicedial[obs3]. Adv. de profundis[Lat]; les larmes aux yeux[Fr]. Int. heigh-ho! alas! alack[obs3]! O dear! ah me! woe is me! lackadaisy[obs3]! well a day! lack a day! alack a day[obs3]! wellaway[obs3]! alas the day! O tempora O mores[obs3]! what a pity! miserabile dictu[Lat]! O lud lud[obs3]! too true! Phr. tears standing in the eyes, tears starting from the eyes; eyes suffused, eyes swimming, eyes brimming, eyes overflowing with tears; "if you have tears prepare to shed them now" [Julius Caesar]; interdum lacrymae pondera vocis habent [Lat][Ovid]; "strangled his language in his tears" [Henry VIII]; "tears such as angels weep" [Paradise Lost].

<— p. 284 —> <— separate out entertainers which do not have their own entry, e.g. musician. Need singer, dancer, comedian = wit —> #840. Amusement. — N. amusement, entertainment, recreation, fun, game, fun and games; diversion, divertissement; reaction, solace; pastime, passetemps[Fr], sport; labor of love; pleasure &c. 827. relaxation; leisure &c. 685. fun, frolic, merriment, jollity; joviality, jovialness[obs3]; heyday; laughter &c. 838; jocosity, jocoseness[obs3]; drollery, buffoonery, tomfoolery; mummery, pleasantry; wit &c. 842; quip, quirk. [verbal expressions of amusement: list] giggle, titter, snigger, snicker, crow, cheer, chuckle, shout; horse laugh, belly laugh, hearty laugh; guffaw; burst of laughter, fit of laughter, shout of laughter, roar of laughter, peal of laughter; cachinnation[obs3]; Kentish fire; tiger. play; game, game at romps; gambol, romp, prank, antic, rig, lark, spree, skylarking, vagary, monkey trick, gambade, fredaine[obs3], escapade, echappee[Fr], bout, espieglerie[Fr]; practical joke &c. (ridicule) 856. dance; hop, reel, rigadoon[obs3], saraband[obs3], hornpipe, bolero, ballroom dance; minuet[ballroom dances: list], waltz, polka, fox trot, tango, samba, rhumba, twist, stroll, hustle, cha-cha; fandango, cancan; bayadere[obs3]; breakdown, cake-walk, cornwallis [U.S.], break dancing; nautch-girl; shindig* [U.S.]; skirtdance[obs3], stag dance, Virginia reel, square dance; galop[obs3], galopade[obs3]; jig, Irish jig, fling, strathspey[obs3]; allemande[Fr]; gavot[obs3], gavotte, tarantella; mazurka, moriscol, morris dance; quadrille; country dance, folk dance; cotillon, Sir Roger de Coverley; ballet &c. (drama) 599; ball; bal, bal masque, bal costume; masquerade; Terpsichore. festivity, merrymaking; party &c. (social gathering) 892; blowout [U.S.], hullabaloo, hoedown, bat* [U.S.], bum* [U.S.], bust*, clambake [U.S.], donation party [U.S.], fish fry [U.S.], jamboree*, kantikoy[obs3], nautch[obs3], randy, squantum [obs3][U.S.], tear *, Turnerfest[obs3], yule log; fete, festival, gala, ridotto[obs3]; revels, revelry, reveling; carnival, brawl, saturnalia, high jinks; feast, banquet &c. (food) 298; regale, symposium, wassail; carouse, carousal; jollification, junket, wake, Irish wake, picnic, fete champetre[Fr], regatta, field day; treat. round of pleasures, dissipation, a short life and a merry one, racketing, holiday making. rejoicing &c. 838; jubilee &c. (celebration) 883. bonfire, fireworks, feu-de-joie, firecracker. holiday; gala day, red letter day, play day; high days and holidays; high holiday, Bank holiday; May day, Derby day; Saint Monday, Easter Monday, Whit Monday; Bairam[obs3]; wayz-goos[obs3], bean feast; Arbor Day, Declaration Day, Independence Day, Labor Day, Memorial Day, Thanksgiving Day; Mardi gras[Fr],mi-careme[Fr], feria[Lat], fiesta. place of amusement, theater; hall, concert room, ballroom, assemblyroom[obs3]; music hall. park, plaisance[obs3]; national park, national forest, state park, county park, city park, vest-pocket park, public park (public) 737a; arbor; garden &c. (horticulture) 371; pleasure ground, playground, cricketground, croquet ground, archery ground, hunting ground; tennis court, racket court; bowling alley, green alley; croquet lawn, rink, glaciarum[obs3], skating rink; roundabout, merry-go-round; swing; montagne Russe[Fr]. game of chance, game of skill. athletic sports, gymnastics; archery, rifle shooting; tournament, pugilism &c. (contention) 720; sports &c. 622; horse racing, the turf; aquatics &c. 267; skating, sliding; cricket, tennis, lawn tennis; hockey, football, baseball, soccer, ice hockey, basketball; rackets, fives, trap bat and ball, battledore and shuttlecock, la grace; pall-mall; tipcat[obs3], croquet, golf, curling, pallone[obs3], polo, water polo; tent pegging; tilting at the ring, quintain[obs3][medieval]; greasy pole; quoits, horseshoes, discus; rounders, lacrosse; tobogganing, water polo; knurr and spell[obs3]. [childrens' games] leapfrog, hop skip and jump; mother may I; French and English, tug of war; blindman's bluff, hunt the slopper[obs3], hide and seek, kiss in the ring; snapdragon; cross questions and crooked answers.; crisscross, hopscotch; jacks, jackstones[obs3], marbles; mumblety-peg, mumble-the-peg, pushball, shinney, shinny, tag &c. billiards, pool, pingpong, pyramids, bagatelle; bowls, skittles, ninepins, kain[obs3], American bowls[obs3]; tenpins [U.S.], tivoli. cards, card games; whist, rubber; round game; loo, cribbage, besique[obs3], euchre, drole[obs3], ecarte[Fr], picquet[obs3], allfours[obs3], quadrille, omber, reverse, Pope Joan, commit; boston, boaston[obs3]; blackjack, twenty-one, vingtun[Fr]; quinze[Fr], thirty-one, put, speculation, connections, brag, cassino[obs3], lottery, commerce, snip-snap-snoren[obs3], lift smoke, blind hookey, Polish bank, Earl of Coventry, Napoleon, patience, pairs; banker; blind poker, draw poker, straight poker, stud poker; bluff, bridge, bridge whist; lotto, monte, three-card monte, nap, penny-ante, poker, reversis[obs3], squeezers, old maid,

fright, beggar-my-neighbor; baccarat. [cards: list] ace, king, queen, knave, jack, ten, nine, eight, seven, six, five, four, trey, deuce; joker; trump, wild card. [card suits: list] spades, hearts, clubs, diamonds; major suit, minor suit. bower; right bower, left bower; dummy; jackpot; deck. [hands at poker: list] pair, two pair, three of a kind, straight, flush, full-house, four of a kind, royal flush; misere &c. [board games: list] chess, draughts, checkers, checquers, backgammon, dominos, merelles[obs3], nine men's morris, go bang, solitaire; game of fox and goose; monopoly; loto &c. [obs3] scrabble[word games: list], scribbage, boggle, crossword puzzle, hangman. morra[obs3]; gambling &c. (chance) 621. toy, plaything, bauble; doll &c. (puppet) 554; teetotum[obs3]; knickknack &c. (trifle) 643; magic lantern &c. (show) 448; peep show, puppet show, raree show, gallanty show[obs3]; toy shop; "quips and cranks and wanton wiles, nods and becks and wreathed smiles" [Milton]. entertainer, showman, showgirl; dancer, tap dancer, song-and-dance man; vaudeville act; singer; musician &c. 416. sportsman, gamester, reveler; master of ceremonies, master of revels; pompom girl[obs3]; arbiter elegantiarum[Lat]; arbiter bibendi[Lat], archer, fan [U.S.], toxophilite[obs3], turfman[obs3]. V. amuse, entertain, divert, enliven; tickle the fancy; titillate, raise a smile, put in good humor; cause laughter, create laughter, occasion laughter, raise laughter, excite laughter, produce laughter, convulse with laughter; set the table in a roar, be the death of one. recreate, solace, cheer, rejoice; please &c. 829; interest; treat, regale. amuse oneself, game; play a game, play pranks, play tricks; sport, disport, toy, wanton, revel, junket, feast, carouse, banquet, make merry, drown care; drive dull care away; frolic, gambol, frisk, romp; caper; dance &c. (leap) 309; keep up the ball; run a rig, sow one's wild oats, have one's fling, take one's pleasure; paint the town red*; see life; desipere in loco[Lat], play the fool. make holiday, keep holiday; go a Maying. while away the time, beguile the time; kill time, dally. smile, simper, smirk; grin, grin like a Cheshire cat; mock, laugh in one's sleeve; laugh, laugh outright; giggle, titter, snigger, crow, snicker, chuckle, cackle; burst out, burst into a fit of laughter; shout, split, roar. shake one's sides, split one's sides, hold both one's sides; roar with laughter, die with laughter. Adj. amusing, entertaining, diverting &c. v.; recreational, recreative, lusory[obs3]; pleasant &c. (pleasing) 829; laughable &c. (ludicrous) 853; witty &c. 842; fun, festive, festal; jovial, jolly, jocund, roguish, rompish[obs3]; playful, playful as a kitten; sportive, ludibriousl. funny; very funny, hilarious, uproarious, side-splitting. amused &c. v.; "pleased with a rattle, tickled with a straw" [Pope]; laughing &c. v.; risible; ready to burst, ready to split, ready to die with laughter; convulsed with laughter, rolling in the aisles. Adv. "on the light fantastic toe" [Milton], at play, in sport. Int. vive la bagatelle[Fr]! vogue la galere[Fr]! Phr. deus nobis haec otia fecit[Lat]; dum vivimus vivamus[Lat]; dulce est desipere in loco [Lat][Horace]; "(every room) hath blazed with lights and brayed with minstrelsy" [Timon of Athens]; misce stullitiam consiliis brevem [Lat][Horace].

<— p. 285 —>

#841. Weariness. — N. weariness, defatigationl; lassitude &c. (fatigue) 688; drowsiness &c. 683. disgust, nausea, loathing, sickness; satiety &c. 869; taedium vitae &c. (dejection) 837; boredom, ennui. wearisomeness, tediousness &c. adj.; dull work, tedium, monotony, twice-told tale. bore, buttonholer, proser[obs3], wet blanket; pill*, stiff*; heavy hours, "the enemy" [time]. V. weary; tire &c. (fatigue) 688; bore; bore to death, weary to death, tire to death, bore out of one's skull, bore out of one's life, weary out of one's life, tire out of one's life, bore out of all patience, weary out of all patience, wear out one's patience, tire out of all patience; set to sleep, send to sleep; buttonhole. pall, sicken, nauseate, disgust. harp on the same string; drag its slow length along, drag its weary length along. never hear the last of; be tired of, be sick of, be tired with &c. adj.; yawn; die with ennui. [of journalistic articles] MEGO, my eyes glaze over. Adj. wearying &c. v.; wearing; wearisome, tiresome, irksome; uninteresting, stupid, bald, devoid of interest, dry, monotonous, dull, arid, tedious, humdrum, mortal, flat; prosy, prosing; slow, soporific, somniferous. disgusting &c. v.; unenjoyed[obs3]. weary, tired &c. v.; drowsy &c. (sleepy) 683; uninterested, flagging, used up, worn out, blase, life-weary, weary of life; sick of. Adv. wearily &c. adj.; usque ad nauseam[Lat]. Phr. time hanging heavily on one's hands; toujours perdrix[Fr]; crambe repetita[Lat][obs3].

<— p. 286 —>

#842. Wit. — N. wit, humor, wittiness; sense of humor; attic wit, attic salt; atticism[obs3]; salt, esprit, point, fancy, whim, drollery, pleasantry. farce, buffoonery, fooling, tomfoolery; shenanigan [U.S.], harlequinade &c. 599[obs3]; broad farce, broad humor; fun, espieglerie[Fr]; vis comica[Lat]. jocularity; jocosity, jocoseness[obs3]; facetiousness; waggery, waggishness; whimsicality; comicality &c. 853. banter, badinage, retort, repartee, smartness, ready wit, quid-pro- quo; ridicule &c. 856. jest, joke, jape, jibe; facetiae[Lat], levity, quips and cranks; capital joke; canorae nugae[Lat]; standing jest, standing joke, private joke, conceit, quip, quirk, crank, quiddity, concetto[obs3], plaisanterie[Fr], brilliant idea; merry thought, bright thought, happy thought; sally; flash of wit, flash of merriment; scintillation; mot[Fr], mot pour rire [French]; witticism, smart saying, bon-mot,jeu d'esprit[Fr],epigram; jest book; dry joke, quodlibet, cream of the jest. word-play, jeu de mots[Fr]; play of words, play upon words, pun, punning; double entente, double entendre &c. (ambiguity) 520[Fr]; quibble, verbal quibble; conundrum &c. (riddle) 533; anagram, acrostic, double acrostic, trifling, idle conceit, turlupinadel. old joke, tired joke, flat joke, Joe Millerl!. V. joke, jest, crack a joke, make a joke, jape, cut jokes; perpetrate a joke; pun, perpetrate a pun; make fun of, make merry with; kid, kid around, fool around; set the table in a roar &c. (amuse) 840. retort. banter &c. (ridicule) 856; ridentem dicere verum[Lat]; joke at one's expense. take in jest. [make a joke which is not funny] bomb, fall flat; go over like a lead balloon. Adj. witty, attic; quick-witted, nimble-witted; smart; jocular, jocose, humorous; facetious, waggish, whimsical; kidding, joking, puckish; playful &c. 840; merry and wise; pleasant, sprightly, light, spirituel[obs3], sparkling, epigram-matic, full of point, ben trovato[It]; comic &c. 853. zany, madcap. funny, amusing &c. (amusement) 840. Adv. jokingly, in joke, in jest, in sport, in play. Phr. adhibenda est in jocando moderatio[Lat][obs3]; "gentle dullness ever loves a joke" [Pope]; "leave this keen encounter of our wits" [Richard III]; just joking, just kidding; "surely you jest!".

#843. Dullness. — N. dullness, heaviness, flatness; infestivity [obs3] &c. 837, stupidity &c. 499; want of originality; dearth of ideas.
    prose, matter of fact; heavy book, conte a dormir debout[Fr]; platitude.
    V. be dull &c. adj.; prose, take au serieux[Fr], be caught napping.
    render dull &c. adj.; damp, depress, throw cold water on, lay a wet blanket on; fall flat upon the ear.
    no joke, serious matter (importance) 642.
    Adj. dull, dull as ditch water; unentertaining, uninteresting, flat, dry as dust; unfunny, unlively[obs3], logy [U.S.]; unimaginative; insulse[obs3]; dry as dust; prosy, prosing, prosaic; matter of fact, commonplace, pedestrian, pointless; "weary stale flat and unprofitable" [Hamlet].
    stupid, slow, flat, insipid, vapid, humdrum, monotonous; melancholic &c. 837; stolid &c. 499; plodding.
    boring, tiresome, tedious &c. 841.
    Phr. davus sum non Aedipus[obs3]; deadly dull and boring, DDB[abbr].
#844. Humorist. — N. humorist, wag, wit, reparteeist[obs3], epigrammatist, punster; bel esprit, life of the party; wit-snapper, wit- cracker, wit-worm; joker, jester, Joe Millerl!, drole de corps[obs3], gaillard[obs3], spark; bon diable[Fr]; practical joker. buffoon, farceur[French], merry-andrew, mime, tumbler, acrobat, mountebank, charlatan, posturemaster[obs3], harlequin, punch, pulcinella[obs3], scaramouch[obs3], clown; wearer of the cap and bells, wearer of the motley; motley fool; pantaloon, gypsy; jack-pudding, jack in the green, jack a dandy; wiseacre, wise guy, smartass [coll.]; fool &c. 501. zany, madcap; pickle-herring, witling[obs3], caricaturist, grimacier[obs3]; persifleur[obs3].

<— p. 287 —> %

2. Discriminative Affections

%

#845. Beauty. — N. beauty, the beautiful, <gr/to kalon/gr>[Grk], le beau ideal. [Science of the perception of beauty] aesthetics, callaestheticsl!. [of people] pulchritude, form elegance, grace, beauty unadorned, natural beauty; symmetry &c. 242; comeliness, fairness &c. adj.; polish, gloss; good effect, good looks; belle tournure[obs3]; trigness[obs3]; bloom, brilliancy, radiance, splendor, gorgeousness, magnificence; sublimity, sublimificationl. concinnity[obs3], delicacy, refinement; charm, je ne sais quoi[Fr], style. Venus, Aphrodite[obs3], Hebe, the Graces, Peri, Houri, Cupid, Apollo[obs3], Hyperion, Adonis[obs3], Antionous[obs3], Narcissus. peacock, butterfly; garden; flower of, pink of; bijou; jewel &c. (ornament) 847; work of art. flower, flow'ret gay[obs3], wildflower; rose[flowers: list], lily, anemone, asphodel, buttercup, crane's bill, daffodil, tulip, tiger lily, day lily, begonia, marigold, geranium, lily of the valley, ranunculus[ISA:herb@flowering], rhododendron, windflower. pleasurableness &c 829. beautifying; landscaping, landscape gardening; decoration &c. 847; calisthenicsl!. [person who is beautiful] beauty; hunk [of men]. V. be beautiful &c. adj.; shine, beam, bloom; become one &c. (accord) 23; set off, grace. render beautiful &c. adj.; beautify; polish, burnish; gild &c. (decorate) 847; set out. "snatch a grace beyond the reach of art" [Pope]. Adj. beautiful, beauteous; handsome; gorgeous; pretty; lovely, graceful, elegant, prepossessing; attractive &c. (inviting) 615; delicate, dainty, refined; fair, personable, comely, seemly; bonny [Scottish]; good- looking; well-favored, well-made, well-formed, well-proportioned; proper, shapely; symmetrical &c. (regular) 242; harmonious &c. (color) 428; sightly. fit to be seen, passable, not amiss. goodly, dapper, tight, jimp[obs3]; gimp; janty[obs3], jaunty; trig, natty, quaint, trim, tidy,neat, spruce, smart, tricksy[obs3]. bright, bright eyed; rosy cheeked, cherry cheeked; rosy, ruddy;
245

blooming, in full bloom. brilliant, shining; beamy[obs3], beaming; sparkling, splendid, resplendent, dazzling, glowing; glossy, sleek. rich, superb, magnificent, grand, fine, sublime, showy, specious. artistic, artistical[obs3]; aesthetic; picturesque, pictorial; fait a peindre[Fr]; well-composed, well grouped, well varied; curious. enchanting &c. (pleasure-giving) 829; becoming &c. (accordant) 23; ornamental &c. 847. undeformed, undefaced, unspotted; spotless &c. (perfect) 650. Phr. auxilium non leve vultus habet [Lat][Ovid]; "beauty born of murmuring sound" [Wordsworth]; "flowers preach to us if we will hear" [C.G. Rossetti]; gratior ac pulchro veniens in corpore virtus [Lat][Vergil]; "none but the brave deserve the fair" [Dryden]; "thou who hast the fatal gift of beauty" [Byron].

#846. Ugliness. — N. ugliness &c. adj.; deformity, inelegance; acomia[obs3]; disfigurement &c. (blemish) 848; want of symmetry, inconcinnity[obs3]; distortion &c. 243; squalor &c. (uncleanness) 653. forbidding countenance, vinegar aspect, hanging look, wry face, "spretae injuria formae" [Vergil]. [person who is ugly] eyesore, object, witch, hag, figure, sight, fright; monster; dog[coll.], woofer[coll.], pig[coll.]; octopus, specter, scarecrow, harridan!!, satyr!!, toad, monkey, baboon, Caliban, Aesop[obs3], "monstrum horrendum informe ingens cui lumen ademptum" [Latin][Vergil]. V. be ugly &c. adj.; look ill, grin horribly a ghastly smile, make faces. render ugly &c. adj.; deface; disfigure, defigure!; distort &c. 23; blemish &c. (injure) 659; soil &c. (render unclean) 653. Adj. ugly, ugly as sin, ugly as a toad, ugly as a scarecrow, ugly as a dead monkey; plain, bald (unadorned) 849; homely; ordinary, unornamental[obs3], inartistic; unsightly, unseemly, uncomely, unlovely; unshapely; sightless, seemless[obs3]; not fit to be seen; unbeauteous[obs3], unbeautiful; beautiless[obs3], semibeautiful; shapeless &c. (amorphous) 241. misshapen, misproportioned[obs3]; monstrous; gaunt &c. (thin) 203; dumpy &c. (short) 201; curtailed of its fair proportions; ill-made, ill- shaped, ill-proportioned; crooked &c. (distorted) 243; hard featured, hard visaged; ill-favored, hard-favored, evil-favored; ill-looking; unprepossessing, unattractive, uninviting, unpleasing. graceless, inelegant; un-graceful, ungainly, uncouth, stiff; rugged, rough, gross, rude, awkward, clumsy, slouching, rickety; gawky; lumping, lumpish[obs3]; lumbering; hulky[obs3], hulking; unwieldy. squalid, haggard; grim, grim faced, grim visaged; grisly; ghastly; ghost like, death like; cadaverous, grewsome[obs3], gruesome. frightful, hideous, odious, uncanny, forbid-ding; repellant, repulsive, repugnant, grotesque, bizarre; grody [coll.], grody to the max [coll.]; horrid, horrible; shocking &c. (painful) 830. foul &c. (dirty) 653; dingy &c. (colorless) 429; gaudy &c. (color) 428; disfigured &c. v.; discolored.

<— p. 288 —>

#847. Ornament. — N. ornament, ornamentation, ornamental art; ornature[obs3], ornateness; adornment, decora-tion, embellishment; architecture; jewelry &c. 847a. [surface coatings for wood: list] garnish, polish, varnish, French polish, veneer, japanning, lacquer. [surface coatings for metal] gilding, plating, ormolu, enamel, cloisonn. [surface coatings for human skin] cosmetics[in general], makeup; eye shadow[list], rouge, face powder, lipstick, blush. [ornamental surface pattern: list] pattern, diaper, powdering, paneling, graining, pargeting[obs3]; detail; repousse (convexity) 250; texture &c. 329; richness; tracery, molding, fillet, listel[obs3], strapwork[obs3], coquillage[Fr], flourish, fleur-de-lis[Fr], arabesque, fret, anthemion[obs3]; egg and tongue, egg and dart; astragal[obs3], zigzag, acanthus, cartouche; pilaster &c. (projection) 250; bead, beading; champleve ware[Fr], cloisonne ware; frost work, Moresque[Lat], Morisco, tooling. [ornamental cloth] embroidery; brocade, brocatelle[obs3], galloon, lace, fringe, trapping, border, edging, trimming; hanging, tapestry, arras; millinery, ermine; drap d'or[Fr]. wreath, festoon, garland, chaplet, flower, nosegay, bouquet, posy, "daisies pied and violets blue" tassel[L.L.L.], knot; shoulder knot, apaulette[obs3], epaulet, aigulet[obs3], frog; star, rosette, bow; feather, plume, pompom[obs3], panache, aigrette. finery, frippery, gewgaw, gimcrack, tinsel, spangle, clinquant[obs3], pinchbeck, paste; excess of ornament &c. (vulgarity) 851; gaud, pride. [ornamentation of text] illustration, illumination, vignette. fleuron[obs3]; head piece[Fr], tail piece[Fr]; cul-de-lampe[Fr]; flowers of rhetoric &c. 577; work of art. V. ornament, embellish, enrich, decorate, adorn, bead, beautify, adonize[obs3]. smarten, furbish, polish, gild, varnish, whitewash, enamel, japan, lacquer, paint, grain. garnish, trim, dizen[obs3], bedizen, prink[obs3], prank; trick out, fig out; deck, bedeck, dight[obs3], bedight[obs3], array; begawd[obs3], titivate[obs3]; dress, dress up; spangle, bespangle, powder; embroider, work; chase, emboss, fret, emblazon; illuminate; illustrate. become &c. (accord with) 23. Adj. ornamented, beautified &c. v.; ornate, rich, gilt, begilt[obs3], tesselated, festooned; champleve[Fr], cloisonne, topiary. smart, gay, trickly[obs3], flowery, glittering; new gilt, new spangled; fine as a Mayday queen, fine as a fivepence[obs3], fine as a carrot fresh scraped; pranked out, bedight[obs3], well-groomed. in full dress &c. (fashion) 852; dressed to kill, dressed to the nines, dressed to advantage; in Sunday best, en grand tenue[Fr], en grande toilette[Fr]; in best bib and tucker, endimanche[Fr]. showy, flashy, gaudy &c. (vulgar) 851; garish, gairish!!; gorgeous. ornamental, decorative; becom-ing &c. (accordant) 23.

#847a. Jewelry — N. jewel[ornaments worn by people on the body][general], jewelry, jewellery[obs3]; bijoutry!!; bijou, bijouterie[Fr]; trinket; fine jewelry; costume jewelry, junk jewelry; gem, gemstone, precious stone. [forms of jewelry: list] necklace, bracelet, anklet; earring; locket, pendant, charm bracelet; ring, pinky ring; carcanet[obs3]; chain, chatelaine; broach, pin, lapel pin, torque. [gemstones: list] diamond, brilliant, rock[coll.]; beryl, emerald; chalcedony, agate, heliotrope; girasol[obs3], girasole[obs3]; onyx, plasma; sard[obs3], sardonyx; garnet, lapis lazuli, opal, peridot[ISA:gemstone], tourmaline, chrysolite; sapphire, ruby, synthetic ruby; spinel, spinelle; balais[obs3]; oriental, oriental topaz; turquois[obs3], turquoise; zircon, cubic zirconia; jacinth, hyacinth, carbuncle, amethyst; alexandrite[obs3], cat's eye, bloodstone, hematite, jasper, moonstone, sunstone[obs3]. [jewelry materials derived from living organisms] pearl, cultured pearl, fresh-water pearl; mother of pearl; coral. [person who sells jewels] jeweler. [person who studies gemstones] gemologist; minerologist. [person who cuts gemstones] lapidary, lapidarian. [study of gemstones] gemology, gemmology; minerology. V. shine like a diamond. Adj. bejeweled; diamond &c. n[gemstones].. gemological.

    #848. Blemish. — N. blemish, disfigurement, deformity; adactylism[obs3]; flaw, defect &c. (imperfection) 651; injury &c. (deterioration) 659; spots on the sun!!; eyesore.

    stain, blot; spot, spottiness; speck, speckle, blur.

    tarnish, smudge; dirt &c. 653.

    [blemish on a person's skin: list] freckle, mole, macula[Anat], patch, blotch, birthmark; blobber lip[obs3], blubber lip; blain[obs3], maculation, ; scar, weml; pustule; whelk; excrescence, pimple &c. (protuberance) 250.

    V. disfigure &c. (injure) 659; speckle.

    Adj. pitted, freckled, discolored; imperfect &c. 651; blobber-lipped, bloodshot; injured &c. (deteriorated) 659.

    #849. Simplicity. — N. simplicity; plainness, homeliness; undress, chastity.

    V. be simple &c. adj.

    render simple &c. adj.; simplify, uncomplicate.

    Adj. simple, plain; homely, homespun; ordinary, household.

    unaffected; ingenuous, sincere (artless) 703; free from affectation, free from ornament; simplex munditiis [Lat][Horace]; sans facon[Fr], en deshabille[Fr].

    chaste, inornate[obs3], severe.

    unadorned, bare, unornamented, undecked[obs3], ungarnished, unarranged[obs3], untrimmed, unvarnished.

    bald, flat, dull.

    Phr. veritatis simplex oratio est[Lat].

<— p. 289 —>

    #850. [Good taste.] Taste. — N. taste; good taste, refined taste, cultivated taste; delicacy, refinement, fine feeling, gust, gusto, tact, finesse; nicety &c. (discrimination) 465; <gr/to prepon/gr>[Grk]; polish, elegance, grace.

    judgment, discernment &c. 465.

    dilettantism, dilettanteism; virtu; fine art; culture, cultivation.

    [Science of taste] aesthetics.

    man of taste &c.; connoisseur, judge, critic, conoscente, virtuoso, amateur, dilettante, Aristarchus[obs3], Corinthian, arbiter elegantiarum[Lat], stagirite[obs3], euphemist.

    "caviare to the general" [Hamlet].

    V. appreciate, judge, criticise, discriminate &c. 465

    Adj. in good taste, cute, tasteful, tasty; unaffected, pure, chaste, classical, attic; cultivated, refined; dainty; esthetic, aesthetic, artistic; elegant &c 578; euphemistic.

    to one's taste, to one's mind; after one's fancy; comme il faut[Fr]; tire a quatre epingles[Fr].

    Adv. elegantly &c. adj.

    Phr. nihil tetigit quod non ornavit [Lat][from Johnson's epitaph on Goldsmith]; chacun a son gout[Fr]; oculi pictura tenentur aures cantibus [Lat][Cicero].

#851. [Bad taste.] Vulgarity. — N. vulgarity, vulgarism; barbarism, Vandalism, Gothicisml!; mauvis gout[Fr], bad taste; gaucherie, awkwardness, want of tact; ill-breeding &c. (discourtesy) 895. courseness &c. adj[obs3].; indecorum, misbehavior. lowness, homeliness; low life, mauvais ton[Fr], rusticity; boorishness &c. adj.; brutality; rowdyism, blackguardism[obs3]; ribaldry; slang &c. (neology) 563. bad joke, mauvais plaisanterie[Fr]. [Excess of ornament] gaudiness, tawdriness; false ornament; finery, frippery, trickery, tinsel, gewgaw, clinquant[obs3]; baroque, rococo. rough diamond, tomboy, hoyden, cub, unlicked cub[obs3]; clown &c. (commonalty) 876; Goth, Vandal, Boeotian; snob, cad, gent; parvenu &c. 876; frump, dowdy; slattern &c. 653. V. be vulgar &c. adj.; misbehave; talk shop, smell of the shop. Adj. in bad taste vulgar, unrefined. coarse, indecorous, ribald, gross; unseemly, unbeeming[obs3], unpresentable[obs3]; contra bonos mores[Lat]; ungraceful &c. (ugly) 846. dowdy; slovenly &c. (dirty) 653; ungenteel, shabby genteel; low, common, hoi polloi[Grk] &c. (plebeian) 876; uncourtly[obs3]; uncivil &c. (discourteous) 895; ill bred, ill mannered; underbred; ungentlemanly, ungentlemanlike; unladylike, unfeminine; wild, wild as an unbacked colt. untutored, unschooled (ignorant) 491. unkempt. uncombed, untamed, unlicked[obs3], unpolished, uncouth; plebeian; incondite[obs3]; heavy, rude, awkward; homely, homespun, home bred; provincial, countrified, rustic; boorish, clownish; savage, brutish, blackguard, rowdy, snobbish; barbarous, barbaric; Gothic, unclassical[obs3], doggerel, heathenish, tramontane, outlandish; uncultivated; Bohemian. obsolete &c. (antiquated) 124; unfashionable; newfangled &c. (unfamiliar) 83; odd &c. (ridiculous) 853. particular; affected &c. 855; meretricious; extravagant, monstrous, horrid; shocking &c. (painful) 830. gaudy, tawdry, overornamented, baroque, rococo; bedizened, tricked out, gingerbread; obtrusive.

#852. Fashion. — N. fashion, style, ton, bon tonl!, society; good society, polite society; monde[Fr]; drawing-room, civilized life, civilization, town, beau monde[Fr], high life, court; world; fashionable world, gay world; Vanity Fair; show &c. (ostentation) 822. manners, breeding &c. (politeness) 894; air, demeanor &c. (appearance) 448; savoir faire[Fr]; gentlemanliness[obs3], gentility, decorum, propriety, biensance[Fr]; conventions of society; Mrs. Grundy; punctilio; form, formality; etiquette, point of etiquette; dress &c. 225. custom &c. 613; mode, vogue, go; rage &c. (desire) 865; prevailing taste; fad, trend, bandwagon, furore[obs3], thing, in thing, craze, chic, last word. man of fashion, woman of fashion, man of the world, woman of the world; height of fashion, pink of fashion, star of fashion, glass of fashion, leader of fashion; arbiter elegantiarum &c. (taste) 850[Lat]; the beautiful people, the fashion set, upper ten thousand &c. (nobility) 875; elite &c. (distinction) 873; smart set; the four hundred [U.S.]; in crowd. V. be fashionable &c. adj., be the rage &c. n.; have a run, pass current. follow the fashion, conform to the fashion, fall in with the fashion, follow the trend, follow the crowd &c. n.; go with the stream &c. (conform) 82; savoir vivre[Fr], savoir faire[Fr]; keep up appearances, behave oneself. set the fashion, bring in the fashion; give a tone to society, cut a figure in society; keep one's carriage. Adj. fashionable; in fashion &c. n.; a la mode, comme il faut[Fr]; admitted in society, admissible in society &c. n.; presentable; conventional &c. (customary) 613; genteel; well-bred, well mannered, well behaved, well spoken; gentlemanlike[obs3], gentlemanly; ladylike; civil, polite &c. (courteous) 894. polished, refined, thoroughbred, courtly; distingue[Fr]; unembarrassed, degage[Fr]; janty[obs3], jaunty; dashing, fast. modish, stylish, chic, trendy, recherche; newfangled &c. (unfamiliar) 83; all the rage, all the gol!; with it, in, faddish. in court, in full dress, in evening dress; en grande tenue[Fr] &c. (ornament) 847. Adv. fashionably &c. adj.; for fashion's sake. Phr. a la francaise, a la parisienne; a l' anglaise[Fr], a l' americaine[Fr]; autre temps autre mauers[Fr]; chaque pays a sa guise[Fr].

<— p. 290 —>

#853. Ridiculousness. — N. ridiculousness &c. adj.; comicality, oddity &c. adj.; extravagance, drollery. farce, comedy; burlesque &c. (ridicule) 856; buffoonery &c. (fun) 840; frippery; doggerel verses; absurdity &c. 497; bombast &c. (unmeaning) 517; anticlimax, bathos; eccentricity, monstrosity &c. (unconformity) 83; laughingstock &c. 857. V. be ridiculous &c. adj.; pass from the sublime to the ridiculous; make one laugh; play the fool, make a fool of oneself, commit an absurdity. Adj. ridiculous, ludicrous; comical; droll, funny, laughable, pour rire, grotesque, farcical, odd; whimsical, whimsical as a dancing bear; fanciful, fantastic, queer, rum, quizzical, quaint, bizarre; screaming; eccentric &c. (unconformable) 83; strange, outlandish, out of the way, baroque, weird; awkward &c. (ugly) 846. extravagant, outre, monstrous, preposterous, bombastic, inflated, stilted, burlesque, mock heroic. drollish; seriocomic, tragicomic; gimcrack, contemptible &c. (unimportant) 643; doggerel; ironical &c. (derisive) 856; risible. Phr. risum teneatis amici [Horace]; rideret Heraclitus; du sublime au ridicule il n'y a qu'un pas [Napoleon].

#854. Fop. — N. fop, fine gentleman; swell; dandy, dandipratl!; exquisite, coxcomb, beau, macaroni, blade, blood, buck, man about town, fast man; fribble, millinerl!; Jemmy Jessamyl!, carpet knight; masher, dude. fine lady, coquette; flirt, vamp.

#855. Affectation. — N. affectation; affectedness &c. adj.; acting a part &c. v.; pretense &c. (falsehood) 544, (ostentation) 882; boasting &c. 884. charlatanism, quackery, shallow profundity; pretension, airs, pedantry, purism, precisianism, euphuism; teratology &c. (altiloquence) 577. mannerism, simagree, grimace. conceit, foppery, dandyism, man millinery, coxcombry, puppyism. stiffness, formality, buckram; prudery, demureness, coquetry, mock modesty, minauderie, sentimentalism; mauvais honte, false shame. affector, performer, actor; pedant, pedagogue, doctrinaire, purist, euphuist, mannerist; grimacier; lump of affectation, precieuse ridicule[Fr], bas bleu[Fr], blue stocking, poetaster; prig; charlatan &c. (deceiver) 548; petit maitre &c. (fop) 854; flatterer &c. 935; coquette, prude, puritan. V. affect, act a part, put on; give oneself airs &c. (arrogance) 885; boast &c. 884; coquet; simper, mince, attitudinize, pose; flirt a fan; overact, overdo. Adj. affected, full of affectation, pretentious, pedantic, stilted, stagy, theatrical, big-sounding, ad captandum; canting, insincere. not natural, unnatural; self-conscious; maniere; artificial; overwrought, overdone, overacted; euphuist &c. 577. stiff, starch, formal, prim, smug, demure, tire a quatre epingles, quakerish, puritanical, prudish, pragmatical, priggish, conceited, coxcomical, foppish, dandified; finical, finikin; mincing, simpering, namby-pamby, sentimental. Phr. "conceit in weakest bodies strongest works" [Hamlet].

<− p. 291 −>

#856. Ridicule. — N. ridicule, derision; sardonic smile, sardonic grin; irrision[obs3]; scoffing &c. (disrespect) 929; mockery, quiz!!, banter, irony, persiflage, raillery, chaff, badinage; quizzing &c. v.; asteism[obs3].

squib, satire, skit, quip, quib[obs3], grin.

parody, burlesque, travesty, travestie[obs3]; farce &c. (drama) 599; caricature.

buffoonery &c. (fun) 840; practical joke; horseplay.

scorn, contempt &c. 930.

V. ridicule[transitive], deride, mock, taunt; snigger; laugh in one's sleeve; tease[ridicule lightly], badinage, banter, rally, chaff, joke, twit, quiz, roast; haze [U.S.]; tehee[obs3]; fleer[obs3]; show up.

[i.p.] play upon, play tricks upon; fool to the top of one's bent; laugh at, grin at, smile at; poke fun at.

satirize, parody, caricature, burlesque, travesty.

turn into ridicule; make merry with; make fun of, make game of, make a fool of, make an April fool of[obs3]; rally; scoff &c. (disrespect) 929.

raise a laugh &c. (amuse) 840; play the fool, make a fool of oneself.

Adj. derisory, derisive; mock, mocking; sarcastic, ironic, ironical, quizzical, burlesque, Hudibrastic[obs3]; scurrilous &c. (disrespectful) 929.

Adv. in ridicule &c. n.

#857. [Object and cause of ridicule.] Laughingstock. — N. laughingstock, jestingstock[obs3], gazingstock[obs3]; butt, game, fair game; April fool &c. (dupe) 547[obs3].

original, oddity; queer fish, odd fish; quiz, square toes; old monkey, old fogey, fogey monkey, fogy monkey; buffoon &c. (jester) 844; pantomimist &c. (actor) 599.

schlemiel.

jest &c. (wit) 842.

Phr. dum vitant stulti vitia in contraria currunt[Lat].

% 3. PROSPECTIVE AFFECTIONS %

#858. Hope. — N. hope, hopes; desire &c. 865; fervent hope, sanguine expectation, trust, confidence, reliance; faith &c. (belief) 484; affiance, assurance; secureness, security; reassurance.

good omen, good auspices; promise, well grounded hopes; good prospect, bright prospect; clear sky.

assumption, presumption; anticipation &c. (expectation) 507.

hopefulness, buoyancy, optimism, enthusiasm, heart of grace, aspiration.

[person who is hopeful] optimist, utopian, utopist[obs3].

castles in the air, castles in Spain, chateaux en Espagne[Fr], le pot aut lait[Fr], Utopia, millennium; day dream, golden dream; dream of Alnaschar[obs3]; airy hopes, fool's paradise; mirage &c. (fallacies of vision) 443; fond hope. beam of hope, ray of hope, gleam of hope, glimmer of hope, flash of hope, dawn of hope, star of hope; cheer; bit of blue sky, silver lining, silver lining of the cloud, bottom of Pandora's box, balm in Gilead; light at the end of the tunnel. anchor, sheet anchor, mainstay; staff &c. (support) 215; heaven &c. 981. V. hope, trust, confide, rely on, put one's trust in; lean upon; pin one's hope upon, pin one's faith upon &c. (believe) 484. feel hope, entertain hope, harbor hope, indulge hope, cherish hope, feed hope, foster hope, nourish hope, encourage hope, cling to hope, live in hope, &c. n.; see land; feel assured, rest assured, feel confident, rest confident &c. adj. presume; promise oneself; expect &c. (look forward to) 507. hope for &c. (desire) 865; anticipate. be hopeful &c. adj.; look on the bright side of, view on the sunny side, voir en couleur de rose[Fr], make the best of it, hope for the best; put a good face upon, put a bold face upon, put the best face upon; keep one's spirits up; take heart, take heart of grace; be of good heart, be of good cheer; flatter oneself, "lay the flattering unction to one's soul" catch at a straw[hamlet], hope against hope, reckon one's chickens before they are hatched, count one's chickens before they are hatched. [cause hope] give hope, inspire hope, raise hope, hold out hope &c. n.; promise, bid fair, augur well, be in a fair way, look up, flatter, tell a flattering tale; raise expectations[sentient subject]; encourage, cheer, assure, reassure, buoy up, embolden. Adj. hoping &c. v.; in hopes &c. n.; hopeful, confident; secure &c. (certain) 484; sanguine, in good heart, buoyed up, buoyant, elated, flushed, exultant, enthusiastic; heartsome[obs3]; utopian. unsuspecting, unsuspicious; fearless, free from fear, free from suspicion, free from distrust, free from despair, exempt from fear, exempt from suspicion, exempt from distrust, exempt from despair; undespairing[obs3], self reliant. probable, on the high road to; within sight of shore, within sight of land; promising, propitious; of promise, full of promise; of good omen; auspicious, de bon augure[Fr]; reassuring; encouraging, cheering, inspiriting, looking up, bright, roseate, couleur de rose[Fr], rose-colored. Adv. hopefully &c. adj. Int. God speed! Phr. nil desperandum [Lat][Horace]; never say die, dum spiro spero[Lat], latet scintillula forsan[Lat], all is for the best, spero meliora[Lat]; every cloud has a silver lining; "the wish being father to the thought" [Henry IV]; "hope told a flattering tale"; rusticus expectat dum defluat amnis[Lat][obs3]. at spes non fracta[Lat]; ego spem prietio non emo [Lat][Terence]; un Dieu est ma fiance[Fr]; "hope! thou nurse of young desire" [Bickerstaff]; in hoc signo spes mea[Lat]; in hoc signo vinces[Lat]; la speranza e il pan de miseri[It]; l'esperance est le songe d'un homme eveille[Fr]; "the mighty hopes that make us men" [Tennyson]; "the sickening pang of hope deferred" [Scott].

<— p. 292 —>

#859. [Absence, want or loss of hope.] Hopelessness. — N. hopelessness &c. adj.; despair, desperation; despond-ency, depression &c. (dejection) 837; pessimism, pessimist; Job's comforter; bird of bad omen, bird of ill omen. abandonment, desolation; resignation, surrender, submission &c. 725. hope deferred, dashed hopes; vain expecta-tion &c. (disappointment) 509. airy hopes &c. &c 858; forlorn hope; gone case, dead duck, gone coon* [U.S.]; goner*; bad job, bad business; enfant perdu[Fr]; gloomy horizon, black spots in the horizon; slough of Despond, cave of Despair; immedicabile vulnus[Lat]. V. despair; lose all hope, give up all hope, abandon all hope, relinquish all hope, lose the hope of, give up the hope of, abandon the hope of, relinquish the hope of; give up, give over; yield to despair; falter; despond &c. (be dejected) 837; jeter le manche apres la cognee[Fr]. inspire despair, drive to despair &c. n.; disconcert; dash one's hopes, crush one's hopes, destroy one's hopes; hope against hope. abandon; resign, surrender, submit &c. 725. Adj. hopeless, desperate, despairing, gone, in despair, au desespoir[Fr], forlorn, desolate; inconsolable &c. (dejected) 837; broken hearted. unpromising, unpropitious; inauspicious, ill-omened, threatening, clouded over. out of the question, not to be thought of; impracticable &c. 471; past hope, past cure, past mending, past recall; at one's last gasp &c. (death) 360; given up, given over. incurable, cureless, immedicable, remediless, beyond remedy; incorrigible; irreparable, irremediable, irrecoverable, irreversible, irretrievable, irreclaimable, irredeemable, irrevocable; ruined, undone; immitigable. Phr. "lasciate ogni speranza voi ch'entrate" [Dante]; its days are numbered; the worst come to the worst; "no change, no pause, no hope, yet I endure" [Shelley]; "O dark, dark, dark, amid the blaze of noon" [Milton]; "mene mene tekel upharson" [Old Testament].

#860. Fear. — N. fear, timidity, diffidence, want of confidence; apprehensiveness, fearfulness &c. adj.; solicitude, anxiety, care, apprehension, misgiving; feeze [obs3][U.S.]; mistrust &c. (doubt) 485; suspicion, qualm; hesitation &c. (irresolution) 605. nervousness, restlessness &c. adj.; inquietude, disquietude, worry, concern; batophobia[obs3]; heartquake[obs3]; flutter, trepidation, fear and trembling, perturbation, tremor, quivering, shaking, trembling, throb-bing heart, palpitation, ague fit, cold sweat; abject fear &c. (cowardice) 862; mortal funk, heartsinking[obs3], de-spondency; despair &c. 859. fright; affright, affrightment[obs3]; boof alarm[obs3][U.S.], dread, awe, terror, horror, dismay, consternation, panic, scare, stampede [of horses]. intimidation, terrorism, reign of terror. [Object of fear] bug bear, bugaboo; scarecrow; hobgoblin &c. (demon) 980; nightmare, Gorgon, mormo[obs3], ogre, Hurlothrumbo[obs3], raw head and bloody bones, fee-faw-fum, bete noire[Fr], enfant terrible[Fr]. alarmist &c. (coward) 862. V. fear, stand in awe of; be afraid &c. adj.; have qualms &c. n.; apprehend, sit upon thorns, eye askance; distrust &c. (disbelieve)

485. hesitate &c. (be irresolute) 605; falter, funk, cower, crouch; skulk &c. (cowardice) 862; "let 'I dare not' wait upon 'I would'"; take fright, take alarm; start, wince, flinch, shy, shrink; fly &c. (avoid) 623. tremble, shake; shiver, shiver in one's shoes; shudder, flutter; shake like an aspen leaf, tremble like an aspen leaf, tremble all over; quake, quaver, quiver, quail. grow pale, turn pale; blench, stand aghast; not dare to say one's soul is one's own. inspire fear, excite fear, inspire awe, excite awe; raise aprehensions[obs3]; be in a daze, bulldoze [U. S.]; faze, feeze [obs3][U. S.]; give an alarm, raise an alarm, sound an alarm; alarm, startle, scare, cry "wolf," disquiet, dismay; fright, frighten, terrify; astound; fright from one's propriety; fright out of one's senses, fright out of one's wits, fright out of one's seven senses; awe; strike all of a heap, strike an awe into, strike terror; harrow up the soul, appall, unman, petrify, horrify; pile on the agony. make one's flesh creep, make one's hair stand on end, make one's blood run cold, make one's teeth chatter; take away one's breath, stop one's breath; make one tremble &c. haunt; prey on the mind, weigh on the mind. put in fear, put in bodily fear; terrorize, intimidate, cow, daunt, overawe, abash, deter, discourage; browbeat, bully; threaten &c. 909. Adj. fearing &c. v.; frightened &c. v.; in fear, in a fright &c. n.; haunted with the fear of &c. n.; afeard[obs3]. afraid, fearful; timid, timorous; nervous, diffident, coy, faint- hearted, tremulous, shaky, afraid of one's shadow, apprehensive, restless, fidgety; more frightened than hurt. aghast; awe-stricken, horror-stricken, terror-stricken, panic- stricken, awestruck, awe-stricken, horror-struck; frightened to death, white as a sheet; pale, pale as a ghost, pale as death, pale as ashes; breathless, in hysterics. inspiring fear &c. v.; alarming; formidable, redoubtable; perilous &c. (danger) 665; portentous; fearful; dread, dreadful; fell; dire, direful; shocking; terrible, terrific; tremendous; horrid, horrible, horrific; ghastly; awful, awe-inspiring; revolting &c. (painful) 830; Gorgonian. Adv. in terrorem[Lat]. Int. "angels and ministers of grace defend us!" [Hamlet]. Phr. ante tubam trepidat[Latin]; horresco referens[Latin], one's heart failing one, obstupui steteruntque comae et vox faucibus haesit [Lat][Vergil]. "a dagger of the mind" [Macbeth]; expertus metuit [Lat][Horace]; "fain would I climb but that I fear to fall" [Raleigh]; "fear is the parent of cruelty" [Froude]; "Gorgons and hydras and chimeras dire" [Paradise Lost]; omnia tuta timens [Latin] [Vergil]; "our fears do make us traitors" [Macbeth].

<— p. 293 —>

#861. [Absence of fear.] Courage. — N. courage, bravery, valor; resoluteness, boldness &c. adj.; spirit, daring, gallantry, intrepidity; contempt of danger, defiance of danger; derring-do; audacity; rashness &c. 863; dash; defiance &c. 715; confidence, self-reliance. manliness, manhood; nerve, pluck, mettle, game; heart, heart of grace; spunk, guts, face, virtue, hardihood, fortitude, intestinal fortitude; firmness &c. (stability) 150; heart of oak; bottom, backbone, spine &c. (perseverance) 604a. resolution &c. (determination) 604; bulldog courage. prowess, heroism, chivalry. exploit, feat, achievement; heroic deed, heroic act; bold stroke. man, man of mettle; hero, demigod, Amazon, Hector; lion, tiger, panther, bulldog; gamecock, fighting-cock; bully, fire eater &c. 863. V. be courageous &c. adj.; dare, venture, make bold; face danger, front danger, affront danger, confront danger, brave danger, defy danger, despise danger, mock danger; look in the face; look full in the face, look boldly in the face, look danger in the face; face; meet, meet in front; brave, beard; defy &c. 715. take courage, muster courage, summon up courage, pluck up courage; nerve oneself, take heart; take heart, pluck up heart of grace; hold up one's head, screw one's courage to the sticking place; come up to scratch; stick to one's guns, standfire[obs3], stand against; bear up, bear up against; hold out &c. (persevere) 604a. put a bold face upon; show a bold front, present a bold front; show fight; face the music. bell the cat, take the bull by the horns, beard the lion in his den, march up to the cannon's mouth, go through fire and water, run the gantlet. give courage, infuse courage, inspire courage; reassure, encourage, embolden, inspirit, cheer, nerve, put upon one's mettle, rally, raise a rallying cry; pat on the back, make a man of., keep in countenance. Adj. courageous, brave; valiant, valorous; gallant, intrepid; spirited, spiritful[obs3]; high-spirited, high-mettled[obs3]; mettlesome, plucky; manly, manful; resolute; stout,.stout-hearted; iron-hearted, lion- hearted; heart of oak; Penthesilean. bold, bold-spirited; daring, audacious; fearless, dauntless, dreadless[obs3], aweless; undaunted, unappalled, undismayed, unawed, unblanched, unabashed, unalarmed, unflinching, unshrinking[obs3], unblanching[obs3], unapprehensive; confident, self-reliant; bold as a lion, bold as brass. enterprising, adventurous; venturous, venturesome; dashing, chivalrous; soldierly &c. (warlike) 722; heroic. fierce, savage; pugnacious &c. (bellicose) 720. strong-minded, hardy, doughty; firm &c. (stable) 150; determined &c. (resolved) 604; dogged, indomitable &c. (persevering) 604a. up to, up to the scratch; upon one's mettle; reassured &c. v.; unfeared[obs3], undreaded[obs3].

Phr. one's blood being up; courage sans peur [Fr];fortes fortuna adjuvat [Lat][Terence]; "have I not in my time heard lions roar" [Taming of the Shrew]; "I dare do all that may become a man" [Macbeth]; male vincetis sed vincite [Lat] [Ovid]; omne solum forti patria[Lat]; "self- trust is the essence of heroism" [Emerson]; stimulos dedit oemula virtus [Lat][Lucan]; "strong and great, a hero" [Longfellow]; teloque animus proestantior omni [Lat][Ovid]; "there, is always safety in valor" [Emerson]; virtus ariete fortier[Lat][obs3].

<— p. 294 —>

#862. [Excess of fear.] Cowardice. — N. cowardice, pusillanimity; cowardliness &c. adj.; timidity, effeminacy. poltroonery, baseness; dastardness[obs3], dastardy[obs3]; abject fear, funk; Dutch courage; fear &c. 860; white feather, faint heart; cold feet * [U. S.], yellow streak*. coward, poltroon, dastard, sneak, recreant; shy cock, dunghill cock; coistril[obs3], milksop, white liver, lily liver, nidget[obs3], one that cannot say "bo" to a goose; slink; Bob Acres, Jerry Sneak. alarmist, terroristl!, pessimist; runagate &c. (fugitive) 623. V. quail &c. (fear) 860; be cowardly &c. adj., be a coward &c. n.; funk; cower,skulk, sneak; flinch, shy, fight shy, slink, turn tail; run away &c. (avoid) 623; show, the white feather. Adj. coward, cowardly; fearful, shy; timid, timorous; skittish; poor- spirited, spiritless, soft, effemi-nate. weak-minded; infirm of purpose &c. 605; weak-hearted, fainthearted, chickenhearted, henhearted[obs3], lilyhearted, pigeon-hearted; white- livered[obs3], lily-livered, milk-livered[obs3]; milksop, smock-faced; unable to say "bo" to a goose. dastard, dastardly; base, craven, sneaking, dunghill, recreant; unwarlike, unsoldier-like. "in face a lion but in heart a deer". unmanned; frightened &c. 860. Int. sauve qui peut[Fr]! [French: every man for himself]; devil take the hindmost! Phr. ante tubam trepidat[Lat], one's courage oozing out; degeneres animos timor arguit [Lat] [Vergil].

#863. Rashness. — N. rashness &c. adj.; temerity, want of caution, imprudence, indiscretion; overconfidence, presumption, audacity. precipitancy, precipitation; impetuosity; levity; foolhardihood[obs3], foolhardiness; heedless-ness, thoughtlessness &c. (inattention) 458; carelessness &c. (neglect) 460; desperation; Quixotism, knight-errantry; fire eating. gaming, gambling; blind bargain, leap in the dark, leap of faith, fool's paradise; too many eggs in one basket. desperado, rashling[obs3], madcap, daredevil, Hotspur, fire eater, bully, bravo, Hector, scapegrace, enfant perdu[Fr]; Don Quixote, knight- errant, Icarus; adventurer; gambler, gamester; dynamitard[obs3]; boomer [obs3][U. S.]. V. be rash &c. adj.; stick at nothing, play a desperate game; run into danger &c. 665; play with fire, play with edge tools. carry too much sail, sail too near the wind, ride at single anchor, go out of one's depth. take a leap in the dark, buy a pig in a poke. donner tete baissee [Fr]; knock, one's bead against a wall &c. (be unskillful) 699; rush on destruction; kick against the pricks, tempt Providence, go on a forlorn hope, go on a fool's errand. reckon one's chickens before they are hatched, count one's chickens before they are hatched, reckon without one's host; catch at straws; trust to a broken reed, lean on a broken reed. Adj. rash, incautious, indiscreet; imprudent, improvident, temerarious; uncalculating[obs3]; heedless; careless &c. (neglectful) 460; without ballast, heels over head, head over heels; giddy &c. (inattentive) 458; wanton, reckless, wild, madcap; desperate, devil-may-care. hot-blooded, hotheaded, hotbrained[obs3]; headlong, headstrong; breakneck; foolhardy; harebrained; precipitate, impulsive. overconfident, overweening; venturesome, venturous; adventurous, Quixotic, fire eating, cavalier; janty[obs3], jaunty, free and easy. off one's guard &c. (inexpectant) 508[obs3]. Adv. post haste, a corps perdu[Fr], hand over head, tete baissee[Fr], headforemost[obs3]; happen what may, come what may. Phr. neck or nothing, the devil being in one; non semper temeritas est felix [Lat][Livy]; paucis temeritas est bono multis malo [Lat][Phaedrus].

<— p. 295 —>

#864. Caution. — N. caution; cautiousness &c. adj.; discretion, prudence, cautell, heed, circumspection, calculation, deliberation. foresight &c. 510; vigilance &c. 459; warning &c. 668. coolness &c. adj.; self-possession, self-com-mand; presence of mind, sang froid[Fr]; well-regulated mind; worldly wisdom, Fabian policy. V. be cautious &c. adj.; take care, take heed, take good care; have a care mind, what one is about; be on one's guard &c. (keep watch) 459; "make assurance doubly sure" [Macbeth]. bespeak &c. (be early) 132. think twice, look before one leaps, count the cost, look to the main chance, cut one's coat according to one's cloth; feel one's ground, feel one's way; see how the land lies &c. (foresight) 510; wait to see how the cat jumps; bridle one's tongue; reculer pour mieux sauter &c. (prepare) 673[Fr]; let well alone, let well enough alone; let sleeping dogs lie, ne pas reveiller le chat qui dort [French: don't wake a sleeping cat]. keep out of harm's way, keep out of troubled waters; keep at a respectful distance, stand aloof; keep on the safe side, be on the safe side. husband one's resources &c. 636. caution &c. (warn) 668. Adj. cautious, wary, guarded; on one's guard &c. (watchful) 459; cavendo tutus[Lat]; in medio tutissimus[Lat]; vigilant. careful, heedful; cautelousl, stealthy, chary, shy of, circumspect, prudent, discreet, politic; sure-footed &c. (skillful) 698. unenterprising, unadventurous, cool, steady, self-possessed; overcautious. Adv. cautiously &c. adj. Int. have a care! Phr. timeo Danaos [Lat][Vergil]; festina lente[Lat]. ante victoriam ne canas triumphum [Lat: don't sing out victory before the triumph]; "give, every man thine ear but few thy voice" [Hamlet]; he who laughs last laughs best, il rit bien qui rit le dernier[Fr]; ni firmes carta que no leas ni bebas agua que no veas [Sp]; nescit vox missa reverti [Lat] [Horace]; "love all, trust a few" [All's Well]; noli irritare leones [obs3][Lat]; safe bind safe find; "if it ain't broke, don't fix it" [Bert Lance].

<— p. 296 —>

#865. Desire. — N. desire, wish, fancy, fantasy; want, need, exigency. mind, inclination, leaning, bent, animus, partiality, penchant, predilection; propensity &c. 820; willingness &c. 602; liking, love, fondness, relish. longing, hankering, inkling; solicitude, anxiety; yearning, coveting; aspiration, ambition, vaulting ambition; eagerness, zeal, ardor, empressement[Fr], breathless impatience, overanxiety; impetuosity, &c. 825. appetite, appetition[obs3], appetence[obs3], appetency[obs3]; sharp appetite, keenness, hunger, stomach, twist; thirst, thirstiness; drouth, mouthwatering; itch, itching; prurience, cacoethes[Lat], cupidity, lust, concupiscence. edge of appetite, edge of hunger; torment of Tantalus; sweet tooth, lickerish tooth[obs3]; itching palm; longing eye, wistful eye, sheep's eye. [excessive desire for money] greed &c. 817a. voracity &c. (gluttony) 957. passion, rage, furore[obs3], mania, maniel; inextinguishable desire; dipsomania, kleptomania. [Person who desires] lover, amateur, votary, devotee, aspirant, solicitant, candidate, applicant, supplicant; cormorant &c. 957. [Object of desire] desideratum; want &c. (require-ment) 630; "a consummation devoutly to be wished"; attraction, magnet, allurement, fancy, temptation, seduction, fascination, prestige, height of one's ambition, idol; whim, whimsy, whimsey[obs3]; maggot; hobby, hobby-horse. Fortunatus's cap; wishing cap, wishing stone, wishing well. V. desire; wish, wish for; be desirous &c. adj. have a longing &c. n.; hope &c. 858. care for, affect, like, list; take to, cling to, take a fancy to; fancy; prefer &c. (choose) 609. have an eye, have a mind to; find it in one's heart &c. (be willing) 602; have a fancy for, set one's eyes upon; cast a sheep's eye upon, look sweet upon; take into one's head, have at heart, be bent upon; set one's cap at, set one's heart upon, set one's mind upon; covet. want, miss, need, feel the want of, would fain have, would fain do; would be glad of. be hungry &c. adj.; have a good appetite, play a good knife and fork; hunger after, thirst after, crave after, lust after, itch after, hanker after, run mad after; raven for, die for; burn to. desiderate[obs3]; sigh for, cry for, gape for, gasp for, pine for, pant for, languish for, yearn for, long, be on thorns for, hope for; aspire after; catch at, grasp at, jump at. woo, court, solicit; fish for, spell for, whistle for, put up for; ogle. cause desire, create desire, raise desire, excite desire, provoke desire; whet the appetite; appetize[obs3], titillate, allure, attract, take one's fancy, tempt; hold out temptation, hold out allurement; tantalize, make one's mouth water, faire venir l'eau a la bouche [Fr]. gratify desire &c. (give pleasure) 829. Adj. desirous; desiring &c. v.; inclined &c. (willing) 602; partial to; fain, wishful, optative[obs3]; anxious, wistful, curious; at a loss for, sedulous, solicitous. craving, hungry, sharp-set, peckish[obs3], ravening, with an empty stomach, esurient[obs3], lickerish[obs3], thirsty, athirst, parched with thirst, pinched with hunger, famished, dry, drouthy[obs3]; hungry as a hunter, hungry as a hawk, hungry as a horse, hungry as a church mouse, hungry as a bear. [excessively desirous] greedy &c. 817a. unsatisfied, unsated, unslaked; unsaturated. eager, avid, keen; burning, fervent, ardent; agog; all agog; breathless; impatient &c. (impetuous) 825; bent on, intent on, set on, bent upon, intent upon, set upon; mad after, enrage, rabid, dying for, devoured by desire. aspiring, ambitious, vaulting, skyaspiring, high-reaching. desirable; desired &c. v.; in demand; pleasing &c. (giving pleasure) 829; appetizing, appetible[obs3]; tantalizing. Adv. wistfully &c. adj.; fain. Int. would that, would that it were! O for! esto perpetual Phr[Lat]. the wish being father to the thought; sua cuique voluptas[Lat]; hoc erat in votis[Lat], the mouth watering, the fingers itching; aut Caesar aut nullus[Lat]. "Cassius has a lean and hungry look" [Jul. Caesar]; "hungry as the grave" [Thomson]; "I was born to other things" [Tennyson]; "not what we wish but what we want" [Merrick]; "such joy ambition finds" [P. L.]; "the sea hath bounds but deep desire hath none" [Venus and Adonis]; ubi mel ibi apes[Lat].

#866. Indifference. — N. indifference, neutrality; coldness &c. adj.; anaphrodisia[obs3]; unconcern, insouciance, nonchalance; want of interest, want of earnestness; anorexy[obs3], anorexia, inappetency[obs3]; apathy &c. (insensibility) 823; supineness &c. (inactivity) 683; disdain &c. 930; recklessness &c. 863; inattention &c. 458. anaphrodisiac[obs3], antaphrodisiac[obs3]; lust-quencher, passion- queller[obs3]. V. be indifferent &c. adj.; stand neuter; take no interest in &c. (insensibility) 823; have no desire for &c. 865,have no taste for, have no relish for; not care for; care nothing for, care nothing about; not care a straw about, not care a fig for, not care a whit about &c. (unimportance) 643; not mind. set at naught &c. (make light of) 483; spurn &c. (disdain) 930. Adj. indifferent, cold, frigid, lukewarm; cool, cool as a cucumber; unconcerned, insouciant, phlegmatic, pococurante[obs3], easygoing, devil- may-care, careless, listless, lackadaisical; half-hearted; unambitious, unaspiring, undesirous[obs3], unsolicitous[obs3], unattracted. [indifferent toward people] aloof, unapproachable, remote; uncaring. unattractive, unalluring, undesired, undesirable, uncared for, unwished[obs3], unvalued, all one to. insipid &c. 391; vain. Adv. for aught one cares. Int. never mind; Who cares? whatever you like, whatever. Phr. I couldn't care less; I could care less; anything will do; es macht nichts [German].

<— p. 297 —>

#867. Dislike. — N. dislike, distaste, disrelish, disinclination, displacency[obs3]. reluctance; backwardness &c. (unwillingness) 603. repugnance, disgust, queasiness, turn, nausea, loathing; averseness[obs3], aversationl, aversion; abomination, antipathy, abhorrence, horror; mortal antipathy, rooted antipathy, mortal horror, rooted horror;

253

hatred, detestation; hate &c. 898; animosity &c. 900; hydrophobia; canine madness; byssa[obs3], xenophobia. sickener[obs3]; gall and wormwood &c. (unsavory) 395; shuddering, cold sweat. V. mislike misrelish[obs3], dislike, disrelish; mind, object to; have rather not, would rather not, prefer not to, not care for; have a dislike for, conceive a dislike to, entertain a dislike for, take a dislike to, have an aversion to, have an aversion for; have no taste for, have no stomach for. shun, avoid &c. 623; eschew; withdraw from, shrink from, recoil from; not be able to bear, not be able to abide, not be able to endure; shrug the shoulders at, shudder at, turn up the nose at, look askance at; make a mouth, make a wry face, make a grimace; make faces. loathe, nauseate, abominate, detest, abhor; hate &c. 898; take amiss &c. 900; have enough of &c. (be satiated) 869. wish away, unwish cause dislike, excite dislike; disincline, repel, sicken; make sick, render sick; turn one's stomach, nauseate, wamble[obs3], disgust, shock, stink in the nostrils; go against the grain, go against the stomach; stick in the throat; make one's blood run cold &c. (give pain) 830; pall. Adj. disliking &c. v.; averse from, loathe, loathe to, loth, adverse; shy of, sick of, out of conceit with; disinclined; heartsick, dogsick[obs3]; queasy. disliked &c. v.; uncared for, unpopular; out of favor; repulsive, repugnant, repellant; abhorrent, insufferable, fulsome, nauseous; loathsome, loathful[obs3]; offensive; disgusting &c. v.; disagreeable c. (painful) 830. Adv. usque ad nauseam[Lat]. Int. faugh! foh[obs3]! ugh! Phr. non libet[Lat].

#868. Fastidiousness. — N. fastidiousness &c. adj.; nicety, hypercriticism, difficulty in being pleased, friandise[Fr], epicurism, omnia suspendens naso[Lat].
    epicure, gourmet.
    [Excess of delicacy] prudery.
    V. be fastidious &c. adj.; have a sweet tooth.
    mince the matter; turn up one's nose at &c. (disdain) 930; look a gift horse in the mouth, see spots on the sun.
    Adj. fastidious, nice, delicate, delicat[obs3], finical, finicky, demanding, meticulous, exacting, strict, anal[vulg.], difficult, dainty, lickerish[obs3], squeamish, thin-skinned; squeasy[obs3], queasy; hard to please, difficult to please; querulous, particular, straitlaced, scrupulous; censorious &c. 932; hypercritical; overcritical.
    Phr. noli me tangere[Lat].

#869. Satiety. — N. satiety, satisfaction, saturation, repletion, glut, surfeit; cloyment[obs3], satiation; weariness &c. 841. spoiled child; enfant gete[Fr], enfant terrible[Fr]; too much of a good thing, toujours perdrix[Fr]; crambe repetita[Lat][obs3]. V. sate, satiate, satisfy, saturate; cloy, quench, slake, pall, glut., gorge, surfeit; bore &c. (weary) 841; tire &c. (fatigue) 688; spoil. have enough of, have quite enough of, have one's fill, have too much of; be satiated &c. adj. Adj. satiated &c. v.; overgorged[obs3]; blase, used up, sick of, heartsick. Int. enough! hold! eheu jam satis[Lat]! basta[obs3]!

<— p. 298 —> % 4. CONTEMPLATIVE AFFECTIONS %

#870. Wonder. — N. wonder, marvel; astonishment, amazement, wonderment, bewilderment; amazedness &c. adj[obs3].; admiration, awe; stupor, stupefaction; stoundl, fascination; sensation; surprise &c. (inexpectation) 5O8[obs3]. note of admiration; thaumaturgy &c.(sorcery) 992[obs3]. V. wonder, marvel, admire; be surprised &c. adj.; start; stare; open one's eyes, rub one's eyes, turn up one's eyes; gloarl; gape, open one's mouth, hold one's breath; look aghast, stand aghast, stand agog; look blank &c. (disappointment) 509; tombe des nues[Fr]; not believe one's eyes, not believe one's ears, not believe one's senses. not be able to account for &c. (unintelligible) 519; not know whether one stands on one's head or one's heels. surprise, astonish, amaze, astound; dumfound, dumfounder; startle, dazzle; daze; strike, strike with wonder, strike with awe; electrify; stun, stupefy, petrify, confound, bewilder, flabbergast, stagger, throw on one's beam ends, fascinate, turn the head, take away one's breath, strike dumb; make one's hair stand on end, make one's tongue cleave to the roof of one's mouth; make one stare. take by surprise &c. (be unexpected) 508. be wonderful &c. adj.; beggar description, beggar the imagination, baffle description; stagger belief. Adj. surprised &c. v.; aghast, all agog, breathless, agape; open- mouthed; awestruck, thunderstruck, moonstruck, planet-struck; spellbound; lost in amazement, lost in wonder, lost in astonishment; struck all of a heap, unable to believe one's senses, like a duck ion thunder. wonderful, wondrous; surprising &c. v.; unexpected &c. 508; unheard of; mysterious &c. (inexplicable) 519; miraculous. indescribable, inexpressible, inaffable[obs3]; unutterable, unspeakable. monstrous, prodigious, stupendous, marvelous; inconceivable, incredible; inimaginable[obs3], unimaginable; strange &c. (uncommon) 83; passing strange. striking &c. v.; overwhelming; wonder-working. Adv. wonderfully, &c. adj.; fearfully; for a wonder, in the name of wonder; strange to say; mirabile dictu[Lat], mirabile visu[Lat]; to one's great surprise. with wonder &c. n., with gaping mouth; with open eyes, with upturned eyes. Int. lo, lo and behold! O! heyday! halloo! what! indeed! really! surely! humph! hem! good lack, good heavens, good gracious! Ye gods! good Lord! good grief! Holy cow! My word! Holy shit![vulg.], gad so! welladay[obs3]! dear me! only think! lackadaisy[obs3]! my stars, my goodness! gracious goodness! goodness gracious! mercy on us! heavens and earth! God bless me! bless us, bless my heart! odzookens[obs3]! O gemini! adzooks[obs3]! hoity-toity! strong! Heaven save the mark, bless the mark! can such things be! zounds! 'sdeath! what on earth, what in the world! who would have thought it! &c. (inexpectation) 508[obs3]; you don't say so! You're kidding!. No kidding? what do you say to that! nous verrons[Fr]! how now! where am I? Phr. vox faucibus haesit[Lat]; one's hair standing on end.

#871. [Absence of wonder.] Expectance. — N. expectance &c.
(expectation) 507.
    example, instance (conformity) 82.
    normality (habit) 613
    nine days' wonder.
    V. expect &c. 507; not be surprised, not wonder &c. 870; nil admirari[Lat], make nothing of.
    Adj. expecting &c. v.; unamazed, astonished at nothing; blase &c.
(weary) 841; expected &c. v.; foreseen; unsurprising.
    common, ordinary, normal, typical, usual &c. (habitual) 613.
    Adv. naturally, as a matter of course.
    Int. no wonder; of course.
#872. Prodigy. — N. prodigy, phenomenon; wonder, wonderment; marvel, miracle; monster &c. (unconformity) 83; curiosity, lion, sight, spectacle; jeu de theatre[Fr], coup de theatre; gazingstock[obs3]; sign; St. Elmo's fire, St. Elmo's light; portent &c. 512. bursting of a shell, bursting of a bomb; volcanic eruption, peal of thunder; thunder-clap, thunder-bolt. what no words can paint; wonders of the world; annus mirabilis[Lat]; dignus vindice nodus[Lat]. Phr. natura il fece e poi roppe la stampa [Ital.].

<— p. 299 —> % 5. EXTRINSIC AFFECTIONS % <— Or personal affections derived from the opinion or feelings of others. —>

#873. Repute. — N. distinction, mark, name, figure; repute, reputation; good repute, high repute; note, notability, notoriety, eclat, "the bubble reputation" [As You Like It], vogue, celebrity; fame, famousness; renown; popularity, aura popularis[Lat]; approbation &c. 931; credit, succes d'estime[Fr], prestige, talk of the town; name to conjure with. glory, honor; luster &c. (light) 420; illustriousness &c. adj. account, regard, respect; reputableness &c. adj[obs3].; respectability &c. (probity) 939; good name, good report; fair name. dignity; stateliness &c. adj.; solemnity, grandeur, splendor, nobility, majesty, sublimity. rank, standing, brevet rank, precedence, pas, station, place, status; position, position in society; order, degree, baccalaureate, locus standi[Lat], caste, condition. greatness &c. adj.; eminence; height &c. 206; importance &c. 642; preeminence, supereminence; high mightiness, primacy; top of the ladder, top of the tree. elevation; ascent &c. 305; superaltation[obs3], exaltation; dignification[obs3], aggrandizement. dedication, consecration, enthronement, canonization, celebration, enshrinement, glorification. hero, man of mark, great card, celebrity, worthy, lion, rara avis[Lat], notability, somebody; classman[obs3]; man of rank &c. (nobleman) 875; pillar of the state, pillar of the church, pillar of the community. chief &c. (master) 745; first fiddle &c. (proficient) 700; cynosure, mirror; flower, pink, pearl; paragon &c. (perfection) 650; choice and master spirits of the age; elite; star,. sun, constellation, galaxy. ornament, honor, feather in one's cap, halo, aureole, nimbus; halo of glory, blaze of glory, blushing honors; laurels &c. (trophy) 733. memory, posthumous fame, niche in the temple of fame; immortality, immortal name; magni nominis umbra [Lat][Lucan]. V. be conscious of glory; be proud of &c. (pride) 878; exult &c. (boast) 884; be vain of &c. (vanity) 880.

be distinguished &c. adj.; shine &c. (light) 420; shine forth, figure; cut a figure, make a dash, make a splash. rival, surpass; outshine, outrival, outvie[obs3], outjump; emulate, eclipse; throw into the shade, cast into the shade; overshadow. live, flourish, glitter, flaunt, gain honor, acquire honor &c. n.; play first fiddle &c. (be of importance) 642, bear the palm, bear the bell; lead the way; take precedence, take the wall of; gain laurels, win laurels, gain spurs, gain golden opinions &c. (approbation) 931; take one's degree, pass one's examination. make a noise, make some noise, make a noise in the world; leave one's mark, exalt one's horn, blow one's horn, star it, have a run, be run after; come into vogue, come to the front; raise one's head. enthrone, signalize, immortalize, deify, exalt to the skies; hand one's name down to posterity. consecrate; dedicate to, devote to; enshrine, inscribe, blazon, lionize, blow the trumpet, crown with laurel. confer honor on, reflect honor on &c. v.; shed a luster on; redound to one's honor, ennoble. give honor to, do honor to, pay honor to, render honor to; honor, accredit, pay regard to, dignify, glorify; sing praises to &c. (approve) 931; lock up to; exalt, aggrandize, elevate, nobilitate[Lat]. Adj. distinguished, distingue[Fr], noted; of note &c. n.; honored &c. v.; popular; fashionable &c. 852. in good odor in; favor, in high favor; reputable, respectable, creditable. remarkable &c. (important) 642; notable, notorious; celebrated, renowned, ion every one's mouth, talked of; famous, famed; far-famed; conspicuous, to the front; foremost; in the front rank, in the ascendant. imperishable, deathless, immortal, never fading, aere perennius[Lat][obs3]; time honored. illustrious, glorious, splendid, brilliant, radiant; bright &c. 420; full-blown; honorific. eminent, prominent; high &c. 206; in the zenith; at the head of, at the top of the tree; peerless, of the first water.; superior &c. 33; supereminent, preeminent. great, dignified, proud, noble, honorable, worshipful, lordly, grand, stately, august, princely. imposing, solemn, transcendent, majestic, sacred, sublime, heaven-born, heroic, sans peur et sans reproche[Fr]; sacrosanct. Int. hail! all hail! ave! viva! vive[Fr]! long life to! banzai![Jap.]; glory be to, honor be to? Phr. one's name being in every mouth, one's name living for ever; sic itur ad astra[Lat], fama volat[Lat], aut Caesar aut nullus[Lat]; not to know him argues oneself unknown; none but himself could be his parallel; palmam qui meruit ferat [Lat][Nelson's motto]. "above all Greek above all Roman fame" [Pope]; - cineri gloria sera est [Lat][Martial]; "great is the glory for the strife is hard" [Wordsworth]; honor virtutis praemium [Lat][Cicero]; immensum gloria calcar habet [Lat][obs3][Ovid]; "the glory dies not and the grief is past" [Brydges]; vivit post funera virtus[Lat].

<— p. 300 —>

#874. Disrepute. — N. disrepute, discredit; ill repute, bad repute, bad name, bad odor, bad favor, ill name, ill odor, ill favor; disapprobation &c. 932; ingloriousness, derogation; abasement, debasement; abjectness &c. adj.; degradation, dedecoration[obs3]; a long farewell to all my greatness [Henry VIII]; odium, obloquy, opprobrium, ignominy. dishonor, disgrace; shame, humiliation; scandal, baseness, vileness[obs3]; turpitude &c. (improbity) 940[obs3]; infamy. tarnish, taint, defilement, pollution. stain, blot, spot, blur, stigma, brand, reproach, imputation, slur. crying shame, burning shame; scandalum magnatum[Lat], badge of infamy, blot in one's escutcheon; bend sinister, bar sinister; champain[obs3], point champain[obs3]; byword of reproach; Ichabod. argumentum ad verecundiam[Lat]; sense of shame &c. 879. V. be inglorious &c. adj.; incur disgrace &c. n.; have a bad name, earn a bad name; put a halter round one's neck, wear a halter round one's neck; disgrace oneself, expose oneself. play second fiddle; lose caste; pale one's ineffectual fire; recede into the shade; fall from one's high estate; keep in the background &c. (modesty) 881; be conscious of disgrace &c. (humility) 879; look blue, look foolish, look like a fool; cut a poor figure, cut a sorry figure; laugh on the wrong side of the mouth; make a sorry face, go away with a flea in. one's ear, slink away. cause shame &c. n.; shame, disgrace, put to shame, dishonor; throw dishonor upon, cast dishonor upon, fling dishonor upon, reflect dishonor upon &c. n.; be a reproach &c. n. to; derogate from. tarnish, stain, blot sully, taint; discredit; degrade, debase, defile; beggar; expel &c. (punish) 972. impute shame to, brand, post, stigmatize, vilify, defame, slur, cast a slur upon, hold up to shame, send to Coventry; tread under foot, trample under foot; show up, drag through the mire, heap dirt upon; reprehend &c. 932. bring low, put down, snub; take down a peg, take down a peg lower, take down a peg or two. obscure. eclipse, outshine, take the shine out of; throw into the shade, cast into the shade; overshadow; leave in the background, put in the background; push into a corner, put one's nose out of joint; put out, put out of countenance. upset, throw off one's center; discompose, disconcert; put to the blush &c. (humble) 879. Adj. disgraced &c. v.; blown upon; "shorn of its beams" [Milton], shorn of one's glory; overcome, downtrodden; loaded with shame &c. n.; in bad repute &c. n.; out of repute, out of favor, out of fashion, out of countenance; at a discount; under a cloud, under an eclipse; unable to show one's face; in the shade, in the background; out at elbows, down at the elbows, down in the world. inglorious; nameless, renownless[obs3]; obscure; unknown to fame; unnoticed, unnoted[obs3], unhonored, unglorified[obs3]. shameful; disgraceful, discreditable, disreputable; despicable; questionable; unbecoming, unworthy; derogatory; degrading, humiliating, infra dignitatem[Lat], dedecorous[obs3]; scandalous, infamous, too bad, unmentionable; ribald, opprobrious; errant, shocking, outrageous, notorious. ignominious, scrubby, dirty, abject, vile, beggarly, pitiful, low, mean, shabby base &c. (dishonorable) 940. Adv. to one's shame be it spoken. Int. fie! shame! for shame! proh pudor[Lat]! O tempora[obs3]! O mores! ough! sic transit gloria mundi[Lat.]! - <— p. 301 —>

#875. Nobility. — N. nobility, rank, condition, distinction, optimacy[obs3], blood, pur sang[Fr], birth, high descent, order; quality, gentility; blue blood of Castile; ancien regime[Fr]. high life, haute monde[Fr]; upper classes, upper ten thousand; the four hundred [U. S.]; elite, aristocracy, great folks; fashionable world &c. (fashion) 852. peer, peerage; house of lords, house of peers; lords, lords temporal and spiritual; noblesse; noble, nobleman; lord, lordling[obs3]; grandee, magnifico[Lat], hidalgo; daimio[obs3], daimyo, samurai, shizoku [all Japanese]; don, donship[obs3]; aristocrat, swell, three-tailed bashaw[obs3]; gentleman, squire, squireen[obs3], patrician, laureate. gentry, gentlefolk; *squirarchy[obs3], better sort magnates, primates, optimates[obs3]; pantisocracy[obs3]. king &c. (master) 745; atheling[obs3]; prince, duke; marquis, marquisate[obs3]; earl, viscount, baron, thane, banneret[obs3]; baronet, baronetcy[obs3]; knight, knighthood; count, armiger[obs3], laird; signior[obs3], seignior; esquire, boyar, margrave, vavasour[obs3]; emir, ameer[obs3], scherif[obs3], sharif, effendi, wali; sahib; chevalier, maharaja, nawab, palsgrave[obs3], pasha, rajah, waldgrave[obs3]. princess, begum[obs3], duchess, marchioness; countess &c.; lady, dame; memsahib; Dona, maharani, rani. personage of distinction, man of distinction, personage of rank, man of rank, personage of mark, man of mark; notables, notabilities; celebrity, bigwig, magnate, great man, star, superstar; big bug; big gun, great gun; gilded rooster* [U. S.]; magni nominis umbra [Lat][Lucan]; "every inch a king" [Lear]. V. be noble &c. adj. Adj. noble, exalted; of rank &c. n.; princely, titled, patrician, aristocratic; high-, well-born; of gentle blood; genteel, comme il faut[Fr], gentlemanlike[obs3], courtly &c. (fashionable) 852; highly respectable. Adv. in high quarters. Phr. Adel sitzt im Gemuthe nicht im Gebluete[Ger.]; adelig und edel sind zweierlei[obs3][Ger.]; noblesse oblige[Fr.].

#876. Commonalty. — N. commonalty, democracy; obscurity; low condition, low life, low society, low company; bourgeoisie; mass of the people, mass of society; Brown Jones and Robinson; lower classes, humbler classes, humbler orders; vulgar herd, common herd; rank and file, hoc genus omne[Lat]; the many, the general,the crowd, the people, the populace, the multitude, the million, the masses, the mobility, the peasantry; king Mob; proletariat; fruges consumere nati[Lat], demos, hoi polloi [Grk][Grk][Grk], great unwashed; man in the street. mob; rabble, rabble rout; chaff, rout, horde, canaille; scum of the people, residuum of the people, dregs of the people, dregs of society; swinish multitude, foex populi[obs3]; trash; profanum vulgus[Lat], ignobile vulgus[Lat]; vermin, riffraff, ragtag and bobtail; small fry. commoner, one of the people, democrat, plebeian, republican, proletary[obs3], proletaire[obs3], roturier[obs3], Mr. Snooks, bourgeois, epicier[Fr], Philistine, cockney; grisette[obs3], demimonde. peasant, country-man, boor, carle[obs3], churl; villain, villein; terrae filius[Latin: son of the land]; serf, kern[obs3], tyke, tike, chuff[obs3], ryot[obs3], fellah; longshoreman; swain, clown, hind; clod, clodhopper; hobnail, yokel, bog-trotter, bumpkin; plowman, plowboy[obs3]; rustic, hayseed*, lunkhead [U. S.], chaw-bacon*[obs3], tiller of the soil; hewers of wood and drawers of water, groundling[obs3]; gaffer, loon, put, cub, Tony Lumpkin[obs3], looby[obs3], rube* [U. S.], lout, underling; gamin; rough; pot-wallopper[obs3], slubberdegullionl; vulgar fellow, low fellow; cad, curmudgeon. upstart, parvenu, skipjack[obs3]; nobody, nobody one knows; hesterni quirites[Lat], pessoribus orti[Lat]; bourgeois gentilhomme[Fr], novus homo[Lat], snob, gent, mushroom, no one knows who, adventurer; man of straw. beggar, gaberlunzie[obs3], muckworm[obs3], mudlark[obs3], sans culotte, raff[obs3], tatterdemalion, caitiff, ragamuffin, Pariah, outcast of society, tramp, vagabond, bezonian[obs3], panhandler*, sundowner[obs3], chiffonnier, Cinderella, cinderwench[obs3], scrub, jade; gossoon[obs3]. Goth, Vandal, Hottentot, Zulu, savage, barbarian, Yahoo; unlicked cub[obs3], rough diamondl!. barbarousness, barbarism; boeotia. V. be ignoble &c. adj., be nobody &c. n. Adj. ignoble, common, mean, low, base, vile, sorry, scrubby, beggarly; below par; no great shakes &c. (unimportant) 643; homely, homespun; vulgar, low-minded; snobbish. plebeian, proletarian; of low parentage, of low origin, of low extraction, of mean parentage, of mean origin, of mean extraction; lowborn, baseborn, earthborn[obs3]; mushroom, dunghill, risen from the ranks; unknown to fame, obscure, untitled. rustic, uncivilized; loutish, boorish, clownish, churlish, brutish, raffish; rude, unlicked[obs3]. barbarous, barbarian, barbaric, barbaresque[obs3]; cockney, born within sound of Bow bells. underling, menial, subaltern. Adv. below the salt. Phr. dummodo sit dives barbarus ipse placet [Lat][Ovid].

<— p. 302 —>

#877. Title. — N. title, honor; knighthood &c. (nobility) 875. highness, excellency, grace; lordship, worship; rever-ence, reverend; esquire, sir, master, Mr., signor, senor, Mein Herr[Ger], mynheer[obs3]; your honor, his honor; serene highness; handle to one's name. decoration, laurel, palm, wreath, garland, bays, medal, ribbon, riband, blue ribbon, cordon, cross, crown, coronet, star, garter; feather, feather in one,s cap; epaulet, epaulette, colors, cockade; livery; order, arms, shield, scutcheon; reward &c. 973.

#878. Pride. — N. dignity, self-respect, mens sibi conscia recti [Lat][Vergil]. pride; haughtiness &c. adj.; high notions, hauteur; vainglory, crest; arrogance &c. (assumption) 885. proud man, highflier[obs3]; fine gentleman, fine lady. V. be proud &c. adj.; put a good face on; look one in the face; stalk abroad, perk oneself up; think no small beer of oneself; presume, swagger, strut; rear one's head, lift up one's head, hold up one's head; hold one's head high, look big, take the wall, "bear like the Turk no rival near the throne" [Pope], carry with a high hand; ride the high horse, mount on one's high horse; set one's back up, bridle, toss the head; give oneself airs &c. (assume) 885; boast &c. 884. pride oneself on; glory in, take a pride in; pique oneself, plume oneself, hug oneself; stand upon, be proud of; put a good face on; not hide one's light under a bushel, not put one's talent in a napkin; not think small beer of oneself &c. (vanity) 880. Adj. dignified; stately; proud, proud-crested; lordly, baronial; lofty-minded; highsouled; high-minded, high-mettled[obs3], high-handed, high-plumed, high-flown, high-toned. haughty lofty, high, mighty, swollen, puffed up, flushed, blown; vainglorious; purse-proud, fine; proud as a peacock, proud as Lucifer; bloated with pride. supercilious, disdainful, bumptious, magisterial, imperious, high and mighty, overweening, consequential; arrogant &c. 885; unblushing &c. 880. stiff, stiff-necked; starch; perked stuck-up; in buckram, strait- laced; prim &c.

(affected) 855. on one's dignity, on one's high horses,on one's tight ropes, on one's high ropes; on stilts; en grand seigneur [Fr]. Adv. with head erect. Phr. odi profanum vulgus et arceo [Lat][Horace]. "a duke's revenues on her back" [Henry VI]; "disdains the shadow which he treads on at noon" [Coriolanis]; "pride in their port, defiance in their eye" [Goldsmith].

#879. Humility. — N. humility, humbleness; meekness, lowness; lowliness, lowlihood[obs3]; abasement, self-abasement; submission &c. 725; resignation. condescension; affability &c. (courtesy) 894. modesty &c. 881; verecundityl, blush, suffusion, confusion; sense of shame,sense of disgrace; humiliation, mortification; let down, set down. V. be humble &c. adj.; deign, vouchsafe, condescend; humble oneself, demean oneself; stoop, stoop to conquer; carry coals; submit &c. 725; submit with a good grace &c. (brook) 826; yield the palm. lower one's tone, lower one's note; sing small, draw in one's horns, sober down; hide one's face, hide one's diminished head; not dare to show one's face, take shame to oneself, not have a word to say for oneself; feel shame, be conscious of shame, feel disgrace, be conscious of disgrace; drink the cup of humiliation to the dregs. blush for, blush up to the eves; redden, change color; color up; hang one's head, look foolish, feel small. render humble; humble, humiliate; let down, set down, take down, tread down, frown down; snub, abash, abase, make one sing small, strike dumb; teach one his distance; put down, take down a peg, take down a peg lower; throw into the shade, cast into the shade &c. 874; stare out of countenance, put out of countenance; put to the blush; confuse, ashame[obs3], mortify, disgrace, crush; send away with a flea in one's ear. get a setdown[obs3]. Adj. humble, lowly, meek; modest &c. 881; humble minded, sober-minded; unoffended[obs3]; submissive &c. 725; servile, &c. 886. condescending; affable &c. (courteous) 891. humbled &c. v.; bowed down, resigned; abashed, ashamed, dashed; out of countenance; down in the mouth; down on one's knees, down on one's marrowbones, down on one's uppers; humbled in the dust, browbeaten; chapfallen[obs3], crestfallen; dumfoundered[obs3]. flabbergasted. shorn of one's glory &c. (disrepute) 874. Adv. with downcast eyes, with bated breath, with bended knee; on all fours, on one's feet. under correction, with due deference. Phr. I am your obedient servant, I am your very humble servant; my service to you; da locum melioribus [Lat] [Terence]; parvum parva decent [Lat][Horace].

<— p. 303 —>

#880. Vanity. — N. vanity; conceit, conceitedness; self-conceit, self-complacency, self-confidence, self-sufficiency, self-esteem, self- love, self-approbation, self-praise, self-glorification, self-laudation, self-gratulation[obs3], self-applause, self-admiration; amour propre[Fr]; selfishness &c. 943. airs, affected manner, pretensions, mannerism; egotism; priggism[obs3], priggishness; coxcombry, gaudery[obs3], vainglory, elation; pride &c. 878; ostentation &c. 882; assurance &c. 885. vox et praeterea nihil[Lat]; cheval de bataille[Fr]. coxcomb &c. 854 Sir Oracle &c. 887. V. be vain &c. adj., be vain of; pique oneself &c. (pride) 878; lay the flattering unction to one's soul. have too high an opinion of oneself, have an overweening opinion of oneself, have too high an opinion of one's talents; blind oneself as to one's own merit; not think small beer of oneself, not think vin ordinaire of oneself[Fr]; put oneself forward; fish for compliments; give oneself airs &c. (assume) 885; boast &c. 884. render vain &c. adj.; inspire with vanity &c. n.; inflate, puff up, turn up, turn one's head. Adj. vain, vain as a peacock, proud as a peacock; conceited, overweening, pert, forward; vainglorious, high-flown; ostentatious &c. 882; puffed up, inflated, flushed. self-satisfied, self-confident, self-sufficient, self-flattering, self-admiring, self-applauding, self-glorious, self-opinionated; entente &c. (wrongheaded) 481; wise in one's own conceit, pragmatical[obs3], overwise[obs3], pretentious, priggish; egotistic, egotistical; soi-disant &c. (boastful) 884[Fr]; arrogant &c. 885. unabashed, unblushing; unconstrained, unceremonious; free and easy. Adv. vainly &c. adj. Phr. "how we apples swim!" [Swift]; "prouder than rustling in unpaid-for silk" [Cymbeline].

#881. Modesty. — N. modesty; humility &c. 879; diffidence, timidity; retiring disposition; unobtrusiveness; bashfulness &c. adj.; mauvaise honte[Fr]; blush, blushing; verecundityl; self-knowledge. reserve, constraint; demureness &c. adj.; "blushing honors" [Henry VIII]. V. be modest &c. adj.; retire, reserve oneself; give way to; draw in one's horns &c. 879; hide one's face. keep private, keep in the background, keep one's distance; pursue the noiseless tenor of one's way, "do good by stealth and blush to find it fame" [Pope], hide one's light under a bushel, cast a sheep's eye. Adj. modest, diffident; humble &c. 879; timid, timorous, bashful; shy, nervous, skittish, coy, sheepish, shamefaced, blushing, overmodest. unpretending[obs3], unpretentious; unobtrusive, unassuming, unostentatious, unboastful[obs3], unaspiring; poor in spirit. out of countenance &c. (humbled) 879. reserved, constrained, demure. Adv. humbly &c. adj.; quietly, privately; without ceremony, without beat of drum; sans fa on. Phr. "not stepping o'er the bounds of modesty" [Romeo and Juliet]; "thy modesty's a candle to thy merit" [Fielding].

<— p. 304 —>

#882. Ostentation. — N. ostentation, display, show, flourish, parade, etalage[Fr], pomp, array, state, solemnity; dash, splash, splurge, glitter, strut, pomposity; pretense, pretensions; showing off; fuss. magnificence, splendor; coup d'oeil[Fr]; grand doings. coup de theatre; stage effect, stage trick; claptrap; mise en scene[Fr]; tour de force; chic. demonstration, flying colors; tomfoolery; flourish of trumpets &c. (celebration) 883; pageant, pageantry; spectacle, exhibition, exposition, procession; turn out, set out; grand function; fte, gala, field day, review, march past, promenade, insubstantial pageant. dress; court dress, full dress, evening dress, ball dress, fancy dress; tailoring, millinery, man millinery, frippery, foppery, equipage. ceremony, ceremonial; ritual; form, formality; etiquette; puncto[Lat], punctilio, punctiliousness; starched stateliness, stateliness. mummery, solemn mockery, mouth honor. attitudinarian[obs3]; fop &c. 854. V. be ostentatious &c. adj.; come forward, put oneself forward; attract attention, star it. cut a figure, make a dash, make a splash, make a splurge, cut a dash, cut a splash, cut a splurge; figure, figure away; make a show, make a display; glitter. show off, show off one's paces; parade, march past; display, exhibit, put forward, hold up; trot out, hand out; sport, brandish, blazon forth; dangle, dangle before the eyes. cry up &c. (praise) 931; proner[Fr], flaunt, emblazon, prink[obs3], set off, mount, have framed and glazed. put a good face upon, put a smiling face upon; clean the outside of the platter &c. (disguise) 544. Adj. ostentatious, showy, dashing, pretentious; janty[obs3], jaunty; grand, pompous, palatial; high-sounding; turgid &c. (big-sounding) 577; gairish[obs3], garish; gaudy, gaudy as a peacock, gaudy as a butterfly, gaudy as a tulip; flaunting, flashing, flaming, glittering; gay &c. (ornate) 847. splendid, magnificent, sumptuous. theatrical, dramatic, spectacular; ceremonial, ritual. solemn, stately, majestic, formal, stiff, ceremonious, punctilious, starched. dressed to kill, dressed to the nines, decjed out, all decked out, en granite tenue[Fr], in best bib and tucker, in Sunday best, endimanch, chic. Adv. with flourish of trumpet, with beat of drum, with flying colors. ad captandum vulgus[Lat.]. Phr. honores mutant mores[Lat].

#883. Celebration. — N. celebration, solemnization, jubilee, commemoration, ovation, paean, triumph, jubilation, ceremony (rite) 998; holiday, fiesta, zarabanda[obs3], revelry, feast (amusement) 840; china anniversary, diamond anniversary, golden anniversary, silver anniversary, tin anniversary, china jubilee, diamond jubilee, golden jubilee, silver jubilee, tin jubilee, china wedding, diamond wedding, golden wedding, silver wedding, tin wedding. triumphal arch, bonfire, salute; salvo, salvo of artillery; feu de joie[Fr], flourish of trumpets, fanfare, colors flying, illuminations. inauguration, installation, presentation; coronation; Lord Mayor's show; harvest-home, red-letter day; trophy &,:c. 733; Te Deum &c. (thanksgiving) 990[Lat]; fete &c. 882; holiday &c. 840; Forefathers' Day [U. S.]. V. celebrate keep, signalize, do honor to, commemorate, solemnize, hallow, mark with a red letter. pledge, drink to, toast, hob and nob[obs3]. inaugurate, install, chair. rejoice &c. 838; kill the fatted calf, hold jubilee, roast an ox. Adj. celebrating &c. v.; commemorative, celebrated, immortal. Adv. in honor of, in commemoration of. Int. hail! all hail! io paean, io triumphe[obs3]! "see the conquering hero comes!".

#884. Boasting. — N. boasting &c. v.; boast, vaunt, crakel; pretense, pretensions; puff, puffery; flourish, fanfaronade[obs3]; gasconade; blague[obs3], bluff, gas*; highfalutin, highfaluting[obs3]; hot air, spread-eagleism [obs3][U. S.]; brag, braggardism[obs3]; bravado, bunkum, buncombe; jactitation[obs3], jactancy[obs3]; bounce; venditationl, vaporing, rodomontade, bombast, fine talking, tall talk, magniloquence, teratologyl, heroics; Chauvinism; exaggeration &c. 549. vanity &c. 880; vox et praeterea nihil[Lat]; much cry and little wool, brutum fulmen[Lat]. exultation; gloriationl, glorification; flourish of trumpets; triumph &c. 883. boaster; braggart, braggadocio; Gascon[Fr], fanfaron[obs3], pretender, soi-disant[Fr]; blower [U. S.], bluffer, Foxy Quiller[obs3]; blusterer &c. 887; charlatan, jack-pudding, trumpeter; puppy &c. (fop) 854. V. boast, make a boast of, brag, vaunt, Puff, show off, flourish, crakel, crack, trumpet, strut, swagger, vapor; blague[obs3], blow, four- flush *, bluff. exult, crow, crow over, neigh, chuckle, triumph; throw up one's cap; talk big, se faire valoir[Fr], faire claquer son fouet[obs3][Fr], take merit to oneself, make a merit of, sing lo triumphe[obs3], holloa before one is out of the wood[obs3]. Adj. boasting &c. v.; magniloquent, flaming, Thrasonic, stilted, gasconading, braggart, boastful, pretentious, soi-disant[Fr]; vainglorious &c. (conceited) 880; highfalutin, highfaluting[obs3]; spread-eagle [U. S.*]. elate, elated; jubilant, triumphant, exultant; in high feather; flushed, flushed with victory; cock-a-hoop; on stilts. vaunted &c. v. Adv. vauntingly &c. adj. Phr. "let the galled jade wince" [Hamlet]; facta non verba[Lat].

<— p. 305 —>

#885. [Undue assumption of superiority.] Insolence. — N. insolence; haughtiness &c. adj.; arrogance, airs; overbearance[obs3]; domineering &c. v.; tyranny &c. 739. impertinence; sauciness &c. adj.; flippancy, dicacityl, petulance, procacity[obs3], bluster; swagger, swaggering &c. v.; bounce; terrorism. assumption, presumption; beggar on horseback; usurpation. impudence, assurance, audacity, hardihood, front, face, brass; shamelessness &c. adj.; effrontery, hardened front, face of brass. assumption of infallibility. saucebox &c. (blusterer) 887[obs3]. V. be insolent &c. adj.; bluster, vapor, swagger, swell, give oneself airs, snap one's fingers, kick up a dust; swear &c. (affirm) 535; rap out oaths; roister. arrogate; assume, presume; make bold, make free; take a liberty, give an inch and take an ell. domineer, bully, dictate, hector; lord it over; traiter de haut en bas[Fr], regarder de haut en bas[Fr];

exact; snub, huff., beard, fly in the face of; put to the blush; bear down, beat down; browbeat, intimidate; trample down, tread down, trample under foot; dragoon, ride roughshod over. out face, outlook, outstare, outbrazen[obs3], outbrave[obs3]; stare out of countenance; brazen out; lay down the law; teach one's grandmother to suck eggs; assume a lofty bearing; talk big, look big; put on big looks, act the grand seigneur[Fr]; mount the high horse, ride the high horse; toss the head, carry, with a high hand. tempt Providence, want snuffing. Adj. insolent, haughty, arrogant, imperious, magisterial, dictatorial, arbitrary; high-handed, high and mighty; contumelious, supercilious, overbearing, intolerant, domineering, overweening, high-flown. flippant, pert, fresh [U. S.], cavalier, saucy, forward, impertinent, malapert. precocious, assuming, would-be, bumptious. bluff; brazen, shameless, aweless, unblushlng[obs3], unabashed; brazen, boldfaced-, barefaced-, brazen-faced; dead to shame, lost to shame. impudent, audacious, presumptuous, free and easy, devil-may-care, rollicking; jaunty, janty[obs3]; roistering, blustering, hectoring, swaggering, vaporing; thrasonic, fire eating, "full of sound and fury" [Macbeth]. Adv. with a high hand; ex cathedra[Lat]. Phr. one's bark being worse than his bite; "beggars mounted run their horse to death" [Henry VI]; quid times? Caesarem vehis [Lat][Plutarch]; wagahai wa [Jap: I (expressing superiority)].

#886. Servility. — N. servility; slavery &c. (subjection) 749; obsequiousness &c. adj.; subserviency; abasement; prostration, prosternationl; genuflection &c. (worship) 990; fawning &c. v.; tuft- hunting, timeserving[obs3], flunkeyism[obs3]; sycophancy &c. (flattery) 933; humility &c. 879. sycophant, parasite; toad, toady, toad-eater; tufthunter[obs3]; snob, flunky, flunkey, yes-man, lapdog, spaniel, lickspittle, smell-feast, Graeculus esuriens[Lat], hanger on, cavaliere servente[It], led captain, carpet knight; timeserver, fortune hunter, Vicar of Bray, Sir-Pertinax, Max Sycophant, pickthank[obs3]; flatterer &c. 935; doer of dirty work; ame damnee[Fr], tool; reptile; slave &c. (servant) 746; courtier; beat*, dead beat*, doughface * [obs3][U. S], heeler [U. S.], homme de cour[Fr], sponger, sucker*, tagtail[obs3], truckler. V. cringe, bow, stoop, kneel, bend the knee; fall on one's knees, prostrate oneself; worship &c. 990. sneak, crawl, crouch, cower, sponge, truckle to, grovel, fawn, lick the feet of, kiss the hem of one's garment, kiss one's ass[vulg.], suck up. pay court to; feed on, fatten on, dance attendance on, pin oneself upon, hang on the sleeve of, avaler les couleuvres[Fr], keep time to, fetch and carry, do the dirty work of. go with the stream, worship the rising sun, hold with the hare and run with the hounds. Adj. servile, obsequious; supple,supple as a glove; soapy, oily, pliant, cringing, abased, dough-faced, fawning, slavish, groveling, sniveling, mealy-mouthed; beggarly, sycophantic, parasitical; abject, prostrate, down on ones marrowbones; base, mean, sneaking; crouching &c. v. Adv. hat in hand, cap in hand.

<— p. 306 —>

#887. Blusterer. — N. blusterer, swaggerer, vaporer, roisterer[obs3], brawler; fanfaron[obs3]; braggart &c. (boaster) 884; bully, terrorist, rough; bulldozer [U. S.], hoodlum, hooligan*, larrikin[obs3], roarer*; Mohock, Mohawk; drawcansir[obs3], swashbuckler, Captain Bobadil, Sir Lucius O'Trigger, Thraso, Pistol, Parolles, Bombastes Furioso[obs3], Hector, Chrononhotonthologos[obs3]; jingo; desperado, dare-devil, fire eater; fury, &c. (violent person) 173; rowdy; slang-whanger*[obs3], tough [U. S.]. puppy &c. (fop) 854; prig; Sir Oracle, dogmatist, doctrinaire, jack- in-office; saucebox[obs3], malapert, jackanapes, minx; bantam-cock.

%
SECTION III. SYMPATHETIC AFFECTIONS
1. SOCIAL AFFECTIONS %

#888. Friendship.— N. friendship, amity; friendliness &c. adj.; brotherhood, fraternity, sodality, confraternity; harmony &c. (concord) 714; peace &c. 721. firm friendship, staunch friendship, intimate friendship, familiar friendship, bosom friendship, cordial friendship, tried friendship, devoted friendship, lasting friendship, fast friendship, sincere friendship, warm friendship, ardent friendship. cordiality, fraternization, entente cordiale[Fr], good understanding, rapprochement, sympathy, fellow-feeling, response, welcomeness. affection &c. (love) 897; favoritism; good will &c. (benevolence) 906. acquaintance, familiarity, intimacy, intercourse, fellowship, knowledge of; introduction. V. be friendly &c. adj., be friends &c. 890, be acquainted with &c. adj.; know; have the ear of; keep company with &c. (sociality) 892; hold communication with, have dealings with, sympathize with; have a leaning to; bear good will &c. (benevolent) 906; love &c. 897; make much of; befriend &c. (aid) 707; introduce to. set one's horses together; have the latchstring out [U. S.]; hold out the right hand of friendship, extend the right hand of friendship, hold out the right hand of fellowship; become friendly &c. adj.; make friends &c. 890 with; break the lee, be introduced to; make acquaintance with, pick acquaintance with, scrape acquaintance with; get into favor, gain the friendship of. shake hands with, fraternize, embrace; receive with open arms, throw oneself into the arms of; meet halfway, take in good part. Adj. friendly; amicable, amical[obs3]; well-affected, unhostile[obs3], neighborly, brotherly, fraternal, sympathetic, harmonious, hearty, cordial, warm-hearted. friends with, well with, at home with, hand in hand with; on good terms, on friendly terms, on amicable terms, on cordial terms, on familiar terms, on intimate terms, on good footing; on speaking terms, on visiting terms; in one's good graces, in one's good books. acquainted, familiar, intimate, thick, hand and glove, hail fellow well met, free and easy; welcome. Adv. amicably &c. adj.; with open arms; sans ceremonie[Fr]; arm in arm. Phr. amicitia semper prodest [Lat][Seneca]; "a mystic bond of brotherhood makes all men one" [Carlyle]; "friendship is love without either flowers or veil" [Hare]; trulgus amicitias utilitate probat [Lat][Ovid].

#889. Enmity.— N. enmity, hostility; unfriendliness &c. adj.; discord &c. 713; bitterness, rancor.
alienation, estrangement; dislike &c. 867; hate &c. 898.
heartburning[obs3]; animosity &c. 900; malevolence &c. 907.
V. be inimical &c. adj.; keep at arm's length, hold at arm's length; be at loggerheads; bear malice &c. 907; fall out; take umbrage &c. 900; harden the heart, alienate, estrange.
[not friendly, but not hostile see indifference 866].
Adj. inimical, unfriendly, hostile; at enmity, at variance, at daggers drawn, at open war with; up in arms against; in bad odor with.
on bad terms, not on speaking terms; cool; cold, cold hearted; estranged, alienated, disaffected, irreconcilable.
<— p. 307 —>

#890. Friend. — N. friend, friend of one's bosom; alter ego; best friend, bosom friend, soulmate, fast friend; amicus[Lat]; usque ad aras[Lat]; fidus Achates[Lat][obs3]; persona grata. acquaintance, neighbor, next-door neighbor, casual acquaintance, nodding acquaintance; wellwisher. favorer, fautor[obs3], patron, Mecaenas; tutelary saint, good genius, advocate, partisan, sympathizer; ally; friend in need &c. (auxiliary) 711. comrade, mate, companion, familiar, confrere, comrade, camarade[obs3], confidante, intimate; old crony, crony; chum; pal; buddy, bosom buddy; playfellow, playmate, childhood friend; bedfellow, bedmate; chamber fellow. associate, colleague, compeer. schoolmate, schoolfellow[obs3]; classfellow[obs3], classman[obs3], classmate; roommate; fellow-man, stable companion. best man, maid of honor, matron of honor. compatriot; fellow countryman, countryman. shopmate, fellow-worker, shipmate, messmate[obs3]; fellow companion, boon companion, pot companion; copartner, partner, senior partner, junior partner. Arcades ambo Pylades and Orestes Castor and Pollux[obs3], Nisus and Euryalus[Lat], Damon and Pythias, par nobile fratrum[Lat]. host, Amphitryon[obs3], Boniface; guest, visitor, protg. Phr. amici probantur rebus adversis[Lat]; ohne bruder kann man leben nicht ohne Freund[Ger]; "best friend, my well-spring in the wilderness" [G. Eliot]; conocidos muchos amigos pocos[Sp]; "friend more divine than all divinities" [G. Eliot]; vida sin amigo muerte sin testigo[Sp].

#891. Enemy. — N. enemy; antagonist; foe, foeman[obs3]; open enemy, bitter enemy; opponent &c. 710; back friend. public enemy, enemy to society. Phr. every hand being against one; "he makes no friend who never made a foe" [Tennyson]. with friends like that, who needs enemies?; Lord protect me from my friends; I can protect myself from my enemies.

#892. Sociality. — N. sociality, sociability, sociableness &c. adj.; social intercourse; consociation[obs3]; intercourse, intercommunity[obs3]; consortship[obs3], companionship, comradeship; clubbism[obs3]; esprit de corps. conviviality; good fellowship, good company; joviality, jollity, savoir vivre[Fr], festivity, festive board, merrymaking; loving cup!; hospitality, heartiness; cheer. welcome, welcomeness; greeting; hearty welcome, hearty reception, warm reception; urbanity &c. (courtesy) 894; familiarity. good fellow, jolly fellow; bon enfant[Fr], bawcock[obs3]. social circle, family circle; circle of acquaintance, coterie, society, company. social gathering, social reunion; assembly &c. (assemblage) 72; barbecue [U. S.], bee; corn-husking [U. S.], corn-shucking [U. S.]; house raising, barn raising; husking, husking-bee [U. S.]; infare[obs3]. party, entertainment, reception, levee, at, home, conversazione[It], soiree, matine; evening party, morning party, afternoon party, bridge party, garden party, surprise party; kettle, kettle drum; partie carre[Fr], dish of tea, ridotto[obs3], rout!; housewarming; ball, festival &c; smoker, smoker-party; sociable [U.S.], stag party, hen party, tamashal!; tea-party, tea-fight*. (amusement) 840; "the feast of reason and the flow of soul" [Pope]. birthday party[parties for specific occasions], Christmas party, New Year's Eve party, Thanksgiving Day Dinner; bonenkai[Japan]; wedding reception. visiting; round of visits; call, morning call; interview &c. (conversation) 588; assignation; tryst, trysting place; appointment. club &c. (association) 712. V. be sociable &c. adj.; know; be acquainted &c. adj.; associate with, sort with, keep company with, walk hand in hand with; eat off the same trencher, club together, consort, bear one company, join; make acquaintance with &c. (friendship) 888; make advances, fraternize, embrace. be at home with, feel at home with, make oneself at home with; make free with; crack a bottle with; receive hospitality, live at free quarters; find the latchstring out [U.S.]. visit, pay a visit; interchange visits, interchange cards;

call at, call upon; leave a card; drop in, look in; look one up, beat up one's quarters. entertain; give a party &c. n.; be at home, see one's friends, hang out, keep open house, do the honors; receive, receive with open arms; welcome; give a warm reception &c. n. to kill the fatted calf. Adj. sociable, companionable, clubbable, conversable[obs3], cosy, cosey[obs3], chatty,, conversational; homiletical. convivial; festive, festal; jovial, jolly, hospitable. welcome, welcome as the roses in May; fted, entertained. free and easy, hall fellow well met, familiar, on visiting terms, acquainted. social, neighborly; international; gregarious. Adv. en famille[Fr], in the family circle; sans fa on, sans ceremonie[Fr]; arm in arm. Phr. "a crowd is not company" [Bacon]; "be bright and jovial among your guests tonight" [Macbeth]; "his worth is warrant for his welcome" [Two Gentlemen]; "let's be red with mirth" [Winter's Tale]; "welcome the coming speed the parting guest" [Pope].

<— p. 308 —>

#893. Seclusion. Exclusion. — N. seclusion, privacy; retirement; reclusion, recess; snugness &c. adj.; delitescence[obs3]; rustication, rus in urbe[Lat]; solitude; solitariness &c. (singleness) 87; isolation; loneliness &c. adj.; estrangement from the world, voluntary exile; aloofness. cell, hermitage; convent &c. 1000; sanctum sanctorum[Lat]. depopulation, desertion, desolation; wilderness &c. (unproductive) 169; howling wilderness; rotten borough, Old Sarum. exclusion, excommunication, banishment, exile, ostracism, proscription; cut, cut direct; dead cut. inhospitality[obs3], inhospitableness &c. adj.; dissociability[obs3]; domesticity, Darby and Joan. recluse, hermit, eremite, cenobite; anchoret[obs3], anchorite; Simon Stylites[obs3]; troglodyte, Timon of Athens[obs3], Santon[obs3], solitaire, ruralist[obs3], disciple of Zimmermann, closet cynic, Diogenes; outcast, Pariah, castaway, pilgarlic[obs3]; wastrel, foundling, wilding[obs3]. V. be secluded, live secluded &c. adj.; keep aloof, stand, hold oneself aloof, keep in the background, stand in the background; keep snug; shut oneself up; deny oneself, seclude oneself creep into a corner, rusticate, aller planter ses choux[Fr]; retire, retire from the world; take the veil; abandon &c. 624; sport one's oak*. cut, cut dead; refuse to associate with, refuse to acknowledge; look cool upon, turn one's back upon, shut the door upon; repel, blackball, excommunicate, exclude, exile, expatriate; banish, outlaw, maroon, ostracize, proscribe, cut off from, send to Coventry, keep at arm's length, draw a cordon round. depopulate; dispeople[obs3], unpeople[obs3]. Adj. secluded, sequestered, retired, delitescent[obs3], private, bye; out of the world, out of the way; "the world forgetting by the world forgot" [Pope]. snug, domestic, stay-at-home. unsociable; unsocial, dissocial[obs3]; inhospitable, cynical, inconversablel, unclubbable, sauvage[Fr]; troglodytic. solitary; lonely, lonesome; isolated, single. estranged; unfrequented; uninhabitable, uninhabited; tenantless; abandoned; deserted, deserted in one's utmost need; unfriended[obs3]; kithless[obs3], friendless, homeless; lorn[obs3], forlorn, desolate. unvisited, unintroduced[obs3], uninvited, unwelcome; under a cloud, left to shift for oneself, derelict, outcast. banished &c. v. Phr. noli me tangere[Lat]. "among them but not of them" [Byron]; "and homeless near a thousand homes I stood" [Wordsworth]; far from the madding crowd's ignoble strife [Gray]; "makes a solitude and calls it peace" [Byron]; magna civitas magna solitudo [Lat]; "never less alone than when alone" [Rogers]; "O sacred solitude! divine retreat!" [Young].

<— p. 309 —>

#894. Courtesy. — N. courtesy; respect &c. 928; good manners, good behavior, good breeding; manners; politeness &c. adj.; bienseance, urbanity, comity, gentility, breeding, polish, presence; civility, civilization; amenity, suavity; good temper, good humor; amiability, easy temper, complacency, soft tongue, mansuetude; condescension &c. (humility) 879; affability, complaisance, prvenance, amability[obs3], gallantry; pink of politeness, pink of courtesy. compliment; fair words, soft words, sweet words; honeyed phrases, ceremonial; salutation, reception, presentation, introduction, accueil[obs3], greeting, recognition; welcome, abordl, respects, devoir, regards, remembrances; kind regards, kind remembrances; love, best love, duty; empty encomium, flattering remark, hollow commendation; salaams. obeisance &c. (reverence) 928; bow, courtesy, curtsy, scrape, salaam, kotow[obs3], kowtow, bowing and scraping; kneeling; genuflection &c. (worship) 990; obsequiousness &c. 886; capping, shaking hands, &c. v.; grip of the hand, embrace, hug, squeeze, accolade, loving cup, vin d'honneur[Fr], pledge; love token &c. (endearment) 902; kiss, buss, salute. mark of recognition, nod; "nods and becks and wreathed smiles" [Milton]; valediction &c. 293; condolence &c. 915. V. be courteous &c. adj.; show courtesy &c. n. mind one's P's and Q's, behave oneself, be all things to all men, conciliate, speak one fair, take in good part; make the amiable, do the amiable; look as if butter would not melt in one's mouth; mend one's manners. receive, do the honors, usher, greet, hail, bid welcome; welcome, welcome with open arms; shake hands; hold out the hand, press the hand, squeeze the hand, press the flesh; bid Godspeed; speed the parting guest; cheer, serenade. salute; embrace &c. (endearment) 902; kiss, kiss hands; drink to, pledge, hob and nob[obs3]; move to, nod to; smile upon. uncover, cap; touch the hat, take off the hat; doff the cap; present arms; make way for; bow; make one's bow, make a leg; scrape, curtsy, courtesy; bob a curtsy, bob a courtesy; kneel; bow the knee, bend the knee. visit, wait upon, present oneself, pay one's respects, pay a visit &c.

(sociability) 892; dance attendance on &c. (servility) 886; pay attentions to; do homage to &c. (respect) 928. prostrate oneself &c. (worship) 990. give one's duty to, send one's duty to, &c. n. render polite &c. adj.; polish, civilize, humanize. Adj. courteous, polite, civil, mannerly, urbane; well-behaved, well- mannered, well-bred, well-brought up; good-mannered, polished, civilized, cultivated; refined &c. (taste) 850; gentlemanlike &c. (fashion) 852[obs3]; gallant; on one's good behavior. fine spoken, fair spoken, soft-spoken; honey-mouthed, honey-tongued; oily, bland; obliging, conciliatory, complaisant, complacent; obsequious &c. 886. ingratiating, winning; gentle, mild; good-humored, cordial, gracious, affable, familiar; neighborly. diplomatic, tactful, politic; artful &c. 702. Adv. courteously &c. adj.; with a good grace; with open arms, with outstretched arms; a bras ouverts[Fr]; suaviter in modo[Fr], in good humor. Int. hail! welcome! well met! ave! all hail! good day, good morrow! Godspeed! pax vobiscum[Lat]! may your shadow never be less! Phr. Tien de plus estimable que la ceremonie[Fr]; "the very pink of courtesy" [Romeo and Juliet].

#895. Discourtesy.— N. discourtesy;ill breeding; ill manners, bad manners, ungainly manners; insuavity[obs3]; uncourteousness &c.adj[obs3].; rusticity, inurbanity[obs3]; illiberality, incivility displacency[obs3]. disrespect &c. 929; procacity[obs3], impudence; barbarism, barbarity; misbehavior, brutality, blackguardism[obs3], conduct unbecoming a gentleman, grossieret, brusquerie[obs3]; vulgarity, &c. 851. churlishness &c. adj.; spinosity[obs3], perversity; moroseness &c. (sullenness) 901a. sternness &c. adj.; austerity; moodishness[obs3], captiousness &c. 901; cynicism; tartness &c. adj.; acrimony, acerbity, virulence, asperity. scowl, black looks, frown; short answer, rebuff; hard words, contumely; unparliamentary language, personality. bear, bruin, brute, blackguard, beast; unlicked cub[obs3]; frump, crosspatch[obs3]; saucebox &c. 887[obs3]; crooked stick; grizzly. V. be -rude &c. adj.; insult &c. 929; treat with discourtesy; take a name in vain; make bold with, make free with; take a liberty; stare out of countenance, ogle, point at, put to the blush. cut; turn one's back upon, turn on one's heel; give the cold shoulder; keep at a distance, keep at arm's length; look cool upon, look coldly upon, look black upon; show the door to, send away with a flea in the ear. lose one's temper &c. (resentment) 900; sulk &c. 90la; frown, scowl, glower, pout; snap, snarl, growl. render rude &c. ad.; brutalize, brutify[obs3]. Adj. discourteous, uncourteous[obs3]; uncourtly[obs3]; ill-bred, ill- mannered, ill-behaved, ill-conditioned; unbred; unmannerly, unmannered; impolite, unpolite[obs3]; unpolished, uncivilized, ungenteel; ungentleman- like, ungentlemanly; unladylike; blackguard; vulgar &c. 851; dedecorous[obs3]; foul-mouthed foul-spoken; abusive. uncivil, ungracious, unceremonious; cool; pert, forward, obtrusive, impudent, rude, saucy, precocious. repulsive; uncomplaisant[obs3], unaccommodating, unneighborly, ungallant; inaffable[obs3]; ungentle, ungainly; rough, rugged, bluff, blunt, gruff; churlish, boorish, bearish; brutal, brusque; stern, harsh, austere; cavalier. taint, sour, crabbed, sharp, short, trenchant, sarcastic, biting, doggish, caustic, virulent, bitter, acrimonious, venomous, contumelious; snarling &c. v.; surly, surly as a bear; perverse; grim, sullen &c. 901a; peevish &c. (irascible) 901. untactful, impolitic, undiplomatic; artless &c. 703; Adv. discourteously &c. adj.; with discourtesy &c. n., with a bad grace.

<— p. 310 —>

    #896. Congratulation. — N. congratulation, gratulation[obs3]; felicitation; salute &c. 894; condolence &c. 915; compliments of the season.
    V. congratulate, gratulate[obs3]; felicitate; give one joy, wish one joy; compliment; tender one's congratulations, offer one's congratulations; wish many happy returns of the day, wish a merry Christmas and a happy new year.
    praise,laud (commendation) 931.
    congratulate oneself &c. (rejoice) 838.
    Adj. congratulatory, gratulatory[obs3].
    Phr. "I wish you all the joy that you can wish" [Merchant of Venice]; best wishes.

#897. Love. — N. love; fondness &c. adj.; liking; inclination &c. (desire) 865; regard, dilectionl, admiration, fancy. affection, sympathy, fellow-feeling; tenderness &c. adj.; heart, brotherly love; benevolence &c. 906; attachment. yearning, <gr/eros/gr>, tender passion, amour; gyneolatry[obs3]; gallantry, passion, flame, devotion, fervor, enthusiasm, transport of love, rapture, enchantment, infatuation, adoration, idolatry. Cupid, Venus; myrtle; true lover's knot; love token, love suit, love affair, love tale, love story; the, old story, plighted love; courtship &c. 902; amourette[obs3]; free love. maternal love, <gr/storge/gr>[Grk], parental love; young love, puppy love. attractiveness; popularity; favorite &c. 899. lover, suitor, follower, admirer, adorer, wooer, amoret[obs3], beau, sweetheart, inamorato[It], swain, young man, flame, love, truelove; leman[obs3], Lothario, gallant, paramour, amoroso[obs3], cavaliere servente[It], captive, cicisbeo[obs3]; caro sposo[It]. inamorata, ladylove, idol, darling, duck, Dulcinea, angel, goddess, cara sposa[It]. betrothed, affianced, fiancee. flirt, coquette; amorette[obs3]; pair of turtledoves; abode of love, agapemone[obs3]. V. love, like, affect, fancy, care for, take an interest in, be partial to, sympathize with; affection; be in love &c. with adj.; have a love &c. n. for, entertain a love &c. n. for, harbor cherish a love &c. n. for; regard, revere; take to, bear love to, be wedded to; set one's affections on; make much of, feast one's eyes on; hold dear, prize; hug, cling to, cherish. pet. burn; adore, idolize, love to distraction, aimer eperdument[Fr]; dote on, dote upon; take a fancy to, look sweet upon; become enamored &c. adj.; fall in love with, lose one's heart; desire &c. 865. excite love; win the heart, gain the heart, win the affections, gain the affections, secure the love, engage the affections; take the fancy of have a place in the heart, wind round the heart; attract, attach, endear, charm, fascinate, captivate, bewitch, seduce, enamor, enrapture, turn the head. get into favor; ingratiate oneself, insinuate oneself, worm oneself; propitiate, curry favor with, pay one's court to, faire l'aimable[Fr], set one's cap at, flirt. Adj. loving &c. v.; fond of; taken with, struck with; smitten, bitten; attached to, wedded to; enamored; charmed &c. v.; in love; love-sick; over head and ears in love, head over heels in love. affectionate, tender, sweet upon, sympathetic, loving; amorous, amatory; fond, erotic, uxorious, ardent, passionate, rapturous, devoted, motherly. loved &c. v. beloved well beloved, dearly beloved; dear, precious, darling, pet, little; favorite, popular. congenial; after one's mind, after one's taste, after one's fancy, after one's own heart, to one's mind, to one's taste, to one's fancy, to one's own heart. in one's good graces &c. (friendly) 888; dear as the apple of one's eye, nearest to one's heart. lovable, adorable; lovely, sweet; attractive, seductive, winning; charming, engaging, interesting, enchanting, captivating, fascinating, bewitching; amiable, like an angel. Phr. amantes amentes [Lat][Terence]; credula res amor est [Lat][Ovid]; militat omnis amasius [Lat][Ovid]; love conquers all, omnia vincit amor [Lat][Vergil]; si vis amari ama [obs3][Lat][Seneca]; "the sweetest joy, the wildest woe" [Bailey].

<— p. 311 —>

#898. Hate. — N. hate, hatred, vials of hate. disaffection, disfavor; alienation, estrangement, coolness; enmity &c. 889; animosity &c. 900. umbrage, pique, grudge; dudgeon, spleen bitterness, bitterness of feeling; ill blood, bad blood; acrimony; malice &c. 907; implacability &c. (revenge) 919. repugnance &c. (dislike) 867; misanthropy, demonophobia[obs3], gynephobia[obs3], negrophobia[obs3]; odium, unpopularity; detestation, antipathy; object of hatred, object of execration; abomination, aversion, bete noire; enemy &c. 891; bitter pill; source of annoyance &c. 830. V. hate, detest, abominate, abhor, loathe; recoil at, shudder at; shrink from, view with horror, hold in abomination, revolt against, execrate;scowl &c. 895; disrelish &c. (dislike) 867. owe a grudge; bear spleen, bear a grudge, bear malice &c. (malevolence) 907; conceive an aversion to, take a dislike to. excite hatred, provoke hatred &c. n.; be hateful &c. adj.; stink in the nostrils; estrange, alienate, repel, set against, sow dissension, set by the ears, envenom, incense, irritate, rile; horrify &c. 830; roil. Adj. hating &c. v.; abhorrent; averse from &c. (disliking) 867; set against. bitter &c. (acrimonious) 895 implacable &c. (revengeful) 919. unloved, unbeloved, unlamented, undeplored, unmourned[obs3], uncared for, unendeared[obs3], un-valued; disliked &c. 867. crossed in love, forsaken, rejected, lovelorn, jilted. obnoxious, hateful, odious, abominable, repulsive, offensive, shocking; disgusting &c. (disagreeable) 830; reprehensible. invidious, spiteful; malicious &c. 907. insulting, irritating, provoking. at daggers drawn[Mutual hate]; not on speaking terms &c. (enmity) 889; at loggerheads. Phr. no love lost between.

#899. Favorite. — N. favorite, pet, cosset, minion, idol, jewel, spoiled child, enfant gat[Fr]; led captain; crony; fondling; apple of one's eye, man after one's own heart; persona grata.
love[person who is a favorite (terms of address)], dear, darling, duck, duckey, honey, sugar, jewel; mopsey[obs3], moppet, princess; sweetheart, sweetie &c. (love) 897.
teacher's pet.
general favorite, universal favorite; idol of the people.

<— p. 312 —>

#900. Resentment. — N. resentment, displeasure, animosity, anger, wrath, indignation; exasperation, bitter resentment, wrathful indignation. pique, umbrage, huff, miff, soreness, dudgeon, acerbity, virulence, bitterness, acrimony, asperity, spleen, gall; heart-burning, heart- swelling; rankling. ill humor, bad humor, ill temper, bad temper; irascibility &c. 901; ill blood &c. (hate) 898; revenge &c. 919. excitement, irritation; warmth, bile, choler, ire, fume, pucker, dander, ferment, ebullition; towering passion, acharnement[Fr], angry mood, taking, pet, tiff, passion, fit, tantrums. burst, explosion, paroxysm, storm, rage, fury, desperation; violence &c. 173; fire and fury; vials of wrath; gnashing of teeth, hot blood, high words. scowl &c. 895; sulks &c. 901a. [Cause of umbrage] affront, provocation, offense; indignity &c. (insult) 929; grudge, crow to pluck, bone to pick, sore subject, casus belli[Lat]; ill turn, outrage. Furies, Eumenides. buffet, slap in the face, box on the ear, rap on the knuckles. V. resent; take amiss, take ill, take to heart, take offense, take umbrage, take huff, take exception; take in ill part, take in bad part, take in dudgeon; ne pas entendre raillerie[Fr]; breathe revenge, cut up rough. fly into a rage, fall into a rage, get into a rage, fly into a passion; bridle up, bristle up, froth up, fire up, flare up; open the vials of one's wrath, pour out the vials of one's wrath. pout, knit the brow, frown, scowl, lower, snarl, growl, gnarl, gnash, snap; redden, color; look black, look black as thunder, look daggers; bite one's thumb; show one's teeth, grind one's teeth; champ the bit, champ at the bit. chafe, mantle, fume, kindle, fly out, take fire; boil, boil over; boil with indignation, boil with rage; rage, storm, foam, vent one's rage, vent one's spleen; lose one's temper, stand on one's hind legs, stamp the foot, stamp with rage, quiver with rage, swell with rage, foam with rage; burst with anger; raise Cain. have a fling at; bear malice &c. (revenge) 919. cause anger, raise anger; affront, offend; give offense, give umbrage; anger; hurt the feelings; insult, discompose, fret, ruffle, nettle, huff, pique; excite &c. 824; irritate, stir the blood, stir up bile; sting, sting to the quick; rile, provoke, chafe, wound, incense, inflame, enrage, aggravate, add fuel to the flame, fan into a flame, widen the breach, envenom, embitter, exasperate, infuriate, kindle wrath; stick in one's gizzard; rankle &e. 919; hit on the raw, rub on the raw, sting on the raw, strike on the raw. put out of countenance, put out of humor; put one's monkey up, put one's back up; raise one's gorge, raise one's dander, raise one's choler; work up into a passion; make one's blood boil, make the ears tingle; throw, into a ferment, madden, drive one mad; lash into fury, lash into madness; fool to the top of one's bent; set by the ears. bring a hornet's nest about one's ears. Adj. angry, wrath, irate; ireful, wrathful; cross &c. (irascible) 901; Achillean[obs3]; sulky, &c. 901a; bitter, virulent; acrimonious &c. (discourteous) &c. 895; violent &c. 173. warm, burning; boiling, boiling over; fuming, raging; foaming, foaming at the mouth; convulsed with rage. offended &c. v.; waxy, acharne; wrought, worked up; indignant, hurt, sore; set against. fierce, wild, rageful[obs3], furious, mad with rage, fiery, infuriate, rabid, savage; relentless &c. 919. flushed with anger, flushed with rage; in a huff, in a stew, in a fume, in a pucker, in a passion, in a rage, in a fury, in a taking, in a way; on one's high ropes, up in arms; in high dudgeon. Adv. angrily &c. adj.; in the height of passion; in the heat of passion, in the heat of the moment. Int. tantaene animis coelestibus irae [Lat][Vergil]! marry come up! zounds! 'sdeath! Phr. one's blood being up, one's back being up, one's monkey being up; fervens difficili bile jecur[Lat]; the gorge rising, eyes flashing fire; the blood rising, the blood boiling; haeret lateri lethalis arundo [Lat][Vergil]; "beware the fury of a patient man" [Dryden]; furor arma ministrat [Lat][Vergil]; ira furor brevis est [Lat][Horace]; quem Jupiter vult perdere dementat prius[Lat]; "What, drunk with choler?" [Henry IV].

#901. Irascibility. — N. irascibility, irascibleness, temper; crossness &c. adj.; susceptibility, procacity, petulance, irritability, tartness, acerbity, protervity; pugnacity &c. (contentiousness) 720. excitability &c. 825; bad temper, fiery temper, crooked temper, irritable &c. adj. temper; genus irritabile[Lat], hot blood. ill humor &c. (sullenness) 901a; asperity &c., churlishness &c. (discourtesy) 895. huff &c. (resentment) 900; a word and a blow. Sir Fretful Plagiary; brabbler[obs3], Tartar; shrew, vixen, virago, termagant, dragon, scold, Xantippe; porcupine; spitfire; fire eater &c. (blusterer) 887; fury &c. (violent person) 173. V. be irascible &c. adj.; have a temper &c. n., have a devil in one; fire up &c. (be angry) 900. Adj. irascible; bad-tempered, ill-tempered; irritable, susceptible; excitable &c. 825; thin-skinned &c. (sensitive) 822; fretful, fidgety; on the fret. hasty, overhasty, quick, warm, hot, testy, touchy, techy[obs3], tetchy; like touchwood, like tinder; huffy; pettish, petulant; waspish, snappish, peppery, fiery, passionate, choleric, shrewish, "sudden and quick in quarrel" [As You Like It]. querulous, captious, moodish[obs3]; quarrelsome, contentious, disputatious; pugnacious &c. (bellicose) 720; cantankerous, exceptious[obs3]; restiff &c. (perverse) 901a[obs3]; churlish &c. (discourteous) 895. cross, cross as crabs, cross as two sticks, cross as a cat, cross as a dog, cross as the tongs; fractious, peevish, acaritre[obs3]. in a bad temper; sulky &c. 901a; angry &c. 900. resentful, resentive[obs3]; vindictive &c. 919. Int. pish! Phr. a vieux comptes nouvelles disputes[Fr]; quamvis tegatur proditur vultu furor [Lat][Seneca]; vino tortus et ira [Lat][Horace].

<— p. 313 —>

#901a. Sullenness. — N. sullenness &c. adj.; morosity[obs3], spleen; churlishness &c. (discourtesy) 895; irascibility &c. 901. moodiness &c. adj.; perversity; obstinacy &c. 606; torvityl, spinosity[obs3]; crabbedness &c. adj. ill temper, bad temper, ill humor, bad humor; sulks, dudgeon, mumps[obs3], dumps, doldrums, fit of the sulks, bouderie[Fr], black looks, scowl; grouch; huff &c. (resentment) 900. V. be sullen &c. adj.; sulk; frown, scowl, lower, glower, gloam[obs3], pout, have a hangdog look, glout[obs3]. Adj. sullen, sulky; ill-tempered, ill-humored, ill-affected, ill- disposed; grouty [obs3][U. S.]; in an ill temper, in a bad temper, in a shocking temper, in an ill humor, in a bad humor, in a shocking humor; out of temper, out of humor; knaggy[obs3], torvous[obs3], crusty, crabbed; sour, sour as a crab; surly &c. (discourteous) 895. moody; spleenish[obs3], spleenly[obs3]; splenetic, cankered. cross, crossgrained[obs3]; perverse, wayward, humorsome[obs3]; restiff[obs3], restive; cantankerous, intractable, exceptious[obs3], sinistrous[obs3], deaf to reason, unaccommodating, rusty, froward; cussed [U. S.]. dogged &c. (stubborn) 606. grumpy, glum, grim, grum[obs3], morose, frumpish; in the sulks &c. n.; out of sorts; scowling, glowering, growling; grouchy. peevish &c. (irascible) 901.

#902. [Expression of affection or love.] Endearment. — N. endearment, caress; blandishment, blandimentl; panchement, fondling, billing and cooing, dalliance, necking, petting, sporting, sparking, hanky-panky; caressing. embrace, salute, kiss, buss, smack, osculation, deosculationl; amorous glances. courtship, wooing, suit, addresses, the soft impeachment; lovemaking; serenading; caterwauling. flirting &c. v.; flirtation, gallantry; coquetry. true lover's knot, plighted love; love tale, love token, love letter; billet-doux, valentine. honeymoon; Strephon and Chloe[obs3]. V. caress, fondle, pet, dandle; pat, pat on the head, pat on the cheek; chuck under the chin, smile upon, coax, wheedle, cosset, coddle, cocker, cockle; make of, make much of; cherish, foster, kill with kindness. clasp, hug, cuddle; fold in one's arms, strain in one's arms; nestle, nuzzle; embrace, kiss, buss, smack, blow a kiss; salute &c. (courtesy) 894; fold to the heart, press to the bosom. bill and coo, spoon, toy, dally, flirt, coquet; gallivant, galavant; philander; make love; pay one's court to, pay one's addresses to, pay one's attentions to; serenade; court, woo; set one's cap at; be sweet upon, look sweet upon; ogle, cast sheep's eyes upon; faire les yeux doux[Fr]. fall in love with, win the affections &c. (love) 897; die for. propose; make an offer, have an offer; pop the question; plight one's troth, plight one's faith. Adj. caressing &c. v.; "sighing like furnace" [Shakespeare]; love- sick, spoony. caressed &c. V. Phr. "faint heart neer won fair lady"; "kisses honeyed by oblivion" [G. Eliot].

<— p. 314 —>

#903. Marriage. — N. marriage, matrimony, wedlock, union, intermarriage, miscegenation, the bonds of marriage, vinculum matrimonii[Lat], nuptial tie. married state, coverture, bed, cohabitation. match; betrothment &c. (promise) 768; wedding, nuptials, Hymen, bridal; espousals, spousals; leading to the altar &c. v.; nuptial benediction, epithalamium[obs3]; sealing. torch of Hymen, temple of Hymen; hymeneal altar; honeymoon. bridesmaid, bridesman[obs3], best man; bride, bridegroom. married man, married woman, married couple; neogamist[obs3], Benedict, partner, spouse, mate, yokemate[obs3]; husband, man, consort, baron; old man, good man; wife of one's bosom; helpmate, rib, better half, gray mare, old woman, old lady, good wife, goodwife. feme[Fr], feme coverte[Fr]; squaw, lady; matron, matronage, matronhood[obs3]; man and wife; wedded pair, Darby and Joan; spiritual wife. monogamy, bigamy, digamy[obs3], deuterogamy[obs3], trigamy[obs3], polygamy; mormonism; levirate[obs3]; spiritual wifery[obs3], spiritual wifeism[obs3]; polyandrism[obs3]; Turk, bluebeard[obs3]. unlawful marriage, left-handed marriage, morganatic marriage, ill- assorted marriage; mesalliance; mariage de convenance[Fr]. marriage broker; matrimonial agency, matrimonial agent, matrimonial bureau, matchmaker; schatchen[Ger]. V. marry, wive, take to oneself a wife; be married, be spliced; go off, pair off; wed, espouse, get hitched[U.S. slang], lead to the hymeneal altar, take "for better for worse", give one's hand to, bestow one's hand upon. marry, join, handfast[obs3]; couple &c. (unit) 43; tie the nuptial knot; give away, give away in marriage; seal; ally, affiance; betroth &c. (promise) 768; publish the banns, bid the banns; be asked in church. Adj. married &c. v.; one, one bone and one flesh. marriageable, nubile. engaged, betrothed, affianced. matrimonial, marital, conjugal, connubial, wedded; nuptial, hymeneal, spousal, bridal. Phr. the gray mare the better horse; "a world-without-end bargain" [Love's Labor's Lost]; "marriages are made in Heaven" [Tennyson]; "render me worthy of this noble wife" [Julius Caesar]; si qua voles apte nubere nube pari [Lat][Ovid].

#904. Celibacy. — N. celibacy, singleness, single blessedness; bachelorhood, bachelorship[obs3]; misogamy[obs3], misogyny.

virginity, pucelage[obs3]; maidenhood, maidenhead.

unmarried man, bachelor, Coelebs, agamist[obs3], old bachelor; misogamist[obs3], misogynist; monogamist; monk.

unmarried woman, spinster; maid, maiden;virgin, feme sole[Fr], old maid; bachelor girl, girl-bachelor; nun.

V. live single, live alone.

Adj. unmarried, unwed, unwedded[obs3]; wifeless, spouseless[obs3]; single.

#905. Divorce. — N. divorce, divorcement; separation; judicial separation, separate maintenance; separatio a mensa et thoro[Lat], separatio a vinculo matrimonii [Lat].

trial separation, breakup; annulment.

widowhood, viduity[obs3], weeds.

widow, widower; relict; dowager; divorcee; cuckold; grass widow, grass widower; merry widow.

V. live separate; separate, divorce, disespouse[obs3], put away; wear the horns.

<— p. 315 —> % 2. DIFFUSIVE SYMPATHETIC AFFECTIONS %

#906. Benevolence. — N. benevolence, Christian charity; God's love, God's grace; good will; philanthropy &c. 910; unselfishness &c. 942. good nature, good feeling, good wishes; kindness, kindliness &c. adj.; loving-kindness, benignity, brotherly love, charity, humanity, fellow- feeling, sympathy: goodness of heart, warmth of heart; bonhomie; kind- heartedness; amiability, milk of human kindness, tenderness; love &c. 897; friendship &c. 888. toleration, consideration, generosity; mercy &c. (pity) 914. charitableness &c. adj.; bounty, almsgiving; good works, benefi- cence, "the luxury of doing good" [Goldsmith]. acts of kindness, a good turn; good offices, kind offices good treat- ment, kind treatment. good Samaritan, sympathizer, bon enfant[Fr]; altruist. V. be benevolent &c. adj.; have one's heart in the right place, bear good will; wish well, wish Godspeed; view with an eye of favor, regard with an eye of favor; take in good part; take an interest in, feel an interest in; be interested in, feel interested in; sympathize with, empathize with, feel for; fraternize &c. (be friendly) 888. enter into the feelings of others, do as you would be done by, meet halfway. treat well; give comfort, smooth the bed of death; do good, do a good turn; benefit &c. (goodness) 648; render a service, be of use; aid &c. 707. Adj. benevolent; kind, kindly; well-meaning; amiable; obliging, accom- modating, indulgent, gracious, complacent, good-humored. warm-hearted, kind-hearted, tender-hearted, large-heart- ed, broad- hearted; merciful &c. 914; charitable, beneficent, humane, benignant; bounteous, bountiful. good-natured, well-natured; spleenless[obs3]; sympathizing, sympathetic; complaisant &c. (courteous) 894; well-meant, well-inten- tioned. fatherly, motherly, brotherly, sisterly; paternal, maternal, fraternal; sororal[obs3]; friendly &c. 888. Adv. with a good intention, with the best intentions. Int. Godspeed! much good may it do! Phr. "act a charity sometimes" [Lamb]; "a tender heart, a will inflexible" [Longfellow]; de mortuis nil nisi bonum [Lat: say only good things about the dead, don't speak ill of the dead]; "kind words are more than coronets" [Tennyson]; quando amigo pide no hay manana[Lat]; "the social smile, the sympathetic tear" [Gray].

#907. Malevolence. — N. malevolence; bad intent, bad intention; unkindness, diskindness[obs3]; ill nature, ill will, ill blood; bad blood; enmity &c. 889; hate &c. 898; malignity; malice, malice prepense[obs3]; maliciousness &c. adj.; spite, despite; resentment &c. 900. uncharitableness &c. adj.; incompassionateness &c. 914a[obs3]; gall, venom, rancor, rankling, virulence, mordacity[obs3], acerbity churlishness &c. (discourtesy) 895. hardness of heart, heart of stone, obduracy; cruelty; cruelness &c. adj.; brutality, savagery; ferity[obs3], ferocity; barbarity, inhumanity, imman- ityl, truculence, ruffianism; evil eye, cloven foot; torture, vivisection. ill turn, bad turn; affront &c. (disrespect) 929; outrage, atrocity; ill usage; intolerance, persecution; tender mercies [ironical]; "unkindest cut of all" [Julius Caesar]. V. be malevolent &c. adj.; bear spleen, harbor spleen, bear a grudge, harbor a grudge, bear malice; betray the cloven foot, show the cloven foot. hurt &c. (physical pain) 378; annoy &c. 830; injure., harm, wrong; do harm to, do an ill office to; outrage; disoblige, malign, plant a thorn in the breast. molest, worry, harass, haunt, harry, bait, tease; throw stones at; play the devil with; hunt down, dragoon, hound; persecute, oppress, grind; maltreat; illtreat, ill-use. wreak one's malice on, do one's worst, break a butterfly on the wheel; dip one's hands in blood, imbrue one's hands in blood; have no mercy &c. 914a. Adj. malevolent, unbenevolent; unbenign; ill-disposed, ill- intentioned, ill-natured, ill-conditioned, ill-contrived; evil-minded, evil-disposed; black-browed[obs3]. malicious; malign, malignant; rancorous; despiteful, spiteful; mordacious, caustic, bitter, envenomed, acrimonious, virulent; unamiable, uncharitable; malefi- cent, venomous, grinding, galling. harsh, disobliging; unkind, unfriendly, ungracious; inofficious[obs3]; invidious; uncandid; churlish &c. (discourteous) 895; surly, sullen &c. 901a. cold, cold-blooded, cold-hearted; black-hearted, hard-hearted, flint- hearted, marble-hearted, stony-hearted; hard of heart, unnatural; ruthless &c. (unmerciful) 914a; relentless &c. (revengeful) 919. cruel; brutal, brutish; savage, savage as a bear, savage as a tiger; ferine[obs3], ferocious; inhuman; barbarous, barbaric, semibarbaric, fell, untamed, tameless, truculent, incendiary; bloodthirsty &c. (murderous) 361; atrocious; bloodyminded[obs3]. fiendish, fiendlike[obs3]; demoniacal; diabolic, diabolical; devilish, infernal, hellish, Satanic; Tartaran. Adv. malevolently &c. adj.; with bad intent &c. n. Phr. cruel as death; "hard unkindness' alter'd eye" [Gray]; homo homini lupus [Lat][Plautus]; mala mens[Lat], malus animus [Lat][Ter- ence].; "rich gifts wax poor when givers prove unkind" [Hamlet]; "sharp-tooth'd unkindness" [Lear].

<— p. 316 —>

#908. Malediction. — N. malediction, malison[obs3], curse, imprecation, denunciation, execration, anathema, ban, proscription, excommunication, commination[obs3], thunders of the Vatican, fulmination, maranatha[obs3]; asper- sion, disparagement, vilification, vituperation. abuse; foul language, bad language, strong language, unparliamentary language; billingsgate, sauce, evil speaking; cursing &c. v.; profane swearing, oath; foul invective, ribaldry, rude reproach, scurrility. threat &c. 909; more bark than bite; invective &c. (disapprobation) 932. V. curse, accurse[obs3], imprecate, damn, swear at; curse with bell book and candle; invoke curses on the head of, call down curses on the head of; devote to destruction. execrate, beshrew[obs3], scold; anathematize &c. (censure) 932; bold up to execra- tion, denounce, proscribe, excommunicate, fulminate, thunder against; threaten &c. 909. curse and swear; swear, swear like a trooper; fall a cursing, rap out an oath, damn. Adj. cursing, cursed &c. v. Int. woe to! beshrew[obs3]! ruat coelum[Lat]! ill betide, woe betide; confusion seize! damn! damn it! damn you! damn you to hell! go to hell! go to blazes! confound! blast! curse! devil take! hang! out with! a plague upon! out upon! aroynt[obs3]! honi soit[Fr]! parbleu[Fr]! Phr. delenda est Carthago[Lat].

#909. Threat. — N. threat, menace; defiance &c. 715; abuse, minacity[obs3], intimidation; denunciation; fulmination; commination &c. (curse) 908[obs3]; gathering clouds &c. (warning) 668. V. threat, threaten; menace; snarl, growl, gnarl, mutter, bark, bully. defy &c. 715; intimidate &c. 860; keep in terrorem[Lat], hold up in terrorem[Lat], hold out in terrorem[Lat]; shake the fist at, double the fist at, clinch the fist at; thunder, talk big, fulminate, use big words, bluster, look daggers, stare daggers. Adj. threatening, menacing; minatory, minacious[obs3]; comminatory[obs3], abusive; in terrorem[Lat]; ominous &c. (predicting) 511 ; defiant &c. 715; under the ban. Int. vae victis[Lat]! at your peril! do your worst!

#910. Philanthropy. — N. philanthropy, humanity, humanitarianism universal benevolence; endaemonism[obs3], deliciae humani generis[Lat]; cosmopolitanism, utilitarianism, the greatest happiness of the greatest number, social science, sociology. common weal; socialism, communism, Fourierisml!, phalansterianism[obs3], Saint Simonianism[obs3]. patriotism, civism[obs3], nationality, love of country, amor patriae[Lat], public spirit. chivalry, knight errantry[obs3]; generosity &c. 942. philanthropist, endaemonist[obs3], utilitarian, Benthamite, socialist, communist, cosmopolite, citizen of the world, amicus humani generis[Lat]; knight errant; patriot. Adj. philanthropic, humanitarian, utilitarian, cosmopolitan; public- spirited, patriotic; humane, large-hearted &c. (benevolent) 906; chivalric; generous &c. 942. Adv. pro bono publico[Lat], pro aris et focis [Lat][obs3][Cicero]. Phr. humani nihil a me alienum puto [Lat][Terence]; omne solum forti patria [Lat][Ovid]; un bien fait n'est jamais perdu[Fr].

#911. Misanthropy. — N. misanthropy, incivism; egotism &c. (selfishness) 943; moroseness &c. 901a; cynicism.
misanthrope, misanthropist, egotist, cynic, man hater, Timon, Diogenes.
woman hater, misogynist.
Adj. misanthropic, antisocial, unpatriotic; egotistical &c.(selfish) 943; morose &c. 901a.
<— p. 317 —>

#912. Benefactor. — N. benefactor, savior, good genius, tutelary saint, guardian angel, good Samaritan; pater patriae[Lat]; salt of the earth &c. (good man); 948; auxiliary &c. 711.

#913. [Maleficent being] Evil doer — N. evil doer, evil worker; wrongdoer &c. 949; mischief-maker, marplot; oppressor, tyrant; destroyer, Vandal; iconoclastl!.
firebrand, incendiary, fire bug [U. S.], pyromaniac; anarchist, communistl!, terrorist.
savage, brute, ruffian, barbarian, semibarbarian[obs3], caitiff, desperado; Apache[obs3], hoodlum, hood, plug-ugly*, pug-ugly* [U.S.], Red Skin, tough [U. S.]; Mohawk, Mo-hock, Mo-hawk; bludgeon man, bully, rough, hooligan, larrikin[obs3], dangerous classes, ugly customer; thief &c. 792.
cockatrice, scorpion, hornet.
snake, viper, adder, snake in the grass; serpent, cobra, asp, rattlesnake, anacondal!.
canker-worm, wire-worm; locust, Colorado beetle; alacran[obs3], alligator, caymon[obs3], crocodile, mosquito, mugger, octopus; torpedo; bane &c. 663.
cutthroat &c. (killer) 461.
cannibal; anthropophagusl!, anthropophagistl!; bloodsucker, vampire, ogre, ghoul, gorilla, vulture; gyrfalconl!, gerfalconl!.
wild beast, tiger, hyena, butcher, hangman; blood-hound, hell-hound, sleuth-hound; catamount [U. S.], cougar, jaguar, puma.
hag, hellhag[obs3], beldam, Jezebel.
monster; fiend &c. (demon) 980; devil incarnate, demon in human shape; Frankenstein's monster.
harpy, siren; Furies, Eumenides.

Hun, Attila[obs3], scourge of the human race.
Phr. faenum habet in cornu [Lat].

% 3. SPECIAL SYMPATHETIC AFFECTIONS %

#914. Pity. — N. pity, compassion, commiseration; bowels, of compassion; sympathy, fellow-feeling, tenderness, yearning, forbearance, humanity, mercy, clemency; leniency &c. (lenity) 740; charity, ruth, long- suffering. melting mood; argumentum ad misericordiam[Lat], quarter, grace, locus paenitentiae[Lat]. sympathizer; advocate, friend, partisan, patron, wellwisher. V. pity; have pity, show pity, take pity &c. n.; commiserate, compassionate; condole &c. 915; sympathize; feel for, be sorry for, yearn for; weep, melt, thaw, enter into the feelings of. forbear, relent, relax, give quarter, wipe the tears, parcere subjectis[Lat], give a coup de grace, put out of one's misery. raise pity, excite pity &c. n..; touch, soften; melt, melt the heart; propitiate, disarm. ask for mercy &c. v.; supplicate &c. (request) 765; cry for quarter, beg one's life, kneel; deprecate. Adj. pitying &c. v.; pitiful, compassionate, sympathetic, touched. merciful, clement, ruthful; humane; humanitarian &c. (philanthropic) 910; tender, tender hearted, tender as a chicken; soft, soft hearted; unhardened[obs3]; lenient &c. 740; exorable[obs3], forbearing; melting &c. v.; weak. Int. for pity's sake! mercy! have mercy! cry you mercy! God help you! poor thing! poor dear! poor fellow! woe betide! "quis talia fando temperet a lachrymiss!" [Lat][Vergil]. Phr. one's heart bleeding for; haud ignara mali miseris succur- rere disco [Lat][Vergil]; "a fellow feeling makes one wondrous kind" onor di bocca assai giova e poco costa[Garrick] [It].

#914a. Pitilessness. — N. pitilessness &c. adj.; inclemency; severity &c. 739; malevolence &c. 907.
V. have no mercy, shut the gates of mercy &c. 914; give no quarter.
Adj. pitiless, merciless, ruthless, bowelless; unpitying, unmerciful, inclement; grim-faced, grim-visaged; incompassionate[obs3], uncompassionate; inexorable; harsh &c. 739; unrelenting &c. 919.
<— p. 318 —>

#915. Condolence. — N. condolence; lamentation &c. 839; sympathy, consolation. V. condole with, console, sympathize express pity, testify pity; afford consolation, supply consolation; lament &c. 839 with; express sympathy for; feel grief in common with, feel sorrow in common with; share one's sorrow.

% 4. RETROSPECTIVE SYMPATHETIC AFFECTIONS %

#916. Gratitude. — N. gratitude, thankfulness, feeling of obligation, sense of obligation. acknowledgment, recogni- tion, thanksgiving, thanksgiving, giving thanks; thankful good will. thanks, praise, benediction; paean; Te Deum &c. (worship) 990[Lat]; grace, grace before meat, grace after meat, grace before meals, grace after meals; thank offering. requital. V. be grateful &c. adj.; thank; give thanks, render thanks, return thanks, offer thanks, tender thanks &c. n.; acknowledge, requite. feel under an obligation, be under an obligation, lie under an obligation; savoir gr[Fr]; not look a gift horse in the mouth; never forget, overflow with gratitude; thank one's stars, thank one's lucky stars, bless one's stars; fall on one's knees. Adj. grateful, thankful, obliged, beholden, indebted to, under obligation. Int. thanks! many thanks! gramercy[obs3]! much obliged! thank you! thank you very much! thanks a lot! thanks a heap, thanks loads [coll.]; thank Heaven! Heaven be praised! Gott sei Dank[Ger]!.

#917. Ingratitude. — N. ingratitude, thanklessness, oblivion of benefits, unthankfulness[obs3].
"benefits forgot"; thankless task,thankless office.
V. be ungrateful &c. adj.; forget benefits; look a gift horse in the mouth.
Adj. ungrateful, unmindful, unthankful; thankless, ingrate, wanting in gratitude, insensible of benefits.
forgotten; unacknowledged, unthanked[obs3], unrequited, unrewarded; ill-requited.
Int. thank you for nothing! thanks for nothing! "et tu Brute!" [Julius Caesar].
Phr. "ingratitude! thou marble-hearted fiend" [Lear].
#918. Forgiveness. — N. forgiveness, pardon, condonation, grace, remission, absolution, amnesty, oblivion; indulgence; reprieve.
conciliation; reconcilement; reconciliation &c. (pacification) 723;

propitiation.

excuse, exoneration, quittance, release, indemnity; bill of indemnity, act of indemnity, covenant of indemnity, deed of indemnity; exculpation &c. (acquittal) 970.

longanimity[obs3], placability; amantium irae[Lat]; locus paenitentiae[Lat]; forbearance.

V. forgive, forgive and forget; pardon, condone, think no more of, let bygones be bygones, shake hands; forget an injury. excuse, pass over, overlook; wink at &c. (neglect) 460; bear with; allow for, make allowances for; let one down easily, not be too hard upon, pocket the affront.

let off, remit, absolve, give absolution, reprieve; acquit &c. 970.

beg pardon, ask pardon, implore pardon &c. n.; conciliate, propitiate, placate; make up a quarrel &c. (pacify) 723; let the wound heal.

Adj. forgiving, placable, conciliatory,.

forgiven &c. v.; unresented[obs3], unavenged, unrevenged[obs3].

Adv. cry you mercy.

Phr. veniam petimusque damusque vicissim [Lat][Horace]; more in sorrow than in anger; comprendre tout c'est tout pardonner[Fr]; "the offender never pardons" [Herbert].

#919. Revenge. — N. revenge, revengement[obs3]; vengeance; avengement[obs3], avengeancel, sweet revenge, vendetta, death feud, blood for blood retaliation &c. 718; day of reckoning. rancor, vindictiveness, implacability; malevolence &c. 907; ruthlessness &c. 914a. avenger, vindicator, Nemesis, Eumenides. V. revenge, avenge; vindicate; take one's revenge, have one's revenge; breathe revenge, breathe vengeance; wreak one's vengeance, wreak one's anger. have accounts to settle, have a crow to pluck, have a bone to pick, have a rod in pickle. keep the wound green; harbor revenge, harbor vindictive feeling; bear malice; rankle, rankle in the breast. Adj. revengeful, vengeful; vindictive, rancorous; pitiless &c. 914a; ruthless, rigorous, avenging. unforgiving, unrelenting; inexorable, stony-hearted, implacable; relentless, remorseless. aeternum servans sub pectore vulnus[Lat]; rankling; immitigable. Phr. manet ciratrix[Lat], manet alid mente repostum[Lat][obs3]; dies irae dies illa[Lat]; "in high vengeance there is noble scorn" [G. Eliot]; inhumanum verbum est ultio [Lat][Seneca]; malevolus animus abditos dentes habet [Lat] [obs3][Syrus]; "now infidel I have thee on the hip" [Merchant of Venice].

<— p. 319 —>

#920. Jealousy. — N. jealousy,jealousness; jaundiced eye; envious suspicion, suspicion; "green-eyed monster" [Othello]; yellows; Juno.

V. be jealous &c. adj.; view with jealousy, view with a jealous eye.

Adj. jealous, jealous as a barbary pigeon[obs3]; jaundiced, yellow-eyed, envious, hornmad.

#921. Envy. — N. envy; enviousness &c. adj.; rivalry; jalousie de milier[Fr]; illwill, spite.

V. envy, covet, burst with envy.

Adj. envious, invidious, covetous; alieni appetens[Lat].

Phr. "base envy withers at another's joy" [Thomson]; caeca invidia est [Lat][Livy]; multa petentibus desunt multa [Lat][Horace]; summa petit livor [Lat][Ovid].

%
SECTION IV. MORAL AFFECTIONS
1. MORAL OBLIGATIONS %

#922. Right. — N. right; what ought to be, what should be; fitness &c. adj.; summum jus[Lat]. justice, equity; equitableness &c. adj.; propriety; fair play, impartiality, measure for measure, give and take, lex talionis[Lat]. Astraea[obs3], Nemesis, Themis. scales of justice, evenhanded justice, karma; suum cuique[Lat]; clear stage, fair field and no favor, level playing field. morals &c. (duty) 926; law &c. 963; honor &c. (probity) 939; virtue &c. 944. V. be right &c. adj.; stand to reason. see justice done, see one righted, see fair play; do justice to; recompense &c. (reward) 973; bold the scales even, give and take; serve one right, put the saddle on the right horse; give every one his due, give the devil his due; audire alteram partem[Lat]. deserve &c. (be entitled to) 924. Adj. right, good; just, reasonable; fit &c. 924; equal, equable, equatable[obs3]; evenhanded, fair. legitimate, justifiable, rightful; as it should be, as it ought to be; lawful &c. (permitted) 760, (legal) 963. deserved &c. 924. Adv. rightly &c. adj.; bon droit[Fr], au bon droit[Fr], in justice, in equity,, in reason. without distinction of persons, without regard to persons, without respect to persons; upon even terms. Int. all right! fair's fair. Phr. Dieu et mon droit[Fr]; "in equal scale weighing delight and dole" [Hamlet]; justitia cuum cuique distribuit [Lat][Cicero]; justitiae soror incorrupta fides[Lat]; justitia virtutem regina[Lat]; "thrice is he armed that hath his quarrel just" [Henry VI].

#923. Wrong. — N. wrong; what ought not to be, what should not be; malum in se[Lat]; unreasonableness, grievance; shame.

injustice; tort [Law]; unfairness &c. adj.; iniquity, foul play.

partiality, leaning, bias; favor, favoritism; nepotism, party spirit, partisanship; bigotry.

undueness &c. 925; wrongdoing (vice) 945; unlawfulness &c. 964.

robbing Peter to pay Paul &c. v.; the wolf and the lamb; vice &c. 945.

"a custom more honored in the breach than the observance" [Hamlet].

V. be wrong &c. adj.; cry to heaven for vengeance.

do wrong &c. n.; be inequitable &c. adj.; favor, lean towards; encroach upon, impose upon; reap where one has not sown; give an inch and take an ell, give an inch and take an mile; rob Peter to pay Paul.

Adj. wrong, wrongful; bad, too bad; unjust, unfair; inequitable, unequitable[obs3]; unequal, partial, one-sided; injurious, tortious[Law].

objectionable; unreasonable, unallowable, unwarrantable, unjustifiable; improper, unfit; unjustified &c. 925; illegal &c. 964; iniquitous; immoral &c. 945.

in the wrong, in the wrong box.

Adv. wrongly &c. adj.

Phr. it will not do.

<— p. 320 —>

#924. Dueness. — N. due, dueness; right, privilege, prerogative, prescription, title, claim, pretension, demand, birthright. immunity, license, liberty, franchise; vested interest, vested right. sanction, authority, warranty, charter; warrant &c. (permission) 760; constitution &c. (law) 963; tenure; bond &c. (security) 771. claimant, appellant; plaintiff &c. 938. V. be due &c. adj. to, be the due &c. n. of; have right to, have title to, have claim to; be entitled to; have a claim upon; belong to &c. (property) 780. deserve, merit, be worthy of, richly deserve. demand, claim; call upon for, come upon for, appeal to for; revendicate[obs3], reclaim; exact; insist on, insist upon; challenge; take one's stand, make a point of, require, lay claim to, assert, assume, arrogate, make good; substantiate; vindicate a claim, vindi-cate a right; fit for, qualify for; make out a case. give a right, confer a right; entitle; authorize &c. 760; sanctify, legalize, ordain, prescribe, allot. give every one his due &c. 922; pay one's dues; have one's due, have one's rights. use a right, assert, enforce, put in force, lay under contribution. Adj. having a right to &c. v.; entitled to; claiming; deserving, meriting, worthy of. privileged, allowed, sanctioned, warranted, authorized; ordained, prescribed, constitu-tional, chartered, enfranchised. prescriptive, presumptive; absolute, indefeasible; unalienable, inalienable; imprescriptible[obs3], inviolable, unimpeachable, unchallenged; sacrosanct. due to, merited, deserved, condign, richly deserved. allowable &c. (permitted) 760; lawful, licit, legitimate, legal; legalized &c. (law) 963. square, unex-ceptionable, right; equitable &c. 922; due, en r gle; fit, fitting; correct, proper, meet, befitting, becoming, seemly; decorous; creditable, up to the mark, right as a trivet; just the thing, quite the thing; selon les r gles[Fr]. Adv. duly, ex officio, de jure[Lat]; by right, by divine right; jure divino[Lat], Dei gratia[Lat], in the name of. Phr. civis Romanus sum [Lat][Cicero]; chaque saint sa chandelle[Fr].

#925. [Absence of right.] Undueness. — N. undueness &c. adj.; malum prohibitum[Lat]; impropriety; illegality &c. 964.

falseness &c. adj.; emptiness of title, invalidity of title; illegitimacy.

loss of right, disfranchisement, forfeiture.

usurpation, tort, violation, breach, encroachment, presumption, assumption, seizure; stretch, exaction, imposition, lion's share.

usurper, pretender.

V. be undue &c. adj.; not be due &c. 924.

infringe, encroach, trench on, exact; arrogate, arrogate to oneself; give an inch and take an ell; stretch a point, strain a point; usurp, violate, do violence to.

disfranchise, disentitle, disqualify; invalidate.

relax &c. (be lax) 738; misbehave &c. (vice) 945; misbecome[obs3].

Adj. undue; unlawful &c. (illegal) 964; unconstitutional; illicit;
unauthorized, unwarranted, disallowed, unallowed[obs3], unsanctioned,
unjustified; unentitled[obs3], disentitled, unqualified, disqualified;
unprivileged, unchartered.

illegitimate, bastard, spurious, supposititious, false; usurped.

tortious [Law].

undeserved, unmerited, unearned; unfulfilled.

forfeited, disfranchised.

improper; unmeet, unfit, unbefitting, unseemly; unbecoming,
misbecoming[obs3]; seemless[obs3]; contra bonos mores[Lat]; not the thing,
out of the question, not to be thought of; preposterous, pretentious,
would-be.

Phr. filius nullius.

<— p. 321 —>

#926. Duty. — N. duty, what ought to be done, moral obligation, accountableness[obs3], liability, onus, responsibility;
bounden duty, imperative duty; call, call of duty; accountability. allegiance, fealty, tie engagement &c. (promise) 768;
part; function, calling &c. (business) 625. morality,, morals, decalogue; case of conscience; conscientiousness &c.
(probity) 939; conscience, inward monitor, still small voice within, sense of duty, tender conscience, superego; the
hell within [P. L.]. dueness &c. 924; propriety, fitness, seemliness, amenability, decorum, <gr/to prepon/gr>; the thing,
the proper thing; the right thing to do, the proper thing to do. [Science of morals] ethics, ethology.; deontology[obs3],
aretology[obs3]; moral philosophy, ethical philosophy; casuistry, polity. observance, fulfillment, discharge, performance, acquittal, satisfaction, redemption; good behavior. V. be the duty of; be incumbent &c. adj. on, be responsible &c. adj.; behoove, become, befit, beseem; belong to, pertain to; fall to one's lot; devolve on; lie upon, lie on one's
head, lie at one's door; rest with, rest on the shoulders of. take upon oneself &c. (promise) 768; be bound to,
become bound to, be sponsor for, become sponsor for; incur a responsibility &c. n.; be under an obligation, stand
under an obligation, lie under an obligation; have to answer for, owe to it oneself. impose a duty, &c. n.; enjoin,
require, exact; bind, bind over; saddle with, prescribe, assign, call upon, look to, oblige. enter upon a duty, perform a
duty, observe a duty, fulfill a duty, discharge a duty, adhere to a duty, acquit oneself of a duty, satisfy a duty, enter
upon an obligation, perform an obligation, observe an obligation, fulfill an obligation, discharge an obligation, adhere
to an obligation, acquit oneself of an obligation, satisfy an obligation; act one's part, redeem one's pledge, do justice
to, be at one's post; do duty; do one's duty &c. (be virtuous) 944. be on one's good behavior, mind one's P's and Q's.
Adj. obligatory, binding; imperative, peremptory; stringent &c. (severe) 739; behooving &c. v.; incumbent on,
chargeable on; under obligation; obliged by, bound by, tied by; saddled with. due to, beholden to, bound to, indebted
to; tied down; compromised &c. (promised) 768; in duty bound. amenable, liable, accountable, responsible, answerable. right, meet &c. (due) 924; moral, ethical, casuistical, conscientious, ethological. Adv. with a safe conscience, as
in duty, bound, on one's own responsibility, at one's own risk, suo periculo[Lat]; in foro conscientiae[Lat]; quamdiu se
bene gesserit[Lat]. Phr. dura lex sed lex[Lat]; dulce et decorum est pro patria mori[Lat]; honos habet onus[Lat]; leve
fit quod bene fertur onus [Lat][Ovid]; loyaute m'oblige[Fr]; "simple duty bath no place for fear" [Whittier]; "stern
daughter of the voice of God" [Wordsworth]; "there is a higher law than the Constitution" [Wm. Seward].

#927. Dereliction of Duty. — N. dereliction of duty; fault &c. (guilt) 947; sin &c. (vice) 945; non-observance, non-
performance; neglect, relaxation, infraction, violation, transgression, failure, evasion; dead letter. V. violate; break,
break through; infringe; set aside, set at naught; encroach upon, trench upon; trample on, trample under foot; slight,
neglect, evade, renounce, forswear, repudiate; wash one's hands of; escape, transgress, fail. call to account &c.
(disapprobation) 932.

#927a. Exemption. — N. exemption, freedom, irresponsibility, immunity, liberty, license, release, exoneration,
excuse, dispensation, absolution, franchise, renunciation, discharge; exculpation &c. 970. V. be exempt &c. adj.
exempt, release, acquit, discharge, quitclaim, remise, remit; free, set at liberty, let off, pass over, spare, excuse,
dispense with, give dispensation, license; stretch a point; absolve &c. (forgive) 918; exonerate &c. (exculpate) 970;
save the necessity. Adj. exempt, free, immune, at liberty, scot-free; released &c. v.; unbound, unencumbered;
irresponsible, unaccountable, not answerable; excusable. Phr. bonis nocet quisquis pepercerit malis [Lat][Syrus].

<— p. 322 —>

#928. Respect. — N. respect, regard, consideration; courtesy &c. 894; attention, deference, reverence, honor, esteem, estimation, veneration, admiration; approbation &c. 931. homage, fealty, obeisance, genuflection, kneeling prostration; obsequiousness &c. 886; salaam, kowtow, bow, presenting arms, salute. respects, regards, duty, devoirs, egards. devotion &c. (piety) 987. V. respect, regard; revere, reverence; hold in reverence, honor, venerate, hallow; esteem &c. (approve of) 931; think much of; entertain respect for, bear respect for; look up to, defer to; have a high opinion of, hold a high opinion of; pay attention, pay respect &c. n. to; do honor to, render honor to; do the honors, hail; show courtesy &c. 894; salute, present arms; do homage to, pay homage to; pay tribute to, kneel to, bow to, bend the knee to; fall down before, prostrate oneself, kiss the hem of one's garment; worship &c. 990. keep one's distance, make room, observe due decorum, stand upon ceremony. command respect, inspire respect; awe, inspire awe, impose, overawe, dazzle. Adj. respecting &c.v.; respectful, deferential, decorous, reverential, obsequious, ceremonious, bareheaded, cap in hand, on one's knees; prostrate &c. (servile) 886. respected &c.v.; in high esteem, in high estimation; time-honored, venerable, emeritus. Adv. in deference to; with all respect, with all due respect, with due respect, with the highest respect; with submission. saving your grace, saving your presence; salva sit reverentia[Lat]; pace tanti nominis[Lat]. Int. hail! all hail! esto perpetua[Lat]! may your shadow never be less! Phr. "and pluck up drowned honor by the locks" [Henry IV]; "his honor rooted in dishonor stood" [Tennyson]; "honor pricks me on" [Henry IV].

#929. Disrespect. — N. disrespect, disesteem, disestimation[obs3]; disparagement &c. (dispraise) 932, (detraction) 934. irreverence; slight, neglect, spretae injuria formae [Lat][Vergil], superciliousness &c. (contempt) 930. vilipend-encyl, vilification, contumely, affront, dishonor, insult, indignity, outrage, discourtesy &c. 895; practical joking; scurrility, scoffing, sibilance, hissing, sibilation; irrision[obs3]; derision; mockery; irony &c. (ridicule) 856; sarcasm. hiss, hoot, boo, gibe, flout, jeer, scoff, gleekl, taunt, sneer, quip, fling, wipe, slap in the face. V. hold in disrespect &c. (despise) 930; misprize, disregard, slight, trifle with, set at naught, pass by, push aside, overlook, turn one's back upon, laugh in one's sleeve; be disrespectful &c. adj., be discourteous &c. 895; treat with disrespect &c.n.; set down, put down, browbeat. dishonor, desecrate; insult, affront, outrage. speak slightingly of; disparage &c. (dispraise) 932; vilipend[obs3], vilify, call names; throw dirt, fling dirt; drag through the mud, point at, indulge in personalities; make mouths, make faces; bite the thumb; take by the beard; pluck by the beard; toss in a blanket, tar and feather. have in derision; hold in derision; deride, scoff, barrack, sneer, laugh at, snigger, ridicule, gibe, mock, jeer, hiss, hoot, taunt, twit, niggle[obs3], gleekl!, gird, flout, fleer[obs3]; roast, turn into ridicule; burlesque &c. 856; laugh to scorn &c. (contempt) 930; smoke; fool; make game of, make a fool of, make an April fool of[obs3]; play a practical joke; lead one a dance, run the rig upon, have a fling at, scout; mob. Adj. disrespectful; aweless, irreverent; disparaging &c. 934; insulting &c.v.; supercilious, contemptuous, patronizing &c. (scornful) 930; rude, derisive, sarcastic; scurrile, scurrilous; contumelious. unrespected[obs3], unworshiped[obs3], unenvied[obs3], unsaluted[obs3]; unregarded[obs3], disregarded. Adv. disrespectfully &c. adj.

<— p. 323 —>

#930. Contempt. — N. contempt, disdain, scorn, sovereign contempt; despisal[obs3], despiciency[obs3]; despisement[obs3]; vilipendencyl!, contumely; slight, sneer, spurn, by-word; despect[obs3]. contemptuousness &c. adj.; scornful eye; smile of contempt; derision &c. (disrespect) 929. despisedness[obs3][State of being despised]. V. despise, contemn, scorn, disdain, feel contempt for, view with a scornful eye; disregard, slight, not mind; pass by &c. (neglect) 460. look down upon; hold cheap, hold in contempt, hold in disrespect; think nothing of, think small beer of; make light of; underestimate &c. 483; esteem slightly, esteem of small or no account; take no account of, care nothing for; set no store by; not care a straw, sneeze at &c. (unimportance) 643; set at naught, laugh in one's sleeve, laugh up one's sleeve, snap one's fingers at, shrug one's shoulders, turn up one's nose at, pooh-pooh, "damn with faint praise" [Pope]; whistle at, sneer at; curl up one's lip, toss the head, traiter de haut enbas[Fr]; laugh at &c. (be disrespectful) 929. point the finger of scorn, hold up to scorn, laugh to scorn; scout, hoot, flout, hiss, scoff at. turn one's back upon, turn a cold shoulder upon; tread upon, trample upon, trample under foot; spurn, kick; fling to the winds &c. (repudiate) 610; send away with a flea in the ear. Adj. contemptuous; disdainful, scornful; withering, contumelious, supercilious, cynical, haughty, bumptious, cavalier; derisive. contemptible, despicable; pitiable; pitiful &c. (unimportant) 643; despised &c.v.; downtrodden; unenvied[obs3]. unrespectable (unworthy) 874. Adv. contemptuously &c. adj. Int. a fig for &c. (unimportant) 643; bah! never mind! away with! hang it! fiddlededee! Phr. "a dismal universal hiss, the sound of public scorn" [Paradise Lost]; "I had rather be a dog and bay the moon than such a Roman" [Julius Caesar].

<— p. 324 —>

#931. Approbation. — N. approbation; approval, approvement[obs3]; sanction, advocacy; nod of approbation; esteem, estimation, good opinion, golden opinions, admiration; love &c. 897; appreciation, regard, account, popularity, <gr/kudos/gr>, credit; repute &c. 873; best seller. commendation, praise; laud, laudation; good word; meed of praise, tribute of praise; encomium; eulogy, eulogium[obs3]; eloge[Fr], panegyric; homage, hero worship; benediction, blessing, benison. applause, plaudit, clap; clapping, clapping of hands; acclaim, acclamation; cheer; paean, hosannah; shout of applause, peal of applause, chorus of applause, chorus of praise &c.; Prytaneum. V. approve; approbate[obs3][1], think good, think much of, think well of, think highly of; esteem, value, prize; set great store by, set great store on. do justice to, appreciate; honor, hold in esteem, look up to, admire; like &c. 897; be in favor of, wish Godspeed; hail, hail with satisfaction. stand up for, stick up for; uphold, hold up, countenance, sanction; clap on the back, pat on the back; keep in countenance, indorse; give credit, recommend; mark with a white mark, mark with a stone. commend, belaud[obs3], praise, laud, compliment; pay a tribute, bepraise[obs3]; clap the hands; applaud, cheer, acclamate[obs3], encore; panegyrize[obs3], eulogize, cry up, proner[Fr], puff; extol, extol to the skies; magnify, glorify, exalt, swell, make much of; flatter &c. 933; bless, give a blessing to; have a good word for, say a good word for; speak well of, speak highly of, speak in high terms of; sing the praises of, sound the praises of, chaunt the praises of; resound the praises of; sing praises to; cheer to the echo, applaud to the echo, applaud to the very echo, cheer to the very echo. redound to the honor, redound to the praise, redound to the credit of; do credit to; deserve praise &c.n.; recommend itself; pass muster. be praised &c.; receive honorable mention; be in favor with, be in high favor with; ring with the praises of, win golden opinions, gain credit, find favor with, stand well in the opinion of; laudari a laudato viro[Lat]. Adj. approving &c.v.; in favor of; lost in admiration. commendatory, complimentary, benedictory[obs3], laudatory, panegyrical, eulogistic, encomiastic, lavish of praise, uncritical. approved, praised &c.v.; uncensured, unimpeached; popular, in good odor; in high esteem &c. (respected) 928; in favor, in high favor. deserving of praise, worthy of praise &c.n.; praiseworthy, commendable, of estimation; good &c. 648; meritorious, estimable, creditable, plausible, unimpeachable; beyond all praise. Adv. with credit, to admiration; well &c. 618; with three times three. Int. hear hear! bully for you! * well done! bravo! bravissimo! euge[Ger]! macte virtute[Lat]! so far so good, that's right, quite right; optime[obs3]! one cheer more; may your shadow never be less! esto perpetua[Lat]! long life to! viva! enviva[obs3]! Godspeed! valete et plaudite[Lat]! encore! bis[obs3]! Phr. probatum est[Lat]; tacent satis laudant[Lat]; "servant of God, well done!" [Paradise Lost].

[note 1][Obsolete in England except in legal writings, but surviving in the United States chiefly in a technical sense for license. C.O.S.M.]. <— p. 324 —>

#932. Disapprobation. — N. disapprobation, disapproval; improbation[obs3]; disesteem, disvaluation[obs3], displacency[obs3]; odium; dislike &c. 867. dispraise, discommendation[obs3]; blame, censure, obloquy; detraction &c. 934; disparagement, depreciation; denunciation; condemnation &c. 971; ostracism; black list. animadversion, reflection, stricture, objection, exception, criticism; sardonic grin, sardonic laugh; sarcasm, insinuation, innuendo; bad compliment, poor compliment, left-handed compliment. satire; sneer &c. (contempt) 930; taunt &c. (disrespect) 929; cavil, carping, censoriousness; hypercriticism &c. (fastidiousness) 868. reprehension, remonstrance, expostulation, reproof, reprobation, admonition, increpation[obs3], reproach; rebuke, reprimand, castigation, jobation[obs3], lecture, curtain lecture, blow up, wigging, dressing, rating, scolding, trimming; correction, set down, rap on the knuckles, coup de bec[Fr], rebuff; slap, slap on the face; home thrust, hit; frown, scowl, black look. diatribe; jeremiad, jeremiade; tirade, philippic. clamor, outcry, hue and cry; hiss, hissing; sibilance, sibilation, catcall; execration &c. 908. chiding, upbraiding &c.v.; exprobation[obs3], abuse, vituperation, invective, objurgation, contumely; hard words, cutting words, bitter words. evil-speaking; bad language &c. 908; personality. V. disapprove; dislike &c. 867; lament &c. 839; object to, take exception to; be scandalized at, think ill of; view with disfavor, view with dark eyes, view with jaundiced eyes; nil admirari[Lat], disvalue[obs3]; improbate[obs3]. frown upon, look grave; bend the brows, knit the brows; shake the head at, shrug the shoulders; turn up the nose &c. (contempt) 930; look askance, look black upon; look with an evil eye; make a wry face, make a wry mouth at; set one's face against. dispraise, discommend[obs3], disparage; deprecate, speak ill of, not speak well of; condemn &c. (find guilty) 971. blame; lay blame upon, cast blame upon; censure, fronder[Fr], reproach, pass censure on, reprobate, impugn. remonstrate, expostulate, recriminate. reprehend, chide, admonish; berate, betongue[obs3]; bring to account, call to account, call over the coals, rake over the coals, call to order; take to task, reprove, lecture, bring to book; read a lesson, read a lecture to; rebuke, correct. reprimand, chastise, castigate, lash, blow up, trounce, trim, laver la tete[Fr], overhaul; give it one, give it one finely; gibbet. accuse &c. 938; impeach, denounce; hold up to reprobation, hold up to execration; expose, brand, gibbet, stigmatize; show up, pull up, take up; cry "shame" upon; be outspoken; raise a hue and cry against. execrate &c. 908; exprobate[obs3], speak daggers, vituperate; abuse, abuse like a pickpocket; scold, rate, objurgate, upbraid, fall foul of; jaw; rail, rail at, rail in good set terms; bark at; anathematize, call names; call by hard names, call by ugly names; avilel, revile, vilify, vilipend[obs3]; bespatter; backbite; clapperclaw[obs3]; rave against, thunder against, fulminate against; load with reproaches. exclaim against, protest against, inveigh against, declaim against, cry out against, raise one's voice against. decry; cry down, run down, frown down; clamor, hiss, hoot, mob, ostracize, blacklist; draw up a round robin, sign a round robin. animadvert upon, reflect upon; glance at; cast reflection, cast reproach, cast a slur upon; insinuate, damn with faint praise; "hint a fault and hesitate dislike"; not to be able to say much for. scoff at, point at; twit, taunt &c. (disrespect) 929; sneer at &c. (despise) 230; satirize, lampoon; defame &c. (detract) 934; depreciate, find fault with, criticize, cut up; pull to pieces, pick to pieces; take exception; cavil; peck at, nibble at, carp at; be censorious &c. adj.; pick holes, pick a hole, pick a hole in one's coat; make a fuss about. take down, take down a peg, set down; snub, snap one up, give a rap on the knuckles; throw a stone at, throw a stone in one's garden; have a fling, have a snap at; have words with, pluck a crow with; give one a wipe, give one a lick with the rough side of the tongue. incur blame, excite disapprobation, scandalize, shock, revolt; get a bad name, forfeit one's good opinion, be under a cloud, come under the ferule, bring a hornet's nest about one's ears. take blame, stand corrected; have to answer for. Adj. disapproving &c.v.; scandalized. disparaging, condemnatory, damnatory[obs3], denunciatory, reproachful, abusive, objurgatory[obs3], clamorous, vituperative; defamatory &c. 934. satirical, sarcastic, sardonic, cynical, dry, sharp, cutting, biting, severe, withering, trenchant, hard upon; censorious, critical, captious, carping, hypercritical; fastidious &c. 868; sparing of praise, grudging praise. disapproved, chid &c.v.; in bad odor, blown upon, unapproved; unblest[obs3]; at a discount, exploded; weighed in the balance and found wanting. blameworthy, reprehensible &c. (guilt) 947; to blame, worthy of blame; answerable, uncommendable, exceptionable, not to be thought of; bad &c. 649; vicious &c. 945. unlamented, unbewailed[obs3], unpitied[obs3]. Adv. with a wry face; reproachfully &c. adj. Int. it is too bad! it won't do, it will never do! marry come up! Oh! come! 'sdeath! forbid it Heaven! God forbid, Heaven forbid! out upon, fie upon it! away with! tut! O tempora[obs3]! O mores! shame! fie, fie for shame! out on you! tell it not in Gath!

<— p. 325 —>

#933. Flattery. — N. flattery, adulation, gloze; blandishment, blandiloquence[obs3]; cajolery; fawning, wheedling &c.v.; captation[obs3], coquetry, obsequiousness, sycophancy, flunkeyism[obs3], toadeating[obs3], tuft-hunting; snobbishness. incense, honeyed words, flummery; bunkum, buncombe; blarney, placebo, butter; soft soap, soft sawder[obs3]; rose water. voice of the charmer, mouth honor; lip homage; euphemism; unctuousness &c. adj. V. flatter, praise to the skies, puff; wheedle, cajole, glaver[obs3], coax; fawn upon, faun upon; humor, gloze, soothe, pet, coquet, slaver, butter; jolly [U.S.]; bespatter, beslubber[obs3], beplaster[obs3], beslaver[obs3]; lay it on thick, overpraise; earwig, cog, collogue[obs3]; truckle to, pander to, pandar to[obs3], suck up to, kiss the ass of [vulgar], pay court to; court; creep into the good graces of, curry favor with, hang on the sleeve of; fool to the top of one's bent; lick the dust. lay the flattering unction to one's soul, gild the pill, make things pleasant. overestimate &c. 482; exaggerate &c. 549. Adj. flattering &c.v.; adulatory; mealy-mouthed, honey-mouthed; honeyed; smooth, smooth-tongued; soapy, oily, unctuous, blandiloquent[obs3], specious; fine-spoken, fair spoken; plausible, servile, sycophantic, fulsome; courtierly[obs3], courtier-like. Adv. ad captandum[Lat].

#934. Detraction. — N. detraction, disparagement, depreciation, vilification, obloquy, scurrility, scandal, defamation, aspersion, traducement, slander, calumny, obtrectation[obs3], evil-speaking, backbiting, scandalum magnatum[Lat]. personality, libel, lampoon, skit, pasquinade; chronique scandaleuse[Fr]; roorback [U.S.]. sarcasm, cynicism; criticism (disapprobation) 932; invective &c. 932; envenomed tongue; spretae injuria formae[Lat]. personality, libel, lampoon, skit, pasquinade; chronique scandaleuse[Fr]; roorback [U.S.]. detractor &c. 936. V. detract, derogate, decry, deprecate, depreciate, disparage; run down, cry down; backcap [obs3][U.S.]; belittle; sneer at &c. (contemn) 930; criticize, pull to pieces, pick a hole in one's coat, asperse, cast aspersions, blow upon, bespatter, blacken, vilify, vilipend[obs3]; avilel; give a dog a bad name, brand, malign; muckrake; backbite, libel, lampoon, traduce, slander, defame, calumniate, bear false witness against; speak ill of behind one's back. fling dirt &c. (disrespect) 929; anathematize &c. 932; dip the pen in gall, view in a bad light. impugn[disparage the motives of]; assail, attack &c. 716; oppose &c. 708; denounce, accuse &c. 938. Adj. detracting &c.v.; defamatory, detractory[obs3], derogatory, deprecatory; catty; disparaging, libelous; scurrile, scurrilous; abusive; foul-spoken, foul-tongued, foul-mouthed; slanderous; calumnious, calumniatory[obs3]; sarcastic, sardonic; sarcastic, satirical, cynical. critical &c. 932. Phr. "damn with faint praise, assent with civil leer; and without sneering, teach the rest to sneer" [Pope]; another lie nailed to the counter; "cut men's throats with whisperings" [B. Jonson]; "foul whisperings are abroad" "soft-buzzing slander" [Macbeth][Thomson]; "virtue itself 'scapes not calumnious strokes" [Hamlet].

<— p. 326 —>

#935. Flatterer. — N. flatterer, adulator; eulogist, euphemist; optimist, encomiast, laudator[Lat], whitewasher. toady, toadeater[obs3]; sycophant, courtier, Sir Pertinax MacSycophant; flaneur[Fr], proneur[Fr]; puffer, touter[obs3], claqueur[Fr]; clawback[obs3], earwig, doer of dirty work; parasite, hanger-on &c. (servility) 886. yes-man, suckup, ass-kisser [vulgar], brown-noser [vulgar], teacher's pet. Phr. pessimum genus inimicorum laudantes [Lat][Tacitus].

#936. Detractor. — N. detractor, reprover; censor, censurer; cynic, critic, caviler, carper, word-catcher, frondeur; barracker[obs3].

defamer, backbiter, slanderer, Sir Benjamin Backbite, lampooner, satirist, traducer, libeler, calumniator, dawplucker[obs3], Thersites[obs3]; Zoilus; good-natured friend [satirically]; reviler, vituperator, castigator; shrew &c. 901; muckraker.

disapprover, laudator temporis acti [Lat][Horace].

Adj. black-mouthed, abusive &c. 934.

<— vindication and advocacy together?? —>

#937. Vindication. — N. vindication, justification, warrant; exoneration, exculpation; acquittal &c. 970; whitewashing.

extenuation; palliation, palliative; softening, mitigation.

reply, defense; recrimination &c 938.

apology, gloss, varnish; plea &c. 617; salvo; excuse, extenuating circumstances; allowance, allowance to be made; locus paenitentiae[Lat].

apologist, vindicator, justifier; defendant &c. 938.

justifiable charge, true bill.

v. justify, warrant; be an excuse &c. n.for; lend a color, furnish a handle; vindicate; exculpate, disculpate[obs3]; acquit &c. 970; clear, set right, exonerate, whitewash; clear the skirts of.

extenuate, palliate, excuse, soften, apologize, varnish, slur, gloze; put a gloss, put a good face upon; mince; gloss over, bolster up, help a lame dog over a stile.

advocate, defend, plead one's cause; stand up for, stick up for, speak up for; contend for, speak for; bear out, keep in countenance, support; plead &c, 617; say in defense; plead ignorance; confess and avoid, propugn[obs3], put in a good word for.

take the will for the deed, make allowance for, give credit for, do justice to; give one his due, give the Devil his due.

make good; prove the truth of, prove one's case; be justified by the event.

Adj. vindicated, vindicating &c v.; exculpatory; apologetic.

excusable, defensible, pardonable; venial, veniable[obs3]; specious, plausible, justifiable.

Phr. "honi sot qui mal y pense"; "good wine needs no bush."

#938. Accusation. — N. accusation, charge, imputation, slur, inculpation, exprobration[obs3], delation; crimination; incrimination, accrimination[obs3], recrimination; tu quoque argument[Lat]; invective &c. 932. denunciation, denouncement; libel, challenge, citation, arraignment; impeachment, appeachment[obs3]; indictment, bill of indictment, true bill; lawsuit &c. 969; condemnation &c. 971. gravamen of a charge, head and front of one's offending, argumentum ad hominem[Lat]; scandal &c. (detraction) 934; scandalum magnatum[Lat]. accuser, prosecutor, plaintiff; relator, informer; appellant. accused, defendant, prisoner, perpetrator, panel, respondent; litigant. V. accuse, charge, tax, impute, twit, taunt with, reproach. brand with reproach; stigmatize, slur; cast a stone at, cast a slur on; incriminate, criminate; inculpate, implicate; call to account &c. (censure) 932; take to blame, take to task; put in the black book. inform against, indict, denounce, arraign; impeach, appeach[obs3]; have up, show up, pull up; challenge, cite, lodge a complaint; prosecute, bring an action against &c. 969; blow upon. charge with, saddle with; lay to one's door, lay charge; lay the blame on, bring home to; cast in one's teeth, throw in one's teeth; cast the first stone at. have a rod in pickle for, keep a rod in pickle for; have a crow to pluck with. trump up a charge. Adj. accusing &c.v.; accusatory, accusative; imputative, denunciatory; recriminatory, criminatory[obs3]. accused &c.v.; suspected; under suspicion, under a cloud, under surveillance; in custody, in detention; in the lockup, in the watch house, in the house of detention. accusable, imputable; indefensible, inexcusable; unpardonable, unjustifiable; vicious &c. 845. Int. look at home; tu quoque &c. (retaliation) 718[Lat]. Phr. "the breath of accusation kills an innocent name" [Shelley]; "thou can'st not say I did it" [Macbeth].

<— p. 327 —> % 3. MORAL CONDITIONS %

#939. Probity. — N. probity, integrity, rectitude; uprightness &c. adj.; honesty, faith; honor; bonne foi[Fr], good faith, bona fides[Lat]; purity, clean hands. fairness &c. adj.; fair play, justice, equity, impartiality, principle, even-handedness; grace. constancy; faithfulness &c. adj.; fidelity, loyalty; incorruption, incorruptibility. trustworthiness &c. adj.; truth, candor, singleness of heart; veracity &c. 543; tender conscience &c. (sense of duty) 926. punctilio, delicacy, nicety; scrupulosity, scrupulousness &c. adj.; scruple; point, point of honor; punctuality. dignity &c, (repute) 873; respectability, respectableness &c. adj; gentilhomme[Fr], gentleman; man of honor, man of his word; fidus Achates[Lat][obs3], preux chevalier[Fr], galantuomo[It]; truepenny[obs3], trump, brick; true Briton; white man * [U.S.]. court of honor, a fair field and no favor; argumentum ad verecundiam[Lat]. V. be honorable &c. adj.; deal honorably, deal squarely, deal impartially, deal fairly; speak the truth &c. (veracity) 543; draw a straight furrow; tell the truth and shame the Devil, vitam impendere vero[Lat]; show a proper spirit, make a point of; do one's duty &c. (virtue) 944. redeem one's pledge &c. 926; keep one's promise, be as good as one's promise, be as good as one's word; keep faith with, not fail. give and take, audire alteram partem[Lat], give the Devil his due, put the saddle on the right horse. redound to one's honor. Adj. upright; honest, honest as daylight; veracious &c. 543; virtuous &c. 944; honorable; fair, right, just, equitable, impartial, evenhanded, square; fair and aboveboard, open and aboveboard; white * [U.S.]. constant, constant as the northern star; faithful, loyal, staunch; true, true blue, true to one's colors, true to the core, true as the needle to the pole; "marble-constant" [Antony and Cleopatra]; true-hearted, trusty, trustworthy; as good as one's word, to be depended on, incorruptible. straightforward &c. (ingenuous) 703; frank, candid, open-hearted. conscientious, tender-conscienced, right-minded; high-principled, high-minded; scrupulous, religious, strict; nice, punctilious, correct, punctual; respectable, reputable; gentlemanlike[obs3]. inviolable, inviolate; unviolated[obs3], unbroken, unbetrayed; unbought, unbribed[obs3]. innocent &c. 946; pure, stainless; unstained, untarnished, unsullied, untainted, unperjured[obs3]; uncorrupt, uncorrupted; undefiled, undepraved[obs3], undebauched[obs3]; integer vitae scelerisque purus [Lat][Horace]; justus et tenax propositi [Lat][Horace]. chivalrous, jealous of honor, sans peur et sans reproche[Fr]; high- spirited. supramundane[obs3], unworldly, other-worldly, overscrupulous[obs3]. Adv. honorable &c. adj.; bona fide; on the square, in good faith, honor bright, foro conscientiae[Lat], with clean hands. Phr. "a face untaught to feign" [Pope]; bene qui latuit bene vixit [Lat][Ovid]; mens sibi conscia recti[Lat]; probitas laudatur et alget [Lat][obs3][Juvenal]; fidelis ad urnam[Lat]; "his heart as far from fraud as heaven from earth" [Two Gentlemen]; loyaute m'oblige[Fr]; loyaute n'a honte[Fr]; "what stronger breastplate than a heart untainted?" [Henry VI].

<— p. 328 —>

#940. Improbity. — N. improbity[obs3]; dishonesty, dishonor; deviation from rectitude; disgrace &c. (disrepute) 874; fraud &c. (deception) 545; lying &c. 544; bad faith, Punic faith; mala fides[Lat], Punica fides[Lat]; infidelity; faithlessness &c. adj.; Judas kiss, betrayal. breach of promise, breach of trust, breach of faith; proditionl, disloyalty, treason, high treason; apostasy &c. (tergiversation) 607; nonobservance &c. 773. shabbiness &c. adj.; villainy, villany[obs3]; baseness &c. adj.; abjection, debasement, turpitude, moral turpitude, laxity, trimming, shuffling. perfidy; perfidiousness &c. adj.; treachery, double dealing; unfairness &c. adj.; knavery, roguery, rascality, foul play; jobbing, jobbery; graft, bribery; venality, nepotism; corruption, job, shuffle, fishy transaction; barratry, sharp practice, heads I win tails you lose; mouth honor &c. (flattery) 933. V. be dishonest &c. adj.; play false; break one's word, break one's faith, break one's promise; jilt, betray, forswear; shuffle &c. (lie) 544; live by one's wits, sail near the wind. disgrace oneself, dishonor oneself, demean oneself; derogate, stoop, grovel, sneak, lose caste; sell oneself, go over to the enemy; seal one's infamy. Adj. dishonest, dishonorable; unconscientious, unscrupulous; fraudulent &c. 545; knavish; disgraceful &c. (disreputable) 974; wicked &c. 945. false-hearted, disingenuous; unfair, one-sided; double, double-hearted, double-tongued, double-faced; timeserving[obs3], crooked, tortuous,insidious, Machiavelian, dark, slippery; fishy; perfidious, treacherous, perjured. infamous, arrant, foul, base, vile, ignominious, blackguard. contemptible, unrespectable, abject, mean, shabby, little, paltry, dirty, scurvy, scabby, sneaking, groveling, scrubby, rascally, pettifogging; beneath one. low-minded, low-thoughted[obs3]; base-minded. undignified, indignl; unbecoming, unbeseeming[obs3], unbefitting; derogatory, degrading; infra dignitatem [Latin: beneath one's dignity]; ungentlemanly, ungentlemanlike; unknightly[obs3], unchivalric[obs3], unmanly, unhandsome; recreant, inglorious. corrupt, venal; debased, mongrel. faithless, of bad faith, false, unfaithful, disloyal; untrustworthy; trustless, trothless[obs3]; lost to shame, dead to honor; barratrous. Adv. dishonestly &c. adj.; mala fide[Lat], like a thief in the night, by crooked paths. Int. O tempora[obs3]! O mores! [Cicero]. Phr. corruptissima respublica plurimae leges [Lat][Tacitus].

#941. Knave. — N. knave, rogue; Scapin[obs3], rascal; Lazarillo de Tormes; bad man &c. 949; blackguard &c. 949; barrater[obs3], barrator[obs3]; shyster [U.S..]. traitor, betrayer, archtraitor[obs3], conspirator, Judas, Catiline; reptile, serpent, snake in the grass, wolf in sheep's clothing, sneak, Jerry Sneak, squealer*, tell-tale, mischief-maker; trimmer, fence-sitter, renegade &c. (tergiversation) 607; truant, recreant; sycophant &c. (servility) 886.

#942. Disinterestedness. — N. disinterestedness &c. adj.; generosity; liberality, liberalism; altruism; benevolence &c. 906; elevation, loftiness of purpose, exaltation, magnanimity; chivalry, chivalrous spirit; heroism, sublimity. self-denial, self-abnegation, self-sacrifice, self-immolation, self- control &c. (resolution) 604; stoicism, devotion, martyrdom, suttee. labor of love. V. be disinterested &c. adj.; make a sacrifice, lay one's head on the block; put oneself in the place of others, do as one would be done by, do unto others as we would men should do unto us. Adj. disinterested; unselfish; self-denying, self-sacrificing, self- devoted; generous. handsome, liberal, noble, broad-minded; noble-minded, high-minded; princely, great, high, elevated, lofty, exalted, spirited, stoical, magnanimous; great-hearted, large-hearted; chivalrous, heroic, sublime. unbought, unbribed[obs3]; uncorrupted &c. (upright) 939. Phr. non vobis solum[Lat].

#943. Selfishness. — N. selfishness &c. adj.; self-love, self- indulgence, self-worship, self-interest; egotism, egoism; amour propre[Fr],&c. (vanity) 880; nepotism. worldliness &c. adj.; world wisdom. illiberality; meanness &c. adj. time-pleaser, time-server; tuft-hunter, fortune-hunter; jobber, worldling; egotist, egoist, monopolist, nepotist; dog in the manger, charity that begins at home; canis in praesepi[Lat], "foes to nobleness," temporizer, trimmer. V. be selfish &c. adj.; please oneself, indulge oneself, coddle oneself; consult one's own wishes, consult one's own pleasure; look after one's own interest; feather one's nest; take care of number one, have an eye to the main chance, know on which side one's bread is buttered; give an inch and take an ell. Adj. selfish; self-seeking, self-indulgent, self-interested, self- centered; wrapped up in self, wrapt up in self[obs3], centered in self; egotistic, egotistical; egoistical[obs3]. illiberal, mean, ungenerous, narrow-minded; mercenary, venal; covetous &c. 819. unspiritual, earthly, earthly-minded; mundane; worldly, worldly- minded; worldly-wise; timeserving[obs3]. interested; alieni appetens sui profusus[Lat]. Adv. ungenerously &c. adj.; to gain some private ends, from interested motives. Phr. apres nous le deluge[Fr].

<— p. 329 —>

#944. Virtue. — N. virtue; virtuousness &c. adj.; morality; moral rectitude; integrity &c. (probity) 939; nobleness &c. 873. morals; ethics &c. (duty) 926; cardinal virtues. merit, worth, desert, excellence, credit; self-control &c. (resolution) 604; self-denial &c. (temperance) 953. well-doing; good actions, good behavior; discharge of duty, fulfillment of duty, performance of duty; well-spent life; innocence &c. 946. V. be virtuous &c. adj.; practice virtue &c.n.; do one's duty, fulfill one's duty, perform one's duty, discharge one's duty; redeem one's pledge, keep one's promise &c. 926; act well, act one's part; fight the good fight; acquit oneself well; command one's passions, master one's passions; keep in the right path. set an example, set a good example; be on one's good behavior, be on one's best behavior. Adj. virtuous, good; innocent &c. 946; meritorious, deserving, worthy, desertful[obs3], correct; dutiful, duteous; moral; right, righteous, right- minded; well-intentioned, creditable, laudable, commendable, praiseworthy; above all praise, beyond all praise; excellent, admirable; sterling, pure, noble; whole-souled[obs3]. exemplary; matchless, peerless; saintly, saint-like; heaven-born, angelic, seraphic, godlike. Adv. virtuously &c, adj.; e merito[Lat]. Phr. esse quam videri bonus malebat [Lat][Sallust]; Schonheit vergeht Tugend besteht[Ger]; "virtue the greatest of all monarchies" [Swift]; virtus laudatur et alget [Lat][obs3][Juvenal]; virtus vincit invidiam[Lat].

#945. Vice. — N. vice; evil-doing, evil courses; wrongdoing; wickedness, viciousness &c. adj.; iniquity, peccability[obs3], demerit; sin, Adaml!; old Adam[obs3], offending Adam[obs3]. immorality, impropriety, indecorum, scandal, laxity, looseness of morals; enphagy[obs3], dophagy[obs3], exophagy[obs3]; want of principle, want of ballast; obliquity, backsliding, infamy, demoralization, pravity[obs3], depravity, pollution; hardness of heart; brutality &c. (malevolence) 907; corruption &c. (debasement) 659; knavery &c. (improbity) 940[obs3]; profligacy; flagrancy, atrocity; cannibalism; lesbianism, Sadism. infirmity; weakness &c. adj.; weakness of the flesh, frailty, imperfection; error; weak side; foible; failing, failure; crying sin, besetting sin; defect, deficiency; cloven foot. lowest dregs of vice, sink of iniquity, Alsatian den[obs3]; gusto picaresco[It]. fault, crime; criminality &c. (guilt) 947. sinner &c. 949. [Resorts] brothel &c. 961; gambling house &c. 621; joint*, opium den, shooting gallery, crack house. V. be vicious &c. adj.; sin, commit sin, do amiss, err, transgress; misdemean oneself[obs3], forget oneself, misconduct oneself; misdo[obs3], misbehave; fall, lapse, slip, trip, offend, trespass; deviate from the line of duty, deviate from the path of virtue &c. 944; take a wrong course, go astray; hug a sin, hug a fault; sow one's wild oats. render vicious &c. adj.; demoralize, brutalize; corrupt &c. (degrade) 659. Adj. vicious[1]; sinful; sinning &c.v.; wicked, iniquitous, immoral, unrighteous, wrong, criminal; naughty, incorrect; unduteous[obs3], undutiful. unprincipled, lawless, disorderly, contra bonos mores[Lat], indecorous, unseemly, improper; dissolute, profligate, scampish; unworthy; worthless; desertless[obs3]; disgraceful, recreant; reprehensible, blameworthy, uncommendable; discreditable, disreputable; Sadistic. base, sinister, scurvy, foul, gross, vile, black, grave, facinorousl, felonious, nefarious, shameful, scandalous, infamous, villainous, of a deep dye, heinous; flagrant, flagitious; atrocious, incarnate, accursed. Mephistophelian, satanic, diabolic, hellish, infernal, stygian, fiendlike[obs3], hell-born, demoniacal, devilish, fiendish. miscreated[obs3], misbegotten; demoralized, corrupt, depraved. evil-minded, evil-disposed; ill-conditioned; malevolent &c. 907; heartless, graceless, shameless, virtueless; abandoned, lost to virtue; unconscionable; sunk in iniquity, lost in iniquity, steeped in iniquity. incorrigible, irreclaimable, obdurate, reprobate, past praying for; culpable, reprehensible &c. (guilty) 947. unjustifiable; indefensible, inexcusable; inexpiable, unpardonable, irremissible[obs3]. weak, frail, lax, infirm, imperfect; indiscrete; demoralizing, degrading. Adv. wrong; sinfully &c. adj.; without excuse. Int. O tempora[obs3]! O mores! Phr. alitur vitium vivitque tegendo [Lat][obs3][Vergil]; genus est mortis male vivere [Lat] [Ovid]; mala mens malus animus [Lat][Terence]; nemo repente fuit turpissimus[Lat]; "the trail of the serpent is over them all" [Moore]; "to sanction vice and hunt decorum down" [Bryon].

[Note 1 - Most of these adjectives are applicable both to the act and to the agent.]. <— p. 330 —>

#946. Innocence. — N. innocence; guiltlessness &c. adj.; incorruption, impeccability.

clean hands, clear conscience, mens sibi conscia recti [Lat][Vergil].

innocent, lamb, dove.

V. be innocent &c. adj; nil conscire sibi nulla pallescere culpa [Lat][Horace].

acquit &c. 970; exculpate &c. (vindicate) 937.

Adj. innocent, not guilty; unguilty[obs3]; guiltless, faultless, sinless, stainless, bloodless, spotless; clear, immaculate; rectus in curia[Lat]; unspotted, unblemished, unerring; undefiled &c. 939; unhardened[obs3], Saturnian; Arcadian &c. (artless) 703[obs3].

inculpable, unculpable[obs3]; unblamed, unblamable[obs3]; blameless, unfallen[obs3], inerrable[obs3], above suspicion; irreproachable, irreprovable[obs3], irreprehensible[obs3]; unexceptionable, unobjectionable, unimpeachable; salvable[obs3]; venial &c. 937.

harmless; inoffensive, innoxious[obs3], innocuous; dove-like, lamb-like; pure, harmless as doves; innocent as a lamb, innocent as the babe unborn; "more sinned against than sinning" [Lear].

virtuous &c. 944; unreproved[obs3], unimpeached, unreproached[obs3].

Adv. innocently &c. adj.; with clean hands; with a clear conscience, with a safe conscience.

Phr. murus aeneus conscientia sana [Lat][obs3][Horace].

#947. Guilt. — N. guilt, guiltiness; culpability; criminality, criminousness[obs3]; deviation from rectitude &c. (improbity) 940[obs3]; sinfulness &c. (vice) 945. misconduct, misbehavior, misdoing, misdeed; malpractice, fault, sin, error, transgression; dereliction, delinquency; indiscretion, lapse, slip, trip, faux pas[Fr], peccadillo; flaw, blot, omission; failing, failure; break, bad break !![U.S.], capital crime, delictum[Lat]. offense, trespass; misdemeanor, misfeasance, misprision; malefaction, malfeasance, malversation; crime, felony. enormity, atrocity, outrage; deadly sin, mortal sin; "deed without a name" [Macbeth]. corpus delicti. Adj. guilty, to blame, culpable, peccable[obs3], in fault, at fault, censurable, reprehensible, blameworthy, uncommendable, illaudable[obs3]; weighed in the balance and found wanting; exceptionable. Adv. in flagrante delicto[Lat]; red-handed, in the very act, with one's hand in the cookie jar. Phr. cui prodest scelus in fecit [Lat][Seneca]; culpam paena premit comes [Lat][Horace]; "O would the deed were good!" [Richard II]; "responsibility prevents crimes" se judice nemo nocens absolvitur [Lat][Burke;][Juvenal]; "so many laws argues so many sins" [Paradise Lost]. <— p. 331 —>

#948. Good Man. — N. good man, honest man, worthy. good woman, perfect lady, Madonna.

model, paragon &c. (perfection) 650; good example; hero, heroine, demigod, seraph, angel; innocent &c. 946; saint &c. (piety) 987; benefactor &c. 912; philanthropist &c. 910; Aristides[obs3]; noble liver!, pattern.

brick*, trump*, gem, jewel, good fellow, prince, diamond in the rough, rough diamond, ugly duckling!!.

salt of the earth; one in ten thousand; one in a million; a gentleman and a scholar; pillar of society, pillar of the community, a man among men.

Phr. si sic omnes[Lat]!

#949. Bad Man. — N. bad man, wrongdoer, worker of iniquity; evildoer &c. 913; sinner; the wicked &c. 945; bad example. villain, rascal, scoundrel, miscreant, budmash[obs3], caitiff!!; wretch, reptile, viper, serpent, cockatrice, basilisk, urchin; tiger!!, monster; devil &c. (demon) 980; devil incarnate; demon in human shape, Nana Sahib; hellhound, hellcat; rakehell[obs3]. bad woman, jade, Jezebel. scamp, scapegrace, rip, runagate, ne'er-do-well, reprobate, scalawag, scallawag. rou[French], rake; Sadist; skeesicks*[obs3], skeezix* [obs3][U.S.]; limb; one who has sold himself to the devil, fallen angel, ame damnee[Fr], vaurien[obs3], mauvais sujet[Fr], loose fish, sad dog; rounder*; lost sheep, black sheep; castaway, recreant, defaulter; prodigal &c. 818. rough, rowdy, hooligan, tough, ugly customer, mean mother [coll.], ruffian, bully, meanie [jocular]; Jonathan Wild; hangman. incendiary, arsonist, fire bug [U.S.]. thief &c. 792; murderer, terrorist &c. 361. [person who violates the criminal law] culprit, delinquent, crook, hoodlum, hood, criminal, thug, malefactor, offender, perpetrator, perp [coll.]; disorderly person, misdemeanant[Law]; outlaw; scofflaw; vandal; felon[convicted criminal]; convict, prisoner, inmate, jail bird, ticket of leave man; multiple offender. blackguard, polisson[obs3], loafer, sneak; rapscallion, rascallion[obs3]; cullion[obs3], mean wretch, varlet, kern[obs3], ame-de- boue[Fr], drole[obs3]; cur, dog, hound!!, whelp!!, mongrel!!; lown!!, loon, runnion[obs3], outcast, vagabond; rogue &c. (knave) 941; ronian[obs3]; scum of the earth, riffraff; Arcades ambo[obs3]. Int. sirrah[obs3]! Phr. Acherontis pabulum[obs3]; gibier de potence[Fr].

#950. Penitence. — N. penitence, contrition, compunction, repentance, remorse; regret &c. 833. self-reproach, self-reproof, self-accusation, self-condemnation, self- humiliation; stings of conscience, pangs of conscience, qualms of conscience, prickings of conscience[obs3], twinge of conscience, twitch of conscience, touch of conscience, voice of conscience; compunctious visitings of nature[obs3]. acknowledgment, confession &c. (disclosure) 529; apology &c. 952; recantation &c. 607; penance &c. 952; resipiscence!!. awakened conscience, deathbed repentance, locus paenitentiae[Lat], stool of repentance, cuttystool[obs3]. penitent, repentant, Magdalen, prodigal son, "a sadder and a wiser man" [Coleridge]. V. repent, be sorry for; be penitent &c. adj.; rue; regret &c. 833; think better of; recant &c. 607; knock under &c. (submit) 725; plead guilty; sing miserere[Lat], sing de profundis[Lat]; cry peccavi; own oneself in the wrong; acknowledge, confess &c, (disclose) 529; humble oneself; beg pardon &c. (apologize) 952; turn over a new leaf, put on the new man, turn from sin; reclaim; repent in sackcloth and ashes &c, (do penance) 952; learn by experience. Adj. penitent; repenting &c.v.; repentant, contrite; conscience- smitten, conscience-stricken; self-accusing, self-convicted. penitential, penitentiary; reclaimed, reborn; not hardened; unhardened[obs3]. Adv. mea culpa. Phr. peccavi; erubuit[Lat]; salva res est [Lat][Terence]; Tu l'as voulu[Fr], Georges Dandin; "and wet his grave with my repentant tears" [Richard III].

#951. Impenitence. — N. impenitence, irrepentance[obs3], recusance[obs3]; lack of contrition.
hardness of heart, seared conscience, induration, obduracy.
V. be impenitent &c. adj.; steel the heart, harden the heart; die game, die and make no sign, die unshriven, die without benefit of clergy.
Adj. impenitent, uncontrite, obdurate; hard, hardened; seared, recusant; unrepentant; relentless, remorseless, graceless, shriftless[obs3].
lost, incorrigible, irreclaimable.
unreconstructed, unregenerate, unreformed; unrepented[obs3], unreclaimed[obs3], unatoned.
<— p. 332 —>

#952. Atonement. — N. atonement, reparation; compromise, composition; compensation &c. 30; quittance, quits; expiation, redemption, reclamation, conciliation, propitiation; indemnification, redress. amends, apology, amende honorable[obs3], satisfaction; peace offering, sin offering, burnt offering; scapegoat, sacrifice. penance, fasting, maceration, sackcloth and ashes, white sheet, shrift, flagellation, lustration[obs3]; purgation, purgatory. V. atone, atone for; expiate; propitiate; make amends, make good; reclaim, redeem, repair, ransom, absolve, purge, shrive, do penance, stand in a white sheet, repent in sackcloth and ashes, wear a hairshirt. set one's house in order, wipe off old scores, make matters up; pay the forfeit, pay the penalty. apologize, beg pardon, fair l'amende honorable[Fr], give satisfaction; come down on one's knees, fall down on one's knees, down on one's marrow bones.

% 4. MORAL PRACTICE %

#953. Temperance. — N. temperance, moderation, sobriety, soberness.
forbearance, abnegation; self-denial, self-restraint, self-control &c.
(resolution) 604.
frugality; vegetarianism, teetotalism, total abstinence; abstinence, abstemiousness; Encratism[obs3], prohibition; system of Pythagoras, system

of Cornaro; Pythagorism, Stoicism.

vegetarian; Pythagorean, gymnosophist[obs3].

teetotaler &c. 958; abstainer; designated driver; Encratite[obs3], fruitarian[obs3], hydropotl!.

V. be temperate &c. adj.; abstain, forbear, refrain, deny oneself, spare, swear off.

know when one has had enough, know one's limit.

take the pledge, go on the wagon.

Adj. temperate, moderate, sober, frugal, sparing; abstemious, abstinent; within compass; measured &c. (sufficient) 639.

on the wagon, on the water wagon.

[re locations where alcoholic beverages are prohibited] dry. Pythagorean; vegetarian; teetotal.

Phr. appetitus rationi obediant [Lat][Cicero]; l'abstenir pour jouir c'est l'epicurisme de la raison [Fr][Rousseau]; trahit sua quemque voluptas [Lat][Vergil].

#954. Intemperance. — N. intemperance; sensuality, animalism, carnality; tragalism[obs3]; pleasure; effeminacy, silkiness; luxury, luxuriousness; lap of pleasure, lap of luxury; free living. indulgence; high living, wild living, inabstinence[obs3], self- indulgence; voluptuousness &c. adj.; epicurism, epicureanism; sybaritism; drug habit. dissipation; licentiousness &c. adj.; debauchery; crapulence[obs3]. revels, revelry; debauch, carousal, jollification, drinking bout, wassail, saturnalia, orgies; excess, too much. Circean cup. [drugs of abuse: list] bhang, hashish, marijuana, pot [coll.], hemp [coll.], grass [coll.]; opium, cocaine, morphine, heroin; LSD[abbr], lysergic acid diethylamide[Chem][Chem]; phencyclidine, angel dust, PCP; barbiturates; amphetamines, speed [coll.]. V. be intemperate &c. adj.; indulge, exceed; live well, live high, live high on the fat of the land, live it up, live high on the hog; give a loose to indulgence &c. n.; wallow in voluptuousness &c. n.; plunge into dissipation. revel; rake, live hard, run riot, sow one's wild oats; slake one's appetite, slake one's thirst; swill; pamper. Adj. intemperate,inabstinent[obs3]; sensual, self-indulgent; voluptuous, luxurious, licentious, wild, dissolute, rakish, fast, debauched. brutish, crapulous[obs3], swinish, piggish. Paphian, Epicurean, Sybaritical; bred in the lap of luxury, nursed in the lap of luxury; indulged, pampered; full-fed, high-fed. Phr. "being full of supper and distempering draughts" [Othello].

#954a. Sensualist. — N. Sybarite, voluptuary, Sardanaphalus, man of pleasure, carpet knight; epicure, epicurean, gourmet, gourmand; pig, hog; votary of Epicurus, swine of Epicurus; sensualist; Heliogabalus; free liver, hard liver; libertine &c. 962; hedonist; tragalist[obs3].

#955. Asceticism. — N. asceticism, puritanism, sabbatarianism[obs3]; cynicisml!, austerity; total abstinence; nephalism[obs3].

mortification, maceration, sackcloth and ashes, flagellation; penance &c. 952; fasting &c. 956; martyrdom.

ascetic; anchoret[obs3], anchorite; martyr; Heautontimorumenos[obs3]; hermit &c. (recluse) 893; puritan, sabbatarian[obs3], cynic, sanyasi[obs3], yogi.

Adj. ascetic, austere, puritanical; cynical; over-religious; acerbic.

<— p. 333 —>

#956. Fasting. — N. fasting; xerophagy[obs3]; famishment, starvation. fast, jour maigre[Fr]; fast day, banyan day; Lent, quadragesima[obs3]; Ramadan, Ramazan; spare diet, meager diet; lenten diet, lenten entertainment; soupe maigre[Fr], short commons, Barmecide feast[obs3]; short rations. V. fast, starve, cleml, famish, perish with hunger; dine with Duke Humphrey[obs3]; make two bites of a cherry. Adj. lenten, quadragesimal[obs3]; unfed[obs3]; starved &c.v.; half- starved; fasting &c. v.; hungry &c. 865.

#957. Gluttony. — N. gluttony; greed, avarice; greediness &c. adj.; voracity.

epicurism; good living, high living; edacity[obs3], gulosity[obs3], crapulence[obs3]; guttling[obs3], guzzling; pantophagy[obs3].

good cheer, blow out; feast &c. (food) 298; gastronomy, batterie de cuisine[Fr].

epicure, bon vivant, gourmand; glutton, cormorant, hog, belly god,

Apicius[obs3], gastronome; gourmet &c. 954a, 868.

v. gormandize, gorge; overgorge[obs3], overeat oneself; engorge, eat one's fill, cram, stuff; guttle[obs3], guzzle; bolt, devour, gobble up; gulp &c. (swallow food) 298; raven, eat out of house and home.

have the stomach of an ostrich; play a good knife and fork &c. (appetite) 865.

pamper.

Adj. gluttonous, greedy; gormandizing &c.v.; edacious[obs3], omnivorous, crapulent[obs3], swinish.

avaricious &c. 819; selfish &c. 918.

pampered; overfed, overgorged[obs3].

Phr. jejunus raro stomachus vulgaria temnit [Lat][Horace].

#958. Sobriety. — N. sobriety; teetotalism.

temperance &c. 953.

water-drinker; hydropotl!; prohibitionist; teetotaler, teetotalist; abstainer, Good Templar, band of hope.

V. take the pledge.

Adj. sober, sober as a judge.

#959. Drunkenness. — N. drunkenness &c. adj.; intemperance; drinking &c. v.; inebriety[obs3], inebriation; ebriety[obs3], ebriosity[obs3]; insobriety; intoxication; temulency[obs3], bibacity[obs3], wine bibbing; comtation[obs3], potation; deep potations, bacchanals, bacchanalia, libations; bender* [U.S.]. oinomania[obs3], dipsomania; delirium tremens; alcohol, alcoholism; mania a potu[Fr]. drink; alcoholic drinks; blue ruin*, grog, port wine; punch, punch bowl; cup, rosy wine, flowing bowl; drop, drop too much; dram; beer &c. (beverage) 298; aguardiente[obs3]; apple brandy, applejack; brandy, brandy smash [U.S.]; chain lightning*, champagne, cocktail; gin, ginsling[obs3]; highball [U.S.], peg, rum, rye, schnapps [U.S.], sherry, sling [U.S.], uisquebaugh[Irish], usquebaugh, whisky, xeres[obs3]. drunkard, sot, toper, tippler, bibber[obs3], wine-bibber, lush; hard drinker, gin drinker, dram drinker; soaker*, sponge, tun; love pot, toss pot; thirsty soul, reveler, carouser, Bacchanal, Bacchanalian; Bacchal[obs3], Bacchante[obs3]; devotee to Bacchus[obs3]; bum* [U.S.], guzzler, tavern haunter. V. get drunk, be drunk &c. adj.; see double; take a drop too much, take a glass too much; drink; tipple, tope, booze, bouse[Fr], guzzle, swill*, soak*, sot, bum* [U.S.], besot, have a jag on, have a buzz on, lush*, bib, swig, carouse; sacrifice at the shrine of Bacchus[obs3]; take to drinking; drink hard, drink deep, drink like a fish; have one's swill*, drain the cup, splice the main brace, take a hair of the dog that bit you. liquor, liquor up; wet one's whistle, take a whet; crack a bottle, pass the bottle; toss off &c. (drink up) 2198; go to the alehouse, go to the public house. make one drunk &c. adj.; inebriate, fuddle, befuddle, fuzzle[obs3], get into one's head. Adj. drunk, tipsy; intoxicated; inebrious[obs3], inebriate, inebriated; in one's cups; in a state of intoxication &c.n.; temulent[obs3], temulentive[obs3]; bombed, smashed; fuddled, mellow, cut, boozy, fou[obs3], fresh, merry, elevated; flustered, disguised, groggy, beery; top-heavy; potvaliant[obs3], glorious; potulentl; squiffy*[obs3]; overcome, overtaken; whittled, screwed*, tight, primed, corned, raddled[obs3], sewed up*, lushy*[obs3], nappy[obs3], muddled, muzzy[obs3], obfuscated, maudlin; crapulous[obs3], dead drunk. woozy[1][slightly drunk], buzzed, flush, flushed. inter pocula[obs3]; in liquor, the worse for liquor; having had a drop too much, half seas over, three sheets in the wind, three sheets to the wind; under the table. drunk as a lord, drunk as a skunk, drunk as a piper, drunk as a fiddler, drunk as Chloe, drunk as an owl, drunk as David's sow, drunk as a wheelbarrow. drunken, bibacious[obs3], sottish; given to drink, addicted to drink, addicted to the bottle; toping &c.v. Phr. nunc est bibendum[Lat]; "Bacchus ever fair and young" [Dryden]; "drink down all unkindness" [Merry Wives]; "O that men should put an enemy in their mouths to steal away their brains" [Othello].

<— p. 334 —>

#960. Purity. — N. purity; decency, decorum, delicacy; continence, chastity, honesty, virtue, modesty, shame; pudicity[obs3], pucelage[obs3], virginity.

vestal, virgin, Joseph, Hippolytus; Lucretia, Diana; prude.

Adj. pure, undefiled, modest, delicate, decent, decorous; virginibus puerisque[Lat]; simon-pure; chaste, continent, virtuous, honest, Platonic.

virgin, unsullied; cherry [coll.].

Phr. "as chaste as unsunn'd snow" [Cymbeline]; "a soul as white as heaven" [Beaumonth & Fl.]; "'tis Chastity, my brother, Chastity" [Milton]; "to the pure all things are pure" [Shelley].

#961. Impurity.— N. impurity; uncleanness &c. (filth) 653; immodesty; grossness &c. adj.; indelicacy, indecency;

impudicity[obs3]; obscenity, ribaldry, Fescennine, smut, bawdry[obs3], double entente, equivoque[Fr]. concupiscence, lust, carnality, flesh, salacity; pruriency, lechery, lasciviency[obs3], lubricity; Sadism, sapphism[obs3]. incontinence, intrigue, faux pas[Fr]; amour, amourette[obs3]; gallantry; debauchery, libertinish[obs3], libertinage[obs3], fornication; liaison; wenching, venery, dissipation. seduction; defloration, defilement, abuse, violation, rape; incest. prostitution, social evil, harlotry, stupration[obs3], whoredom, concubinage, cuckoldom[obs3], adultery, advoutry[obs3], crim[abbr]. con.; free love. seraglio, harem; brothel, bagnio[obs3], stew, bawdyhouse[obs3], cat house, lupanar[obs3], house of ill fame, bordel[obs3], bordello. V. be impure &c. adj.; intrigue; debauch, defile, seduce; prostitute; abuse, violate, deflower; commit adultery &c.n. Adj. impure; unclean &c. (dirty) 653; not to be mentioned to ears polite; immodest, shameless; indecorous, indelicate, indecent; Fescennine; loose, risque [French], coarse, gross, broad, free, equivocal, smutty, fulsome, ribald, obscene, bawdy, pornographic. concupiscent, prurient, lickerish[obs3], rampant, lustful; carnal, carnal-minded; lewd, lascivious, lecherous, libidinous, erotic, ruttish, salacious; Paphian; voluptuous; goatish, must, musty. unchaste, light, wanton, licentious, debauched, dissolute; of loose character, of easy virtue; frail, gay, riggish[obs3], incontinent, meretricious, rakish, gallant, dissipated; no better than she should be; on the town, on the streets, on the pave, on the loose. adulterous, incestuous, bestial.

#962. Libertine. — N. libertine; voluptuary &c. 954a; rake, debauchee, loose fish, rip, rakehell[obs3], fast man; intrigant[obs3], gallant, seducer, fornicator, lecher, satyr, goat, whoremonger, paillard[obs3], adulterer, gay deceiver, Lothario, Don Juan, Bluebeard[obs3]; chartered libertine. adulteress, advoutress[obs3], courtesan, prostitute, strumpet, harlot, whore, punk, fille de joie[Fr]; woman, woman of the town; streetwalker, Cyprian, miss, piece[Fr]; frail sisterhood; demirep, wench, trollop, trull[obs3], baggage, hussy, drab, bitch, jade, skit, rig, quean[obs3], mopsy[obs3], slut, minx, harridan; unfortunate, unfortunate female, unfortunate woman; woman of easy virtue &c. (unchaste) 961; wanton, fornicatress[obs3]; Jezebel, Messalina, Delilah, Thais, Phryne, Aspasia[obs3], Lais, lorette[obs3], cocotte[obs3], petite dame, grisette[obs3]; demimonde; chippy* [obs3][U.S.]; sapphist[obs3]; spiritual wife; white slave. concubine, mistress, doxy[obs3], chere amie[Fr], bona roba[It]. pimp, procurer; pander, pandar[obs3]; bawd, conciliatrix[obs3], procuress[obs3], mackerel, wittoll.

<— p. 335 —>

% 5. INSTITUTIONS

%

#963. Legality. — N. legality; legitimacy, legitimateness.
legislature; law, code, corpus juris[Lat], constitution,
pandect[obs3], charter, enactment, statute, rule; canon &c. (precept) 697;
ordinance, institution, regulation; bylaw, byelaw; decree &c. (order) 741;
ordonnance[obs3]; standing order; plebiscite &c. (choice) 609.
legal process; form, formula, formality; rite, arm of the law; habeas
corpus; fieri facias[Lat].
[Science of law] jurisprudence, nomology[obs3]; legislation,
codification.
equity, common law; lex[Lat], lex nonscripta[Lat][obs3]; law of
nations, droit des gens[Fr], international law, jus gentium[Lat]; jus
civile[Lat]; civil law, canon law, crown law, criminal law, statute law,
ecclesiastical law, administrative law; lex mercatoria[Lat].
constitutionalism, constitutionality; justice &c. 922.
[institution for deciding questions of law] court, tribunal &c. 966.
[person who presides at a court or tribunal] judge &c. 967.
[specialist in questions of law] lawyer, attorney, legal counsel &c.
968.
V. legalize; enact, ordain; decree &c. (order) 741; pass a law, enact
a regulation; legislate; codify, formulate; regulate.
Adj. legal, legitimate; according to law; vested, constitutional,
chartered, legalized; lawful &c. (permitted) 760; statutable[obs3],
statutory; legislatorial, legislative; regulatory, regulated.
Adv. legally &c. adj.; in the eye of the law; de jure[Lat].
Phr. ignorantia legis neminem excusat[Latin: ignorance of the law is

no excuse]; "where law ends tyranny begins" [Earl of Chatham].

#964. [Absence or violation of law.] Illegality. — N. lawlessness; illicitness; breach of law, violation of law, infraction of the law; disobedience &c. 742; unconformity &c. 83.

arbitrariness &c. adj.; antinomy, violence, brute force, despotism, outlawry.

mob law, lynch law, club law, Lydford law, martial law, drumhead law; coup d'etat[Fr]; le droit du plus fort[Fr]; argumentum baculinum[obs3][Lat].

illegality, informality, unlawfulness, illegitimacy, bar sinister.

trover and conversion[Law]; smuggling, poaching; simony.

[person who violates the law] outlaw, bad man &c. 949.

v. offend against the law; violate the law, infringe the law, break the law; set the law at defiance, ride roughshod over, drive a coach and six through a statute; ignore the law, make the law a dead letter, take the law into one's own hands.

smuggle, run, poach.

Adj. illegal[contrary to law], unlawful, illegitimate; not allowed, prohibited &c. 761; illicit, contraband; actionable.

unwarranted, unwarrantable; unauthorized; informal, unofficial; injudicial[obs3], extrajudicial.

lawless, arbitrary; despotic, despotical[obs3]; corrupt, summary, irresponsible; unanswerable, unaccountable.

[of invalid or expired law] expired, invalid; unchartered, unconstitutional; null and void; a dead letter.

[in absence of law] lawless, unregulated

Adv. illegally &c. adj.; with a high hand, in violation of law.

#965. Jurisdiction. [Executive.] — N. jurisdiction, judicature, administration of justice, soc; executive, commission of the peace; magistracy &c. (authority) 737. judge &c. 967; tribunal &c. 966; municipality, corporation, bailiwick, shrievalty[Brit]; lord lieutenant, sheriff, shire reeve, shrieve[obs3], constable; selectman; police, police force, the fuzz [sarcastic]; constabulary, bumbledom[obs3], gendarmerie[Fr]. officer, bailiff, tipstaff, bum-bailiff, catchpoll, beadle; policeman, cop [coll.], police constable, police sergeant; sbirro[obs3], alguazil[obs3], gendarme, kavass[obs3], lictor[obs3], mace bearer, huissier[Fr], bedel[obs3]; tithingman[obs3]. press gang; exciseman[obs3], gauger, gager[obs3], customhouse officer, douanier[Fr]. coroner, edile[obs3], aedile[obs3], portreeve[obs3], paritorl; posse comitatus[Lat]. bureau, cutchery[obs3], department, secretariat. [extension of jurisdiction] long arm of the law, extradition. V. judge, sit in judgment; extradite. Adj. executive, administrative, municipal; inquisitorial, causidical[obs3]; judicatory[obs3], judiciary, judicial; juridical. Adv. coram judice[Lat].

<— p. 336 —>

#966. Tribunal. — N. tribunal, court, board, bench, judicatory[obs3]; court of justice, court of law, court of arbitration, administrative court; inquisition; guild. justice seat; judgment seat, mercy seat; woolsack[obs3]; bar of justice; dock; forum, hustings, bureau, drumhead; jury box, witness box. senate house, town hall, theater; House of Commons, House of Lords; statehouse [U.S.], townhouse. assize, eyre; wardmote[obs3], burghmote[obs3]; barmote[obs3]; superior courts of Westminster; court of record, court oyer and terminer[Law], court assize, court of appeal, court of error; High court of Judicature, High court of Appeal; Judicial Committee of the Privy Council; Star Chamber; Court of Chancery, Court of King's or Queen's Bench, Court of Exchequer, Court of Common Pleas, Court of Probate, Court of Arches, Court of Admiralty; Lords Justices' court, Rolls court, Vice Chancellor's court, Stannary court[obs3], Divorce court, Family court, Palatine court, county court, district court, police court; sessions; quarter sessions, petty sessions; court-leet[Fr], court-baron, court of pie poudre[Fr], court of common council; board of green cloth. court martial; drumhead court martial; durbar[obs3], divan; Areopagus[obs3]; Irota. Adj. judicial &c. 965; appellate. Phr. die Weltgeschichte ist das Weltgericht[Ger].

#967. Judge. — N. judge; justice, justiciar[obs3], justiciary[obs3]; chancellor; justice of assize, judge of assize; recorder, common sergeant; puisne judge, assistant judge, county court judge; conservator of the peace, justice of the peace; J.P.; court &c. (tribunal) 966; magistrate, police magistrate, beak*; his worship, his honor, his lordship. jury, twelve men in a box. Lord Chancellor, Lord Justice; Master of the Rolls, Vice Chancellor; Lord Chief Justice, Chief Baron; Mr. Justice, Associate Justice, Chief Justice; Baron, Baron of the Exchequer. jurat[Lat], assessor;

arbiter, arbitrator; umpire; referee, referendary[obs3]; revising barrister; domesman[obs3]; censor &c. (critic) 480; barmaster[obs3], ephor[obs3]; grand juror, grand juryman; juryman, talesman. archon, tribune, praetor, syndic, podesta[obs3], mollah[obs3], ulema, mufti, cadi[obs3], kadi[obs3]; Rhadamanthus[obs3]. litigant &c. (accusation) 938. V. adjudge &c. (determine) 480; try a case, try a prisoner. Adj. judicial &c. 965. Phr. "a Daniel come to judgment" [Merchant of Venice].

#968. Lawyer. — N. lawyer, attorney, legal counsel; counsel, counsellor, counsellor at law, attorney at law; jurist, legist[obs3], civilian, pundit, publicist, juris consult[Lat], legal adviser, advocate; barrister, barrister at law; King's or Queen's counsel; K.C.; Q.C.; silk gown, leader, sergeant-at-law, bencher; tubman[obs3], judge &c. 967. bar, legal profession, bar association, association of trial lawyers; officer of the court; gentleman of the long robe; junior bar, outer bar, inner bar; equity draftsman, conveyancer, pleader, special pleader. solicitor, proctor; notary, notary public; scrivener, cursitor[obs3]; writer, writer to the signet; S.S.C.; limb of the law; pettifogger; vakil[obs3]. legal beagle [coll.]. [persons accessory to lawyers] legal secretary; legal assistant; law student. V. practice law, practice at the bar, practice within the bar; plead; call to the bar, be called to the bar, be called within the bar; take silk; take to the law. give legal counsel, provide legal counsel. Adj. learned in the law; at the bar; forensic; esquire, esquired. Phr. banco regis[Lat].

#969. Lawsuit.— N. lawsuit, suit, action, cause; litigation; suit in law; dispute &c. 713.

citation, arraignment, prosecution, impeachment; accusation &c. 938; presentment, true bill, indictment.

apprehension, arrest; committal; imprisonment &c. (restraint) 751.

writ, summons, subpoena, latitat[obs3], nisi prius[Lat]; venire, venire facias

pleadings[Lat]; declaration, bill, claim; proces verbal[Fr]; bill of right, information, corpus delicti; affidavit, state of facts; answer, reply, replication, plea, demurrer, rebutter, rejoinder; surrebutter[obs3], surrejoinder[obs3].

suitor, party to a suit; plaintiff, defendant, litigant &c. 938.

hearing, trial; verdict &c. (judgment) 480; appeal, appeal motion; writ of error; certiorari[Lat].

case; decision, precedent; decided case, reports (legal reference works, see reference books).

V. go to law, appeal to the law; bring to justice, bring to trial, bring to the bar; put on trial, pull up; accuse &c. 938; prefer a claim, file a claim &c.n.; take the law of, inform against.

serve with a writ, cite, apprehend, arraign, sue, prosecute, bring an action against, indict, impeach, attach, distrain, commit; arrest; summon, summons; give in charge &c. (restrain) 751.

empanel a jury, implead[obs3], join issue; close the pleadings; set down for hearing.

try, hear a cause; sit in judgment; adjudicate &c. 480.

Adj. litigious &c. (quarrelsome) 713; qui tam; coram judice[Lat], sub judice[Lat].

Adv. pendente lite[Lat].

Phr. adhuc sub judice lis est[Lat]; accedas ad curiam[Lat]; transeat in exemplum[Lat].
<— p. 337 —>

#970. Acquittal.— N. acquittal, acquitment[obs3]; clearance, exculpation; acquittance, clearance, exoneration; discharge &c. (release) 750; quietus, absolution, compurgation[obs3], reprieve, respite; pardon &c. (forgiveness) 918.

[Exemption from punishment] impunity; diplomatic immunity; immunity; plea bargain, deal with the prosecutor.

[in civil suits] no cause for action; no damages.

V. acquit, exculpate, exonerate, clear; absolve, whitewash, assoil[obs3]; discharge, release; liberate &c. 750.

reprieve, respite; pardon &c. (forgive) 918; let off, let off scot-free.

drop the charges.

plea bargain, strike a deal.

no-cause[in civil suits][transitive]; get no-caused[intransitive].

Adj. acquitted &c. v.; uncondemned, unpunished, unchastised.

not guilty; not proven.

not liable.

Phr. nemo bis punitur pro codem delicto[Lat][obs3].

#971. Condemnation.— N. condemnation, conviction, judgment, penalty, sentence; proscription, damnation; death warrant.

attainder, attainture[obs3], attaintment[obs3].

V. condemn, convict, cast, bring home to, find guilty, damn, doom, sign the death warrant, sentence, pass sentence on, attaint, confiscate, proscribe, sequestrate; nonsuit[obs3].

disapprove &c. 932; accuse &c. 938.

stand condemned.

Adj. condemnatory, damnatory[obs3]; guilty, condemned &c.v.; nonsuited &c. (failure) 732[obs3]; self-convicted.

Phr. mutato nomine de te fabula narratur[Lat]; "unrespited, unpitied, unreprieved" [P.L.].

#972. Punishment.— N. punishment,punition[obs3]; chastisement, chastening; correction, castigation. discipline, infliction, trial; judgment; penalty &c. 974; retribution; thunderbolt, Nemesis; requital &c. (reward) 973; penology; retributive justice. lash, scaffold &c. (instrument of punishment) 975; imprisonment &c. (restraint) 751; transportation, banishment, expulsion, exile, involuntary exile, ostracism; penal servitude, hard labor; galleys &c. 975; beating &c.v.; flagellation, fustigation[obs3], gantlet, strappado[obs3], estrapade[obs3], bastinado, argumentum baculinum[Lat] [obs3], stick law, rap on the knuckles, box on the ear; blow &c. (impulse) 276; stripe, cuff, kick, buffet, pummel; slap, slap in the face; wipe, douse; coup de grace; torture, rack; picket, picketing; dragonnade[obs3]. capital punishment; execution; lethal injection; the gas chamber; hanging &c.v.; electrocution, rail-riding, scarpines[obs3]; decapitation, decollation[obs3]; garrotte, garrotto[It]; crucifixion, impalement; firing squad; martyrdom; auto-da-fe[Fr]; noyade[obs3]; happy dispatch. [suicide as punishment] hara-kiri, seppuku [Japanese]; drinking the hemlock. V. punish; chastise, chasten; castigate, correct, inflict punishment, administer correction, deal retributive justice; cowhide, lambaste*. visit upon, pay; pay out, serve out; do for; make short work of, give a lesson to, serve one right, make an example of; have a rod in pickle for; give it one. strike &c. 276; deal a blow to, administer the lash, smite; slap, slap the face; smack, cuff, box the ears, spank, thwack, thump, beat, lay on, swinge[obs3], buffet; thresh, thrash, pummel, drub, leather, trounce, sandbag, baste, belabor; lace, lace one's jacket; dress, dress down, give a dressing, trim, warm, wipe, tund[obs3], cob, bang, strap, comb, lash, lick, larrup, wallop, whop, flog, scourge, whip, birch, cane, give the stick, switch, flagellate, horsewhip, bastinado, towel, rub down with an oaken towel, rib roast, dust one's jacket, fustigate[obs3], pitch into, lay about one, beat black and blue; beat to a mummy, beat to a jelly; give a black eye. tar and feather; pelt, stone, lapidate[obs3]; masthead, keelhaul. execute; bring to the block, bring to the gallows; behead, decapitate, guillotine; decollate; hang, turn off, gibbet, bowstring, hang draw and quarter; shoot; decimate; burn; break on the wheel, crucify; empale[obs3], impale; flay; lynch; electrocute; gas, send to the gas chamber. torture; put on, put to the rack; picket. banish, exile, transport, expel, ostracize; rusticate; drum out; dismiss, disbar, disbench[obs3]; strike off the roll, unfrock; post. suffer, suffer for, suffer punishment; be flogged. be executed, suffer the ultimate penalty; be hanged &c., come to the gallows, mount the gallows, swing [coll.], twist in the wind, dance upon nothing, die in one's shoes; be rightly served; be electrocuted, fry [coll.], ride the lightning [coll.]; face the firing squad. Adj. punishing &c. v.; penal; punitory[obs3], punitive; inflictive, castigatory; punished &c.v. Int. a la lanterne[Fr]! Phr. culpan paena premit comes [Lat][Horace]; "eating the bitter bread of banishment" [Richard II]; gravis ira regum est semper [Lat][Seneca]; sera tamen tacitis paena venit pedibus [Lat][Tibullus]; suo sibi gladio hunc jugulo [Lat][Terence].

<— p. 338 —>

#973. Reward. — N. reward, recompense, remuneration, meed, guerdon[obs3], reguerdon|; price.

[payment for damage or debt] indemnity, indemnification; quittance; compensation; reparation, redress, satisfaction; reckoning, acknowledgment, requital, amends, sop; atonement, retribution; consideration, return, quid pro quo.

salvage, perquisite; vail &c. (donation) 784[obs3].

douceur[Fr], bribe; hush money, smart money!; blackmail, extortion; carcelage!; solatium[obs3].

allowance, salary, stipend, wages, compensation; pay, payment; emolument; tribute; batta[obs3], shot, scot; bonus, premium, tip; fee, honorarium; hire; dasturi[obs3], dustoori[obs3]; mileage.

crown &c. (decoration of honor) 877.

V. reward, recompense, repay, requite; remunerate, munerate[obs3]; compensate; fee; pay one's footing &c. (pay) 807; make amends, indemnify, atone; satisfy, acknowledge.

get for one's pains, reap the fruits of.

tip.

Adj. remunerative, remuneratory; munerary[obs3], compensatory, retributive, reparatory[obs3]; rewarding; satisfactory.

Phr. fideli certa merces[Lat]; honor virtutis praemium [Lat][Cicero]; tibi seris tibi metis[Lat].

#974. Penalty. — N. penalty; retribution &c. (punishment) 972; pain, pains and penalties; weregild[obs3], wergild; peine forte et dure[Fr]; penance &c. (atonement) 952; the devil to pay. fine, mulct, amercement; forfeit, forfeiture; escheat[Law], damages, deodand[obs3], sequestration, confiscation, premunire[Lat]; doomage [obs3][U.S.]. V. fine, mulct, amerce, sconce, confiscate; sequestrate, sequester; escheat[Law]; estreat[obs3], forfeit.

#975. [Instrument of punishment.] Scourge. — N. scourge, rod, cane, stick; ratan[obs3], rattan; birch, birch rod; azote[obs3], blacksnake[obs3], bullwhack [obs3][U.S.], chicote[obs3], kurbash[obs3], quirt, rawhide, sjambok[obs3]; rod in pickle; switch, ferule, cudgel, truncheon. whip, bullwhip, lash, strap, thong, cowhide, knout; cat, cat o'nine tails; rope's end. pillory, stocks, whipping post; cucking stool[obs3], ducking stool; brank[obs3]; trebuchet[obs3], trebuket[obs3]. triangle[instruments of torture: list], wooden horse, iron maiden, thumbscrew, boot, rack, wheel, iron heel; chinese water torture. treadmill, crank, galleys. scaffold; block, ax, guillotine; stake; cross; gallows, gibbet, tree, drop, noose, rope, halter, bowstring; death chair, electric chair; gas chamber; lethal injection; firing squad; mecate[obs3]. house of correction &c. (prison) 752. goaler, jailer; executioner; electrocutioner[obs3]; lyncher; hangman; headsman[obs3]; Jack Ketch.

<— p. 339 —> % SECTION V. RELIGIOUS AFFECTIONS

1. SUPERHUMAN BEINGS AND REGIONS %

#976. Deity. — N. Deity, Divinity; Godhead, Godship[obs3]; Omnipotence, Providence; Heaven [metonymically]. [Quality of being divine] divineness[obs3], divinity. God, Lord, Jehovah, Jahweh, Allah[obs3]; The Almighty, The Supreme Being, The First Cause, the Prime Mover; Ens Entium[Lat]; Author of all things, Creator of all things; Author of our being; Cosmoplast[obs3]; El; The Infinite, The Eternal; The All-powerful, The All-wise, The All- merciful, The All-holy. [Attributes and perfections] infinite power, infinite wisdom, infinite goodness, infinite justice, infinite truth, infinite mercy; omnipotence, omniscience, omnipresence; unity, immutability, holiness, glory, majesty, sovereignty, infinity, eternity. The Trinity, The Holy Trinity, The Trinity in Unity, The Triune God, God the Father Son and Holy Ghost. God the Father; The Maker, The Creator, The Preserver. [Functions] creation, preservation, divine govern- ment; Theocracy, Thearchy[obs3]; providence; ways of Providence, dealings of Providence, dispensations of Providence, visitations of Providence. [Christian God: second person] God the Son, Jesus, Christ; The Messiah, The Anointed, The Saviour, the Redeemer, The Mediator, The Intercessor, The Advocate, The Judge; The Son of God, The Son of Man, The Son of David; The Lamb of God, The Word; Logos; Emmanuel; Immanuel; The King of Kings and Lord of Lords, The King of Glory, The Prince of Peace, The Good Shepherd, The Way, The Truth, The Life, The Bread of Life, The Light of the World; The Lord our, The Sun of Righteousness; "The Pilot of the Galilean lake" [Milton]. The Incarnation, The Hypostatic Union. [Functions] salvation, redemption, atonement, propitiation, media- tion, intercession, judgment. [Christian God: third person] God the Holy Ghost, The Holy Spirit, Paraclete[Theol]; The Comforter, The Spirit of Truth, The Dove. [Functions] inspiration, unction, regeneration, sanctification, consolation. eon, aeon, special providence, deus ex machina[Lat]; avatar. V. create, move, uphold, preserve, govern &c. atone, redeem, save, propitiate, mediate &c. predestinate, elect, call, ordain, bless, justify, sanctify, glorify &c. Adj. almighty, holy, hallowed, sacred, divine, heavenly, celestial; sacrosanct; all-knowing, all-seeing, all-wise; omniscient. superhu- man, supernatural; ghostly, spiritual, hyperphysical[obs3], unearthly; theistic, theocratic; anointed; soterial[obs3]. Adj. jure divino[Lat], by divine right. Phr. Domine dirige nos[Lat]; en Dieu est ma fiance[Fr]; et sceleratis sol oritur [Lat]

[Seneca]; "He mounts the storm and walks upon the wind" [Pope]; "Thou great First Cause, least understood" [Pope]; sans Dieu rien[Fr].

#977. [Beneficent spirits] Angel. — N. angel, archangel; guardian angel; heavenly host, host of heaven, sons of God; seraph, seraphim; cherub, cherubim.
　　ministering spirit, morning star.
　　saint, patron saint, Madonna; invisible helpers.
　　Adj. angelic, seraphic, cherubic; saintly.

#978. [Maleficent spirits.] Satan. — N. Satan, the Devil, Lucifer, Mephistopheles, Ahriman[obs3], Belial; Samael, Zamiel, Beelzebub, the Prince of the Devils. the tempter[1]; the evil one, the evil spirit; the Adversary; the archenemy; the author of evil, the wicked one, the old Serpent; the Prince of darkness, the Prince of this world, the Prince of the power of the air; the foul fiend, the arch fiend; the devil incarnate; the common enemy, the angel of the bottomless pit; Abaddon[obs3], Apollyon[obs3]. fallen angels, unclean spirits, devils; the rulers, the powers of darkness; inhabitants of Pandemonium; demon &c. 980. diabolism; devilism[obs3], devilship[obs3]; diabolology[obs3]; satanism, devil worship; manicheism; the cloven foot. Adj. satanic, diabolic, devilish; infernal, hellborn[obs3]. [1-The slang expressions "the deuce, dickens, old Gentleman; old Nick, old Scratch, old Horny, old Harry, old Gooseberry," have not been inserted in the text.].

<— p. 340 —> <— I'm not sure whether this is supposed to be number two, but I can't find any other piece for it (previous 1., next 3.). Sampo Niskanen <sampo.niskanen@iki.fi> —> % 2. Mythological and other fabulous Deities and Powers

% <— break this into serious deities and fairies —>

#979. Jupiter. — N. god, goddess; heathen gods and goddesses; deva[obs3]; Jupiter, Jove &c.; pantheon. Allah[obs3], Bathala[obs3], Brahm[obs3], Brahma[obs3], Brahma[obs3], cloud-compeller, Devi, Durga, Kali, oread[obs3], the Great Spirit, Ushas; water nymph, wood nymph; Yama, Varuna, Zeus; Vishnu[Hindu deities], Siva, Shiva, Krishna, Juggernath[obs3], Buddha; Isis[Egyptian deities], Osiris, Ra; Belus, Bel, Baal[obs3], Asteroth &c. [obs3]; Thor[Norse deities], Odin; Mumbo Jumbo; good genius, tutelary genius; demiurge, familiar; sibyl; fairy, fay; sylph,, sylphid; Ariel[obs3], peri, nymph, nereid, dryad, seamaid, banshee, benshie[obs3], Ormuzd; Oberon, Mab, hamadryad[obs3], naiad, mermaid, kelpie[obs3], Ondine, nixie, sprite; denizens of the air; pixy &c. (bad spirit) 980. mythology; heathen-mythology, fairy-mythology; Lempriere, folklore. Adj. god-like, fairy-like; sylph-like; sylphic[obs3]. Phr. "you moonshine revelers and shades of night" [Merry Wives].

#980. Demon. — N. demon, daemon, demonry[obs3], demonology; evil genius, fiend, familiar, daeva[obs3], devil; bad spirit, unclean spirit; cacodemon[obs3], incubus, Eblis, shaitan[obs3], succubus, succuba; Frankenstein's monster; Titan, Shedim, Mephistopheles, Asmodeus[obs3], Moloch, Belial, Ahriman[obs3]; fury, harpy; Friar Rush. vampire, ghoul; afreet[obs3], barghest[obs3], Loki; ogre, ogress; gnome, gin, jinn, imp, deev[obs3], lamia[obs3]; bogie, bogeyman, bogle[obs3]; nis[obs3], kobold[obs3], flibbertigibbet, fairy, brownie, pixy, elf, dwarf, urchin; Puck, Robin Goodfellow; leprechaun, Cluricaune[obs3], troll, dwerger[obs3], sprite, ouphe[obs3], bad fairy, nix, nixie, pigwidgeon[obs3], will-o'-the wisp. [Supernatural appearance] ghost, revenant, specter, apparition, spirit, shade, shadow, vision; hobglobin, goblin, orc; wraith, spook, boggart[obs3], banshee, loup-garou[Fr], lemures[obs3]; evil eye. merman, mermaid, merfolk[obs3]; siren; satyr, faun; manito[obs3], manitou, manitu. possession, demonic possession, diabolic possession; insanity &c.503. [in jest, in science] Maxwell's demon. [person possessed by a demon] demoniac. Adj. demonic, demonical, impish, demoniacal; fiendish, fiend-like; supernatural, weird, uncanny, unearthly, spectral; ghostly, ghost-like; elfin, elvin[obs3], elfish, elflike[obs3]; haunted; pokerish [obs3][U.S.]. possessed, possessed by a devil, possessed by a demon. Adv. demonically.

#981. Heaven. — N. heaven; kingdom of heaven, kingdom of God; heavenly kingdom; throne of God; presence of God; inheritance of the saints in light. Paradise, Eden, Zion, abode of the blessed; celestial bliss, glory. [Mythological heaven] Olympus; Elysium[paradise], Elysian fields, Arcadia[obs3], bowers of bliss, garden of the Hesperides, third heaven; Valhalla, Walhalla (Scandinavian); Nirvana (Buddhist); happy hunting grounds; Alfardaws[obs3], Assama[obs3]; Falak al aflak "the highest heaven" (Mohammedan)[Arabic][Arab]. future state, eternal home, eternal reward. resurrection, translation; resuscitation &c. 660. apotheosis, deification. Adj. heavenly, celestial, supernal, unearthly, from on high, paradisiacal, beatific, elysian. Phr. "looks through nature up to the nature's god" [Pope]; "the great world;s altarstairs, that slope through darkness up to God" [Tennyson]; "the treasury of everlasting joy" [Henry VI]; vigeur de dessus[Fr].

288

#982. Hell. — N. hell, bottomless pit, place of torment; habitation of fallen angels; Pandemonium, Abaddon[obs3], Domdaniel; jahannan[obs3], sheol[obs3].

hell fire; everlasting fire, everlasting torment, eternal damnation; lake of fire and brimstone; fire that is never quenched; worm that never dies.

purgatory, limbo, gehenna, abyss.

[Mythological hell] Tartarus, Hades, Avernus[Lat], Styx, Stygian creek, pit of Acheron[obs3], Cocytus; infernal regions, inferno, shades below, realms of Pluto.

Pluto, Rhadamanthus[obs3], Erebus[Lat]; Tophet.

Adj. hellish, infernal, stygian.

Phr. dies irae dies illa[Lat]; "the hue of dungeons and the scowl of night" [Love's Labor's Lost].

<— p. 341 —>

#983. [Religious Knowledge.] Theology. — N. theology (natural and revealed); theogony[obs3], theosophy; divinity; hagiology, hagiography; Caucasian mystery; monotheism; religion; religious persuasion, religious sect, religious denomination; creed &c. (belief) 484; article of faith, declaration of faith, profession of faith, confession of faith. theologue, theologian; scholastic, divine, schoolman[obs3], canonist, theologist[obs3]; the Fathers. Adj. theological, religious; denominational; sectarian &c. 984.

#983a. Orthodoxy. — N. orthodoxy; strictness, soundness, religious truth, true faith; truth &c. 494; soundness of doctrine. Christianity, Christianism[obs3]; Catholicism, Catholicity; "the faith once delivered to the saints"; hyperorthodoxy &c. 984[obs3]; iconoclasm. The Church; Catholic Church, Universal Church, Apostolic Church, Established Church; temple of the Holy Ghost; Church of Christ, body of Christ, members of Christ, disciples of Christ, followers of Christ; Christian, Christian community; true believer; canonist &c. (theologian) 983; Christendom, collective body of Christians. canons &c. (belief) 484; thirty nine articles; Apostles' Creed, Nicene Creed, Athanasian Creed[obs3]; Church Catechism; textuary[obs3]. Adj. orthodox, sound, strick[obs3], faithful, catholic, schismless[obs3], Christian, evangelical, scriptural, divine, monotheistic; true &c. 494. Phr. of the true faith.

#984. Heterodoxy. [Sectarianism.] — N. heterodoxy; error &c. 495; false doctrine, heresy, schism; schismaticism[obs3], schismaticalness; recusancy, backsliding, apostasy; atheism &c. (irreligion) 989[obs3]. bigotry &c. (obstinacy) 606; fanaticism, iconoclasm; hyperorthodoxy[obs3], precisianism[obs3], bibliolatry[obs3], sabbatarianism[obs3], puritanism; anthropomorphism; idolatry &c. 991; superstition &c. (credulity) 486; dissent &c. 489. sectarism[obs3], sectarianism; noncomformity[obs3]; secularism; syncretism[obs3], religious sects. protestant-ism, Arianism[obs3], Adventism, Jansenism, Stundism[obs3], Erastianism[obs3], Calvinism, quakerism[obs3], methodism, anabaptism[obs3], Puseyism, tractarianism[obs3], ritualism, Origenism, Sabellianism, Socinianism[obs3], Deism, Theism, materialism, positivism, latitudinarianism &c. High Church, Low Church, Broad Church, Free Church; ultramontanism[obs3]; papism, papistry; monkery[obs3]; papacy; Anglicanism, Catholicism, Romanism; popery, Scarlet Lady, Church of Rome, Greek Church. paganism, heathenism, ethicism[obs3]; mythol-ogy; polytheism, ditheism[obs3], tritheism[obs3]; dualism; heathendom[obs3]. Judaism, Gentilism[obs3], Islamism, Islam, Mohammedanism, Babism[obs3], Sufiism, Neoplatonism, Turcism[obs3], Brahminism, Hinduism, Buddhism, Sabianism, Gnosticism, Hylotheism[obs3], Mormonism; Christian Science. heretic, apostate, antichrist[obs3]; pagan, heathen; painim[obs3], paynim[obs3]; giaour[obs3]; gentile; pantheist, polytheist; idolator. schismatic; sectary, sectarian, sectarist[obs3]; seceder, separatist, recusant, dissenter; nonconformist, nonjuror[obs3]. bigot &c. (obsti-nacy) 606; fanatic, abdal[obs3], iconoclast. latitudinarian, Deist, Theist, Unitarian; positivist, materialist; Homoiousian[obs3], Homoousian[obs3], limitarian[obs3], theosophist, ubiquitarian[obs3]; skeptic &c. 989. Protes-tant; Huguenot; orthodox dissenter, Congregationalist, Independent; Episcopalian, Presbyterian; Lutheran, Calvinist, Methodist, Wesleyan; Ana[obs3], Baptist; Mormon, Latter-day Saint[obs3], Irvingite, Sandemanian, Glassite, Erastian; Sublapsarian, Supralapsarian[obs3]; Gentoo, Antinomian[obs3], Swedenborgian[obs3]; Adventist[obs3], Bible Christian, Bryanite, Brownian, Christian Scientist, Dunker, Ebionite, Eusebian; Faith Curer[obs3], Curist[obs3]; Familist[obs3], Jovinianist, Libadist[obs3], Quaker, Restitutionist[obs3], Shaker, Stundist, Tunker &c.[obs3]; ultra-montane; Anglican[obs3], Oxford School; tractarian[obs3], Puseyite, ritualist; Puritan. Catholic, Roman, Catholic, Romanist, papist. Jew, Hebrew, Rabbinist, Rabbist[obs3], Sadducee; Babist[obs3], Motazilite; Mohammedan, Mussulman, Moslem, Shiah, Sunni, Wahabi, Osmanli. Brahmin[obs3], Brahman[obs3]; Parsee, Sufi, Buddhist; Magi, Gymnosophist[obs3], fire worshiper, Sabian, Gnostic, Rosicrucian &c. Adj. heterodox, heretical; unorthodox, unscriptural, uncanonical; antiscriptural[obs3], apocryphal; unchristian, antichristian[obs3]; schismatic, recusant, iconoclastic; sectarian; dissenting, dissident; secular &c, (lay) 997. pagan; heathen, heathenish; ethnic, ethnical; gentile, paynim[obs3]; pantheistic, polytheistic. Judaical, Mohammedan, Brahminical[obs3], Buddhist &c.n.; Romish, Protestant &c.n. bigoted &c. (prejudiced) 481, (obstinate) 606; superstitious &c. (credulous) 486; fanatical; idolatrous &c. 991; visionary &c. (imaginative) 515. Phr. "slave to no sect" [Pope]; superstitione tollenda religio non tollitur [Lat] [Cicero].

<— p. 342 —>

#985. Judeo-Christian Revelation.— N. revelation, inspiration, afflatus; theophany[obs3], theopneusty[obs3]. Word, Word of God; Scripture; the Scriptures, the Bible; Holy Writ, Holy Scriptures; inspired writings, Gospel. Old Testament, Septuagint, Vulgate, Pentateuch; Octateuch; the Law, the Jewish Law, the Prophets; major Prophets, minor Prophets; Hagiographa, Hagiology; Hierographa[obs3]; Apocrypha. New Testament; Gospels, Evangelists, Acts, Epistles, Apocalypse, Revelations. Talmud; Mishna, Masorah. prophet &c. (seer) 513; evangelist, apostle, disciple, saint; the Fathers, the Apostolical Fathers[obs3]; Holy Men of old, inspired penmen. Adj. scriptural, biblical, sacred, prophetic; evangelical, evangelistic; apostolic, apostolical[obs3]; inspired, theopneustic[obs3], theophneusted[obs3], apocalyptic, ecclesiastical, canonical, textuary[obs3].

#986. Pseudo-Revelation.— N. the Koran, the Alcoran[obs3];
Lyking[obs3], Vedas, Zendavesta, Avesta[obs3], Sastra, Shastra,
Tantra[obs3], Upanishads, Purana, Edda; Book of Mormon.
    [Non-Biblical prophets and religious founders] Gautama, Buddha;
Zoroaster, Confucius, Bab-ed-Din[obs3], Mohammed.
    [Idols] golden calf &c. 991; Baal[obs3], Moloch, Dagon.
% 3. RELIGIOUS SENTIMENTS %

#987. Piety.— N. piety, religion, theism, faith; religiousness, holiness &c. adj.; saintship[obs3]; religionism[obs3]; sanctimony &c. (assumed piety) 988; reverence &c. (respect) 928; humility, veneration, devotion; prostration &c. (worship) 990; grace, unction, edification; sanctity, sanctitude[obs3]; consecration. spiritual existence, odor of sanctity, beauty of holiness. theopathy[obs3], beatification, adoption, regeneration, conversion, justification, sanctification, salvation, inspiration, bread of life; Body and Blood of Christ. believer, convert, theist, Christian, devotee, pietist[obs3]; the good, the righteous, the just, the believing, the elect; Saint, Madonna, Notre Dame[Fr], Our Lady. the children of God, the children of the Kingdom, the children of the light. V. be pious &c. adj.; have faith &c. n.; believe, receive Christ; revere &c. 928; be converted &c. convert, edify, sanctify, keep holy, beatify, regenerate, inspire, consecrate, enshrine. Adj. pious, religious, devout, devoted, reverent, godly, heavenly- minded, humble, pure, holy, spiritual, pietistic; saintly, saint-like; seraphic, sacred, solemn. believing, faithful, Christian, Catholic. elected, adopted, justified, sanctified, regenerated, inspired, consecrated, converted, unearthly, not of the earth. Phr. ne vile fano[It]; "pure-eyed Faith . . . thou hovering angel girt with golden wings" [Milton].

<— p. 343 —>

#988. Impiety.— N. impiety; sin &c. 945; irreverence; profaneness &c. adj.; profanity, profanation; blasphemy, desecration, sacrilege; scoffing &c.v. [feigned piety] hypocrisy &c. (falsehood) 544; pietism, cant, pious fraud; lip devotion, lip service, lip reverence; misdevotion[obs3], formalism, austerity; sanctimony, sanctimoniousness &c. adj; pharisaism, precisianism[obs3]; sabbatism[obs3], sabbatarianism[obs3]; odium theologicum[Lat], sacerdotalism[obs3]; bigotry &c. (obstinacy) 606, (prejudice) 481; blue laws. hardening, backsliding, declension, perversion, reprobation. sinner &c. 949; scoffer, blasphemer; sacrilegist[obs3]; sabbath breaker; worldling; hypocrite &c. (dissembler) 548; Tartufe[obs3], Mawworm[obs3]. bigot; saint [ironically]; Pharisee; sabbatarian[obs3], formalist, methodist, puritan, pietist[obs3], precisian[obs3], religionist, devotee; ranter, fanatic, juramentado[obs3]. the wicked, the evil, the unjust, the reprobate; sons of men, sons of Belial, the wicked one; children of darkness. V. be impious &c. adj., profane, desecrate, blaspheme, revile, scoff; swear &c. (malediction) 908; commit sacrilege. snuffle; turn up the whites of the eyes; idolize. Adj. impious; irreligious &c. 989; desecrating &c.v.; profane, irreverent, sacrilegious, blasphemous. un-hallowed, un-sanctified, un-regenerate; hardened, perverted, reprobate. hypocritical &c. (false) 544; canting, pietistical[obs3], sanctimonious, unctuous, pharisaical, overrighteous[obs3], righteous over much. bigoted, fanatical; priest-ridden. Adv. under the mask of religion, under the cloak of religion, under the pretense of religion, under the form of religion, under the guise of religion. Phr. giovane santo diavolo vecchio[It].

#989. Irreligion.— N. irreligion[obs3], indevotion[obs3];

godlessness, ungodliness &c. adj.; laxity, quietism.

skepticism, doubt; unbelief, disbelief; incredulity, incredulousness &c. adj[obs3].; want of faith, want of belief; pyrrhonism; bout &c. 485; agnosticism.

atheism; deism; hylotheism[obs3]; materialism; positivism; nihilism.

infidelity, freethinking, antichristianity[obs3], rationalism; neology.

[person who is not religious] atheist, skeptic, unbeliever, deist, infidel, pyrrhonist; giaour[obs3], heathen, alien, gentile, Nazarene; espri fort[Fr], freethinker, latitudinarian, rationalist; materialist, positivist, nihilist, agnostic, somatist[obs3], theophobist[obs3].

V. be irreligious &c. adj.; disbelieve, lack faith; doubt, question &c. 485.

dechristianize[obs3].

Adj. irreligious; indevout[obs3]; undevout[obs3]; devoutless[obs3], godless, graceless; ungodly, unholy, unsanctified[obs3], unhallowed; atheistic, without God.

skeptical, freethinking; unbelieving, unconverted; incredulous, faithless, lacking faith; deistical; unchristian, antichristian[obs3].

worldly, mundane, earthly, carnal; worldly &c. minded.

Adv. irreligiously &c. adj.

% 4. ACTS OF RELIGION %

#990. Worship.— N. worship, adoration, devotion, aspiration, homage, service, humiliation; kneeling, genuflection, prostration. prayer, invocation, supplication, rogation, intercession, orison, holy breathing; petition &c. (request) 765; collect, litany, Lord's prayer, paternoster[Lat]; beadroll[obs3]; latria[obs3], dulia[obs3], hyperdulia[obs3], vigils; revival; cult; anxious meeting, camp meeting; ebenezer, virginal. thanksgiving; giving thanks, returning thanks; grace, praise, glorification, benediction, doxology, hosanna; hallelujah, allelujah[obs3]; Te Deum[Lat], non nobis Domine[Lat], nunc dimittis[Lat]; paean; benschen[Ger]; Ave Maria, O Salutaris, Sanctus[Lat], The Annunciation, Tersanctus, Trisagion. psalm, psalmody; hymn, plain song, chant, chaunt, response, anthem, motet; antiphon[obs3], antiphony. oblation, sacrifice, incense, libation; burnt offering, heave offering, votive offering; offertory. discipline; self-discipline, self-examination, self-denial; fasting. divine service, office, duty; exercises; morning prayer; mass, matins, evensong, vespers; undersong[obs3], tierce[obs3]; holyday &c. (rites) 998. worshipper, congregation, communicant, celebrant. V. worship, lift up the heart, aspire; revere &c. 928; adore, do service, pay homage; humble oneself, kneel; bow the knee, bend the knee; fall down, fall on one's knees; prostrate oneself, bow down and worship. pray, invoke, supplicate; put up, offer up prayers, offer petitions; beseech &c. (ask) 765; say one's prayers, tell one's beads. return thanks, give thanks; say grace, bless, praise, laud, glorify, magnify, sing praises; give benediction, lead the choir, intone; deacon, deacon off propitiate[U.S.], offer sacrifice, fast, deny oneself; vow, offer vows, give alms. work out one's salvation; go to church; attend service, attend mass; communicate &c. (rite) 998. Adj. worshipping &c.v.; devout, devotional, reverent, pure, solemn; fervid &c. (heartfelt) 821. Int. hallelujah, allelujah[obs3]! hosanna! glory be to God! O Lord! pray God that! God grant, God bless, God save, God forbid! sursum corda [Lat]. Phr. "making their lives a prayer" [Whittier]; ora et labora[Lat]; "prayers ardent open heaven" [Young].

<— p. 344 —>

#991. Idolatry. — N. idolatry, idolism[obs3]; demonism[obs3], demonolatry[obs3]; idol-worship, demon-worship, devil-worship, fire-worship; zoolatry, fetishism, fetichism; ecclesiolatry[obs3], heliolatry, Mariolatry, Bibliolatry[obs3].

deification, apotheosis, canonization; hero worship.

sacrifices, hecatomb, holocaust; human sacrifices, immolation, mactation[obs3], infanticide, self-immolation, suttee.

idol, golden calf, graven image, fetich, avatar, Juggernath[obs3], lares et penates[Lat]; Baal &c. 986[obs3].

V. worship idols, worship pictures, worship relics; deify, canonize.

Adj. idolatrous.

Phr. adorer le veau d'or[Fr].

#992. Sorcery.— N. sorcery; occult art, occult sciences; magic, the black art, necromancy, theurgy, thaumaturgy[obs3]; demonology, demonomy[obs3], demonship[obs3]; diablerie[Fr], bedevilment; witchcraft, witchery; glamor; fetishism, fetichism, feticism[obs3]; ghost dance, hoodoo; obi, obiism[obs3]; voodoo, voodooism; Shamanism [Esquimaux], vampirism; conjuration; bewitchery, exorcism, enchantment, mysticism, second sight, mesmerism, animal magnetism; od force, odylic force[obs3]; electrobiology[obs3], clairvoyance; spiritualism, spirit rapping, table turning. divination &c. (prediction) 511; sortilege[obs3], ordeal, sortes Virgilianae[obs3]; hocus-pocus &c. (deception) 545. V. practice sorcery &c.n.; cast a nativity, conjure, exorcise, charm, enchant; bewitch, bedevil; hoodoo, voodoo; entrance, mesmerize, magnetize; fascinate &c. (influence) 615; taboo; wave a wand; rub the ring, rub the lamp; cast a spell; call up spirits, call up spirits from the vasty deep; raise spirits from the dead. Adj. magic, magical; mystic, weird, cabalistic, talismanic, phylacteric[obs3], incantatory; charmed &c. v.; Circean, odylic[obs3], voodoo.

#993. Spell.— N. spell, charm, incantation, exorcism, weird, cabala[obs3], exsufflationl, cantrap[obs3], runes, abracadabra, open sesame, countercharm[obs3], Ephesian letters, bell book and candle, Mumbo Jumbo, evil eye, fee-faw-fum. talisman, amulet, periapt[obs3], telesm[obs3], phylactery, philter; fetich, fetish; agnus Dei[Latin: lamb of God]; furcula[obs3], madstone[obs3]; mascot, mascotte[obs3]; merrythought[obs3]; Om, Aum[obs3]; scarab, scarabaeus[obs3]; sudarium[obs3], triskelion, veronica, wishbone; swastika, fylfot[obs3], gammadion[obs3]. wand, caduceus, rod, divining rod, lamp of Aladdin[obs3]; wishing-cap, Fortunatus's cap.

#994. Sorcerer.— N. sorcerer, magician; thaumaturgist[obs3], theurgist; conjuror, necromancer, seer, wizard, witch; hoodoo, voodoo; fairy &c. 980; lamia[obs3], hag. warlock, charmer, exorcist, mage[obs3]; cunning man, medicine man; Shaman, figure flinger, ecstatica[obs3]; medium, clairvoyant, fortune teller; mesmerist; deus ex machina[Lat]; soothsayer &c. 513. Katerfelto, Cagliostro, Mesmer, Rosicrucian; Circe, siren, weird sisters.

<— p. 345 —>

% 5. RELIGIOUS INSTITUTIONS %

#995. Churchdom.— N. church, churchdom; ministry, apostleship[obs3], priesthood, prelacy, hierarch[obs3], church government, christendom, pale of the church. clericalism, sacerdotalism[obs3], episcopalianism, ultramontanism[obs3]; theocracy; ecclesiology[obs3], ecclesiologist[obs3]; priestcraft[obs3], odium theologicum[Lat]. monachism[obs3], monachy[obs3]; monasticism, monkhood[obs3]. [Ecclesiastical offices and dignities] pontificate, primacy, archbishopric[obs3], archiepiscopacy[obs3]; prelacy; bishopric, bishopdom[obs3]; episcopate, episcopacy; see, diocese; deanery, stall; canonry, canonicate[obs3]; prebend, prebendaryship[obs3]; benefice, incumbency, glebe, advowson[obs3], living, cure; rectorship[obs3]; vicariate, vicarship; deaconry[obs3], deaconship[obs3]; curacy; chaplain, chaplaincy, chaplainship; cardinalate, cardinalship[obs3]; abbacy, presbytery. holy orders, ordination, institution, consecration, induction, reading in, preferment, translation, presentation. popedom[obs3]; the Vatican, the apostolic see; religious sects &c. 984. council &c. 696; conclave, convocation, synod, consistory, chapter, vestry; sanhedrim, conge d'elire[Fr]; ecclesiastical courts, consistorial court, court of Arches. V. call, ordain, induct, prefer, translate, consecrate, present. take orders, take the tonsure, take the veil, take vows. Adj. ecclesiastical, ecclesiological[obs3]; clerical, sacerdotal, priestly, prelatical, pastoral, ministerial, capitular[obs3], theocratic; hierarchical, archiepiscopal; episcopal, episcopalian; canonical; monastic, monachal[obs3]; monkish; abbatial[obs3], abbatical[obs3]; Anglican[obs3]; pontifical, papal, apostolic, Roman, Popish; ultramontane, priest-ridden.

#996. Clergy.— N. clergy, clericals, ministry, priesthood, presbytery, the cloth, the desk. clergyman, divine, ecclesiastic, churchman, priest, presbyter, hierophant[obs3], pastor, shepherd, minister; father, father in Christ; padre, abbe, cure; patriarch; reverend; black coat; confessor. dignitaries of the church; ecclesiarch[obs3], hierarch[obs3]; ebdomarius[Lat]; eminence, reverence, elder, primate, metropolitan, archbishop, bishop, prelate, diocesan, suffragan[obs3], dean, subdean[obs3], archdeacon, prebendary, canon, rural dean, rector, parson, vicar, perpetual curate, residentiary[obs3], beneficiary, incumbent, chaplain, curate; deacon, deaconess; preacher, reader, lecturer; capitular[obs3]; missionary, propagandist, Jesuit, revivalist, field preacher. churchwarden, sidesman[obs3]; clerk, precentor[obs3], choir; almoner, suisse[Fr], verger, beadle, sexton, sacristan; acolyth[obs3], acolothyst[obs3], acolyte, altar boy; chorister. [Roman Catholic priesthood] Pope, Papa, pontiff, high priest, cardinal; ancient flamen[obs3], flamen[obs3]; confessor, penitentiary; spiritual director. cenobite, conventual, abbot, prior, monk, friar, lay brother, beadsman[obs3], mendicant, pilgrim, palmer; canon regular, canon secular; Franciscan, Friars minor, Minorites; Observant, Capuchin, Dominican, Carmelite; Augustinian[obs3]; Gilbertine; Austin Friars[obs3], Black Friars, White Friars, Gray Friars, Crossed Friars, Crutched Friars; Bonhomme[Fr], Carthusian, Benedictine[obs3], Cistercian, Trappist, Cluniac, Premonstratensian, Maturine; Templar, Hospitaler; Bernardine[obs3], Lorettine, pillarist[obs3], stylite[obs3]. abbess, prioress, canoness[obs3]; religieuse[Fr], nun, novice, postulant. [Under the Jewish dispensation] prophet, priest, high priest, Levite; Rabbi, Rabbin, Rebbe; scribe. [Mohammedan &c.] mullah, muezzin, ayatollah; ulema, imaum[obs3], imam, sheik; sufi; kahin[obs3], kassis[obs3]; mufti, hadji, dervish; fakir, faquir[obs3]; brahmin[obs3], guru, kaziaskier[obs3], poonghie[obs3], sanyasi[obs3]; druid, bonze[obs3], santon[obs3], abdal[obs3], Lama, talapoin[obs3], caloyer[obs3]. V. take orders &c. 995. Adj. the Reverend, the very Reverend, the Right Reverend; ordained, in orders, called to the ministry.

#997. Laity. — N. laity, flock, fold, congregation, assembly, brethren, people; society [U.S.].

temporality, secularization.

layman, civilian; parishioner, catechumen; secularist.

V. secularize.

Adj. secular, lay, laical, civil, temporal, profane.

#998. Rite. — N. rite; ceremony, ritual, liturgy, ceremonial; ordinance, observance, function, duty; form, formulary; solemnity, sacrament; incantation &c. (spell) 993; service, psalmody &c. (worship) 990. ministration; preaching, preachment; predication, sermon, homily, lecture, discourse, pastoral. [Christian ritual for induction into the faith] baptism, christening, chrism; circumcision; baptismal regeneration; font. confirmation; imposition of hands, laying on of hands; ordination &c. (churchdom) 995; excommunication. [Jewish rituals] Bar Mitzvah, Bas Mitzvah[Fr], Bris. Eucharist, Lord's supper, communion; the sacrament, the holy sacrament; celebration, high celebration; missa cantata[Lat]; asperges[obs3]; offertory; introit; consecration; consubstantiation, transubstantiation; real presence; elements; mass; high mass, low mass, dry mass. matrimony &c. 903; burial &c. 363; visitation of the sick. seven sacraments, impanation[obs3], subpanation[obs3], extreme unction, viaticum, invocation of saints, canonization, transfiguration, auricular confession; maceration, flagellation, sackcloth and ashes; penance &c. (atonement) 952; telling of beads, processional; thurification[obs3], incense, holy water, aspersion. relics, rosary, beads, reliquary, host, cross, rood, crucifix, pax[Lat], pyx, agnus Dei[Lat], censer, thurible, patera[obs3]; eileton[obs3], Holy Grail; prayer machine, prayer wheel; Sangraal[obs3], urceus[obs3]. ritualism, ceremonialism; sabbatism[obs3], sabbatarianism[obs3]; ritualist, sabbatarian[obs3]. holyday, feast, fast. [Christian holy days] Sabbath, Pentecost; Advent, Christmas, Epiphany; Lent; Passion week, Holy week; Easter, Easter Sunday, Whitsuntide; agape, Ascension Day, Candlemas[obs3], Ash Wednesday, Good Friday, Holy Thursday; Lammas, Martinmas, Michaelmas; All SAint's DAy, All Souls' Day [Moslem holy days] Ramadan, Ramazan; Bairam &c.[obs3], &c. [Jewish holy days] Passover; Shabuoth; Yom Kippur, Day of Atonement; Rosh Hashana, New Year; Hanukkah, Chanukkah, Feast of Lights; Purim, Feast of lots. V. perform service[ritual actions of clergy], do duty, minister, officiate, baptize, dip, sprinkle; anoint, confirm, lay hands on; give the sacrament, administer the sacrament; administer extreme unction; hear confession, administer holy penance, shrive; excommunicate, ban with bell book and candle. [ritual actions of believers] attend services, attend mass, go to mass, hear mass; take the sacrament, receive the sacrament, receive communion, attend the sacrament, partake of the sacrament, partake of communion; communicate; receive extreme unction; confess, go to confession, receive penance; anele[obs3]. [teaching functions of clergy] preach, sermonize, predicate, lecture. Adj. ritual, ritualistic; ceremonial; baptismal, eucharistical; paschal. Phr. "what art thou, thou idol ceremony?" [Henry V].

#999. Canonicals. — N. canonicals, vestments; robe, gown, Geneva gown frock, pallium, surplice, cassock, dalmatic[obs3], scapulary[obs3], cope, mozetta[obs3], scarf, tunicle[obs3], chasuble, alb[obs3], alba[obs3], stole; fanon[obs3], fannel[obs3]; tonsure, cowl, hood; calote[obs3], calotte[obs3]; bands; capouch[obs3], amice[obs3]; vagas[obs3], vakas[obs3], vakass[obs3]; apron, lawn sleeves, pontificals[obs3], pall; miter, tiara, triple crown; shovel hat, cardinal's hat; biretta; crosier; pastoral staff, thurifer[obs3]; costume &c. 225.

#1000. Temple. — N. place of worship; house of God, house of prayer. temple, cathedral, minster[obs3], church, kirk, chapel, meetinghouse, bethel[obs3], tabernacle, conventicle, basilica, fane[obs3], holy place, chantry[obs3], oratory. synagogue; mosque; marabout[obs3]; pantheon; pagoda; joss house[obs3]; dogobah[obs3], tope; kiosk; kiack[obs3], masjid[obs3]. [clergymen's residence] parsonage, rectory, vicarage, manse, deanery, glebe; Vatican; bishop's palace; Lambeth. altar, shrine, sanctuary, Holy of Holies, sanctum sanctorum[Lat], sacristy; sacrarium[obs3]; communion table, holy table, Lord's table; table of the Lord; pyx; baptistery, font; piscina[obs3], stoup; aumbry[obs3]; sedile[obs3]; reredos; rood loft, rood screen. [parts of a church: list] chancel, quire, choir, nave, aisle, transept, vestry, crypt, golgotha, calvary, Easter sepulcher; stall, pew; pulpit, ambo[obs3], lectern, reading desk, confessional, prothesis[obs3], credence, baldachin, baldacchino[obs3]; apse, belfry; chapter house; presbytery; anxious-bench, anxious-seat; diaconicum[Lat], jube[obs3]; mourner's bench, mourner's seat. [exterior adjacent to a church] cloisters, churchyard. monastery, priory, abbey, friary, convent, nunnery, cloister. Adj. claustral, cloistered; monastic, monasterial; conventual. Phr. ne vile fano[It]; "there's nothing ill can dwell in such a temple" [tempest].

of Roget's Thesaurus, by Peter Mark Roget

Lightning Source UK Ltd.
Milton Keynes UK
UKOW07f2035250315

248537UK00009B/363/P